Beyond Kushnapur

Mark Flawn-Thomas

MAY 2020

by
Peter & Mark Flawn-Thomas

BROCKWELL PRESS

www.brockwellpress.com

Copyright © Mark Flawn-Thomas 2019
The moral right of the author has been asserted.

ISBN paperback: 978-1-9161440-0-2
ISBN hardcover: 978-1-9161440-2-6
ISBN ebook: 978-1-9161440-1-9

A CIP catalogue record for this book is available from the British Library.

This paperback can be ordered from all bookstores as well as from Amazon, and the ebook is available on online platforms such as Amazon and iBooks.

Cover illustration by Mark Flawn-Thomas
Cover design by Caroline Mills

For further information and updates visit
www.beyondkushnapur.com

We would like to dedicate this book to Janet,
wife to Peter and mother to Mark,
whose untiring support has made it all possible.

Map of India

The Debrahm Family Tree

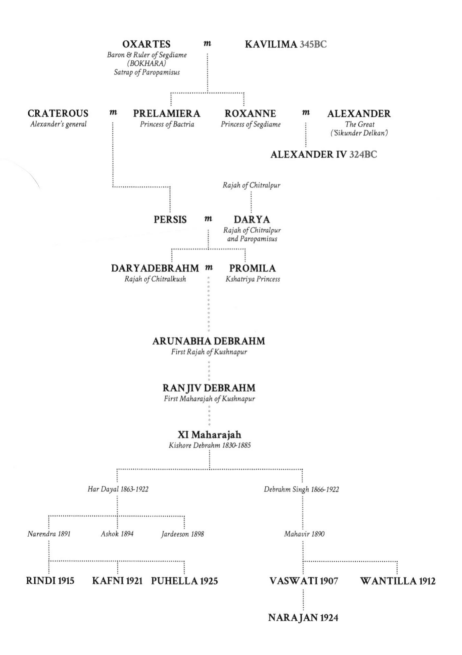

OXARTES *m* KAVILIMA 345BC
Baron & Ruler of Segdiame
(BOKHARA)
Satrap of Paropamisus

CRATEROUS *m* PRELAMIERA   ROXANNE *m* ALEXANDER
Alexander's general   Princess of Bactria   Princess of Segdiame   The Great
('Sikunder Delkan')

ALEXANDER IV 324BC

Rajah of Chitralpur

PERSIS *m* DARYA
Rajah of Chitralpur
and Paropamisus

DARYADEBRAHM *m* PROMILA
Rajah of Chitralkush   Kshatriya Princess

ARUNABHA DEBRAHM
First Rajah of Kushnapur

RANJIV DEBRAHM
First Maharajah of Kushnapur

XI Maharajah
Kishore Debrahm 1830-1885

Har Dayal 1863-1922   Debrahm Singh 1866-1922

Narendra 1891   Ashok 1894   Jardeeson 1898   Mahavir 1890

RINDI 1915   KAFNI 1921   PUHELLA 1925   VASWATI 1907   WANTILLA 1912

NARAJAN 1924

The significance of the Lingam.

Central to this story is the significance of the Lingam in Hinduism. In the Hindu scripts the Lingam or Shiva-Linga, is described as -the cosmic pillar of fire, the cause of all causes from which Lord Shiva emerges proving his superiority over the gods Brahma and Vishnu.

In the ancient Hindu text, the Mahabharata, the Lingam is unequivocally designated as the sexual organ of Shiva.

More than just a phallic symbol the Lingam is worshipped because it is the cosmic symbol of unity and completeness. Together the masculine and feminine are complete, holistic, divinely unified and endless. Just as the Yin-Yang is a circle of life which is complete, the Lingam is a symbol of eternity and symmetry. The Lingam emerges from the female Yoni, symbolizing fertility, life, indivisibility, indestructibility, and creation.

Kushnapur Palace, North East India, December 1941.

The sound of tumbling water was stronger now. Adam raked his torch around the cave and found its source; a small waterfall cascading into a channel about eight feet wide. On the other side of the stream, the beam now illuminated a statue set into a deep alcove. He recognised it as the God Shiva and knew he was in a temple. Curiosity impelled him to take a closer look at this magnificent effigy. At first he could see no obvious way to cross the channel but then noticed the line of stepping-stones just below the surface of the water. These appeared to be the heads of deep stone pillars and, even though the water was crystal-clear, the light from the torch could not reach the bottom. Adam slipped off his shoes and stepped across the stones. The water was freezing so it probably came from a mountain stream. He paused before the great statue to admire the intricate carvings of the smaller figures on either side and realised that he was in the *Gardha-griha*, the sanctum: the most sacred part of this ancient temple.

Adam could now see in detail the girdle of plaited gold, and the interlaced loin apron that hung down, overlaid with thick shining cords. The arms and ankles carried broad bangles inset with rows of diamonds, their facets scattering his torchlight into a thousand reflections. A brilliant headband lent a final air of triumph to the image. Beside Shiva, and slightly further back, was the smaller figure of Parvati, his consort, also generously adorned and, discerningly, revealing only one of her breasts. On her face was an expression of great contentment as she tightly clasped one of Shiva's hands.

The fear that had gripped Adam a minute or two earlier was now subsiding. He decided to return the way he had come but found himself drawn by an imperceptible force. Directing his torch around the sanctum the brilliant aura of a sculpture radiated its powerful presence even before the light had reached it.

Standing about two feet high, sculpted in gold was a lingam; a sacred phallus. Rubies and diamonds adorned the length of its shaft, and even more spectacular blood red stones formed the head. Beneath the phallus was a platinum scrotum encrusted with dazzling sapphires. Adam stood in awe as he traced the magnificent gold base studded with row upon row of white diamonds and emeralds, some the size of a pigeon's egg.

Although the opening to the sky Adam had seen earlier provided a gentle flow of mountain air there was a slightly pungent odour that he could not identify. An odd sound, like a chain being dragged, made him shiver and a cold sweat came over him. Should I be here? he thought. His overwhelming desire to touch this beautiful object overcame any trepidation he felt. As he walked forward with his fingers outstretched towards the gleaming sculpture, something very heavy hit his shoulder. He felt a stinging, excruciating pain, and then lurched forward. Whatever it was that had attached itself to his back now flung him sideways onto the marble floor. Fear-driven adrenaline suppressed the pain and as Adam wrestled to free himself from the creature they fell into the freezing stream. Fur crushed against him and the shock of the icy water caused it to detach its snarling jaws from his shoulder.

Adam swam to the other side of the channel; no stepping stones to help him this time. Oblivious to the pain, he climbed out and crawled several yards, but he had lost his torch. He turned his head and saw its beam, casting a strip of light on the marble floor where it had fallen. In the gloom of the great chamber he could now make out the lithe body of a cheetah, its eyes glowing and teeth glinting as it climbed out of the water. Why had it not pursued him? Then he saw the chain attached to the base of the statue of Shiva, with just enough spare leash to reach the phallic sculpture.

Adam somehow made his way back up to his room in the palace. The freezing water had relieved some of the searing pain in his shoulder but his mind spun with conflicting feelings of wonderment, anger and guilt. He knew he shouldn't have entered this inner sanctum but why had they not shown him the temple? How could the family, he had shared such confidences and intimacies with, think he was unworthy of knowing about this place and that magnificent sculpture? Had he not made one of the greatest of all sacrifices for them?

CHAPTER ONE

Rockton School, Bristol, May 1932.

Adam Cullworthy had been at Rockton School for over two years before he came to know Rindi Debrahm. Adam was in the year below and in a different house which made fraternising difficult. He had seen him many times in the dining hall and at morning assembly and he was particularly aware of his talent on the cricket pitch.

Late one afternoon Adam was in the library reading when the large panelled door opened abruptly. Heads lifted and curious eyes quickly assessed the source of the intrusion. Paper shuffled, a chair scraped, a throat was cleared and then silence descended once more. The figure at the door now struck out with a purposeful tread getting steadily closer and finally came to a halt beside Adam's desk. He looked up and staring down at him was a dark, stern face.

'Cullworthy?' he said.

'Yes,' Adam replied hesitantly.

'Debrahm, Rindi Debrahm,'

Adam knew exactly who he was. Head of Gascoigne House, Captain of the 1st XI and, if rumour were to be believed, an Indian prince.

'I see that we've both made it to the quarter-finals of the Peploe Cup. If we each manage to beat our opponents, we might well meet over the chessboard.'

Adam had never imagined he would get so far in the school chess tournament and now before him stood his likely demise. He must have looked in dread at the prospect because Rindi said, 'I am fallible you know, old boy,' and gave him a broad, disarming smile.

It was 1932, fourteen years after the end of the First World War, a conflict that had not only reduced the Old Boys by 83 but had severely depleted the teaching staff at Rockton.

Spanish flu had inflicted a further toll on numbers and the masters were now either very young or very old. Consequently, the school prefects, already a powerful body, assumed responsibilities and a level of authority far greater than at any time in the school's history. Rindi Debrahm was athletic, bright, charming and exotically good looking. He may have been a prince in India but he was more like a god at Rockton.

The day following their encounter in the library a first-year boy arrived to tell Adam that he was bidden to Debrahm's study on the chapel side of King's Quad. Debrahm greeted Adam formally, directed him silently to one of the chairs, and then sat down opposite him. He looked enquiringly at Adam, his long eyelashes softening the intensity of his stare.

'I understand that you're something of a demon bowler, Cullworthy.'

Adam sat slightly sideways in his chair clearly intimidated by his interviewer.

'I open the bowling for the 3rd XI,' Adam said in modest acknowledgement.

'Good. Leonard has twisted his ankle and we need a first change bowler in the 1st XI and there is no one with real pace in the 2nd XI. We're playing away at Blundells next week,' said Rindi taking it for granted that Adam would want play for him.

Debrahm studied the boy in front of him. For someone who was a good athlete he was ungainly, coltish with big hands and long limbs. His school blazer hung loose on a broad frame, yet to be filled out. His hair, a shade lighter than chestnut and longer than regulation stipulated, was parted in the middle. From time to time he gave his hair a sweeping flick with his hand. This action revealed piercing blue-green eyes and a long thin boyish face tapering to a firm jaw.

He looked at his watch. 'It's getting a bit late; you must be hungry. Will you join me for tea?'

He treated Adam to a sumptuous tea of boiled eggs, buttered muffins and strawberry jam, all prepared for them in the prefects modest kitchen by Rogers, a plump boy whose head looked as if it had not quite made it through his stiff collar.

'Lovely brown eggs,' Adam observed.

'Ah yes. The Boiled Pink One procures them for me,' He said, looking mockingly at the blushing Rogers. 'I'm not sure he doesn't boil them in coffee to get them brown just to please me.'

Adam laughed, then regretted it as the unfortunate boy shot him a resentful glance and then shuffled hurriedly from the room.

'You think I am cruel?' he said, his pronunciation almost too perfect.

'Maybe a little harsh. He looks the sensitive type.' Adam responded.

'Nonsense. Behind his defenceless rabbit exterior lurks a budding Machiavelli and one day he will no doubt turn on his prince.'

'So it is true that you are a prince.' Adam responded rather impertinently.

'Don't believe everything you hear, old boy.' He paused, looked at Adam conspiratorially, then raising one eyebrow and folding his arms with pride said, 'I'll have you know my family is descended from ruthless Punjabi thieves.'

'That still doesn't mean you aren't a prince.'

'Quite so,' he said and laughed.

'So what about you, Cullworthy? Any skeletons in your closet?'

'Oh, the odd Celtic pirate.'

'I thought there might be some remnant of the Armada in the blood,' he said, but did not look disappointed.

Adam returned to his rather cramped study feeling that he had briefly stepped into a different world. Debrahm's study was not only considerably larger than his but everywhere he looked there were intriguing Indian artefacts. The small but exquisite silk carpet which hung on one of the walls. Adam had never seen a carpet displayed like this. On another wall a mirror with a wooden frame which on closer examination had intricate carvings of erotic scenes.

Debrahm as Adam preferred to call him, despite having been asked to call him Rindi, had made him feel totally at ease by the end of his visit. He had an aura about him that exuded confidence and privilege but had a disarming charm which made Adam feel for the hour he had spent with him that perhaps this person could even become a friend. Now back in his room and assessing the difference in their lives this now seemed something of a fantasy to him.

The cricket match was away at Tiverton, about sixty miles from Bristol. They travelled by train and the journey on that warm summer day gave Adam the opportunity to study Rindi more closely. At five feet eleven, he was a trifle taller than Adam, a difference that would reverse itself in the next two years. He had clear, pale brown skin and refined features, a straight nose and firm mouth, showing white, even teeth when he smiled. His eyes were striking: they appeared to be amber, yet, when caught at a certain angle by the rays of the morning sun, they were distinctly violet. He exuded confidence and it was difficult for Adam not to be in awe of him.

Their conversation for the first half hour revolved round cricket and the general, dismal state of the school food.

'I really miss Indian food. Have you ever tried an Indian curry, Cullworthy?'

'No, I can't say I have.'

'My father had his own Brahmin cook when he was at Harrow,' Debrahm continued. 'Sadly they wouldn't allow me to have one at Rockton.'

'Why did you not go to Harrow?'

'Ah, that's a long story, maybe one for another day.'

'Have any of your family ever been to India?' he asked, moving on.

'Only one, as far as I know. My late Uncle Alfred was in India for some years with the Hampshire's. I would love to go there one day,'

Debrahm liked Adam's straightforward manner. He found most English boys difficult to fathom. They were either arrogant and opinionated like Fortescue or understated and self-deprecating. He had been brought up to say things as they were not overstate them or indulge in false modesty. There was a charming youthful uncertainty about Adam and he found himself drawn to him.

'India is a very demanding mistress, Adam,' he said, gazing pensively out onto the passing fields and hedgerows of rural Somerset.

He had not called him Adam before which seemed to add weight to his statement, which he delivered almost as a warning.

'What do you mean by that?'

'India is not green and clean and well-ordered like your England. It is, at its worst, hot, foul smelling and poverty-stricken and a boiling pot of political and religious intolerance. But it is also a most beautiful and fascinating country of intriguing contrasts. Once you are in the grasp of her seductive powers you will surrender your soul to her.'

Adam stared at him in awe and waited childlike for a magical story to unfold.

'Where in India do you live Debrahm?'

'I would like you to call me Rindi when we are alone together if you are not uncomfortable with that.' Adam nodded not entirely convinced that he was comfortable with that level of familiarity. He had only recently stopped calling his father 'sir'.

'In answer to your question we live in the foothills of the

Himalayas. One day you must visit us in Kushnapur; you will love our sweet mangoes, and the women are more beautiful and alluring than you can possibly imagine.'

Adam's imagination was fuelled to bursting with questions to be answered. He wanted to know more about Rindi's family. Then, as though to break the spell, Rindi said, 'Now we have ten minutes before we arrive in Tiverton. So tell me, how would you like me to set your field? Do you want three slips or two?'

'I think we should try three slips, a gully and a long man,' Adam replied, 'and see what plunder that brings us.'

* * *

Adam was not aware that their friendship had attracted any attention until one afternoon shortly before the end of term. Leaving the changing room, he found his way blocked by the hefty frame of Hawkins, a boy in the form above him. A cricketer manqué, his sport was limited to intimidating new boys.

'So, Cullworthy! You've managed to hang on in the 1st XI.' He spoke with a sneering tone. 'Has the captain taken his *droit de seigneur* and buggered you yet?'

Adam's anger was triggered as much by the insult to someone that he had come to respect, as to any personal affront. He should have responded with a clever retort, but discretion was abandoned as he drove his right fist into the jaw of Hawkin's smug face followed by a left uppercut of such force that his victim fell to the ground swearing profusely and threatening dire retribution. That this never came was probably as much due to Hawkins's wish not to acknowledge the encounter as to any degree of cowardice.

During the next seven weeks, Adam justified his place in Rindi's team, but the encounter with Hawkins had made him realise that a little more discretion was appropriate in his dealings with Rindi. Their earlier conversation had left him wanting on the subject of India but with no opportunity to pursue it further. Adam was also curious to find out why Rindi had ended up at Rockton. It was about this time that Adam, looking out of his study window, noticed a tall turbaned Indian man hovering around the entrance gates of the school. This was an unusual sight in the West of England. The man appeared to be staring up at Adam's window. Having gathered his books for his next lesson Adam looked back towards the gates but the man was no longer anywhere to be seen. He felt unsettled by this event but wondered if he had perhaps imagined the idea that his window was the focus of the man's attention.

Adam thought to mention this to Rindi but never did. The summer term ended and his new acquaintance was then on his way back to India for the long summer vacation. Adam conjured thoughts of the smells, sights and sounds of the sub-continent and longed to be going with him. He looked forward to seeing him in the autumn term but wondered how they might continue their friendship in the absence of cricket.

* * *

The start of the Michaelmas term and the new school year was occupied with moving up to new forms and settling into a new curriculum. Rindi had become head of his house in the previous term had now been made a school prefect. These changes, the intensity of studies and the fact that Rindi did not play rugby restricted opportunities to spend time together.

At the beginning of December, Rindi mentioned that he would be spending part of his Christmas break with his uncle and aunt at their home in London. His absence during the summer vacation had made Adam crave more of his stimulating company. There was so much that he wanted to know about Rindi. He knew that he had applied for a place to read history at Balliol College, Oxford, and with his academic record he would doubtless be starting there the following autumn. This set Adam thinking and during the Christmas holidays he resolved to ask his parents if they would invite Rindi down to Sussex for Easter. Thus it was that as Adam sat down to breakfast a few days after returning to school for the Lent term, a letter was waved over his shoulder and he turned to see Rindi wearing a mischievous grin.

'So this is what you've been hatching. I've just received an invitation for Easter from your mother.'

'Well, I thought it's about time you came down to Fletching to meet my family. If you feel brave enough.'

'Excellent idea. I'll write back straight away. If you are going to inflict me on your family I think it is only fair for me to introduce you to some of mine.'

'Oh? What had you in mind?'

'Come and stay with my aunt and uncle in London. We might even introduce you to the delights of the Westbury *bibis*.'

'What on earth are the Westbury *bibis*?'

'Well, *larkis* more accurately. Girls to you dear boy. Actually they are great family friends and I am sure they will meet with your approval.'

Adam was curious at the way Rindi referred to these girls almost as if they were chattels. Nevertheless, this was an interesting invitation.

Easter, April 1933. Fletching, East Sussex.

Adam had been a trifle mischievous when telling his parents about Rindi, not so much by what he had told them, but what he had omitted. He knew that his mother would conjure up a vision of a dark and mysterious Indian.

She was a little reassured when Adam's elder sister Daphne said, 'These Indians can be very handsome. There are several at Cambridge; one or two of them are stunning.'

'Yes, darling, I'm sure you're right, though I can't say I really approve of foreigners. I hope you're not being distracted from your studies.'

Adam's mother was a handsome woman with refined features but was otherwise solidly built. She was very much the mistress of her own domain only deferring to her husband's authority on matters of law, finance and discipline.

'Really, Mummy, you're so conventional.' She put an arm round her mother and kissed her on the cheek. 'Don't worry I'm determined to finish my degree.' This was heartening for her mother, as she had not really approved of Daphne going to Cambridge in the first place. But having got there, she wanted her to complete the course.

The nearest station to Adam's home was Sheffield Park. It hardly justified a station, though doubtless access to the mansion of the eponymous earl had influenced the routing of the railway line to the end of his drive. Adam's mother met them off the train and drove them to Fletching at considerable speed with surprisingly little to say. Adam sensed that she was already falling under Rindi's spell even in the absence of conversation. On arriving at the house Adam's twelve year old sister, Sue, put her head out of the upstairs window and then, seconds later, was standing beside them waiting to be introduced.

'Susie, this is Mr Debrahm,' said Adam's mother very formally.

Rindi shook her hand and said, 'Please call me Rindi.'

'Mummy, is Mr Debrahm in the Willow room?' ignoring his request for informality, 'No, in the Blue room, darling,' replied her mother.

'Oh, good, that means we're sharing a bathroom,' and then grabbing Rindi's bag disappeared through the front door.

'I am sorry, Rindi,' said Mrs Cullworthy, 'she's been in a state of high excitement about your coming to stay.'

Rindi laughed. 'Don't worry, I have a younger sister just like her.'

Over dinner that night Rindi chatted to Adam's mother about how late the daffodils were and how much he liked English formal gardens. Sue sat transfixed like a rabbit in the headlights and was obviously bursting to say something.

'Mr Debrahm?' she said.

'Rindi, please,' he responded more insistently.

'Rindi?' she said hesitantly, 'do you have your own elephant?'

'Oh, Susie!' her mother interjected, 'not everyone in India has an elephant,' and then to Rindi, 'I am so sorry, Rindi, she is completely obsessed with elephants.'

But with their curiosity aroused they all waited for Rindi's response.

'Yes, I do have an elephant, four in fact. Well, actually they belong to my father.'

'Golly, he must be very important.' Sue said deeply impressed.' Is he a maharajah?'

Rindi hesitated for a moment, looked across at Adam and then back to Sue and said, 'Yes, actually my father is a maharajah. The Maharajah of Kushnapur and, yes, he is important to me.' He smiled across at Adam, knowing that this was an answer that would leave many further questions still to be answered.

'Well, when I grow up I would like to come and ride on one of your elephants,' said Sue.

'And so you shall,' replied Rindi with a new air of authority.

Adam knew that his father's division on the Western Front had included two Indian infantry battalions. Their fighting ability had gained his respect and, as they chatted together, a mutual rapport was evident.

'Adam tells me that your home is in the foothills of the Himalayas?'

'Yes, I think it's one of the best parts of India. But I'm biased of course.'

'What is the climate like there?'

'The winters can be chilly but we live well below the snow line and, for most of the year, the climate is comfortably hot but without the scorching heat of the plains.'

'Sounds like England at the height of summer.'

'For most of the year, rather hotter I'd say.'

'Are you part of a large family?'

'Oh no, I just have two younger sisters who are both still being tutored.'

'It must be strange being so far from home, you must miss them dreadfully,' said Mrs Cullworthy.

'Yes, I do and in all my years at Rockton I've only been home twice. However, this summer, before I go up to Oxford in October, I shall have a long vacation. This will enable me to stay longer at home and attend to certain responsibilities that I have to take on.' He did not elaborate, and went on, 'life is so very different here in England, but in many respects it is less complicated than my life in Kushnapur.'

'Well, at least you'll be able to show them a thing or two about cricket,' Adam cut in.

'You're wrong there, Adam. India has some of the finest cricketers in the world.' Then with a mischievous smile he added, 'like many things that we have adopted from the British, I believe we may have improved on it.'

Adam's mother and Daphne and Sue retired early – the latter with protest. 'Why do we always have to leave when the conversation starts getting interesting?'

'She has a point,' said Rindi and then, after they had left he added, 'I think she'll break a few hearts one day.'

'Yes,' said Adam's father, adding with a wry smile, 'but I'm not sure that most men like them quite as strong-willed as that one. Now, Rindi, we didn't offer you wine earlier on because I wasn't sure whether it was against your religion?'

'Well, under strict Hindu code, we should not drink strong alcohol. My family don't totally observe this rule. Within reason, we respect the wishes of a guest, or the host if we are guests, although we never drink in public or if there are those present who might be offended.'

'That sounds a practical and honest approach. I have some Sandemans '04 decanted. Could I tempt you to a glass?'

'Ah yes, I must confess I have developed a taste for vintage port since my uncle introduced me to it.'

Adam could not recall ever having discussed his father's writing with Rindi and was surprised when he asked, 'Have your views changed, Sir, since you wrote *Futile Heroes?*'

Adam's father rarely spoke about his experiences in the war although Adam knew he had been mentioned in dispatches. He had lost so many friends that it was almost too painful to talk about, although it was probably never very far from his thoughts. His elder brother Alfred, a regular soldier, had been killed at Passchendaele in 1917. Adam often wondered whether his writing was his way of talking about these events but through someone else.

Slow to respond he smiled at Rindi and replied rather pensively.

'We English have a strange, perhaps even illogical disposition and character. In war we fight with pride and resolution in the belief that we are defending our homeland and way of life. Yet we appear incapable of applying that same determination to solve the problems of the peace that follows our victories. Our expectations are seldom fulfilled. Many who contributed so much to our success in battle, have felt obliged to emigrate. After Waterloo thousands of disillusioned and jobless men were forced to seek a tough new life in South Africa.'

'They probably weren't satisfied with their way of life, even before going to war,' Adam interjected.

'Possibly. Though it's more likely that the very experience of war raised their expectations of what their country would do for them. I think that some form of elitism is beneficial to a nation as long as we don't get bogged down with a lot of petty ideals and conventions. That was a weakness of us Victorians. We were brought up to be proud of our empire, yet we could never reconcile this with the fact that we are an island race.'

Rindi nodded, though Adam was not sure that he agreed.

'Well, that's enough about us. Tell me about India, and your family. 'He paused and then asked hesitantly, 'Did any of your family fight in the Great War?'

'Sadly or perhaps fortunately not, we were either too old or too young. We did send soldiers from Kushnapur to France. Tragically most of them were lost on the battlefields of the Somme,'

'That was a great sacrifice, fighting so far from home in a war that must have seemed even more pointless than to our own soldiers,' Adam contributed.

Adam's father gave him an admonishing look, as if to convey that he was not qualified to trivialise it as 'pointless', and suddenly he looked rather tired.

'Well, Rindi, I think I'll turn in but you and Adam probably have much to catch up on,' he said, passing the decanter. 'By the way, if you'd like to ride in the morning, we'll see if we can find you a mount. I might even let you ride Harry.'

'I'd enjoy that very much, although I may have to borrow some kit from Adam.'

'That won't be a problem; we'll sort that all out in the morning.'

'Good night, Sir,' said Rindi rather formally as he stood up, but Adam knew his father would appreciate this act of respect.

They were finally alone and Adam felt relieved that the family so obviously approved of Rindi, although slightly resentful that they had monopolised his company. 'So, you sly fox, you are a prince after all. What's with all the secrecy?'

'It's complicated and I apologise for not telling you sooner but our family has been under grave threat for some time.'

'Really? From whom?'

'A Hindu faction of fundamentalists who were in disagreement with the progressive policy of our family. They vowed to castrate all male offspring of my grandparents unless they fell into line with the policy and wishes of their faction.'

"But that doesn't make much sense. You are also Hindu.'

'Indeed we are. However, Hindus follow a polytheistic religion. They worship several gods, all embraced by the religion. Over the last five thousand years, many dogmas have emerged, all supposedly adhering to the original concepts of our Vedas.'

'It all sounds quite complicated.'

'Hinduism is a total way of life. Although it may appear alien to you, I believe its basic concepts are sound and practical. Only when the system itself is challenged, do problems arise.'

'So have these fanatics ever carried out any of their threats? They clearly did not castrate your father.'

'No they didn't. But thinking his younger brother Ashok was the first born they kidnapped him instead.'

'My God, how terrible, so what happened?'

'At the age of five he was found castrated and screaming at the end of the drive in Kushnapur.'

Adam stared at him in disbelief. 'And where is he now?'

'He now lives a quiet life in Kushnapur, his six foot six inches an unfortunate testament to his lost manhood.'

'Are you in danger in England?'

'Hopefully not, but as the only son we could not take any chances. Unless I undertake to abandon our liberal policies when I succeed to the *gaddi*, the inference is that I can expect the same treatment as my uncle. Since then the family have taken security measures very seriously. Amongst these was the decision that when I came to school in England, it would be wiser to be an ordinary Indian private citizen.'

'Was that why you were not sent to Harrow like your father?'

'Partly, although Rockton was also chosen for its academic standards, especially in history.'

'Didn't you feel that I could be trusted with that information?'

'Yes, I did and I have often thought about telling you but I didn't want to burden you unnecessarily. Only my uncle and aunt in London, my housemaster and the Westburys know my true identity and they are aware of the threats. Perhaps our friendship is stronger for your not knowing who I was?'

'You may be right, but I think my family thought it a bit strange that I didn't know that my best friend was the son of a maharajah.'

'Yes, I can understand that and perhaps you should tell them the reason and ask them if they could be circumspect with the information.'

'Of course. So what exactly is your title?'

'*Maharajkuma.* It means crown prince, but of course I never use it outside India. In fact, my great-grandfather started a tradition at the end of the nineteenth century that, unless on an official or state visit, we leave our titles behind in Kushnapur. He felt that as we are a state of only one and a half million people it would teach us a little humility.'

'No more questions,' said Rindi with yawn. 'If we are riding in the morning I'll need some sleep.'

As Adam lay in bed he pondered Rindi's revelations. It now seemed so obvious that he was from a grand family. Would it have made a difference if he had known who he was? He certainly felt more anxious about his friend now. How might a threat manifest itself? He remembered the tall Indian he had seen at the gates of Rockton.

Adam and Rindi greeted each other in the morning with the mutual sense of relief that a shared confidence can bring. It was a glorious spring morning, and the clip-clop of their horses' hooves echoed from the buildings as they passed the village pub and houses whose doors opened right onto the street. Once clear of the village, the hedges, farm gates and streams seemed to pass under their mounts with ease. The sounds and sights of the country felt good. Squirrels scurried across the road, cock pheasants screeched at their rivals in a nearby copse, a fallow deer, heavy in fawn, lolloped up a bank, cunning wood pigeons, seemed aware that no gun was carried, inquisitive heads peeped above the water as otter and cubs were disturbed in a shallow stream. The problems of the world seemed a million miles away.

CHAPTER TWO

Kensington, London

Adam and Rindi arrived at Victoria Station late in the afternoon.

Rindi hailed a cab: 'Queen's Gate Gardens please'. Ten minutes later, they drew up outside an imposing mid-Victorian terraced house with grand pillars. Rindi paid the driver and Adam turned to see a tall Indian wearing a cream turban and a black silk coat down to below the knee with a lilac coloured high collar.

He addressed Rindi: '*Namaste, Rindiji-sahib, Ap kaise hain.*' Then with a slight tilt forward of the head, he gave Adam a similar greeting in English: 'Good evening, Sir.' Deferential but not obsequious, he then picked up their cases and led the way into the house.

'Guest room on first floor is ready for Cullworthy-sahib. I will show the sahib.' There was a gentle movement of the head to give emphasis to his statement. It was polite, though not like the charming side-to-side shake of the head that Adam would experience years later in Bombay.

'Memsahib-Jardeeson is ordering dinner at quarter-past eight.'

'*Shukriya, Jandah,*' acknowledged Rindi,

'Right, Adam, I suggest we meet in the drawing room at quarter to eight for an aperitif.'

Adam wondered what an aperitif for a schoolboy would consist of in an Indian household, albeit an Anglicised one.

They followed Jandah up a wide, elegant staircase and along the first floor landing to the foot of the second floor stairs. 'I'm up here, see you later,' called Rindi, as he took his bags and continued up to the next floor.

Jandah led the way along a short passage to a tall, white door with a crystal handle and motioned Adam to enter

'If there is anything the sahib needs, Sir, please ring this bell.' He pointed to a large ceramic button sunk into the wall.

Adam had encountered butlers before but there was something rather superior about Jandah that would have made him hesitate to ring that bell.

Beyond Kushnapur

A small, ornate travelling clock on the mantelpiece showed the time at half-past six. Time to take a leisurely bath and change for dinner. The house was so quiet that he wondered just where everyone was, especially the servants. There was a well proportioned window in keeping with the early Victorian architecture. This gave a bird's eye view of the garden square opposite the house. The daffodils were past their prime but a fine magnolia tree was bursting into bloom its blushing pink and purple canopy adding a grandeur to the view.

Turning back to survey the bedroom, he noticed that, to the left of the window, was an attractive escritoire, delicately carved and inlaid with silver and ivory. Across the top was writing in what Adam presumed to be Indian Sanskrit letters. There was writing paper that although tastefully embossed, was in a pale purple colour. His Aunt Emma would not have approved: personal letters she said, 'should always be written on pale blue notepaper.'

Further round the room was a large double bed with the head and foot fashioned in brass. The sheets and pillowcases were made of the finest Egyptian linen, cream in colour and bordered with a discreet band of the same pale purple as the notepaper and Jandah's collar. Was this an insight into the type of life that Rindi led in India, or just his aunt's caprice?

Adam lay down to test the bed. It was so comfortable he nearly dozed off. On the bedside table was an impressive-looking book entitled *The Debrahms of Kushnapur*. He opened it at the back, thinking this was where he was most likely to find a picture of Rindi. Sure enough, there perched on top of a very small elephant in his full princely regalia was, judging by the date on the photograph, a twelve-year-old Rindi. Beside the elephant were two beautifully dressed young girls of about five and seven looking rather disgruntled. Tucked into a pouch on the back cover was a family tree that traced the family back to General Craterous, notated as a close military adviser to Alexander the Great. The last four entries, all handwritten, were of Rindi, his sisters Kafni and Puhella and a cousin. It was hard to connect this impressive history to his friend Rindi but it did explain why he had a fascination for genealogy.

Adam had been so engrossed that he had almost forgotten about his bath. Opening the door to the left of the bed, he found a capacious bathroom infused with a welcome fragrance of jasmine. As he lay in the hot scented water he started to wonder about Rindi's uncle. Would he have a beard, or wear a turban like Jandah? Was there just one wife in the household or several extra concubines? They probably did not call them that any more. He had heard of one maharajah that had a mistress in his harem for every night of the year. Rindi had mentioned nothing of his uncle beyond the fact that he was his legal guardian whilst he was at school in England. As Adam entered the drawing room Rindi was sitting in a wing-backed chair, half facing the door, drinking what looked like a dark cordial. He was wearing an immaculate green smoking jacket.

'Ah, so you've finally surfaced. You're looking very smooth.'

'Yes, I had a wonderful bath. What's that cocktail you're drinking?

'Try some' said Rindi. He walked over to the table, picked up a jug, filled a glass and handed it to Adam. 'It's a fruit punch that Jandah prepares. Being a strict Brahmin he doesn't approve of alcohol, so what he puts in it I daren't ask'

Adam took a good draught, and then stopped abruptly to take a breath. 'Wow! That has a hell of a kick.'

Rindi laughed, and was pleased that his friend had come to stay. Over the last year he had seen him grow from a lanky, slightly awkward boy into a strong, handsome young man. He had always been manifestly modest, which Rindi attributed to his very British upbringing which he had now witnessed at first hand. Adam was clearly the blue-eyed boy of the family which accounted for his quiet self-belief, but Rindi had also seen growing seeds of self-doubt which reflected an increasing awareness that there was a different world beyond the security of his family and school. He felt sure that the girls he would be meeting the following day would fall for his good looks and charm but would they appreciate the vulnerability behind his confident façade?

A clock in the hall struck eight and Adam began to wonder when Rindi's uncle would appear. Was it going to be a bore to entertain a school friend of his nephew? Perhaps he had decided to leave them to their own devices. Then he remembered that it was *he* who had specifically invited Adam. It might have been telepathy, for at that moment, the door was opened by Jandah and in walked *Shri* Jardeeson Debrahm.

Adam was immediately struck by his elegance. He was probably in his late forties and about the same height as Rindi. He was clean-shaven with very dark hair, flecked with grey on the sides. The Debrahm features were immediately distinguishable: a high broad brow and the distinctive, deep violet eyes which twinkled in the light of the chandelier. Perfect teeth revealed themselves as he gave Adam a beguiling smile. The cut of his charcoal suit, with a barely visible dark red pinstripe, was clearly Savile Row.

Jardeeson greeted his nephew, and then paused to allow Rindi to introduce him to Adam.

'Welcome to Queen's Gate Gardens. I hope you enjoy your stay here.' His handshake was firm, but unlike the English, who shake hands almost dismissively, he held the handshake and his eyes engaged Adam's throughout his greeting.

'I suppose you're quite familiar with London?' He spoke without the slightest Indian inflection.

'No, Sir, not very, just the well-known streets and famous places.'

'And Richmond?'

'I was there some years ago when my father went to the Star and Garter Home to visit a wartime colleague who'd suffered permanent wounds.'

'So not a happy association for you, then?'

'Not really. I didn't know the man, or even see him.'

'So what would you say about going over to Richmond tomorrow? Some old friends of ours, the Westburys, have invited us for lunch.'

'That sounds a capital idea.'

The smile on Rindi's face told him that this might be where they would meet his *bibis* or was it *larkis*.

'Sir Julian came back last year from his secondment to the judiciary in India. He asked to return to England when his father died and he's now taken over the family home.' He looked over to Rindi. 'You remember going there when the old boy was alive?'

Rindi nodded. 'I certainly do and especially playing on that immaculate croquet lawn.'

'Yes, fortunately they've still got that, though the gardener's cottage, stables and paddocks had to be sold off to pay death duties.'

The sound of a deep, resonating gong announced dinner and the double doors at the far end of the drawing room were opened from the inside. Adam glanced at his watch. It was exactly eight-fifteen. This household was clearly run with precision.

The dining room ran the depth of the house, with four tall windows at each end heavily curtained with pale coffee-coloured velvet. The table was the longest Adam had seen in a private home, capable of seating at least thirty people. Three chandeliers and a dozen wall lights gave it a certain grandeur.

Adam was directed to a dark, hide-covered chair on Rindi's uncle's right at the end of the highly polished, mahogany table. Rindi sat on his left. A tall Indian of about twenty-five, wearing a turban and dressed in a long waisted white jacket with high collar and cream trousers, drew back the uncle's chair. Rindi and Adam were not accorded this formality. The room felt slightly austere with only the three of them dining and Adam was curious as to why Rindi's aunt had not joined them. The good humour of both Rindi and his uncle soon warmed the atmosphere and then Adam was treated to a feast of Indian food such as he had never experienced.

'Rindi tells me your father is an author.'

'Well, his career was as a solicitor but since he retired he has devoted much of his time to writing.'

'Your parents obviously prefer living in the country. I always enjoy visiting friends in the country but wouldn't choose to live there myself. I prefer living in London. It is where I was brought up and went to school. '

Adam nodded but was gazing around the room at the family portraits. In one of them, a faded sepia photograph, there was a posed family group which looked like it was Rindi's father and mother in full regalia with their two daughters standing on either side. In front of them were stretched three huge tigers for all intents and purposes they could have just been sleeping. A diminutive Rindi was sitting on one of the tigers trying unsuccessfully to look triumphant and at ease.

'It might appear to be a very English residence but we try to maintain our family traditions here and, as you have no doubt noticed most of our servants are from India. Rindi's aunt came here as a young bride-to-be and, as is our usual custom, we had never met until the week before the wedding.'

'Was the wedding in London?'

'It was, and in this very house. Two Brahmins came and conducted the Marriage ceremony and the receptions went on for more than a year.'

'Good Heavens! Why was that, Sir?'

'Indian families have an obligation to invite not only their friends, but also every single relative, however distant. Many of them we had never seen before and probably would never see again. Fortunately many of them decided not to make the journey from India but for those who came later we arranged private parties.' And then he added with a chuckle: 'The real challenge was what to do with all the presents.'

'Have your family always been educated at Rockton?' he said

returning the subject to Adam.

'No, my great grandfather was at Winchester,' Adam said.

'Was that the one who became a bishop?' Rindi asked.

'No, that was his son, my grandfather. My great-grandfather was an Oxford scholar, but seems never to have done a proper day's work in his life. He spent much of his time researching our family tree but it isn't as impressive as the one of the Debrahm family that I found in my bedroom.'

'Ah yes, well our archivist managed to skip over some of the more colourful episodes in our past.'

Rindi smiled and nodded in agreement.

Later, in his room Adam opened *The Debrahms of Kushnapur* once more, his interest having been rekindled by his meeting with Uncle Jardeeson. He couldn't help thinking about his poor, emasculated brother and looking at the photographs he wondered which one he was. Probably the tall one at the back with the rather doleful look in his eyes. But what really fascinated Adam was the picture of Rindi and his sisters and thinking how handsome Rindi had become he wondered how the girls might also blossom as teenagers.

'Good morning, it's eight o'clock sir. I hope you slept well.'

Too sleepy to hear her knock, Adam raised his head to see the curtains being drawn back and the maid carrying a breakfast tray.

Breakfast at his home was a substantial meal and was only served in bed if one was ill. It felt opulent being waited upon in a style that was clearly taken for granted in this household.

'Would you like anything else sir? Egg and bacon, or a kipper? I've brought coffee, but I can easily bring tea, if you would prefer it.' Adam had never been called sir before and was expecting something less English for breakfast. He wondered if this was a concession to him.

He looked at the tray and saw fruit, cereal, a pot of coffee and what he presumed to be hot rolls wrapped in a napkin. 'No, this is fine, thank you.'

She smiled, making her look much prettier. She was about to leave then paused and said, 'I was told to inform you that Mister Rindi has gone for a ride on *Rotten Row*. He should be back shortly. He thought you would prefer to sleep on.'

'Did he? the devil.' Adam then smiled to let her know that he was not annoyed.

'He said I was to remind you that you're all leaving for Richmond at half past eleven.'

Tucked in beside the coffee pot was a copy of 'The Times' and, as Adam ate the fruit and cereal, he scanned the news. On page two was a photograph of a judge, taken at Buckingham Palace, following his investiture by the king. He would not normally have given it a second glance since many judges were knighted but the name 'Westbury' caught his eye. He was probably the very person that they were due to meet that day. He read the article with greater interest.

"Sir Julian Westbury had a narrow escape, shortly before leaving India: A man threw a knife at him when he was getting into his car. Fortunately, in bending down to enter the vehicle, he had avoided being killed, and had sustained only a gash on the neck. The attempt on Judge Westbury's life was thought to have been an act of revenge for his sentencing of seven members of the *Kushdin* movement to lengthy stretches in prison."

After Adam had bathed and shaved he stood at the window looking down into the street and across into the square. Once more he admired the magnolia and the emerging cherry blossom. He watched the bowler hatted gentlemen with rolled umbrellas making their way to work but his attention was drawn to a thin Indian man leaning on the railings opposite the house. He presumed this was a member of the Debrahm household but the man suddenly moved hastily off towards Gloucester Road. Adam could not be sure but there was something strangely familiar about this man. Shortly afterwards, the distinctive figure of Jandah emerged from the house and crossed to where the man had been standing. Looking up and down the street he appeared very agitated but after a few minutes returned to the house.

Just after nine, Rindi came into Adam's room still in his jodhpurs and carrying a crop.

'Good morning, old boy. I trust you slept well?'

'Ah, you sod, you thought you were going to whip me out of bed.'

'It looks as though I nearly did. Mollie told me that you've only just had your breakfast'

'How was your ride in Hyde Park?'

'Absolutely marvellous except the Household Cavalry were preparing for some ceremonial work so we had to go a different route to our normal one.'

'Who is we?'

'Oh, Uncle Jardesson always insists I take his *syce* with me.'

'Rindi I saw something rather strange from my window.'

'Oh, what was that?'

'Well it may be nothing but there was a slightly suspicious looking man standing over there looking at the house.' Adam pointed to the railings next to the square.

'Was he an Indian?' Rindi asked earnestly.

'Yes, he was, and he shot off down the road when he saw Jandah coming out of the house.' Adam didn't mention that he had previously seen a similar character loitering outside the school.

'Could have been a relative of one of the staff but I will ask Jandah when I see him,' Rindi replied unconvincingly.

'By the way, I saw an item in the Times this morning about a Sir Julian Westbury. Is that who we're having lunch with today?'

'Yes, that's him.' Rindi appeared preoccupied.

'What's wrong, the trip's not off, is it?'

'No, no,' he shook his head. 'I was just thinking that our family was involved with that incident Sir Julian had to deal with. I ought to fill you in really.'

'Let's meet in the library for a coffee in twenty minutes. Oh, you'll find it on the ground floor next to the dining room.'

Although not a large room, the library had French windows with access to a small rear garden and courtyard. There was ample daylight but no direct sunlight. Two walls were covered with glass-fronted bookcases reaching to the ceiling. The titles of a number of the books were written in oriental characters, probably Sanskrit, and were beautifully bound in leather. The third wall had shelves only up to halfway, filled with recent editions of novels and biographies. Above these hung two large maps, one of the British Isles, the other of the Indian sub-continent and its neighbours. It was the latter that Adam was examining when Rindi came in.

'Good, you're studying the territory.'

Rindi stood before the map of India contemplating where to start.

'This is Delhi our capital but the seat of government and the Viceroy's House is in New Delhi, here, south of the old Moghul Capital.' Adam followed Rindi's elegant finger. 'The buildings of New Delhi are very impressive and were designed on a grand scale by Sir Herbert Baker and Sir Edwin Lutyens.'

Rindi then moved his hand upwards from Delhi to a point where the contours changed colour to show the rapid rise in altitude. 'This is Simla, which becomes the summer imperial capital for five months each year. The Viceroy and his entire government move up here when the heat of the plains becomes unbearable.'

Running his finger further up the map he stopped and said, 'And here in the foothills of the Himalayas is where we live.'

The map was largely coloured imperial pink but scattered the length and breadth of the country were both large and small patches of yellow.

'So what are the yellow bits?'

'They are the Princely states, some of them the size of Britain and with considerable armies of their own.'

'And why do the British tolerate that?'

'These rulers have no external powers and have all signed treaties of loyalty to the British Crown. Many of these states have different religions and sects which are incomprehensible to foreigners. So as long as they keep the peace and abide by the rules the British seem perfectly happy with the arrangement.'

'What goes on in Kushnapur?'

'We follow a Hindu sect known as *Sardarji*. We believe the British cannot remain in control of India indefinitely and that we should prepare ourselves for the time when they leave. However, unlike the *Kushdins,* we do not think militancy is the right solution. Last year they mounted a massive demonstration in the British-ruled United Provinces that adjoin our state. They wanted greater autonomy in their part of the country. Our family is not without influence and, because we did not support them, they were extremely angry.'

'So where does Sir Julian fit in?' Adam asked.

'In the violence that followed, many people were seriously injured, and several were killed. The authorities took a serious view of the matter. Thirty of the troublemakers and leaders were arrested and charged. When the case was brought to court, it was Sir Julian who tried them. He gave seven of them prison sentences and the rest were fined. Because it was a political matter he requested to be excused from any future cases of this kind. Had they known this they might not have bothered to make an attempt on his life.'

'Good morning, boys.' They looked up to see Jardeeson stride into the library. He wore an immaculate blue suit with a white shirt and a bow tie in what looked like club colours. He was the essence of an English gentleman and were it not for the colour of his skin Adam would not have considered him as the likely brother of the grand Indian maharajah in the photograph in the dining room.

'Good morning, Uncle, I've just been telling Adam about the *Kushdins* case.'

'Yes, nasty business. I wish those damn fools would not go and muck it all up. They'll ruin everything we're trying to do.'

He turned and smiled at the woman who had just entered the room. She was short and neat and wore her hair up which made her neck appear unusually long. Probably in her late thirties she was light skinned with refined features. She wore a pale pink sari traced through with mother-of-pearl that shimmered as she walked. For a small person she had remarkable presence.

Rindi went forward to greet her. '*Namaste, Ninaji,*'

'Adam, let me introduce my Aunt Nina.'

'How do you do, Mrs Debrahm?'

She placed the palms of her hands together and held them for a moment in front of her, as she quietly gave the traditional Indian greeting. '*Namaste*, Adam.'

This was the extent of her concession to Indian formality; her next words were in English and, unlike Jardeeson, she had a slight Indian inflection. 'I hope you're comfortable in your room.'

There was no explanation as to why she had not made an appearance the evening before.

'Yes, very comfortable, thank you.'

'Well, I suppose we had better be on our way to Richmond,' said Jardeeson.

Jandah came in to announce that the car was waiting. Outside the front door the liveried chauffeur held open the rear door of a gleaming Bentley. Nina got in and then beckoned Adam to sit beside her. Jardeeson joined her on the other side whilst Rindi sat upfront beside the chauffeur.

The sun was shining as they crossed Putney Bridge. The blades of a rowing eight cut through the calm waters of the Thames. Six swans, necks stretched forward, flew low above them as if in salute. The beat of their great white wings slowing as they landed on the sparkling water like a squadron of flying boats.

They turned west into Upper Richmond Road then past Barnes Common and East Sheen. A mile further on they left the highway to travel south, and after a few minutes turned into the entrance of a drive. Surmounted on the pillars of the wide gateway was a pair of stone griffins, symbolic of the Anglo-Indian name for a newly arrived European in India. Sir Julian's father had, with some humility, bought them to remind him of his early days with the Indian Civil Service. Some fifty yards from the gateway, the gravel drive took a gentle bend through a short avenue of yew trees which opened up to reveal a beautiful red brick Tudor country house with mullioned windows and tall brick chimneys. It seemed a fitting residence for the tall, distinguished-looking man who emerged through the front doorway and raised his hand in greeting. There was nothing stilted about the reception; the families were obviously old friends with a deep mutual regard. Sir Julian's manner was neither deprecating nor patronizing. He looked much younger than Adam had anticipated and was certainly still in his early fifties.

Nina was the first to enter the house, with Jardeeson and Sir Julian in leisurely pursuit, discussing what sounded like a legal point. Rindi and Adam followed them into a spacious hall panelled in oak, mellowed over four centuries with well-worn quarry tiles on the floor. It might have been gloomy were it not for the generous long windows each side of the front door, and another at the top of a wide staircase.

Nina responded to a woman's voice, just discernible above the conversation of the two men in front of them.

'Bridget, we've not seen you since Ascot last year, how have you been?' and then turning she said, 'You haven't met Rindi's school friend Adam Cullworthy.'

As Adam took her proffered hand, she seemed distracted, observing Adam's face with a look of recognition as if she had met him before. 'Of course, yes, how do you do, Adam, please come in.'

She had the authoritative manner of the wife of a *Burra sahib* but her broad smile was unexpected and disarming.

At that moment there was a clatter of shoes on the oak stairs and the sound of excited female voices. Two girls appeared nearly tripping over the last few stairs and ran straight over to Nina embracing her in turn.

'Mrs. Debrahm! It's ages since we've seen you, and Mr. Debrahm.' Jardeeson, bent down, to receive a similar welcome.

They had each taken one of Rindi's arms and were propelling him out of the hall. The taller of the girls then stopped and turned around.

'We're being very rude; we have another guest. Please introduce us, Rindi.'

'Adam, this is Pauline.' She shook his hand whilst still holding on to Rindi with the other arm. 'And this is Tina.' This time there was no hand, only a coy smile and a shy tilt of the head.

'Come on through with us,' said Pauline. 'We want to show Rindi our new ping pong table.'

Lady Westbury looked at Adam, then said with a tone of despair, 'Those girls! Lunch in half an hour' she called out to the disappearing trio.

'Adam, you should have a look round the house' said Jardeeson. 'Sir Julian has a marvellous collection of military prints which I am sure he will be pleased to show you.' Sir Julian nodded approvingly.

'Yes, I would like that', said Adam suppressing his desire to go and play table tennis with Rindi and the girls.

Sir Julian led Adam up the main staircase. The tour took in many interesting things including a rare collection of stamps, two model galleons and a regiment of lead soldiers which Adam admired enthusiastically.

'If you are interested in soldiers you had better come and see the prints in my study,' he said.

Sir Julian's study was on the first floor and on one of the walls were six fine prints of scenes from the Battle of Waterloo. 'Wellington won his spurs in India you know. He was nearly killed several times. It's amazing he made it back at all really. Have you ever thought about joining the army?'

This was a surprisingly direct question, and slightly unexpected, coming from a senior lawyer. 'Yes,' Adam said. 'I rather hope to join my father's regiment after I leave school.'

'Good idea', he said as if Adam had given him the correct answer. Then, changing the subject rather abruptly, he said, 'I think Rindi has told you a bit about his family. He clearly trusts and respects you.'

'I would like to think so, Sir.'

'Well, I am an old friend of his father's and a trustee of the Kushnapur estate.' He paused and Adam wondered if he needed to comment. 'This largely concerns their legal and financial matters,' the judge continued, leaning back in his chair.

'In due course Rindi will need to assume more responsibility.

You may have gathered the Debrahms are complete anglophiles and like there to be an English trustee to serve each generation. Rindi has indicated that he thinks you would be ideal. Of course you will need to visit Kushnapur at some stage to see what the responsibilities entail.'

'I'm not sure how well qualified I am for such a role,' Adam replied, a little surprised by the rather serious direction the conversation had taken, 'but I would be happy to assist Rindi and his family in any way...'

The last few words were lost as Tina came through the open door, calling excitedly: 'Adam! Papa! There you are. Mummy's been waiting simply ages. You said you'd show the Debrahms your orchids.'

'Oh, yes, you're quite right I'll come straight away.' Then turning to Adam he said, 'Perhaps we can finish this conversation later.'

Sitting between the two girls at lunch Adam had the opportunity to get to know them a little better. Pauline, the older sister, had long dark brunette hair and penetrating sky-blue eyes. Her earlier skittish behaviour belied the serious side of her nature.

Tina at sixteen had quite different looks. She was fair-haired, with darker blue eyes and a faultless alabaster complexion with pinched pink cheeks. She wore a knee-length, blue cotton dress and with her long legs silhouetted against the low angle of the spring sunshine she was a becoming sight. Her spontaneous and infectious laugh prevented anything from being taken too seriously.

After lunch Tina said, 'What should we do now? We could go for a walk in the park and see if there are any deer around.'

'What about this famous croquet pitch?' Adam suggested.

'Good idea', said Rindi. 'Pauline and I will take on you and Tina.'

It proved to be an uneven contest as Rindi was clearly an old hand at the game. The girls decided it was more fun jogging Rindi's arm in an attempt to disrupt his play. His revenge was to wrap Pauline's skirt round her legs, tumbling them all in the process into a youthful carefree heap of laughing bodies. Tina's sweet-smelling hair lay across Adam's face and he didn't care about the discomfort of the buttons on her dress pressing into his ribs.

When the time came for them to leave Adam was clearly smitten and wondered how he might contrive to see Tina again. He never did finish his conversation with Sir Julian but was curious as to why Rindi had not mentioned anything to him about a possible future role in the Debrahm family's affairs.

CHAPTER THREE

Fletching, Sussex, April 1933.

Adam conspired with his mother and Rindi to invite Pauline and Tina down to Sussex for the weekend towards the end of the Easter holiday. Mrs Cullworthy had written to Lady Westbury inviting the girls to stay, tactfully mentioning that her older daughter Daphne would be around to keep an eye on them.

Rindi and the two girls arrived on the Friday. Adam's father had generously offered them the use of his Lanchester on condition that only Daphne drove it. Sue, much to her annoyance, had been dispatched to stay with a school friend so there was room enough for five in the car. It was a glorious afternoon and they drove up to Ashdown Forest for a long ramble in the woods recently carpeted with bluebells as far as the eye could see. Adam noticed that Rindi never held Pauline's hand and that their relationship seemed more like brother and sister whilst by contrast Adam took every opportunity to hold Tina's hand or wrap an arm round her.

On the way home Adam sat in the back with Tina. He flicked the travelling rug across her knees and moved in closer. 'Home, James,' He said jokingly, 'and please *do* spare the horses. There's plenty of time.'

'Plenty of time for what?' said Pauline, laughing mischievously. Taking a cue from her sister Tina whispered in Adam's ear, 'plenty of time for this,' and she kissed him on the cheek. Her hands slipped round his shoulders. They slid back on the seat and he brushed her ear with his lips, and then buried his face into her neck, blissfully breathing in the fragrance of her skin. Tina pressed her lips firmly yet softly against his. Then, as they arrived back at the house she broke away, tightly squeezed his hand and hopped out of the car. Adam was in love and in a glow of euphoria and happiness, had little doubt that it was requited.

Sue returned in time for lunch on the Sunday and it was very apparent that she was infatuated with Rindi.

'Is Pauline your girlfriend?' she asked very directly

'We are good friends,' he replied

This seemed to satisfy her curiosity. She adjusted the broad pink Alice band holding her hair back from her pretty face.

'Rindi, you did say I could come and ride your elephant one day.'

'I did, didn't I? Well, all you have to do is get yourself out to India.'

'Will Pauline be there?'

'You all have an open invitation to Kushnapur,' Rindi replied with a twinkle in his eye which Adam knew was a suppressed urge to laugh. Sue seemed disappointed that her invitation was not exclusive.

'I am not sure she would be brave enough to go on an elephant,' Sue opined.

'You're quite right' said Pauline also trying not to laugh at the very earnest comments of this twelve year old.

'Susie, can you leave Rindi alone?' Daphne pleaded.

'Well I am definitely coming to India. As soon as I leave school,' Sue responded and left the room.

After lunch Daphne and Adam took Rindi and the girls to the station. As the train moved slowly down the platform Tina leant out of the window, waving goodbye to Adam until it finally disappeared under the bridge and she was gone. Almost as soon as she was out of sight Adam was wondering how he might manage to see her again.

The start of the summer term always brought with it the excitement of the new cricket season mixed with the apprehension of looming year-end exams.

This serious side of life was relieved by a letter from Tina, ending with, "*Heaps of love*". Adam had hoped to see "darling" written somewhere, but it was sufficiently encouraging for him to think of her now as his girlfriend. When writing back it was the fear of the letter being seen by her mother that restrained him from any overt declaration of affection.

Adam's reserve may have acted to his advantage, because the contents of Tina's next two letters were much more enthusiastic. She then wrote suggesting that they meet in Salisbury on the Sunday of her short half-term.

Adam should have asked her parents' permission but Pauline had volunteered to be a chaperone.

'Don't worry, Adam,' Pauline said on arrival, 'I've got a good book so if you and Tina want to explore the countryside, that's fine by me.'

They left Pauline in cathedral close and took a bus out to Alderbury.

They got off outside the village and walked as far as a small signpost that read, *Public Footpath to Avon Valley.*

'Let's explore this way,' Adam said.

She stood on the first cross-plank of the style, swung her leg over the top bar and just sat there. Her summer dress in pale yellow had drawn up, revealing long elegant legs, but she did not move on.

'Now you'll have to carry me over.'

The request was a challenge, but she was already halfway across and Adam slipped one arm under her legs and the other round her waist. Her arms came tightly round his neck and held his face against her. She was not wearing a brassiere, and had only a shaped petticoat to cradle her roundness. Adam released his hold, and as Tina slipped down on the far side of the style, she turned to offer inviting lips and he responded willingly. Only when he was about to over-balance did their embrace end.

Cows were grazing in the first meadow they walked through. In the second field, long lines of cut hay stretched out, obscuring the footpath, and they flicked the golden grass as they wandered away from the path to where the field sloped down to a stream. Adam gathered armfuls of hay and then removed his linen jacket and lay it over the hay.

'Your country seat, my lady.'

'Thank you, Sir Galahad.' Tina sat down, then lay back, drawing up her dress and petticoat to let the sun reach her thighs. Adam dropped down beside her and they kissed tenderly and he stroked her hair, damp with perspiration where it left the temples. He caressed one leg then the other, the fine golden hairs on the lower part of her legs glistened in the afternoon sun. Her eyes were closed and her deep gentle breathing conveyed her pleasure with his attentions. Now lying very close to her, Adam realised his state of arousal must have been obvious to Tina as well. He could feel the smoothness of her skin under his caress and his hand followed the outer line of her leg, intent upon reaching the lace on her knickers. Then he seemed lost and was fumbling, not knowing where to search. The soft dip into her waist and the downy triangle which brushed against the inside of his arm confirmed his fast forming realisation. Under her petticoat, Tina was quite naked. He moved his hand away, not wishing to take advantage of her.

Adam moved over on top of Tina, his leg falling between hers; in retrieving his hand, he had lifted her dress even further. Still kissing, he felt the tip of her tongue dart in and out of his mouth whilst her hand held his neck. They were both breathing heavily, oblivious to everything except themselves. A ripple ran through Adam, causing an exquisite sensation. Tina's gentle rocking beneath him became more urgent, and he felt the delicious taste of her tongue again and her fingers digging into his shoulder. Clinging tightly against him she murmured with pleasure. They lay locked in an embrace whilst their breathing slowly returned to normal.

When Adam finally lifted his head and slid his leg away, Tina still had her eyes closed. She was bare up to her navel. For a moment Adam admired her wonderful contours and then gently pulled her dress back down to cover her.

Tina sat up and shielded her eyes from the glare of the sun.

'What time is it?' she asked as Adam glanced at his watch.

Perhaps because it was Sunday, there were no labourers in the fields. The only sounds were the voices of children in the distance, the low chatter of the stream tumbling over stones and the buzz of insects. To be in love on a perfect English summer's day, what else could they wish for? How could Adam hold on to this moment of blissful contentment? This was a memory that would sustain him through some of his darkest hours.

They hardly spoke on their way back to Salisbury; it was enough just to hold hands and exchange meaningful glances.

Pauline greeted them with a knowing look and said, 'Not wishing to hurry you love birds but we'd better get a move on if we are going to catch our train.'

He saw them off on their train back to London and as Adam waited for his train to Bristol his euphoria became tempered with a feeling of vulnerability. His mind filled with conflicting thoughts. Why, he wondered, had she not worn any underwear? He was sure that he had glimpsed the lace edge of her knickers when they had crossed the style. Was this the innocent act of a young girl on a very hot summer's day? Or had she planned their amorous encounter? And even if she had, why should he care? She had become so important to him that he felt he should be master of her innocence but he began to realise that she was the one in control. When would he see her again? How would their feelings translate into the letters that would follow? For the moment he could still taste her and smell her and just the thought of her made him feel surrounded in a mellow blissfulness.

That summer term passed in a haze of youthful contentment. Tina and Adam wrote to each other from time to time. His letters became ever more imaginative and, although he didn't want to admit it, hers became increasingly matter of fact. Rindi and Adam were the stars of the 1st XI cricket team which gave them privileges and a degree of freedom to indulge in such illicit pleasures as drinking bottles of beer and smoking Turkish cigarettes down by the lake. This was to be their last summer together at Rockton. Rindi would be going up to Oxford in the autumn and if Adam succeeded in passing his army entrance exam he would be joining the officer training course at Sandhurst in the New Year. Little did they appreciate how quickly their cocooned lives would change and become embroiled in the mounting turmoil of the world outside. But for the moment they occupied their thoughts with such weighty matters as who would win the house cricket cup.

December 1933. Fletching, Sussex.

For Adam the autumn term had been a demanding one. There was the normal pressure of the School Certificate and then, of greater importance for his intended career, preparation for his Army Entrance exams.

His housemaster 'Banger' Barnes, so named because his family were famous for producing rather fine sausages, had served in the war and was well placed to prepare Adam for what the army expected of its officer recruits.

'Well done, Cullworthy, you deserve to do well in the exams. But you should be aware that having only just finished shedding the wartime officers they are only looking for the cream in peacetime.'

Confident that he had done his best in the exams Adam headed home for Christmas. The family all descended from different parts and everyone had their allocated tasks. Adam was responsible for choosing and cutting the right size and best shaped tree for the hallway. Sue would always be in charge of decorating it although she had to sit on Adam's shoulders to position the star on top and the lighting of the candles was left to Daphne.

'I don't know why I can't light the candles? 'Sue protested.

'Maybe next year' her mother replied.

'You always say that.'

As they had all been away from each other for months there were remarkably few disputes. There was a warm familiarity about their mother's preparations which meant that everyone was made to feel special.

'Isn't Rindi coming for Christmas mother? Sue asked.

'No, but he is coming down on Boxing Day so you will need to be on your best behaviour. No more talk of elephants please.

And no more interrogation about his love life. I want to see some lady-like behaviour.'

Sue scowled and went back to hanging baubles on the tree.

Rindi had been to India and back and also completed his first term at Oxford since Adam had last seen him. He couldn't wait to catch up on all his news. Rindi had told Adam rather insistently not to bother with picking him up from the station. 'Don't worry, old boy, I'll get there under my own steam. I should be with you well before lunch.'

At nine o'clock the front doorbell rang and Sue scrambled out of the dining room into the hall only to find that it was Bert the postman with a special delivery. Adam had followed her.

'It's only boring old Bert,' said Sue.

'Mornin, Adam, I reckon I got a special one 'ere for yer.' He blew on his fingers before dipping into the deep bag. 'I reckon us might get snow tonight.' He said looking at the sky. He handed Adam a formal looking buff envelope addressed to him with O.H.M.S. on the top in large letters. Adam hastily ripped it open.

'Can't be good news, surely? Usually no one wants those 'Majesty Service letters.'

'Well, Bert its actually wonderful news. I've passed my exams and been accepted for the Army.'

He shook his head. 'I can't understand how a bloke could actually *volunteer* for a job like that. Course if you can get sent to a place like Armiens.'

Adam cut off, not wishing to hear details of Bert's amorous exploits in the brothels of the Somme.

'Thank you, Bert.' and giving him half a crown for his trouble he wished him a good day.

Adam watched him weave his way unsteadily up the drive on his bicycle. Then from the direction of the road there came the growl of an engine followed by the steady crunch of wheels on the gravel drive.

Emerging from behind the clipped box hedge was a cream coloured sports car. At the wheel, wearing a tweed cap and goggles and heavily wrapped up in a purple and cream silk scarf was Rindi. Bert stopped and gazed in amazement as much at the spectacle of Rindi as of the car itself.

He came to a halt in front of the house and Adam walked over to greet him.

'So this is what you call arriving under your own steam, you dark horse!'

'It's a Morgan Aero. What do you think?'

'I think it's magnificent but you must be frozen. Have you driven all the way from London?'

'No, only from Haywards Heath and don't get too excited it's only on loan for two days.'

'Well, come inside and warm up'

Rindi noticed the envelope in Adam's hand.

'So what's your news? Rindi said, pointing to the envelope. 'Anything I should know about?'

The rest of the Cullworthy family had gathered in the hall to greet Rindi.

'Well, you should all know that I have passed my army exams.'

'Bravo, Adam' said his father. 'Well done, darling' his mother added and gave him a congratulatory hug.

'Now, Rindi let's get you something to drink and come and sit by the fire.'

Sue hopped nervously from one leg to the other until Rindi took notice of her. 'Hello young lady. Do I get a hug?' No second invitation needed she shot over and threw her arms round him.'

'Susie,' her mother said in a cautionary tone. 'What did I say?'

'I'm not allowed to ask you about elephants but maybe you could take me for a drive in your new car?'

'I am sure I can, provided your parents agree, and anyone else who fancies a spin for that matter. It will have to be one at a time though because there are only two seats' Sue looked delighted at this prospect but fearing that her mother would not approve she gave her a silent pleading look.

'Well, I am sure Rindi is a very sensible driver so maybe this afternoon. Now come on I want you and Daphne to help with the lunch and I am sure Adam and Rindi have a lot to catch up on.'

Adam poured Rindi a glass of Madeira and they settled down in front of the drawing-room fire.

'So I suppose you'll be off to Sandhurst at the end of the summer?'

'Yes, I am really looking forward to it. Although the first few weeks will be hell, I'm told.'

'Nothing you can't cope with I'm sure.'

'What about you? How is Balliol?'

'Marvellous, in fact the whole of Oxford is wonderful. One can feel centuries of history all around. It's a great privilege for me, an Indian, to be amongst the British elite.'

'Now you're exaggerating. You are heir to a grand title and an estate probably larger than one of the Home Counties. How much more elite can you get?'

'You only think that because you and I have been doing exactly the same things for several years. I have an English accent, and we have many interests in common. When you come to India, you'll realize the differences between our two cultures.'

'Surely your Oxford acquaintances treat you as one of their own'

'You'd be surprised. Many of them will join the Indian Civil Service and they will then consider themselves superior to even the most revered maharajah.'

'The Indian Civil Service doesn't sound very important.'

'You're wrong there. For a start the entrance exams are fiendishly difficult and if these chaps get through that and become part of the Raj system and they have to abide by rules that demand a certain detachment. Bear in mind that there are only twelve hundred of these British civil servants who rule the whole of India. You will understand this better when you come and see for yourself.'

'And that can't be soon enough for me. You and Jardeeson and Nina have already made me feel I know quite a lot about India and your family.'

'That might be misleading. We are not typical Indians. Jardeeson was born and educated here and Nina has lived in England for most of her life. Some say they are more English than the English.'

'What do you think I will find most different about India?'

'You may think that English society is complicated but the social divisions in India are far wider, much more numerous and generally unfathomable to Europeans. Race, religion and caste divide society and that is before you even consider education and wealth.'

The more Rindi spoke about his home country the more fascinated Adam became and also frustrated that he couldn't start this new adventure immediately.

'And by the way my parents have written to say that they would like you to come and stay with them in India.'

'I would love to. That reminds me' said Adam 'I had a rather curious conversation with Sir Julian when we went to lunch with the Westburys.'

'Yes, I can guess what that was about.'

'Well, I didn't think I was very qualified to be a trustee and couldn't really see how I could be of much assistance to your family'

'I am sure you will be and in more ways than you know. But it will become more apparent when you come to Kushnapur.'

'So do you have to go back tomorrow?'

'I am afraid so. Apart from needing to return the Morgan I have a mountain of reading to do before I go back to Oxford. But why don't you come and stay at Queen's Gate Gardens next week? Nina has said you are always welcome.'

'I would love to see them again.'

'Well, that's fixed then. I still haven't told you about the boat trip back.'

'No, you haven't. Was it eventful?'

'Yes, you could say that, but I'll tell you all about it in London.'

CHAPTER FOUR

North-Eastern India, September 1933.

The steady rain of the mid-monsoon season was falling as Rindi walked through the tall entrance arch to Saharanpur station, in the early hours of the morning. What a relief to feel the rain after the long hot and humid six-hour journey by road from Kushnapur. A wave of tiredness came over him as he looked up at the station clock. One o'clock in the morning. Plenty of time for an early breakfast at Spencers, the ubiquitous and efficient railway restaurant service.

An hour later, back on the platform Rindi found his bearer Gulap, waiting to direct three coolie porters who stood next to his trunks like guardians of a treasure. Two coolies would have been ample. Typically, in the conditions of the oversupply of labour, three accorded more prestige, especially to the bearer himself.

Two blasts of a distant train's whistle cut through the night air, above the hubbub of anticipation that was fast developing on the platform. The express had now cleared the tiny Pickhani Station up the line, and was on the straight less than two miles from the junction.

At precisely 2.32am the Frontier Mail steamed into the station. Outside his office, the Anglo-Indian station foreman had appeared and flicked open the cover of his official timepiece. As the hissing locomotive drew level he nodded to the driver with an air of satisfaction, and then snapped the watch-cover closed.

Gulap had already taken Rindi's ticket and was racing up the platform to the front of the train to find the reserved compartment number. It had, after all, been useful to bring Gulap with him. For Gulap this journey also meant the opportunity to visit his aging aunt in Delhi before returning to Kushnapur.

As Rindi waited in his compartment he watched the last of the passengers hurriedly boarding. One of them was a young English gentleman dressed in a cream-coloured linen suit and a well-worn panama hat. He reminded Rindi of Adam and those final heady summer days at Rockton. Rindi had told his family so much about Adam and for many different reasons they were keen to meet him. How different their summer vacations would have been. He wondered whether Adam and Tina had seen each other again. He knew that Adam was besotted with her and he could hardly blame him for that, she was rapidly becoming a very alluring young woman.

By the time the train slowly pulled out, the rain was spattering on the windows. Rindi knew from experience not to waste sleeping time. In less than four hours, he would be awoken in Delhi for the two-hour breakfast and marshalling stop, when bedding would be collected. But his mind was preoccupied by thoughts of his own romantic situation. By sending him to school in England his parents had encouraged him to become anglicised but they also made it clear that he would be expected to marry a high caste Indian one day and someone of their choosing. The subject of marriage had been raised with him on this visit home and three possible future brides had been suggested, none of whom he was acquainted with.

He had enjoyed the admiration of several English girls but he wondered whether he wasn't just a novelty for them. Perhaps the cultural divide was too great and marriage to a European would not survive the test of time. He took comfort in the knowledge that for the next three years he would be able to follow his heart. With this agreeable thought in mind, sleep finally overtook him.

Nine hundred miles away to the south east, in Calcutta, Lady Hawkswood and her twenty-one-year old daughter Virginia were also starting their journey to Bombay where they would board the SS Strathclyde back to England.

They had spent the last three months at their elegant summer residence in the hills in Simla. Built on two terraced levels, on the road to Jakoo Hill, the house had a commanding view of the town to the east. To the south, one could see for miles down the valley. The prestige that Sir Arthur Hawkswood, her late husband, had sought when he had built the place three years earlier had only been partially achieved. Lady Hawkswood had been quite satisfied with her position and her husband's achievements. Sir Arthur had not. For Virginia, this period in the hills had been blessed with only rare snatches of enjoyment. Her mother was suffering from the trauma of losing her husband so suddenly. Nine months earlier, at the age of fifty-eight, and nearing the peak of his career, he had been killed in a shooting accident during a tiger hunt.

Beyond Kushnapur

Sir Arthur's family connections with India stretched back to 1840, when the aristocratic forebear of his great grandmother had served the Governor of Bengal. It was at a time when few European women lived in India and an Indian wife or mistress for an English official was tacitly accepted without censure. Secrecy was not demanded, provided that the liaison was discreetly conducted. These unions were often with Indian women of high caste, and it was one such union that produced Emily, Sir Arthur's great-grandmother. It was unfortunate for the progeny of mixed marriages that the codes of acceptance changed dramatically over the following half-century. With the opening of the Suez Canal, and halving of the sailing time to Europe, it became the custom for British Officers serving in India to seek their brides from England. Thereafter, with a few notable exceptions, only those in the lower social strata would take an Indian or Eurasian wife or mistress.

The result of this was that high-caste Indian women themselves now shunned such liaisons. That the early mixed unions of high breeding and beauty had produced some remarkably handsome offspring was beyond doubt. Those with these good looks, like Emily, integrated easily into the middle-class English society of mid-nineteenth century India. And, whilst European women were still unavailable, a good marriage with an English junior official was not too difficult to achieve. For the rest, a new racial segment of life in India came into being, the *Eurasians,* who later became known as Anglo-Indians.

By the time Arthur Hawkswood was born, only the most knowledgeable in such matters would have suspected his distant Indian ancestry. He had been born and brought up in England and given a good education at Rugby school and Imperial College, in London. He then joined the London, Midland and Scottish Railway and five years later was offered an executive administrator's appointment with the Indian Railways. Though handsome of feature, he was short and stocky in stature and displayed a steely determination early in life. He enjoyed considerable success in his career, and by the time he was thirty-five he was sufficiently well established to consider marriage. During a long leave in England he met Elizabeth Kenton, the youngest daughter of the Bishop of Tonbridge. They were married three months later and spent their honeymoon on board ship returning to India. A year later, in Simla, Elizabeth gave birth to their daughter Virginia.

Arthur had been knighted at the age of fifty-three. Two years later, whilst still remaining a non-executive director of the Railways

Control Board, he decided to devote himself to politics which, he believed, offered a better avenue to further his ambitions. This decision had been taken partly as the result of a conversation overheard at a reception in Delhi. A senior member of the Viceroy's staff had referred to him as a box-wallah. Whilst Sir Arthur had not passed through the ranks of the Indian Civil Service he was not a box-wallah, a derogatory term for people engaged in trade. He became further disillusioned when he discovered that he had been overlooked for a provincial governorship.

Thwarted ambition had turned to bitterness and he found himself resenting the impenetrable snobbery of the British establishment. He decided a different strategy was needed. He discreetly conspired with the Indian *Swaraj* supporters who were intent on ridding India of their British rulers. He had assumed, mistakenly, that Rindi's father, Narendra, was one such Indian. Sir Arthur contrived to get himself invited on a tiger *shikar* arranged at the Debrahm estate in Kushnapur. Lady Hawkswood knew nothing of his plans and intrigues, treating the visit to Rindi's parents at Kushnapur as a purely social occasion. When it ended in tragedy, she was devastated.

Lady Hawkswood and Virginia were now returning to England to celebrate Virginia's official engagement to Simon, Viscount Duffell, the twenty-eight year old son and heir to the Earl of Chalvington. For the past week they had been staying at Government House in Calcutta. The invitation had been issued as a gesture of condolence by the Governor of Bengal, following a memorial service for Sir Arthur in St. Paul's Cathedral, Calcutta. With the dank stifling heat of that city in August, and the torrential rain, it was not the best time of the year to experience the Governor's hospitality. The reversion to sleeping under mosquito nets, from which the ladies had been free whilst living in the hills, was particularly irksome.

The governor's wife had wisely elected to remain at their summer lodge in the Darjeeling hills. The governor had himself returned there the day after the memorial service. Lady Hawkswood also wished to be away, as soon as possible, from the city reputed to be 'the most revolting in Asia'.

Formalities for the official departure of Lady Hawkswood and her daughter had been placed in the hands of the governor's senior A.D.C., Captain Beardmore of the Grenadier Guards. In this instance, the duty proved to be more formal than functional. The Indian Railways had claimed their right to take charge of the arrangements. They wished to accord the widow of their late director all the privileges that Sir Arthur had enjoyed before he died.

Virginia had not felt her father's death to the same degree as her mother. She had spent most of her recent life in England and even when in India had seen little of him. They had never been close. She found his tenacious ambition slightly embarrassing. Her last memory of him was the discussion they had had shortly before his death. Sir Arthur had received a letter from Simon Duffell, requesting permission to marry his daughter. Sir Arthur looked upon it only as a courteous formality to ask for Virginia's agreement. That she did not immediately consent came as a shock to him. He had greatly favoured the match, concluding that even if he was to be denied a peerage himself, at least his future grandson could have one.

Although Virginia had initially agreed to Simon's marriage proposal, subsequent events had made her think twice about whether this was the right course for her.

The first of these was at Viceregal Lodge, where His Excellency the Viceroy had held a formal banquet. Included in the guest list were four Indian princes. Since few of the Indian guests would bring their wives, additional unattached ladies who could, like Virginia, accompany their parents, were also invited. An invitation from the Viceroy was always treated as a royal command, and despite her reservations that it might be a starchy affair Virginia was duty-bound to attend.

The Army officers were immaculate in their red and blue uniforms and the ladies and civilians wore formal evening dress. The princes looked splendid in their silk *achkans*, over-draped with their orders and decorations. Their *puggarees* wound in a variety of styles were embellished with jewels. It was a glittering gathering.

On her right at dinner sat an English cavalry major, the very elite of the Indian Army. He might have developed into an amusing dinner companion had the order of precedence, so rigidly adhered to in India, not overridden the normal convention that avoids placing a woman opposite her husband at dinner. Instead, whenever the major looked like engaging Virginia in an interesting anecdote, his wife eyed him disapprovingly from across the table.

Before dinner Virginia had spotted a tall Indian of about her own age who surpassed the elegance of all the other guests. She had been struck by his handsome, aristocratic looks. As fortune would have it the same order of precedence in which the guests took their places had positioned him beside her on the other side. His dark eyes showed glints of indigo as they caught the sparkle from the chandeliers. His full black moustache was brushed down at the sides, and no hair showed beneath his *puggaree*. Her fears that his rather arrogant bearing might prove him difficult to converse with were dispelled by the smooth charm with which he introduced himself.

'Wantilla Mahavir Debrahm, delighted to make your acquaintance.'

Virginia felt a frisson of excitement and arousal that she had not experienced before. Emotions which had lain dormant in her began to stir. She was entranced.

In the weeks that followed the banquet, life in Simla, which had previously proved tedious and socially repetitive, developed new meaning for Virginia. She and Wantilla conducted a discreet correspondence and with the aid of his bearer, they sent each other amorous notes that were then carefully destroyed.

It was whilst Virginia was in this state of mind that another encounter occurred that would sow further seeds of doubt in her mind. She was walking in the Mall in Simla, with her *ayah* discreetly following, when she met Mrs. Felicity Gilbert, an older woman to whom she had been introduced at her parents' house.

Having left behind in England the few friends she had made at school Virginia led a lonely existence with often only her mother to share her thoughts with. This made her receptive to flattery and attention from the likes of Wantilla and also made her more gullible and vulnerable. She was on the whole a poor judge of peoples' true intentions.

Mrs. Gilbert was married to a captain in Probyn's Horse, and she had discovered early in her eight-year marriage that her husband paid far more attention to his regiment and his horses than to her needs. With a husband so inattentive and regularly absent, Mrs Gilbert had a great deal of spare time to seek amusement and pleasure.

Her favourite activity was to take part in plays put on by the Simla Amateur Dramatic Society. These productions at the small Gaiety Theatre were of a high standard, and Felicity Gilbert was no mean actress. When she took the lead in plays like 'Love in a Mist', her interpretation of amorous roles would ensure full houses. Among the audience there was sure to be a scattering of lonely subalterns on leave at the hill station, who would later queue up at the stage door with bouquets and lunch invitations. The post-prandial encounter that followed these leisurely repasts would sometimes involve a discreetly shared couch where appetites whetted by stage performances could be acted out to their climax.

Mrs Gilbert also relished the dissemination of scandal. Whilst she was quite capable of ingenious embellishment of a simple indiscretion, she was careful to convey that nothing originated from herself. 'My dear, wild horses wouldn't drag from me the name of the person who told me. I'm only telling you because I know it will go no further.'

She liked to cultivate the confidence of young unmarried or recently married women as they were not only more receptive to her gossip but more effective at spreading the word when it suited her purpose. She had arranged to meet Virginia for coffee at Davico's a much favoured restaurant on the Mall in Simla.

'So Virginia how are you finding life in Simla?'

'Well Mrs Gilbert.'

'Felicity please.'

'Well Felicity,' she said slightly hesitantly, 'to be honest I find the social scene a bit of a challenge.'

'Let me speculate my dear. You find the women a bit frosty and the men a bit over friendly.'

Virginia looked surprised at the acute perception of this comment.

'How did you guess?'

'You're just too pretty my dear. You see the 'fishing fleet' that come out to find a husband tend to be the ones that are unsuccessful in finding a catch in Engand. Hence they find you a threat, even the married ones. For the same reason the men are all dying to win your favour.'

'So what is the solution?'

'You need to get engaged as quickly as possible, even if you have no intention of marrying the man.'

'I don't think that's very honourable.'

'Maybe not, but until you do you will find youself excluded from many social gatherings by the hostesses and pursued relentlessly by all the randy men in the district.' Virginia was shocked by this assessment mainly because it had more than a ring of truth to it.

'You must understand Virginia, dear, that being a wife in India is not the same as being a wife in England. We have to spend many lonely months each year in the hill-stations, away from our beloved husbands. Without physical affection, our bodies would shrink into barren shells, and we'd become unattractive to our spouses. Those of us that wish to maintain our libido must covertly indulge in amorous affairs'.

As she listened, Virginia's mind vacillated between disgust and fascination. Her imagined interpretation of amorous affairs could well have limited itself to a kiss on the cheek or caress of the neck by Wantilla, had not Mrs. Gilbert delivered her 'coup de grace'.

'There is one vital rule,' she said. 'Make sure that you only ever fall pregnant by your husband.'

The look of incredulity on Virginia's face was ample reward for Mrs. Gilbert.

The bewildered Virginia had still not resolved her dilemma when her father had spoken to her about the marriage proposal. When, soon after this he had been killed, without having received her affirmation, she had been filled with remorse. She had immediately written to Simon saying that her father had verbally given his consent to the marriage. Partly as an act of respect for his future mother-in-law and partly to reaffirm his feelings for Virginia, Simon had taken leave from the Army and come to India.

Virginia's decision to accept Simon's proposal had been motivated more by a sense of duty, and what Felicity Gilbert had said, than by any strong affection for Simon. As she sat beside her mother in the Governor's Daimler, her misgivings pervaded. But it was certainly not the time to convey these doubts, least of all to her mother. Her melancholy state had been tempered by the message she had received from Wantilla that he would also be sailing on the SS Strathclyde.

The governor's limousine drew up in front of Howrah Station, Calcutta and Lady Hawkswood and Virginia were greeted by the station master, complete with tailcoat and top hat. For him it was a sad duty for a popular lady. In deference to her bereavement, he had arranged that she should travel with the minimum exposure to the general public. The special coach previously reserved for Sir Arthur's personal use, and which by custom he was entitled to attach to almost any train, had been shunted into position. It now stood gleaming red and cream in the afternoon sun at the front of the Imperial Express.

At twenty past four the stationmaster asked Lady Hawkswood's permission for the train to proceed on its twelve hundred mile journey to Bombay.

Wantilla had not mentioned in his message to Virginia that he would also be travelling on the same train. Despite being in a First Class coupé only two coaches away his plot to surprise her was frustrated by the fact that the Hawkswood state coach was not accessible from his part of the train. Furious that his plan had been scuppered, he took his rage out on the unfortunate steward who had delivered the bad news.

'What sort of a bloody ridiculous arrangement is that?'

'My apologies, sir. If you would you like I can inform her Ladyship that you wish to see them at the next stop?'

'No, I bloody well wouldn't.' And fearing the consequences of such an action he said. 'Never mind, it really doesn't matter' then gave the bewildered man a tip and retreated into his cabin. Wantilla would now have to wait until they were on-board the SS Strathclyde to pursue his lascivious intentions.

Although tall and dignified Simon Duffell was rather effete and his father had always feared that he would not be up to producing a son and heir. It was therefore without equivocation that on meeting Virginia, whom the Earl considered to be excellent breeding material, he instructed his son to propose at the earliest opportunity. It was with a sense of triumph, in the knowledge that he would finally have earned his father's approval, that he cabled him from Simla with the happy news that Lady Hawkswood had given her consent to their marriage.

Despite his aristocratic background Duffell was not socially confident. He tended to shy away from major social gatherings unless instructed to attend them by his father. Thus it was that he was sent to represent his father at the Court of Baroda rather than attend Sir Arthur's memorial service. The *Gaekwad* as the Maharajah of Baroda was known, had been at school with the Earl of Chalvington. He was amongst only five princes deemed worthy of a twenty-one gun salute and the celebrations for the marriage of his second daughter were suitably spectacular. Amongst the many events laid on for his guests the Maharajah had organised a tiger *shikar*. Having never been that keen on hunting and even less so after Sir Arthur's death Duffell declined this invitation in favour of watching an exhibition cricket match.

After a week of celebrations it was something of a relief for him to board the Frontier Mail to Bombay. Even though it was one-thirty in the morning Baroda Station was still a sweltering eighty degrees. He undressed by the dim bulkhead light, put on his pyjamas, and eased himself into bed. He wondered where Virginia might be now and how it would be between them when he saw her next. Most of all he felt a sense of relief that at last he was heading home.

In the next coach down, sleeping soundly, was Rindi, who had boarded the same train seven-hundred-and-thirty miles away, twenty-four hours earlier.

The night before the Strathclyde was to sail from Ballard Pier in Bombay, Ali Abdullah, the ship's senior steward, was sitting in the back room of a general store in Hornby Road. The serious nature of his bargaining with the *banian,* a trader, did not concern the shop's hardware. Ali wished to take the shop owner's daughter as his second wife. Agreement now depended upon the provision of a second home for the bride, equal in quality to the dwelling of his first wife. The shop owner remained unconvinced that Ali would be able to deliver on this undertaking. It was therefore agreed that when he returned from his next voyage, he would produce evidence of his ability to purchase rooms of a suitable standard for the trader's daughter.

CHAPTER FIVE

The SS Strathclyde

As Rindi entered the upper starboard lounge, he noticed Lady Hawkswood sitting by the window. She was staring pensively into the distance as if hopeful that a brighter future lay beyond the horizon. As he approached her she turned and greeted him with enthusiasm.

'Good morning, Rindi. What a lovely surprise.'

Rindi was relieved that she seemed pleased to see him. Considering that her husband had died in such unfortunate circumstances whilst staying with his parents in Kushnapur she might well have felt differently.

'Good morning, Lady Hawkswood. I trust you had a good journey from Calcutta?'

'Yes, very comfortable, thank you.'

'I am so sorry about Sir Arthur's tragic death. My parents wrote to me at school and told me what a ghastly accident it was.'

Lady Hawkswood drew a deep breath and turned her head once more to the horizon. Her widow black dress severe against her gaunt neck and pale face.

'How was Sir Arthur's memorial service?' Rindi asked, moving the subject quickly on. 'I am sorry none of the Debrahms were able to be there.'

'It was a lovely service and considering the sweltering heat it was remarkably well attended,' she replied having composed herself once more.

'Is Virginia travelling with you?'

'Yes, she is. You know she's engaged?'

'Yes, I saw the announcement in the 'Times of India', or to be more accurate, mother did. A captain in the 17th/21st Lancers I think?'

'Yes. He's called Simon Duffell.' She paused. 'He's the perfect gentleman. I am sure she will be very comfortable.'

By which Rindi inferred that he was rich and well connected but that this was no love match.

'He's on board as well. In fact we are all travelling back together to celebrate their engagement with his parents, Lord and Lady Chalvington.'

'Have you a date set for the wedding?'

'No, not yet, Virginia seems in no hurry.'

Rindi was not aware until the next morning that his cousin Wantilla was on board, and then only by coincidence when taking the air on the poop deck.

'Ah, Wantilla I hadn't expected to see you on this boat.'

Wantilla looked less than delighted to see his cousin. The last thing he wanted was his activities being reported back to his family.

'Well, all a bit last minute, old boy.'

'So what takes you back to England?'

'Oh this and that,' he replied rather tetchily.

'Business or pleasure?'

'I've been invited to a shoot on a friend's grouse moor if you must know.' This sounded improbable to Rindi. It was a long way to go to shoot grouse and given his reputation for stealing other people's girlfriends it was surprising he had any friends. In fact because of a trip to Brighton with the bursar's daughter Wantilla had had an untimely departure from Harrow.

'So it wouldn't involve a liaison with a woman?'

'None of your bloody business you nosy bastard!' he hissed.

Rindi knew he had come close to the mark.

'Did you know that Lady Hawkswood and Virginia are on board?'

'Oh really? Last I heard was that Virginia had got engaged to some prat in the Lancers. Now if you don't mind I think it's time for my breakfast.'

Wantilla turned and stalked off towards the bow of the ship.

Two levels below this deck, Lady Hawkswood was sipping her early morning cup of Darjeeling tea. The morning sun beamed at a low angle into the cabin. In another hour, when its intensity had increased, it would have passed round towards the stern. Lady Hawkswood appreciated the consideration she had been accorded of being provided with a *stateroom* on the starboard quarter. Port out starboard home, the origin of Posh and one of the privileges Sir Arthur had enjoyed as a director of the shipping line.

The stateroom was luxuriously appointed: the central day-cabin was furnished for comfort with armchairs, tables, and a writing bureau that all appeared to float on a pale blue deep-pile Axminster carpet. The bathroom led off the day-cabin, and on either side were the night-cabins for Lady Hawkswood and Virginia.

Virginia occupied the first days out from Bombay by carefully observing a routine. In the morning she would sit on deck reading until coffee was served at eleven, followed by a stroll on the promenade deck and a chat with some of the ship's officers.

She had received a note from Wantilla confirming he was on board and voicing his frustration at not being able to get access to her coach on the train from Calcutta. She too was disappointed but also relieved that she had not had to manage an illicit encounter within the confines of the train. She was now keen to see him, but they needed to be very discreet.

After lunch, Lady Hawkswood would take a long siesta in her cabin, leaving her refreshed for a two-hour game of bridge after dinner, when Simon Duffell would dutifully partner his future mother-in-law. Virginia would tactfully remain to see a few hands played, and then excuse herself to go and watch table horseracing, or to write letters. She would never be seen with Wantilla so it was only the unfortunate fiancé who had to be watched to ensure his attendance on Virginia was within the bounds of decorum.

From Bombay more than sixteen hundred miles of the Arabian Sea lay ahead before the ship would reach Aden. The heavy monsoons of June, July and early August, were giving way to the more moderate rains that would last until mid-September. Day temperatures were now bearable. The only break in this crossing was a call at the port of Karachi; a bustling dusty mercantile city that held few attractions for visitors, but was an essential pick up point for passengers coming down from Lahore.

For Ali Abdullah this stop provided an important opportunity to visit a locksmith of his acquaintance. On the previous morning, whilst fulfilling his duties as steward to Lady Hawkswood, he had taken a wax impression of the key for her jewellery box, which she had unwisely left open whilst bathing.

The locksmith had produced a duplicate at a cost but with no questions asked. Ali Abdullah tested the key at the first opportunity. It worked perfectly, and his plan was then put into operation. The jewellery box had two tiers. The pieces on the top would seem to be used more frequently because they were not wrapped in tissue paper like the fine brooch on the second tier. He thought there was less chance of this piece being missed and decided he would remove it after dinner on the night before they docked at Aden.

A pale reflection of moonlight flickered up from the sea through the porthole of Virginia's cabin. On the bunk lay a figure stretched out. Wantilla was relaxing, hands behind his head, contemplating the pleasure that lay ahead. It had all been too easy. Virginia had given him her key and after taking an early dinner he had made his way to her cabin, where he awaited her arrival. The following morning they would be docking in Aden. There was no telling what the arrangements would be once they left that port. In any case, the stifling humidity of the three day journey through the Red Sea was not the ideal environment for amorous indulgence. Wantilla intended to make the best use of their last night in the Arabian Sea.

He was quite content to lie and let his lustful thoughts anticipate the sensuous embraces that he hoped for. Wantilla had no false modesty about his masculine appeal to women. Virginia, he was sure, would not be late. So deep in hedonistic thought was he, that above the hum of the ship's engines he did not hear Virginia enter the stateroom, but he did smell her scent.

'Wanty are you there?' She spoke softly as she walked through to her cabin and kicked off her shoes.

'Any problem getting away?' he asked.

'No, but I thought I'd better stay and watch the first rubber,' she replied. 'Have you got my key?'

'Yes, don't worry, I'll go and lock the door.'

He climbed off the bunk, walked through the main cabin, locked the outer door and returned to drop the key on the dressing table.

'There's your key, *bibi*.'

'Hey, I'm not *your woman*,' Virginia protested lightly.

Virginia left the door ajar just in case Lady Hawkswood should return. This would permit conversation without the necessity of her coming into Virginia's cabin.

'Don't you despise yourself for deceiving that fiancé of yours?'

'At first I did but after a few months in Simla I realised that he'd have no physical need of me beyond producing an heir. I could just become a frustrated woman, with unfulfilled needs.'

'And what needs might those be?' Wantilla now stood behind

Virginia, kissing her tenderly on the neck. As he embraced her he slid off one shoulder strap of her evening gown whilst his other hand unzipped the back.

She quickly lifted her hand to hold on to her dress as misgivings arose at how fast things were happening. But her qualms began to dissolve as she felt his hands cupping her breasts and the pressure of his virile body, coaxing her to murmur in acquiescence. In the last few weeks, she had fantasized about them being together, safe from prying eyes or wagging tongues. Now for a few moments she stood bathed in euphoria, oblivious to what might be expected of her as Wantilla's moustache brushed against her cheek and he moved to nibble her earlobe. Strong fingers moved across her bosom caressing the nipples now firm beneath the material of her dress. Virginia felt his strong masculine body against hers and experienced a sensation of excitement that she had never known before. Savouring the moment, as he drew her tighter against him.

With eager anticipation overcoming her token resistance, Wantilla slipped off her dress. His experienced fingers removed her brassiere and he then paused to feast his eyes on the sensuous figure that stood there in the moonlight. 'You really are ravishing, Ginny.'

The last two words were muffled as he kissed her navel and lifted her on to the bunk. He moved his face along her body sending a frisson of pleasure through her. He then slid his hand down until it reached her knickers, where he flicked the waistband.

'I think we can do without these.'

'No, absolutely not.' There was a breathless concern in her voice.

'Come on, you know you're longing to have me.'

Virginia suddenly became anxious that the romantic petting was going beyond where she felt comfortable. A conflict of conscience and desire surged through her mind. Wantilla, however, had no such moral dilemma.

'Well, are they coming off? Or am I going to take them off?'

He slid the knickers down on one side. Virginia's hands instantly went down and pulled them back up. She then moved her hands to cover her breasts.

'You know jolly well what the code is, Wanty. If there's no wedding ring, the knickers stay on.'

'I suppose that's another of Mrs. Gilbert's dictums. Well, we'll have to see about that.'

He moved to kiss her behind the ear whilst one hand slid beneath her ineffectual shielding of herself. Her head now turned to meet his lips and her breathing and warmth of response told him that the first layer of her will to resist had been breached. There was plenty of time to achieve his objective. The sweetest fruit was always the hardest to obtain.

The rattle of a key in the lock of the outer door alerted them both. Virginia's mouth was close to Wantilla's as she whispered.

'Shhh, mother must be coming back for something. She won't stay.'

They heard the outer door open and close. Someone moved quietly across into Lady Hawkswood's cabin and switched on an interior light.

Virginia quite expected her mother to call out, 'Are you asleep darling?' and had prepared to answer sleepily: 'Not quite, mother', or make no reply, to convey that she was asleep. They heard what sounded like a drawer being opened.

'What the hell's she doing?' Wantilla whispered impatiently, his words muffled by Virginia's hand as she gently held it across his mouth. Her left hand gripped his shoulder, signalling him to keep quiet. She hardly dared to breathe and her heart was thumping. She was nonplussed. What was of sufficient importance to cause her mother to leave her beloved game of bridge?

The light in Lady Hawkswood's cabin was switched off and Virginia felt a surge of relief, which was almost immediately overtaken by a fresh anxiety that her mother might still call as she passed her door. A ray of reflected light came through from the passageway as the outer-door was opened once more, but almost instantly it was closed again and the cabin plunged back into darkness. Whoever had opened it had changed their mind about leaving. Something was not quite right. Footsteps could be heard moving quickly back across the carpeted stateroom floor. 'Oh my God,' thought Virginia, she's going to come and speak to me after all. But nothing was said. Instead, the bathroom door was opened and quickly closed.

Rindi was finishing his second cup of coffee in the Reading Room after a late dinner. 'Getting to be a bad habit,' he thought, his head buzzing. He closed his book, *The Aryanization of India* by N.K. Dutt. Rindi had been lucky to discover a copy in the ship's library, as it had long been out of print. He stood up and left the room to continue reading in his cabin.

At the bottom of the companionway leading from the boat-deck, he noticed movement at the far end of the corridor. A figure in white had emerged from a cabin, then hurriedly retreated back inside again. The furtive way that it was done made Rindi suspicious. The *puggaree* indicated that it was an Indian and possibly a steward, but this was very late for him to be attending to his duties.

Keeping his eye on the cabin, he walked along the corridor, and nearing the door, he realised that it was the Hawkswood's stateroom. He hesitated, not wishing to interfere, then remembered that he had seen Lady Hawkswood playing bridge as he passed the card-room. The door was very slightly ajar and there was no light on which made him more suspicious. He pushed the door open so that light from the passage enabled him to survey the room.

'Is anyone there?' he said. There was no response. Ahead of him was a closed door, which, Rindi presumed, led to the bathroom and to his left was a door partly open. To the right was another internal door wide open. Turning on the light he closed the outer cabin door behind him and made straight for the open door on the right. He pushed back the door as far as it would go to see if anyone was hiding there. The whole of the room, even the space beneath the bed, was now open to his view. With the possible exception of the wardrobe, there was no one in the room.

He closed the door and turned to the cabin opposite, the door was latched open with the hook. Rindi flipped up the hook with his left foot and pushed the door open. He stepped inside to the right, keeping his back hard against the wood panelling. He could see a figure with their head bent over the bed leaning against the bunk. He was about to tackle the figure when he became aware of a near-naked female lying on the bunk.

Wantilla was not one to remain passive in such a situation. He had been in too many tight corners, evading many a cuckolded husband. Without hesitation, he kicked viciously towards the groin of this intruder. His foot moved with such force, that had it found its mark it would have done Rindi a severe injury. However, having sensed what was coming Rindi sidestepped the blow which only glanced off his thigh.

Wantilla now flung himself forward and drew up his fists and then realised it was Rindi.

'You bastard! What do you mean by bursting in here?'

'Wantilla? what the hell are you doing in here?'

'I might ask you the same bloody question.' He spat back at him.

Rindi felt a surge of embarrassment. He was in Virginia's cabin and she was there lying on the bed. Whatever the morality of the situation he realized that he should not be there.

'I am so sorry,' he spluttered. 'I thought I saw an intruder come in to your cabin.'

'Yes, well the only intruder is you.' Wantilla responded.

Virginia sat up covering herself with a sheet. She was still wondering where her mother was and why she had not emerged from the bathroom. 'What do you mean by an intruder? I thought it was my mother.'

'No, this was an Indian. And anyway your mother is still upstairs playing bridge.'

As he spoke, he looked at Wantilla. His cousin was not wearing a *puggaree*; he was not the intruder. With a burst of anger Rindi spat out, 'Where is the swine?' He shot back into the stateroom and seeing the bathroom door and the main door now both open, he rushed into the corridor. He looked in both directions but there was no one in sight.

He returned to the cabin to apologise to Virginia. Wantilla seemed quite composed and was running his fingers through his long black hair.

'Who was it? Did you see anyone?'

'No, he got clean away.'

'Well, I don't like it,' Wantilla growled. 'I don't like it at all, I shan't be satisfied till I know who the bastard was.'

'I'd keep quiet about the whole incident if I were you, cousin. I'm not sure how well you'd come out of this.'

'It's bad enough having one's privacy invaded, but when some bugger comes snooping around eavesdropping, that's another matter.'

To Wantilla's suspicious mind, the possibilities assumed a more sinister aspect. He had been blackmailed before.

'Now switch the bloody light off and get the hell out of here.'

Someone was now knocking firmly on the outer stateroom door. Virginia felt her throat go dry as she heard a man's voice calling,

'Virginia, are you there?'

'Oh my God. It's Simon,' she whispered 'What are we going to do? If I don't answer, he'll come in.'

Wantilla reacted instantly to the situation. He gripped Rindi by one shoulder and whispered in his ear.

'I'm going to hide. You go and talk to Duffell and sort this bloody lot out. If you let on that I'm here, you and your father will regret it. Just remember *Khizarpura!*'

With that, Wantilla stepped into the wardrobe and pulled the door closed behind him. He had spoken close to Rindi's ear in a low register, and Virginia had barely heard what was said but the name *Khizarpura* did momentarily flash her mind back to the tiger hunt and her father's death. But her thoughts were too preoccupied with the nightmare of being discovered by her fiancée, to dwell on anything else.

Rindi was disturbed by this malicious threat, but however disinclined he was to protect his cousin he felt it was his duty to try and preserve Virginia's reputation and any prospect of her future marriage.

Simon Duffell, finding the stateroom cabin door ajar and no light on, had entered the cabin. Receiving no response to his call, he strode across to the open door of Virginia's cabin, and finding it dark, felt for the switch and turned on the light. The spectacle of his fiancé on the bed half-naked, with a handsome Indian in a state of disarray standing beside her bunk, made him gasp in disbelief.

'What on earth is going on here?'

In the look of disdain Duffell gave Virginia, Rindi sensed there was little love lost between them. This was betrayal beyond a mere sexual indiscretion; it was about dignity and the Chalvington family honour.

Duffell moved his head from side to side not wanting to take in the scene. 'I'll ask only one question, Virginia,' he managed to say, as his throat went dry. 'Did you plan for him to come here?'

An almost inaudible, 'No,' accompanied Virginia's shake of the head.

Rindi immediately interjected. 'I was neither invited nor did I expect to find Virginia here. It's not what it seems, Duffell.'

'Well, who were you expecting to find?'

'I was following an intruder.'

There was a moment of silence and by the look of contempt he gave Rindi it was obvious that he didn't believe him.

'Well, you haven't heard the last of this.' And with that he turned and walked out slamming the stateroom door behind him.

Rindi shook his head with genuine concern. 'Poor devil, he doesn't deserve it.'

'But he wasn't supposed to know,' murmured Virginia. 'He

should never have found out. I didn't want to hurt him.' She sat cowed and vulnerable. The sheet had slipped off her shoulder revealing her long beautiful back with her lustrous golden brown hair spread across her shoulders. Rindi was transfixed. He had never seen a European woman undressed before.

'Of course he deserved it.' Wantilla emerged from the wardrobe with a smirk on his face. 'If the bloody fool leaves ripe fruit unplucked, what does he expect?'

Rindi and Wantilla judiciously withdrew from the stateroom, leaving Virginia to contemplate her fate.

The following morning

Simon stood beside Lady Hawkswood's breakfast table nervously fingering his tie. 'Good morning, Lady Hawkswood, may I sit down?'

'Oh hello, Simon. Yes, please do.'

'Isn't Virginia coming down to breakfast this morning?'

'No. She decided she would just take *'chota hazri'* in her cabin.'

Simon was quite sure that it was not concern for her figure that had kept Virginia from taking a normal breakfast. If her distress at their situation were anything like his, she would not have slept much the previous night. He was however relieved that she wasn't there.

'Lady Hawkswood, it's very important that I speak to you.'

'Yes, Simon, please do.' She smiled at him, sensing his disquiet.

'No, not here. May we meet in the salon on the promenade deck after breakfast?'

'Yes, if you wish' she replied wondering what he might have to tell her which could not be said in the dining room. 'Shall we say in half-an-hour?'

Simon got up and gave a token bow of the head. He had always respected Lady Hawkswood and he hoped that this very unfortunate incident would not cause her too much distress. She had already suffered a great deal in the last year.

He was also deeply concerned as to how his father would react to this incident and wondered how he would expect his son to handle it. Would he, like Simon, think that this was a terrible affront to the Chalvington family honour? To have his fiancé cheat on him even before they were married and with an Indian to boot. But he could also hear his father's voice reprimanding him. 'You complete idiot, how could you let such a prize slip through your fingers, all that girl needed was a firm hand'. He was not sure that he had a firm enough hand for Virginia. He also imagined himself the laughing stock of the officers' mess once the story got out, as he knew it would. No, he had to take a stand.

Simon was already seated in the salon when Lady Hawkswood appeared. He rose and gave her an awkward greeting. She could see how nervous this earnest young man was and she smiled at him, in an attempt to put him at his ease, her clear blue eyes exuding kindness.

'So, tell me Simon, what's troubling you?'

He had spent half the night rehearsing what he would say to her and his formal delivery now seemed stripped of all emotion.

'Lady Hawkswood, I have good reason to believe that Virginia has been unfaithful to me.'

She had realised that Simon wanted to discuss a serious matter, but was clearly taken aback by this statement.

'Simon, I simply cannot believe that. What on earth makes you think so?'

'Last night I went to your cabin to find Virginia to talk to her about today's shore visit. The door was open but no lights were on. I knocked and called out but there was no reply. Thinking there must be something wrong I entered the cabin. I then heard a man's voice in Virginia's cabin and became alarmed and went straight in. Lady Hawkswood, I'm sorry to have to tell you that when I switched on the light I found young Rindi Debrahm standing there beside Virginia ,who was lying on her bunk practically naked.'

Lady Hawkswood sat in stunned silence trying to absorb this information.

'But that cannot be, he's not much more than a schoolboy,' she protested. Simon appeared not to have registered her remark as he continued. 'I asked her only one question and was told that Debrahm had arrived uninvited and presumably took advantage of a not unwilling Virginia.'

'How do you know she was "not unwilling"?'

'Well, there was no sound of objection when I entered the cabin.'

Simon stared out of the window as the crew prepared the ship for docking. He avoided eye contact with Lady Hawkswood in case it weakened his resolve. He no longer felt a part of the life on that ship. He had been plunged into a void from which he must retreat with honour and dignity.

'You'll understand, Lady Hawkswood that I have no alternative but to ask your indulgence to break off our engagement. We are due to dock in Aden in two hours' time. I shall formally advise Virginia after we set sail again tomorrow.'

Lady Hawkswood was devastated. She rose to her feet and steadied herself on the back of the chair. Her hand was trembling.

'I can say nothing, Simon, until I have spoken to Virginia.'

The thought of their engagement breaking was devastating. This union was exactly what Arthur had wanted. Such a suitable match, and her father, the bishop, had been hoping to conduct his beloved granddaughter's wedding ceremony. How was it possible for things to have gone so terribly wrong?

Virginia was sitting in her cabin attempting to read when her mother came in.

'Simon has just told me what he discovered last night in <u>this</u> cabin,' she said sternly. "Whatever possessed you to be so foolish and irresponsible?'

'What did he tell you, Mummy?'

'He said that he came into your cabin and found you and Rindi Debrahm in a distinctly compromising situation.'

'But did he also tell you that Rindi had come in completely uninvited, and that he was in fact looking for an intruder. You must speak to Rindi about it. Please. There is nothing going on between us. He's like my younger brother.'

This statement was true but she also thought how much Rindi had changed since they had last met. No longer the gangly awkward schoolboy, he was a man now both in stature and in self-assurance and obviously a credible lover in Simon's eyes. More importantly, her future now depended on his gallantry outweighing his honesty.

'I have every intention of speaking to him. That charming mother of his would be shocked if she knew that her son had been involved in anything dishonourable.'

After the fracas had broken out in the night cabin, and with its occupants suitably distracted, Ali Abdullah had grabbed the opportunity to escape. He realised that he might have been observed, but was confident that his identity remained unknown.

It might have been wiser for him to have abandoned his intent and returned the brooch to the jewel-box. But his consuming lust for that young nubile girl waiting for him in Bombay had overridden reason and he went ashore with the brooch as planned. Within a few hours a local jeweller he knew, a Mr Alexis Garabedienne, had removed the precious stones and skilfully remounted the brooch with fake gemstones. Ali was rewarded for his effort and re-embarked satisfied that he would now be able to fulfil the dowry requirement for his second wife. All he had to do now was to return the brooch and rely on the fact that Lady Hawkswood was unlikely to scrutinise it until long after she had arrived back in England.

Lady Hawkswood, Virginia, Rindi and Simon had gone ashore in three separate parties. Virginia, being unaware of Simon's intentions, did not wish to give him an opportunity to question her further, at least not until an explanation from Rindi had filtered through to him via her mother.

Wantilla had artfully kept out of sight. He was well aware that he must continue to do so if there was to be any hope of Virginia hanging on to the threads of her engagement. The potential liability of a besotted unattached female pursuing him was quite contrary to his plans.

Lady Hawkswood, back from her shore visit, was changing when the dinner gong sounded. She was undecided whether she wanted to go in to dinner. Her indecision was partly due to her desire to seek out Rindi and get some answers. In the end she decided to wait until the next day. Rindi, however, was not content to delay. He found Virginia and they went together to speak to her mother.

'Please tell me what happened last night, Rindi,' she asked.

Rindi related his version of events whilst carefully avoiding any mention of his cousin.

'When you realised the intruder had escaped why didn't you pursue him?' Lady Hawkswood asked trying to make sense of the story.

'Well, by the time I did he had disappeared and I felt Virginia needed an explanation as to why I was in your cabin.'

'And why was the cabin light switched off when Simon came in?'

Virginia decided to answer this. 'When Rindi saw that I was undressed, he switched it off.'

'And why were you undressed?'

'I was about to go to bed.'

'Well, your story sounds feasible, though I don't think Simon believes that's what happened. What I can't understand is why you didn't hear him and respond to his call?'

'Oh, I did, Mummy. It's just that he came into the cabin so quickly.'

'Well, if there really was an intruder, it would be wise to check if anything is missing. Perhaps you would help me go through my valuables, darling.'

Rindi excused himself and left the stateroom.

It was about an hour later that an agitated Virginia found Rindi standing at the rails on the boat deck. He had been watching a distant lighthouse as the ship approached the Straits of Aden.

Virginia spoke breathlessly. 'Oh God, another ghastly development. We've checked Mummy's jewels and there's a valuable brooch missing.'

'This must be the work of the fellow I was following. Maybe now they will believe my story.'

Virginia shook her head and looked very worried. 'It's not going to be that simple. Mummy was so upset that she rushed off to report it to the Chief Purser and have another talk with Simon. Oh hell, what a bloody muddle.'

'Well, there's not much that anyone can do at this late hour. We'd better get to bed and see what can be done in the morning.'

Straight after breakfast Rindi went to see Lady Hawkswood to ask about the jewels.

'I gather from Virginia that something has been stolen.'

'Yes, it's my most precious piece of jewellery. The beautiful brooch that the Maharajah of Khizarpura gave me.'

The very mention of the name Khizarpura made Rindi inwardly shudder. 'Have you told Simon? Surely this explains everything.'

'Yes, Rindi, I've told him. But for some reason, Simon still doesn't accept your explanation. Now that this jewel theft has come to light, he has been to see the captain and insists on a full inquiry. He feels that either his or Virginia's honour is at stake.'

'Whatever does he hope to achieve so far as his honour is concerned?'

Lady Hawkswood looked straight at Rindi. 'I'm afraid he thinks that you stole the brooch and that you are trying to get Virginia, as your innamorata to cover up for you.'

'How ridiculous! The man must be absolutely demented to think such a thing.'

Rindi dearly wished that he could take Lady Hawkswood into his confidence with a fuller explanation but this was impossible without compromising Virginia and Wantilla and placing his father in serious danger. Fearing that the situation was getting out of hand he looked straight at her and said. 'Unless this whole matter and the proposed inquiry is terminated immediately, something very unpleasant, something you would not wish to hear, something very distressing to you, will come to light.' The gravity of his words was unmistakeable.

The blood drained from Lady Hawkswood's face. She was in an obvious state of shock. In that brief moment, she had sifted through any facts that she would not wish to become known. The one that now thudded in her brain was the knowledge that her late husband had descended from Anglo-Indian stock. That revelation, she was sure, would completely alter Lord Chalvington's enthusiasm for his son's marriage to Virginia. She caught her breath, 'Surely you wouldn't do that?'

Rindi realised that he had already said too much, and that she may have reached the wrong conclusion. He had been clumsy in his choice of words. To attempt to say more now would only worsen the situation. He stood up and took his leave of her.

Ali Abdullah had had a sleepless night tormented with the thought that at any moment he might be called on to account for his movements. He had somehow to return the brooch to the jewel-box without being observed. He had seen Lady Hawkswood talking to the purser in an agitated fashion the previous evening and realised he could not overlook the possibility that the theft had already been discovered. He resolved that his only course of action was to pretend to discover the jewel whilst cleaning the bathroom and removing the laundry. He could only hope that if this was done first thing in the morning his manifest honesty might divert any suggestion of his involvement in the theft. He also prayed that Mr Garabedienne's 'alterations' would go undetected.

Virginia heard a gentle knock at the door. She opened it to find Ali Abdullah bearing a large pile of clean linen. 'Please, *memsahib*, your laundry.'

'Oh thank you, please come in,' she said.

Ali proceeded with crisp efficiency to distribute the clean towels and then disappeared into the bathroom to empty the laundry basket.

He re-emerged almost immediately with a suitably surprised look on his face.

'Please, *memsahib*, something most unusual,' he said. 'I am finding this in the laundry basket.' He unfolded a hand towel to reveal the Khizapura brooch. 'I am thinking it should not be there.'

'Gosh,' blurted Virginia. 'Yes, I mean no, of course not. How wonderful that you found it, Lady Hawkswood will be delighted. Thank you.'

Ali looked appropriately pleased and said, 'Not at all memsahib,' and bobbed deferentially. 'Ali Abdullah at your service, and now I must be taking the laundry for cleaning.' He quietly left the cabin with a stunned Virginia still clutching the recovered brooch.

Would this be the end of the affair she wondered? Would Simon accept that there had been an intruder? Did she even want to salvage her engagement to him? Clearly he mistrusted her. She knew that she must stop her dalliance with Wantilla but she found him irresistible. She was also not convinced he wouldn't cast her aside if he was tempted elsewhere. She longed for a real man but one who was kind as well.

CHAPTER SIX

January 1934. Queens Gate Gardens, Kensington.

Adam sat back and watched a wisp of smoke rise from Rindi's turkish cigarette, absorbed by his account of the incident on board the Strathclyde.

'I can see why you said the voyage was eventful. Did they ever catch the culprit?'

'No, they didn't and given how absent-minded Lady H had become it was entirely possible she had dropped the brooch in the laundry basket herself. But I am still not entirely convinced that the steward was as innocent as he made out.'

'So did the inquiry go ahead?'

'No, after the brooch turned up the captain persuaded Duffell that there was too little evidence to go on and in any event Lady H had become pretty insistent that the matter be dropped.'

'Weren't you keen to clear your name?'

'Frankly, I was finding protecting Virginia and my rascal cousin rather exhausting. I was happy for it just to all go away.'

'Did Duffell break off the engagement?'

'As far as I know he didn't but it would have been a bit churlish to have done so on the evidence he had. It was hardly a case of *in flagrante delicto*, although if Wantilla had had his way it might well have been.'

'What news of your cousin?'

'I saw nothing of him after we landed but I have heard that he is back in India.'

'Tell me, why did Wantilla threaten you with Khizapura?'

Rindi looked at Adam gravely and appeared reluctant to answer his question.

'Was it anything to do with the Khizapura brooch?' Adam added hoping to make it easier for him.

'Yes, indirectly. As you know Sir Arthur was killed whilst on a tiger shoot at Kushnapur. The elephant he was on was attacked by a tiger and it reared up throwing him to the ground. The Maharajah of Khizapura, who was in the same howdah, attempted to shoot the tiger to stop it mauling Sir Arthur but when the elephant lurched again he accidentally shot him instead. At least everyone, including the Maharajah himself, thought that he had shot him.'

'So where does the Khizapura brooch come in to it?'

'These accidents are not that uncommon and it is not unusual for substantial sums to be paid in compensation to the victim's family. In this instance money was not thought appropriate and the Maharajah offered Lady Hawkswood one of his most valuable jewels, the Khizapura brooch, as a token of his remorse.'

'But hold on you said everyone *thought* he had shot Sir Arthur?'

'The truth, Adam, is that it was not an accident and Wantilla is one of the few people who knows that.'

Adam sat stunned by this revelation.

'It is very complicated and I have probably told you too much already. It is best, not least for your own safety that you continue to believe it was an accident.'

Adam was frustrated by this incomplete answer but clearly Rindi had no intention of elaborating any further.

***

Adam lay quite still, listening to a clock striking in the direction of St. Mary Abbots Hospital. He counted the chimes as they came across the crisp January air. Twelve, midnight. With such a comfortable bed he would normally have been asleep long since, had not the affairs of the Debrahms' been flooding through his head. There was much more to his friend and his family than met the eye.

After dinner that evening, attended by both Jardeeson and Nina on this occasion, Adam and Rindi had played chess and reminisced about the first time they had met at Rockton.

'You looked terrified when I approached you in the library.'

'Understandably, you were a prefect and I was a squit!'

'You exaggerate.' Rindi replied and laughed.

Adam was pleased to see his friend in good humour as recently he had had a habit of shutting down a subject when it started becoming too sensitive.

'May I ask about your uncle?'

Rindi pondering his next move said, 'Which one?'

'Jardeeson.'

'Do you like him?' he asked.

'I find him fascinating; talking to him is like flicking through the pages of an encyclopaedia of India. But I am puzzled why he seems to have taken up residence in England when all his family live in India?'

Rindi placed his finger on the king's bishop. His next move would threaten Adam's queen.

Without making his move he said, 'It's a fair observation.'

'So when was he last in India?'

Rindi moved his bishop, then looked up, smiled and replied. 'He's never been to India.'

He paused to allow Adam to absorb this statement.

'He must have been to India. Wasn't he born in Kushnapur?'

'No, he wasn't. My grandparents came over as official guests for Queen Victoria's Diamond Jubilee. Whilst they were here, my grandmother discovered that she was pregnant. Her doctor advised against the long sea voyage back to India and she remained in England for the birth. My Uncle Jardeeson was the child that she bore.'

'Surely your grandmother returned to India?'

'She did, but without Jardeeson.'

'Did that have anything to do with his older brother's abduction?'

'Precisely so. After that it was thought prudent to keep him safe in England as a provision against anything happening to my father.' Rindi spoke matter of factly and Adam wondered at this seeming lack of emotion at what must have been a traumatic decision for both child and mother.

'And where does Jandah fit into this picture?' Adam asked.

'When my grandfather arrived back in India, he arranged for Jandah, who was the son of one of his most loyal servants, to be sent to London. At the time he had been working in the household of the Maharajah of Gwalior. From the moment he arrived in London, until my uncle was old enough to go to boarding school, Jandah was his constant protector.'

Adam recalled the time he had seen Jandah patrolling the pavement opposite the house after he had spotted the stranger loitering by the entrance to the square. He could feel his presence even when he couldn't see him, like a resident ghost.

Adam sat up in bed, anxious to break the train of thought that was keeping him awake. He flicked on the light and picked up the book he had earlier selected from the library downstairs: James Hilton's 'Knight without Armour'. After several pages he started to drift into sleep, the character of Ainsley Fothergill becoming fuzzy and merging bizarrely with the spectre of a giant eunuch wandering around an Indian palace.

After their stay at Queens Gate Gardens, Rindi returned to Oxford and Adam to Rockton knowing that he would be starting his officer cadet course at Sandhurst at the end of the summer. Adam visited Rindi in Oxford from time to time and was always surprised at how little work seemed to take place at this august centre of learning. On one of these occasions Rindi had arranged for Tina to come and stay at the same time. She had left school early and gone to the Slade College of Art and her new life could not have been more different from the intense discipline of Adam's daily routine. They still wrote to each other in sufficiently affectionate terms that Adam remained hopeful of a future together but to his disappointment this affection did not manifest itself in any physical sense. She didn't mention other boyfriends but perhaps he would be the last to know. Her letters frequently mentioned a fellow student called Nancy Singleton who had introduced her to the work of the Cubists. Adam didn't really understand this form of art and that made him feel all the more alienated from her world.

Later that year she came with Pauline and Rindi to the Sandhurst Ball where she spent more time dancing with Rindi and other officers than with himself. He had hoped to rekindle the passion of that summer's day near Salisbury but neither the opportunity nor her inclination presented itself. Curious as to why she had cooled since their original encounter Adam asked her whether she thought there was any future for them. She said something very strange to him.

'Adam, my father said I shouldn't get too fond of you and that it was unlikely that I would ever be able to marry you.'

'Who's even thinking about marriage? And, anyway why on earth not?'

'He wouldn't tell me. Just said it was difficult to explain.'

'I thought I got on rather well with him.'

'That's the funny thing, he couldn't speak more highly of you.'

She then paused and said, 'Whatever happens, Adam, I will always be very fond of you,' and squeezed his hand.

This conversation had left Adam frustrated and wondering if Tina wasn't just using her father as an excuse to end their relationship. He tried to comfort himself with the thought that she was still very young and he should not impose his future hopes onto her.

Egypt, October 1937

Adam passed out from his officers' training course at the Royal Military College in the spring of 1935 and was promptly sent to China for two years with the Second Battalion of the Royal Wessex Regiment. Adam and Rindi corresponded regularly but it wasn't until Adam was posted to Egypt in October 1937 that an opportunity arose for them to see each other again.

Rindi had returned to India after graduating from Oxford in June 1936. On arriving in Cairo Adam received a letter from Rindi pressing him to spend his leave in Kushnapur. His only expense would be the return passage to Bombay. This was an attractive proposition for a lieutenant on a low income, and Adam could not have been keener to go to India. However, the limited availability of leave forced him to decline the offer. Instead it was arranged that Rindi would come and see him in Egypt. Rindi based himself at Shepheard's Hotel which allowed them to meet in considerable comfort away from army quarters.

His apprehension about seeing Rindi after so long was unfounded and they spent ten days exploring the sights of ancient Egypt and enjoying the cosmopolitan night life of Cairo. They talked about how life had treated them in the intervening years and developments in Europe. But having missed out on the opportunity to go to India Adam had an urge to hear more of life in Kushnapur.

'So, what news of that rascal Wantilla?'

'He's even worse than before if that's possible. He's now taken to pestering my father about his desire to marry my sister.'

'Has he indeed. But I thought he was already married?'

'Oh, yes, but that would not prevent him. Hindus are permitted plural marriages. Admittedly, they are less common nowadays.'

'I presume your father showed him the door.'

'He certainly did, though the situation was not as easily dealt with as that. Wantilla's motives are complex, and for several reasons he will not let the matter rest.'

'By the way whatever happened to Virginia?'

'She married Duffell a year after the boat incident.'

'So, did the affair with Wantilla end?'

'Well, I saw her for lunch in London shortly after she got married and she was quite evasive when I asked whether she had seen him or not. I have to say she really is poor at picking her men.'

'From what you have told me she does sound absolutely gorgeous.'

'Yes, and I am not sure if Duffell is really ringing her bell, if you know what I mean.'

'What about romance in your life?' Adam probed.

'My parents would like me to choose a wife. They have a more relaxed approach to arranged marriage but it still doesn't stop them inviting suitable ladies to Kushnapur in the hope that I will eventually find one of them agreeable.'

'I suppose you got to sow your wild oats at Oxford.'

'Yes. I did have some fun but I think I was something of an exotic novelty to English girls. There was this very pretty Somerville College girl who I was particularly taken with. But what about you?'

'Not much to report really. I still burn a candle for Tina but she didn't seem that interested when she came to that ball at Sandhurst.'

'She's a lovely girl.'

'She said a curious thing. That her father had said she would be wise not to grow too fond of me.'

'Well maybe you're better to move on. Other fish in the sea.'

Rindi didn't seem to be that surprised by Tina's comment.

'As it so happens the Westbury's are coming out to stay in Kushnapur. He has retired now and they haven't been back for a while. There was some suggestion that Tina might also come with them.'

'Oh really. What happened to the painting career?'

'Last I heard she was up for some hush hush job in Whitehall but if she is coming to India maybe that never came to anything.'

Adam felt faintly jealous that Rindi clearly knew much more about Tina's life than he did but after all their families had been friends for a long time. All too soon it was time for Rindi's return journey to Bombay.

'Now don't go following intruders into other people's cabins, will you.'

'No, I think I've learnt that lesson. And Adam don't leave it too long before you come and visit us in Kushnapur', he said in a plaintive tone. 'There is so much that I want to show you and need you to understand.'

April 1939

Adam had hoped that after a year or two in Egypt he would have accrued sufficient leave for a trip to India. Unfortunately, developments in Europe were to deem otherwise. Hitler had rendered the Munich Agreement a meaningless scrap of paper and on 16th March 1939, the Bohemia and Monrovia provinces of Czechoslovakia were annexed and declared German Protectorates. A week later, under duress, the city and port of Memel on the Baltic were ceded to Germany by Lithuania. Britain had seen enough and by the end of April, conscription was introduced.

Soldiering now became deadly serious; training was stepped up and officers were told to be conscious of espionage. Cairo was a hotbed of intrigue and rumour. Under War Office instructions, Adam was one of a party of four officers and two sergeants sent back to England to join a new Wessex battalion of the rapidly expanding Army. They sailed from Port Said on 1st September 1939, the same day that massive German air and land forces invaded Poland. Great Britain and France mobilised and a few hours later all men in Britain aged 18 to 41 became liable for compulsory military service.

On 3rd September, at 11 a.m. war with Germany was declared. Any thoughts of travelling to India would have to be delayed indefinitely and he wondered what the implications of war in Europe would have for Rindi in the Kushnapur.

CHAPTER SEVEN

September 1939. London.

The drab hand of war lay everywhere. There were no street lamps or neon signs illuminated. On dark nights, one had to almost grope one's way home. Out of town, where there were no pavements, a hooded flashlight was essential. Car headlights were masked, leaving a pathetic little slot for the light to shine a short way ahead. 'Put that light out!' was a common cry in the early days, as the air-raid wardens and police did their rounds.

Just before dark every night, it was routine to put up blackout boards or thick material over all windows and outside doors. Getting in and out, through the double curtains at the entrance to public buildings, became a new skill. If self-preservation against enemy bombers were not motive enough, the thought of a heavy fine would deter the careless from showing any chink of light.

The sky was a different matter. Great searchlights swept the heavens, piercing the autumn night, converging from point to point, before plunging everything back into darkness. The church bells no longer rang. Evacuation schemes were put into motion in England and Wales. Within a few days, 1,200,000 people were on the move. Men and women in uniform proliferated. The Army, Navy, Air Force, Fire Service, women ambulance drivers and wardens. Every week more of the population appeared in a variety of uniforms. Everyone seemed determined to play his or her part. Hitler's forces would be crushed in weeks.

On their way to the War Office Adam's contingent from Egypt drove over Westminster Bridge and into Parliament Square. London looked and felt very different. Everywhere there were thousands of sand bags piled round doorways and windows. Large 'S' signs, indicating Air Raid Shelters, were ubiquitous. A number of barrage balloons appeared to be tethered in Green Park and St. James's Park. The cab waited for the lights to change and two girls in Air Force uniform, with gas masks slung over their shoulders, walked across in front of them. In the opposite direction four sailors passed, their caps, denuded of the proud name of their ship, now bore an uninformative 'H.M.S.' On the top of some buildings the muzzles of Anti-Aircraft guns were poised on alert. Along Victoria Street, there was the occasional sign pasted over a shop window saying, 'Closed for the Duration'. More often, the signs said 'Business as Usual.'

At the War Office they were given seven day's leave, and told to report to the barracks in Salisbury to join the recently mustered Third Battalion of the Royal Wessex Regiment. Adam's leave was spent saying hello and good-bye to family and friends, the cheerful optimism of these visits obscuring underlying anxieties. Although Adam had told them he would probably be back within a few weeks, he had said goodbye in expectation of not seeing them for some time. It was just as well, because upon arriving at the barracks in Salisbury, he found himself reporting to a Major Mercer in charge of the rear party.

'Didn't they tell you we were leaving for France?' was almost his first comment.

'No, Sir. I suppose they couldn't really. I hadn't even reported for duty.'

'Huh, I suppose not. Maybe just as well. You might have gone off and done something stupid, like getting pissed, or engaged. Come and have a drink.'

It was only four o'clock in the afternoon. A drink at this time of the day would normally confound all the rules of sobriety taught at Sandhurst but it was not for Adam to contradict this genial, self-assured, field officer as they strode to the officers' mess.

'You'll be coming with me tomorrow, Cullworthy. Your two sergeants arrived this morning and are now with a squad cleaning-up the place before we leave.' As if to emphasise the point he gave his trouser leg a thwack with his leather swagger stick, and made a sort of snort, then said, 'This place is being taken-over by a company of 'flat-cocks'.

The expression was new to Adam, but he nodded in acknowledgement as if he had understood. They entered the mess and walked through into the anteroom where a lieutenant of their regiment was talking to a company commander of the Auxiliary Territorial Service. Her short hair was neatly pinned back to fit into the soft service cap which they had seen on the table in the entrance hall.

The lieutenant introduced himself as Willie Ashford, and

introduced them to Company Commander Jennifer Davenport. Adam was grateful she was wearing only three pips on her shoulders and not a crown. He would not have known whether to call her ma'am, or something else. He realised they had met the first of the 'flat-cocks'. Major Mercer had obviously not expected to see the A.T.S officer in the mess and now changed his mind about ordering the bar to be opened-up.

'Steward, bring some tea. Enough for four.' Then addressing Davenport he asked, 'What are you people going to do with this place?'

'We're making it a transport driving and maintenance centre, Sir. We have to supply staff-car drivers to all static headquarters throughout Southern Command. We shall also be getting quite a few First Aid Nursing Yeomanry sent here for training to drive ambulances.'

"Ah, the Fanys,' said Ashford with a chuckle.

'Just so,' said Davenport crisply, not sharing in his amusement at their nick name.

Adam was alone in the mess that night when Major Mercer walked in.

'Hello, Cullworthy, still up. Have a night-cap?'

'Thank you, Sir.'

'Never mind the 'sir'. In the Mess, I'm 'Bob'.'

Bob ordered two pink gins and told the steward to close the bar. An hour later, they went off to their beds knowing rather more about each other. Bob had been a don at Oxford and it transpired that he had known Rindi who had attended his tutorials. It soon became apparent to Adam that this was no ordinary army major but a man with an incisive mind and a wealth of anecdotes.

A few days later they were shipped over to France, sailing all the way round to Nantes on the French northwest coast in the mistaken belief that the Germans would not be aware of their movements.

Northern France, April 1940.

They had been stationed at Flixecourt north-west of Amiens for six months undergoing intensive training, but with little evidence of enemy action this period became known as the 'phoney war'. British and Commonwealth troops continued to pour into their sector and at the height of the campaign forces had built up to fourteen divisions.

Including the R.A.F., there were about three hundred thousand men in the British Expeditionary Force in France. Although this was a considerable army, the French with their enormous Maginot Line garrisons had ten times this number of armed men in service.

Bob Mercer advised the CO that his officers and men were now at the peak of their training and were looking for deployments to keep them fit and fully occupied. One of the responses that came back informed them that their brigade would be in the operations sector beside a French Army Corps and that a liaison officer was to be appointed and sent to their HQ. In the hope of seeing some action, Adam immediately volunteered and was on his way within the week.

Fortunately, he was able to keep his staff car and more importantly, Tom Johnson, his faithful driver. Adam's farewell party in the mess was to be the last he would see of Bob and his fellow officers on French soil.

He did not have long to wait to fulfil his wish to find action. In the early hours of 10th May the unexpected storm broke. Three German Army Groups launched a massive offensive. The greatest and best-prepared military force ever assembled in history and they had the advantage of starting from their own territory.

On May 11th, a National Government was formed under Winston Churchill. In the following days Queen Wilhelmina arrived in London, Holland ceased fighting and the Belgian army capitulated on the orders of King Leopold. Ypres, Lille and other Belgian and French towns were lost to the Germans.

Ahead of the retreating armies, came the human flotsam: the refugees. At first, just a trickle, then a flood. Although they did not know it at the time, the number of civilians who left their homes to flee from the advancing German Army rose to over eight million.

At first, Adam personalised this human tragedy. Seeing a Belgian girl of no more than ten, bewildered, clinging to her mother with one hand and clutching a well-worn doll in the other, his only thought was that this could have been his sister Sue and he felt tears welling in his eyes.

As the weeks went by he became inured to the individual circumstances of these people and came to treat them as a logistical problem. They clogged the roads and made advance or retreat virtually impossible. Any military objective they may have had, had to be abandoned. The British Expeditionary Force scrambled for the Channel realising that the pincers of the German machine were snapping at their heels.

* * *

At Corps HQ, Adam had been joined by a French captain who introduced himself as Maurice Perrier. Within days of the German breakthrough, he and his driver in their light armoured vehicle had been cut off from their unit further up the line. German planes were constantly overhead and next day orders were issued to evacuate Corps HQ. They were told to form small mobile groups capable of defending themselves and ready to travel west. Adam and Perrier found cover off the road and took up defensive positions ready to move on at dawn. They took it in turns to keep watch and enable each other to get some sleep.

Alas, not for long. Shortly after midnight, a French lieutenant drove up and told them that a general order had been given to withdraw. To their dismay, they saw some British units already passing them on their way back.

'*Mon Dieu, Mon Dieu*, what's happening?' Perrier was muttering. 'We were doing so well.'

Still in their wooded cover, they got into their respective vehicles and sat waiting, ready for one of the motorcycle escorts to tell them when to join the retreating column. About a dozen of the Corps HQ trucks had already gone back past their position, when suddenly they heard machine gun fire. For a few moments, there was nothing on the road. Then, peering through the leaves, they could just make out four armoured cars with headlights dipped.

'Holy fuck,' Johnson ejaculated, 'they're Gerries!' His next utterance was masked by a burst from the German guns, as they raced along the road.

'Good God,' Adam muttered, 'they're chasing our troops.' Another three German armoured fighting vehicles with half-tracks followed, and then the road was clear. They waited a full five minutes. No more vehicles came and Adam walked over to Perrier.

'What the hell do we do now, Maurice? Looks like we're trapped. Have you any idea where we are?'

'Yes, we're a few kilometres outside Peronne. The *Boche* must be all around, so we must quickly get off this route. There is only one main bridge over the River Somme in this area, and that means going through the town. The *Boche* may be using it already, so it could be tricky. If we go whilst it's still dark, we might get through.'

'Then you had better lead the way.'

'What do you think, Johnson?'

'Christ! If you ask me, Sir, the whole thing's bloody dodgy. I promised the old woman that I wouldn't take any chances but, bugger it, Sir, this "frog" officer seems a clever cunt, he ought to be able to get us through'.

Adam gave a wry smile at Johnson's colourful language. Fortunately, Perrier was out of earshot, talking to his own driver.

'I hope so Johnson, but we're going to need a bit of luck.'

Adam gave a thumbs up and Perrier's armoured car roared off into the night with them in pursuit. Fifteen minutes later, he branched off along a track, stopped and switched off the lights. Johnson followed suit.

Perrier put his head out of the turret and whispered. 'Wait here whilst I do a reccy.'

Suddenly he stopped speaking as they heard the clank of an ancient bicycle chain and the faint scuffle of tyres on the road. It certainly was not a German.

'*Quis allez la?*' Perrier called out.

The cyclist recognised the accent, dismounted and came to where we were parked. Perrier briefly shone his torch on the figure of an elderly farm labourer, and then questioned him. '*Qu'est que c'est la situation en ville?*'

'*Tres mauvaise messieurs. Les Boches sont arrivés depuis trois jours.*'

He went on to tell them that the Germans had taken the town and hundreds of tanks had poured across the town bridge. They had also taken the town of Albert, only twenty-four kilometres away, and had captured many British soldiers.

'Do you still want to go on, Adam? We could just abandon our vehicles and try to get away disguised as peasants.' Maurice sounded disheartened.

'How far would we get without transport or weapons, Maurice? It's worse than I thought, but if we don't take our chance to slip through tonight, we are almost certain to be captured. As I see it, there are two factors in our favour. Firstly, in the confusion, the Germans could mistake our small vehicles for captured transport. Secondly, they will, hopefully, be too preoccupied with getting their armour across the Somme to worry about an odd camion and a scout car.'

'Well, whatever we do, we've got to be quick,' said Perrier. 'If dawn breaks, *c'est finis!*

'Agreed. Let's get moving now. I suggest we drive into the town using back streets, wait near the bridge and then slip over with one of the German convoys. If we only use sidelights they might not be able to see us very well and certainly won't be expecting us.'

They stopped near a small intersection that lay away to their left about a hundred yards from the bridge. They then had a rare piece of luck. Ahead were six fuel tankers waiting to cross the bridge. Perrier got out of his vehicle and crept round to whisper to Adam.

'It's fairly dark; do you think we can slip in between these tankers?'

'We haven't got much choice if we don't want to be taken prisoner. At least they won't be expecting us. No allied troops would be mad enough to get mixed up with their tankers.'

'*Exactement*. Then you go first, Adam. If there's any shooting, it's likely to come from behind. I have armour protection and can cover you with my Chatellerault.'

'*D'accord*, Maurice. When those tankers drive off, I'll get in between the second and third. You can then get in between the fourth and fifth. The drivers will at least be able to see one of their convoy either in front or behind them and give them confidence. They will probably travel at the regulation minimum distance of forty metres apart. They'll be used to having small vehicles cutting into the convoy. With all that valuable fuel, the last thing they will want, is to get involved with any shooting.'

Perrier nodded.

Just then, a German motorcyclist drove up, stopped beside the cab of the leading tanker and spoke to the driver. Perrier crept back to his vehicle and it was none too soon. Almost immediately, the leading tanker started to follow the motorcyclist.

Johnson already had the engine running and timed it perfectly. The right gear, the right speed and the exact moment. The tankers were travelling on the right hand side of the road and they joined from the left as if they were overtaking. A minute later, they were on the bridge and Adam prayed that Maurice's driver Dupreez had also timed it well. So great was the tension, that all fear was suppressed. They had a right-hand drive vehicle so Adam had to tell Johnson when to overtake. At least Perrier and Dupreez did not have that problem.

Two minutes later, they had reached the far side of the bridge and Adam thought their luck had run out when he saw ahead to their right that a German military policeman was holding up the traffic to let their tanker convoy pass. He knew that even in that street lit only by a few sidelights he would get a good a view of them as they slowly passed and they must convey confidence and not attract his attention

Adam could see that there was no oncoming traffic, and without re-checking, he shouted, 'Overtake! Now, Johnson!' They managed to screen themselves with the tanker as they were passing the military policeman. Adam preferred to risk being thought a mad driver than one of the enemy. Johnson knew what to do, and keeping up the engine revs, he passed the leading tanker of the convoy and then the motorcycle escort. A few seconds later the increased rip from his exhaust left them in no doubt that he was in pursuit.

Johnson was straining every ounce out of his vehicle and had drawn a hundred yards clear of the convoy. However, the superior acceleration of the powerful B.M.W. motorcycle quickly brought the German up close behind them. He peered through his goggles, as if to identify them; hesitated briefly, then drew his Luger. No fool this. He lined himself behind the blind corner in the vehicle, and Adam knew that Johnson was his target. At the speed they were travelling, there was little chance of the German getting an accurate shot but Adam was taking no chances. He fingered the trigger of his French M29, waiting for the German to come into view.

Adam was about to tell Johnson to brake hard or swerve, to bring the motorcyclist into his sights, when he called out, 'Cross-roads ahead, Sir!' This time Johnson, who knew exactly where they were, slightly reduced speed to make sure that the road was clear.

'We're coming up to the Amiens-St.Quentin Road. Roye is about 14k south of here. Let's hope the sods haven't got there yet.'

As he spoke Adam heard machine-gun fire, and in the mirror saw the motorcyclist slew across the road out of control and crash into a tree. The German, unaware that the vehicle behind him was also his enemy, had been a sitting duck for Perrier in his light armoured car.

Dawn was breaking as they shot over the crossroads, passing two Germans with a motorcycle combination. They had seen their comrade crash and were kick-starting their engines. They quickly gained on them and the soldier in the sidecar opened fire, his accuracy fortunately impaired by the swaying of his vehicle and the poor early light.

Perrier, however, with his mounted machine gun and the stability of four-wheel drive, had no such problem. But Johnson knew there was a danger of them also being hit and as they approached a bend in the road he swerved out to give him a clear shot. The Chatellerault stammered and almost immediately found its mark. The German side car combination careered wildly, then spun off the road, crashed through a fence, ran down a short bank and tipped upside down in the ditch, its wheels spinning aimlessly.

Their early luck in evading the enemy did not hold out; the following day they were strafed by low flying fighters. As the swathe of bullets ripped through the staff car, Johnson was killed instantly and Adam later discovered Maurice and Dupreez had also been killed when his armoured car veered out of control and crashed into a burnt-out tank. Adam was more fortunate, being flung out before their vehicle hit a tree and survived with only a bullet wound in the thigh.

Rescued unconscious from a gully by a local farmer, he was tended by a local doctor too old for military service. Delirious with morphine for several days he was nursed back to health by the farmer's daughter, Annette.

As Adam's strength returned he became aware of her angular features and high cheekbones. With her sallow skin, piercing blue eyes and brown hair tied up in a simple red scarf, she reminded him of the gypsy girls he had seen near his home in Sussex. They hardly spoke at all but developed an understanding and intimacy borne of the vulnerability of their situation.

One night she came to administer the medication Adam needed to help him sleep and to re-dress his wound, but on this occasion she was not wearing her scarf and her hair hung loose. She drew back the sheets to tend to his wound. Her hands were rough from her labours on the farm but her touch was gentle and as she caressed Adam's leg he became aroused. Her normally melancholy eyes now looked at him with a very different intent. Without saying anything she unbuttoned the front of her dress to reveal small firm breasts and generous hips. Her hair smelt of lavender and her skin faintly of garlic, but with the scent of her aroused body she exuded an almost primitive sexuality. She had told Adam how she feared the arrival of the German army and what might happen to her. Adam also wondered if he would ever make it out of France. She bore down on him, her full red lips met his and they kissed. Not tenderly but with a voracious passion of two people for whom there was no tomorrow. As they made love there was a wanton urgency in her, as if she wished to defy the enemy by mating before they could defile her. To be so desired by a woman was wonderful and even the pain in Adam's leg was erased for those few ecstatic moments.

In the morning the farmer woke Adam and told him that

Annette had gone to the local market and said he should prepare to leave immediately. Adam's fear that he had overheard their night of lust was allayed when he told him a German patrol had been spotted in the next village.

Although still limping, he was sufficiently recovered to travel. He hid Adam underneath a tarpaulin in the back of his ancient farm vehicle and drove him for what seemed like days. As he lay there in some discomfort he rather guiltily thought about Tina. He had always imagined that he would lose his virginity with her and, even in the afterglow of his night with Annette, he thought of how they might one day consummate their love.

Somewhere south of Rouen the farmer left Adam in the company of two sergeants from the Royal Engineers that had been tasked with blowing the bridges as the Allies retreated. Before he left the farmer shook Adam's hand with an iron grasp and holding his arm with his other hand he said, *'Bonne chance, mon fils.'* The look of both affection and apprehension in his eyes made Adam feel like a parting son. He knew that he could never repay the kindness of this man and his daughter.

At les Andelys Adam and his party rendezvoused with the French Corps of Engineers, with whose help they planned to blow the town bridge over the River Seine at midnight. As soon as their teams had set the explosives, Adam ordered the British sergeants to move on with their truck load of equipment to meet another team of Royal Engineers. He would stay with the French to co-ordinate the blasting. Desperate to reach other bridges in time, the sergeants readily complied.

The deadline had been set to allow Allied transport to get across the bridge, but Adam was determined to take his own retribution. He told the French lieutenant, a Pierre Montreuil, his plan to ambush some of the leading German vehicles on the bridge and that it might mean delaying the detonation for a couple of hours. Montreuil looked apprehensive saying he didn't want to risk his men unnecessarily and that he would like to be well clear by the time the Germans reached the river.

'Look Pierre, as this is my plan I suggest I stay back with one of your drivers if one will volunteer and you push on with the rest of your men,'

'Non'. He spoke emphatically and Adam feared a contretemps. 'I will stay myself,' he added. 'I cannot ask my men to take a risk I am not prepared to take myself, and besides anything an English officer can do, a French officer can do just as well. You blow the bridge and I will be ready with our escape vehicle.'

Waiting with mounting tension, they finally heard the clatter of the German tanks just after half-past one.

The charges and wires had been so skilfully concealed that the triumphant Germans in their reconnaissance scout car, had failed to detect them. Following close behind were the panzers with their cupolas open, headlights on, racing to secure bridgeheads over the Seine, the last great obstacle to the west. Confident that they could take this bridge intact, the tanks surged forward. Adam's heart was thumping as the leading tank reached the halfway point and he detonated the first charge. Two seconds later the ground shuddered as the charge on the far side of the bridge exploded in front of the headlights of the tanks waiting to cross. He saw the framework twist and a great gap open up. 'That's for Maurice,' he muttered.

The leading tank stopped instantly and Adam gave his second signal. The sappers must have placed enormous charges under their side of the bridge and had they known the Germans would be within firing range when the charges were detonated they would certainly have run the wires back into the woods. A blast went off like a dozen cannons, knocking Adam sideways, even from a hundred yards away. The centre section of the bridge lurched as it was blown out and four Mark III tanks slid ignominiously into the deep flowing waters of the Seine, followed by tons of masonry and steel showering down. 'And that's for Johnson!' Adam spat out. Then, ignoring the searing pain in his leg, he ran as fast as he could over the road towards the trees.

Machine gun fire rattled around him. Montreuil's Citroën shot out of its hiding place, barely halting to let Adam scramble aboard. A further hail of erratic bullets followed them as they tore up the road, not waiting for the panzers to find their range. Within the hour they were many miles away.

'Well done,' said Montreuil, 'you English really are crazy.'

'Well driven,' Adam replied. 'I don't know how you can drive like that without headlights.'

As the dawn broke Adam felt a sense of elation that at last he had done something worthwhile for the Allies in France. Two days later, still limping, he was shipped out through the port of Cherbourg with hundreds of French soldiers and airmen, hoping to join the Free French in London under General de Gaulle.

Adam often wondered what became of Annette and whether there had been any fruit of their union. Those six months in France experiencing both the havoc of war and the kindness of that farmer and his daughter took with it the innocence and optimism of his youth and replaced it with maturity and knowledge of the worst and the best that humanity could offer.

CHAPTER EIGHT

June 1940. London.

After disembarking at Portsmouth, British personnel were issued with a seven-day leave pass and a rail warrant and told where to report at the end of their leave. The French were interrogated by their own officers to sift out any spies, and then enlisted with the Free French Forces.

Arriving by the boat train at Waterloo station, Adam made for a row of red telephone boxes.

His first call was to his mother. 'Where are you, darling? Thank God you're back. Are you alright?'

'I'm fine, mother, they've given me seven day's leave so I'll be down the day after tomorrow.'

'Wonderful! What time?'

'Not till early evening, I'm afraid. I've a few things to do in London but I'll give you a ring to let you know what train I'm coming on.'

Adam wanted to see Nina and Jardeeson to get news of Rindi and he also had a burning desire to see Tina. He dialled the Debrahm's number, and Jandah answered. Within a few seconds Nina came on the line.

'Adam! This is wonderful. You've made it back from France? Are you in London? Is there any chance of seeing you?'

'I am in London and I was planning to stay at Brown's Hotel.'

'Nonsense, you're to come and stay with us. Come across now and you will be in time for lunch.'

Arriving at Queen's Gate Gardens, Adam was greeted by Jandah. 'Your room is ready, captain sahib. Let me take your bag.'

There was something very reassuring about the permanence of this household in these uncertain times.

'The captain sahib was injured?' He said noticing Adam's limp as he led the way up to the guest bedroom.

'Oh, just a stray bullet from a Gerry fighter plane, nothing serious, Jandah.'

Everything was the same in the bedroom: the paintings of the great house and the young girl with the wistful eyes. Only the heavy blackout curtains had been added.

Nina was waiting downstairs to greet him. 'I'm afraid lunch will be very simple, Adam. You probably know that we're rationed now.'

'I am sure it will be better than anything I have eaten in the last six months.'

'Let's hope so. Now tell be about you. You seem to be limping. How was France?'

'Oh, long periods of hanging around doing nothing followed by a few rather terrifying skirmishes.'

Nina sensed that Adam didn't really want to talk about it and changed the subject. 'Well, the good news from Rindi is that he has passed out of the Indian Military Academy at Dehra Dun and has been given a king's commission in the Third Punjab Regiment.'

'I sometimes wish I could be in the Indian Army with him, and far away from this bloody conflict in Europe.'

'I fear it won't be long, Adam, before they are embroiled.'

'Yes, I know, the Japanese look as threatening as Hitler.'

Of course if you joined the Indian Army you would need to learn Hindi, Urdu and Punjabi,' she said with an amused twinkle, 'as they only speak English in the officers' mess.'

'Rindi has already taught me to swear in Urdu so I am probably well equipped to communicate with the men,' Adam responded and Nina laughed.

'Nina, would you mind terribly if I used your telephone?'

'Of course not, whenever you wish, it's best to use the one in the study.'

Adam dialled the number of Tina's flat, not really expecting her to be at home at that time of the day but he thought he would try anyway. There was a short delay, then the unmistakable voice of Nancy Singleton. He had never met her but she invariably answered their telephone.

'Hello, Nancy, it's Adam here.'

'Oh .....' she drawled in her distinctive Roedean accent, 'I thought you were in France.'

'Well, I was, but I got back this morning.'

'Did you have a good crossing?' From the way she said it, he might have been returning from a weekend in Paris. 'I'm afraid Tina's out. Don't know what time she'll be back, all very hush hush, you know.' She spoke dismissively.

Adam knew Tina was working at The Air Ministry but he did not appreciate Nancy's attitude. She had always appeared resentful of him for some reason and never disguised her disapproval of their relationship.

'Perhaps you could tell her I rang and I will try to call again later?'

'Yes, if I see her but she's a very busy girl these days,' she said, taunting him.

Adam wondered if it was her work or her social life that was keeping her busy.

To distract himself from this rather unsatisfactory conversation he took a piece of Nina's headed notepaper and wrote a letter to Johnson's wife. He'd been loyal beyond the call of duty and kept Adam amused with his irreverent cockney sense of humour. He missed him terribly. He hoped that his letter would be of some comfort to his twenty-five-year-old widow.

Adam went out to post the letter, and by the time he had returned it had gone 6 o'clock. He called Tina's number again. Once more the languid voice answered

'I'm afraid she's still not here,' came that same bored contralto voice.

Adam's disappointment turned to annoyance. 'Then when will she be there?'

'I've really no idea what time she'll be back. She sometimes doesn't come back at all.'

This statement, clearly designed to goad his feelings of jealousy, had succeeded in its aim. Adam now considered the possibility that Tina was having an affair with someone else. He hated the thought but she was a lovely girl and why should she wait for him. After all he had been with another woman albeit only a brief physical encounter. Was it unreasonable to hope that she should remain faithful to him?

After a period of silence from Adam she said, 'Why don't you leave me your number and I will ask her to call you?' This seemed an obvious thing to do but he wasn't sure he could trust Nancy to pass the message on to her.

'Ask her to call me tomorrow at my parents' house in Sussex. She knows the number.'

The next day Adam's father picked him up at the station using some of their meagre petrol ration. Concrete tank traps now stretched for mile after mile in every direction. Freshly erected pillboxes manned by machine-gunners, and Anti-Aircraft artillery batteries, tucked into the woods at frequent intervals made Adam realise that far from being out of harm's way in the country his parents would be in the first line of defence of any likely invasion route.

'So how were things in France?'

Adam told him about their narrow escape after blowing the bridge over the Seine.

His father, deep in thought, shook his head. 'Did you ever report the incident?'

'No. It was Montreuil's operation and his privilege to inform his own French headquarters.'

'Quite so. Any idea where they are going to send you next?'

'None I'm afraid, apart from the fact that I have to report to Salisbury barracks in five days' time.'

'Did you get our letter about Aunt Adeline?'

'No, haven't had a letter for weeks.'

'I am afraid she died last month.'

'Oh, that is sad news; I thought she'd have lived on for donkey's years.'

'Yes, it was quite unexpected. There is however some good news. She has left you £10,000 in her will.'

'Good heavens! That is good news. Why me?'

'Well, she was a bit old fashioned about boys needing money and knew you wouldn't get much from us for a while.'

'What about you and the girls?'

'They'll get £5,000 each and I'm to get her pictures and what's left of Uncle Gerald's cellar. And before you think I have been too hard done by, he had over a thousand bottles of claret and port laid down, also some very good champagne.'

As they arrived at the house his father said, 'Oh, by the way, I'd go light on the details of France to your mother.'

Next morning Adam was woken with the news that Tina was on the telephone.

'Adam, how wonderful, you're back, and in one piece. I am so sorry to have missed you the last times you've called.' The enthusiasm of her greeting made him almost forget the frustrations of his conversations with Nancy.

'When can I see you? Why don't you come up to Richmond next weekend? My parents would love to see you.'

From what she had said all those years ago, he was not sure that

Sir Julian would be that pleased to see him, but he was encouraged that Tina thought differently.

'Sadly I need to be in Salisbury on Thursday so my timetable is quite tight. Perhaps we could have dinner on Tuesday? I've had a bit of a windfall and I thought we might go to the Ritz.'

'That would be lovely but it may be difficult,' she said 'There's a lot going on at the moment and the Ministry quite often needs me to work until midnight.'

After what Nancy had said about her being a busy girl, Adam couldn't help wondering if this was all about work.

'I will be at the flat on Tuesday afternoon so call me and I'll be able to tell you whether I am needed that night. It would be good to see you, it's been far too long.'

After his conversation with Rindi in Egypt, Adam had begun to think he should be a bit clearer about his intentions to Tina. Aunt Adeline's bequest had removed one of the obstacles to his getting married, and if he was not careful he would find her engaged to someone else by the time the war was over. He so wanted to believe that the beautiful passionate girl he had glimpsed in the hayfield was the true reflection of how she felt and that any subsequent coolness was in deference to her father's words. He knew he could only find that out face to face.

London

Adam arrived back in London after lunch on the Tuesday and tried Tina's number from a telephone box in Victoria Station but there was no response. He often wondered how different his life might have been had she answered that call.

Despite a few threatening clouds it was a lovely day and Adam thought he would walk up Grosvenor Place and across Hyde Park to Tina's flat in Bayswater. It would take about forty-five minutes, by which time she would hopefully be back and they could have afternoon tea together. He managed to find some flowers in a florist on the Bayswater Road and with a spring in his step headed along the wide street towards Tina's Victorian mansion block.

He reached the large front door and pressed the bell of her flat number, once. There was no answer. He was about to try again when he heard footsteps coming along the street and turning saw Pamela, Tina's other flatmate, approaching.

'Adam! What a wonderful surprise,' she said breathlessly as she reached the steps and embraced him with enthusiasm.

'I am afraid the bell doesn't work,' she said, and then smelling the flowers. 'Mmm, how lovely. Are those for me? No, of course not, they're for that silly Tina.'

Adam had only met Pamela once before but she had made it gratifyingly clear that if ever things did not work out with Tina, she was next in line for his affections.

'I'm not sure whether Tina's back but come in anyway and have a cup of tea.'

In the absence of a lift, they walked up six flights of stairs arm in arm. They arrived on the third floor landing and as Pamela unlocked the door there was a great clap of thunder and the heavens opened. Leading the way into the kitchen, she pulled out a tall stool and manoeuvred Adam to sit down, using an excess of body contact. Her tight-fitting Wren's uniform emphasised her full figure and he was flattered by her flirtation. Adam had always had boyish good looks and a winning smile but five years in the army had given him a new self-assurance which women seem to find so attractive in a man.

'Make yourself comfortable. I'll get the tea', said Pamela, filling the kettle. Adam stood up. 'Will you excuse me a minute, I'd like to wash my hands. Shall I use Tina's bathroom?'

'Yes, do you know where it is?'

Adam had been to the flat once before and knew that Tina had her own connecting bathroom. Nancy and Pamela shared the other bathroom; an arrangement that gave Nancy the largest bedroom with its north-facing window for her painting.

Leaving the kitchen, he could hear the rain beating down hard with occasional rumbles of thunder. 'Poor Tina,' Adam thought, I hope she's not caught out in this lot.

A wide hallway gave access to all the rooms except Tina's bathroom. Opposite the kitchen was the sitting room and to its right, Tina's bedroom. Further down the corridor were Pamela and Nancy's bedrooms. Tina's door was ajar and through it Adam could see the rain bouncing off the stone windowsill. Tina's bed was behind the door, almost hidden.

Pausing in the doorway, Adam saw Tina's clothes hanging on the wardrobe door. Even the sight of her lingerie gave him a frisson of excitement. He hesitated to enter her room as he felt this would be an intrusion on her privacy.

The rain was now driving down harder than ever, and he paused sensing something was wrong; a miasma pervaded him and he realised there was someone in her room. Above the sound of the rain, he could hear Tina's voice. Indistinctly at first, as if her head was buried beneath a pillow; then clearer as he realised that it was right beside him on the other side of the door.

'Oh God,' she screamed, 'yes!' Her wanton cry, a fusion of urgency and ecstasy.

Adam could hardly breathe as his mind grappled with the thought that there was someone making love to her only feet away from him. What a fool he was. How could he have let another man usurp his position? Defiling his beautiful girl.

'Yes, yesss!' she screamed and a spiralling moan announced her approaching orgasm. Adam's feeling of nausea was rapidly followed by uncontrollable anger and he burst into the room.

Expecting to find a man in bed with Tina, he was at first relieved that she was lying alone on the bed completely naked. It was only then that he noticed Nancy kneeling beside the bed, her hair hanging down each side of her face, her eyes glowering at him. She too was naked and as she stood up she made no attempt to cover her body.

'Oh my God,' said Tina, burying herself under a sheet.

Nancy stood in a defiant pose, her hands on her hips and her small breasts pointing insolently towards him as if guarding her property. Behind her, he could see only Tina's tousled hair on the pillow. It took him a few moments to overcome his total disbelief of what he was witnessing and then he mustered, 'What the hell is going on here?'

This was the signal for Nancy to unleash her invective. 'You filthy bloody Peeping Tom; you dirty little keyhole sneaking bastard; piss-off before you learn anything more that your mother never intended you to know.' She gave a mocking laugh. 'Haven't you yet learnt that only a woman really knows how to pleasure a woman?'

His feeling of relief that there was no man in Tina's bed now turned to revulsion at this woman who had abused the love of his life. His desire to defend Tina as an innocent led astray slowly turned to realisation that she was obviously a happy participant of this lesbian tryst.

He could not remember seeing Pamela, but she subsequently told him that he had pushed her roughly aside as he rushed out of the flat, nor could he recall going down the six flights of stairs. The first thing he remembered was standing behind a bush in Hyde Park being violently sick. There were not many people about and he had mustered sufficient innate dignity to choose a secluded spot.

Adam emerged unsteadily from this retreat. The rain had stopped and the warm evening air was drying the grass. He wandered on, having no objective or purpose. At Lancaster Gate, he bought an Evening Standard and sat down to read it. But it was hopeless, the words blurred over. He got up and wandered towards the Serpentine, now void of boats. On the far side, some bell tents had been pitched and two searchlights lurked beneath their camouflage netting.

He debated whether to head towards Queen's Gate Gardens where he knew he would receive a warm welcome, but had so much to resolve in his own mind before he could share his feelings with anyone else. He carried on to Hyde Park Corner, out through the gates past Apsley House, and down Piccadilly. He turned into Dover Street and found himself at the door of Brown's Hotel. He asked the porter if he would call the Ritz and cancel the reservation for dinner and then sat at the bar, contemplating how differently things should have turned out that evening.

It was almost incomprehensible that a tender love affair which had appeared to blossom for so many years, could be shattered in one moment. Maybe he had allowed himself to believe there was more between them than there was? In many ways, he could have coped better with her being unfaithful with a man, as devastating as it still would have been, but to see her under the spell of that dominatrix left him floundering to make sense of her actions.

He remembered Rindi rebuking him for his attitude to homosexuals. He understood the revulsion Adam felt towards the sexual predators at school but thought it was too simplistic a view. 'The Ancient Greeks believed that this type of love was as worthy as normal love and was often a pathway to heterosexual love,' was the view he had proffered.

Did his beautiful girl really prefer the attentions of that sexless bitch? Had her nubile body desperately needed fulfilment? Was he to blame for having not asserted his desires more boldly or was it a different satisfaction that she sought? Perhaps it was, as Rindi had theorised, a journey rather than the destination. Whatever the real answer was, he felt betrayed and humiliated and could not contemplate forgiving her. It was over.

He slept fitfully and woke early hoping that it was all a bad dream. However, the memory of Nancy's scrawny frame and rude posture challenging his sexuality returned to torment him. He resolved to expunge this event from his mind and to move on. But even if he could succeed in blocking out that memory of sexual betrayal, only time would heal the aching pain of having lost his first real love.

Adam took an early train to Salisbury where a sprawling camp had been hastily constructed a few months earlier. The hive of military activity there was a comforting diversion from the turbulence of his memories of the previous afternoon. He walked up the wooden steps to the Adjutant's Office and knocked on the door with far more confidence than he had done nine months before.

'Come in.' There was something familiar about the voice; he stepped inside and gave a courtesy salute. 'Cullworthy reporting for duty, Sir.'

The head looked up from the desk, and then its owner leapt to his feet.

'Good God! Adam! I don't believe it. How bloody marvellous. We thought you hadn't made it out of France.' It was the enthusiastic welcome of Willie Ashford.

'So what's the news of Bob Mercer? I suppose the poor bastard's now in the bag.'

'Amazingly not, Adam. He managed to get out from Dunkirk on one of those hundreds of pleasure boats. I only learnt about what happened from the staff captain. When some of his company were shot-up on the beach and wounded, Bob stayed to get them onto a Navy Corvette. It was only when the brigadier ordered him to leave, that he waded out and got into a boat himself.'

'That's about typical of Bob. So where is he now?'

'He's away on a commanding officer's course. He'll be back in three weeks' time and will almost certainly be promoted to "half-colonel" and given his own battalion.'

August 1940

The whole country was now in state of tension awaiting the inevitable invasion by the Germans. Defences along the coast from Kent to Hampshire were heavily reinforced, steel barriers erected along the high tide line and razor-sharp barbed wire laid to a depth of several yards on the beaches. The Luftwaffe was intent upon destroying the RAF, leaving Britain defenceless and clearing the way for the invasion.

Wave after wave of German bombers, protected by hundreds of Messerschmitt 109 fighters, crossed the Channel. The RAF was in position at a higher altitude, ready to engage them in Spitfire and Hurricane fighters. Dogfights proliferated and despite heavy losses the RAF were able to display superiority and destroyed enemy aircraft in considerable numbers. This was the beginning of the Battle of Britain.

The threat of imminent invasion remained and the camp commandant called together about a dozen officers who had been engaged in fighting in France. They were briefed, ready to be sent to areas in Britain that might be used by the Germans as airborne landing sites. Their assignment was to pass on to regiments protecting those areas, the experience of the possible tactics of the enemy.

Adam was despatched to Craigellachie in Aberdeenshire where an important strategic road and railway bridge crossed the River Spey. He reported to the C.O. of the Eighth Gordon Highlanders. They had made their own preparations for the invasion. Acre upon acre of flat fields were peppered with thousands of hastily erected tall poles, designed to frustrate any airborne landing craft. The effect was to make it look more like a hop farm. Adam was glad to be well away from London not only because of the nightly raids but because of the painful memories it aroused. It was no surprise to him that he had heard nothing from Tina since that afternoon but he still had many unresolved questions in his mind.

After eight months in the Highlands in a training capacity Adam was pleased to be recalled to the Salisbury transit camp with the prospect of active service with the battalion.

Adam reported to Bob Mercer, now deputy commandant of the depot, to be given his posting orders.

'Good morning, Sir; you sent for me.'

'Yes, sit down, Adam. How do you fancy a posting overseas?'

'The Virgin Islands are said to be rather agreeable at this time of year, Sir, or maybe the Duke of Windsor needs another A.D.C. in the Bahamas?'

'I see you haven't lost your sense of humour, old boy' Mercer replied giving him a wry smile and then went on. 'As you know, our regiment has one battalion permanently stationed in India; it never totally comes home, or hasn't since the last war, but the officers and men are changed periodically. The C.O. of that battalion has been brought home and promoted to brigadier, to serve in the India department at the War Office. It seems they want to replace him with someone who's seen some real action in Europe, and I've been given the command.'

'Congratulations, Sir. When does the promotion come through?'

'Oh, not until I get to India.'

'That is excellent news. When do you expect to go?'

'As soon as they can get us on a boat, and that may take three or four weeks. The ships all have to be made up into convoys with adequate warship protection against German "U" Boats.'

'Yes, I gather things are pretty treacherous out in the Atlantic.'

'How would you like to come with me to India? There are some vacancies and the Adjutant General's Branch say that I can take two or three officers.'

It would be difficult to fully describe Adam's emotions and thoughts over those next few seconds. India was somewhere he had wanted so very much to go ever since he had made a friend of Rindi Debrahm. All the stories he had told him: the adventures; the fascinating buildings; the people; bazaars, peacocks, palaces, elephants and tigers loomed before him, as his imagination ran riot. But perhaps it would be all different in wartime.

'I can think of nowhere I'd rather be posted, Sir, and it would be good to get some sun on my back.'

'Splendid. I can't promise there'll be much action but from what I've heard you've probably had your fill of that over in France.'

'Well, I had a lucky escape Sir.'

'Rather more heroic than that if the despatches are to be believed. There may even be something in the pipeline for you.'

Adam looked surprised but nodded in acknowledgement.

'I'll inform them that you will be joining us on the boat. Hopefully we will be away within three weeks.'

CHAPTER NINE

August 1941. Convoy to India

The sun was just disappearing into the Indian Ocean when the sharp strident blasts of the ship's siren summoned them to their allocated fire stations. Adam was sitting in the lounge on 'A' deck, wondering whether to get himself a long drink.

'Christ, not another god damn fire drill; you'd think that we had a gang of arsonists on board, the way this bunch of tits behave.' Captain Hugh Archibald was never at a loss to express himself.

He was an American who had come over to Oxford before the War as a Rhodes Scholar to take his master's degree in archaeology. Having an English mother, he had given up his studies and volunteered for the British Army and was given a direct commission into the Royal Artillery. He was a bear of a man with a mop of blond hair which even with a regulation haircut he never managed to tame fully. He was not a tidy soldier but his intelligence, charm and enthusiasm usually got him through. His success at the School of Gunnery had resulted in an instructor's posting to India. Archie, as he was known to friends, had made a long journey almost bearable with his irrepressible banter.

Everyone was scurrying for their life jackets. Emergency drill had become a regular feature and in the event of an attack would no doubt have saved many lives but had become extremely tedious. It did, however, have the benefit of providing an opportunity to meet the women officers on board.

On reaching his lifeboat station, it was still light enough for Adam to see the attractive face of Junior Commander Sarah Roberts leaning against the rail, chatting to another A.T.S. officer.

She smiled at him. 'Cheer up, Adam. In less than two weeks we'll be sailing into Bombay.'

Sarah was one of only a dozen A.T.S. officers on the ship. The women were accommodated in two large cabins at the end of a corridor on 'A' deck. Although tacitly out of bounds, there were other inhibiting factors to venturesome males. First, it was necessary to run the gauntlet of a number of cabins occupied by colonels and brigadiers, then skilfully avoid the formidable guardian of the seraglio: a chief commander A.T.S., whose equivalent rank was lieutenant-colonel. Even if one had succeeded in overcoming these obstacles, the expedition would have been fruitless since a cabin of six women confers no privacy.

Their ship, The Strathallan, may have been the pride of the P & O fleet when launched four years earlier, but now, having been eviscerated and refitted as a troopship, she was far from luxurious. Major Mercer and Adam, together with several hundred officers and over 2000 men, had boarded the vessel in late July at Gourock, twenty miles west of Glasgow. It had been pouring with rain, and to add to their displeasure they had embarked by *lighter*. Sailing down the Firth of Clyde, they were joined by one troopship after another, until out in the Irish Sea warships that were to protect them began to marshal the convoy. There were corvettes, destroyers, battleships and, far in the background, an aircraft carrier.

With such a mixed fleet, it must have been a nightmare for the convoy commander. Little wonder that one night in the fog the blacked-out 'Sterling' and the 'Windsor Castle' had collided; thereafter displaying their crumpled bows for all to see.

The 'U' boats chased them across the Atlantic to the coast of America, which they then followed down to the Bahamas, then south-east back across the Atlantic to Freetown. There, late at night, the 'Strathallan' had its narrowest escape. It was saved by the vigilance of the lookouts and the seamanship of the captain and officers on the bridge, taking instant action to evade a torpedo heading straight for them.

It was in the euphoria of the brief celebration following this fortunate deliverance and the antics of 'Crossing the Equator' that Sarah and Adam had become better acquainted. They had met frequently on fire and boat drill and in the mess where she was usually surrounded by several officers jockeying for her company. Although they always greeted each other amiably, Adam had never actively sought her favour. Whether this arose through the thought of a rebuff or his disillusionment with females in general, he could not honestly say. Whatever the reason may have been, his apparent disinterest in her acted in his favour.

Adam was standing by the rail, looking through his binoculars at the distant island of St. Helena, when he became aware of Sarah standing beside him. Even in her dull khaki uniform she looked remarkably pretty.

'It must have been rather lonely there for Napoleon,' she said. 'Although they do say he had two or three secret mistresses.'

'We studied Napoleon's operations at Sandhurst, but I can't say it extended to his prowess in bed.' Adam responded.

'Well, Josephine seemed to like it.'

Adam detected facetiousness in her manner, but she gave him such a disarming smile.

'How old are you, Sarah?'

'My, my Captain Cullworthy, you are getting personal.' She gave a mock curtsy. 'Six and twenty good years, Sir.'

Sarah swung round with her back to the rail and looked at him as he stared out to sea. 'Adam, would you like to sleep with me?' she asked.

'What sort of chap do you think I am?' Adam said with the pretence of indignation masking his astonishment.

Her coy look made him realise she was serious.

'When had you in mind?' he replied, giving her a cheeky smile.

At that moment, Adam saw Bob Mercer walking towards them, precluding further discussion on this subject.

Although they saw each other frequently during the next four days, Sarah did not mention this conversation again. Adam could not work out whether she was manipulative or merely someone who expected to get her own way. She was very desirable and he now looked at her in a completely different light but he was still licking his wounds from the Tina debacle.

After six weeks in confined conditions the sight of Table Mountain as they entered the bay at Cape Town was very uplifting and made the prospect of getting ashore even more tantalising. The first message that the Cape Town reception committee signalled was, 'are there any Australians aboard your ships?' A reply in the negative was signalled, and the Capetonians then welcomed them ashore. The apparent reason for this precaution was that earlier in the year a full Australia and New Zealand Expeditionary Force bound for England had arrived in the Cape. With their training still to come, they lacked discipline and made nonsense of all the welcoming arrangements of the City. The canteens were in full swing and held dances every night. During the day cars and buses lined up along Dock Road to take the men sightseeing, but these unruly men were looking for more adventurous exploits. A girl waiting in her car for her mother outside the Post Office expressed regret that she could not give them a lift. Four disgruntled burly Aussies lifted up her car and carried it up the steps and into the Post Office, stuck a stamp on the windscreen and said 'Now go home!'

Others intercepted four great carthorses pulling a dray laden with crated bottles of beer. They took the horses out of their harness and had bareback races up the main street, whilst their friends took beer from the brewer's dray. Some of this beer was happily accepted by onlookers who found themselves in the magistrate's court the next day for accepting stolen goods. Although the citizens of Cape Town took the whole escapade in good spirit, they were not keen to expose the city to a repeat performance.

Sarah was still keeping Adam guessing, but her comment the night before they docked aroused his curiosity. 'I've a cousin who lives out beyond Chapman's Peak, I wondered if you'd like a trip out there with me?'

Adam had no idea where Chapman's Peak was, but the invitation was timely because, as soon as the ship berthed, shore leave procedures were put into action. Everyone had to be back on board by midnight. He was, therefore, surprised when Sarah came to him with an overnight pass signed not only by her own 'Queen Bee', but also by the brigadier O.C. Troops on their ship. She had with her another special pass, unsigned.

'This is for you, Adam. I'm only being let out overnight on condition that I have a male officer escort, so I hope you'll agree to come with me. The least I can promise you is that you'll be well fed and entertained.'

'But who's going to sign my overnight pass? And how on earth..?'

'That won't be a problem,' she said with an air of confidence.

* * *

They took a suburban train along the coast of False Bay, and after an hour they arrived at the cliff-side station of Simonstown.

Sarah's cousin Fiona was two years older than her. She was married to Henry Lombard, a South African. Fiona's father was a Royal Navy captain stationed at the Naval Base in Simonstown. It became apparent to Adam that he was the source of influence for the special overnight passes.

After lunch at the captain's residence Fiona drove them to her home on the other side of the Peninsula. The ten-mile trip took them through countryside quite different from any Adam had seen in Europe. The Lombard residence was an extensive single storey building set high on the hillside, capturing views of the Atlantic on three sides. Sarah and Adam were given adjacent bedrooms with French windows leading on to a terrace where they could look out across the bay to another shoreline. Each bedroom had its own bathroom with a plentiful supply of hot water which, after six weeks of salt-water showers, was a great luxury.

As she lay in her bath Sarah wondered what is was about Adam that had attracted her. He was not her normal type, she usually liked older men who tended to be more at ease with themselves. She had had younger men pursue her and their attentiveness was initially very flattering but their overzealous spaniel approach soon became a bore. Adam's coolness interested her. There was a worldliness about him which she had seen in other men who had been in the frontline. She liked the warrior in him but there was also a vulnerability about him which she found appealing.

Sarah appeared for dinner in a close fitting red dress, cut low to reveal the top of her cleavage. A fine woollen cardigan covered her shoulders to protect her from the chill of the South African late winter evening and she had let her hair down making her look much younger. A pair of high heels emphasised her elegant ankles and shapely legs. She really was a vision, a complete contrast to the uniformed officer Adam had arrived with an hour before.

Henry arrived shortly before dinner and mixed them a 'sundowner'. The food and the wine which followed had none of the constraints of rationing and the whole experience seemed far removed from the war they were fighting.

After dinner, they followed the South African custom of retiring early. Adam was thinking about bed but not about sleep as he walked out onto the terrace. Above the sound of the surf driven by the huge Atlantic waves that thundered far below he could hear the insistent chirp of the crickets, then more faintly, the call of a nightjar. He wondered whether the rest of the household was asleep. Having barely been able to take his eyes off her all evening he imagined Sarah slipping her lithe figure out of that dress. One of the French windows to her room was open and the golden glow of the light within seemed very inviting. Emboldened by the wine, and at the risk of his advances being dismissed, he popped his head round the door. There was no one there. Then from outside a voice said. 'Looking for me?'

He turned to see Sarah sitting in a wicker chair at the edge of the terrace looking out on the moonlit sea. She was still wearing the red dress and her eyes sparkled in the moonlight. As he walked towards her she smiled revealing her lovely straight teeth.

'I just came to deliver this,' he said and bent down to kiss her gently on the neck, 'and to tell you how beautiful you looked this evening.'

Sarah stood up, put her arms round his neck and kissed him passionately.

'Wow,' he said when they stopped to draw breath, 'that was worth waiting for.'

She squeezed his hand then turned and walked back towards her room, the soft cool grass caressing her bare feet. 'Give me five minutes,' she said with a mischievous twinkle.

Adam did not know why he was so surprised at the warmth of her embrace, after all this was the woman who a few days earlier had asked if he would like to sleep with her, but this invitation was more than he had hoped for.

The main light in Sarah's bedroom had gone out and Adam took this as a signal that the five minutes was up. Sarah was already in bed when he walked through the door, and with a puckish smile, she pulled the sheet down to reveal a fine lace negligee. With shameless relish she watched Adam undress and climb into bed beside her. Although she had probably planned this encounter carefully, now lying there, she looked vulnerable. Adam's lustful gaze must have made her feel self-conscious because she then reached across and turned out the bedside light.

In those few moments whilst his eyes adjusted, she had dispensed with the negligee and now lay naked allowing the moonlight to emphasise her beautiful curves. As they caressed each other he felt sure that he was probably not her first lover but this did not concern him and anyway he was also not a beginner. But this time it would be different. Not the impulsive urgent coupling of two people who feared for their lives. This time there would be no need to rush their love making.

Sarah was sleeping soundly when Adam left her room in the early hours of the morning. It seemed almost a waste to go to sleep, at least not immediately. He knew that as wonderful as the last few hours had been, Sarah had used him for her own pleasure. Yet he had seen a tender side of her that had touched him more than just physically.

Beyond Kushnapur

The fresh salty smell of the sea drifted in on the night air as Adam walked to the edge of the terrace. He found himself thinking about Tina. She had been his first love but had left him tormented and disillusioned. Looking back on that afternoon in London, he realised how naive he had been and wondered whether he had overreacted to finding her in bed with Nancy. It had been such an assault on his early manhood. For so long he had dreamed of making love to her but felt her beauty and innocence were a wonder to be saved for some special moment in the future. Now he felt a sense of relief that perhaps he could move on.

His thoughts returned to Sarah. Although strong willed, she was a sensual woman who had reassured him once more of his masculine attraction. He was now glowing with the glorious feeling of complete romantic fulfilment. He returned to his own room and climbed into bed. Cocooned in the warmth of her scent, still on his skin, and with the blissful thought of possibly having her in his arms again soon, he drifted into a contented sleep.

CHAPTER TEN

Bombay, September 1941.

Major Mercer leant forward and smiled having just enjoyed an excellent *tandoori murg* in the dining room of the Willingdon Club.

'I'm sure you'll agree, Adam, it would be the worst possible start for you to arrive with me at the battalion. The last thing you need is your fellow officers thinking you are chummy with the C.O.'

'I understand completely, Sir, and thank you for taking the trouble to get me on the training course at Mhow at such short notice.'

'Nominally it's for junior staff officers', so you'll need to raise your game.'

'It should be a good experience,' Adam confirmed.

'Yes, you'll enjoy Mhow. You might find them a bit behind the times. I gather they haven't even clocked the fact that we are at war down there.'

'Yes, well, Europe does seem a long way away.'

'I think we should probably be off if we are going to catch our trains. I'll see you in Rawalpindi in about a month, Adam.' They parted; Adam to Victoria Terminus to catch the Punjab Mail and the major to Bombay Central to pick up the Frontier Mail to New Delhi and then on to Rawalpindi.

The first stop for the Punjab Mail was the Transit Camp at Deolali where Adam spent two days. Then a twelve-hour onward journey to Mhow including a half-hour wait at Khandwa to change trains and move on to the metre gauge single line. The train hurtled through Kipling country, the engine roaring and leaving a billowing trail of steam and smoke. The sights and smells of India pervaded. Open air sanitation and dung fires; then in the evening, as temperatures abated, the scent of jasmine blossom.

Mhow proved an interesting and comfortable introduction to life in India for Adam. The accommodation was an ancient barracks paved with solid stone floors which helped keep the place cool. The Officers'

Mess had the trappings of colonial splendour with immaculate silver, glass and linen, and paintings of past and present monarchs on every wall. Well-drilled servants catered to every whim with obvious enthusiasm. Garments and items of uniform were laundered and polished within hours of being discarded. Sporting activity was encouraged once the daily coursework was completed. This consisted of polo for those that rode and even the occasional cricket match against a local team.

As Adam lay in his bath at the end of the day savouring a mint julep he thought about the hordes of scruffy undernourished children that had plagued the train whenever it stopped, hoping for a hand-out of food or clothing. Would he ever be able to adjust to the extreme social differences in this country?

Rindi had talked to him about the *Kushdins* and their plots to rid India of British rule. Maybe they had a point. Maybe it was time for India to face its own problems for better or for worse. Wallowing in the warmth of his scented bath it was difficult to imagine an India without its colonial masters and where would independence leave families like the Debrahms of Kushnapur?

Adam had written to Rindi via his home address informing him that he would be joining his regiment in Rawalpindi within three weeks and that it might be possible for them to meet somewhere on his journey through to the north.

One evening a week later, the mess steward called Adam to the telephone. It was surely too soon for Rindi to have received his letter, so who else could possibly know where to contact him?

'Hello, Adam, it's Sarah.'

'How on earth did you know where to find me? I didn't even know myself that I was coming here until the day after we landed. And you'd already left by then.'

'Ah, well, we A.T.S. girls have a way of finding these things out.'

'You certainly do.'

'It's alright, Adam; I'll put you out of your misery. By chance I saw Colonel Mercer at GHQ when he called at the Women's Army Corps unit for a car.'

'So what's your news, Sarah? Do you know where they're sending you?'

'Yes, I'm moving down to Agra tomorrow. And I've also been given some weekend leave to spend with my parents.'

'I didn't realize they were in India. Is your father still in the army?'

'He certainly is; he's doing a staff job. I hope you'll get to meet him one day. '

'So what will you be doing in Agra?'

'I'm training the Women's' Army Corps Indian.'

'Ah, yes, the Wackeyes.'

'That's right. A few of the Anglo-Indian girls could shape-up well as future officers. And when do you finish your course?'

'Within a week and then I should be coming through Agra on my way north. Any chance of seeing you?'

'Yes, I'd like that. When you know what train you're on call me there.'

She rang off and Adam thought it a pity he wasn't going to be stationed near Agra, instead of in Rawalpindi, five hundred miles away.

Rindi's reply arrived a few days later and Adam learnt that he was stationed at Ambala Cantonment, north of Delhi and nine hundred miles from Mhow. He'd given a telephone number and that evening, after several abortive attempts by the operator and frequent requests 'to please holding-on, sahib,' Adam's patience was rewarded.

'Rindi! Is that really you? Do you realise it's been two years since we last spoke. My God, so much has happened since we last saw each other.'

'Adam, you old sod, this is marvellous. How the hell did you fix it? Nina said in a letter that you were coming to India, but I just couldn't believe it.'

'Yes, it really was a stroke of luck getting out here, but it's a long story.'

'Never mind that, just give me the short answer.'

'Well, Colonel Mercer arranged the posting. He was our second-in-command in France. He was transferred to India with promotion and asked me if I'd like to join him. He's now my new C.O.'

'From your letter I gather your course ends soon, so what train can you take? I can meet you at Ambala station. I'll arrange for you to stay at the Mess.'

'That all sounds fine. I'll check on the trains.' He wonderd if he should he go straight through to Ambala or stopover in Agra to meet up with Sarah. After all she had rung him and sounded pleased at the prospect of seeing him. The thought of revisiting their romantic encounter in Cape Town was irresistible. He felt sure that Rindi would understand.

'I may have to go via Agra but I'll telephone you from New Dehli to confirm what time I'll get to Ambala.'

'That's fine; I'll stand by for your call. I know most of the train times.'

Adam then telephoned Sarah to tell her he would be on the Jhelum Express arriving in Agra at 13.00 the following day.

'Oh, that's excellent, Adam, and that's the Poona train which is much faster than the Punjab Mail. We'll meet you at the station and have lunch at the Club.'

That was about the limit of their telephone conversation. A warm welcome seemed in prospect.

October 1941. Central India.

The monsoons had now ended, and Adam had chosen to travel at night as the temperature was thirty-degrees lower than during the day.

Dawn was breaking as the train steamed into Bhopal, its white walled houses and red tile roofs appeared like a shimmering mirage as the low red sun rose from the East. After Hyderabad, Bhopal was the most important Muslim State in India and the wailing call to prayer floated across the heavy morning atmosphere. An hour later far beyond that city, the peasant farmers could be seen tending their lands, bursting with the benefits of the recent rains. It was hard to conceive how they were able to scratch an existence on these small strips of land, yet the villagers appeared to accept their plight with a gentle dignity. Probably, thought Adam, in the firm belief that they would be treated better in the next life.

Three hours later the train drew slowly into Agra Cantonment Station. On the opposite platform Adam admired the diligence with which the driver of a great steam locomotive was polishing a section of brass in his cab. The train had barely halted before a flood of khaki disgorged onto the platform merging uneasily with the press of fresh passengers waiting to board for Delhi and beyond. Uniforms were everywhere and even the distinctive headgear of the A.T.S. was not easy to spot. Then Adam caught sight of Sarah waving in the distance. A warm feeling came over him as her smiling face approached his carriage. His spirit was lifted and it felt good to be in India.

'Sarah, how lovely of you to come and meet me.'

'Oh, but I said we would. Did you have a good journey? How was the course?'

It was difficult to answer amid the hubbub on the crowded platform with steam hissing in the background.

'I'll tell you when we get out of here', Adam said, and was about to steer her through the milling throng when he became aware of another officer standing beside her. Sarah glanced at him then back to Adam.

'Let me introduce James Pendleton. James, this is Adam Cullworthy.'

A hand came forward and Adam found himself greeting a major of the 7th Queen's Own Hussars. He was about the same height as himself, though some years older, probably in his mid-thirties and with a fuller figure. His skin had the tanned look of one who has been in the tropics for many years. Despite a receding hairline he was handsome of face. Adam was not sure whether he was going to like him; at least not until he knew where he fitted in the picture.

'As you've probably discovered, Adam, officers are not allowed to drive army vehicles in India so James brought me down in his staff car. We've given him one of our top women drivers, so I have to make him show his appreciation from time to time.'

The appealing way Sarah looked at Adam assuaged some of the resentment he felt that she had not come alone.

'When are you going on to Delhi?'

'That slightly depends.' Adam said keeping his options open 'but probably this same train tomorrow would be the fastest.'

'Oh, not much time then,' she said, sounding disappointed but not questioning the uncertainty in Adam's reply.

'At least you'll be able to join us for dinner tonight; James has a table booked at the Grand Hotel.' She looked at Pendleton who seemed a little surprised to hear his name, but then responded enthusiastically to the questioning tilt of her head.

'Oh rather, yes, everything's laid on.'

Clearly, Sarah was the one calling the tune, and Adam's company at dinner did not appear to be of his choosing.

It seemed unlikely that Adam would have Sarah to himself that evening, and disguising his disappointment he asked, 'Do you think I could get a room at the Agra Club tonight?'

'They're always pretty full, but James knows the secretary so I'm sure he can fix it.'

Pendleton smiled, without comment, in acknowledgement of her compliment.

The driver was waiting beside a Humber Snipe staff car and saluted them smartly before directing the coolies to Adam's bags. Adam had hoped to ride in the back with Sarah, but whilst he was paying the porters Pendleton slipped into the rear seat beside her, leaving Adam to sit beside the driver.

'You ought to see the Taj whilst you're here and Agra Fort if you have time.'

'I had hoped for the VIP tour,' Adam said cheekily, looking at Sarah over his shoulder.

'Well, that could probably be arranged,' she said, turning to Pendleton for approval.

'Yes, by all means, darling,' he replied. 'Would you like to take the car?'

'That would be very kind.'

Hearing him call her "darling" made Adam feel both jealous and uncomfortable. He had been naïve to think that someone as attractive as Sarah would remain unescorted for long and there had never been any talk of any commitment between them.

They drove east along Station Road for about a mile-and-a-quarter, then as they entered the Mall the driver slowed down. For a moment it looked as if she intended to stop at the General Post Office; instead, she turned the car in a gentle arc into an entrance between two small red-roofed buildings.

'Stop here,' Pendleton instructed the driver.

He got out of the car and walked through a door marked "Secretary". Two minutes later he returned, having organised a room for Adam.

'All fixed, old boy,' he said in an over friendly but slightly patronising manner.

There was something about Pendleton that made Adam feel awkward but he couldn't quite put his finger on it. Further down the gravel drive, they stopped at the Club building which was fronted by pairs of imposing white pillars supporting the roof of a curved veranda.

After lunch Sarah and Pendleton left together.

'I'll pick you up, say in about an hour?' said Sarah.

'That would be lovely.' Then, turning to Pendleton, Adam said, 'and thank you for arranging the room and the car.'

'No problem, old boy, see you later.'

Adam's hope of seeing the Taj Mahal in the moonlight with Sarah was not to be but it was no less impressive by daylight and he still had her to guide him.

'Shahjahan built this for his great love Muntaz. Sadly she died bearing his fourteenth child. I find it difficult to imagine even having one child.'

'I'm sure you'll make a wonderful mother one day.'

'Do you think so?' she said squeezing his arm.

Encouraged by this Adam ventured, 'So how long have you been seeing Pendleton?'

'Oh, it's not like that. We're just good friends,' she said defensively.

'Well, he seems quite taken with you.'

'No, believe me he is not.'

'Why does he call you darling?'

'Mainly because he's my cousin. Adam, you really are jealous aren't you?'

'You looked like the perfect couple to me, arm in arm on the platform.'

'Well, let's just say it suits both of us if people think that. Besides which he will report back to my parents and I'm just not sure I am ready for an inquisition from my mother.'

'I had rather hoped that we might...' Adam began but was not bold enough to follow through with his statement.

'Yes, I know' she responded with a meaningful look, 'it would be lovely but it just isn't going to be possible this time.'

Adam was still not convinced. He knew Sarah was inclined to use men for her own purpose. Perhaps Pendleton was just friend or a cousin but he sensed that Sarah was not giving him the full story. At that moment she leaned across and kissed him with unexpected tenderness. Adam drew her to him and the fragrant smell of her hair and the softness of the skin on her neck made him feel like they were holding back a tide of passion.

Holding his hand possessively she said, 'Where are you heading to after Delhi?'

'I'll catch the Jhelum Express right through to Ambala Cantonment. There I'm meeting Rindi Debrahm.'

'Oh, yes, that's your Indian pal from school. So you're still in touch?'

'Yes, you must meet him sometime.' As Adam said this he wondered what they would make of each other. If Sarah was reluctant to introduce Adam as anything significant to her family he also felt strangely protective of his relationship with Rindi.

As his train sped north towards the Punjab the next day, Adam sat staring out of the window at the green fields and the Yamuna River swollen by the monsoons. In the distance he could see the great diversity of traffic on the Grand Trunk road: the highway which stretched for six hundred miles up to the North-West Frontier of India.

What was he to make of Sarah? Perhaps his expectations of their reunion had been unrealistic. She had been very affectionate when they were alone together. But was he prepared to show unguarded emotions? He had been there before. Putting aside this tangle of feelings about Sarah he occupied himself instead with thoughts of what lay ahead.

There was a forty-five minute stop at New Delhi Station and Adam tried to put a call through to Rindi but he was not available so he left a message with the duty clerk. Back on board the train, the "chai-wallah" brought a tray of tea and toast and when three Indian *King's Commissioned* officers joined his compartment he thought of his friend. How much would he have changed in the two years since he had seen him in Cairo? So much had changed in his own life that he felt a completely different person.

The train finally pulled into Ambala at twenty-past eight. Adam scanned the platform for Rindi. In England he had stood out from the crowd but here amongst a mass of uniformed Indians he was less distinctive. He must have checked on the number of the carriage, because as soon as Adam stepped off the train he saw him carving his way through the sea of humanity.

'Adam,' he shouted above the noisy crowd, 'welcome to the Punjab.'

The Punjab

Rindi took Adam to his officer's mess where he had reserved a room for him.

'When do you have to be in Rawalpindi?' Can you break your journey for a bit longer? Stay an extra night?

Having hoped to spend the weekend with Sarah, Adam now had more time before he needed to join the battalion. 'I'd love to, and we've a quite a bit to catch up on.'

The mess waiter delivered two "burra-pegs" of scotch.

'So where do we start? How's the love life?' said Rindi.

'I'm afraid it all ended rather disastrously with Tina.'

'Oh, I'm sorry to hear that,'Rindi said rather disingenuously.

Adam related the Nancy saga and Rindi tried to feign surprise at his revelation although he had already heard Tina's account.

Rindi leant back in his chair and considered how much Adam had changed. He had always been tall but he had now filled out his lean frame. A fine moustache provided definition to his handsome face and gave him a look of maturity beyond his years. Despite a self-confidence born of years in the army and the experience of conflict, his eyes, sometimes blue sometimes green, could not disguise a certain vulnerability when it came to talking about romance. It was this vulnerability which prevented him from revealing to Adam his involvement with Tina.

It had all been so innocent at first. She had come up to Oxford to visit the Ashmolean Museum as part of her coursework. Rindi had always fancied Tina more than Pauline but she was so young and then Adam had taken a shine to her and so she was off limits. Tina likewise had always idolised Rindi but she knew she was too young and unsophisticated for him. On that glorious June afternoon he had taken her punting on the river. He remembered the comic scene of him being left clinging to the pole whilst the punt drifted steadily away on the current. The punt and Tina were eventually retrieved but not before he had taken a soaking. Whether it was the laughter, the heat of the sun or the champagne which broke down the barriers of their hidden desire, they ended up in a passionate embrace. Even though Tina had told Rindi that her youthful romance with Adam was over they were both tormented by the guilt of betraying him. Rindi longed to share all his feelings with Adam but he couldn't conceive how this might ever be possible.

Adam broke Rindi's reverie. 'Any news of that scoundrel Wantilla?'

'Still making trouble, I'm afraid.'

'How is Virginia by the way? Have you seen her since that boat incident?'

'Yes, I saw her once or twice in London. She had managed to salvage the situation with Simon although I can't really understand what she sees in him.'

'Apart from the title?'

'Oh, I think that is more for her mother's benefit.'

With each new mouthful of scotch Rindi felt he was getting closer to confessing to Adam, but for reasons beyond the survival of their friendship he needed to hold his tongue.

'So, Adam, any other romantic involvements?'

'Well, there is this ATS officer who I had a fling with on the way out, but you know what it's like in these turbulent times.'

'Yes, *carpe diem* eh?'

Adam looked pensive.

'Ah, I sense more than a passing interest. So does she have a name?'

'Sarah.'

'Any plans to see her in India?'

'Actually I have just seen her in Agra but it was rather frustrating. I can't see much future in it to be honest.'

'I'm sorry to hear that,' Rindi replied, 'but probably for the best. You never know what tomorrow will bring.'

Rindi touched a nerve and Adam found it difficult to make light of his recent experience.

'So I guess I am pretty fancy free now,' he said trying to sound convincing. 'What about you? Any news of Pauline?'

'Oh, we still keep in touch but as you know she's more like a sister to me.'

Rindi had always kept his cards quite close to his chest about his romantic life and Adam had wondered whether he might already have a bride chosen for him but he had never felt he could ask. His looks and charm made him very desirable to English girls and Adam knew the effect he had had on his sisters and mother.

'Adam, how soon can you get leave? I want you to come up to Kushnapur and meet my family.'

'Well, I think that's a marvellous idea, but as I haven't even reported to my regiment I can hardly ask for leave as soon as I get there, although I must admit that I am due some.'

'Look, Adam, the position is this. I am in this Tactical Warfare training unit and I have been told that I am not likely to be here more than a year. Kushnapur is only a hundred and forty miles from here, so I'm conveniently placed to get home.'

Adam smiled. He was getting used to the relaxed attitude to distances in India. Anything less than a thousand miles seemed just up the road.

'When I next go home on leave I would like you to come with me.'

'Right, I'll see what can be done. Who will be there when we visit?'

'Apart from my parents, my two sisters, Kafni and Puella.'

'How old are they now?'

'Kafni is nineteen and Puella fifteen.'

'Both unmarried?'

'Yes, but Wantilla has his mind set on marrying Kafni and is not beyond conniving to get his way.'

'Surely she can refuse to marry him?'

'It's not quite as simple as that. Wantilla's branch of the family is extremely rich and has considerable influence. She would be consulted on the matter, but as you must be aware, families almost always arrange marriages in India. My sister is bright and well educated and certainly not the submissive type but she would place the interests of our family above other considerations.'

'Wouldn't it be better if Wantilla didn't marry his first cousin?'

'Indeed, my thoughts entirely but by marrying the oldest daughter of the senior branch of the family it would confer great honour on him and may even give him claim to the *gaddi*.'

'What is that?'

'It's the throne of Kushnapur.'

'Rightfully yours.'

'Yes, but to the constant irritation and envy of the Mahavir Debrahms.'

'And what do your parents think?'

'For several reasons they are dead set against it.'

'So it won't happen?'

'Again not that simple. My father has refused to consent to the marriage and it won't surprise you to know that he has my support but, unfortunately, Wantilla has a few more tricks up his sleeve.'

Two days later Adam left Rindi and Lahore and headed further north. From the train he observed a gradual change in the people and the scenery. The clothing of the women became more sombre. Fewer saris and more of the modest salwar kameez, and mosques with their distinguishing minarets were now a constant feature. Islam was the dominant religion of this part of the country.

Rawalpindi

'How long have you been in India, Cullworthy?'

'A few months now.'

'Never let these chaps see anything but your best side.' He nodded towards two Indian N.C.O.s outside the window.

'Respect, Cullworthy. That's what we've earned in our two hundred years in India. We've established it, and must not let it slip through our fingers.'

Major Claude Williams, Adam's new company commander, was fulminating on his favourite theme. He liked it to be known that he was an authority on the British Raj and took great relish in passing on his opinions to *griffins* like Adam.

'Surely, Sir, India can't always remain under British rule? We can't keep the country in permanent subjection.'

'That's the very attitude which invites failure. The Americans would love to see us trip up and fall on our arses in India; they've always resented our successful Empire. It's not a question of subjection. Without the stability that the British provide, this country would be in chaos. With all these religions, they'd be at each other's throats in no time if we weren't here to keep order. Just imagine the blood-bath.'

'When this war is finally over, do you think that Britain will have the desire, or indeed the ability to carry on? The Indian Congress Party is already causing problems, and this fellow Ghandi seems very awkward and determined to get his way.'

Major Williams leaned back in his chair.

'He appears awkward, Cullworthy, because some people let him be awkward. They're playing into his hands. All he needs is firm handling. That will stop his nonsense. Churchill called him a half-naked fakir, so *he* won't put up with his nonsense I can tell you. Take it from me, Cullworthy; if you want to succeed in India, you must adapt all the time. The Indian is as cunning as an organ grinder's monkey and will constantly seek a chink in your armour.'

The North West Frontier, November 1941.

In November Adam's company was moved up to patrol the frontier. At first this had a certain thrill and romance. Many a conquering army had crossed this border, including Alexander the Great twenty-three centuries before. Adam remembered the book at Queens Gate Gardens that had somehow linked the Debrahm's to one of his generals.

After a few weeks the daily routine and lack of action began to pall and Adam was glad to get back to headquarters in Rawalpindi. He felt having done some duty this may be a good moment to request the leave he wanted.

December 1941.

'Leave in the army is a privilege, Cullworthy' Williams said.

Adam was not finding this abrasive manner easy to deal with. For some reason Williams felt the constant need to exert authority, but finally, having implied that he was making a major concession, he signed Adam's application for fourteen day's leave.

Once more he found himself on the twelve-hour train journey back to Ambala. The British had built the Indian Railways for their own convenience. Travelling vast distances by road was not an option and this impressive network was the only way they stood any chance of controlling the sub-continent.

He spent a day in Ambala with Rindi before setting off on the next leg of their journey to Saharanpur. Everything had been carefully planned.

'We get there at 6.30am which is quite civilised. My father's chauffeur will meet us there and drive us the final leg to Kushnapur.'

'Are your parents expecting me?'

'The family can't wait to meet you, old boy.' Then with a mischievous grin he added. 'After the glowing reports they've had from London you're bound to be a disappointment.'

Adam laughed. He had missed his friend's wit.

CHAPTER ELEVEN

Kushnapur, December 1941

As the first faint rays of dawn filtered through the slatted shutters their train drew into Saharanpur station. Adam had some expectations of the lifestyle of a maharajah but he was not prepared for the reception they received.

A bearer, in an immaculate uniform, met them off the train and directed two coolie porters to take their baggage. Once outside the station, they were greeted by two smartly dressed chauffeurs who snapped to attention and saluted. They were standing beside a Rolls Royce landau.

'*Namaste, Rajkumar-sahib*'. Adam didn't need to understand Hindi to know that they were addressing a prince. Adam admired the bonnet that seemed to stretch on endlessly only stopping to accommodate the gleaming silver chrome figure of the Spirit of Ecstasy. The doors were embellished with a discreet family crest, although the body finished in a pale purple combined with cream hide upholstery did add a certain folly to this fine automobile.

They sank back into the comfort and luxury of the leather seats.

'Feel like *chota hazri*?' Rindi asked, lifting the lid of the "tiffin box" stored in a compartment in front of them.

'Yes, that would be excellent. I'm feeling rather peckish,' Adam replied admiring the carefully prepared sandwiches, portions of cold chicken and fresh fruit, and the flasks of tea and coffee.

They purred along the tarred highway which after about half an hour gave way to a gravel road.

'We are now leaving the India of the British Raj.' Rindi declared.

'What does that mean?'

'No more tarmac for a start. We are now in what they call a Princely State, ruled in this case my father.'

'So is it independent of British rule and influence?'

'Rule, officially yes. But behind the scenes, the watchful influence of the Raj sits in judgement in the person of the British Resident. His authority is paramount in matters like succession. He would have the final word in the event of a major dispute.'

'Who is the British Resident here?'

'Sir Iain MacDonald. You are unlikely meet him, but if you do you will find he has quite a high opinion of himself.'

The gentle pink morning glow was now beginning to give way to a stronger warmer light. New scenery unfolded. Recently harvested rice and maize lay spread out for drying before being ladled with big wooden shovels into sacks. Loaded ox carts trundling along on their solid wooden wheels, a scene unchanged for hundreds if not thousands of years.

'That's the last of the *kela* and *khajur* trees you'll see on this trip.' Rindi pointed to a plantation of banana and date palms. 'It gets too cold as we climb to a higher altitude.'

'By the way, how do I address your father? Do I say your highness, or your grace?'

'Good Lord, no. He gets quite enough of that from his petitioners. The British Army gave him the rank of full colonel so I suggest you treat him like you would your senior officers.'

'They must think highly of him.'

'They may well do so, but that's not exactly why they did it. My grandfather raised and supported a brigade of troops in the First World War and I think they're hoping that my father may be encouraged to do something similar this time.'

'Is there any likelihood he will?'

'None, I'm afraid; for two reasons. In the first place, although my father, as a Rajput, admires honour in battle, he felt that many of my grandfather's brigade had been coerced by patriotism to volunteer. And, secondly, a thousand widows and twice as many orphans was too high a price to pay.'

Rindi sat for a full minute, as if weighing up the facts, then said, 'There could be a third reason. My father could enlist a force greater than a brigade strong, but if he did so his cousin, Mahavir - that's Wantilla's father - could make trouble.'

'Why would he do that? Surely he must be loyal to his cousin as the state ruler?'

'I can see how little you know of the nature and temperament of high caste Hindus, especially the Kshatriya or warrior class. For us to fight and rule is a way of life.'

Rindi added nothing further. There was much that Adam did not understand, and as he sat trying to seek his own answers he was lulled into a deep sleep by the gentle movement of the car.

Adam must have slept for at least an hour, because when he awoke the sun was high and the shadows shorter. They were in a village, the car was moving very slowly; villagers and children were calling, a baby was crying and cattle were lowing. Looking out, Adam saw a small group of cows standing in the middle of the road ahead of them, and as they reached them the chauffeur brought the car to a standstill. At least five minutes must have elapsed before the cows moved to the side of the road, and they were able to skirt round them.

'Doesn't anyone look after those beasts?'

'Oh yes, they probably belong to that wallah over there.' Rindi flicked a finger in the direction of a middle-aged Indian with a red turban. 'He doesn't bother to move them off the road, because he knows full well that no one will harm them. They are Brahmin cattle and sacred to all Hindus. No one would venture to harass them, they're free to wander wherever they wish. As for killing such a creature it would be sacrilege for a Hindu to do so.'

'And the Muslims?'

'They have quite different ideas. They will slaughter and eat oxen, but they do have their own taboos.'

'Are most Hindus vegetarian?'

'It varies in different parts of India, but it's probably correct to say that half of the Hindus hold beliefs akin to the Sardarji. We have no prohibitions about eating meat, provided it is not beef.'

'Now I know where the expression "holy cow" comes from. No disrespect to your religion, but isn't it a bit absurd to make such a fuss over these cattle?'

'It might seem that way to you, but there are sound practical reasons, as well as religious justification for the tenet. Thousands of years ago when the Hindu religion was developing, the Brahmins came to realize that not only was the cow a valuable beast of burden, it was a provider of life. It produced milk, cream, butter, cheese, yoghurt and most prized of all, ghee. They knew that in time of famine cattle would be liable to be slaughtered for food and consequently valuable breeding stock would be lost. The only sure way to preserve them was to say they were a God-sent gift. This became part of the Hindu vedas which made them sacred.'

'Why didn't they slaughter only the bulls?'

'Well, at first they did allow that. Then it was found that a farmer, whose needs for the family or village community had become pressing, would not always discriminate. Remember, the flesh of a cow cannot be distinguished from that of a bull. A half-way compromise was not possible.'

With the cows safely behind them, they moved gently forward and some of the bystanders were peering inside. Then as the limousine picked up speed, several of the older men and women raised their hands in *namaste* greeting as they recognised their maharajah's landau.

Suddenly a young bearded man launched himself onto the bonnet of the car and clinging to the windscreen wiper he hurled abuse at them in Urdu. Two other men joined in and started to hammer on the passenger windows.

'Drive on,' shouted Rindi to the chauffeur who was about to get out and remove the man from the bonnet.

They left the crowd behind and looking back Adam could see they had turned on the two men and a fight had broken out. After a few hundred yards the chauffeur stopped the car and the two drivers leapt out of the car. The man on the bonnet let go and ran off into the bushes.

'What was that all about?' Adam asked.

'Pilgrims,' replied Rindi.

'Pilgrims? I thought they were meant to be peace loving.'

'They normally are but there are a few who are resentful that we have denied them access to the temple.'

'You've lost me completely.'

'Long before Kushnapur became a palace and the seat of the Debrahm family it was a place of pilgrimage. Not just a stopping point on the way to Tibet but a destination in its own right.'

'I remember you telling me that Buddha came here on his way to Tibet.'

'That certainly helped but it is actually the Hindus who believe that a visit to Kushnapur will enhance their fertility.'

'A bit like Veranasi?'

'Not really; more like Amarnath. Pilgrims come to see a stalagmite in the shape of a phallus, or lingam as it is called. This is a symbol of Shiva, the God of war and fertility. But more than just conveying increased fertility the Kushnapur lingam is thought to give rise to male offspring.'

'I can see that would be popular. So is it still a place of pilgrimage?'

'Yes, it is, but pilgrims are now denied access to the temple which is now in the bowels of the palace itself. My great grandfather had the present palace built over the temple because that was the most suitable site from an architectural point of view. It caused an uproar at the time and for many years pilgrims were given continued access on certain days in the year.'

'But not anymore?'

'Thousands visited every year and when the railway reached Saharanpur this turned into tens of thousands. We couldn't charge to visit the temple so it became very costly to maintain and a security nightmare. When some important religious artefacts went missing he finally put an end to the visits. You will only fully understand the magnitude of the problem when you visit the temple.'

'So where do the pilgrims go now?'

'A replica of the temple was built near the city but although it is still on the ancient path to Tibet it is not quite the same thing. The pilgrims believe it is the water from the mountain stream that passes through the temple and beside the lingam that imbues them with greater fertility. There is continuing resentment that they are denied access to the waters.'

'What do you and your father think about the pilgrims?'

'Father is a traditionalist. He believes that people's long-held beliefs should be respected but he also believes that as the ruler of Kushnapur his word should be final. I think that ever since his brother was abducted he has been fearful of allowing strangers to have access to the palace. As for myself, I am not sure that denying access doesn't fuel the fanatics whilst denying the peaceful worshippers a long-held right to visit the temple.'

'A tricky dilemma, I can see. I suppose it only takes one lunatic to completely ruin your family's lives.'

'Kushnapur is the most beautiful and serene place but sometimes it feels like we are forcing her to keep the world at bay and I am not sure that is the way we should live our lives in a changing India.'

'You refer to Kushnapur as "*her*"?'

'We believe that Kushnapur is a living entity with powers to influence her own destiny.'

'Surely you don't really believe that?'

Rindi raised an eyebrow in acknowledgement of Adam's ridicule of him.

'Adam, as you know, Indians are highly superstitious and the Debrahm family is no exception. Kushnapur has an aura which I am sure you will feel when you are there. Things happen that cannot be easily put down to human influence or fate.'

It was hard for Adam to accept that his Oxford educated friend still held such arcane beliefs. Adam had always been known as 'Doubting Thomas' in his family because he needed practical or scientific explanations for everything remotely spiritual but he refrained from voicing his cynicism further.

'Well, I look forward to meeting *"her"*.

'In any event I certainly believe our family have suffered our fair share of bad karma since we stopped the pilgrims visiting the temple.'

Rindi had said in London and again in Cairo that there were things that would be easier to understand when Adam visited Kushnapur. This journey had the feeling of a pilgrimage to him but the closer Adam came to the destination the wider the cultural gap between himself and Rindi seemed to become.

'Have we much further to go?'

'About another hour and we should be there, so you can relax.'

Adam was still shaken by the earlier attack on the car but it was a relief to sit back and absorb the changing landscape. Hills were all around them, and ahead in the distance there was a range of mountains with an even higher snow-capped range beyond.

They passed through a village which appeared to hang on the mountainside; then another village with cultivated terraces stretching down into the valley. A few minutes later, they were running along near the top of a small escarpment. Looking down the steep rocky slope to their left, Adam could see a torrent glinting in the sunlight, at least three hundred feet below them. A sweeping bend in the road, and the river passed completely from view. For ten, perhaps fifteen minutes they were in the shadow of the mountain, then as they rounded another bend Adam saw that they were unexpectedly only fifty feet above the water.

This river, sparkling and clear as it surged over its rocky course, was unlike any other Adam had seen in India. On the far bank, the land rose steeply for at least two thousand feet. Ahead, the distant skyline was freely covered with small groups of tall deodar trees with their majestic spires and spreading branches.

Adam's first view of the palace came when they were about ten miles from Kushnapur City. They had reached the crest of a long hill and saw the massive pale stone building extending along the mountainside, occupying the whole length of a small plateau. The facade was broken at intervals by great trees, some of which were clearly leafless.

'Well, there it is.'

It was imposing by any standards, with its ornate stonework reflecting the afternoon sun. It had grandeur and a feeling of permanence. Yet Adam was not quite sure of its beauty.

'Is this what you expected, Adam?'

'It must be vast. From here, it gives me the impression of a citadel.'

'Not a bad observation. It was once just that. The third Great Moghul Emperor, Akbar, sent his troops to besiege the place in 1588, just about the time of the Spanish Armada. Akbar mistakenly believed that Kushnapur could command an alternative summer route into Tibet. He correctly deduced that during the sixth century B.C. Gautama Buddha and his followers had often travelled this way. The Buddha had been a Kshatriya prince from the Indo-Nepal region and knew these mountain areas well. But that's another story.'

'Presumably the siege was raised?'

'Yes, but at a price.'

'Intelligence had reached the Akbar that the Rajah of Kushnapur had three beautiful daughters.' Rindi laughed, then continued. 'Of course, they had to be beautiful; it would have hardly been worthwhile otherwise. The emperor demanded that Nilima, the youngest daughter, should be presented to take up residence in the royal seraglio at Delhi. The Rajah refused; no daughter of a Rajput would be permitted to join the harem of concubines at the Moghul's palace. He eventually agreed on the condition that she became one of the Emperor's official wives.'

'Surely it was unthinkable for a high-caste Hindu princess to become the wife of a Muslim?'

'Traditionally this would have been the case, but there were a number of important differences here. In the first place Akbar was a Great Emperor. In the second place, although earlier Muslim rulers had married Hindu wives, these women had been obliged to follow Muslim customs; at least to all outward appearances. Akbar was the first Muslim ruler to allow his Hindu wives to practice their rites within the walls of the harem.'

Another important consideration was that Akbar, twenty-six years earlier, had taken in marriage, a Rajput princess, the daughter of the Rajah of Amber or Jaipur as they now call it. The son of that princess was to become the next Moghul Emperor. So you see, the position of the young Princess Nilima was reasonably well assured.'

'Was that the end of the matter?'

'Not quite, The Rajah had to enter into a treaty never to fight against the Emperor, and also to maintain an army which would defend India against attacks from Tibet, an unlikely event as the mountain passes were almost impenetrable.'

'I thought your father was a maharajah?'

'Ah yes. A few years after Nilima had married the Emperor, a rich Zemindar, who owned extensive lands adjoining Kushnapur, unwisely clashed with Akbar's tax collectors. In consequence, his lands and small principality were seized and given to the children of Princess Nilima. It so happened that for two generations these were all girls. The Emperor built a beautiful summer residence for these daughters on the newly acquired lands at Khanate so that they could escape the scorching heat of Delhi each year in May. The fact that the early heirs were all girls had an interesting consequence - which also answers your question about the royal title. The granddaughter of Nilima, who had then inherited the principality, married her cousin, Harish Debrahm, Rajah of Kushnapur, taking with her the lands of Khanate; henceforth to be incorporated into Kushnapur. Not only was the domain of the Rajah greatly extended; he became, by the wish of the new Emperor Jahangir, the Maharajah of Kushnapur.'

'Does this Khanate still exist?'

'It certainly does. My father's cousin Mahavir Debrahm, and his family live there. They have a married daughter, Vaswati, and a son, who you already know about.'

'Wantilla?'

'I'm afraid so. If you like, we can drive over and see them during your stay.' He said with an ironic smile.

'Now speaking of beautiful daughters, tell me about your sisters?'

'You might find them rather shy at first. You will certainly like Kafni but I don't want you getting any ideas.' He raised an eyebrow in mock disapproval.

The broad view of the countryside had now gone. The palace could only be seen in glimpses as they rounded each of the sharp bends on the steep ascent. Then came a complete change. A straight avenue lined with closely planted conifers spreading either side of a shallow valley. It was about a mile long, and ahead Adam could see the road disappearing into a narrow gap between the hills. A few minutes later they were in a gorge with rock faces rising almost vertically on both sides. It must have followed a contour, because the slight bend in the road obstructed a clear view from one end to the other.

Leaving the defile, they climbed steeply for a short distance, and then came an open, level area in the centre of which stood a massive stone archway with long high walls abutted to either side. They drove on through this great entrance, passing two sentries who saluted. They were now in a great courtyard the size of a hockey pitch, but there was still no sign of the palace. Neither did the road carry on, for in front of them rose the sharp crags of the hillside. As the car came to a halt Adam looked around scrutinising the single storey buildings on both sides. Adam was somewhat baffled. This seemed like some elaborate Indian rope trick, where the whole of the edifice is swallowed up into the mountain and mist.

If it was an illusion, he thought with some amusement, at least some of the staff had been left behind, for there were dozens of people moving around the quadrangle. Some hope of the reappearance of the palace came when two uniformed attendants hurried forward to simultaneously open the car doors, whilst two coolies were being directed by the driver to pick up the baggage. Here, as in the rest of India, everyone knew his or her place.

A *chaprassi* in an immaculate uniform of pale purple and cream emerged from the building, his brilliantly polished *chapras* badge of office gleaming on his belt. A salute to Rindi and a few words in Hindi and then he hurried away.

'He's off to tell the family we've arrived. Would you like to look over the *pilkhannas* and the stables, whilst we're down here?'

'Elephants,' he said in response to Adam's quizzical look.

'Ah yes, I'd better see them. Sister Sue will want a full report.'

He led the way through an opening between the buildings where a pair of huge doors hung. It was not just their size and construction that was remarkable. The prominent feature was the series of long steel spikes that protruded from them. The doors themselves were set well back into a recess in the wall and a light wrought iron fence had been slid across in front of the lower half of the door for obvious protection of those walking past.

'What the hell are those grisly looking things for?'

'They're elephant spikes. They were to prevent the enemy using elephants to crash through the gates.'

'Bloody nasty and very effective, I imagine.'

They had now passed into another smaller courtyard. On one side was a row of about a dozen tall doors, the top sections of which were inset with well-spaced heavy iron bars. Only four of the stalls were occupied, the others were empty and their doors stood open. An inquisitive trunk protruded through the bars of one of the stables. A mahout appeared, clearly anxious to bring out one of the beasts for inspection. Rindi shook his head and waved his hand to decline. He had acquired a dignified air of authority and a presence that Adam hadn't seen in him before.

'That chap will take hours to prepare and mount the howdahs. If you're interested, I'll lay on a trip for us in a day or two.'

'How many elephants do you have?' Adam indicated the empty stalls.

'Only four now. At the beginning of the Great War we had a dozen, but my father loaned the rest to the Forestry Department. I doubt if we'll ever have them back; we don't need them. In the eighteenth and nineteenth centuries there were up to twenty elephants here. Now we only keep them for ceremonial occasions and the tiger *shikars*. The citizens of any Indian state would feel ashamed if their ruler did not have at least four elephants. Before the war, each of the 560 rulers had an average of nine elephants.'

Adam smiled, then thought of the fabulous lives that some of these princes must lead in stark contrast to the abject, grinding poverty of their subjects.

'And what about your father?'

'He's well up to average with the Rolls Royces and railway stock, but lets the side down a bit by having only one spouse.'

'What do you use railway carriages for?'

'We keep them in a private covered siding in Saharanpur and only use them when a party is travelling with their servants. It is useful when a number of female members of the family and staff are on a long journey, as they are able to observe the limited degree of purdah which is expected of them.'

'Rajkumar sahib.' The mahout was no longer alone. Three *pilkhanna-wallahs* had appeared and stood in attendance, apparently hoping for some instructions from the mahout. He in turn was clearly hoping to retain the attention of his prince for a little longer. Inspiration must have come to him because a glimpse of satisfaction passed over his face as he addressed Rindi.

'He's suggested that we inspect the caparisons, the "tack room".'

'That would be interesting.'

A nod of consent from Rindi and the mahout produced an oversized key, with which he unlocked a door at the end of the building. His assistants ceremoniously drew back the door and they were ushered into what at first looked like a long dark storeroom. It was dimly lit by a single window at the end of the room.

The *pilkhanna-wallahs* drew back a series of heavy curtains and illuminated rows of howdahs with magnificent brocades and brilliantly coloured fabrics embroidered with gold and silver thread. Adam was intrigued by a hunting howdah that, in sharp contrast to the immaculate condition of the others, looked distinctly battle-scarred.

'I'm afraid my great-great-grandfather was killed in that one. He was on a *shikar* with the Maharajah of Gwalior whose jungles were teeming with tiger at the time. The attention of the hunting party was concentrated on a magnificent feline specimen and as guest of honour he was to be given first shot. In the excitement of the hunt, his mahout made the classic error of passing too close to a tree-covered ledge where another tiger was lurking. The beast sprang onto the elephant's head and flung the mahout to the ground, where he was trampled to death. The tiger then turned to deal with my great-great grandfather who just managed to get one shot into its neck, before his head was crushed by its powerful jaws.'

Adam shuddered. 'These *shikars* sound bloody dangerous.'

'I think that's part of their attraction. It was considered that he had died honourably and as a mark of respect the howdah was brought back here from Gwalior – three hundred and fifty miles by rail and road.'

Rindi had made no mention of the Sir Arthur Hawkswood incident and Adam felt it was politic not to raise the subject.

A palace official, elegantly dressed in achkan and jodhpurs, appeared to ascertain the reason for the delay in their arrival. He shook hands with Rindi and was introduced to Adam as the equerry. He spoke excellent, if somewhat stilted English, and announced that the reception party was awaiting them.

They returned to the main courtyard and walked towards a low covered archway that appeared to lead straight into the mountainside. This was deceptive, for the passageway turned left almost as soon as they had passed under the entrance arch. It was here that Adam saw the conveyance for the last stage of their journey. Three bright red *dhoolies* were lined up, each attended by four uniformed coolies. These were far superior to the open "dandy" litters he had seen elsewhere. Rindi directed Adam into the second "dhooly" and took the leading one himself and the equerry took the last one.

Much to Adam's surprise, the *dhooly-wallahs* set off at a gentle trot, and although the carriages could have accommodated two persons, the reason for having only one passenger in each palaquin was evident when the tilt of the carriage indicated a steep ascent, despite the coolies' attempts to adjust for the slope.

They all looked young, and from the effort, muscle and strain involved, they needed to be. They were obviously proud of their feats of strength and endurance and Adam realised, not for the last time, what an important part pride and saving face played in life in India.

He felt far removed from the other India, the British Raj, the Army and the War.

It had taken ten minutes to make the climb along the wide, well-kept pathway that wound back and forth along the hillside. Each hairpin bend had changed the view from one side of the carriage to the other. Long before they reached the top Adam had seen in the distance the tarred road they had travelled on, and curving away from it, the gravel road to Kushnapur City. His view of the landscape was lost as they entered a covered area, corbelled against a basement of the palace. The last incline of the trip had taken them up through a paved tunnel and onto a broad terrace. Here they alighted and were greeted by a small reception party. Adam was a little surprised that none of Rindi's family was in attendance at this minor levee. Protocol, it seemed, was as important here as amongst the nobility of Europe.

Although Rindi introduced each of the reception party in turn, Adam could only recall the identity of four of the officials. With these they had shaken hands. The others had greeted them only with the traditional *'Namaste'* and polite touch of their foreheads. At the head of the line was the *Dewan:* chief minister of the state. He was a *sirdar* with aristocratic bearing who must have looked upon the little ceremony as a slightly tiresome duty. The next two were characters who could have stepped straight out of a medieval court: the *hakim,* who was reputed to have spent a year at Edinburgh University - though probably better versed in ancient rites than in modern medicine - and then the court astrologer who took Adam's hand with long sinuous fingers that evinced no strength, yet were reluctant to release it, conveying the strange sensation to Adam that he was already being scrutinised.

Last but not least was the Commander of the Guard who was about forty and the same height as Adam. A product of the Indian Military Academy in Dehra Dun with a proud military bearing. He snapped to attention and saluted them.

'Adam, I would like you to meet Major Harish Ram Chandra.' Rindi clearly had a closer rapport with this man. 'We were lucky enough to recruit him from the Indian Army to take charge of our state forces.'

By the time the reception formalities had been completed, the sun was setting. Rindi looked at his watch. 'It's eighteen hundred. How about dinner at nineteen-thirty?'

'Sounds perfect, I'm getting rather peckish.'

'Your case has already been taken up to your room and your bearer is here waiting to show you the way. Incidentally, he'll be looking after you throughout your stay. Tell him anything you need and he'll lay it on. He'll show you the way down to the anteroom when you're ready. Come in time to have a drink before dinner. Please excuse me now, I must go and see Mother.'

This implied she would not be joining them for dinner, a custom Adam had become familiar with when dining with the Debrahm's for the first time in London.

He followed the bearer up a series of staircases and along wide corridors, noting with slight surprise that there was electric lighting installed everywhere. He was ushered into a spacious bedroom, brightly lit, with curtains already drawn. A log-fire was burning in the fireplace. To his right was a large bed with a scarlet cover interwoven with gold filigree. Above the bed, a brightly decorated canopy protruded from the wall, draped with matching silk curtains. His suitcase had been unpacked for him and his service dress laid-out on an armchair. The bearer drew Adam's attention to two curtained wardrobes set into deep alcoves. Between these, a door led out to a covered balcony overlooking a large open courtyard, two storeys below. Adam observed that they had come up three staircases to reach his room, so there must be other rooms below the courtyard.

Back in the room, on a wall at one side was a further line of curtains. After the bearer had left Adam pulled them aside and was surprised to find a heavy, carved wooden door. He tried the handle and found it locked. At first he concluded that it must lead into another bedroom but on reflection, its position so close to an outside wall meant this was unlikely.

Whilst Adam could see why Kushnapur had been a good site in the past for both a monastery and a fortress, its transformation into a palace within the last hundred years had left little evidence of its former life. The natural masonry gave it a sense of permanence. The honey-coloured plain dressed stonework provided a perfect backdrop for the beautiful tapestries and brocades that decorated the walls and the fine oriental rugs that were strewn across the floor.

When Adam had changed for dinner he called for his bearer. He appeared so quickly that he must have been poised outside the door awaiting his command. He escorted Adam back down the three flights of stairs, along a hallway and into the anteroom, where Rindi was standing with his back to a blazing log fire.

'Good, you've made it. I hope that chap is looking after you alright.' He raised the glass in his hand. 'Try some of this excellent sherry.'

Although he should have expected it, Adam was momentarily taken aback to see Rindi in complete Indian dress. His close fitting *kurta* in cream silk, with a broad neckband of pale mauve, was complimented by a pair of fine cotton twill trousers. He was wearing a cream *puggaree* with the ubiquitous band of light purple folded into the material and all secured by a brightly jewelled clasp. Compared to the dress he would see him in on later occasions it was modest, yet he looked every inch the Maharajkumar. Adam felt distinctly underdressed.

Rindi nodded to the *khansama*, who came forward with a glass of sherry on a silver tray.

'Rather good. I didn't know you could still get Spanish sherry, with the war going on.'

'Well, I must admit, it is rather difficult. This came from the Resident; he gave father a case last Christmas. I think he wanted to emphasise that a British regime is still in charge in this country.'

'Well I'll drink to that because otherwise I wouldn't be here.'

'Quite so and it would be our loss' Rindi responded.' If you'd like to borrow some clothes whilst you're here, you're more than welcome. It'll be a change from your army uniform.'

The prospect of dressing like a maharajah made Adam smile.

'I would like that. Have you got anything that will fit me?'

'Oh, don't worry about that. My clothes might be a trifle short in the leg and a bit tight round the chest, but I'll lay on Prem Vijay, our head *derzi*. He'll come and measure you up in the morning. I am sure he will come up with something that will appeal to you.'

The sound of a deep-noted gong prompted Adam to glance at the clock on the mantelpiece. Seven-thirty on the dot.

Rindi led the way through a pair of cream doors with gold mouldings, held open by a servant, into a dining room of relatively moderate proportions. The furnishings of this dining room were simple but elegant and the only concession to the ornate was the intricate carving of the eight chairs set around the table.

There were just the two of them for dinner which surprised Adam as he was anticipating meeting some of the rest of the family.

As they were finishing dinner the door at the far end of the room opened and from the reaction of the servants, someone of importance was about to enter. Rindi stood up and Adam followed his example. He thought for a moment that it was Rindi's Uncle Jardeeson, the likeness was so strong, but then he realised that it must be Rindi's father. The same handsome features and strong brow. Only the *puggaree* made him look different. His tunic was similar to the one Rindi wore, his broad cuffs were also of pale purple, and like the collar, edged with gold. He was shorter than Rindi but his deliberate stride and dignified bearing made it clear that he was the maharajah.

Rindi looked over to his father. 'Good evening, Sir. *Namaste papaji.*' He then turned to Adam and said, 'Father, I would like to introduce Adam Cullworthy.'

Adam felt an inclination to give at least a token bow, but before this could be manifested, a hand came towards him. 'My dear boy, delighted to meet you. Do sit down.'

As he said this, he took the chair beside Adam. His voice was not unlike that of Rindi or Jardeeson, with the tone of a cultured Oxford accent, but perhaps a trifle too refined to be taken for that of an Englishman.

'I trust your rooms are comfortable, Adam?'

'Yes, Sir. Thank you. In fact beyond my expectation.'

'Ah, and what were you expecting?' Rindi's father responded with a twinkle in his eye.

'Well, I suppose given your remote location I wasn't expecting electricity.'

'Yes, you are quite right that is an unexpected luxury. In fact we have our own little power generator. In the late 1920s we had a Scottish electrical engineer visiting and he spotted the hydro potential of the mountain stream which passes beneath the palace. Under his supervision we constructed a powerhouse, and installed a water-turbine.'

'But I am surprised we cannot hear it.'

'That was the clever part. The turbine was sited at the lowest point of the palace grounds, buried deep into the hillside. If you're interested I am sure Rindi will take you down there.' The maharajah stood up. 'Now I hope you don't mind me leaving you but I have to be up early tomorrow. Please take your time in the morning, although I know Rindi is keen to give you a full tour.'

Adam was in no doubt that he had met someone with considerable presence and immense intellect.

CHAPTER TWELVE

Kushnapur Palace, December 1941.

Only when the bearer drew back the heavily lined curtains the next morning did Adam realize that his bedroom faced east. The early morning winter sun streamed in through the shutters

Chota hazri, Captain sahib.'

Adam looked up to see a silver tray had been placed on the polished teak table beside his bed. The silver teapot, hot water jug, milk jug, sugar basin and fruit bowl were gleaming in evidence of the labours of a *masalchee* in the kitchens below. The bearer poured the tea and then withdrew.

Adam got out of bed and carrying his cup of tea he walked over to the window and folded back one section of the shutters. His eyes were drawn to the rosy hue of the mountaintops in the far distance where the snow lines zigzagged like badly drizzled icing. The slopes facing him were still in deep shadow; only the occasional high ridge was illuminated as fingers of sunlight crept down over the Himalayas. The tracery of thousands of treetops and the tips of their branches glistening with the morning dew, gave evidence of vast forests stretching for mile upon mile until being swallowed up by the blue haze of the upper rock faces. He felt a sense of wonder at this scene that must have barely changed in a millennium.

The oriel window of his room was set on large Hindu brackets, and constructed to protrude from the building. Yet so thick were the walls that it was necessary to stand on tiptoe to gain a wider view. To the left, the palace stretched back for about one hundred yards, then merged into the hillside. The chasm that separated the building from the land to the north could not be detected from his window.

A shout from below directed his attention to the gardens extending in long terraces from the building. A party of ten *mali* were being allocated their tasks in the garden. There must have been a garden passageway or tunnel with steps down, because some of these gardeners reappeared about thirty yards further on, at a much lower level, in an orchard beyond a neat cypress hedge. The gardens, like all parts of the palace, had an abundance of servants. When Adam later questioned Rindi about this extravagance, he pointed out that the six hundred staff they employed supported at least five times that number of people. It was the obligation of the maharajah to employ as many servants as possible.

The previous evening Rindi had said, 'If you feel like a swim in the morning, there's a pool on the lower level, heated by a natural hot spring. You can get down there by the stairs that lead off your balcony.'

Adam thought a swim before breakfast would set him up well for the day. He slipped on the cream bathing robe with its distinctive purple edging that was hanging in the bathroom, opened the balcony door and stepped outside. Despite the sunshine there was a chill in the air and he was glad of the warmth of the generous towelling robe.

He descended three flights of stairs and then passed through a covered area where the air felt distinctly warmer. At the bottom of the next flight an arched wrought iron gate led into an enclosed garden where the scent of jasmine filled the morning air. Ahead of him he saw a pool with wisps of steam rising and as he approached it he was surprised to hear a splash. A girl emerged from the rippling water wrapped in pale green wet muslin which clung to her body revealing a perfect figure beneath. She paused at the top step and then turned to face him. He stood motionless, transfixed by her beauty. Adam knew by the surprised look on her face that he had invaded her privacy and should not have been there. For a moment he considered a tactful retreat to save her any embarrassment but the bewitching smile she gave him as she raised her elegant hands with a gesture of 'namaste' dismissed the thought. Her striking violet eyes left him in no doubt that this was Rindi's sister.

'You must be Adam,' she said.

'Yes,' he replied hesitantly.

'Hello, I'm Kafni.'

Adam wanted to express his pleasure at meeting her but this wish was frustrated by the appearance of an anxious ayah carrying a bathrobe, similar to his own.

Kafni, seeing her servant's concern, allowed the ayah to quickly wrap the gown round her shoulders and restore her modesty. Kafni now looked straight at him and placed an elegant finger on her lips which Adam took to denote a secret shared. She then turned and disappeared through a gate at the far end, leaving him wondering just when he would see her again.

He took off his gown and dived into the warm water. He was overwhelmed; something incredible had happened in those brief minutes that would change him forever.

Back in his room, still elated by the entrancing encounter, he stood gazing out of the oriel widow reliving the fleeting introduction. There was something enchantingly conspiratorial about her parting gesture of discretion.

A knock at the door interrupted his reverie. He turned back from the window and called, 'Come in.'

It was the bearer and as he entered, he looked back and called out 'thaharna,' thereby instructing someone to wait in the corridor.

'The Captain-sahib is ready to take bath?'

'Oh. Yes, thank you.'

The bathroom adjoining the bedroom had no running water, a fact that almost passed without notice since two jugs of water were always at hand. Two large marble hand-basins and a framed mirror, each exquisitely decorated, stood on a raised slab near the window at the end of the bathroom. The bath itself, partially sunken into the marble floor, was lined with a pale green mosaic, relieved with bright patterns traced in red and blue.

The tableau of filling the bath was pure theatre. The bearer directed, principally by hand movements, three *masalchee* with huge water jugs of different temperatures. Each was dispensed with the care of an alchemist. Their efforts to achieve the precise temperature and the final test by the elbow of the bearer, would have satisfied the most exacting memsahib about to bathe her precious *baba-log*.

Near the hand-basins stood a well-padded chair, the obvious comfort and purpose of which seemed a trifle superfluous. Unless perhaps a *rajkumar* wished to sit and enjoy the sight of his mistress bathing. Its true purpose became evident when he stepped out of the bath to dry himself. The bearer must have been carefully listening to determine his progress, because Adam heard him call in the corridor outside, 'Hajjam ko idhar bulao'. The barber had been sent for.

A few minutes later he was languishing in the chair enjoying being shaved by the Indian barber, using his open razor with some dexterity. Yes, this was an excellent start to the day.

Adam went through to the bedroom to contemplate what clothes he should wear. Rindi had mentioned that they would be riding, so perhaps jodhpurs would be the order of the day. A courtesy knock, then came the cheery voice of Rindi as he walked through the first of the two doors that led into Adam's room. 'Sleep well, Cullworthy?'

'Like a top.'

'Good, because we have a full schedule of activities for you today. How was your swim by the way?'

Adam wondered how he knew he had been for a swim but then saw that his wet swimming trunks were still hooked over the bathroom door. 'Wonderful, the water was the perfect temperature.'

Respecting Kafni's silent entreaty, he did not mention seeing her by the pool.

Adam looked at Rindi in his tweed riding jacket and jodhpurs.

'I was wondering just what I should wear but it looks like we are off for a hack.'

'Yes, we need to get you sorted out with some clothes for your stay. The *derzi* will be along shortly to measure you up. In the meantime I suggest you wear your battle dress jacket and you will find some jods that should fit you in the wardrobe. It will be chilly in the hills until mid-morning. One of the *syce* can bring your khaki drill so you can change when it warms up later.'

Remembering the hidden door Adam crossed the room and pulled back the curtain and said, 'I wanted to ask you where this rather impressive door leads to?'

'Oh, that leads to a back staircase.'

Adam did not query the significance of where it might lead, but just said, 'Might I need to use it?'

'There'll probably be an occasion or two,' he said without further explanation.

'But it's locked.'

'Ah yes, I'll show you where the key is kept.'

Rindi walked over to an ornate writing bureau that stood beneath a small window on the east wall. Lifting the carved inner lid, he exposed a number of small compartments holding writing paper and envelopes. Below these was a line of miniature drawers, and others that looked like dummy drawers. He pressed the centre one of these and at the same time pulled open the extreme left-hand drawer. 'There's your key.'

Adam was now standing beside him and looked into the small velvet-lined compartment from where he had taken the key.

'It's quite heavy, and an interesting shape.' He ran his fingers over the handle which was fashioned in the pattern of a woman's head in profile. 'Very interesting. '

Adam repeated the procedure that Rindi had followed, replacing the key and snapping the drawer closed again.

'Quite neat,' he said. But before Adam could ask more questions Rindi moved the conversation on. 'Now how about some *jalpan?*'

'What's on offer?'

'Almost anything except bacon.'

'Then I'll have fried brinjals and an omelette.'

'Hey, I'm not the *khitmagar*. They'll take your order in the dining room.'

After breakfast I've laid on a little *shikar*. Nothing spectacular, but the beaters should be able to put up plenty of *kallege*, pheasant, partridge and jungle fowl. They're very plump now after the monsoon. Sometime, possibly not today, we'll think about the duck. There are thousands on the lake that have flown in from their Russian breeding grounds.

Adam welcomed the distraction of a day out hunting as Kafni had totally pre-occupied his thoughts since their encounter.

An hour later Rindi and Adam went down to the stables where two fine stallions were saddled and ready for them. Adam was offered the choice but as soon as he was mounted he realised that he had a high-spirited beast. The special twisted bit confirmed that it would be a challenge to establish who was master.

There were six other mounted members of their party: two *shikari*, who carried a selection of guns for Rindi and Adam; a *syce* with the tiffin boxes and spare clothes; and another whose task it was to bring back the 'bag'. The last two horsemen had service rifles slung across their backs; they were well spurred and carried no whip, clearly conveying their purpose.

'Is that our escort?' Adam smiled as he looked over at Rindi.

'Yes, I'm afraid so. The old man insists that we take them whenever we go to the remoter parts of the *zemindari*. I suppose it's a wise precaution, although it may seem a little excessive.'

'I don't know this part of the country, but do they expect to have to use those rifles?'

'I shouldn't think so for one minute, but the fact that they have them ensures that there's unlikely to be any trouble.'

After their previous conversations about fanatics and their

encounter with the pilgrims Adam wondered what he meant by trouble.

'We are more likely to encounter some big cats,' Rindi said.

'Tigers?'

'Yes, and we also have quite a few leopard up here as well.'

As he spoke, the two armed horsemen came alongside. Their fine physique and alert eyes left no doubt that they could handle any incident. The two *shikari* now led the way across the courtyard and as they approached the gatehouse two *chokidars* swung back the tall reinforced wooden doors. Adam wondered whether these were for security or privacy.

They rode for about half an hour until they could no longer see the palace.

'Where are we heading, Rindi?'

'We'll head up into the grasslands. There should be some pheasant and partridge near the woods.' Rindi used his crop and his horse broke into a gallop. Adam set off in pursuit, although he did not catch him up until he drew up by a large chenah tree, where Rindi had a brief discussion with the *shikari.*

'They're going to do a drive through those woods.' Rindi indicated an extensive area of trees about a quarter of a mile away.

'There's cover for us to the east, so we should be able to pick off a few birds as they flush them. Let's go.' He gave his mount a flick with his crop and they headed towards a secluded spot behind a row of low bushes. Four of the escort rode off to the far end of the covert.

With one of the *shikari* and one of the armed men in attendance, Rindi and Adam proceeded slowly, allowing the beaters to get in place. As they approached the line of bushes the *shikari* held his hand up signalling them all to stop. There was then an animated exchange.

'What was that about? Adam asked.

'Can you smell that?'

A strong pungent odour assaulted their nostrils in sharp contrast to the crisp freshness of the morning air.

'Tiger,' said Rindi, with remarkable composure.

Adam looked nervously around him. He felt unprepared for this type of unseen danger.

'Don't worry, old boy. If he is still in there' - he pointed towards the covert 'he will not hang around once the shooting starts.'

The *shikari* dismounted and unsheathed two twelve-bore shotguns from the saddle holsters on his horse. Rindi, who had also dismounted, took one of the guns. Adam followed suit but with a continuing sense of apprehension. He would have preferred to be on top of an elephant at this point, not that that had been much use to poor Sir Arthur. He felt more comfortable once he had the gun in his grasp, a fine weapon which he noticed had the distinctive markings of James Purdey & sons.

An exchange of whistles signalled that the guns were loaded and in position. They waited in silence for about ten minutes and then heard the sound of the escort beating the trees as they drove whatever prey was in the woods towards them. Suddenly the bushes in front of them parted and a flash of orange and black shot past them and disappeared equally rapidly into the long grass behind them. Adam lay sprawled on the grass where he had thrown himself aside to avoid the big cat. His heart was beating furiously and above the agitated shouting of the men he heard two shots ring out. Looking up he was amazed to see that Rindi was on his feet shooting at a covey of partridges which had followed the tiger out of the woods. He stood up, still wondering where the tiger had got to.

In awe of the coolness with which his friend had carried on with the shoot, Adam managed to compose himself sufficiently before the next flush of birds came over. This time it was pheasants, protesting furiously as they flew out of the woods. With one of the men loading with swift efficiency behind him he was able to contribute four brace of birds to the bag. One of the *shikari* whistled, indicating the end of the drive. The beaters then emerged from the bushes rather more slowly than the tiger before them and an animated conversation in Hindi ensued.

'I think that's enough excitement for one morning' said Rindi, handing his gun to the *shikari* for safe keeping.

'I'll say,' Adam replied, his palms still sweating.

They remounted their horses and left the *syce* behind to retrieve the birds.

'How about some tiffin? I'll race you to the Lodge.'

'What Lodge?'

'If you can catch me, you'll find out.' Rindi spurred his mount, and this time Adam was not taken unawares but was obliged to follow until about a mile in the distance a building came into view. Their objective now in sight, Adam gave a touch of the whip for encouragement, and his horse lengthened its stride and took the lead. They came to a halt beside the Lodge, their horses snorting and breathing steamily into the cold morning air.

'By the look of things someone's in good riding fettle.'

'I can't let you get away with it all the time, even on your own turf!'

A *chokidar* ran out from the Lodge to greet them and take the tiffin boxes. One of the *syces* led their horses away to the rear of the building and in almost comic contrast to the wild setting a uniformed bearer appeared with a silver tray and two glasses of a dark liquid.

'Sloe gin?' said Rindi, proffering a glass to Adam.

'My God, do I need that,' said Adam lowering himself onto a wickered tea planter's chair. 'Tell me, is it normal to have tigers making an entrance like that?'

'No, not normal. It's more likely to be a wild boar actually and they can be much more dangerous. One of the reasons we don't use dogs any more is that too many of them were getting killed by the boar.'

'Well if it comes to choosing an adversary I would rather have a German patrol any day. At least you know when and where the buggers are coming from.'

'It's all a matter of what you're accustomed to. Personally I would prefer something that hasn't set out that morning with deliberate intent to kill me. Speaking of which, I really admire you for blowing that bridge Adam. That took a lot of guts.'

'That all seems a lifetime away from this.'

'Yes, you're right' replied Rindi, gazing at the serenity of the landscape before them, the valley lined with fluffy pockets of low hanging cloud.

'Do you ever wonder how long it can last? Your privileged life here under the protection of the British Raj?'

'We've lived through many turbulent times in the past and we have survived by facing each challenge as it arrives.'

'Do you have a long-term plan?'

'We do have a sense of dynasty and feel a responsibility to future generations. I hope that maybe you will play a part in that.'

'What, like Sir Julian, as a trustee?'

'Rather more significant than that I think but that discussion can wait.'

Once more Adam found Rindi's reluctance to elaborate somewhat frustrating.

'So when am I going to meet the rest of your family?'

'All in good time.'

Adam hadn't stopped thinking about Kafni since their meeting and longed to share these thoughts with his friend but knew this was not possible. In fact given what Rindi had said about his sisters being off limits he wondered if he would ever be able to share his thoughts about Kafni with him. Her own manifest desire to keep their early morning encounter a secret only confirmed in his mind the forbidden nature of his thoughts. He also wondered whether he hadn't just been seduced by the beauty and romance of Kushapur itself. Perhaps this was all just a fantasy.

Rindi broke Adam's reverie

'Now, let's see if we can add to our bag. Maybe even a peacock!'

That evening they dined alone again and Adam wondered when he would finally get to meet Rindi's mother and sisters. Whatever the reason for delaying this introduction might have been it had succeeded in fuelling his anticipation whilst also frustrating his desire to see Kafni once more. Perhaps he would see her again in the morning by the pool. With this happy prospect in mind and exhausted from the excitements of the day, he excused himself shortly after dinner and retired early.

Adam slipped on a fine pair of silk pyjamas edged in purple and laid out on his bed. To his amazement these, together with a small wardrobe of other garments, had all been hand-sewn by the *derzi*, Prem Vijay and his team of the tailors in the few hours since he had been measured up that morning. Such was the industry behind the scenes in this Indian nobleman's household.

Too weary to read, Adam reached to turn off the bedside lamp. As he did so, there was a tap on the door. Expecting Rindi's head to appear round the corner to say goodnight he did not bother to respond. Only when the knock was repeated did he say, 'Come in'.

The door opened and closed so quickly that he was hardly aware that anyone had entered. He had been looking at the lamp so it took a few seconds for his eyes to adjust to the figure that had entered the room. To his surprise he saw that it was a young woman.

He had seen many servants in the corridors of the palace, but few of them had been women. All these servants had remained respectfully remote, and none had attended upon Rindi or Adam. It appeared quite out of character for this woman to now be in his room. She was carrying a tray which she placed on the table and put her hands together in the traditional gesture of *namaste*.

'Good evening, Captain Sahib. I am Mandira. I am a servant of the palace'. She kept her eyes below his as she spoke. It did not occur to Adam that this was a rather vague identification in an establishment with hundreds of servants and staff.

'Would the Sahib like this *'simkin'* for night drink?'

It was clearly not *'simkin'*, the Indian type champagne, but no doubt, it sounded more impressive to call it that.

She was an attractive girl, wearing a sari of pale green tulle edged with a broad gold band. It was pulled across the top of her head, leaving her pretty face uncovered. She must have been holding the material in place, because when she put the tray down and lowered her hands in her *'namaste'*, one end of the sari fell straight down and revealed part of her breast. The other end of her sari was loosely draped over her right shoulder and then drawn down to her left thigh where it was somehow secured and kept low enough to show her navel.

Adam glanced at the glass and thanked her, endeavouring to display nonchalance. Possibly this was part of the palace routine for visitors, and he felt sure this was no ordinary palace servant. Perhaps she was going to dance for him. Possibly she was a *'nautch*-girl', who, he knew, were professional dancers trained to entertain in the temples and palaces. But her only movement was to come closer to the bed. She had such a graceful innocence about her that Adam thought it unlikely that she was a courtesan. A sweeping movement of her hand released the sari from below her left thigh, and it now hung down straight from each shoulder. Beneath, was a gossamer thin *choli*, affording the barest covering of her small well-shaped breasts, and Adam could now see the curve of her hip. She was alluring but there was nothing erotic about her manner. She turned and deftly picked up one of the large cushions that lay on the rugs around the bedroom, placed it beside the bed and sat down facing him. She made no effort to re-arrange her sari as she spoke in a gentle melodious voice.

'Would Captain Sahib be sleeping better if I sang Hindu love song of *Punjab*?'

The way she was sitting allowed Adam to see that she was wearing very little under her sari and he was now becoming aroused. His hesitation in replying evoked an unexpected suggestion.

'I will stay all night, if the Sahib wishes.'

So this was it. There was no ambiguity about the invitation. Adam could feel his pulse quicken and a physical desire surged through him.

She was young, beautiful and very seductive. Adam sought to convince myself that it might be impolite to his host to refuse. Rindi must have known about this girl's visit. Since he no longer held out hope for an ongoing amorous affair with Sarah, perhaps he should be grateful for the offer of this gentle submissive girl. Would it be churlish of him to decline?

However, there was something not quite right about the situation.

Adam turned and picked up the drink that Mandira had brought, wanting time to ponder, and given her offer to stay the night there was no urgency. He took a sip of the drink: a warm *negus* with nuts sprinkled on it. It was stimulating and tangy and he drank it slowly, relishing each sip. Replacing the half-empty glass on the table he looked straight at her. She then smiled at him in a way that clearly invited a decision. It then struck him that maybe Rindi didn't know about this visit and that maybe it was Kafni who had sent her. Perhaps he was reading too much into it.

As he looked at this sensual Indian girl he could only think of Kafni emerging from the steaming pool. It was she whom Adam desired and this girl would only be a proxy for what Rindi had already implied was forbidden fruit.

'I'm very tired, Mandira, but I'd love to hear one of your songs, just one.'

She got up, unobtrusively adjusted her sari and turned quickly to the door. 'The Sahib will excuse me.'

Adam thought for one moment that he had offended her as she quietly slipped out of the door, but she returned after a few seconds with a small sitar and again sat down on the cushion.

She dextrously plucked the strings of the sitar, sending a haunting twang echoing round the room as she softly sang; her slight form deceptive of the canorous quality of her voice. Adam did not understand the words which were either in Sanskrit or Hindi, but the melody and variations were entrancing and left him with a feeling of deep contentment.

'Thank you, Mandira, I will now sleep well.' She gathered up her sari, and with a polite tilt of her head, turned and left the room.

Adam lay back on the pillow trying to make sense of his turbulent feelings but nevertheless glad he had resisted temptation. He switched off the light and drifted into sleep, dreaming of Kafni.

CHAPTER THIRTEEN

Kushnapur Palace, December 1941.

Adam awoke early and made his way down to the pool at the same time as the previous morning in the anticipation that he might coincide with what he hoped would be Kafni's regular morning swim. Alas there was no sign of her. On returning to his room Adam found his newly tailored silk suit laid out for him on the chair. Beside his bed he found a note from Rindi saying that he would come and collect him at 9.15 and they would then meet his father in his study at 9.30. Adam wondered if this was the moment that he would get to meet the rest of the family.

'Good morning old boy, I trust you slept well.'

'Yes, thank you, all that activity really took it out of me.'

Adam had expected Rindi to refer to Mandira's visit to his room but he made no mention of it. This left Adam wondering whether he even knew about it. Perhaps this was a standard courtesy afforded to all male guests of the palace.

When they arrived at the maharajah's study Adam was greeted with a broad smile of approval by Rindi's father. 'Good morning, Adam,' and gesturing his hand towards his suit he said, 'Superb fit I must say! We'll make an Indian sahib of you yet. Now, dear chap, we wondered if you would care to join us for morning prayers? It's an informal gathering and you are not obliged to join in the worship but it will give you an opportunity to meet the rest of the family.'

'I would be honoured, Sir.' Adam replied, excited at the prospect of meeting Kafni again.

The maharajah led them down a series of colonnaded hallways into a part of the building with an entirely different type of architecture. At the end of a long wide terrace, they walked down a flight of marble steps that widened as they descended. At the bottom it opened out into a capacious chamber with a lower ceiling than those in the palace rooms. A series of arches mounted on pillars stretched across in front of them obscuring parts of the room. In the centre, on the floor, were a number of large cushions. Faint music could be heard as they walked towards them and sat down. Rindi's father took the centre, front cushion.

A few moments later a *Brahmin* priest entered, chanting and reciting prayers in Sanskrit that he obviously knew by heart. To the side of the chamber, well removed from them, was another group, who looked like members of the household staff. Beyond them, the ceiling rose to a considerable height, and at the rear of this lofty section was a *triforlum*, a gallery, screened by a perforated marble *jali*. Adam noticed the movement of people behind the fretted masonry screen.

'That is a private balcony where the women conduct their prayers,' said Rindi in hushed tones. Adam nodded in acknowledgement and felt a frisson of pleasure at the thought that Kafni might be watching him from the seclusion of this private place.

Behind the *Brahmin* priest, beneath the gallery, was a statue of the God *Vishnu*, and nearby was an image of his consort *Laksmi*, the Goddess of Wealth and Bliss. Although the images appeared to be embraced by the service, at no time did the priest bow or pay obeisance to them. It was as if their presence was merely a symbol.

The prayers lasted little more than half an hour. Towards their end, a second *Brahmin* came in carrying a bowl of rose water and sprinkled each of them with this delicate perfume. In the cool atmosphere, without the heat of the sun to evaporate the fine oils, the whole chamber took on the fragrance of an evening flower garden. As they left Adam had a great feeling of tranquillity and although he had understood none of the Sanskrit ceremony he felt that a profound change had taken place within him.

This was the first time since his arrival that he had felt a sense of real cultural difference between himself and Rindi. But whether it was because of his friendship with Rindi or possible presence of his sister, he felt drawn in by this experience and a desire to embrace it rather than reject it as something alien.

After prayers Rindi took him on a tour of the palace. They were accompanied by a servant who opened doors and turned on lights where necessary to show the ornate beauty of the decoration.

'When was this place built?' Adam asked.

'It's hard to put an exact date on it; construction took place over many centuries.'

They were on the third floor, and had now come to an open area near the centre of the palace. It reached up from a cloistered courtyard at ground floor level, to the open blue sky above the fourth storey. Looking down Adam saw that the enclosed courtyard was paved with a pale marble, reflecting light into the surrounding rooms, thus augmenting the daylight reaching the internal rooms. On each floor, a balcony gave access to other rooms on the same level. However, he noticed that the balcony below them, was enclosed with stone latticework.

'I suppose that's reserved for the distaff side of the family.'

'Yes, spot on. That's the *zenana*. It has extensive rooms, not many of which are used today but useful when the maharajah had several wives and concubines.'

'Sounds interesting.'

'Yes, but sadly that won't be part of our tour.'

'So, which is the oldest part of the Palace?'

'It starts from there,' Rindi indicated a section of the second floor below them. 'It then goes down to the ground floor and back into the rock. As you know the original building on this site was a Buddhist temple. It had been blocked off by an earthquake and massive rock fall hundreds of years before we arrived. It was not until excavations were started for the foundations that the temple was discovered, in almost perfect condition.'

'Will we get to see that?'

'In due course but probably not today. Come on, let's go up on to the roof.'

He led the way up a long staircase that spiralled round an enormous stone pillar. Only when they were actually on the roof did he realise that they had bypassed the fourth floor without seeing any apparent access at that level. They came out onto a flat roof covered with large stone slabs, and he wondered how they had managed to lift them into place. Then he noticed that a viaduct ran from the rear of the building into the hillside quite close to this point. It would have been reasonably easy to slide the flagstones along this viaduct together with other building materials. It really was a triumph of engineering. A parapet about four feet in height surrounded the whole of the roof. At the rear, it rose straight off the roof, but on the other side, four steps led down to a wide gully. Across the roof at intervals were small channels designed to take away the rainwater and discharge it into ducts at the rear.

'Come and look at this.' Rindi beckoned as he looked down between the rear of the building and the hillside. 'Now you can see how each level of the building was constructed. The soil was first pushed forward when the rooms were constructed, then dug away again when roof height was reached, leaving a protective valley between the hillside and the actual building. This enables light to reach the rooms below'. Rindi suddenly stopped talking and looked at his watch.

'It's nearly midday. We must hurry. We've got an appointment with my mother.' And with that he hastened across to a raised turret with a doorway. Taking a key from his pocket, he unlocked and opened the door, revealing another stairway, similar to the one they had ascended, but even longer. Down and down they went, bypassing both the fourth and the third floors to arrive at the second floor. Adam realised that the servant was no longer with them.

'This is the floor reserved for the women,' said Rindi, 'so there is no access from this staircase.'

They were now walking along a veranda opening onto the central courtyard that they had been viewing earlier. It was a strange feeling passing behind the carved stone latticework screen designed to protect the women's modesty. A short way along, Rindi stopped outside one of the doors, knocked and then entered. He followed him into a fair sized room, on the far side of which were double doors. The room was sparsely furnished. In two of the chairs sat elderly Indian women sewing brightly coloured materials - perhaps saris. Rindi greeted them, and then spoke in Hindi. One of them answered and Rindi turned to Adam.

'Wait here a minute, I'll see if Mother is ready to receive us.'

Whilst Rindi was gone Adam noticed that the two women had covered their faces but continued to chat to each other. Rindi returned after five minutes smiling as he came out and held the door open.

'Come in, Adam. Mother is looking forward to meeting you.'

Adam walked through, not knowing what to expect, but was instantly charmed by the beauty of the room: a blend of Georgian elegance with the glorious colours of India. Each aspect of the decor, every object, confirmed the taste of its designer. Warm rose-coloured panels, edged with cream and dove-grey, covered the walls from floor to ceiling. Interspersing these panels at intervals were square fluted columns, headed by gold lotus leaf capitals in harmony with the intricate mouldings of the ceiling. A line of five windows, with splendid scalloped Hindu arches, gave out to the front of the Palace, commanding a magnificent panorama of the valley. They walked across the luxuriant carpet, the deep pile absorbing sound, creating a hushed feeling of tranquillity.

The room was so large that at first glance he saw no one. Then a movement drew his eye to the far left window. Nearby, set at an angle was a sofa. It was obvious from her dignified stature that this was the *maharani*.

Rindi walked briskly over to her, then turned and looked at Adam.

'Adam, I would like you to meet my mother.'

'How nice of you to come and visit us, Captain Cullworthy. Do sit down.'

Adam gave a token bow. 'Your Highness.'

She smiled graciously and then said, 'I hope Rindi has been looking after you?'

'Yes, thank you, he has been the perfect host.'

'Please tell me about your mother. Has she ever been to India?'

'No, Ma'am.'

'Then when this dreadful war is over, she must come and stay with us.'

'That's very kind of you, your Highness. I'm sure she'd like that very much.' He was curious as to why she had only asked after his mother as if it were unseemly for her to enquire after a man's life.

Adam was now able to study the maharani. She was much shorter than Rindi and her loose-fitting sari disguised a heavier figure than her daughter, but she was still a fine looking woman, and on his reckoning must have been in her mid-forties. A red and gold scarf drawn over gently waved hair framed her face and fell to her shoulders. When speaking, she moved her hands with the expression and grace of a dancer and the dignity of an aristocrat. Her diction was precise with a marked Indian inflection, consistent with the content of her next remark.

'I have never been to England. I would love to go one day. My governess, who came from Hampshire, told me so much about it. It really must be a lovely country.'

'My parents think so, Ma'am, but like all countries, it just depends where you live.'

'Are you married, Captain Cullworthy?' Adam found this a surprising question, it was as if she knew nothing of her son's best friend.

'No, I am not. As a regular officer I am not permitted to get married until I'm over thirty.'

Rindi's mother looked beyond his shoulder and gave a beckoning gesture with her hand to a woman standing by the door. A few minutes later she returned followed by two younger women, one of whom Adam recognised as Kafni. She looked entirely different dressed in a striking yellow sari and beside her dressed in a green sari was a younger girl that Adam took to be Puhella. Rindi stood up as they entered the room and greeted his sisters fondly.

'Adam, I would like you to meet my sisters.'

They both greeted him with '*namaste*'.

'Kafni, I would like you to meet Captain Cullworthy.'

She held out her hand. Taking it gently, Adam felt her long slim fingers and his pulse quickened. He wanted to kiss her hand but overcame this temptation knowing how shockingly over-familiar that would be in front of her mother. Instead he just said, 'How do you do?'

'Delighted to meet you, Captain Cullworthy.' She replied, her voice not betraying any emotion or indication of their previous encounter, but there was a warmth in her violet eyes.

'Please, I would prefer it if you all called me Adam,' he said, looking across to the maharani, who with a gracious tilt of her head acknowledged his request.

Kafni's beautiful oval face with faultless pale brown skin broke into a lovely gentle smile revealing perfect white teeth peeping between her full lips. As she turned to move away he was able to admire her striking profile with long curving eyelashes.

'And, finally, this is Puhella.'

Whereas Kafni was definitely all woman Puhella was still very much a girl and although she was pretty in a precocious way she did not possess the beauty and stature of her sister. There was a youthful sparkle about her and she seemed to have no inhibitions about squeezing Adam's hand flirtatiously.

'Please tell us about London, Adam. Rindi never tells us anything. Is it bigger than Delhi?'

'Oh, about three times as big I should think.'

'Good heavens. And is that where the King lives?'

'Yes, the King and Queen live in Buckingham Palace and last year they survived a German air raid.'

'Have you ever met the King?'

'No, I haven't.'

'I would like to meet the King. Did you know that my grandfather met Queen Victoria?'

'Yes. I did know that.'

Puhella's impulsive questions reminded him of his sister Sue.

She turned to her mother. 'Please, please, Mamaji, can we go to London when the war is over. Adam will show us round. And we can stay with Uncle Jardeeson.'

The girls both spoke perfect English but unlike Rindi's Oxford accent they had a charming Indian intonation. Her mother smiled with her eyes. 'Of course, we had planned just that for you - for both of you.'

A look of sadness then came across her face. 'We must all be very patient and hope that this war won't last too long.'

Puhella pouted in disappointment and she finally released Adam's hand. 'Why do those beastly Germans want to go on fighting? I hope they never come to India.'

In this serene setting it was hard to imagine the horror of the war in Europe. Adam thought of the last time he had been in France and how very different things must be now.

In the distance, a gong sounded for luncheon and Rindi's mother rose to her feet. 'Run along now girls. Rindi and Captain Cullworthy have more important things to talk about.' Turning to Adam, and ignoring his previous request she said, 'We do keep some English customs, Captain Cullworthy so I hope you'll join us later for afternoon tea.'

'Of course, ma'am. I'd be delighted to.'

Afternoon tea with Rindi's mother was incongruously British. A ritual that would not have been out of place in the grand houses of Kensington. The maharajah joined them briefly and for the first time Adam was able to observe the whole family together. He detected a degree of remoteness between the girls and their father, in contrast to the close affinity he clearly held with Rindi. The maharajah did not stay long, his attendance appeared to be more of a formality and it was clear that this was the maharani's domain. This was the Debrahms at ease and he felt honoured to be treated as a close friend of the family.

'Are you interested in Indian art, Adam? Perhaps you would like to see some of Kafni's tapestries.' This was the first time the maharani had addressed him informally.

'Yes - I'd like that very much,' Adam replied hoping this might be an opportunity to be alone with Kafni. But this was not to be. A servant was dispatched to fetch the works, and returned carrying two small brightly coloured tapestries and with motionless shoulders, she walked over to him. Her tapestries were intricately detailed; they must have taken weeks to complete. Numerous small figures had been worked into the fabric and, no doubt, each had some significance.

'These are beautiful, Kafni. Who drew the cartoons?'

'They come from books and pictures that I find. Sometimes I draw them myself.' She gave a modest smile.

One tapestry depicted a part of the palace. Another showed elephants and a tiger appearing through long grass. Was this, Adam thought, the *shikar* where Sir Arthur Hawkswood had been killed? Did the two girls know that his death was not an accident? And Rindi's mother; did she know? Of course, Wantilla would be ready to make mischief with that information whenever it suited his purpose.

Kafni admired Adam's strong elegant hands. As he handled her needlework their fingers briefly touched and they both felt the electricity pass between them. She longed to hold his hand but knew her mother was watching and would strongly disapprove.

Adam's absorption with Kafni and her work was curtailed by Rindi who said rather abruptly. 'Will you excuse us, Mamaji? Adam and I have things to discuss.'

'Of course, Rindi, I understand.'

His mother looked at Adam. 'We hope you'll join us again soon.'

'Thank you, I look forward to that.' Within this household nothing seemed to be taken for granted and he was getting accustomed to being invited to join the family for even trivial meetings.

Rindi led the way, not to the study as Adam expected, but to his own rooms. It was considerably larger than his own room, grander and more lavishly furnished but unlike his room it had windows only on the east side.

'Make yourself comfortable. By the way I hope you don't mind I've asked for supper to be sent up here. We've quite a lot to talk about.'

'That's fine with me.'

'Adam, you probably think I have been rather evasive in some of my answers to your questions for some time now and I hope my reasons for this will become apparent. Much of what I need to tell you depended on your coming to Kushnapur and meeting the family and understanding that complete discretion is essential.'

The implication to Adam was that meeting the family was part of a vetting process but one which he could assume that he had passed. Rindi paced the room holding his hand to his chin. Whatever his revelation was going to be, he appeared to be thinking hard.

'As you know we are descended from the Indo-Aryans, themselves a product of Alexander the Great's armies interbreeding with the local Indian people. This Hindu population were a light skinned, vigorous and dynamic people who remained in control of northern India until the arrival of the Moghuls in the sixteenth century. By that stage our family had been established for fourteen centuries in a small state in the Hindu Kush. Their reluctance to be ruled by the Turkish invaders led to them moving to where we now live.' Rindi took a moment to drink from a glass of water.

'Shortly after this one of my forebears became concerned about the deterioration in the hereditary characteristics of the Debrahm family. Centuries of interbreeding to maintain control of the territory had taken its toll. Occasionally new blood had been introduced when the daughter of one of the noble Sardarji families married the heir, but too often these were cousins. Unfortunately, it was not possible to introduce a male from another branch of the ruling castes without the risk of having our small state taken over by another ruler. It would also have been quite impossible for any member of the Debrahm family to marry outside the caste. The whole credibility of the family would have been destroyed by such action.'

'So what was his solution?' Adam asked, intrigued at where this was all leading to.

'His first idea was that the daughter of the family would marry into another family. If this marriage produced a son who was not already heir to a princedom he would be invited to marry a granddaughter of the Debrahm family.'

'That would still be one of his cousins.'

'Yes, again the relationship was rather closer than was desirable.'

'It sounds rather complicated. What about the natural heir? I bet he wouldn't take kindly to being usurped by a cousin.'

'He certainly would not and this often led to bitter clashes and even murder.'

'So did they abandon that idea?'

'Let's say it was modified considerably and refined further.'

Adam made no comment as Rindi continued his explanation.

'It then occurred to the maharajah at the time that the introduction of Aryan blood into the Indian breeding stock had been a great success in Alexander's day and it might be worth trying the same idea again.

'The logical solution was to find a suitable female of Aryan stock and introduce her to the Debrahm family. Her first male heir would then provide fresh Aryan blood to the line.'

'Did they do that?'

'No they didn't.It proved almost impossible. Apart from the fact that there were almost no European women in India at the time that met the criteria, those that might have done were unlikely to go along with such a scheme. Marriage outside the Hindu high caste would not have been allowed for a Debrahm so she would have become an unmarried, pregnant, European woman. Not an enviable position in society.'

'So what solution did they come up with?'

'They decided it would be easier for a "sire" to remain anonymous. So it was decided that the only safe way to introduce new blood into the family was through the female line.'

A detailed list of desirable family and personal attributes of the suitable man was drawn up: good health and physique, good features, intelligence and a natural ability to command.'

'A demanding list, and not that easy to find a willing participant like that in India I imagine.' Adam suggested his curiousity ignited.

'There were quite a few candidates but as you say not that easy to get them to play ball, so to speak.'

'What about the child? would it not have an unusually light skin? Was that not a problem?'

'That was not such a big issue, many of the original Indo-Aryans were blue-eyed and light skinned and the lighter skinned members of Indian families always contract the best marriages.'

'So how did they set about this? It must have been quite a challenge to keep it quiet.'

'No one, other than those involved, was permitted to know of the arrangement and they were all sworn to absolute secrecy.'

Adam felt beads of sweat forming on his brow, realising what an extraordinary family secret had been revealed to him.

'And where did they find their first "sire"?' he asked tentatively.

'A search was made for a suitable person and the family learnt of a Portuguese naval captain living in Goa, who fitted the bill. They persuaded him to visit Kushnapur Palace on the pretence of wanting to hire him for maritime services. Once here he was effectively held prisoner not being allowed to leave but detained in the most comfortable of conditions and with discreet access to one of the princesses. Unbeknown to him she became pregnant and disappeared from the palace. He was eventually allowed to leave but given the luxury he had become accustomed to he did so reluctantly. And that was the start of what became known as the Alexander project. The successful introduction of reinvigorating stock into the Debrahm dynasty.'

'So they didn't marry?'

'Absolutely not. In fact he never saw the princess again and nor was he ever aware of the resulting child.'

'How was the child explained to her family?'

'She had previously been betrothed to the third son of a suitable Indian prince and as soon as she became pregnant the marriage was hastily arranged. The prince assumed the baby was his and as it was a girl with abnormally light skin she was considered a blessing.'

Adam took a mango from the fruit bowl on Rindi's desk. He held it up to his nose to smell it contemplating whether he wanted to eat it or just enjoy the comfort of its shape and smell.'

'Surely they needed a son for him to become the heir to Kushnapur?'

'Well, the problem with a son is that he could only inherit if there was no natural male heir from the direct line. On the other hand a girl could marry and then herself produce offspring that could marry the heir to the Maharajah a generation later.'

'Sounds complicated and must have taken careful long-term planning.'

'It is and does,' Adam noticed Rindi's use of the present tense, 'and is also subject to the perils of childbirth which is made more uncertain by hundreds of years of inbreeding. On more than one occasion either the mother or the baby has died.'

'So how often does this process take place?'

'Once every four generations.'

'And when did it last take place?'

'Three generations ago,' he said and paused.

Adam sat contemplating the significance of what Rindi had just told him. Not only had been made privy to a great Debrahm family secret but it would appear that, if he wasn't mistaken, he was about to play a leading role in the next chapter of their genetic plan.

The tension in the room was broken with the arrival of supper and Adam used this interruption as an opportunity to get up and walk around the room trying to make sense of this whole conversation. As he stood by the window deep in thought he noticed a pile of letters on Rindi's writing desk but his attention was drawn to the distinctive handwriting of the top letter which was unmistakeable.

'I see you've had correspondence from Tina. More than I've had.'

Rindi tried not to look flustered by this comment. 'Yes, she writes to tell me that Pauline is engaged.'

'You didn't tell me. Who's the lucky fellow?'

'Some barrister she met in her chambers.' At least that part was true. Adam stood gazing at the envelope suppressing a desire to pick it up. How he had loved receiving her letters but this was not addressed to him. Had he realised that the whole pile of letters were from Tina the conversation may have been considerably more awkward.

'Well, where had we got to?' Rindi said bringing the discussion back to where they had left off.

Adam began to think he might be mistaken in his conjecture. Could Rindi really be about to propose what he was thinking? If so, it crossed Adam's mind that he was not obliged to take part in this arcane scheme. He could just say no.

They couldn't keep him prisoner. Perhaps he was allowing his imagination to run away with itself and the end of the story would be quite different. But if his assumption was correct, how long he wondered had he been in the frame as a potential sire.

'When did you decide that it was to be me?' Adam said abruptly.

Rindi looked across at Adam, his manner and tone now almost apologetic.

'The final decision was only made this afternoon after you had met the family. But the original proposal came from Uncle Jardeeson when he first met you.'

Adam's mind wrestled with conflicting thoughts. After the shock of realising that he had been singled out to fulfil this extraordinary task his initial reaction was to feel flattered that he had been chosen by the family as having all the desired attributes. This was followed swiftly by a sense of outrage that he had been the subject of their secret scrutiny for at least ten years.

'Jardeeson! Is that why you took me to his house in London?' All this time he had been just a pawn in their great game. What of the affection and friendship he had for Nina and Jardeeson and that which he believed they had for him? Had it all been a charade? And what about Rindi's involvement? Had their friendship been just a cynical ploy to secure his participation in their scheme?

'Not at all, Adam, you came with me to London as my friend. At the time, I was only vaguely aware there had been arrangements in the previous generations to strengthen our bloodline. In the past these participants had always been found in India. The possibility of someone agreeing to travel to India from Europe for this purpose was considered extremely unlikely. It was only after our visit to Richmond to see Sir Julian that Jardeeson informed me that they thought you had many of the qualities they were looking for.

'What was Sir Julian's involvement?'

'Genealogy is one of his great interests and given his position within the establishment he was well positioned to research your antecedents.'

Rindi could see that Adam was finding these revelations difficult to reconcile. He poured a glass of port from the decanter on the tray and gave it to him. Adam took it silently and welcomed the strength and sweet warmth of the alcohol.

'At what stage did he decide I would be suitable?'

'About a year after our lunch in Richmond. But at that point you were only one of several candidates deemed acceptable.'

'Acceptable? But obviously not for his own daughter. Was that why he warned Tina off getting involved with me?'

Rindi wondered how he would ever be able to reveal to Adam how he and Tina had become romantically involved. So much had happened in all their lives that he felt maybe he could now come clean. Part of his reservation about telling Adam about Tina in the past was that it may have come to nothing and the hurt would have been unnecessary. But things had panned out differently.

'He should not have said anything to her but like any father he didn't want his daughter to get hurt. He was well aware how complicated things might become if you were to be *so* involved with the Debrahm family.'

Adam wondered how fate might have dealt him a different hand. His plans to marry Tina, the perfect English rose, and settle down in England had been all that he had aspired to. Now life had become much more complicated but also, without doubt, more interesting.

He began to see that maybe there was honour in his selection and that perhaps he should feel proud of having passed such rigorous scrutiny. But he felt manipulated and the extent of his involvement was still far from clear.

'I hope you can now see why it was impossible to reveal any of this to you before you came to Kushnapur. Please believe me when I say that you are first and foremost my friend and that if you do not wish to participate in our plan you must feel free to say so.'

Adam knew that Rindi was right. Had he not been enchanted by the Debrahm family and seduced by the magic of Kushnapur itself he would never have willingly contemplated the role they had planned for him. They had played a perfect game of chess and they must have felt confident that they were close to check mating him.

'I assume it would be Kafni as the oldest?' Adam asked, barely able to disguise his enthusiasm.

'Yes, that's correct. But Adam I have to say to you in all seriousness; there can never be any romantic involvement with her. I realise this may affect your decision, but she will marry a Hindu of our family's choice and my father will not change his mind on that.'

Rindi felt hypocritical warning Adam off involvement with Kafni but it was as it would need to be and this was not the moment to waiver in their plans.

'If that is the case perhaps it would be better if I <u>was</u> involved with someone else.'

'Perhaps and in principle it would have made little difference to us but I knew that you personally would object on moral grounds and I would never have compromised you in that way.'

Adam nodded to acknowledge the brutal reality of Rindi's statement.

'How does Kafni feel about all this?'

'She considers it both an honour and her duty to fulfil the needs of the family.'

Adam realised that the disappointment he felt could not be justified by anything but his own romantic imaginings. Kafni had not given him any expectation of something more between them.

'And Adam, nothing would give me greater pleasure than to share my bloodline with my closest friend.'

Put like that Adam suddenly felt the weight of destiny upon him. He walked over to the table and picked out the mango he had previously returned to the bowl of fruit and now began peeling it. His mind filling in recent events like pieces in a puzzle.

Sleep eluded Adam for a long time that night. The thought that he was being offered a licence to make love to this beautiful woman was tempered with the disappointment of knowing that that would be the extent of his involvement with her.

CHAPTER FOURTEEN

Kushnapur Palace, 6ᵗʰ December 1941.

When Adam arrived down for breakfast Rindi was listening to the news on the BBC World Service. In this rarefied atmosphere of palace life in the far flung reaches of Northern India it would have been easy to forget that there was a bloody conflict taking place the other side of the world. As serving soldiers they were acutely aware of the need to keep up with fast moving events taking place. That morning's news was that the Russians had halted the German advance on Moscow, and in the United States the government was having strong words with the Japanese Ambassador.

'I don't like the look of things in the Far East,' said Rindi.

'Yes, I wonder how long it will be before the Japanese start realising their territorial ambitions.'

'Well, the Americans seem to think they can contain them with diplomacy but that didn't get us very far with Mr Hitler.'

'All too depressing,'.Rindi said with a sigh.' How about a ride down to see the old fort? I also promised to show you the hydro generator.'

'Where are they?'

'The fort is on the hill overlooking the approach road from the gorge and the power station is underneath it.'

'Sounds well protected.'

'Yes, well we've become rather accustomed to enjoying electricity. Life would not be the same without the generator.'

Neither of them mentioned their discussion of the previous evening. Rindi for fear that Adam might have had second thoughts about his participation in their plan. Adam because he still couldn't quite believe what they were asking him to do and had mixed emotions about the limitations placed on his involvement with Kafni. He had many questions to ask, not least of which was how the whole scheme would work in practice. But he knew that until he could unravel these thoughts in his own mind, his questions might seem indelicate.

Twenty minutes later booted, spurred and mounted, they trotted out through the main entrance and onto the road away from the Palace. They had been riding for less than ten minutes when they heard the sound of a car approaching at speed. They barely had time to draw their horses on to the verge when round the bend, appeared the bonnet of a Bentley. If Adam had expected the car to slow down as it passed the horses, he was to be disappointed. Instead, the magnificent pale blue drop-head shot by spitting stones and gravel from the road, leaving a trail of dust in its wake, and the horses in a very agitated state.

'Arrogant bastard!' Rindi spat the words out.

'Who was that? He certainly doesn't respect horses.'

'That's Wantilla and he doesn't have respect for anyone. God knows what he wants. He won't be welcome; Father can't stand him.'

They had turned their horses off the road into the shade of a *neem* tree, whilst the dust settled.

'Why does your father agree to see him? Or even permit him to visit the palace?'

'He seldom does consent to see him. A senior servant is usually as far as he gets. If there's an official matter to discuss, the Assistant Dewan will deal with him. However, we are in a difficult position. My father and Mahavir, Wantilla's father, are first cousins. Next to ours, they are the most important family in the state. They are also extremely rich. Their wealth derives from a fabulous dowry, brought by a princess from another state when she married my great uncle. They used it to buy vast estates, a silver mine and other assets all producing huge revenues.'

'I can see the problem.'

'Yes, money can buy influence and support. And, there's a political dimension. You will remember the attack on Sir Julian Westbury some years ago, when he was a Judge here in India. Well suffice it to say wealth not only creates power, it also attracts undesirable elements.'

'On our journey from Saharanpur you mentioned that he wants to marry Kafni. Perhaps that is what he is here about.'

'It could be, but father gave him short shrift last time he raised that subject.'

On returning to the Palace they entered the outer courtyard. The first thing they saw was the blue Bentley. Pacing up and down beside it was Wantilla puffing furiously on a cigarette. Two *syces* ran up and held their horses as they dismounted. Wantilla was leaning against the long bonnet of his car, with an expression like thunder.

Rindi walked over to him, shook hands in a perfunctory manner, and then turned to introduce Adam to his cousin.

'How do you do?' Wantilla said with studied indifference.

When Adam shook his hand he noticed that it was cold and slippery and that Wantilla winced slightly at Adam's firm grip.

It was a strange feeling meeting someone of whom he had heard a great deal but who almost certainly knew very little about him. He was taller than he expected and he could see how his handsome features and arrogant bearing would appeal to the ladies. He wondered whether the slightly sinister look he perceived in Wantilla's eyes was of his own imagining or a genuine manifestation of evil.

'You've taken your time getting back, I must say.'

Rindi clearly knew the man too well to be baited by such a remark and showed remarkable equanimity in not mentioning how his car had nearly swept them off the road.

'I came to see that father of yours, but he lacks the manners to greet me.'

'I'm sure he's very busy. Did you have an appointment?'

'No! None should be necessary when the Mahavir Debrahms come visiting. I need to know when he will confirm my betrothal to your sister.'

'Which one? Rindi responded mischievously.

'You know very well. Kafni of course. Don't treat me like an idiot.'

Adam's hackles rose to hear him mention Kafni's name.

'And even she won't agree to see me, the stuck up bitch!'

'I know she has music lessons about this time.' Rindi replied trying to keep a lid on Wantilla's ferocious temper.

'Instead of giving me a proper reply, one of his flunkies hands me this, written by some bloody palace *babu*.' Wantilla took a folded sheet of writing paper from its envelope and thrust it forward.

Rindi opened it, and having read it handed it to Adam. Written on palace headed notepaper it read:

"His Highness presents his compliments, and wishes to inform his esteemed Cousin Wantilla, that he does not consider it appropriate at this time that any formalities should be set in motion in pursuance of the proposal that he has made in respect of his daughter, The Princess Kafni. Nevertheless, his Highness is not unaware of the benefits which could emerge from a nuptial arrangement within the compass of our two families at some stage in the future."

Adam barely had time to read the letter before Wantilla snatched it back.

'What bloody business is this of his?' he said furiously with a contemptuous glance towards Adam.

'Captain Cullworthy is a future trustee of the Kushnapur estate.'

'I warn you my father simply will not stand for this bullshit. If I don't get my way, someone is going to regret it.'

Flinging open the door of the Bentley, he swung his heavy frame into the driver's seat, scarcely giving his unfortunate chauffeur time to climb aboard before he raced off at high speed.

This brief encounter had confirmed Adam's previously held opinion of Wantilla. He resented the matter of fact way Kafni's future had been discussed with him. But hadn't Adam's conversation with Rindi the previous night been even more calculated? Adam longed to see her, to just hold her hand but after Rindi's comments he feared there would be no familiarity. Would she have even been aware of their discussion? Of course she would. But no formal decision had been made. In not rejecting the idea out of hand it had been assumed that he would be a willing participant.

Neither Rindi's mother nor either of his sisters were in evidence that day and although the Maharajah did appear briefly for a drink he did not join them for dinner.

The deep sense of anti-climax Adam was feeling must have been apparent to Rindi because he announced that he had laid on a little entertainment for them after dinner. 'I thought it was about time you experienced some of our traditional dancing.'

He led the way through the hallways, down well-worn broad stone steps, into a chamber where columns and arches surrounded an open area of patterned marble. This led into the *natamandap*, a spectacular dancing chamber.

'This was exposed during excavations for the palace. We think it is at least a thousand years old.'

A woman in a gold sari came forward to greet them, and indicated to the cushions that had been set out on a dais. The moment they were seated, four musicians entered the room, followed by a girl who bowed her head, gave a *namaste*, and started to sing. Judging by Rindi's broad smiles, her first song must have been amusing.

'I'll explain it to you later,' he said.

The second ballad needed no translation. The pathos in her voice clearly indicated a lost love and her gesticulations, a broken heart. At no time did she look directly at Rindi and Adam; her eyes were either demurely cast downwards or occasionally joyously lifted towards the ceiling. This created the illusion that the players were totally apart from them.

Two of the musicians played long flutes; another provided the refrain to the melody with a *saraugi* - a small portable harmonium; the fourth was a *sitar* player; and then finally a drummer with his twin *tabla*. Following her second ballad, the singer withdrew. The musicians then moved to a livelier score, and six girls dancing in perfect unison swept into the room. Their turquoise skirts swirling one way then the other as they twisted and turned to the repeated beat of the music. Sometimes their fingers were cupped together, at other times extended singly. Then, with arms outstretched and palms held flat, they accelerated their graceful spinning movements. Skirts were flung higher, like giant umbrellas, revealing deep blue pyjamas matching their *choli*. Bells on the dancers' ankles moved in rhythm with the *tabla*, articulating the rhythms of the feet.

'These movements are the *angas*,' said Rindi as Adam watched in fascination. 'There are almost a dozen different movements of the arms, head, chest, waist, thigh, calves, wrists and elbows.'

The girls danced for a further fifteen minutes, their bare feet apparently tireless. In a blend of colours, they weaved in and out of each formation of the dance with exquisite grace.

'How do they achieve such perfection?' Adam asked.

'Years of training,' said Rindi. 'They think nothing of practising fourteen hours a day and it takes up to ten years before they are permitted to perform in public. Of course they start very young.'

'Dancing must be considered important.'

'It's far more than that; it's a vital part of the life of India. It is the very soul of Hinduism. It has been for thousands of years. Girls were dancing in the temples in India when your ancient Britons were dancing round stone circles.' He laughed.

A few moments later, the girls fanned out, facing them in a semi-circle, and then settled on to the floor with the grace of a swan tending its cygnets. 'This dance is called the *adavus*,' said Rindi, as a particularly stunning girl swept into the room. Her deep cream dress, patterned with gold peacock eyes, was edged with purple. So too was the long headscarf. A diamond-studded clasp ran through the parting of her hair and held a heart-shaped brooch above her forehead. Reaching the centre of the room, she stood erect in an elegant pose, and then began a rhythmic swaying movement of the neck followed at first only by the body, then by the arms and hands and delicate movements of the eyes and eyebrows. A series of remarkable dance flexions followed, with expressive mime woven into the dance.

'This is the dalliance with the Gods,' said Rindi. 'She alternately depicts the lover and the beloved, passing from one role to the other by means of the *palta* - that spiral turn from side to side.'

Adam watched as the dance reached a frenzied climax as the other dancers leapt to their feet and joined in the dazzling finale.

CHAPTER FIFTEEN

Kushnapur Palace, 6ᵗʰ December 1941

Adam had been given no hint of a chosen time. He might have attached some significance to the fact that fresh pyjamas had been laid out for him, but linen and clothes were changed so frequently at the palace that this in itself was not significant. He should have deduced something from the fact that although, as before, the pyjamas were of cream silk with purple facings, the style was now an Indian high neck and the trimming was delicately interwoven with gold thread and the ubiquitous family colours.

He had gone to bed soon after ten, and had been reading for less than half an hour, when there was a gentle knock at the door.

To his surprise, it was Mandira, the girl who had come to his room three nights earlier.

'*Namaste Huzoor.* Good evening, Captain-sahib.'

'*Namaste*, Mandira.'

She walked over and stood beside his bed. Her deep blue sari edged in russet and decorated with small leaf motifs conveyed a demure and charming quality. Each pleat, fold and gather was carefully arranged to protect vital areas of the body and obstruct evil. Her dress was in sharp contrast to the emerald green sari she had worn on her previous visit.

She smiled and with a twinkle in her eye said. 'No songs tonight. Would the Captain-sahib please be coming with me.' Then, to allay suspicion, she added, 'The Rajkumari Kafni is wishing to see you.'

The words sounded strange to Adam as if he was taking part in a play. He had a sudden urge to assert himself, but under the present circumstances there would have been no point. She gracefully picked up his dressing gown from the chair and laid it on the bed.

'I shall get the key,' she said with an appealing tilt of her head.

She turned and walked over to the writing bureau, her fumbling operation of the secret device indicating that although she knew where the key was hidden she was not entirely familiar with the mechanism itself.

Adam slipped on the dressing gown and slippers whilst she pulled aside the curtain. She then unlocked and opened the heavy oak door and removed the key once more.

Adam followed her out of the bedroom; there was now no turning back even if he had wished to do so. An oil lamp burning brightly stood on a plinth on the covered stone landing. Things had been well prepared. Pausing at the top of a flight of stone steps, he felt a slight chill in the night air as the scent of jasmine drifted up from the gardens four floors below. Neither of them spoke, but there was complicity in their silence.

Adam considered the significance of the fact that Kafni's personal ayah had been sent to tempt him. If he had succumbed to her how much more difficult would this arrangement have been, if indeed it had happened at all. She picked up the lamp to lead the way casting an eerie shadow as she moved gracefully down two flights and round several corners, her soft leather slippers soundless beneath her gown. They passed several levels and Adam calculated that they had now reached the second floor. The walls here were brightly decorated with murals of dancing girls and other colourfully dressed women whose heavily made-up eyes seemed to follow him auspiciously.

He felt the aura that Rindi had talked about. Was Kushnapur the living entity now using him as an instrument of its destiny? Two more long passages brought them to a studded oak door like the one leading from his room. Mandira unlocked this door with the same key and Adam followed her through into a wide entrance hall well-lit with electric lanterns.

There was now a marked change in the ambience and he felt warmth rising from the spectacular mosaic floor. Vividly coloured rugs hung on either side and ahead, at the end of the hall, a blue and gold brocade drape reached from the high ceiling to the floor. He watched with expectancy as Mandira drew the curtain to one side revealing a pale cream door with azure panels. She turned the handle and beckoned him, provoking a surge of exhilaration as he thought of what might lie ahead.

He knew instinctively from its intimacy that this was Kafni's apartment. The delicate perfume that pervaded his senses, the feminine touch of the pale rose pink walls with their intricate patterns of leaves and flowers. His inquisitive fingertips lightly touching the wall revealed that they were not painted on plaster as he had thought but onto brightly coloured silk interlaced with silver and gold threads.

On the blue marble floor lay a Heriz carpet, its soft pallet colours of rust, green, yellow and orange, exhibiting centuries of blending.

To one side of this elegant chamber the wall was completely curtained and Mandira walked past him to pull back one section, disclosing a line of windows. Beyond these lay a moonlit balcony. 'Chandi Sitari', she said, looking out into the night, as if expecting him to know its astrological significance. A graceful hand gesture invited him to look out at the three-quarter moon and starlit sky. It was an exhilarating view of the heavens. He then remembered that no prudent Hindu would arrange such an occasion without consulting her astrologer.

Turning round, he saw another curtained section, above which the feminine character of the décor was further emphasised by a series of nymphs, exquisitely painted on a celestial blue background.

The Rajkumari Kafni is coming soon. The Captain-sahib would like to rest?' She reached out to touch a switch and an illuminated bedchamber appeared behind a tulle curtain.

It was not rest that interested Adam, it was anticipation of what lay ahead that occupied his active mind.

Mandira drew back the curtain and revealed a large four-poster bed. The cream silk sheets and pillows were once more edged with the pale purple. This was no ordinary place; it was a nuptial bedchamber, prepared with infinite care. Adam walked over to an armchair beside the head of the bed and sank into its luxurious upholstery, taking in a deep breath of satisfaction.

Mandira made a gesture of *namaste*, turned and left. The silence of the bedchamber emphasised its privacy. Surely those hundreds of palace servants could not all be sleeping?

The journey to their rendezvous was itself an adventure, taking Adam into a mysterious world unfamiliar to his occidental background. Rindi had revealed little of how and when Adam would fulfil his part in their plan and he'd been apprehensive that it would be very clinical. These fears were slowly dissipating and although there was something very ceremonial about the proceedings he felt thrilled at the prospect of just seeing Kafni again. There was so much he wanted to ask her about herself and how she felt about being with him. Adam realised he should not impose his western thoughts on this ceremony. But however devoted she might be to her family, Kafni must have been approaching this personal encounter with some anxiety. Although no one else was to be present, this felt more like preparation for a symbolic

Hindu marriage. Yet, other than Adam's silence, no commitment had been asked for or given.

On the far wall was a mural showing clouds floating across a moonlit sky. His eyes were drawn to four Indian pictures hung on the wall to his left. These were Rajasthani scenes set in luxurious bedchambers each portraying a nubile woman in the intimate embrace of a virile noble. The expression on the face of each woman clearly conveyed contentment and bliss and, in one scene, the joy of her orgasm. It was clear that in Hindu love, physical expression was not only acceptable but could indeed be a beautiful act of devotion.

Whatever the intention was of leaving him to contemplate these erotic surroundings it was having the desired effect. His sensual thoughts were now interrupted by a delicate fragrance which seemed to fill the room, as if a window was opening onto a spring garden. He sat up and turned his head to see that a concealed jib door had opened. A moment later, the tulle curtain was drawn aside, and there stood Kafni.

Adam gasped as he gazed at her; she was even lovelier than he had realised. In her beautiful gold and brilliant red sari, - its colours proclaiming love and marriage- he felt that he was truly in the presence of royalty.

'Good evening, Adam-sahib,' she said rather respectfully. She smiled as the delicate silk curtain fell into place behind her.

'Good evening, Rajkumari Kafni,' Adam responded with equal formality. He raised himself ready to stand and greet her but a gentle lift of her hand indicated that he should remain seated.

The complete absence of coquetry as Kafni walked up to the bed was confirmation of her serious approach to the occasion. Her movements, though gentle and unhurried, were also unhesitating and had an air of confidence that many a honeymoon would benefit from.

'Thank you for coming to Kushnapur. My family are most grateful.'

She looked enchanting. Adam could well understand her cousin Wantilla's obsession to claim her as a bride. The light twinkled back from the diamond-encrusted motifs woven into her silken brocade sari. But these were surpassed by her dazzling gold and emerald necklace, and gold and diamond bracelet. Releasing her sari at the waist, the material fell back to reveal a magnificent Benares Cross below the necklace. Adam smiled in amazement and as their glances met he admired her delicate eyebrows that ran almost level, lending definition to her beautiful violet blue eyes. Her dark brown hair, caressed her shoulders and shone in the candlelight. Her complexion, two shades darker than Adam's, was faultless and glowing. He waited entranced and his eyes held her gaze as she gracefully unwound her sari. No pin or needle had touched this dress. Using both hands, she lifted the long length of material and carefully laid it on a stool. The cream silk bodice and pyjamas now revealed, gave her an angelic air. She looked so innocent that Adam felt constrained to protect her modesty. He wanted to say "don't take anything else off, come and get into bed." but the words evaporated on his lips. He could not forego this enchanting scene. As he watched she walked over to the dressing table and sat down in front of the mirror.

As she slowly removed her bracelet Adam realised that she was looking at his reflection in the side mirror. She smiled as their eyes met then tilting her head forward she lifted the hair off her neck to reveal the necklace fastener and waited expectantly in this submissive position. He stood up and crossed to where she was sitting. Slipping his fingers behind the clasp, he felt the warmth of her smooth skin. He leant forward and gently kissed the top of her head breathing in her intoxicating scent. Resting his fingers on her bare shoulders he released the gold necklace into her waiting hands.

With gentle poise, she stood up and turned to face him her arms to her side and her hands facing towards him in a silent invitation to remove the last of her underclothes. As the last delicate piece fell to the floor, he was spellbound by the vision of her naked body. He was quite certain that no man had ever seen Kafni like this before. There was no hesitancy in the way she presented her perfect figure for his exclusive admiration. His eyes rejoiced in the wonder of the female form and his state of arousal was now evident.

Running one hand across her shoulders and the other beneath her bottom, he swept her up in his arms and carried her to the bed. The feel of her body so close to his was exhilarating. Was the grip she now gave his arm, her approval of the response in his loins? Bending his head, seeking to kiss her, she drew his head down to meet her lips. Any doubts he may have had about her desire to submit herself to him were dispelled by the passion in her kiss.

He lay her on the bed and kissed her again. Casting off his pyjamas and with an uncontrollable desire to possess her completely he climbed in beside her.

'You're so beautiful, Kafni... Kafni darling.' The whispered endearment, though spontaneous and heartfelt, had momentarily broken the spell and breached his privilege. Looking at her violet eyes, he felt impelled to further express his feelings. He wanted to say, "I love you," but such utterance, he knew, would have been motivated by transient desire, unfitting for this moment.

Seeing the catch-lights in her eyes, he sensed the need to give her the intimacy of darkness, and he reached to the light switches beside the bed. But as he moved his hand to the last of these, she whispered, 'Wait, please leave it on.'

Adam was happy that she wished to leave this soft light gently illuminating the bedchamber. The scene was so perfect, and could now be savoured and remembered.

They lay side-by-side for a few minutes, holding hands, breathing gently, slowly overcoming the unfamiliar closeness of their bodies.

'I'm glad that they chose you, Adam.' The gentle tone of her voice and the wonderful inflexion in her English was a delight to hear. He just wanted her to go on speaking. To allow her words to flow over him like a soothing balm.

'It is my privilege,' he said, 'at this moment...' she placed a finger on his lips silencing him and reminding him of a similar gesture and the secret they had shared when they first met. Words were now superfluous. She kissed him and drew his body closer. She lifted his hand to her breast; an invitation eagerly accepted as his tongue sought the pleasure of teasing her upturned nipples. The scent of her skin had a delicate aroma of vanilla, jasmine and truffles. He longed to go on and on with the bliss of this intimacy, kissing her, caressing her and exploring each part of her beautiful body; yet he knew that his total possession of her must be only minutes away.

Gently at first, then more ardently, she enticed him with her tongue between parted lips. Her elegant fingers began to explore his body, her touch passing from his face to his chest, then to the flat of his stomach. No Indian woman of culture would be unaware of each detail of the male anatomy and its preparedness to make love. Kafni's brief grasp of his erect member appeared to reassure her. His hand slid down between her legs and caressed her gently but firmly and he realised that she was now in need of him. In an act of urgent submission her knees parted and thighs lifted. Unable to restrain himself any longer he moved on top of her and tenderly entered her, until sensing a restriction, he paused, conscious of causing her pain. 'No! No it's alright.' she said breathlessly and lifted her body, urging him on. With a sudden gasp and muffled cry she surrendered her virginity. The confidence with which Kafni conducted her love making might have suggested to Adam that she had had previous experience but now he was in no doubt that this was her first time.

Her nails dug hard into his flesh, delivering an exquisite sensation of pain and pleasure, urging him to achieve the deep penetration that she so clearly desired. As their passion intensified, he felt her pressing hard against him. The mounting feeling of bliss culminating with a rapturous orgasm as he delivered his seed. Seconds later, with a cry of ecstasy, Kafni reached her own breathless climax.

In the euphoric afterglow, as they remained locked together, reluctant to relinquish those treasured moments, he marvelled at the joy of Indian love. The last time that he had slept with a woman had been on the Cape Peninsular with Sarah. The contrast could not have been greater. On that tempestuous occasion, Sarah's passion seemed more centred on her own satisfaction. Now, Kafni, whilst clearly finding pleasure in submitting herself, had revealed a beguiling desire to give him pleasure. He couldn't really believe what had just happened and given the level of planning and prescribed nature of this mating ritual, how natural it had seemed. Was it just lust that burned within him? As he gazed at her beautiful face serenely sleeping beside him he knew that what he felt was much more than mere physical desire. He longed to tell her he loved her but that would break the rules set out by her family. The thought that he was now required to forget her and never hope for further love of any nature, tormented him.

Their reasons for being together had been fulfilled. It was the realisation that everything which had stood between them the day before would have to be re-established in the morning. Emotional walls re-built, physical desires denied and cultural differences acknowledged. But was this not precisely the kind of relationship he now wanted with women? affairs devoid of all obligations and commitments. That he could view this particular relationship with Kafni in that light was, he would later realize, crass stupidity. Even if for no other reason, that the sworn secrecy placed an enormous obligation upon him; and of course, she was the sister of his best friend.

As if sensing Adam's turbulent thoughts Kafni awoke from her sleep and gazing at him with obvious affection she asked. 'Could you learn to love India?' Adam squeezed Kafni's hand in affirmation, as she continued, 'perhaps it is difficult for you to feel an affinity with our culture and people.'

'I have learnt a lot in the last few days.'

'I am sure you find many of our customs and beliefs strange, Adam.'

'I find it hard to understand how you can set all other considerations aside for the sake of the family.'

She looked at him with measured judgement. 'What is more important than family?'

'Love?' he ventured.

'In India family and suitability in a relationship are more important than love. What you have done for our family is greater than love.'

'Is that all you see it as?' he asked hoping to find a romantic chink in her armour.

She looked at him as if he had disappointed her or perhaps it was she who had disappointed him. 'Adam you will always be special to our family and especially to me.'

Her maturity and eloquence were admirable but this was small consolation as he was still enveloped in the glow of her aura. He hung his head in a moment of sadness.

She reached out and took his hand. 'Don't be sad,' she said, 'we will always have this night' and then drawing him closer she whispered, 'please make love to me again.'

Adam slept deeply and woke three hours later. Kafni was asleep beside him and he wondered when he should return to his room, yet at the same time he knew well enough that this would also have been arranged. As if responding to his thoughts, he heard a gentle voice beyond the curtain. *Hazrat, Hazrat Kafni.*'

Kafni woke and responded. 'Come in, Mandira.'

It was confirmation of Mandira's intimate participation that Kafni made no move to cover herself and Adam beyond the sheet that lay across the lower part of their bodies. Mandira drew back the curtain and came into the bedchamber carrying clothing and clean bed linen. She placed these on another of the stools and to Adam's amazement Kafni asked her to switch on all the lights. He turned to look at Kafni and in the flood of that illumination, devoid of make-up, she looked as beautiful as ever.

'I think it's time for me to go.' he said, moving to his side of the bed.

'Yes, but wait.'

The ambiguous request had a reason to which Mandira was privy. She picked up a dressing gown, and walked over to the bed, where she held it up for Kafni to slip on. Meanwhile, Adam ran his hand under the sheet, to retrieve his pyjama bottoms, but before he had located them, Mandira had handed him a freshly laundered pair. He swung himself out of bed, and, turning his back, put on the fresh pyjamas, and then recovered his slippers and dressing gown.

A quick exodus seemed appropriate, but Mandira made no move to lead Adam from the chamber. Instead, she stripped off the under sheet, and held it up briefly for Kafni and Adam to see. In that bright light, the crimson stain stood out like a camellia blossom. Adam felt remorse at the pain he had caused Kafni. It was a thought immediately dispelled by the look of happiness he saw on her face. She watched contentedly as Mandira carefully folded up the sheet together with the discarded pyjamas and carried them into the main chamber. She returned almost immediately bearing the small oil lamp.

'The Captain-sahib is ready?'

'Yes,' Adam murmured. His mind was totally preoccupied, reluctant to surrender the reverie of the unbelievable night. Barely conscious of their route back, he followed Mandira until they reached the top of the stairs outside his room. There, she handed him the key and by the time he had unlocked and opened the door, she had gone, leaving him pondering just how he had found himself in this situation.

CHAPTER SIXTEEN

Kushnapur Palace, 7th December 1941.

It was five o'clock and still dark when Adam returned to his room. He was feeling thirsty, and as often happened in Kushnapur, his needs had been anticipated: beside his bed was a carafe of fresh juice. He poured out a glass, then went to the wardrobe, took his diary from his service dress pocket and looked at the date: Sunday 7th December. A daze came over him as he stared at the space for Saturday 6th December.

Secrecy precluded him from writing anything with direct reference to what had happened. He needed to write something that would remind him of this night. Something that would capture his feelings that would be only significant to him. But each time he tried to find a phrase or sentences they seemed wholly inadequate and he didn't get beyond "Kafni and I". Strangely there was a power in just those three words that connected them. This was the first time that he had opened his diary since leaving Rawalpindi the previous week. So much had happened, he had been living in another world. He knew this bubble would have to burst sooner or later. After completing entries for the previous days he lay down on the bed and fell into a deep sleep.

'*Chota hazri*, Captain-sahib.' Adam gazed, bleary-eyed at the tray of early morning tea, with delicately cut papaya and mango. His watch showed seven o'clock. He drank a cup of tea and then immediately drifted into sleep again.

Two hours later, he opened his eyes and heard Rindi saying, 'Someone didn't get much sleep last night.'

'Oh dear, is that the time?'

'I thought you might like to go into the city and look round the bazaar.'

'Yes, I'd like that. Is it far?'

'Not as the crow flies. We could go through the Resident's estate, but that means trotting down scores of steps, and we would have to send a car miles round to pick us up. It's better to take the car from the main courtyard and drive back down the Kushnapur City Road.'

Rindi probably knew every detail of the previous night but showed no inclination to talk about it. In contrast Adam longed to share his thoughts and feelings and Rindi was the only other person he could ever discuss this experience with. He had been so willing to discuss things in great detail before the event so why he had become so evasive about it afterwards? In retrospect Adam realised how turbulent Rindi's own feelings must have been. His best friend had slept with his sister and anything he might say would either sound insensitive or sanction deeper feelings towards Kafni.

They spent an interesting day visiting the bazaar and the sites of the ancient city but Adam felt distracted by a longing to see Kafni again. Rindi's striking resemblance to his sister in so many ways and in particular in their eyes, did nothing to relieve this yearning.

Feeling physically and emotionally drained Adam retired early that evening and fell asleep almost immediately. It seemed to be only a few hours later that he was wide awake with vivid thoughts of Kafni filling his mind. The Indian princely states and their heady history had subconsciously swept him into a fantasy. It felt incredible that, in some small measure, he had become part of it. He needed to convince himself that it had really happened. He got out of bed, went over to the cabinet and operated the device to release the drawer. Yes, the key was still there. He picked it up and ran his fingers over the shape of the woman's head, then, reassured, he dropped it back in. He was about to close the drawer when it occurred to him that its continued existence there might be an invitation to use it again. If that was not the intention, why leave it there? He felt not only intrigue and curiosity, but also a pressing desire to be with Kafni again.

He picked up the key once more and drew back the curtain and unlocked the door. The landing was dark, and he returned to collect the electric torch from his kit. As he did so, it occurred to him that a male walking around in a dressing gown would be an object of suspicion if by mistake he stumbled into the women's' quarters. Battledress was the answer, so he went back and changed.

When he had followed Mandira down the steps the night before, the route had appeared quite straightforward. By the light of the oil lamp, he had not noticed any steps other than the ones she had taken. He clearly remembered going down two flights of steps, and then turning to the right a few minutes later, he felt that he was on the right track. Having ignored the steps going to his left, he was now in what looked like the same long corridor with the murals of dancing girls.

At any moment he should come upon the wooden door to Kafni's apartment, and he fingered the figurehead key in his pocket. The corridor seemed interminable and his confidence began to waver. Seconds later, it was restored by the sight of a door to his right. He must have approached the apartment from a different direction. And now the door was open, perhaps it was an indication that he was expected.

He entered and flashed his torch around to inspect. There were carpets on the wall, but no bracket lights, nor was the air warm. He dismissed the apparent absence of these things as a trick of memory, and walked confidently on. Where now were the curtains at the entrance to Kafni's apartments? Instead, ahead of him was a flight of steps leading down. He shone the torch upwards, searching for a clue to his location. The light travelling across the ceiling illuminated beautiful intricate carvings. Now he knew he had come the wrong way. Rather than retrace his route, he decided to continue down the steps in the hope that he would come across something familiar, something that would lead him back to Kafni's suite.

Reaching the bottom of these steps, he paused to examine the decor and began to question the wisdom of his decision not to go back the way he had come. Huge slabs of polished marble covered the floor, stretching along a wide corridor for about thirty yards. On each side, spaced at intervals of about five yards, were a series of columns, headed by ornamented capitals. He walked forward a few yards, only to discover that he was not in a hallway, but on the upper level of a capacious chamber. To his left, beyond the columns, four marble steps ran along the length of the chamber. He flashed his torch to reveal a high vaulted ceiling supported by a pattern of pillars carved with figures of young girls with prominent breasts. Their artistic poses and hand gestures were those of dancers.

He recalled Rindi telling him how the temple dancers had dedicated their whole lives to the service of the holy place. This was the "*natamandap*", the dancing pavilion. These dancing girls must have presented an exquisite spectacle as they performed their rituals for the veneration of the Gods Shiva, Vishnu or Krishna, and no doubt for the pleasure of the temple priests. The ceilings here were beautifully decorated with carvings, and as he examined the detail, he had an eerie feeling that he was not alone, that he was being observed. Conscious of being an intruder, he felt he should leave, but there was a strange magnetism in the chamber compelling him to stay.

He listened for a footfall, but there was none. Then he heard the faint sound of running water. Drawn towards its source, he walked through the *natamandap*, passing row after row of the beautifully carved pillars. Suddenly, he felt a chill air on his face and glancing up, saw the reason. He was beneath a deep shaft cut through the rock, at the top of which was a clear starlit sky. Walking on, there was again a ceiling above him. The open shaft was, he concluded, a means of admitting reflected sunlight.

The sound of tumbling water was stronger now. Adam raked his torch around the cave and found its source; a small waterfall cascading into a channel about eight feet wide. On the other side of the stream, the beam now illuminated a statue set into a deep alcove. He recognised it as the God Shiva and realised he was in a temple. Curiosity impelled him to take a closer look at this magnificent effigy. At first he could see no obvious way to cross the channel but then noticed the line of stepping-stones just below the surface of the water. These appeared to be the heads of deep stone pillars and, even though the water was crystal-clear, the light from the torch did not reach the bottom. Adam slipped off his shoes and stepped across the stones. The water was freezing so it probably came from a mountain stream. He paused before the great statue to admire the intricate carvings of the smaller figures on either side and realised that he was in the *Gardha-griha*, the sanctum: the most sacred part of this ancient temple.

He could now see in detail the girdle of plaited gold, and the interlaced loin apron that hung down, overlaid with thick shining cords. The arms and ankles carried broad bangles inset with rows of diamonds, their facets scattering his torchlight into a thousand reflections. A brilliant headband lent a final air of triumph to the image. Beside Shiva, and slightly further back, was the smaller figure of Parvarti, his consort, also generously adorned and, discerningly, revealing only one of her breasts. On her face was an expression of great contentment as she tightly clasped one of Shiva's hands.

The fear that had gripped Adam a minute or two earlier, was now subsiding. He decided to return the way he had come but found himself drawn by an imperceptible force. Directing his torch around the sanctum the brilliant aura of a sculpture radiated its powerful presence even before the light had reached it.

Standing about two feet high sculpted in gold was a lingam; a sacred phallus. Rubies and diamonds adorned the length of its shaft, and even more spectacular blood red stones formed the head. Beneath the phallus was a platinum scrotum encrusted with dazzling sapphires. Adam stood in awe as he traced the magnificent gold base studded with row upon row of white diamonds and emeralds, some the size of a pigeon's egg.

Although the opening to the sky Adam had seen earlier provided a gentle flow of mountain air there was a slightly pungent odour that he could not identify. A bizarre sound, like a chain being dragged, made him shiver and a cold sweat came over him. Should he be here? He thought. His overwhelming desire to touch this beautiful object overcame any trepidation he felt. As he walked forward with his fingers outstretched towards the gleaming sculpture, something very heavy hit his shoulder. He felt a stinging, excruciating pain, and then lurched forward. Whatever it was that had attached itself to his back now flung him sideways onto the marble floor. Fear driven adrenalin supressed the pain and as Adam wrestled to free himself from the creature they fell into the freezing stream. Fur crushed against him and the shock of the icy water caused it to detach its snarling jaws from his shoulder.

Adam swam to the other side of the channel; no stepping stones to help him this time. Oblivious to the pain, he climbed out and crawled several yards and then realised he had left his torch on the other side. He turned his head and saw its beam, casting a strip of light on the marble floor where it had fallen. In the gloom of the great chamber, he could now make out the lithe body of a cheetah its eyes glowing and teeth glinting as it climbed out of the water. Why had it not pursued him? Then he saw the chain attached to the base of the statue of Shiva, with just enough spare leash to reach the phallic sculpture.

He managed to make his way back up to his room in the palace. The freezing water had relieved some of the searing pain in his shoulder but his mind spun with conflicting feelings of wonderment, anger and guilt. He knew he shouldn't have entered this inner sanctum but why had they not shown him the temple? How could this family, that he had shared such confidences and intimacies with, think that he was unworthy of knowing about this place and that magnificent sculpture? Had he not made one of the greatest of all sacrifices for them?

On reaching his room he took off the battledress top and saw that it was badly ripped. The wound was still bleeding so he took out the oldest of his army khaki shirts and wrapped it round his shoulder and then climbed awkwardly into bed.

There was little hope of going back to sleep. Thoughts of that incredible sculpture were still racing through his head and his shoulder was aching like hell. He struggled to switch on the bedside light and to his alarm, saw that his pyjamas, dressing gown and the sheets all had patches of blood on them; it would be impossible to hide his injury. At least the bleeding had stopped. Now, with a moment of anxiety, he searched in his pockets for the figurehead key. It was missing - he had really cocked things up. His concern was not for his misadventure, but his abuse of hospitality. He could not with sincerity plead contrition.

His bedside light was still burning when Rindi hurried into his room just after seven. He had a grave look as he said, 'I suppose we should have expected it. Eventually it had to happen. We should have known.'

Adam struggled to sit up in bed without drawing attention to his injury. This was going to be more difficult to deal with than he had anticipated. 'I am terribly sorry, Rindi...' he started.

'Oh, have you heard?'

'Heard what?'

'The Japanese bombed Pearl Harbour early yesterday morning. They've sunk several American battleships and thousands of sailors have been killed. The United States is now at war!'

'My God!'

'Yes, and we've now got the Japs against us, Adam. It's no longer just a European war.'

'So, those cunning bastards have joined up with the Germans so they can grab the spoils of the Far East.'

'And you realise they'll want to take over the whole of South-East Asia and to do that they need gain control of India. They must have been planning this for some time. Apparently their fleet is already off the coast of Malaya.'

To Adam, the prospect of invasion by the Japanese seemed remote, but to Rindi it was very real and he had been anxious to give him the news.

'What were you apologising for?'

'I'm afraid I've made a bloody fool of myself. I suppose I should have known better than to poke around in places where I shouldn't be.'

'What's happened to you?' he said pointing at Adam's bloody pyjamas. He looked concerned, but not angry or accusing.

'Oh, it's not as bad as it looks. Last night I decided I would go down and see Kafni again. The only problem was that this time I did not have Mandira to show me the way. I got lost and finished up in the old temple.'

'And you met Sheba?'

'If you mean that creature that guards the temple, yes, I did.' Adam pulled back his dressing gown.

Rindi looked at Adam's shoulder and sucked air through his teeth. 'Hell! That looks awful. Does it hurt much? Surely, you must have heard her. She's supposed to growl when anyone approaches.'

'That's the strange thing, I heard nothing. The first I knew was when she landed on my back. Even when I stood in front of the sculpture, I did not hear her growl. Perhaps it was masked by the sound of the waterfall. She only struck when I actually reached out to touch the sculpture.'

'I'm surprised that your injuries aren't worse. How did you manage to get away?'

'Probably thanks to my thick battledress, and then the shock of the cold water when we fell into the stream made her let go.'

'I hope Sheba's alright.' Rindi said with an expression of concern similar to how Adam's mother would talk about her spaniel.

'You make it sound like she's a pet.'

'Not as such, but she is very precious to us. You may know that, unlike leopards, cheetahs can be trained so when she is with us she is as friendly as a domestic cat but she is also trained to attack any stranger who approaches the lingam.'

'You mean that golden phallus?' Adam asked unable to disguise his disappointment that such a significant treasure had been kept secret from him.

'I am sorry. I had intended to take you to the temple and show it to you earlier. The lingam is a phallic symbol of the God Shiva the God of destruction, regeneration and sexuality; the cosmic force that changes all things. It destroys and then reproduces life.'

'Is it not strange to revere something which destroys?'

'Without constant destruction or decomposition the whole world would cease to function. Change is vital: it occurs constantly in every part of life. You must remember that all Hindus believe in the doctrine of Karma, or predestination. Every soul is thought to be involved in a cycle of births and deaths. Virtue in a previous life brings rewards in the present; whereas a sinner is destined to suffer.'

'So do Hindus worship the lingam?'

'It is quite common in South India, although we in this *pradesh* do not; the Rig Veda specifically condemns it. So whilst we revere the lingam we do not worship it.'

'Where on earth did that sculpture come from? It must be worth a fortune.'

'It certainly is. The Debrahms were very fortunate. Laksmi must have been smiling on us. When the palace was under reconstruction in the last century, a vast quantity of jewels and precious metals were discovered, buried at the side of the temple. It originated from a caravan transporting the state fortune of a Harsha prince, fleeing from the Huns in the seventh century. It had probably been left in the safekeeping of the Buddhist monks, to be retrieved by the prince when a safe haven had been found. This return never took place, because the treasure was entombed during an earthquake and landslide. My forebears deemed it an omen that they had found this treasure and decided to use it to create something of permanent significance.'

'So what made them choose the lingam?'

'They wanted an icon as a unifying symbol of the state and its ruling dynasty and the lingam was already part of Hindu doctrine. A sculpture was created and kept at Paropamisus Castle, in the Hindu Kush, where the Debrahm dynasty was founded.'

'And why was it then brought to Kushnapur?'

'As you know pilgrimages had been made to Kushnapur for thousands of years to revere a stone lingam so it seemed the best place for it.'

'No wonder you have to keep it so well guarded.'

'Yes, without it no maharajah of the state can be legitimately enthroned. The phallic symbol of Shiva is also a perfect permanent reminder of the obligation of the family to introduce fresh Aryan blood into the Debrahm line.'

'So who gets to see it these days?'

'During the centuries that we lived in the Hindu Kush, most of the populace had at some time in their life been able to view the lingam. Now, because of its great worth, only the ruler's family, senior Brahmins and ministers of state are permitted to see it.'

'Then I feel honoured.'

'Now let's get that shoulder seen to. I could get the *hakim* to look at it, but that would mean telling him how it happened. If you don't mind, I'll get Mandira to clean it and dress it.'

'Thanks, that'll be fine, but there is another thing. I'm afraid I've dropped that key somewhere down there.'

'That's unfortunate. Listen, I'm sure no one knows about this yet so it shouldn't be a problem.'

'Surely we can't keep this thing quiet? My bearer will wonder what happened when he sees the state of my battledress.'

'You're right. Well at least we can limit the number of people who need know you've been injured. And we don't have to tell him why.'

'I'll borrow your torch if that's OK? Let me see if I can find that key.'

A short time later there was a knock at the door and Mandira appeared carrying a small basket with bandages and herbal dressings to tend to Adam's shoulder. After she had bandaged him she removed the blood-stained bed linen and clothing, and with a polite *namaste*, left.

After about twenty minutes Rindi returned, holding the lost key.

'Luckily it had not fallen into the stream or we would have been in real trouble. How's that shoulder?'

'Much more comfortable, thank you.'

'I'm sorry you had to learn about the shrine and the lingam in the way you did. We had intended to take you down there earlier but there has been so much going on. You ought to see it in daylight. We will try and put that right before you leave. I know Kafni would love to take you down there herself.'

CHAPTER SEVENTEEN

Kushnapur Palace, *9ᵗʰ December 1941.*

When Adam had filled in his furlough application to request leave, he had given Rindi's postal address, Post Office Box 100X, Saharanpur. Rindi's home was some sixty miles from the city, and the palace Dak van came daily to collect the mail. He had given no thought to the possibility of being contacted during his leave, until a breathless *chaprassi* hurried into the study and handed an envelope to Rindi.

'A telegram for you, Adam.' Rindi said, glancing at the address, 'It has come up from Saharanpur.'

Adam ripped it open and read:

DUE TO SITUATION IN FAR EAST RETURN REGIMENT IMMEDIATELY STOP LEAVE CURTAILED STOP ACKNOWLEDGE "WILLIAMS".

Adam handed the telegram to Rindi who was aware that Williams was his Company Commander. 'Trust that bugger to jump the gun and look for any excuse to call me back.'

'Can't you say you've never received it?'

'Yes, perhaps I could do just that - at least for a day or two. But I imagine they're all panicking about Pearl Harbour.'

Unfortunately, Adam was denied that opportunity. Williams was not leaving anything to chance. A few hours later, he called the special number Adam had given the Adjutant. "In case of a real emergency." It was the direct line to Rindi's private study, not through the palace switchboard.

Rindi answered it.

'Hello, hello, who am I speaking to?' said Williams.

'Captain Debrahm speaking. How can I help you?'

'Cullworthy, Captain Cullworthy. Is he there?'

'Who wishes to speak to him?'

'Major Williams, Royal Wessex Regiment and it's urgent.'

'I'll see if I can locate him.'

Rindi smiled and held his hand over the mouthpiece. 'Don't rush, let him sweat a bit.'

Adam took the telephone, 'Cullworthy here.'

'Where the bloody hell have you been Cullworthy? Swanning around with the natives I bet. And who was that I was speaking to? I didn't like his attitude.'

Adam ignored the question, and Williams continued, 'Did you get my telegram?'

'Yes, I received it today. The telegraph service is quite slow up here.'

'And where exactly is *here?*'

Rindi and Adam had agreed that for a number of reasons this visit to his home should be kept confidential.

'I'm staying in the hills with a friend.'

'In the hills, Cullworthy! Where in the hills? Be more specific, man, I know all the hill stations.'

The man was being very tedious. 'It's a private residence, Sir. The home of an Indian Army officer friend of mine.'

There was a crackle on the line, and Adam heard the operator in a high-pitched voice say,

'Three minutes, sahib, please terminate call; lines very busy.'

Williams was not one to be dictated to by an Indian telephone operator. 'I'm a busy man, Cullworthy. I can't waste time discussing the details of your holiday in the hills, I want you back here within twenty-four hours.'

Adam wanted to object, the travelling time alone would take at least half that time but to have protested would have created more problems and inevitably have involved Adam's C.O. Bob Mercer.

Williams was off the line without further comment and Adam was left with the problem of getting a seat on a train at short notice.

Rindi pulled out a railway timetable and studied it. 'Your best train would be the Howrah-Lahore Mail. It left Calcutta last night so there is no chance of booking a sleeper, but the conductor may find you a bed. Anyway, we'll have to be at the station before 01.10 hours tomorrow morning.'

'What do you mean "we". You don't have to....'

'Oh yes I do. I'm coming with you.'

'Don't be bloody ridiculous, you still have a week's leave.'

'Yes I know but I don't want to stay now. It would be an anti-climax. In any case, with America now in the war, I'd like to get back to my regiment to see what's happening.'

Adam left Kushnapur without seeing Kafni again and with only the pain in his shoulder to remind him it wasn't a dream.

Rawalpindi.

'Sorry to fetch you back, old boy, but it looks as though the balloon's going up. Nothing definite yet, but I don't think it'll be long. Need to be up to full force,' were Williams' first words to him. To Adam's intense frustration, his recall had been entirely motivated by Williams' personal whim. For a small man Williams had an unusually large head which made his self important posturing rather comical and Adam had to supress his desire to laugh.

For the next two weeks, rumours were whizzing around like tips for the Derby. Most of these were highly improbable and were dismissed out of hand. However, Command HQ decided that a jungle warfare school was to be established and that some officers from the Regiment would be sent on one of its courses.

Adam had written to both Rindi and his parents, thanking them for his enjoyable stay at the Palace and apologising for his hasty departure. Rindi's letter of response was, as always, cheery and friendly. The maharajah, whom Adam had not expected to write back, sent a hand-written letter. He understood the reasons for the sudden departure, and hoped that it would not be long before he could return to the Palace. "The maharani and I have seen far too little of you", he wrote. Adam was touched by the personal note, and felt something akin to being a son-in-law.

Adam received a request from the Adjutant to go and see Colonel Mercer.

'Hello, Adam, I hear you've been fraternising with the locals. You've certainly wasted no time in getting your contacts organised.'

'It wasn't exactly that, sir. I was visiting a school friend. Rindi Debrahm I think you taught him at Oxford.'

'Ah yes, nice chap, good historian, pity the war interrupted his studies.It was unfortunate you had to cut short your stay, but Williams felt that under the circumstances he needed you back in the Regiment.' He said this without irony but the raised eyebrow was a good indication of what he thought about Major Williams.

'This is for you, Adam' he said handing him a piece of paper. 'It's a temporary posting to South-Western Army Command Headquarters in Delhi. It's signed by the major-general D.A.G. at GHQ. It looks as though someone has been asking for you, but it might be connected with this notice. 'He picked up another piece of paper. 'Seems you have been gazetted for a Military Cross for an action in France. The citation states that in co-operation with a Lieutenant Montreuil of the French Engineer Corps, you destroyed four German Mark III tanks. Montreuil was awarded the Croix de Guerre. I gather he's now a captain with De Gaulle's Free French forces in England.'

'Good God! I didn't know that incident had been reported.'

'Well, congratulations that was a fine effort.'

'But what about this posting, Sir? Have you any idea what the job will be?'

'Sorry, haven't a clue. The order came through via GHQ. I telephoned the staff colonel and he wasn't sure, but said that he did know that some officers who had seen action were being pulled out for duty as instructors. He said you had to report to a Brigadier Stevenson.'

Adam read through the posting order and must have looked nonplussed, because Colonel Mercer added, 'Perhaps it's a staff job. You did go on that course.'

'If that's what it is, I'm not too keen, Sir.'

'D'you want me to raise an objection? I could say I can't spare you.'

Adam was on the point of saying, " I'd appreciate that", when the thought came to him that this would be an opportunity to get away from Williams, at least for the present.

'It's good of you to offer, Sir, but it might be better not to object. It says it's only a temporary move, so I'll be coming back to the Regiment.'

'You will indeed. I've managed to extract that promise from Army HQ.'

There is always an element of excitement about the unknown and Adam thought this change of job might be interesting. His pleasure contrasted with William's irritation, who seemed convinced that Adam had organised the posting for his own convenience. He left Rawalpindi without regret, but with a genuine wish to return and serve under Bob Mercer again. It was only thanks to him that he was in India.

On arrival at South-Western Army Headquarters, in the cantonment near Delhi, he located Brigadier Stevenson's office, who began by asking about his experiences in France, and how he had come to India. He then dealt in some detail with a number of personal matters, the significance of which eluded Adam but only served to fuel his curiosity further.

'Book in at the HQ Mess, Cullworthy and come and see me about this time tomorrow morning; I may have some news for you.'

When Adam returned next morning the brigadier's door was half-open. He knocked and entered. There was no prevarication now. Stevenson looked up.

'Good morning, Cullworthy, the G.O.C.-in-C will see you now.'

Had he known that he was to meet the General Officer Commanding-in-Chief, he would at least have checked-up on some biographical details. As it was, he found himself shaking hands with Lieutenant-General Sir David Roberts, whose existence until then had been shadowy and remote. The brigadier left the room and closed the door behind him.

The General moved away from his desk and invited him to take a seat on a well-upholstered chair. As he stood with his back to the deep windows of this rather grand first floor office, Adam could see beyond him the headquarters flag drooping from its tall pole dividing two palm trees and the magenta and red bougainvillaea framing the outside of the window.

'You are probably wondering why you've been brought here, Cullworthy,' he paused to see if Adam would respond but he was still trying to absorb the significance of being interviewed by such a senior officer, 'the fact is that I need a new A.D.C., and you've been recommended for the job. How do you feel about that?'

Adam's inclination was to say that he did not want the job, but it isn't every day that a general implies that you may be his personal choice as an aide. He was also intrigued to know why.

'I'm wondering whether I'm qualified for such a position, Sir.'

'Not qualified? Or is it that you don't want the job?'

'Frankly, Sir, I think it's probably a bit of both.' This response may have been a trifle impulsive, but at least it was honest. Even against the light of the window, he could see the general's broad smile beneath his moustache.

'Well done, Cullworthy. That's the kind of reply I wanted. I've had enough of these peacocks strutting around looking for prestige jobs with plenty of perks. I told my Chief of Staff that I wanted an officer who had seen some action and had had the corners rubbed off.

Your name was put forward with half-a-dozen others.'

Adam's apparent lack of enthusiasm for the job appeared to be sufficient qualification. The General walked back from the window and took his seat behind the desk.

'Well then, Cullworthy, that settles it. You'll start in a couple of days' time. By the way, what's your first name?'

January 1942, New Delhi.

The role of A.D.C. to a general could not be described as being dull, but it did mean being almost constantly in the eye of his fellow officers. Perhaps this was why the General had wanted an aide who had seen some action. However, it was still not clear to Adam why he had not chosen an officer from his own Indian Army regiments. It may have been just his wish to show unity with the British Army. India was now on the doorstep of a new theatre of war, and there was no place for rivalries. When Rindi heard about Adam's new appointment, he chided him for getting himself a soft job. Meanwhile, his own unit was fully occupied training the huge intake of Indians and so it was not until late February that he was able to come to New Delhi to spend a weekend with Adam.

There was an air of gloom that hung over headquarters following the terrible shock of the surrender of Singapore on Valentine's Day, the week before. Seventy thousand British, Australian, and Indian troops had been captured. Singapore had always been claimed to be impregnable- the strongest naval base in the world. Unfortunately, its creators did not appear to have entertained the possibility that it could be attacked from the land: all its defences had been built pointing out to sea.

It was therefore something of a relief to have a visit from Rindi But he seemed rather agitated and it was not because of the perilous war situation.

'Could you get back to the palace for a few days, Adam? Soon, if possible.'

His serious tone conflicted with the idea of it being a few days leave.

'Yes, I'd like to, although it may still be difficult for me to get away. Is it urgent?'

'In one way yes. The fact is that Kafni is *not* pregnant.'

Under other circumstances, Adam might have been relieved to hear this news but this situation was quite different, and he knew how seriously the Debrahm family viewed this matter.

'It never happens when you want it to does it?' Adam said trying to make light of the disappointment. His first concern was for Kafni. She was probably thinking it was her fault. An early visit to the palace would, hopefully assuage her concern. This obligation no longer felt like a duty but was now a delightful prospect.

'Look, there may be a solution. General Roberts is going to Calcutta for a conference in two weeks' time. He's taking some staff officers who'll be happy to do any running around for him so I don't think he'll need me. It may be a good opportunity as he'll be away for five days.'

Rindi looked relieved. 'Let me know as soon as you can, and I'll tell father to expect you.'

Two days later, the General agreed to Adam's leave. 'Just let the Chief of Staff know when you'll be away, and don't forget, Adam, there's that *burra-khana* this Saturday; I'd like you to be there. My wife will be making all the arrangements and I know she'll be grateful for your help.'

Adam had met Lady Roberts several times when going to the house to collect the General or calling for a briefing at weekends. She was a good-looking woman in her late forties - some ten years younger than the General. As Miss Alice Elizabeth Scoones, she had come to India thirty years earlier with one of the "fishing fleets" of young ladies looking for husbands.

'The party this weekend is a modest affair,' Lady Roberts had told him. 'A dozen personal guests and some family.' It was due to the late arrival of her son and daughter that Adam found himself with an empty chair beside him at the dinner table.

The first course had already been served when a young Indian Cavalry captain and an A.T.S. officer entered the dining room. The General got up and greeted them warmly, then walked with them over to the vacant chairs either side of Adam. He put down his napkin and stood up and then in astonishment almost sat down again. There standing beside General Roberts was Sarah. He rapidly gathered his wits as he heard the General say, 'Adam, I don't think you've met my son Jonathan and my daughter Sarah.'

Sarah, showing no trace of surprise, held out her hand and smiled.

With considerable restraint Adam confined his response to, 'How do you do?' It all started to fit into place; she had obviously got him the A.D.C. posting. But after their cool departure at the Agra Club this made little sense. The thought that she had somehow planned all of this made him rather irritated. He didn't like the idea that she felt she could influence his army career.

During dinner, Adam confined his conversation to an exchange of generalities and the state of the war in Europe. Sarah did venture a brief foray into the merits of his present job and by the time dessert was served Adam had reached a number of conclusions. The first of these was that he had been naive not to probe deeper into the source of his recommendation for this post. Now it was staring him in the face. He had forgotten that Sarah's name was Roberts, but even if he had remembered, it was highly improbable that he would have associated her with a G.O.C.-in-C. After all there were many officers in the British and Indian Armies with that surname. Sarah had never given a hint that her father was such a senior officer.

Although Adam was indignant at her manipulation he was not quite sure how she had managed to arrange this posting. He now knew the general well enough to realize that a recommendation from his daughter would not have influenced him unduly, if at all. Brigadier Stevenson and the General had reached their own conclusions before offering him the job so at least he had reasonable merit in their eyes. Nevertheless after her performance in the Cape he wouldn't have put it past Sarah to arrange things to suit her purpose.

After dinner he took the opportunity to clear the matter up.

'Come on, Sarah, who did you get to put me up for this?' He recalled that the last time they had met he had felt like the odd man out. Now he was wondering why he had been brought back into the picture.

'Is this my consolation prize for what happened in Agra?'

Sarah still did not answer his questions. Instead, she said, 'Let's go for a walk in the garden, Adam. It's lovely at this time in the evening.' She led the way down the terrace steps, past little lanterns, into the garden where the balmy scent of jasmine wafted up to meet them. They walked side by side not speaking until they were out of sight of the house. Suddenly she stopped, turned and kissed him on the cheek. A mild euphoria came over him as memories of their previous encounter came flooding back. He held her close and kissed her full on the lips. His umbrage of a few minutes earlier had melted. This beautiful girl was once more warm and responsive. Such was her unpredictable nature.

As if to confirm his thoughts, she gently broke away. The curtain that had briefly lifted dropped back into place.

'We'd better go back to the house to join the others, Adam. Don't want people getting ideas.' She turned and walked quickly towards the house. The respectable distance she maintained between them was consistent with an A.D.C. politely escorting the daughter of the host around the garden. Sarah's brother Jonathan was there to greet them as they reached the top of the terrace steps.

'Has my sister been showing you the garden? You'll be needing a drink. Come on, I think the old man wants us to join the other men for brandy and cigars. We'll see you later, Sarah.'

Sarah and Jonathan spent the weekend with their parents, and although Adam was invited to have lunch with them the day after the dinner party, Sarah maintained an attitude that suggested he was a new acquaintance. In this regard, he helped her along. Although in normal circumstances it would have been perfectly natural to let the general know that they had met on board ship, the situation was now quite different. If the General knew, he would be something of a fool not to recognise the significance of the coincidence that he had been recommended for the A.D.C's job. Adam had no wish to undermine his own position, and anyway, now he had learnt the routine, he was enjoying his duties. He wanted to stay on - at least for a few months.

No one at Headquarters had ever asked him the name of the ship that had brought him to India. Fortunately sufficient time had elapsed for it any longer to be of interest. One piece of news that did emerge during Sunday's lunch was that Sarah's training unit had now been moved to the New Delhi Cantonment.

After lunch, there was no further opportunity to talk to Sarah, and Adam left the General's house with a polite goodbye to everyone. That appeared to be the last he would see of Sarah for the time being. However, when he put on his cap and climbed into the rear seat of the staff car, he felt something in the cap lining. A folded note. "Call me tomorrow night, New Delhi Cantonment 7843. S." He shook his head in amazement. Just when he thought he was beginning to understand her better. She obviously liked her little intrigues. Nothing was to be too straightforward or mundane. She could easily have taken him aside and told him the telephone number, or slipped the note into his hand. But Sarah had her own way of doing things. Although Adam was the one who should have been doing the chasing, he was past being annoyed by her caprice. Nevertheless, if she wanted to retain an intimate friendship, it would have to be on his terms. To demonstrate this he did not telephone Sarah. Instead, he waited until the Tuesday night when she rang him.

'Why did you not telephone me yesterday evening?'

Adam did not respond to her question. Nor did she pursue her question. His tacit point had been made.

Sarah now came straight to what she had obviously been planning. 'My father is going away to Calcutta next week.'

'Yes, I know.'

'You're not going with him, he says.'

'No.'

'Good. That means you are free at the weekend?'

'No, not quite. I'm free from official duties, but I have the General's permission to take a few days leave.'

'Ah, then you can come down here for the weekend. I'm sure you'll find it very enjoyable.' There was a tempting emphasis in her voice.

'I'm afraid not, Sarah. I've got something fixed up.'

'Well, can't you unfix it?' She sounded disappointed.

'That would be letting other people down.'

'Oh well, we can always talk about it, but you can at least come down to the cantonment for an hour or two tomorrow evening. Daddy doesn't keep you on a permanent leash does he?'

'I am pretty well on twenty-four-hour call.' Adam thought there was no reason why he shouldn't go, the general always gave him plenty of warning if he was needed in the evening. 'But I'm sure I could get down after dinner tomorrow. I should be able to get to your place by about eight.'

'That's fine, Adam. Your driver will know the way.'

One of the privileges of being an A.D.C. was the use of a staff car with driver - officers were directed not to drive themselves in India. In principle, the General always needed to know where to contact him. He would leave a telephone number with the duty officer at Headquarters. It was seldom further than the garrison theatre, though this time it was the location of a W.A.C. (I) unit. To spell it out may have raised an eyebrow, so he conveniently gave the telephone number that Sarah had supplied.

Sarah was waiting at the rendezvous, and before Adam could get out she had slipped into the back seat beside him. 'Good evening, Adam, I'd like to show you our staff quarters in the cantonment. Shall I tell him where to go?'

'Please do.'

She directed the driver in the fluent Hindustani she had acquired during her childhood. Five minutes later, they turned into the driveway of an impressive looking bungalow. 'I suggest that you ask your driver to come back in two hours. There's an Indian canteen not far from here.'

'Good idea.' Adam pulled out a few *annas* and gave them to the driver, telling him to be back at ten-thirty, and Sarah directed him to the canteen.

The bungalow had a flat roof surrounded by a low stonework guard. The top few feet of the building was painted in a shade of pink ochre below which projected the roof of a deep verandah. This covering extended round three sides of the building and was supported by a line of square pillars. The whole place was completely private and shaded by a number of mature trees. These were no ordinary staff quarters.

'Have a look round,' Sarah said, when they were inside. The bungalow was well furnished, not the ordinary "Army Issue". Four leather armchairs added elegance to the sitting room and two shelves were liberally stacked with books. Several pictures and photographs graced the walls, and in one of these an infantry major was seated in front of his company. The fact that these had not been removed, indicated that he had anticipated an early return. There was an ambience of comfort: plenty of small tables for drinks, a generous scattering of oriental rugs, and reading lamps. A large electric fan hung from the ceiling.

Adam followed Sarah into the dining area where a well-polished refectory table was set out with eight chairs and leading off this was the kitchen.

'Here's the boudoir.' Sarah said, turning back to the sitting room, and taking him through to a room occupied by a wide double bed. Again, there was no sign of austerity. There were bedside lamps, armchairs and rugs, another ceiling fan, and a door leading off to the bathroom.

'This is nice, Sarah. Rather superior for an A.T.S. junior commander. Did you pull the old man's rank?'

She had been hanging up her shoulder bag and had her back to him. The next thing he knew was a well-aimed service cap struck him on the head.

'I can do some things for myself you know. Actually there was a surplus of officers' bungalows when we moved here. My O.C. has even more luxurious quarters at the other end of the enclosure. She's got the colonel's house, but it's not quite so secluded as this one. I've got the second-in-command's bungalow. I'm told he was a bachelor; though judging by this bed, I don't think he was spending too many nights alone.'

Sarah walked over to a small icebox, and took out a bottle of Haywards gin and another of Indian tonic water, poured two drinks, dropped in a slice of lemon and some ice, and then handed one of them to Adam.

'Perfect, just what I need.'

'Chin chin!' she said raising her glass.

They each took a couple of sips, and then she put her glass down and went through into the bathroom. A few minutes later, she reappeared wearing a bright green silk dressing gown.

'Much more comfortable, don't you think, Adam?'

Sarah's lithe body moved seductively beneath the thin silk as she walked over and perched herself on the edge of the bed. Adam sat in one of the armchairs admiring her with barely contained anticipation of what she had planned.

They sat apart on the bed sipping their gin and discussing the issues she had with her Indian women drivers. All of which seemed a strange prelude to what they both knew would be an evening of love making.

Adam put down his drink and stood up. He walked over and gently pushed Sarah back on the bed and untied her dressing gown, exposing her naked contours. The last time they had made love was in the dark and he had not been able to appreciate what a fine figure she had. Her slim waist curved out to wide hips and small but well rounded breasts with prominent nipples. He kissed her tenderly whilst his hands roamed across her silky smooth skin. She responded to his caresses with small wimpers of pleasure. Perhaps he had got better at love making. He tried not to think about Kafni and it helped that the two women were so different in every respect. Any guilt that he might have had was assuaged by the thought that he needed to forget about any romantic association with his Indian princess.

After what seemed like hours of passion they lay together in blissful afterglow and Sarah said 'That was lovely darling.' He responded by kissing her gently on the forehead, 'Yes it was, perhaps we can do it again sometime.' At that moment Adam heard his staff car arriving.

Sarah turned her head towards him. 'Will you come on Saturday?'

Adam felt his pulse quicken. Rindi had arranged for them to travel to the Kushnapur together, and he had no intention of putting it off, but excusing himself from Sarah was not going to be so easy.

'I'm sorry, I shan't be able to come this weekend.'

She pulled away and sat up, looking surprised. 'Why not? Is there something more important going on?'

'I've arranged to go and stay with Rindi and I really can't cancel it now.'

'Oh yes, you must. I have it all planned. We can have a wonderful weekend together. I know a nice hotel where we can stay, we don't have to come here. With Daddy away, we would have lots of time to ourselves. We may not get another opportunity like this.'

'It sounds a lovely idea but I can't change it now.'

'Are you sure the two of you aren't going to Mussorie?'

Adam knew well enough about the reputation of Mussorie, a hill station in the United Provinces frequented by comely Eurasian girls hoping to find husbands.

'No, we're not going to Mussorie.'

'Is it another woman? There's someone else, isn't there, Adam?'

He was surprised at the unexpected concern of this independent-minded young woman. It was not going to be easy to answer her truthfully.

'Don't be so silly. Anyway I never took you for the jealous type.'

She felt suitably admonished. He was right she was normally more sure of herself but Adam had changed, he was more confident and more assertive. Whilst this made him more masculine and more attractive she was not accustomed to him being in command and it made her feel more insecure.

'Are you sure you can't change it?'

'I've been invited by Rindi's parents and it would be very impolite to start messing them about. There will be other opportunities I'm sure, particularly now that you're stationed nearby.'

'Well, I might not be available.' The bathroom light was reflecting through the open door on to her face. She looked beautiful lying there, fragile and strangely vulnerable. He could hardly wish for more desirable company. If their relationship could be kept discreet and she was willing, why should it not continue for as long as he was stationed in Delhi? He was sure that the General, and certainly Lady Roberts, would not approve of the intimacy of their relationship. Discovery would precipitate instant return to his unit. However, in this regard, his conscience was clear. Whilst he had been keenly compliant in the affair, Sarah was the one who had made most of the running.

'So are they a grand Indian family?'

'Yes quite grand. Rindi's father is the Maharajah of Kushnapur.'

'I suppose they live in a palace?'

'Yes they do.'

'My sister Kathleen once spent a weekend at the palace of the Nawab of Bhopal. One of his daughters was a friend from school. She said it was utterly tedious. They spent the whole time confined to the *zenana*, discussing needlework, swimming almost fully clothed and eating piles of sickly *halwa*. Never again she said.'

'Well, if she must choose a Muslim family. Purdah is important to them. Kushnapur is not like that at all. We ride, hunt and shoot. There are masses of wild animals and birds and many interesting things to see and do; there never seems enough time.'

'I doubt whether any of those activities would be available to the women.'

'Yes, you may have a point there.'

'I would be interested to see it one day, if Rindi wouldn't mind.'

'I am sure he wouldn't,' he said, knowing that it was not Rindi who would be uncomfortable with her coming to Kushnapur. Adam had managed to steer his way through this conversation without mentioning that Rindi had two sisters.

Now fully dressed, Adam came back into the bedroom to take his leave, but Sarah had not moved. She was still lying naked, but for a sheet half draped across her. He bent over and kissed her forehead, then left without further ceremony. He resolved not to let love intrude into their relationship. He had learnt his lesson. If this affair were to end tomorrow he would be sorry, but, without the pangs of love to impair his judgement, he could take it in his stride. Meanwhile, the best insurance for its continuance was to keep Sarah guessing about his true feelings and riding back to headquarters in the staff car he decided that, for the present at least, he had succeeded.

CHAPTER EIGHTEEN

Kushnapur Palace, March 1942.

Adam looked forward to his stay at the palace with eager anticipation. He now knew many things about the Debrahms that he had not known before. He had been asked to return for a specific purpose, but had good reason to feel that he would be welcomed as more than just a friend of the family.

Sitting in the train, he pondered his predicament. When Kafni and he had met on that auspicious night in December, he had been 'free of romantic involvement' as Rindi put it. He had then been bowled over by his beautiful, sensual sister and even though he had known her for such a short time he had fallen for her. But he had left with a sense of hopelessness that she could never be his. Since then he had become Sarah's lover once more, albeit only in a physical way.

Now as he headed back to Kushnapur and to Kafni he felt strangely disloyal to both of them.

He wondered how Kafni would feel about their reunion. Would the thought of another visit from him give her pleasure, or was it purely a duty for an obedient daughter? Would she be concerned about her fertility? He wasn't sure that comforting her with the possibility of his own infertility would be any more reassuring. It was probably just a question of timing.

The train hissed its way into Saharanpur Station at ten minutes to one in the morning. The station thermometer showed a comfortable fifty-five degrees. By midday this would soar to eighty-eight, but by then they would be in the hills where the temperature would be twenty degrees lower.

Moments after Adam's train came to a standstill, Rindi's bearer was beside the carriage door and fifteen minutes later, the Janata Express pulled in bearing his master. Adam remembered the splendour of the last time they had arrived at Saharanpur. This time they were travelling much lighter and it was the middle of the night. Whilst their reception was less ceremonious they were still greeted by the immaculate chauffeur standing beside the maharajah's pristine Rolls Royce.

It was before dinner that Adam noticed the change of formalities from his previous visit. Rindi had taken him to see the maharajah in his study, where they exchanged thoughts on the state of the war and Adam's new role as A.D.C.

The maharajah gave an almost imperceptible signal to the *khitmagar*, and then led the way into the hall and across the pink marble floor to the dining room where the maharani and her daughters were waiting. Although Rindi had said that they should be dining with the family, Adam knew from his previous experience that this was an unusual occurrence and had almost certainly been arranged in his honour. The grandeur of the gold settings on the table set his mind thinking about the lingam. When would he officially get to see the temple and its magnificent contents?

The maharani was gracious and charming and involved him in every discussion. He had not seen Kafni since they had parted in the early hours of that auspicious morning and whilst her smile had warmth there was no hint that he was anything more than a good friend of the family. He longed to embrace her or even to hold her hand but this was the first of many reminders that there had to be a defined formality to their relationship.

Puhella was less impish than before, though glimpses of that nature did emerge when she attempted to impress Adam.

'Why can't we have more tiger hunts? I'm sure that Ad ... err, Captain Cullworthy, is an excellent shot. I am sure he would love to ride on one of the elephants.'

In so many ways she reminded him of his sister Sue. In fact for a brief moment he could have been at home surrounded by his own family, but perhaps discussing a less majestic hunting event.

'You know very well, Puhella that Papaji has given up hunting.' Anyway, whilst we're at war, it would be quite contrary to the wishes of the British Resident,' the maharani interjected.

Adam wondered whether the maharajah had given up hunting after the incident with Sir Arthur. As if in confirmation of the sensitivity of this subject, Rindi diverted the conversation. 'There are masses of game birds here now, Adam, and the black buck need culling.'

The name black buck was enough for Puhella. 'Yes! Yes! Rindi.

Why don't you take Captain Cullworthy out with the cheetahs? Wantilla says that is real sport, no buck can outrun them.'

The stern look on the maharani's face made it very apparent that she did not wish to talk about Wantilla. The mention of the cheetah reminded Adam of his painful midnight encounter. He wondered if Kafni even knew of his injuries. Then he thought how she would see his scars soon enough.

'The game birds sounds just the thing, and what about duck? Have they come in yet?'

'Ah yes, the *shikari* tells me there are huge paddlings arriving on the lake every day, especially mallard, shoveller, and tufted duck. We limit the number we shoot, so the birds come back to feed each year in large numbers.'

The maharajah now joined in. 'Rindi, why don't you take Adam up to Mountain Lake? Chandra was up there last week and said that several large flocks of teal had flown in.'

'Do you have many lakes around here?' Adam enquired.

Kafni took up this non-contentious subject. 'Oh yes, we have three beautiful small lakes within five miles, and then there is the *Burra Talab,* the Great Lake which goes back for miles.'

Adam loved hearing her speak and he found it difficult to concentrate on the detail of her words. The gaze he gave her made her flush and the look she gave him dispelled any doubt that she held feelings for him and was sufficient to turn his heart over. The directness and honesty in her eyes were such a contrast to Sarah's cool seductive gaze. Adam's head was telling him these thoughts were absurd but his heart wanted to believe there was hope behind those deep violet eyes.

Next morning, crouching in the undergrowth beside the Mountain Lake, Rindi and Adam watched the magnificent swirling flocks of waterfowl arriving and leaving. The *shikari* handed the loaded Purdeys and the temptation to use them was almost irresistible. But the wonderful sight of those birds convinced them to just admire the spectacle through their binoculars, rather than shoot them. How many thousands of miles had they flown from their breeding grounds in Russia and Scandinavia.

'There's enough killing going on. Shall we leave them in peace?' Rindi said as if reading Adam's thoughts.

On their way back up to the palace, Adam's thoughts returned to Kafni. He wondered what arrangements had been made for them to meet.

It was unlikely that it would be left to his own initiative. Everything seemed to be carefully planned. His reflections were interrupted by Rindi.

'Perhaps you might like to use the private staircase this afternoon, Adam.'

This surprised him, because not only was his expectation that it would be Mandira who would convey any messages from Kafni, but he also expected that such visits would be made during the hours of darkness. The thought of being with her again excited him but he longed for more innocence and less interference in their romance. The joy of his first vision of her emerging from the steaming waters of the pool seemed all too distant.

'Why not?' Adam responded with mustered nonchalance and nothing more was said.

After lunch Adam returned to his room and lay on his bed thinking that what lay ahead of him was every man's dream. He got up and walked over to the wardrobe and quickly took out the figurehead key and unlocked the private door. The staircase was now lit by daylight through a series of *jali*. This fretted masonry was positioned at a height designed to prevent observers from outside seeing into these private quarters. In the absence of Mandira, Adam was hesitant to try and find his way to Kafni's rooms especially after having lost his way on his previous attempt. Would they expect him to make his own way? He thought this unlikely and returned to his room and he decided to write a letter to his parents. He had written just two pages when he heard a tap at the door. He glanced across the bedroom, thinking that it must be his bearer.

'Adam, are you there?'

He swung around and saw Kafni standing at the secret door he had left open. She was dressed in another beautiful sari, shimmering emerald green silk bordered with a band woven from pure gold thread. This was more of a day sari and had less of the splendour of red bridal sari she had worn in her bedchamber. A tulle headscarf in the same colours partly covered her shining black hair. Her long eyelashes gave her that doe-eyed innocence he had first seen down at the pool.

Adam got up and walked towards her drawn like a hopeless moth to this radiant candle.

'Adam, I want to show you the temple. I know you've seen it before, but this time it will be very different.'

At night, when darkness obscures imperfections and skilfully placed lights emphasize features of beauty, the interior of a building can look more magnificent than during the day; this place was quite the reverse. Adam felt that he was entering an architectural wonderland. The first difference was in the colours and patterns of the tiles that formed the staircase. These had been barely discernible by lamplight. Now, as Kafni led him down the steps the sun filtered through the lattice stonework, revealing tiles on the walls each with a different symbol.

They passed into a long hallway. Ahead of them lay a kaleidoscope of shadow and diffused sunlight coming from shafts, lined with white marble, extending to the roof of the building.

Kafni unlocked the door that he had mistaken for her room and descended the steps to the wide corridor paved with the huge marble slabs he had seen before. But this time, it was glints of sunlight that were scattered across the lustred surface.

'There's something special I want you to see,' said Kafni, a little breathlessly. At the end of the corridor, they came to the series of columns of the *natamandap*. He felt her grip tighten on his hand as she led him down the steps into the centre aisle. There, beyond the stream, gleaming in a narrow beam of sunlight was the golden phallus.

'Only at this time in the afternoon during the spring equinox, does the sun strike the lingam,' she said.

She touched him on the shoulder indicating that he should remain where he was. Then after a few minutes she reappeared beyond the water. She walked over and stood in front of the phallic symbol, then remained motionless. Although she did not beckon him, he began to walk towards her, and as he drew nearer, there was something very familiar about this scene. Perhaps he was just recalling his own experience, only this time it was Kafni standing there. Then it came to him. This was the same scene as the hauntingly beautiful painting on the bedroom wall at Queen's Gate Gardens. It was Kafni but as a young girl. Was this her way of showing him that she knew their destinies had been determined many years before? Perhaps the timing was different. They could not have known about the War, but the ultimate situation was now as it had been planned; precisely by whom he no longer cared.

Until that moment the initiative had been with Kafni. It now shifted to Adam. As he approached the stream he felt his throat tighten as he remembered his encounter with the cheetah. He scanned the shadows and to his surprise saw Sheba lying half in the sunlight, with her head half raised. Looking no more threatening than a contented domestic cat. He crossed the stepping-stones warily and came up beside Kafni. Picking her up in his arms he carried her to the edge of the stream. Pausing to judge the distance between the stepping-stones, he was amazed to see that the water was teeming with brilliantly coloured fish. Now sure of his steps, he carried her back across the stream and through to the far side of the dancing pavilion. He lowered her gently on to the marble steps, and then kissed her passionately. Kafni felt a heat surging through her body and grabbing Adam by the hand they started to climb the staircase to the small landing. Intermittently glancing at each other there was suddenly an urgency in their step. Reaching the curtained archway they pushed through into Kafni's apartment. There was none of the ceremony of their first night. They both undressed with undignified haste and once naked fell into each other's arms and then scrambled into Kafni's capacious bed. They made love with uninhibited passion.

Adam couldn't decide whether it was the aura of the lingam or just their well-matched chemistry that had produced this all-consuming desire to be together, but it led to the most blissful evening he had ever spent.

It was more than twelve hours later that Mandira came to wake them and conduct Adam back to his room. No other servant of the palace must find him absent from his bed. Reluctant for this glorious night to finish he drew back the curtains in his room to look down on the gardens slumbering under the soft light of the brilliant full moon. The Court Astrologer had chosen well this third day of March 1942.

Whereas on his previous visit, Adam had not seen Kafni again after their night together, this time he saw her on three more occasions. Twice, when he dined with the whole family, and once when he was invited to be present to meet a distant visiting cousin.

Ever conscious of the necessity for secrecy, Kafni and Adam maintained an outward appearance of polite formality. Kafni had felt confident that she could fulfil her family's requirement of her and still remain emotionally detached but she was finding it increasingly difficult to disguise her feelings for this handsome army officer. The more she saw of him the more she admired his discreet charm and thoughtfulness. But she knew there was no future in it and she decided, as a form of self-defence and to protect Adam from heartbreak that she must discourage any further romantic thoughts he might have. So she put on an act of complete indifference which not only convinced the family that she had no romantic inclinations but also fooled Adam into believing it. Rindi was sufficiently concerned that something might have gone wrong that he felt the need to console Adam when they were alone again.

'Everything alright, old boy?'

'Yes, thank you.'

'I hope things went according to plan? I was just a bit concerned that Kafni seemed a bit frosty towards you.'

'Suffice it to say that there will hopefully be a more fruitful outcome this time.'

'Good, and thank you for doing this for us, we really do appreciate it and know how difficult it must be for you. I can see by the way you look at her that you would like there to be more.'

'Not reciprocated it would appear, so no danger of breeching your sanction.'

Adam could not fathom why Kafni had suddenly cooled towards him. This made his deep yearning to be with her again even stronger. It was also creating tension between himself and Rindi who he felt was not being completely open with him.

Rindi was tormented by the thought that he was standing between his friend and his sister whilst at the same time he was becoming ever more closely involved with Adam's first love. It was only a matter of time before one of the family mentioned Tina in a compromising way. How much worse would that be than just coming clean to Adam himself? Another letter from Tina had arrived that morning. Absence was making their hearts grow fonder. The immediate threat of invasion had diminished but Rindi feared for Tina in London. Whilst the Blitz was over, there was still the constant threat of further strategic bombing by the Luftwaffe. How he would love to share his feelings with Adam, but if he were to reveal it now Adam would probably feel he had not only been used by Rindi but betrayed by him as well. He could not risk losing his closest friend but wasn't he just postponing the problem?

In view of the tepid reception that Wantilla had received on his previous visit, Adam was surprised to learn that his seventeen year old nephew Narajan Ram was in attendance at the palace. The timing of his nephew's visit made Rindi and his father understandably suspicious. It was almost impossible to maintain watertight security in a place with over four hundred servants and no doubt Wantilla would have had at least one spy under his pay. Since his meeting with Adam he would have been alert to any further visits to the palace by him. Rindi having introduced Adam as a future trustee of the Kushnapur Estate was enough to raise Wantilla's hackles.

Despite his youth, Narajan had few reservations when he spoke to Adam.

'You are Mr. Cullworthy. You met my uncle here last year I think?' His tone was truculent, and his emphasis on "mister" may have been deliberate but Adam affected to ignore the comment. Rindi on the other hand had no intention of letting it pass.

'Mr Cullworthy is a captain, Narajan, and should be so addressed.'

The point had been made, but his young cousin appeared unabashed as he posed an apparently meaningless question. 'You seem to be a regular visitor to the palace, Captain Cullworthy?'

'Well it makes a nice change from the heat of New Delhi.' Adam responded and added 'You know, of course, that your cousin Rindi and I were at school together?'

'Oh no, I did not.' Clearly, he was surprised by this information, which Wantilla had not bothered to pass on, probably preferring his nephew to believe that Adam was a recent army acquaintance.

'Cousin Rindi my uncle tells me he will soon be betrothed to Kafni.'

Rindi disliked the familiarity with which this youth was treating him and disliked the subject of his question even more.

'I think your uncle is deluding himself. It is more than likely that my sister will be found a suitable husband outside the immediate family.'

'He will be disappointed.'

'Yes, maybe, but I trust you will convey this information to him.' Rindi knew full well that Narajan would not wish to incur the wrath of his uncle by delivering such bad news.

Adam left Kushnapur in a confused state. He had experienced a roller coaster of emotions over his week with the Debrahm family. He had succeeded in fulfilling the family's expectation of him but rather than feeling a sense of gratitude from them he left feeling they were disappointed with him. What had started so well with the euphoria of his visit to the temple and his joyous afternoon with Kafni, had ended with confusion and disappointment. Once more he found the complexities of the opposite sex baffling. Even his friendship with Rindi seemed to have changed over the period of his stay.

Without making any specific reference to the purpose of his return visit Kafni's parents had been gracious in thanking him for coming to stay and said he would always be welcome at any time. But the two members of the family most dear to Adam had not made him feel they were any closer to him.

CHAPTER NINETEEN

New Delhi, April 1942.

Perhaps because Adam had not sought the job, and in the beginning did not particularly want it, he made no special effort to impress the General. He endeavoured to do his duties efficiently and made sure that Sir David could rely upon him. He knew that there would be no promotion whilst he remained in this post so his main concern was to return to the regiment with a clean slate.

Sarah left him with little doubt that his company was expected to be at her disposal. Their relationship had been rekindled on a physical basis but as time went on Adam found her increasingly good company. Although they conducted their affair with considerable circumspection it became increasingly difficult to hide the fact that they were spending a lot of time together. At some stage the General, or more probably Lady Roberts, would discover their secret and this could be very awkward for Adam. He still felt a mild resentment that Sarah was probably instrumental in his appointment as the General's A.D.C. and had no desire for her to be the cause of any further interference in his career. It would be better if a harmless friendship could be made apparent to her parents. Sarah came up with a solution to the problem.

A dance was to be held at Headquarters, and it was perfectly reasonable that Adam should be invited to join her party. Sarah took the precaution of discussing the arrangements with her mother who raised no objection to including her husband's A.D.C. Adam was formally invited to join their party by Lady Roberts, and during the evening of the dance he and Sarah were able to conduct a charade of openly getting to know each other.

Two weeks later when Sarah came for her fortnightly visit to her parents, she let her mother know that she wanted Adam to be invited to Sunday lunch. Their relationship became less formal, and when the time came to leave Sarah said to her father. 'Daddy, it's horrid travelling back alone at night; do you think that Adam could run me to my quarters?'

Sir David looked from Sarah to Adam and then said, 'I don't know if he's got a car. Have you, Adam?'

'Yes, Sir, the MT sergeant at the transport pool always reserves a car for me.'

'Will he have a driver available at this time of the evening?'

'Oh yes, there are always two drivers on duty; it's Brigadier Stevenson's orders.' Adam was rather relieved by the General's questions. It indicated that he had not taken too much interest in his off-duty activities.

After that, it became routine for Adam to drive Sarah back to her unit, and it was accepted that, as Lady Roberts put it, they were "walking out together".

Despite his increasing closeness with Sarah, Kafni was constantly in Adam's thoughts. Their time together had been so special and it still puzzled him why she had suddenly become so cool towards him before he left the palace. Was it something that her family had said to her? Whatever the reason, he convinced himself that her true feelings were those she had displayed when they were alone together. Even though he knew it was a hopeless pursuit, he could not control a deep yearning for her.

By early May the temperature in Delhi topped the hundred every day. Tempers shortened and fans were speeded-up. In times of peace, the Viceroy and his vast entourage would, some weeks earlier, have decamped to the cool slopes of Simla. For Adam's regiment there was no such relief, and they had to endure the relentless sweat. The usual greeting by the office *chaprassi* was, 'coming hotter sahib, coming much hotter. Without hotter, rains not coming.' He was quite right, and as the thermometer touched one hundred and ten, the first of the monsoon rains fell on New Delhi. It did little to reduce the heat, but it was a great relief during the few minutes that the rain was actually falling. Not until July and August would the heavy showers arrive. Even then, the monthly eight inches of rain would only ease the temperature by just a few degrees.

Adam thought about Kafni back in the palace. It would be a lot cooler up there but he knew that within a few weeks the rains would be falling in earnest on the Himalayas. Kushnapur could expect sixteen inches each month until September and it would become lush and green. Imagining all that fertility made him wonder whether their union had been fruitful. Surely they must know by now? Not being able to communicate with Kafni at all was a torment to him. He was even reluctant to question Rindi lest it be interpreted the wrong way or indeed the right way.

At last it came. Late one evening in June, Rindi called Adam on his private line.

'We have news from Kushnapur.'

Adam held his breath, not wishing to miss a word. His pulse thumped in his ears as he waited for Rindi to put him out of his misery.

'Well, is it good news?' he responded impatiently.

'Yes, everything's fine. Kafni and Puhella will be going up to Rajah's Lodge after the ceremony.' Rindi paused, knowing that Adam would need a moment to absorb the significance of this information.

'What ceremony?'

'Kafni is to be married in a small private ceremony.'

'Who on earth to?' Adam blurted out in astonishment fearing that Wantilla might have got his way.

'Prince Ranjhalla Singh, a distant cousin on my mother's side. She has been betrothed to him for some time but it is only now that it is appropriate for the marriage to proceed.'

'Will a small ceremony suffice for the daughter of a grand family?'

'Even if there was time to make the arrangements father would not sanction a show of opulence with a war going on. And in any case he is a serving officer so will need to return to his regiment straightaway.'

Adam felt relieved that at least she was not marrying Wantilla but could not conceive of this girl he had come to love being married to anyone else. He could not imagine her sharing intimacy with this stranger. He then reminded himself that he too had been a stranger to her just months before. But all of this had been meticulously planned and was happening as Rindi had described it to him all those months ago. Kafni was now pregnant and needed to be married so that the world could accept her forthcoming child as legitimate.

'Will he not suspect anything when the baby is born early?'

'It is not unusual for babies to be born prematurely in India. In fact it is seen as something of a blessing as it increases the chances of the mother surviving.'

Adam shuddered to think of even the smallest possibility that

Kafni could die giving birth to his child.

'So what happens now?' Adam asked still bewildered by Rindi's revelations.

Rindi knew what Adam was hoping to hear. That he could see Kafni in due course and that when the baby was born he would be able to see both mother and child, but he could give him no such reassurance. 'My friend you have played your part and for that we are very grateful but it is time for you to step off the stage and let the Debrahm family fulfil its destiny.'

There was something so final in this statement that Adam wondered whether there was even a future for his friendship with Rindi. Tears welled in his eyes and he was grateful that Rindi was not with him to witness his grief.

'Are you all right, Adam?'

'Yes, yes, absolutely.' He said clearing his throat. 'Please wish Kafni well from me.' This sounded so trite that Rindi knew Adam was hurting.

'You will always be an important part of our family Adam.'

'I feel we should be celebrating,' Adam spluttered trying to be cheery. 'Can you make it down here anytime soon?'

'Sorry, Adam, it's impossible. I have to go off on this jungle training course. I'll be away for a month, but I can apply for a weekend pass immediately I get back.'

Adam was disappointed. Even though Rindi could not give Adam the reassurances he so wanted he was the only person that he could talk to about this major event in his life.

'Well, that sounds the best we can hope for. Where are you going for this course?'

'It's at Mhow. I know that's where you went on a course. What's it like?'

'It's a very comfy billet but given the title of your course I doubt whether you will be treated to the frills I experienced.'

'Yes, I'm told that we'll be roughing it out in the *mofussil* under canvas. Oh, by the way, you might run into Wantilla in New Delhi. He's been promoted to captain and is being sent to your headquarters as an Indian Liaison Officer.'

'Ah, a treat in store. Presumably he doesn't know about Kafni getting married?'

'No and the longer we can keep it that way the better. Reading between the lines, I reckon that with things hotting-up in the

East, he's got himself a cushy job that should keep him out of the fighting.'

When Adam finally ran into Wantilla it was in unexpected circumstances. Sarah was staying with her parents and she asked if Adam could come for dinner. As he walked into the drawing room, he looked in disbelief to see Wantilla, with one hand in his pocket and a glass of scotch in the other, casually chatting to Sir David. The General looked up and beckoned Adam over.

'This is my A.D.C., Adam Cullworthy. Adam, I'd like you to meet Wantilla Debrahm from the A.G.s branch at GHQ. He's now attached to our headquarters.'

'Cullworthy and I have met before, General.'

'Oh really where did you come across each other?'

'I was at school with Debrahm's cousin, Sir.'

Wantilla gave a thinly veiled look of contempt at the mention of his cousin. Sir David gave a knowing smile. 'Excellent! Then you two should get on well together. I am sure Cullworthy will introduce you to some of the officers here.'

Adam could think of nothing he would like to do less than inflict this rascal on his fellow officers.

Wantilla was not the only unexpected guest at the party. Adam looked around to find Sarah and her mother deep in conversation with James Pendleton.

'Good evening Lady Roberts.'

'Oh, good evening, Adam I think you have already met my nephew James.'

'Indeed, yes, you were very helpful to me in Agra.'

'More helpful than you know.'Lady Roberts added, 'it was James's recommendation that led to your appointment as David's A.D.C.'

'Thank you for that.' Adam said with genuine gratitude. 'It has been a very rewarding posting for me.' This was a surpising revelation for Adam who was quietly relieved and felt rather guilty that he had wrongly suspected Sarah all this time. He had long since ceased to regard Pendleton as a threat but was still curious as to Sarah's rather protective manner towards him. When they were alone again he asked her. 'When we were in Agra you said that it served both your purposes for you and James to be seen as a couple. Why was that?'

Sarah looked uncharacteristically restrained. 'I think I know you well enough now and know that you can be trusted to keep a secret.'

'I would hope so.'

'James's dark secret is that he prefers men to women.'

'You're not serious.'

'I am afraid I am.'

'Well, I do see how difficult that must be in his position.'

'It would be the end of his career if anyone suspected him so our little charade just helped to suppress any rumours.'

Adam thought how badly he had judged James Pendleton and felt pity for him in his terrible predicament. Adam's love life was confused and secretive but at least exposure of his secrets wouldn't result in a prison sentence.

The Womens' Army Corps continued to expand at a rapid pace. They were trained to take over from the men wherever they could, and relieve them to join the fighting units of the Fourteenth Army. This battle group, when trained and fully equipped, would invade and endeavour to recapture Burma from the Japanese. Far from using her father's position to gain advancement, Sarah had to prove herself better than her contemporaries. Her promotion came through in August and she was told she was being posted to Poona.

Shortly before leaving, she put up her crown as a senior commander. Her air of confidence and authority was attractive to some men but to most potential admirers this aspect of her character was off-putting. Her desire for independence made it difficult for her to love and be loved but the time Adam had spent with her in Delhi had enabled him to see beyond this outward emotional armour.

They had a tacit agreement that there would be no deep involvement. That they were both regular Army officers and there was a war going on certainly influenced this decision, although for Adam there were other reasons. He knew how much his pre-occupation with the fantasy world of Kafni had constrained his desire to commit himself emotionally to Sarah. But he hadn't realised how important she had become to him until faced with the prospect of being parted from her.

'How long do you think they'll keep you in Poona?'

'I really don't know. It is a permanent posting.' She must have guessed what was on his mind, 'It's an awfully long way away, so we shan't see much of each other.'

'Yes, nearly a thousand miles. You will write, won't you?'

Adam kissed her and held her tightly, 'Good luck, old girl. Hope to see in a couple of months.'

He did not see her again for almost four months, and although they wrote to each other every couple of weeks, their letters never revealed the true extent of their relationship.

CHAPTER TWENTY

New Delhi Cantonment, September 1942.

The rains were still falling in Delhi when Rindi came for a couple of days. His arrival was an opportune boost for Adam's morale. It was more than a month since Sarah had left, depriving him of those indulgent weekends. His mood had not been improved by a letter from Bob Mercer telling him that as the battalion had temporarily been divided for special duties there was no immediate need for him to return.

Rindi had completed his jungle warfare course and Adam knew that it was only a matter of time before that training would be called upon. The Commander-in-Chief was anxious to hit back at the Japs and only the monsoon still raging in Assam and northern Burma was preventing this happening. He was hesitant as ever to ask after Kafni but longed to know how things were going.

'What news from the summer residence?'

Rindi shook his head. 'Not much. They're having tremendous monsoon rains, which rather hampers communications. But when I last heard, all was well.'

'How are things going with the General's daughter? Is she still keeping you amused?'

'Unfortunately not. She's been promoted and was posted to Poona over a month ago.'

'Well absence will make the heart grow fonder.'

This was true but Adam felt curiously uncomfortable when discussing Sarah as though he were being disloyal to Kafni but this was clearly not how Rindi viewed it.

'Have you seen anything of Wantilla?' Rindi enquired.

'He's not been in the mess for a while, but then he doesn't live in. He seems to be lying low.'

'That is never a good sign. His father hasn't heard from him for some time and asked me to contact him if I came to New Delhi but I feel sure he will ask about Kafni and I would rather not have to lie about her getting married.'

'I imagine he will be furious.'

'That is the understatement of the year.'

'Perhaps I could check him out for you, although I doubt he will relish a visit from me.' Adam offered reluctantly.

Three weeks later Adam received a letter from Rindi. He had volunteered for Major-General Wingate's guerrilla force but he gave no indication of its location, nor was any operational activity foreshadowed. However, information gleaned from other sources indicated that he was probably somewhere in Assam. Rindi told him that his prime motive for joining this force was that if the Japanese took India they would be merciless to a very pro-British family like the Debrahms. The dangers were considerable and Adam was not sure whether the pang he felt was from guilt or anxiety.

Rindi's letter prompted him to seek out Wantilla, as he had promised to do. He took the morning off and eventually tracked him down to a fashionable residential district on the outskirts of New Delhi. The houses were large with their own gardens and a servants' bungalow. Wantilla's blue Bentley in the driveway confirmed that he was in residence. Parked behind it were a small Indian Army Austin and a black Morris Twelve. Not expecting to stay long Adam told his driver to come and collect him after half an hour. He got out and walked along the path bordered by a well-groomed grass lawn now lush from the heavy rains. The front door was open and Adam pressed the bell, but no one came. He pushed back the door and walked into the hallway. He could hear a heated altercation coming from the depths of the house. Curiosity got the better of him and he crept down the corridor towards the source of the conversation.

'You bloody idiot. I give you a simple task and you cock it up not once but twice. Now the bastard is up in the jungle we have no chance.' There was a muffled response to Wantilla's outburst but Adam could not hear this part of the conversation. 'No more bloody money till it's done and that goes for that bastard Cullworthy too.'

Adam was shocked to hear his name. He was about to retreat when he heard footsteps approaching the door in front of him. He quickly ducked into a room on his left which turned out to be full of laundry. Through a crack in the door he saw a man emerge from the room opposite, who closed the door behind him and walked briskly past the laundry room heading for the front door. Adam had a clear view and there was something very familiar about him but he was unable to pinpoint where he had seen him before. Adam was relieved that he had sent his driver away as there would be no evidence that he was there but he still had to extricate himself before he was discovered. He wondered what exactly Wantilla was up to and feared the worst. Rindi had warned him that he might be in danger but he hadn't really taken him seriously.

The laundry room was dark because the only window had a blind drawn over it. Adam pulled back the side of the blind enough to see that the room backed on to the rear of the property. About fifteen feet from the side of the house was a thick hibiscus hedge with a small gap in it. If he could get behind that he might be able to skirt round back to the road. He was about to draw the blind when a servant walked straight past the window. Escape was not going to be easy. What if the servant was coming to do the laundry? He waited a couple of minutes then quickly pulled up the blind and opened the window. As he was lowering himself out of it he thought how embarrassing this would look if he was caught but he quickly gained the cover of the hedge and found a path in the neighbouring property which led down to the road. He would now have to wait for his driver and risk being spotted loitering with no obvious reason to be there. Instead he decided to make a new approach to the house and pretend he had only just arrived. As he walked back up the path to the house he saw the man he had seen in the corridor getting into his car. In the daylight he looked even more familiar but Adam still couldn't put his finger on where he had seen him before. He also noticed that the Austin was still parked behind the Bentley. There was obviously a second visitor still in the house.

This time when he rang the bell the servant he had seen passing the laundry room came to the door. As Adam stood in the hallway an Indian girl dressed in a Wackeye officer's uniform descended the elegant staircase curving down from the first floor. She stopped when she saw Adam and looked embarrassed. She appeared undecided whether to proceed or retreat upstairs, then, realising the implied discourtesy in doing so, came down to greet him.

'Hello I'm Parvarti'

'Good afternoon, Adam Cullworthy,' he responded, 'I was hoping to have a word with Wantilla. He knows who I am but is not expecting me.'

The girl was short and neat and looked about twenty. She gave him a rather sheepish smile and looked ill at ease.

'Captain Debrahm has a visitor at the moment. Perhaps you'd like to wait in the sitting room.' She pointed to an open door at the front of the house.

'Thank you.'

The girl disappeared down the corridor he had recently vacated. From the rear of the house, just audible, he heard. 'Cullworthy? What does that bastard want?'

After a couple of minutes Wantilla appeared followed a few steps behind by the Indian girl. As it was approaching midday Adam was surprised to find him wearing a long black dressing gown, cuffed and collared in cream silk with the Harrow crest embossed in silver thread on his breast pocket. Whatever this individual lacked in moral principles and however disagreeable Adam found him, he had to concede that he was not without style.

'Cullworthy, to what do I owe this pleasure?' Then turning to the girl he said. 'Why don't you go and arrange tea for us and bring some of those *mitha* cakes, there's a good girl.'

Wantilla watched Adam's eyes follow the young woman as she left the room.

'A pretty little thing don't you think?'

'Indeed she is,' Adam replied looking a trifle embarrassed at being caught admiring his taste in women.

'Now, you were going to tell me the reason for your visit.'

'Rindi asked if I could look in on you as your family hadn't heard from you for a while.'

'Sent to spy on me more likely.' He seemed unruffled and gave no indication of the venom with which he had expressed his instructions to his previous guest. 'You know, Cullworthy you and I got off to a bad start. I think you'll find we have more in common than you imagine.'

Adam struggled to see what these common interests might be.

'For a start we both have a good eye for the female form. How is the General's daughter by the way?' Wantilla preened his impressive moustache.

'Very well as far as I know.'

'Come now it must be common knowledge that you're bedding her.'

Adam was both disturbed and irritated at how well informed he was.

'Well as you seem such an authority you will know that she has been posted to Poona.'

'And what about my cousin? Any news from the jungle?'

Adam felt he was constantly on the back foot.

'Yes, unlike some of us he is putting his life on the line for King and country.'

A bearer entered the room with a tray of tea and the cakes Wantilla had requested.

'I don't know what you're implying Cullworthy but if you must know I think there are an awful lot of Indian lives being sacrificed unnecessarily for your King and country.'

'And likewise British lives to protect your liberty.'

'Liberty from what? I make no bones about it, Cullworthy, I am behind the Congress Party's move to get independence from the British.'

'Is that just an excuse not to fight the Japs?'

'Enough of this Imperial crap, Cullworthy. If my cousin insists on risking his life I am happy to stand prepared to take on the *gaddi* of Kushnapur. Once I have secured the delectable Kafni as my wife it will be a foregone conclusion.'

'That will never be allowed to happen,' Adam said in an ill-judged retort. How he would have loved to have told this smug bastard the whole truth but his life was evidently in danger already without any further incitement.

'What the hell do you know about it, Cullworthy! You have been sticking your nose in to Debrahm family business for far too long. I think this meeting is over. Next time my cousin and his father wish to spy on me tell them not to send a general's lackey.' He gave Adam a look of contempt which made the sinister conversation he had overheard more worrying.

Tea and cakes forgotten Adam turned and left the room. Walking back to where his driver was now parked it came to him where he had seen the mystery man before. Although he was older and his hair had threads of grey there was something very distinctive about his long thin shape and loping gait. It was definitely the man he had seen behaving suspiciously outside Queen's Gate Gardens in London several years before.

Adam could not take his mind off the conversation he had overheard. What was the simple task the man had failed to execute? It was important that he should speak to Rindi at the earliest opportunity but that would not be easy. Waiting for Rindi to make contact was agonising

It was mid-December when Adam received the call he had been waiting for.

'Hello, old chap how are things going?'

Adam was amazed at how jocular Rindi was given the circumstances of his operational deployment.

'All fine here.'

'I thought you should know that Kafni had a son last night.' For a moment Adam was lost for words. 'They are both doing well and my parents are delighted.'

Adam felt his eyes welling up but took a grip of his emotions.

'That is wonderful news.'

'I am afraid I also have some very sad news. Kafni's husband has been killed in action.'

'Oh, God, how tragic.'

'Yes, he was a very fine man and a great soldier.'

'Where did it happen?'

'Up on the Burmese border. His whole unit was wiped out in an ambush.'

Adam felt a strange sense of relief. This could so easily have been a report of Rindi's death. He then felt remorse for his thoughts about the man he hadn't even met but whose position he had so envied. How difficult for Kafni being widowed so young.

'What happens now?'

'All too early to say. I am not sure they have even recovered his body, but some sort of memorial in due course.'

'I am sorry to hear about that. Will you send my condolences to Kafni? Where is she now?'

'Back at the palace.'

Adam longed to see her and the child but thought it would be too insensitive to ask if this might be possible. He also feared what Rindi's response was likely to be. He wanted to celebrate becoming a father with Rindi but this was not going to happen. The joyous outcome that had taken so much planning and caused him such emotional turmoil was now overshadowed by this tragic event.

'I suppose there is no chance of your coming to Delhi?'

'No, I am afraid not. I don't know exactly what is going on here but all leave has been cancelled. I will be in touch when I get back.'

'Take care, my friend.'

'Of course, and thank you, Adam, for all you have done. We are really very grateful and you should be very proud.'

December 1942.

When Lady Roberts told Adam that Sarah had been given leave and would be coming back for Christmas, he asked the General if he might go and meet her off the train.

'Did Mother not want to come with you?' Sarah asked, 'How did you manage to swing it to come alone?'

'I think she is much cannier than we think and made her excuses.'

'I think you're right. She seems to have a soft spot for you.'

Sarah looked radiant. Poona had clearly been good for her. In the hubbub of the milling crowds it was hard to hear themselves speak. As they passed beneath one of the archways they turned to each other and embraced with urgency. A passion generated by four months apart. As they were leaving the station Adam was reminded that Sarah was now a higher rank than him and as the senior officer she was obliged to return the salutes of passing soldiers.

On Christmas Day, Adam was fully committed to the General's military agenda but he was delighted to accept Lady Roberts's invitation to spend Boxing Day with the family.

'Adam's asked me to go with him to the New Year's Eve dance, so you won't go putting him on duty that night will you?'

The General looked at Sarah with a mock sternness. 'Ah, let me see... Thursday 31st December. Yes, sorry, I have him down as the Orderly Officer that night. Afraid it can't possibly be altered.'

Sarah pouted. 'Well, I'm sorry General, you might find yourself with an insubordinate daughter who takes after her father in getting her own way.'

'I'd say it's more likely that she inherits that tendency from her mother.'

Lady Roberts flicked her napkin towards the general and a wave of spontaneous laughter passed round the table.

Sarah returned to Poona shortly after New Year and Adam was sad to see her go. Her visit had been a welcome diversion from his turbulent thoughts. Rindi and Kafni were constantly on his mind for very different reasons. He longed to know what they were doing.

When the news came in early February, the operation was already over. General Wingate's group had been dropped into the heart of northern Burma and had succeeded in cutting the railway line used by the Japanese to transport army supplies and reinforcements. The operation, whilst of only minor military significance, had a tremendous effect on the morale of the troops in India. At last, there was evidence of a success against the Japanese.

Adam felt frustrated that he had not made any real contribution towards the war effort since he had been in India and was increasingly uncomfortable about his cushy role as the General's A.D.C. He now wanted to return to his regiment and serve under Bob Mercer once more. Whilst he didn't relish the thought of answering to the dreaded Major Williams who would probably still be the second-in-command, it was time he saw some action. But it was not going to be easy negotiating his departure from the General.

The next two weeks were fraught with fears and anxieties. In one nightmare, he was convinced that Rindi was lying dead in a northern Burmese jungle. When his bearer came in next morning carrying his carefully *dhobied* khaki drill uniform, his anguish turned into a troubled conscience. The lovingly laundered garment seemed a symbol of the privilege and security he enjoyed at command headquarters.

His fears were finally relieved when he received a letter from Rindi, written from the General Hospital in Dacca. There was no mention of how he came to be there except that he was recovering from malaria and expected to be discharged soon.

Ten days later he telephoned. 'They're discharging me with a week's sick leave and the doc wants me to spend it at a convalescent centre up in Darjeeling,'

'Sounds just what you need. When are you going?'

'I'm not. I've talked the old quack into letting me spend my sick leave in Calcutta.'

'How on earth did you manage that?'

'I told him that I have an aunt living in the suburbs at Alipore who would be pleased to take care of me.'

'And do you have an aunt in Calcutta?'

'Yes I do, my mother's sister. Anyway, the doctor agreed to it. Look, Adam, the point is I was hoping you could get a week's leave to come and join me?'

'A week's leave! Not a bloody hope. I might be able to talk the old man into a seventy-two hour pass.' The operator cut-in; time was up. Rindi ignored the interruption and gave Adam a Calcutta telephone number to contact him on the following week.

Adam needed a sound reason for this trip and decided to use Rindi's stint with Wingate's force in Burma as an excuse. He knew the General would like to get some first-hand information on this strategically important campaign.

'So who is this chap?'

'An old school friend, Sir. I think I mentioned him to you. He is Captain Debrahm's cousin.'

'Ah yes. Well I suppose I could do without you for a couple of days. Come to think of it you might do a bit of "duck shoving" whilst you're down there. It would be good to know what G.H.Q. are up to.'

'Do you want to make it official?'

'Yes, good for you to have status. I'll tell them that we are sending a liaison officer down for an update on the situation. I doubt whether you will get much out of the official channels but see what you can do by keeping your nose to the ground. I am keen to get our Command involved in some of the action and the better informed we are the better we can play our cards.'

It sounded strange to hear the general musing like this. In Adam's eyes, he was omnipotent.

Calcutta.

Adam had heard the description of Calcutta as "the most revolting city in Asia" but he was still not prepared for the stench and assaulting sea of humanity which confronted him on his arrival. It was the late afternoon and once away from the station he directed the taxi to take him to the Royal Calcutta Turf Club where he had arranged to meet Rindi.

'Adam, welcome to Calcutta.'

Adam gazed at the colonial splendour of the tranquil surroundings he had stepped into, such a contrast to the outside world he had just experienced.

'You look a bit shell-shocked my friend, I imagine it's not quite what you were expecting.'

'So much poverty and so many children begging.'

'Yes, and many of them blind from birth as a result of venereal diseases passed on through the sins of their parents. Some are even mutilated as babies; the more grotesque they appear the better their begging prospects. The money collected by one child beggar can support a whole family. Possession of a valuable patch in Sealdah station is a lifetime's ambition for some of these people.'

'I suppose you get used to it.'

'Sad to say but it's true. But enough of this depressing conversation, who knows where we might be tomorrow. Let's enjoy the trappings of wealth while we can.'

Despite his slightly debilitated appearance, Rindi had lost none of his zest and took relish in relating some of his recent encounters up on the Burmese border.

'If I'm not mistaken it sounds as if you rather enjoyed it.'

'I wouldn't go that far, it was pretty terrifying at times. It's one thing training in jungle warfare but it's another thing completely putting it into practice against an invisible enemy.'

'I should have been with you.'

'Don't fret yourself on that score. There were about twenty volunteers for every vacancy in the force.'

'So you were lucky to be selected?'

'Lucky to get out alive more to the point.'

'Well, I would still prefer to be in the action than stuck behind a desk.' Adam looked disappointed and chewed a finger nail distractedly. It reminded Rindi of the time he had left him out of the first eleven.

'How do you think I felt when you were getting shot up in France before I had even managed to get into uniform? Your chance will come soon enough. The monsoon will break next month so nothing much will happen until October at the earliest. You'd better resign yourself to a few more months of paper shuffling.'

'Yes you're probably right. Speaking of which I went to see that front-line dodger cousin of yours.'

'Oh yes, and what did he have to say for himself?'

Adam gave Rindi a full account of his visit to Wantilla's lodgings.

'What do you think he meant by "simple task"?'

'I fear the worst, Adam. He will stop at nothing to get the *gaddi and* he has powerful friends on his payroll.'

'I think you should mind your back from now on.'

'I am more concerned about you, Adam. I wouldn't like to feel that I was responsible for something happening to you.'

'Why would he bother to harm me? As far as he's concerned I'm just an outsider.'

'That you're certainly not. And I'm afraid, no longer even as far as he's concerned. First of all, if he even suspected the way that you are involved with the family, you'd be lucky to get out of India alive.'

'This is not Chicago!'

'I'm afraid that things are changing. At one time, patriotism, gallantry, honour and love were the motivation for deeds, but now politics and corruption have seeped into our lives. Even though there is a war on, the political parties are tensing their muscles and some would even go as far as making a deal with the Japs.'

'Is he involved in politics?'

'Not overtly. He and his father have politicians in their pay who they manipulate for their own ends. We are pretty sure they were behind the incident that nearly got Sir Julian killed. They are playing a dangerous game which could go badly wrong.'

'What about Hawkswood? Was he connected to them?'

'Not directly.' But before he could elucidate Rindi saw his uncle approaching.

'Rindi, my good fellow, how wonderful to see you and this must be your friend Adam.'

Shri Duttajee was short and portly but exuded bonhomie and his charm filled a bigger space in the room.

'Come now, let's get you both a drink. You are looking terrible my boy, what on earth did they do to you up the jungle?'

Rindi laughed. 'I'm afraid the greatest threat to my health turned out to be the mosquitos.'

'Ah malaria, very nasty, and it will come back to plague you for years to come. So no whisky then?'

'No, but I am told the quinine in Indian tonic has medicinal benefits so one of those, and perhaps a dash of Haywards.'

'I've booked a table for dinner at eight, just a few people you might find interesting.'

'Anyone I know?' Rindi asked.

'I don't think so. Oh, Cooch, I think you may have met him.'

'Ah yes, Cooch Behar, a thirteen-gun-salute prince if I remember rightly. Mad about horses.'

'Yes, that's the chap. Very amusing and well connected.'

'What is a salute prince?' Adam asked.

'The "salute princes" are the three hundred or so rulers of the most important states. Each is entitled to a salute of guns ranking from twenty-one, diminishing in twos, down to nine guns.'

'Who decides how many salutes they get?'

'The "heaven born" British in the political department, like most other matters involving status and given the immense prestige attached to the gun salutes there are very strict criteria. It is officially secret, but most of the princes know the necessary attributes. However, it's extremely difficult for them to bring any influence to bear. The beauty of the British civil servants is that they are incorruptible.'

'I suppose it is all about wealth?'

'Not at all,' said Duttajee. 'Take for example those two gentlemen over there.' He pointed to a table close to the window 'the Maharajahs of Mayurbhanj and Burdwan, both are fabulously wealthy. In fact Burdwan is the biggest individual taxpayer in the British Empire. His wealth, like that of Darbhanga, derives from the Act of Settlement of Bengal in 1793. They were permitted to retain their lands so long as they paid their government dues on time. However, they lost their rights as a local ruler. The advantage of this was that they were no longer obliged to pay for the welfare of their tenant farmers and thus became exceedingly rich!'

'Sounds ideal for them but not for the farmers.'

'Yes, indeed Adam, and their wealth has enabled them to live in the style of Indian royalty but Burdwan is still only ranked with an eleven gun salute and the recent origins of their wealth mean they are not really considered *pukka* princes.'

Rindi smiled at Adam. 'Nothing's straightforward in India my friend. And who else have you got coming for dinner Uncle?'

'Mainly serving officers. They're curious to know more about the Wingate operation.'

The "serving officers" were mainly Colonels and after a few glasses of port they freely gave their prognostications on the future course of the war. Adam was able to glean some very useful information for the General's mission.

When the guests and Duttajee had all left Rindi and Adam found a quiet corner in the member's bar.

'Your uncle has some interesting friends.'

'Yes, there is more to him than meets the eye. My father relies on him heavily to keep him informed. It's not that easy to keep your finger on the pulse up in Kushnapur.'

'You were about to tell me about the Hawkswood incident.'

'You already know it was not an accident, but what you don't know is that it was my father who shot him,' said Rindi.

'Good God! Are you being serious?'

'I am afraid I am. I haven't felt like burdening you with the details until now, but you are already embroiled so it's best you know the full story.'

'Hawkswood had become a bitter man. With his ambitions of becoming a State governor through the normal channels frustrated, he turned to a group of power-hungry Indian politicians. These turned out to be the same people that Mahavir had in his pocket.'

'When did that come to light?'

'No one trusts anyone in those circles so Mahavir had his spies infiltrate the group. Most of the politicians involved were supporters of the *Swaraj* cause who want the British out of India. The spies discovered that Hawkswood had devised a treacherous plot that would need political support.'

'So what was this plot?'

'He planned an invasion of the Punjab.'

'How on earth would he have pulled that off?'

'By involving the Russians. They've coveted the rich agricultural lands of the Punjab and for centuries the Russians have wanted to have a warm water port so access to Karachi would have been their reward. Hawkswood's plan was to use Kushnapur as a secret base and set up a network of cells to create disturbances by inflaming ethnic and religious differences. This unrest would keep the over-stretched British and Indian Armies occupied and then when they were at their most vulnerable, Russia would send their forces down through the Khyber Pass.'

'What would the Afghans have to say about that?'

'They would have been offered the spoils of war; the properties and assets of the Sikhs in the Punjab.'

'I can't imagine the Sikhs would have put up with that without a fight.'

'No, but once the local Muslim population saw that the Sikhs had their backs to the wall they would have mercilessly joined in the rout.'

'And what did Hawkswood hope to get out of it?'

'Once the Russians had taken control of the Punjab he expected to become Commissioner General of the Punjab.'

'It all sounds pretty far-fetched. Could it ever have succeeded?'

'Quite possibly. Remember that at the time, Britain was in a weak state with few allies who would have been willing or able to help.'

'So what Hawkswood was planning was essentially treason.'

'Correct.'

'He really did sound deranged. How was it all uncovered?'

'By sheer luck as it happens.'

'He obviously knew what he was doing was political dynamite so took the papers with him almost everywhere he went. Even when he came to Kushnapur for the tiger *shikar.*'

'But they should have been safe enough whilst he was in the palace?'

'Under normal circumstances, yes, but Wantilla and Mahavir were also staying at the palace for the *shikar.* They must have had their suspicions about Hawkswood so they had someone steal his briefcase whilst he was out. Their chap was disturbed by a palace servant and dropped the briefcase in the corridor. The servant gathered up the papers and took them to the *mistri,* who immediately went to my father.'

'And what was their content?'

'Letters from the Russians and the detailed plan to be implemented.'

'What did he do?'

'Nothing, well apart from replacing the papers and returning the briefcase to Hawkswood's room.'

Rindi leaned back in the large leather chair and scanned the room to make sure no one was eaves-dropping on their conversation. He flagged down the steward and ordered a *burra peg* for Adam and a glass of tonic water for himself.

'Surely it would have been better to hand the information over to the police or the British authorities?'

'That was certainly his first thought but the letters inferred that father had agreed to go along with the plan. There was a good chance that he would be implicated in the plot.'

'What about that Resident fellow? He knows your father well enough.'

'Yes, but he was also an old friend of Sir Arthur's and an Indian trying to contradict the word of an English establishment figure was not a risk he was prepared to take.'

'Why did Hawkswood even think your father would be party to something like this?'

'We can only speculate but I don't think he ever intended to let him in on the actual plot. He knew there was no love lost between father and Mahavir so maybe he thought he could win father's favour by telling him that his cousin was plotting with the *Swaraj* politicians.'

Adam looked bemused and took a long swig of his whisky.

'Before he went off the rails Hawkswood had always been a decent sort of chap, otherwise father would never have invited him to the shoot, and mother got on well with Lady Hawkswood.'

'But it's a big leap from there to using Kushnapur as a base for an invasion.'

'I agree and those blanks in the plot will remain a mystery, but suffice it to say that father thought he needed to take the matter into his own hands.'

'And the *shikar* provided the ideal opportunity?'

'Yes and as fortune would have it the Maharajah of Khizapura thought <u>he</u> was responsible for shooting Sir Arthur.'

'I still don't know how you would not know if you had shot someone.'

'To be honest there was so much confusion at the time that anyone could have shot him. As you have experienced when there is a tiger on the loose rational behaviour is in short supply.'

'But how did Wantilla find out?'

'Hawkswood and Khizapura were on one elephant and Wantilla was with father on another. The only two people who knew what had really happened were Wantilla and my father.'

'And he thinks he can blackmail you?'

Rindi drew heavily on his cigarette and exhaled strongly as if expelling pent up anger. 'I think we are one step ahead of him and I believe the Mahavir Debrahms have good reason to keep this quiet so the blackmail threat doesn't have much bite. But that doesn't stop Wantilla thinking he can get both Kafni and the *gaddi*.'

'To lay claim to the *gaddi* doesn't he have to possess the Lingam?'

'Yes, and you know how much chance there is of that happening.'

'Speaking of Hawkswood, did his daughter ever marry that Duffell fellow?'

'Yes, they married shortly before the war.'

'Has she produced the heir that the old Earl longed for?'

'No such luck. But then they didn't have a lot of opportunity. Soon after the wedding, his regiment was posted to Egypt and she stayed behind in England. I don't think there is much love lost between them and it wouldn't surprise me if Wantilla isn't still lurking in the background.'

Rindi looked exhausted. 'Now my friend I think it's time we both got some sleep.'

'Yes, good idea. By the way I thought you were meant to be

convalescing with your aunt?'

'That was just a smokescreen, my uncle has booked us in here for the next two nights.'

'I'd like to meet your aunt sometime.'

'She is wonderful but she would have mothered us relentlessly given half a chance. I was conscious that we were short for time. Now tomorrow I suggest you go along to the Bengal Club, and also the Tollygunge Club. You should find some good material there for your "duck shoving".'

'What d'you mean, *you*. Aren't you coming?'

'No, they don't allow Indians into those clubs.'

Adam shook his head in disbelief. 'How absurd. So how will I get into them if I am not with a member?'

'Serving British officers can get the club secretary to sign them in.'

'Don't worry, old boy, there are other clubs and plenty of interesting places we can go to together. Anyway, whilst you are doing that, I want to visit some Indian chums at Dum-Dum and Barrackpur, and then we can explore some of the more interesting bits of the city.'

CHAPTER TWENTY ONE

New Delhi, May 1943.

Adam returned to Delhi with enough information to satisfy the General and having had a very enlightening few days with Rindi. Listening to Rindi's reports of his time in Burma and hearing the different views of officers from other regiments had given him a new perspective on the war and he now wanted to be more involved.

His last correspondence with Bob Mercer had made it clear that he would like to return to the regiment. The response had been longer in coming than he had expected but brought good news when it came. Part of the delay was explained by the surprising news that the battalion had moved to Patna, more than a thousand miles from Rawalpindi and that Major Williams was in hospital at base, nursing a broken leg. He had been taking part in a practice river crossing in an assault boat at Bankipore, when one of the underwater detonations had exploded much closer than planned. It would be many weeks before he would be fit enough to return to the battalion, let alone go into active training.

The upshot was that Bob Mercer was offering Williams's post as Company Commander to Adam with the rank of acting major. His only reservation about re-joining the battalion had now been removed. How soon it would be before he moved would now be up to the General. Three weeks later Brigadier Stevenson called him into his office.

'It seems that Colonel Mercer would like to have you back, and if I'm not mistaken there's promotion in the wind. I think the General will be sad to see you go.'

The General did not openly express this sentiment but thanked Adam for his support and with a twinkle in his eye said. 'No doubt I will be seeing you again before long.'

Adam wondered what the future held for him and Sarah. Having been at first upset to find that she was the General's daughter he had enjoyed how their relationship had developed and grown to appreciate her family. With his posting orders in his pocket, and a new crown on his shoulder, he left Delhi on the Benares night express with mixed feelings. It was the end of a good chapter in his life but he felt excited at the prospect of what lay ahead.

The following morning, there was an hour's stop at Lucknow where Spencers served breakfast. Adam took a stroll through what the Army described as the "City of a Thousand Barbers". With its seething crowds swarming around the railway station, the persistent poverty was starkly evident. Having many children, preferably boys, was looked upon as providing more sources of income for a family and an insurance against old age. Girls, however, presented a crushing burden for poor families who were unable to afford their dowries, a fact that sometimes led to the tragedy of female infanticide. Poverty, caste and religion limited the choice of husbands to a succession of close relatives, producing inbreeding and an inherited indolence that the enervating climate would only serve to exacerbate. Adam found it difficult to reconcile the extreme wealth of the salute princes he had met in Calcutta with this crippling level of destitution. Could there ever be a workable solution?

On arrival at Patna, he found the regiment under canvas. Swapping his comfortable room at HQ for a sparsely equipped tent was the reality check he needed. It was good to be serving under Bob Mercer again.

Sometimes at night as Adam lay under his mosquito net reading by the light of a hurricane lamp he would think of the three people in India with whom he was most closely connected: Rindi, Sarah, and Kafni. They were now all far away. Rindi, seven hundred miles to the northwest; Sarah, a thousand miles away in Poona, and Kafni, where was she? Somewhere in the Himalayas nursing a baby: their son; his son; a secret which could not even be revealed to the boy himself.

As the rains tapered off there was an air of expectancy that Adam's regiment would soon be called into action. The first move came towards the end of November when they were sent by train to the Burmese border to take part in the Malaya Peninsula offensive. By Christmas they had heavily engaged the Japanese. Operational conditions were appalling. It was the beginning of a long and bloody jungle campaign.

Near the northeast border of India on the lower slopes of the Barail Range, at a height of 4,800 feet, lay the small town of Kohima. It lay on an important strategic route for an advance into northern India. As the eagle flew, it was fifty miles to the Burma border but by the only road it was 160 miles. Manipur Road, the railhead for the Burma front, was 46 miles back, along a tortuous mountain route. Much of it single track, rising to 4,000 feet and surrounded by steaming jungle. Huge trees encrusted with a moss-like growth were embraced by vigorous creepers. The area averaged 250 inches of rainfall a year and the ground was sodden. Although rainfall since December had been down to its minimum, operating conditions were still atrocious in January.

Miserable though it was, there was a great difference from the last time they had faced the Japanese. They were now prepared and highly trained. It was here, as a company commander, that Adam learnt the value of carefully planned operational tactics. The garrison at Kohima were in desperate need of help.

On 20th January the Japs broke through and overran the divisional hospital and it was there that Adam witnessed the extent of their inhumanity. They moved into the hospital, killed all the patients and shot the doctors. They made the British hospital orderlies carry the Japanese wounded back to their own lines. Then having carried out their task these medical orderlies were killed in cold blood, in complete defiance of the protection afforded them under the Geneva Convention.

The battle for Kohima raged throughout March and April. As Adam's Brigade advanced with bloody engagements, two of his officers and six men were killed and several wounded.

On 18th April they moved forward for the final relief of the Kohima garrison. The troops there were exhausted. Soaked by the incessant rain, the jungle-covered mountains were slippery and treacherous, and there were frequent floods and landslides. The town of Kohima itself was not taken until mid-May.

By June, the monsoon was again raging; battlefields were knee-deep in mud. It took hours to cover even short distances of only a few miles and Adam thought of what his father had had to endure on the Western Front. The Japs were exhausted and starving; most of them dying of hunger. They came across one soldier chewing seeds and grass. He was so weak that he appeared oblivious to Adam's approach. He stopped a few yards short of him, with his service revolver ready to fire. As he caught sight of Adam he fumbled in his ammunition pouch and withdrew a hand grenade. Adam took cover expecting the grenade to come his way. Seconds later he heard it explode. This was the first of many incidents of the Japanese committing suicide rather than be captured.

Beyond Kushnapur

Adam's company travelled south from Kohima along the single-track road between Mao and Maram. The route was reported clear of active Japanese units, but they were still on the lookout for stragglers. Ahead, they saw three bodies lying on a sloping bank beside the road and he instructed his driver to slow down to see if they were still alive. As they passed, one of the Japs curled-up and rolled in front of the vehicle. There was a double explosion. One of the tracks of their Bren Carrier was blown off and the vehicle turned over. Adam vaguely recalled being slid from a stretcher into a field ambulance before he blacked out. He had suffered a fractured femur. As soon as his bones were set in plaster, he and the other wounded were loaded onto a hospital train and shipped well away from the battle zone. After a week in a base hospital in Lucknow he was moved to an Army General Hospital in Delhi to make way for more urgent casualties.

Adam didn't much like being in bed and at every opportunity he swung his one good leg off the bed and with the help of the old wooden crutch they had given him he would manoeuvre himself up and down the ward. The formidable staff nurse appeared unexpectedly beside him.

'Now Major Cullworthy that's quite enough exercise for one day. Shall we get you back into bed?'

'Well if you insist.'

'I do and as a reward I am allowing you to have two visitors outside visiting hours.' Her admonishing look had changed to a mischievous smile.

Adam lay back in bed wondering who might even be aware that he was in hospital. He heard them before he saw them and his heart leapt with joy. Walking towards him were Sarah and Rindi. She looking radiant and sexy in her uniform. Adam always liked the way the edge of her well fitted jacket splayed just above her hips emphasising her fine curves. Rindi had recovered his neat muscular frame and allowed Sarah to kiss Adam before he grabbed his hand with both of his.

'I can't believe this. I didn't even know you knew each other let alone knew where I was.'

'Well, your Sarah is quite resourceful. Not only did she find out where you were but she telephoned me in Ambala and told me to meet her in New Delhi so that we could arrive at the hospital together.'

'I must confess I asked Rindi to come because I was afraid you had been badly shot-up and that I might need some moral support.'

The two hours they spent with Adam flew by and he knew they

would have to return to their duties almost immediately. It was strange to have Sarah sit on the side of the bed holding his hand whilst Rindi looked on inquisitively. Adam longed to hug her and run his fingers through her hair and just to smell the scent on her soft neck. But that would have been awkward for all of them.

'How long are you both in Delhi for?'

'I have to return to Poona tomorrow morning I'm afraid, darling.' It was strange to hear her call him darling and Rindi's glance at Adam had more meaning in it than anything he might have said. Adam was relieved that Sarah and Rindi had finally met and any apprehensions he may have had now seemed inconsequential.

Rindi was glad to see Sarah and Adam's mutual affection for each other. In a strange way it made him feel less uncomfortable about his secret affair with Tina, although he didn't feel he was any closer to telling Adam about it.

'I also have to be back within twenty-four hours.'Rindi said. 'But I am sure you two would like some time alone.'

'Lovely idea, but I see matron approaching so it looks like our time is up.'

After a further three weeks in hospital the Medical Officer told Adam that he was to be given two week's sick leave to recuperate at Kasanli, a convalescent centre in the mountains, about forty miles from Simla. On hearing this news Rindi had a different idea.

'Why go up to Kasanli, when you could spend your leave in greater comfort in Kushnapur?'

'That does sound much more appealing. Would your parents mind?'

'Quite the contrary. I think they would like to see you soon.'

'All is well I hope?' said Adam responding to the "soon" part of Rindi's statement.

'Absolutely. All is fine with the family.'

'Any chance of your joining me up there?'

'Not a hope. Fortescue has been very good with weekend passes but I know he can't spare me for longer. But don't worry; everything will be laid on for you, just telephone to let me know if you have managed to swing it with the Medical Officer. You know the form now. The driver will be there to meet you.' He paused and smiled. 'Oh, and by the way, you may find that Kafni will be there.'

September 1944, Kushnapur.

For weeks Adam had been trapped in the hospital with only the rotating overhead fan to take the edge off the blistering heat so it was a great relief to be heading back into the hills. On a journey of less than four hours, it did not seem worth bedding down in a sleeper, even if he could have got one. He had become accustomed to these long train journeys, they gave him time to reflect.

It seemed an age since Sarah and Rindi had visited him in hospital. It had all ended so quickly. He would have loved to have known what they both had thought of each other on first meeting. Sarah had written to him and jested that she could see why he had not introduced such a handsome devil to her before but Adam knew she had always seen Rindi as competing for his time. Rindi had not written and given that he was at pains to discourage any ongoing relationship between his friend and Kafni, Adam found it curious that he was sending him back to Kushnapur at a time when he knew she would be there.

Shortly before eleven the train came to a jerky halt at Meerut City Station. Adam peered out of the window and saw in odd dark corners of the platform what looked like bundles of rags but were in fact people, struggling to find temporary respite from the unending task of daily survival. The war had done little to mitigate their plight.

Adam thought about the *Swaraj* and their desire to rid India of the British. Sitting in his First Class compartment, he wondered how the Indians would have fared in the absence of the British. The life of each of these people was principally dictated by the accident of their birth, which could have made them the son of a maharajah or a low caste *candela*. The remarkable thing was that most of them seemed to accept their position without rancour or resentment, accepting as a favour any benefits that were scattered their way.

After a thousand years of Muslim domination Indians had grown accustomed to absolute rule, and were surprised to find the British or *"Angrez Log"*, as they called them, actually consulting the people to get their opinion. The British expected and had received, acknowledgement of their authority, and Indians had universally benefitted from the law and order, irrigation canals, roads, bridges, railways and communications, and the schools and hospitals that the British had provided. But now they were hungry for power and self-rule and any gratitude which may have existed had turned to bitter resentment of their presence. How, Adam wondered, could such a massive change be achieved without disastrous consequences?

Hissing steam, the train came to a halt at Saharanpur Station. Adam opened the window and scanned the platform to see if anyone had been sent to meet him. A well-dressed Indian conspicuous by his attire was looking at him intently and then when Adam returned his stare he slipped quickly into a doorway. There was something disturbing about the way he had been looking at Adam and about the way he had hastily disappeared.

Adam opened the compartment door and had barely alighted on the platform when a bearer quickly relieved him of his bags. As they made their way to the car Adam searched the crowd for the man on the platform. He couldn't see him and wondered if he had imagined this mystery figure.

Once in the comfort of the Rolls Royce he took advantage of a pillow that had been provided and dozed off. He must have slept for about three hours because when he opened his eyes dawn was breaking. During the three months of the monsoon, the countryside had blossomed into life. The night's rain had endowed the air with a wonderful freshness. It had been winter on his first visit to Kushnapur and spring on his second. Now it was late summer, and whilst appreciably cooler than Delhi, the temperature was still the wrong side of comfortable.

Adam sat contentedly absorbing the scenery; happy in anticipation of what lay ahead. He would have remained so, had he not thought about the man on the platform and then remembered a remark Rindi had made on the telephone. 'It's unlikely that you would wish to do so, but don't attempt to contact Wantilla again whilst you're in Delhi. Certainly he must not know that you're visiting the palace. He doesn't know that Kafni will be returning to Kushnapur. He's been told that she's been sent to a place of safety whilst there is the threat of a Japanese invasion.'

As they approached the outskirts of Kushnapur City, Adam was a little puzzled that the chauffeur did not turn off the main road and take the normal route to the palace. He tapped the glass partition and the car slowed down. The bearer beside the chauffeur then slid back the glass and asked, 'Yes, major-sahib?'

'Why are we not going the usual way?'

'The dewan-sahib is ordering that major-sahib is coming by rajmarg of Resident-sahib.' So that was it. He was being driven to the other side of the city and would arrive by the avenue used only by the British Resident, visiting princes and dignitaries. It was far less convenient, had no road access to the rest of the palace lands and involved a climb up the wide flight of one hundred-and-one stone steps.

The Rolls Royce came smoothly to a halt at the foot of the steps. Ten sepoys in Kushnapur Guards' uniform lined the bottom five steps, and a sergeant came forward, opened the car door and saluted.

This was an impressive reception but given that his leg was still causing him a certain discomfort, he could have done without the steps to climb. When he reached the flagstone landing at the halfway mark, he looked up and saw the maharajah himself descending the steps towards him. The sergeant, who had been following, asked him to wait. He then stopped and drew himself to attention. As the maharajah reached Adam he also stood to attention and saluted him.

'Adam, how honoured we are to have you visit us again. I am sorry you've been put through this ritual when you are obviously still being troubled by that wound.'

'No it's a great honour, Sir, thank you.'

'I have arranged for a *dhooly* to carry you the rest of the way to the palace.'

Perhaps because Rindi was not at the palace, the maharajah had allocated his senior bearer to attend to Adam's needs. He was afforded every comfort and spent much of the first day asleep. In the morning he went down to the pool to swim partly because this was a good way to strengthen his leg but also secretly hoping he might meet Kafni there. Although her parents confirmed she had arrived in *purdah* the night before they told Adam she would not be available to see him for a few days. There was a strangely austere atmosphere in the palace. The absence of Rindi and the seclusion of Kafni made the palace feel empty and joyless. On the second evening he dined with the maharajah and the maharani.

'How is your leg today, Adam?' the maharani enquired with genuine concern.

'Much improved thank you, your highness,' he exaggerated.

'Please no need for such formality when we are together in private.'

'It must have been ghastly for you in the Burmese jungle.' The maharajah said, a deep frown furrowing his brow.

'We were very fortunate. It was the soldiers in the first Burma campaign who really suffered.'

'India owes a debt of gratitude to your Army. If the Japanese had invaded India, it would have been one of the most barbaric occupations in history.'

'You're right about that, Sir.'

'Unfortunately there are some political activists who would still like to see them succeed,' Adam noticed him grip the arms of his chair.

He looked older and the sparkle was missing from his eyes.

'Your Fourteenth Army has done so well,' said the maharani moving the subject on.

'The Indian regiments also did magnificently,' Adam said with conviction, 'they deserve great credit and I suspect they will get their fair share of bravery medals.'

'Did you hear that Kafni's husband is to receive a posthumous MC?'

'No, I hadn't but Rindi said he had been very courageous and by the way my condolences, it must have been a terrible shock to you all.'

'Yes, it was although we had only met him twice before they were married,' the maharani admitted.

Adam could sense their anxiety and knew how difficult it must be to know that their only son was facing similar dangers.

'But Adam we gather you have also been gazetted for a bar to your MC for your action in the Burma campaign.'

'There were many others in the Regiment more worthy of the award.'

'Your modesty does you credit.' The Maharajah drew a deep breath. 'We will be ever grateful to you, Adam, for what you have done for us and I'm only sorry that you cannot be part of our family.'

Adam found this matter of fact statement tortuous. He longed to ask about his son but felt it was not his place to bring up the subject. The uncomfortable silence which followed was broken by the maharajah standing up. 'Would you please excuse me? I need to prepare for a meeting in the morning.' Adam stood up and bid him good night. After the maharajah had left the maharani diffused the tension of the moment. 'Would you like more coffee, Adam?'

'Yes, please.' The *khitmagar* stepped forward to oblige.

'Now you will be pleased to hear that Kafni will be ready to meet with you tomorrow. We will send someone to fetch you at around eleven.'

The refilled cup had barely touched Adam's lips when the maharajah returned, raising his hand to stop Adam getting up again. He seemed a little agitated as he spoke. 'I must apologise, Adam, something unexpected has arisen. Sir Iain Macdonald, the British Resident has asked to come and see me the day after tomorrow. I'm afraid this means that Kafni must return to Kushnapur Lodge before his visit. It's unlikely that he would wish to pay his compliments to her, but, if he does ask, I want to be able to say that she is not in the palace.'

This puzzled Adam but he knew from Rindi how important the Resident was in the scheme of things and imagined that this was unlikely to be a social call.

'I understand, Sir. Is my being here an inconvenience?'

'Strictly speaking, no, but MacDonald is a wily old bird and little eludes him. Under the circumstances, I would appreciate you remaining in the private guest wing during his visit. Sorry, old chap.'

His attempt at an idiom of cordiality was not entirely successful, but Adam knew he was sincere and concerned that nothing should go awry.

The following morning Mandira came to collect Adam and he was so pleased to see her he felt like embracing her but knew how inappropriate that would be. She took him to the maharani's quarters and left him sitting on his own on one of the large sofas.

It was over two years since he had seen Kafni and he wondered how it would be between them. Before he had left she had shown a measured indifference towards him that he had never been able to reconcile with the passionate hours they had spent together. So much had happened in both their lives in the intervening years, particularly in hers. She had been married, widowed and had a child in that time. Any one of these events could have changed her outlook on life.

He heard her voice before he saw her and his heart leapt. The door opened and there she stood radiant in the diffused light. She strode towards him her pace just slow enough to retain dignity but the strength of her embrace displayed unreserved joy.

'Adam, how wonderful to see you. How is your injury?' She looked down, not knowing which leg had been fractured.

'I'm fine now but how are you? I am so sorry to hear about your husband- I mean him being killed like that. How traumatic for you.'

'Yes, it was very sad but as you probably realise I hardly knew him at all.'

'And may I ask how little Pratap is getting on?'

'You may indeed.'

At that moment Adam heard the sound of small feet running

down the passage way. 'Mama, where is my tiger?' He ran across the room and into Kafni's arms. Looking up at her he said in a quieter voice 'Mama I can't find tiger anywhere.'

She held both his hands and turned him to face Adam. 'Now Pratap I would like you to meet Major Cullworthy who is an old friend of your Uncle Rindi.'

Adam had not prepared himself to meet Pratap. Somehow he imagined he would be kept out of sight or might even have still been up at the winter Bhavan. There standing before him was the most beautiful little boy he had ever seen. He had the Debrahm eyes, huge and inquisitive, his hair was fairer than his mothers and he had a wonderful honey brown complexion. What joy this moment brought to him and glancing at Kafni he beamed with pride and love.

'As Major Cullworthy is a very special friend of the family and has a sore leg you had better give him a hug.'

With complete absence of self-consciousness Pratap walked over and gave Adam a spontaneous hug.

'So what is this tiger you have lost? Not a real one I hope.' Adam asked in jest.

Pratap did not answer and turning he ran back and buried himself in the skirts of Kafni's sari.

'Now if you are very nice to her Mandira might help you find your tiger.'

Mandira scooped him up and walked towards the door. Pratap's little face peeped over her shoulder and gave Adam one last curious look.

In accordance with her father's instructions Kafni moved to Kushnapur Lodge for the period covering Sir Iain's visit. Adam was also confined to the guest wing and so they were unable to meet again for a further two days. Once she had returned to the palace Adam was able to visit her regularly, using the secret door and private corridors.

She was not the shy virgin of their first meeting, nor was she the enthusiastic princess, anxious to fulfil her obligations to the dynasty, of their second encounter. It seemed miraculous to Adam that she said she loved him but maybe this was her way of making their difficult task easier to bear. Whenever he left her he pretended that it was all a dream; that there could be no relationship so why torture himself unnecessarily. He imagined that her upbringing and traditions enabled her to cut off emotionally. But every time they met again there was this spark; a strong physical attraction and a natural bond between them. This time it was different; she was a mature young woman and more importantly a mother. Whilst Pratap was now her priority she treated Adam with the devotion of a loving wife. It felt deceitful towards Kafni's parents when they made love. He had made his way to her apartment with the normal discretion but this time it needed to be their secret alone. As far as her parents were concerned their arrangement was completed and they would not countenance further association. But the embers were hot and it took little to rekindle the flames of passion; only this time they were at pains to prevent her conceiving again.

Adam knew well enough that this intimate relationship was ephemeral and that he must treasure those precious enchanted hours together. Although he could never be her husband or Pratap's acknowledged father, these days gave him a real sense of what it must be like to be a husband and a father and to have a family of one's own.

Yet, despite the intimacies they experienced, Adam was aware of a chasm between them. Kafni had an indefinable aura and grace which served to remind him that she was a princess. He would sometimes look in wonderment at this beautiful woman and realise how deeply privileged he was to have been chosen to mate with her. The only bridge to reality was the knowledge that she was the sister of Rindi whose close affinity had developed out of the many years of their friendship.

As Adam lay beside her listening to her soothing voice he felt the urge to ask her the question he had suppressed for so long.

'Kafni, what would you say if I asked you to be my wife?'

Having spoken it he at once regretted it. He knew the answer and feared by unsettling her it could spoil their last hours together.

'My darling, do not torment yourself with such thoughts. You know it is impossible.'

'But what will become of you? You cannot remain a widow for ever.'

'My parents will no doubt find someone for me to marry. I may even, in time, have to accept that I may become Wantilla's second wife.'

Adam could hardly bring himself to speak. 'Surely you cannot be serious?'

'You know already that his family has asked for my betrothal to him and that my father has always refused. We may now have no choice. As a widow my options are limited. Wantilla doesn't know I was married yet or that I have a child or that my husband is now dead. All of these things will make it more likely that I will have to accept marriage to him and he will know that, when he finds out.'

Adam could not believe that with everything they knew about Wantilla and his family that they would resign themselves to this fate. Why would he be acceptable and Adam not?

'These are matters for parents and families. It must be difficult for you to understand the ways and customs of Hindu life. I am sure you have your own customs and social constraints on who you marry.'

'Yes, within reason, but seldom would parents subject their daughter to a life of misery for the sake of tradition and family ties.'

'Are you sure? And how welcome would I be to your family?' she asked.

'They would love you.'

'You say that but I suspect it would come as quite a shock.'

She was right. As much as Adam's parents liked Rindi they would not expect their son to marry an Indian woman, however well-bred she might be.

'Wantilla is obsessed with you.'

'The more unattainable I appear, the more he pursues me. And for him the uniting of our two families would have great advantages. His family have enormous wealth, and we have the *gaddi*.'

'Of course, the throne.'

'If Wantilla knew about you and me and Pratap all our lives would be in danger. Our greatest fear is that something might happen to Rindi and then the gaddi would end up with Wantilla.'

'Surely it would go to Jardeeson?'

'Yes, assuming he outlives my father, but as you know he has no children. We know who we are dealing with, Adam, and sometimes it is wise to keep close to your enemies.'

'Whoever succeeds to the *gaddi* it is important that our family ensures that Pratap's child carries on the bloodline. You have done our family a great service.'

Kafni could see how distressed this conversation had made Adam and she drew him to her, 'Whatever happens I will always love you.'

For the first time he understood the danger that Rindi, Kafni and Pratap were exposed to. With every move he made thereafter, he would have to exercise caution and would constantly find himself looking for potential informers, spies and poisoners among the Palace staff. Perhaps his fears were exaggerated, but he was not prepared to take any risks.

CHAPTER TWENTY TWO

Poona, October 1944.

When Adam reported to GHQ, he learnt that his post in the battalion had been filled and that he was being sent to Poona. Bob Mercer had written explaining that the brigade commander had insisted that the battalion was quickly made up to strength and that it had not been possible for him to keep his post open. However, as he was regular army, he should be able to re-join the battalion at a later date. His disappointment was mollified by the thought that with Delhi temperatures still in the nineties, Poona would be at a cooler altitude. And, of course, Sarah would be there.

It was more than three years since he had travelled out to India with her and there was a part of him that rather hoped she had acquired a new admirer during her time in Poona. This was probably to assuage his guilt at having spent such a blissful ten days with Kafni. As they were so different in so many ways and geographically miles apart he found it remarkably easy to compartmentalise these two relationships and in his own mind he justified it by the fact that he knew there was no future with Kafni.

Sarah was now Commandant of a W.A.C. I. training group, with the rank of chief commander, equivalent to lieutenant colonel, and Adam had again to go through the charade of saluting her and addressing her as "ma'am." In private they quickly adjusted to being lovers again and Adam was surprised to find Sarah rather more prone to bouts of jealousy.

'Adam, what the devil do you do with yourself when I'm not around?'

'Well, I have to confess I found the nurses in the hospital rather distracting.'

'I bet you did, and did you submit to those distractions?'

Adam gave her a look of mild reproof as if to say he had no intention of answering such a provocative question.

'What about the Indian girls? Some of our Anglo-Indian

Wackeyes are rather beautiful. And what about Rindi's sisters if they are anything like as good looking as him?'

Adam knew she was half-teasing and half-serious. He couldn't remember telling her that Rindi had sisters so he took this for a well judged speculative comment and avoided being drawn on the subject.

'It's all a different world up there. Wonderful in many ways but far removed from reality. The women lead a very protected existence and they don't really fraternise much with the men. Adam felt that that was at least partially true.'

After a month in Poona, Adam was told he had been selected to join a small group of officers being sent to advise the Adjutant-General's Branch at the War Office in London. The idea had arisen out of an incident during a meeting at S.E.A.C. HQ in Delhi when one of Mountbatten's senior staff officers had exploded in frustration, 'Don't those silly bastards at "War Box" understand our situation?' An American major-general who had been present relayed the remark to London. It was passed on to Churchill who promptly issued orders for something to be done about it. The group of eight, mainly half-colonels and majors who had seen front line experience in the Burma campaign and knew the conditions was rapidly pulled together.

Those who had not seen England or their families for years were delighted to be chosen, Adam had more mixed feelings.He was leaving behind so much of the life and people who had become an important part of him. His initial reluctance to accept the posting had been abruptly dismissed by Command Headquarters. Ironically he was almost prevented from leaving India for a quite different reason.

He had been given a week's local leave to wind up his personal affairs in India and to settle any outstanding financial obligations, a matter the Army took very seriously. Three days before he was due to leave a signal was brought to him at breakfast. It read:

"MAJOR DEBRAHM WISHES MEET YOU AT OFFICERS' CLUB POONA
TUESDAY 30 NOV 20.00 HOURS" "TAZA"

Adam was puzzled and delighted. The 30th was that very evening. This short notice could the only mean one thing: that Rindi had received his anticipated promotion and was coming to Poona to say farewell. He had written to Adam a few days earlier, when he heard that he would be leaving India, and said he would try to get away to see him. Now it seemed that was happening.

Adam contacted the signals' duty sergeant to see if he could tell him anything further, but all he could say was that the message had originated in Delhi. In the past they had both used the expression "TAZA", meaning "friend", to sign off their letters and presumably Rindi felt a telegram would be quicker via Delhi than from Ambala.

Adam rang Sarah to give her the good news and asked her to join them for dinner. Sarah and Adam arrived at the Club at 7.30 p.m. and ordered drinks in the Members bar. By 8.30 they were on their third round and had been joined by the two officers from his Unit. They were beginning to wonder what might have happened to Rindi when a steward delivered Adam the message that there was someone asking to see him in the club foyer.

Adam found a well-dressed Indian waiting for him. 'Major Cullworthy-sahib?'

He handed Adam a folded sheet of Club notepaper on which was pencilled in block letters:

MUST SEE YOU PRIVATELY BEFORE JOINING THE OTHERS.

'Is this from Major Debrahm?'

'Indeed, Sir. You will come with me to see him please.'

Adam was keen to see Rindi, and slightly anxious as to what news he might have that could not be discussed in the club. Perhaps it concerned Kafni. He followed the Indian down the steps and along the Club drive. Adjacent to the entrance, near the road was a bungalow, which he knew was occupied by a retired Colonel Clarke. The place was in darkness and in the drive of the bungalow was a locally registered, large black American Ford sedan. The Indian stopped and opened one of the rear doors.

'By car?' Adam asked. 'If Major Debrahm is so near, why can't we walk? If it's a long way, I must go and tell my friends.'

'Is not far, sahib, but easier for major-sahib to talk in car.'

Adam got into the back seat of the spacious saloon. The Indian took the wheel, backed rapidly out of the drive and sped off. After about a mile, Adam became irritated.

'Where the devil are we going? You said it wasn't far.'

'We are coming there just now, Major-sahib.' A few moments later they came to a halt just off the road, beside a large banyan tree. The driver switched off the headlights and kept the engine running.

Beyond Kushnapur

The two of them must have approached the car from behind because the first thing Adam knew was the simultaneous opening of the front and rear doors. Someone in army officer's uniform slipped into the front seat beside the driver and in the faint glimmer of the sidelights, Adam caught sight of a major's crown on his shoulder. From behind the shape looked familiar but was not that of Rindi. His attention was diverted by the hulk of a man thrusting himself against him in the back seat. The headlights were switched on, the doors slammed and the car roared away.

He then recognised the distinctive shape of Wantilla in the front seat who half turned to face him. Adam's anger erupted and he reached out to grab his collar.

'What the bloody hell's going on? Where's Rindi?'

He felt a sharp stab of pain in his arm as the brute beside him chopped at his forearm forcing Adam to release his grip on Wantilla's collar.

'That nasty temper will get you into a lot of trouble, Cullworthy. I've warned you about that before. Now, unless you want my bearer to break your jaw and re-shape your smug face, I want some answers.'

'You'll never get away with this you swine! What have you done with Rindi?'

'You may well ask. I knew you could not resist a request from your pet poodle *rajkumar*. You'll have to wait a long time for an answer to your question. I want to talk about something quite different.' His tone, as usual, was obnoxious, but this time he sounded angry. 'I won't sod around, Cullworthy. Exactly *what* were you doing at Kushnapur Palace last month?'

'It's none of your business and anyway who told you I was there?'

'I have my sources.'

'That creepy nephew of yours no doubt.'

'The Resident himself if you must know.'

'Highly unlikely, he wouldn't have time for the likes of you Wantilla.'

'Well your wrong there, my friend. He was there to discuss our claim to the *gaddi*.'

So that was what had made the maharajah so anxious.

'I imagine he gave that idea short shrift.'

'On the contrary, Sir Iain seemed rather keen on our proposition that we should unite the families by my marrying Princess Kafni.'

'That will never happen and you know it.'

'I think it will. Amazing what a little financial inducement can do.'

'I doubt very much that the Resident would be susceptible to your corrupt ways, Wantilla.'

'We'll see about that, but in the meantime we can do without some jumped up British officer upsetting the applecart. Now stop buggering around and tell me why you were at the Palace. What regimental bullshit did you give McDonald?'

Obviously the meeting had not gone as smoothly as Wantilla was making out. Their mission had been spiked by Rindi's father and now they were looking for a scapegoat. Adam was relieved that so far there was no mention of Kafni. The car was now travelling at speed and his mind was taxed with thoughts of how he might extract himself from this dangerous situation.

'I was convalescing at the palace after I left hospital if you must know. So you can forget your conspiracy theories.'

'That's a likely story. Who invited you? the Maharajah? Or was it my cousin angling for promotion from one of your cronies? You have never been up there without him before, so you probably wormed your way in hoping to get a glimpse of the princesses. Weren't you disappointed that they were not there to see your tin pot medal?

Adam did not respond but was comforted that Wantilla obviously didn't know that Kafni had been there at the time.

'Well, Cullworthy, whatever your reason for being at the Palace, I don't like it. Your days of interfering are over.'

With the windows closed Adam found atmosphere in the car increasingly oppressive. Stale sweat, halitosis and Wantilla's distinctive musky sweet hair lotion combined to produce an unbearable clawing odour.

'What the hell are you up to, Wantilla? Stop this fucking game and take me back to the Club. Now!'

'Not until you tell me *exactly* what you said to that pompous prick McDonald.'

'For God's sake I've never even met the man.'

'I can see we aren't going to get much out of you so I think we'll take you on a little trip to where the vultures will quickly dispose of one extra corpse.'

Adam's mind flashed back to a day trip he and Sarah had taken to Kharakvasla Lake, about twelve miles from Poona. It would be an ideal place to dump a body. Three or four corpses floated down the river and into that lake every week.

They had now left the cantonment and the chance of signalling a passing vehicle became less likely, even if he could have got the window open. Wantilla had timed his plan well. They travelled on south in the direction of Satara and then turned west on the road to Lake Mulshi. Perhaps this was their destination. No, that would be too far. His fears were confirmed when the car swung off on to the Kharakvasla Road.

He was thinking fast; even his training in unarmed combat would do little to protect him from the gorilla sitting beside him.

'I'll give you one last chance to tell me why you were at the palace, you meddlesome bastard.'

As he spoke, they were passing through the narrow street of a village and still travelling at high speed. Frequent blasts of the horn cleared bicyclists out of the way. Adrenalin was now fuelling Adam's senses but he could see no way out. Then in the distance the headlights picked up a white Brahmin bull. This could be his chance but the opportunity would be brief. He prayed that the driver was a Hindu and not a Muslim. To avoid the bull, the driver would have to pull over and steer carefully past the houses and telegraph poles.

As they approached the bull they were still at a good speed but he knew the driver would have to slow down to avoid a collision. Sensing that their attention was now on the bull, Adam clenched his fist. Then, with all the force he could muster, he drove the sharpest part of his knuckles hard into the driver's temple. The driver yelled out in pain and his head jerked to one side as he lost control of the car.

The hubbub of voices ebbed and flowed and Adam felt suffocated by the encroaching crowd. He was aware of being carried by three Indians wearing white dhotis. In their enthusiasm they seemed to disregard the fact that he was a human in a delicate condition. He felt himself pulled in all directions with apparent disregard to any injuries. He heard a voice in the background speaking in English with some attempt at authority. 'Lay sahib down flat, we must check if he is being injured or having bones broken.' This instruction was obeyed somewhat abruptly and he found himself dumped on the ground with a torch flashing in his face. Seeing Adam's eyes open, the holder of the torch moved it to the side of his face, and in the reflection, Adam saw that it was an Indian policeman.

'Sahib has been in accident.' Then, more informatively, 'other major-sahib still in car.'

Raising his head to see what was going on, Adam felt a sharp pain above his left eye, and lifting his hand to his face to investigate found it covered in blood. His head must have struck some part of the car and the impact had knocked him out for a few minutes. A brief inspection confirmed that he was otherwise unhurt.

He put out his hand towards one of the Indians who helped him up. He was unsteady on his feet and took a few moments to orientate himself. Two or three Indians were carrying hurricane lamps and there must have been about fifty people swarming round the crashed car eager to see who was dead or injured. At least a dozen children, pushing each other to get as close as possible, were chattering and gesticulating.

Adam pushed his way through the crowd to the front of the car. There he found a second Indian Police constable shining his torch through the shattered windscreen. The car driver, oblivious of his lacerated hand, was struggling to force open the door with a spade. Wantilla's brute of a bearer had one eye closed and blood running from gashes on his face and hands. Despite his injuries he was working feverishly with a pick-head, in an attempt to lever back the metal fascia that was trapping his rich employer.

Through the glass shards of the broken windscreen Adam saw the bloody face of Wantilla. Half leaning across the car, just an inch or two from his face was the telegraph pole that had taken the full force of the impact. He was crushed against the contorted door and the splintered side window was clearly the source of his lacerations. His head was twisted to one side and one arm was wedged-in beside the steering column. He wasn't moving and his eyes were closed. Adam wondered if he might be dead.

Adam made his way round to where the two men were working to get him free.

'Has anyone checked that he is alive?'

The driver grunted but sounded unconvincing. Adam leant into the car and checked Wantilla's pulse. He was alive but unconscious.

He turned to the senior policeman. 'Has anyone sent for an ambulance?'

'*Han,* major-sahib. Ambulance coming from Poona Military Hospital.'

'Do they know someone is trapped in the car?'

'Fire engine is also coming, major-sahib.'

Adam calculated that that would take at least fifteen minutes. He felt he should stay until the emergency services arrived but he needed to tell Sarah where he was. 'Is there a telephone near here?'

'Not so near, sahib. Outside Post Office one mile away.'

'Then can you get me a taxi?'

'There is man in the village who has small taxi.'

'Can you please ask someone to bring him here? I need transport, urgently.' A five-rupee note quickly dispelled any hesitancy.

'Yes, I know the man and can get him here for major-sahib, *jaldi*.'

Wantilla's two henchmen were still working to get him out; an ambulance and fire crew were on their way, and for the moment there was nothing further he could do. Five minutes later the taxi arrived and took Adam to the telephone.

'What in God's name happened to you, Adam? Where did you disappear to?'

'Sorry, Sarah, I can't stop to explain now. Rindi's not coming tonight and I was abducted by his cousin.'

'Abducted! Where are you now?'

'Out by Kharakvasla Lake.'

'What on earth..?

'You may well ask but suffice it to say that I escaped and I'm OK, and once the ambulance has arrived I will be on my way back.'

'Ambulance? Adam, what is going on?'

Adam realised he was not making much sense and his telephone call would soon be interrupted by the operator.

'Don't worry, I will tell you all when I see you which should be within the hour. Carry on without me and make up some excuse. It's best to keep all this to yourself for the moment.'

By the time Adam returned to the accident, they were removing Wantilla from the wreck. He watched two orderlies lift him on to a stretcher and carry him to the ambulance. Someone was addressing Adam in English and he turned to see an R.A.M.C. Medical Corporal.

'Sir, I believe that you were travelling with the injured major and these two Indians?'

'That's right.'

'Is there anything you'd like to tell me about the accident, sir? I'll have to make a report.'

'The car swerved to avoid a bull and hit the telegraph pole and I can tell you that the major's name is Wantilla Debrahm.'

'Is he a friend of yours, Sir?'

'No, he's just an acquaintance.'

One of the Indian stretcher-bearers came up and saluted. 'Sir, the major is now conscious. He's trying to say something.'

The corporal turned to Adam. 'Would you like to speak to him, Sir?'

'Yes, I think I'd better.'

The interior of the ambulance was well lit, and as Adam climbed in, he saw Wantilla's bearer sitting morosely in one corner. Adam put his head down to Wantilla's face to listen. His eyes were closed and he was breathing heavily through his mouth.

'Wantilla, this is Cullworthy. Do you want to say anything?'

He opened his eyes and stared up at Adam without moving his head. His face was contorted either with pain or fury. He attempted to speak but all that came out was a husky whisper. Adam leant closer to him to see if he could make sense of what he was saying. 'You fucking bastard, Cullworthy, you'll pay for this.'

The effort had drained him and his eyes closed again and he drifted back into unconsciousness.

Adam returned to the taxi where an Indian Police constable was standing. 'Driver has made statement.'

The constable took out his notebook, and read out the signed statement. It tended to be prolix and Adam suspected that the constable himself had suggested much of the wording. It was far from being an accurate account of events but the last thing Adam needed now was a lengthy investigation into why he might have been abducted.

It was gone midnight before Adam returned to Poona by which time Sarah had returned to her quarters. He knew the accident report would filter back to his C.O so first thing the following morning he gave him his own report that he had been a passenger in a car that had had an accident but without any serious consequences. This seemed to satisfy him which was a relief to Adam as he was now keen to drop quietly out of the picture, in the hope that once he was out of the country he would be beyond the reach of Wantilla. Sarah was less easily convinced.

'It all sounds too bizarre for words. Why on earth would Wantilla wish to abduct you? I know you didn't exactly bond when he was in Delhi but why would he wish to harm you?'

'It's really quite complicated, darling.'

'Well, it may have escaped you but I am more than slightly interested in your safety and welfare so if there is something you are not telling me now is the time to put me in the picture.'

Adam knew he couldn't tell her the full story and he wasn't even sure he knew it himself.

'It is all tied up with a feud between the two sides of the Debrahm family. Wantilla's side are laying claim to the *gaddi,* the family throne you might call it. Rindi's father has rejected this out of hand and somehow Wantilla believes I am a conspirator in the whole business.'

'And are you?'

'No more than providing moral support to my friend.' Adam lied.

Sarah still looked unconvinced. 'Well, that hardly sounds like grounds for an attempt on your life. Probably a good thing that you are leaving the country. I'd rather you were alive in England than dead in India.'

Adam managed to speak to Rindi on the telephone.

'What the hell was Wantilla doing in Poona? I knew he was in Delhi when he telephoned my adjutant a couple of days ago.'

Rindi sounded incredulous and Adam was still trying to make sense of it all himself.

'I must see you before you leave, Adam. I'll come on Friday evening's Jhelum Express.'

There was urgency in Rindi's voice that was at variance with the calm way he normally dealt with family affairs. Adam had the feeling this incident had unnerved him, but maybe it was something else.

Rindi arrived in Poona as planned and was able to join Adam's farewell party at the Club. Surrounded by his friends and fellow officers Adam had mixed emotions about the future. With the conflict in Europe and the Far East showing no signs of abating he wondered when he might return to India and to the three people that had become so important to him.

Sarah was conscious of his close friendship with Rindi and tactfully arranged to leave them alone on the Sunday evening. She would have the last three evenings with Adam before he left at the end of the week.

Rindi and Adam dined alone together at the Club.

'That was an excellent dinner, Adam. I doubt whether you'll get anything like that back in London. The Westbury's tell me that rationing is really quite severe now.'

'How are they all? Do you hear from Pauline?'

'No, but Tina writes to me from time to time.'

'Lucky you.' Rindi sensed resentment in Adam's voice.

'I know she wanted to write to you but found it too difficult.'

Adam gave Rindi a puzzled look but accepted that he too had found it impossible to correspond with her after the Nancy incident.

'Adam, I have been meaning to talk to you about something for a long time.'

'Is it about Kafni?'

'No, actually, it's about Tina.'

'What about her?'

'Adam, Tina and I have become romantically involved.'

Adam's brow furrowed in disbelief at what he had heard.

'Sorry, Rindi, can you just say that again?'

'I really wanted to tell you sooner but there never seemed the right moment. I couldn't let you leave India without telling you.'

'Are you telling me that you and Tina are having an affair?'

'More than that Adam, we are in love.'

Adam stared at Rindi then scratched his neck.

'When did this all happen?'

'The Westbury's came to stay at Kushnapur before the war and Tina came with them. Neither of us meant it to happen.'

Rindi was being economical with the truth. Adam was not taking this revelation well. It was hard enough for him to grasp the fact that he and Tina were lovers without inflicting further pain by describing the first heady days of their affair in Oxford.

'Do your family know? Does Kafni know?'

'They know we are close, but that is all.'

There were so many questions tumbling around in Adam's head How could they have carried on for so long without him knowing? He drained his glass of whisky in an attempt to suppress his tormented thoughts. He had no reason to feel betrayed. He had had two love affairs since he'd last seen Tina. But he did feel betrayed. This was not just anyone; this was Tina, his first love. How could his best friend do this to him? There was a silence between them. A giant wave had broken over him and there was little comfort from the surf returning gently to the sea. What had meant to be a fond farewell had turned into rift between them which would not easily mend.

CHAPTER TWENTY THREE

Bombay, December 1944.

As there were no windows in the cabin of the R.A.F. Dakota DC3, the pilot had asked Adam if he would like to join him on the flight deck to have one last glimpse of India. In the early morning sun the coastline stretched out before them, to starboard was the Gulf of Cambay and in the distance the City of Baroda and beneath them the city of Bombay.

'Hard to imagine it as the small island given to Charles the second as part of his dowry from Catherine of Braganza.'

'Yes, and look at it now, the most important port on the sub-continent.'

Adam closed his eyes and listened to the roar of the twin engines. The cold stark interior of the plane was in sharp contrast to the warm comfort of the Taj Hotel where he had spent his last night with Sarah.

Rindi's revelation that he was romantically involved with Tina had shaken Adam. He still found it incredible that they had managed to keep it a secret from him for nearly five years. Rindi had said it had all happened rather unexpectedly when she visited Kushnapur but Adam wondered whether the flames of their affair hadn't been kindled earlier. He remembered how at the Sandhurst Ball she had danced most of the night with Rindi. And then there was the conversation with Tina about her father encouraging her not to get too fond of Adam. Perhaps he had been in denial and in fact their youthful romance had already ended at that stage but he could just not bring himself to see it. What galled Adam most was that whilst carrying on this clandestine affair Rindi had felt no compunction about placing a sanction on Adam's relationship with Kafni.

All these thoughts had made him realise that it was pointless chasing unrealistic romantic dreams but rather he should appreciate the girl he was with. Sarah was beautiful, sexy and clever. She was ambitious, wilful and liked to be in charge but he had learnt to deal with that. Their political views differed somewhat but as they were both army officers their pragmatism quelled any antagonism on this front.

For much of their time together in India Adam had been preoccupied with thoughts of Kafni. Sarah had also treated their relationship as one of convenience. Something had changed, perhaps crystallised by the thought that they would not see each other for many months. Adam had felt this was not the moment to propose marriage but he had needed to affirm his feelings towards her. He had pushed her back onto the bed and kissed her gently. 'I do love you, Sarah.'

'I love you too.'

'I'm going to miss you.'

'We've had a lovely time together.'

'Will you wait for me?'

'Of course,' she said with a tender vulnerability Adam had not seen in her before.

January 1945. Southern England.

Adam wondered whether the tragedy could have been avoided had he returned to England earlier. Within an hour of his arrival on home soil he was on his way to the Kent and Sussex Hospital in Tunbridge Wells.

He sat by his father's bed, reading a week-old copy of the Daily Express, staring with shock at the picture and the headlines: **"Mystery car bomb kills chauffeur."** The photograph showed the burnt-out remains of the beautiful Rolls Royce his father had inherited from his Aunt Adeline. There was an ugly void where the driver's seat should have been and the remains of the chassis hung at an ungainly angle. In the background Adam recognised the corner of their house in Fletching.

'Good to see you old chap. Rotten business this eh.' his father croaked.

He was lying with his head back on his hospital pillow, looking pale and much older than when Adam had left for India.

'Do they have any idea who did it?'

'Nothing more than that reported in the paper,' the old man replied.

'Can you tell me what happened?' Adam asked tentatively.

'Not now old chap, too tired.' His father managed a weak smile before he closed his eyes and fell asleep.

'I think we should leave him to rest now' Adam's mother said 'we will come back and see him in the morning.'

As they drove back through the Sussex countryside scattered with patches of snow and still scarred with the defences against invasion Adam asked his mother for details about the incident.

'So what on earth happened?'

'The Red Cross called to tell us they needed to requisition the Rolls for a day or two. Some emergency or other they told us. They came to collect it the following evening but your father and I were out and so Dalton gave them the keys.'

'Them?'

'Yes two gentleman apparently.'

'So where were you and Pa that evening?'

'We always go to the Barratts on a Thursday they have a regular bridge evening to raise money, ironically for the Red Cross.'

'Is that just a coincidence?'

'Must be, I can't believe anyone in the Red Cross could have been involved.' Adam's mother said with conviction.

'Maybe you're right.'

'Well anyway they returned the car on the Saturday evening when we were all out, so they just posted the keys through the letterbox. We thought it a bit strange. Not so much as a thank you note.'

'Sounds pretty well planned. They must have known you would be out'

'We didn't use the car on the Sunday but Dalton always drives your father into Uckfield on a Monday morning.'

'So what exactly happened?'

'Fortunately I didn't witness it but I gather the bomb was placed under the driver's seat. The detonator was triggered by opening the rear passenger door. Dalton is always' she paused 'was always ready and opened that passenger door when your father came out of the house. Poor old Jack didn't stand a chance.' she choked back her emotion. Adam had never heard her refer to him as Jack; he had always been Dalton.

'How did Pa get off so lightly?'

'Had he not bent down to pick up the hat he'd dropped he would almost certainly have been killed.'

'Is he going to be alright? He seems very withdrawn.'

'He blames himself for Dalton's death. For years he had been trying to get him to retire. We didn't really need a chauffeur.'

'Did he leave a widow?'

'His wife died some years back from TB and they had no children. He shared a cottage with his wife's sister, Celeste. He so loved that Rolls and of course driving your father around.'

'Didn't he have a dog?'

'Yes a Jack Russell. Do you remember, great little chap, the runt of the litter he called him Snip because he was. Susie has said she will take him if Celeste can't cope with him. The girls have been wonderful rallying round and keeping an eye on things whilst I was tending to your father.'

Adam realised that Jack Dalton had just been in the wrong place at the wrong time which was tragic and it was unlikely that he was the target of the attack.But why would anyone want to kill his father. He really had no enemies. It seemed too well planned to be a case of mistaken identity. And then it struck him. Maybe this was revenge for another road accident. Maybe he was meant to be the target. There was only one person sufficiently motivated, well connected and also sufficiently callous to carry out an act like this. The more he thought about it the more he was convinced that the bomb had been intended for him not his father.

Much as he wanted to relieve his parents of some of the guilt of Dalton's death he could not be certain and the last thing he wanted to do was start having to answer questions from the Sussex police about an incident on the other side of the empire.

There was little Adam could do for the present. The Army had given him extended leave for compassionate reasons and after another two days his father was well enough to be taken home. The knowledge that he was probably indirectly responsible for his accident and the death of poor old Dalton haunted Adam for weeks. The police investigation rumbled on but made little progress. Their resources were fully stretched what with thousands of troops returning from various parts of Europe and the Middle East. The only clue that gave Adam reason to think he was on the right track was a report from the local publican that he had seen an Indian gentleman in the area on several occasions prior to the incident but not since. This was sufficiently unusual to warrant mention but was not considered significant by the Sussex police. If Wantilla was responsible there would be a complicated chain of events in both India and England which would be beyond the wit of the local constabulary. He felt sure that it was only he and Rindi who could exact retribution for this crime.

May 1945 London

After two months of assiduous work at the War Office and visits to various weapon training and testing establishments, Adam's assignment was completed and he was given a temporary staff job.

The spring of 1945 saw the Allied armies move forward rapidly and on 4th May 1945, the German Armies in N.W. Germany, Holland and Denmark surrendered to Field Marshal Montgomery. The war against Germany officially ended on 8th May. From the window of his office in Whitehall Adam saw the build-up of the crowds heading for Buckingham Palace. He left his desk, went out onto the streets and joined the euphoric sea of people. This was a mass outpouring of joy at the announcement that the terrible conflict which had affected everyone's lives was finally over. The crowd was so tightly packed that he found himself swept up into Trafalgar Square. The cheering suddenly turned into a roar as a car bearing Churchill sitting half on the roof edged its way through the crowd. How he would have loved Sarah, Rindi and Kafni to be there to share this moment instead of being on the other side of the world.

Once the celebrations had died down the reality that many British troops were still engaged in the ongoing war in the Far East returned to dampen the euphoria. Adam put in a request to return to regimental duty. Whilst waiting for a response he received the offer of a place at the Staff College in Camberley. The opportunity to move up the ranks to Lieutenant Colonel if he successfully completed this course was not to be missed. Although he was excited by this prospect he recalled the comment his house master Banger Barnes had made when he was about to take his Army Board exams at Rockton, that in peacetime they only selected the cream.

June 1945. Fletching, Sussex.

It was a glorious summer's day when Adam drove down to Sussex to visit his parents. His father had made almost a full recovery but although he looked physically well there was a haunted look in his eyes. Adam knew he still bore the heavy burden of Dalton's death. Several times he found him looking absent mindedly into the distance. They sat on the terrace enjoying a glass of Pimms No.1 cup admiring the bursting white blossom of the Blackthorn in the hedgerow. Adam drew in a deep breath of country air. 'Aah, how wonderful to smell freshly cut grass. One could almost forget that we have just fought a five-year war.'

'I'm afraid lunch isn't very exciting' his mother said getting to her feet, 'although we do have some fresh asparagus and new potatoes from the garden, but very little butter.'

'That sounds perfect, Mama.'

'What the devil happened to that lovely girl, Tina Westbury? his father asked, emerging from his reverie, 'I thought you were about to pop the question before you left for India?'

'A delightful girl,' his mother added. 'We liked her very much.'

'And damned pretty too,' his father said with a chuckle.

Adam decided not to tell his parents what had happened to Tina because, despite the deep misgivings he still had about their relationship, he didn't want them to think badly of Tina or Rindi.

'Yes, Tina is a lovely girl, but I'm afraid it just didn't work out. It was just one of those things.'

'So who's this new girl in your life? His father referred to any female younger than his mother as a girl.

'She's not exactly a girl and I've actually known her since we met on the ship going out to India.'

Adam had been granted fourteen days leave before reporting to the Staff College and was surprised that the Army Post Office had tracked him down at the War Office to deliver a letter from Sarah. She was back in London. They had met the following night at Quaglino's, which meant that they could have a dance after a meagre dinner. She wore the same red dress she had worn on that memorable evening on the Cape Peninsula. So much water had passed under the bridge since then. As they danced they clung to each other as if they might suddenly be parted again. When the band stopped for a break Adam guided Sarah back to their table.

'How were things in India?'

'It's a strange atmosphere. The celebration of the news from Europe is rather muted because there seems to be no immediate sign of the Japanese surrendering.'

'How did you manage to get away?'

'I've been given a position as one of the three Assistant Directors of the Auxiliary Territorial Service in the Adjutant-General's Department. I'm not due to take up the role until the end of July but when I heard there was going to be a general election I requested permission to return earlier to help with the campaign.'

'For the Labour Party, I presume?'

'Of course.'

'Not much gratitude to Churchill then.'

'He could still be Prime Minister in a coalition, depending on who holds the most seats.'

'Would you like to be an MP?'he enquired but already knew what her answer would be.

'Certainly, and if I canvas for Labour now they might consider offering me a seat to fight at the next election.'

'Quite tough to get selected as a woman.'

'Yes, but they desperately need women in Parliament to change the thinking about women's role in society.'

'Well, I am not sure the Labour party are in touch with reality.'

'Oh and I suppose the Tories are.'

'I quite like the idea of coalitions where the extreme views get watered down. It seemed to work well during the war so why not in peacetime?'

'No, that won't work. Radical change is needed to tackle social injustice.'

'Socialism is a lovely idea,' Adam said with thinly disguised cynicism, 'giving everyone what they want for free. But without capitalism there would be no money to pay for it.'

'I can see we are not going to see eye to eye on this, Adam.'

'Well for what it is worth I think you will make a very good MP.'

'Thank you, darling. Does that mean you will campaign for me?'

'One thing at a time. Right now I am just delighted that this election has brought you home sooner.'

'I'm not sure that daddy approves of my going into politics.'

'How is the General?'

'Getting bored of shuffling paper and nervous about the rise of the Indian nationalists. They are like vultures watching the death throes of the British Raj. It could all get very messy.'

'Yes, I think you're right. I fear for Rindi and his family. They have done well under British rule.'

'Have you heard from him? Does he know about the bomb in your father's car?'

'Not yet. I was hoping to report some progress on finding the culprits. Now speaking of father, how about coming down to Sussex this weekend? It's about time you saw the Cullworthy's in their natural habitat.'

'That would be lovely. Do your parents even know I exist?'

'They do, but not the extent of our involvement. I am going down tomorrow and intend to tell them about you before you arrive. There wasn't much point in getting them interested if you were still in India.'

Sarah arrived on the Friday afternoon which meant that she had the opportunity to spend time with Adam's parents before Daphne and Sue arrived on the Saturday. The sisters were so taken with Sarah that Adam's parents could not help being carried along by their enthusiasm. Adam's father even found himself being persuaded by some of Sarah's arguments for greater social justice although he was less convinced by her thoughts on how to pay for the changes.

Sarah and Adam returned to London together on the train.

'I really liked your family, Adam.'

'They were embarrassingly fond of you too.'

'I thought your father looked a little sad at times.'

'He's never been quite the same since Jack was killed. He felt it was his fault. In truth it was mine.'

'What do you mean?'

'That attack had all the hallmarks of a Wantilla plot. I am sure I was the intended target but his henchmen blundered it.'

'You will be careful darling, won't you?' She could not suppress the anxiety in her voice. Adam felt sure she loved him, not with the passion Kafni had shown but in a more level-headed way. He knew he would ask her to marry him but he wanted to choose the moment. She had always been in control of their relationship and in a way she still was because she could still decline his offer.

Sarah returned to her canvassing for Labour and Adam headed to Camberley to start his Staff College course.

July 1945

To everyone's amazement Labour won the General Election with a landslide. Churchill was sent packing and Clement Atlee formed a Government with a huge majority. Sarah called Adam at the Staff College.

'Darling, isn't it an incredible result. I know it's probably not what you were hoping for but this will mean real changes for the working classes.'

'Yes, you are probably right but I feel sorry for poor Winston. He really deserved better for what he did for the country. But I am pleased for you. I presume your chap got in?'

'Yes he did, with a comfortable majority. He says he will put me forward to fight a bi-election if one comes up.'

'Now the hard work starts, rebuilding the country.'

'Darling, I wondered if you could get up to London for a couple of days. It's been far too long.'

'Yes, I know. I'll see what I can do but it won't be for at least three weeks.'

Two weeks later on the 6th August, the first atomic bomb was dropped on Hiroshima; three days later another atomic bomb obliterated Nagasaki. Less than a week later, Japan surrendered unconditionally. Their planned weekend in London coincided with the "Victory over Japan" celebrations. These were more restrained than the VE day celebrations but Sarah and Adam found themselves embraced by total strangers and by the time they made it to their hotel they were riding high on hope and optimism for the future.

The following morning Adam paid a visit to SJ Phillips in Bond Street where thanks to Aunt Adeline's legacy he was able to purchase a diamond and sapphire ring. In the evening he took Sarah for dinner at the Savoy and proposed.

'I thought you would never ask.'

'Is that a yes, then?'

'Well, you may have to get clearance from the General and you know how demanding he is,' she said with a mischievous smile.

'Not as demanding as his daughter.'

'Well the "demanding daughter" says yes.'

'How wonderful.'

'You know that means you will have to canvas for me.'

'Oh, I see. Conditions already being laid down.'

Adam leant across and kissed her. 'Thank you darling, you've made me a very happy man.'

The following morning Adam sent a cable to Sir David requesting permission to marry his daughter.

The reply came two days later.

"SPLENDID NEWS STOP
PERMISSION GRANTED STOP
LADY R TO LONDON STOP"

London, October 1945.

After a long flight, with night stops in Karachi and Cairo, Lady Roberts finally arrived at the Hurn Airfield and Sarah was there to meet her.

'Hello, darling, thank you for coming to collect me, that was an exhausting journey.'

'You needn't have come back just because we got engaged.'

'I had planned to come back anyway. Your father's role in India is coming to an end and we need to find somewhere to live back in England.'

Sarah knew that the real reason her mother had returned early was to make sure the wedding arrangements were entirely to her satisfaction.

Their engagement was announced in The Times and The Daily Telegraph and from that moment on Lady Roberts took charge of planning the wedding. Sarah and Adam had favoured a country wedding, an idea summarily dismissed by Lady Roberts. It was to be in London at St. Margaret's, Westminster and the guest list was formidable, both in length and composition.

There weren't many decisions Adam had to make but the important one was who would be his best man. There was an obvious candidate for this role but he found himself nurturing doubts about whether Rindi was the right man. Apart from the fact that he would have to travel from India, Adam had not really come to terms with the revelation of his secret relationship with Tina. He had always considered Rindi to be his best friend, even closer perhaps than a brother, but recent events had made him feel manipulated by him. Were these the actions of a true friend? In his professional life he felt in control of his future but his private life seemed to be directed by others with varying agendas, not always with his best interests at heart. After some thought he decided it would be churlish to choose someone else.

Lady Roberts raised an eyebrow when Adam told her, but then appeared quite content once she had decided that Rindi should be officially referred to as Prince Rindi, Rajkumar of Kushnapur. Years of exposure to *durbars*, *levees* and viceroy's receptions in India had made her a stickler for protocol. Adam knew how much she enjoyed ceremony and pageant, and would delight in having Rindi in the resplendent attire of an Indian prince on one side of the aisle and her husband in the full dress uniform of a general on the other. Two field-marshals: Lord Birdwood and Sir Claud Jacob, both of whom Sir David had served under in the Indian Army, would be among the guests.

In the meantime a cable arrived from Rindi with the news that he had been transferred to the Indian Army Reserve of Officers and was now coming to England with the intention of returning to Oxford to complete his doctorate.

Kensington

'The murderous bastard,' Rindi hissed through gritted teeth. 'Adam, I feel bloody awful about this; it's entirely my fault this has happened' he ran his fingers through his thick, dark, glossy hair in an agitated fashion.'

Why didn't you write and tell me straightaway? I could have done something about this before I left India.'

Adam sat in a high-backed armchair watching his friend shake his head in disbelief.

'I'm not sure what you could have achieved. There is no evidence linking Wantilla to this incident. And in any case, you're not to blame. I'm the one who caused the road accident in Poona. It's a pity he didn't die then.'

Rindi stood up and walked over to the bay window overlooking Queen's Gate Gardens. It had been over five years since he and Adam had visited his Aunt and Uncle's residence.

'He's gone too far this time.' Rindi said pressing his clenched fist into his other hand. 'I can't undo Dalton's death, but I'll make sure Wantilla gets what he deserves.'

'Do you even know where he is?'

'I know he's left the army but I haven't heard what he is up to. I suspect he is probably in the thick of the political manoeuvring going on in Delhi.'

'Could he be in England?'

'It's possible but he doesn't like to be too close to the action when his dastardly deeds are being implemented.'

'How do you think we can stop him?'

'It will not be easy but I now have new means of bringing pressure on him.'

'Sounds uncommonly like blackmail.'

'Bloody right. It's time he had a taste of his own medicine.'

Jandah entered the room with a tray of drinks. Adam was impressed at how upright he still was, although his fine moustache had now started to turn grey.

'Dinner will be at 8.15, sir.'

'Thank you, Jandah.' Rindi waited for the tall servant to leave the room.

'My sources tell me Wantilla has been engaged in a highly dangerous game. He duped two ingénue nieces of the Maharajah of Mysore into believing that somehow by thaumaturgy, he could find prestigious husbands for them, provided they placed themselves completely in his hands. His intention was to crudely amuse himself with the girls. He felt safe in the belief that, provided he was discreet, shame would ensure their silence.'

'So what happened?'

'Over-confidence led him to become careless. What started out as amusing nude titillation, degenerated into lewd acts. The consequences of this are serious enough for any high caste Hindu woman; for a family as distinguished as Mysore, it would be disastrous. Even more so, as it was witnessed by the lower caste maidservant and also Wantilla's girlfriend.'

'How did you hear about this?'

'Through my sister Puhella. The girls had been at school with her at St. Mary's in Poona. They knew she was Wantilla's cousin and that there was no love lost between our families. In desperation they asked for her help. She has their signed witness statements.'

'That is powerful stuff.'

'Yes, it could end his political career. But Wantilla knows that the girls could also not risk the story becoming public.'

'So a bit of high stakes poker going on.'

'Let's just say it's an ace up our sleeve in the event he tries to interfere with our family again. Now enough of my evil cousin. Tell me about your exciting news. Aunt Nina showed me the announcement in the Times.'

'So what do you think?'

'I'd say it's a good match. You both know all about service life, and although I know you've found Sarah unpredictable at times, she's bright, has a good sense of humour and certainly has the looks.'

'I'm glad you approve because I was going to ask you to be my best man.'

'It would be my honour, dear boy.'

'We were thinking of getting married in the spring, will that be OK for you?'

'Yes, that's fine. I won't be going back to India before the summer, unless something unexpected crops up.'

Adam could not bring himself to ask how things were with Tina, and Rindi was not volunteering any information. Instead he decided to ask about his son.

'How is Pratap getting on?'

'He is a bundle of energy driving the palace staff crazy with his mischief. He looks quite the little prince in his turban and jacket.' Then holding Adam's arm he said 'I am glad you are getting married, Adam, it doesn't do any good to think of what might have been.'

Camberley, December 1945.

Adam was relieved when his course at the Staff College ended. It had been a period of intensive study and the s.c. after his name in the Army List was well earned. He now had no wish to re-join the battalion in India. In the first place he wanted to spend more time with Sarah. In the second place, Bob Mercer had been promoted to full colonel and posted to G.H.Q. in Delhi, and Major Williams had taken his place. He was therefore relieved and very grateful to be given the news that he was to be second-in-command of the First Battalion of the Wessex.

After Adam had told Sarah's mother that Rindi had agreed to be his best man, she asked him if he had any friends suitable to be ushers at the wedding. Many of Adam's closest friends were still abroad. He hadn't heard from Hugh Archibald since before VJ day. It always made him nervous when he didn't hear from friends. Having survived the war his friend Willie Ashford had been shot dead by a rogue sniper in Cairo. It was therefore a great relief when he received a call from

Archie saying he was back in London.

'How good to hear from you. Where the devil have you been these last few months?'

'I was demobbed by the Royal Artillery back in June and headed back to Los Angeles.'

'So did you get my letter?'

'I did and that's one of the reasons I am back in England. I couldn't miss giving you a send-off. Who's the best man by the way?'

'My friend from school, Rindi Debrahm.'

'Ah yes, some Indian grandee I seem to remember.'

'So what was the other reason you are here? And how did you manage to get a passage from California?'

'Well, my old buddy, I may be a Yank, but I exploited my service in the British Army. The British Consul-General in Los Angeles appreciated my patriotism, and as I'd interrupted my degree at Oxford to join up, he raked up a geology bursary with a free return passage.'

'So you'll be going back to Oxford?'

'That's it. I thought I'd see a bit of England and Scotland before I start in October. My grandfather came from Aberdeen, he was a Gordon so I thought I might get myself a kilt,' he said mischievously.

The vision of his bear like friend in a kilt made Adam snort with involuntary laughter.

'What? you don't think I have the legs for it?' Archie protested.

'I am sure you will be the pride of the Gordon clan.'

'Mock me not you envious Sassenach!'

'Now you've arrived just in time for our engagement party. Tomorrow night, 6.30 at the Lonsdale Club. Rindi will be there and is also going back to Oxford so you might see more of each other after the wedding.'

Amongst the guests that Lady Roberts had invited was Lady Hawkswood whom she had met at a *durbar* in Delhi before Sir Arthur had been shot. Also invited was her daughter Virginia, who she had once thought a possible match for her son Jonathan, and of course Virginia's husband Lord Chalvington.

'Adam, I don't think you've met Lady Chalvington? Virginia, this is my future son-in-law Adam Cullworthy.'

'Delighted to meet you Lady Chalvington.'

'Please call me Virginia.'

At that moment Rindi appeared through the door dressed in an immaculate white high collared Rajasthani suit.

'Good evening, Adam.'

'Rindi, I'd like you to meet Virginia Chalvington.' To Adam's surprise Rindi stepped forward and kissed her on the cheek.

'We already know each other, Adam.'

'Of course, <u>that</u> Virginia.' Adam blurted out a bit too enthusiastically. Virginia gave him a quizzical look. From the other side of the room her husband shot her a dark glare.

'Well, I won't keep you two I am sure you need to circulate,' she said trying to avoid catching her husband's eye again.

Adam steered Rindi towards the bar. 'So that is the famous Virginia Hawkswood. She's absolutely gorgeous.'

'Now, now old boy you're newly engaged and I'm responsible for keeping you on the straight and narrow.'

'Why is she called Chalvington? I'm sure that wasn't her fiancé's name.'

'No that's because his father died and he inherited the title, Earl of Chalvington.'

'Which one is her husband?'

'That chap over there who looks like he has a plank of wood up the back of his jacket.'

'She didn't seem too keen to talk to us.'

'To me you mean.'

'I thought you had had lunch with her after the boat trip.'

'I did, but her husband Simon still thinks there was something going on between us.'

'Yet more trouble caused by your cousin.'

As if he knew they were talking about him Simon Chalvington gave them a long cheerless stare from where he was standing alone by the ornate marble fireplace.

Across the room Adam heard the distinctive guffaw of his American friend and was amused to see Archie chatting animatedly with Sarah and Virginia. Trust him to corner two of the best looking girls at the party.

'Hey, buddy how are you doing?' Adam looked slightly embarrassed as Archie gave him an all American bear hug.

'Now Archie I don't want you getting any ideas, these two girls are both spoken for.'

'Shucks just when I thought I was in with a chance.' They all laughed.

Salisbury, Wiltshire, March 1946.

Adam was now based with the regiment in Salisbury during the week.

At weekends he would take the train to London. For appearances sake he had joined the Army and Navy Club in Pall Mall and after spending the evening with Sarah, he would go there for the night.

'Darling I've been meaning to tell you that I have asked to be released from the A.T.S. I've served longer than the period I signed up for in 1938, so there should be no problem.'

'Does that mean we can now find a place to live near Salisbury?'

'That was the other thing I wanted to tell you. The chap I campaigned for in the General Election, Ivan Parkinson, has been made the Minister for Industrial Development.'

'What has he got to do with it?'

'Well he's offered me a job as his private secretary.'

'I see. So when would you need to start.'

'It could be as soon as we get back from our honeymoon. He'd like to meet you and by the way he's got a lovely wife.'

'So where do you see us living?'

'It might be a good idea to get a place in Wiltshire in any case. We'll need somewhere with some space when we start a family.'

'Have you discussed that with him?'

'I've already warned Ivan that I'll need to take leave three months before any baby is due. We can have a Norland nanny and after a few weeks, I could go back to Westminster. He's willing to take on a temporary secretary to cover for six months.'

'So where would we be based?'

'I thought you might apply for a job in the Ministry of Defence and then we could both be in London.'

'That would hardly be a good long-term career move for me.'

'Well, I'm sure we will work it out. We've lived apart for short periods in the past.'

Adam did not appreciate being given this revelation as a *fait accompli* but he could not say that she hadn't made it plain that she wanted to pursue a career in politics. 'Well, you've certainly been busy along the corridors of power.'

It was a bright crisp April morning on their wedding day. As they came out of St Margaret's through a Guard of Honour of crossed swords, the bells ringing and a stone's throw from Sarah's future office, the whole world seemed to be going their way. Seeing Sarah looking graceful and beautiful in her wedding dress; her distinguished father leading her up the aisle; her mother who had been so kind; his parents so delighted and guests who had heaped their good wishes upon them, Adam felt the happiest man alive.

Rindi had made a splendid best man, and although Adam had wanted him to be at the ceremony dressed as a *rajkumar,* they had deferred to the Bishop of London and so he came to the church, dressed complete with sword, in the uniform of a major of the Punjabi Regiment. After the service he slipped away during the signing of the register, and by the time the phalanx of the wedding party had reached the Dorchester, he had changed into his princely attire, ready for the wedding photographs. The bridesmaids were delighted, and could not take their eyes off him. A cloak of fresh responsibilities had fallen upon Adam but he felt light headed and full of optimism for the future.

CHAPTER TWENTY FOUR

London, May 1946.

Adam could not share the enthusiasm that Sarah felt for her new job. This was because their opinions diverged on the role of an army wife.

'Things have changed since mother was a bride,' Sarah said. 'There was no opportunity for a woman to take up a career - particularly in India - even if convention had not frowned upon it. If women are to be effective in the post-war years, they must move into the mainstream of affairs.'

'And you believe that is at Westminster?'

Sarah had taken lipstick out of her bag and with the help of a small compact mirror was applying a deep red coating to her lips.

'Not entirely, but it is an epicentre of decision-making. And there are an awful lot of decisions to be made by the Government in the next few years.'

'So when do you start this job?'

'Second of May.'

Adam was due to move to Aldershot in the autumn and with Sarah's new job being based in Westminster there seemed little point in looking for a house near Salisbury. The Roberts' were happy to have Sarah living with them in Bayswater and always made Adam welcome at the weekends. He was therefore surprised when Sarah told him that Ivan had arranged a flat for her in Petty France.

'I'd hardly call going from Bayswater to Westminster a long journey.'

'I know but if Ivan's kept late in the House he likes to give me the next day's work when he comes out, leaving him free to see Department secretaries in the morning.'

'I don't think he should keep you late at night. And you can tell him from me, I don't want you doing it for long. It sounds as if he's exploiting a willing horse.'

'Not really, he knows that I must have my weekends free.'

'I'm glad he's got that message.' Adam folded his arms in defiant attitude.

Rindi's academic year finished in mid-June and as there was a lot going on in India his father had requested he return to Kushnapur for the vacation. He knew his father was slowing down. Doctors had suggested the maharajah should cut down on his consumption of scotch but to no avail. It would not be long before Rindi had to assume a more active role in the familys' affairs.

BOAC had started a new air service from London to Delhi. Although Rindi rather enjoyed the slower pace of the boat trip back to India, flying meant his travelling time was cut by several weeks. As Adam had not seen him since the wedding he decided to go and see Rindi off from the new London Airport out at Heathrow.

'Good of you to come, old boy. How's married life treating you?'

'I seem to see less of Sarah now than before we were married.'

'She was always going to be a career-minded girl. You should be proud of her.'

'Yes, I know, but the army does expect wives to support their husbands, especially as I am to command my own battalion.'

'Wow, you kept that quiet. Congratulations, Colonel Cullworthy.'

'Thank you. I wish Sarah was as enthusiastic. And what about your love life?' Adam asked, not sure he really wanted to know.

'Tina and I see each other from time to time but we both have very busy lives.'

'Well, send her my best wishes when you next talk to her.'

'I will,' said Rindi. He was relieved that Adam seemed to have accepted the situation.

'You must be looking forward to being back in Kushnapur.'

'It will be good to see the family but I do not relish the thought of the politics. Things are really hotting up with all this independence talk.'

'Please send my regards to your parents and love to Kafni and give that boy a big hug from me.'

Rindi gave Adam a knowing look which conveyed more than any words.

'*This is the final call for Flight BO 750, for Tripoli, Cairo, Basra, Karachi, Delhi and Calcutta.*' The urgency of tannoy message brought them back down to earth.

'Safe journey, Rindi.' They shook hands and Adam wished he had

Archie's boldness and had given his friend a hug.

'Send my love to Sarah. She's a good woman, Adam, she just needs a firm hand.'

Bayswater, London, July 1946.

After meeting at the engagement party Sarah and Virginia had become good friends. Both of them had been brought up in India and they had a lot in common. Virginia found life in the English countryside rather dull and took any opportunity to come up to London. They had taken to lunching together on a Thursday.

'No sign of you getting pregnant?' This was a subject which was preoccupying both of them.

'I'm afraid not but Simon isn't too keen on bedroom activity. I've rather given up hoping. How about you?'

'No shortage of enthusiasm in that department from Adam but nothing seems to be happening with me either. Excuse me for being a bit impertinent,' Sarah continued, 'but Adam mentioned to me that you had a fling with Wantilla Debrahm.'

'A harmless dalliance, but it never really came to much. I realised he had several girls on the go.'

'You know he very nearly killed Adam.'

'What?! I know he's a bit of a hothead but I can't see him resorting to murder. What on earth provoked that?'

'Something to do with a feud between the Debrahm families.'

'I do remember Wantilla threatening Rindi when we were on the boat but it seemed to be about some old score.'

'They are devilishly handsome those Debrahms. Rindi in particular.'

'Yes, you're right and, unlike his cousin, Rindi's a gentleman. He really saved my marriage by his gallantry on the boat.'

'Do I detect a certain admiration?' Sarah floated, prompting more a more revealing response.

'We are more like brother and sister but Simon is convinced there is more to it than that.'

'Well I can't say I'd blame you if there was, what with Simon being a bit of a cold fish. We girls have our needs as well.'

'How is your political career coming on?' Virginia asked moving away from analysis of her Debrahm associations.

'Rather well in fact. Ivan my boss has arranged a flat for me and although he makes me work all hours he spoils me with gifts from time to time.'

'Are you sure his intentions are honourable?'

'I'm not an innocent schoolgirl, Virginia,' Sarah said rather defensively.

'No, I'm sure you know what you're doing.'

A few weeks later they met at Simpsons on the Strand.

'Golly, Virginia, you look the picture of health. Perhaps the countryside does have its benefits.'

'Sarah can you keep a secret?'

'Of course I can.'

'I think I might be pregnant.'

'Oh, that's fabulous news. Have you told Simon?'

'Not yet. I am just terrified I will lose it and it will then be a terrible anti-climax. But I am going to see my specialist in Harley Street this afternoon to see what he thinks.'

Kushnapur Palace, July 1946.

The maharajah, formally robed, sat at the judicial table in his Durbar Chamber, ready to receive his weekly petitioners. On one side sat Rindi, and on the other his *Dewan*. As the tall cream and gilt doors were held open, an attendant announced Wantilla Debrahm's arrival. He came strutting through, intent upon flaunting his new found status. Slinking at his heels was his nephew Narajan. Wantilla gave a perfunctory *namaste* to the maharajah, then a nod to the *Dewan* and ignored Rindi.

'Good day to you, Wantilla. Congratulations on your appointment to the State Legislature. Now, to what do we owe the pleasure of your company?'

'In my new capacity as the future political representative of the district, I am here to claim my right.'

'And what right would that be?'

'My right to marry the Princess Kafni.'

'I told you I would consider it, but since then you have taken a wife.'

'Yes, but I now wish to take a second wife.'

'Then you must look elsewhere. My daughters are not available.'

Wantilla's eyes blazed with anger. 'Unless you agree immediately to my marriage to Kafni, I shall start a movement in parliament to strip you of your title and lands. There is considerable discontent in the Congress Party with you meddlesome princes.' The assembled company shuffled uncomfortably at this outburst and Rindi scowled at his cousin.

'So we are meddlesome now,' the maharajah responded coolly, 'I seem to remember you and your father representing yourselves to the Resident as being the rightful heirs to the *gaddi* of Kushnapur. If you can't own it better to destroy it. Is that your thinking? Well, you may be an aspiring politician but you will never sit in the Chamber of Princes in Delhi.' He concluded defiantly.

'The privileges of the Princes will all be swept away in the new democracy, Wantilla countered, 'and you won't have the British Raj to hold your hand much longer. Churchill's gone, and Attlee's government can't wait to get rid of India. Have I made myself clear?'

The maharajah was exercising the utmost restraint. In former times he would have had this insolent scoundrel removed from the palace without hesitation. Now, exercising diplomacy and dignity, he said, 'You have obviously not been informed that my daughter Kafni was married and is now the mother of a fine boy.'

Astonishment and suspicion clouded Wantilla's face. He leapt to his feet and paced up and down. 'Who is this husband? Why was I not informed?'

'Because it was no damn business...' Rindi started to answer but was halted by his father's raised hand.

'His name was Prince Ranjhalla Singh and you may remember,' the maharajah said, 'that he was tragically killed in action on the Burmese border in September 1942. I am sorry that you felt you should be informed, but we have kept this sad news strictly within the immediate family.'

'Very convenient I am sure. So when were they married?'

'They had been betrothed for many years but both felt they would like to get married before he went off on active service. The full celebrations were postponed until after the war. We are of course all delighted that there is a boy to follow in his brave father's footsteps.'

Wantilla realised that derogatory remarks about the marriage or the boy would be in bad taste, even by his standards, but he was not to be defeated.

'A widow, how interesting? And how socially unfortunate. Of course, I could never marry her now. It would be beneath the dignity of the Mahavirs to espouse a widow. No, I shall claim her as a concubine. She must be told. Now!'

His outrageous suggestion and the degrading manner of its delivery was too much for the *Dewan*.

'*Hazrat*, Shall I have him thrown out?'

'No, Dewan-sahib, I have something more to say to my perfidious cousin. Princess Kafni will never be permitted to enter your household. As a royal widow, she and her child will remain permanently under my protection. We are well aware of your unsavoury behaviour with daughters of another Prince and if you persist in this campaign we will have no hesitation in making this information public. This meeting is over. Good day.'

The very composure of the maharajah infuriated his visitor. At a signal from the Dewan, two attendants came forward to escort Wantilla and Narajan from the chamber, but they were not in time to prevent Wantilla thumping his fist on the maharajah's table.

'You have made an extremely unwise decision; one which you will regret. There are many ways of trapping a hind. You obviously force me to use a disagreeable one.' He turned and swept out of the chamber deliberately tipping over a five-hundred-year-old porcelain vase.

Rindi sprung to his feet to intercept Wantilla, but his father stood up to restrain him.

'Not now Rindi, not now.'

'I should have knocked him down, father.'

'Yes, and that would have given the politicians just the kind of incident they are looking for. Already the princes are being blamed for too many of this country's ills.'

Bayswater, London, September 1946.

'Of course we love having you both here at weekends, but this rushing back and forth doesn't seem an ideal way to conduct a marriage. I'm sure Adam would rather have you in Aldershot with him all the time. Isn't that so, Adam?'

'That goes without saying.'

'Has he been talking to you, Mummy?' Sarah said with obvious resentment.

'He's not said a word. I just think you should start looking for a place to settle down so that you can pay attention to some of the more important aspects of marriage.'

'I know just what you mean, Mother. You think it's about time I got pregnant.'

'That's putting it rather bluntly, darling.'

'We like plain speaking in the Labour Party.'

'So it seems, dear,' her mother replied calmly refusing to be drawn into a political exchange.

'You'll get your grandchildren all in good time. When things get a bit quieter I'll come down to Hampshire and look for a place.'

Adam nodded his approval.

'Speaking of children,' he said, 'I bumped into Simon Chalvington the other day and he tells me Virginia's expecting.'

'Yes, I know, she told me about a month ago but asked me to keep it a secret. It should be due at the end of April.'

'That must be exciting for them, an heir for Simon,' said Sarah's mother.

'Not if it's a girl,' Adam said.

'Bloody male rights again. They should let the succession go to the first born, whatever the sex,' Sarah piped up.

'Language darling!' her mother interjected, 'anyway imagine the problems that would cause.'

'Well, the Marlborough and Nelson peerages were passed through the female line.'

'Ah, yes, but they were both great national heroes,' Adam added.

Sarah opened her handbag, took out a cigarette and lit it. Elizabeth looked at her disapprovingly. 'I thought you'd given up that awful habit years ago, Sarah.'

'I had, but they all smoke in my office.' She took a long drag on her cigarette and exhaled in her mother's direction. 'And I find it helps to relieve tension.'

Sarah was as good as her word and a month later she took two week's leave and went down to Aldershot to house-hunt. It took them five days to find an attractive Georgian house on the outskirts of Farnham. The house was to rent but was also available to buy. Adam persuaded Sarah that it would be better to buy it with some of his Aunt Adeline's legacy.

By mid-December the house was theirs.

'Wouldn't it be fun to spend Christmas down there?' Adam asked hopefully.

'We're hardly ready for that.'

'Personally, I'm more than ready after years of living in the Mess.'

'That may be, but I can't leave London yet.'

'Well, why not? There's a fast train every morning that gets to Waterloo within the hour.'

'You *have* done your homework, darling. But I'll need to talk to Ivan.'

'Oh, bugger Ivan, you're married to me, not him.'

'Of course, darling,' She came and gave him a long tender kiss. 'I'll move down here as soon as it's confirmed that I'm pregnant.'

'Well, I suppose that's fair enough.'

'It shouldn't be too long, darling. Now, how about dinner and an early night?'

May 1947.

Sarah had been scouring the births columns of the Times and Telegraph for the announcement of Virginia's baby. They had stopped meeting for lunch when Virginia was seven months pregnant. Sarah felt it would be tiresome to bother her just before the baby was due. Far better to wait until the announcement, then send flowers and congratulations.

However, as the due date passed and there was no news, Sarah began to worry that something was amiss. Her anxiety was not helped by her own inability to get pregnant. She knew how important this baby was for the Chalvingtons. It had taken years for it to happen and she so wanted it to go well for Virginia. Each time she tried to telephone her friend, the butler would answer and always gave the same message. 'I regret that neither Lord nor Lady Chalvington are available.'

CHAPTER TWENTY FIVE

London, Late May 1947.

It was the day after Rindi had returned to Delhi that the startling news broke. It came from the tabloid press.

"Earl disclaims paternity of heir and files for divorce"

The story was soon taken-up by the other newspapers in their later editions. Sarah and Adam were totally perplexed. She tried again to get through to the castle, and on this occasion she managed to convince the butler that she was not the press. He agreed to pass on a message to Lady Chalvington asking her to please telephone Sarah.

'Adam, if I don't hear by the weekend, I'm going to drive down to Lythe Hill. I'll insist upon seeing her. She's obviously in some trouble.'

They agreed a plan, and on the Sunday morning after Sarah had left to go and see Virginia, Adam went up to the Lonsdale Club. He had not expected to see Simon Chalvington there, but spotted him in the distance, reading the notice board. Although he knew no details beyond what he had read in the press, Adam was still baffled as to why Simon thought the child was not his. They had been desperate for an heir so it had to be something quite serious for him to reject the child.

As Adam walked towards him, he was sure Simon would have seen him but as he approached, Simon turned and walked briskly away towards the library. It was possible that he hadn't seen him or that he didn't feel like talking to anyone and Adam decided he should not overreact to this apparent snub.

Chalvington sat in the library scanning the headlines of the previous day's Daily Telegraph. He found it almost impossible to concentrate, his mind being preoccupied with the humiliating state of his personal affairs. What a complete idiot he had been. To be cuckolded was bad enough; but by that Indian! And the swine had not even bothered to disguise his interest in Virginia. He had suspected the worst when he saw them together at Cullworthy's party. At first he hadn't recognised him but then the penny dropped. He was the chap he had found in her cabin on the boat. What a pity the rotter was tied-up with Cullworthy, who had always struck him as a decent chap. Now he would have to avoid him as well.

Chalvington thought of his family motto, "Honour Above All". As the thirteenth earl, he had made a poor job of it. Now he needed to prove that he had the courage to make amends to the family name. He had already taken the first steps by filing for a divorce and disclaiming Virginia's child as his heir. Thank God his father was not alive. The shock would have finished the old boy off.

Various plans for retribution were formulating in his mind, yet none seemed to fit the style or courage that his illustrious forebears would have adopted. One problem was logistics. The scoundrel had slipped back to India and retribution would now have to take place in that country. It was with this in mind that Chalvington's eye caught an item in the personal columns. *"Vernon: Major, Bengal Sappers (retired), recently returned from India seeks engagement."*

An investigation found that Vernon had incurred heavy gambling debts, far beyond his ability to pay, and that his involvement with a married woman had been less than honourable. A charge of conduct unbecoming to an officer was seriously considered. However his military record was otherwise unblemished and the District Commander had decided not to order a case against him. Instead, he suggested that Vernon take early retirement. This was not the sort of chap Chalvington would normally associate with but he seemed perfect for the task he had in mind.

Sarah's trip to Lythe Hill had been unsuccessful, although not entirely fruitless. When she arrived she could see a number of journalists hanging around hoping to catch sight of the Chalvingtons. Recognising Sarah as a friend of Virginia's, the butler had given her entry to the castle. On the strict understanding that she tell no one else, he disclosed that Lady Chalvington and the child had gone to an undisclosed location in Ireland. The butler also confirmed that Sarah's previous telephone message had been passed on to Lady Chalvington. There was nothing more Sarah could do but wait for Virginia to make contact.

'I can't believe Simon would have snubbed you. You seemed to get on perfectly well.'

'Well, he knows you are a close friend of hers so perhaps he thinks that would make me more sympathetic to Virginia.' Adam ventured.

'It's true, I am thinking about her and the baby. I'm itching to know the facts. Why on earth does Simon think the baby isn't his? He seemed so thrilled about the prospect of a son three weeks ago.'

'Maybe he's discovered a lover.'

'I think that's unlikely I am sure she would have given me an inkling of something like that.' Sarah added ponderously.

'Well as I told you she nearly ended her marriage before it had begun.'

'Yes, but that was over ten years ago. She certainly seems to have a penchant for the exotic.'

'You mean Wantilla?'

'Yes, and I think she rather fancied Rindi too.'

'Together with most of the English girls in Oxford,' Adam said with a hint of jealousy.

'I can't say I'd blame her for taking a lover. Simon seems devoid of any emotion and she as much as told me they very rarely make love.'

'Don't go getting any ideas now,' Adam said putting his arm round her waist.

'I've no complaints in that quarter,' she said pecking him on the cheek.

Adam and Sarah were at their house in Farnham the following weekend when Virginia's call came through. 'I've been ringing your number for two days.' She sounded anxious.

'Sorry about that,' Adam responded, 'we're usually only here at weekends. Sarah's been waiting for your call. Where are you now?'

'I'm in Dublin.'

'Are you alright?'

'Not exactly. Is Sarah there?'

Adam called Sarah to the telephone. After a brief conversation she came through to join him in the kitchen.

'Virginia's terribly distressed. She's staying in a place called Fox Rock, in a house belonging to her mother.'

'Fox Rock? Never heard of it.'

'No, and she's hoping the press haven't either. She wants me to go over and spend a few days with her. Would you mind?'

'Huh. Shouldn't you be asking Ivan?'

Sarah ignored his comment. 'I'm serious. Virginia's in an awful state.'

'Why do you have to go? She must have dozens of other friends.

And what about her mother? Surely she's the best person to go.'

'I asked the same question, but most of her friends are chums of Simon and they've made various excuses. As for her mother, she's totally distraught and thinks that what Virginia has done is unforgivable and can barely bring herself to speak to her.'

'You seem determined to play the Good Samaritan. I suppose it would be kind to go and see her; but just for a few days, a week at the absolute limit. You know I'm due to fly to Egypt with the battalion in three weeks' time.'

'Oh Lord. That date has caught up with us.'

Adam drove up to London the following Friday morning, collected Sarah and took her to the airport. He then went on to spend the weekend with her parents in Bayswater.

On Saturday morning he went to the Club to read the papers and use the steam room. He was surprised to see Chalvington there. He normally went down to the country at weekends. But then nothing about Simon's life was normal now and Lythe Hill was probably besieged wilh journalists. He was sitting in a corner of the Oak Room with his back half towards Adam. He was in deep conversation with a middle-aged man whose ruddy complexion was evidence of long over-indulgence and years in the Tropics. Adam had not seen this man before and assumed that he was a guest.

'That's Major Vernon, sir,' Reg, the Club barman confirmed, 'become quite a regular, more of a business acquaintance I'd say, sir,' he said raising an eyebrow as he continued polishing a wine glass.

Adam had taken two day's leave after the weekend to enable him to stay on in London and on the Tuesday afternoon he met Sarah off the Dublin flight. On the way back to her parents' house, Sarah related the startling information she had learnt that weekend.

'So how was Virginia?'

'In a desperate state, but rather grateful to see me. Everyone's deserted her.'

'And the baby?'

'He's a lovely little fellow, but ...' she hesitated.

'What?'

'Nothing, except that he's very dark.'

'Very dark? '

'Yes, you might say- a touch of the tar brush.'

'But Virginia and Simon are both quite fair.'

'Yes I know, but she told me that her great-grandmother was Indian. Did you know that?'

'Yes, actually I did. Rindi had reason to tell me. But I doubt whether Simon knew.'

'No. Virginia was always afraid that he would find out.'

'So has she told him now?'

'Yes, but he refuses to believe the baby's skin colour is just the result of a genetic throwback.'

'But she's sticking to that story?'

'It does happen sometimes.'

'So how dark is the baby?'

'Too dark to be acceptable as Simon's heir and he refuses to believe he is the father.'

'And there is no other possible explanation?'

'If you mean Wantilla, she always insists her fling with him ended some time ago and I felt it was indelicate to bring the subject up again.'

'I wouldn't put anything past that man. Rindi told me he had been back in England.'

'I feel so sorry for her. She's in such a pickle.'

'You seem to think that Virginia is the victim in all of this.'

'She has this lovely little boy that nobody wants and has become a social outcaste as a result.' Sarah replied.

'Yes, and I can't see Wantilla wanting anything to do with it either.'

Adam wanted to voice his disapproval but felt hypocritical that he had his own dark secret. 'Perhaps it's best we keep our distance from Virginia.'

'Oh, Adam don't be such a moralising prig.She needs someone to support her.'

Adam did have some sympathy for Virginia trapped in a cold sexless marriage and she wouldn't have been the first person to have sought solace elsewhere.

Egypt, 10th July 1947.

The camp base for the Second Wessex battalion was a tented desert location about five miles west of Isamilia. This Egyptian town on the Suez Canal, about halfway between Port Said and Suez, had a sizable

French population. These were mainly employees and officials of the Suez Canal Company who had operated the hundred mile long canal since it's opening in 1869.

The Command Headquarters was in the garrison of Moascar, a mile south of Ismailia. There were married quarters for officers with their own gardens; a tennis club; swimming pool, and the ubiquitous Navy, Army & Air Force Institute. Facilities included a Military Families Hospital with a well-equipped maternity wing. With these excellent conditions, all Adam needed was his wife.

When he had said goodbye to Sarah, she had tacitly agreed that she would join him as soon as circumstances were right. From his standpoint circumstances could not have been better. He applied for married accommodation, was allocated officer's quarters near the tennis club and cabled the good news to Sarah.

Adam had, optimistically, expected a cable back the next day, but had to wait over a week for Sarah's letter. Its content was not just disappointing, it was very annoying. She told him that pressures at the Ministry were such that she could not let them down by leaving at present, and since she was not yet pregnant, there was no urgency to move into married quarters.

Adam replied with a strongly worded letter, bordering on an ultimatum. And how did she expect to get pregnant when she was thousands of miles away? He contemplated writing to her mother, but decided that this might be counter-productive. Whilst Adam waited for Sarah's response he received a long and disturbing letter from Rindi.

Rindi had arrived back in India to find the country facing upheaval. Although India had experienced wars and invasions for thousands of years, this was something different. The whole country was involved in bloody conflict as it raced towards the date set for independence. Mohammed Ali Jinnah, the leader of the Muslim League, fought bitterly against Mountbatten's mandate to keep independent India as a single state. He insisted upon, and finally won, the right to a separate Islamic Pakistan. Consequently millions of Hindus and Sikhs - the latter being the most vulnerable - were leaving the northern Punjab. Similarly, millions of Muslims were packing the trains heading north towards Lahore and Rawalpindi.

Throughout India there were reports of atrocities being committed by the rival religions: Sikhs and Hindus on one hand, against Muslims on the other. Those who had lived happily together for many centuries suddenly found themselves embroiled in wanton ethnic slaughter, intent upon inflicting the maximum humiliation and suppression on those of the other religion. Rape, degradation and massacre were a daily occurrence.

The root of the problem was the loss of the authority of the British and Indian Armies. The British were preparing to depart, whilst the Indian battalions were negotiating to join the respective armies of the future independent nations of India and Pakistan. Not least the hectic and acrimonious scramble to secure the maximum quantity of arms and ammunition to take with them. Each Indian Army unit would take it upon themselves to defend the religion and honour of their particular group. Partiality was inevitable.

One of the tragedies was that the Indian troops who had fought so magnificently side by side in Burma, should now indulge in such barbarism. Rindi reported that as their British officers departed, they would turn upon other regiments and defenceless villagers. A Hindu company would move into a predominantly Muslim village, rape every female in the place regardless of age, then murder their victims and leave them lying in the streets. In reprisal, Muslim troops would lay in wait for a troop train carrying soldiers. The engine would be blown-off the rails and as the Hindu soldiers attempted to escape from the overturned carriages, they would be gunned down.

In Kushnapur things had also become strained. Rindi could not forgive himself for staying in England to complete his studies. He felt guilty that he had not been at his father's side in these difficult times. Particularly disturbing was the news that Wantilla had been elected to the Legislative Assembly. Rindi described the details of Wantilla's appearance at the durbar. He might have been odious before but with his new found status he had now become insufferable

The saving grace for Kushnapur was its remoteness. After consultation with Rindi and the dewan, the maharajah agreed that Kushnapur would remain part of the new India. However, there were thousands of Muslims who had come to live in Kushnapur over the centuries. Few of these wished to go to Pakistan and it was important to make them feel secure enough to stay.

Adam had hoped the letter would include news of Kafni and Pratap, but sadly not. Rindi was clearly too preoccupied with the drama unfolding as the British prepared to leave the stage.

When it finally arrived, Sarah's reply offered Adam little

consolation. "I'll resign and come to join you as soon as I can, darling ……" Adam wrote back saying how disappointed he was that she considered being a ministerial secretary as more important than being there to support him in his role as commanding officer. She of all people should understand that. Adam was coming to the realisation that their careers were increasingly incompatible.

CHAPTER TWENTY SIX

Saharanpur, North East India, 21ˢᵗ July 1947.

Three weeks after their final meeting in London, Chalvington joined Vernon in his hotel room in Saharanpur. So far, everything had gone according to plan.

'You appear to have done your part well, Vernon. I must say your local knowledge has been invaluable, albeit that I find some of your contacts are rather unsavoury.'

'Needs must, my lord.' Vernon tugged nervously at the corner of his moustache.

'Indeed. So what news of my quarry?'

'We gather that he left on a trip with his sister, a young cousin called Narajan and one of the senior officers at the Palace.

'Do we know where they were going?'

'As far as we can gather they were heading for Lahore. But I can't think why they would want to go there when all this violence is taking place. Our source tells us they are due back within the week.'

'We'll just have to sit it out and wait.'

'We have another man in a petrol station on the outskirts of town. It's the only one for miles so they are bound to stop there on their way through to Kushnapur. He'll tell us when they're on the way.'

'Will that give you enough time to set the plan in motion?'

'My man with the explosives is already up there and I will join him tomorrow.'

'Are you sure you can trust him?'

'He was my sergeant for many years. Besides, what we're paying him will set him up for a very comfortable retirement.'

'They all know the signals?'

'Yes. We've rehearsed it all several times.'

The Gorge, Kushnapur Palace, 26th July 1947.

The afternoon sun was beginning its descent to the west when Chalvington drove his car off the road and parked it out of sight in a small *jangal* of deodar trees. He opened the boot and took out field glasses, a fishing rod, a fishing bag, and a long canvas bag with a carrying handle. To the casual observer this last item might appear to contain just another rod. In fact the bag concealed an automatic rifle.

Chalvington locked the boot and the car doors, picked up his equipment, walked back to the road and headed north. He felt the scorching heat reflected off the tarred road. The heavy rain of the previous night had now dried out. Only the lush green vegetation and the bank of clouds building-up in the south west gave evidence that the country was in the middle of the monsoon season.

The conifer-lined road ran along the bottom of a shallow valley. At the end, about half a mile ahead, it disappeared into a narrow gorge. Chalvington admired the perfect location Vernon had chosen. This road was only used by traffic to and from the palace, and most of the time it was deserted.

Some minutes after entering the gorge, Chalvington rounded a slight bend, stopped and raised his field glasses. Focusing on a high point at the upper end of the gorge, he could see Vernon's sergeant crouched beside a boulder. He was well positioned to warn and prevent anyone entering that end of the gorge. Lower down, with only the top of his hat visible, Vernon was kneeling beside the blasting generator.

Chalvington positioned himself on the outer curve of the bend, commanding a view in both directions. His "fishing tackle" lay innocently on the opposite side of the road. All he had to do now was wait. A party of chattering *shudra* women, brightly dressed in green and yellow saris, approached from the north and passed by without appearing to notice him. Shortly afterwards, a five-ton truck with several workmen in the back, passed in the same direction. The driver slowed down, but receiving no request to stop, drove on.

Chalvington chain-smoked as the minutes dragged on. He listened intently, frequently consulting his watch. And then he saw it. Even without field glasses, there was no mistaking the Bentley shooting-break as it took the climb up off the main road about a mile away. He raised his right arm high above his head and swept it down, then raised his field glasses to check the response. The sergeant stood up, holding the rifle above his head with his left hand. With his right arm he gave the pre-arranged umpire's boundary-four signal. This confirmed that no one was in his section of the gorge.

Chalvington crossed the road and released the four pre-positioned boulders one after another. They rolled down the slope into the middle of the road. He unzipped the canvas bag and took out the automatic rifle which he held inconspicuously by his side. He heard the car rapidly approaching and, as it rounded the bend the driver braked hard and the vehicle skidded to a standstill a few feet from the rocks.

The passenger's window wound down and Rindi called out, 'What the devil's going on here?' He found himself looking down the barrel of the automatic rifle.

'Get out! Hands on your head.'

Rindi recognised the distinctive features of Simon Chalvington. He did not like the deranged look on his face and did as he was requested. Simultaneously, Narajan opened his door and started to get out.

'Not you!' Chalvington snapped at him. 'Get back in, and tell your driver to turn the car round. Now!'

'Chalvington, what the hell is this? What on earth are you doing here?

'You'll learn soon enough, Debrahm. Tell your driver to get that car out of here.'

Rindi half turned, and, keeping his hands on his head said, 'Do as he says, Narajan. I'll deal with Lord Chalvington here.' Making it clear to his young cousin who his captor was.

'What about the ling....?.'

'Never mind that!' Rindi cut him off. 'Make your way back to the Palace. The *Dewan* will know what to do.'

Narajan looked surprised. He had not encountered an English lord before and this was not what he had imagined them to be like. He nervously got back into the car and the driver started the engine. Less than a minute later they had completed the difficult manoeuvre of turning the Bentley round in the limited space. The other passenger door now opened and Major Chandra who had been biding his time to assess the situation got out.

'Sahib, if you want a hostage please take me instead.'

Chalvington gesticulated with his rifle, and snapped at Chandra.

'Get back in the car, you bloody idiot. We haven't got time for this. I'll give you two minutes to get clear of the gorge.'

'Harish, do as he says,' said Rindi.

Chandra nodded and reluctantly got back into the Bentley. They drove off, leaving Rindi still held at gunpoint and trying to fathom what Chalvington intended to do.

'Just what exactly is the purpose of all of this?' Rindi asked in bewilderment.

'Don't play the innocent with me, Debrahm. You know exactly what you've done.'

'Truly, I haven't the first clue.'

'I knew you weren't innocent on board that boat and now my suspicions have been confirmed.'

'What on earth do you mean?'

'What I mean is the little brown bastard that you and my wife have produced.'

And with that he swung the rifle barrel into the air and fired two clearly spaced single shots. The sound echoed through the gorge. The Bentley had now disappeared from sight.

There was an eerie silence. There was a wild look in Chalvington's eyes and a triumphant smile crept across his face. Suddenly the air was rent by a series of earth-shattering explosions destroying the natural barrier which held the vast Kushnapur lake in-tact. One blast followed another as the detonations reverberated along the sheer rock face of the gorge. The deafening sound of the explosions gave way to a rumbling sound growing ever stronger. 'Nothing can stop it now!' Chalvington spat out the words.

'What have you done, you complete madman?'

'I've blown the dam and within a few minutes we will both be under a torrent of water and my family's honour will be satisfied.'

Rindi stood in total disbelief at what was happening. The rumbling had changed to an urgent gushing sound interspersed with the cracking noise of trees being flattened.

'This is crazy! You've got this all wrong.'

Chalvington was still pointing the gun at Rindi. A startled black buck broke cover and shot past them away from the rumbling noise.

'You might as well admit it Debrahm no point in denying it now.'

At that moment a shot rang out and Chalvington dropped the gun and staggered backwards clutching his chest. From above him on the cliff face Rindi saw Chandra holding a gun.

'Run, sahib, run for your life,' he shouted.

But it was too late. Moments later he and Chalvington were swept away by a tidal wave of water twenty feet high.

Desperate to find Rindi, Chandra raced back along the ridge the way he had come. Anxiously scanning the raging torrent now rushing far ahead of him. In the fast fading light, this became increasingly difficult. There was no sign of Rindi, even at the place where Chandra knew that he might have been able to climb clear of the water.

Despite his exhaustion, Chandra forced himself to go on. He was conscious of the fact that Wantilla's scheming nephew Narajan was now in charge of the lingam. Could he really be relied on to return it to the Palace? The well-laid plan to exchange the Princess Kafni for the lingam and return it to the Kushnapur was unravelling fast and it was now also probable that the Rajkumar Rindi had been swept to his death.

He collapsed with exhaustion as he reached the Dak bungalow which had luckily been far enough from the torrent to avoid any real damage. There he found a distraught *chokidar,* attempting to telephone the police station for help. He took over and seconds later he was speaking to the officer-in-charge.

A series of police patrols were immediately organised to set up roadblocks and comb the hills to make sure that everyone had got out of the area. Chandra then telephoned the palace and ordered his deputy to send out every available guard to scour the domain and arrest anyone not authorised to be there. He spoke to the maharajah and reported the terrible news. He had nothing positive to tell him. Rindi was missing, presumed drowned. The Bentley and Narajan were also missing with the lingam still in the boot of the car.

The following day, Kushnapur Palace.

It was a tormented Chandra who presented himself to his maharajah the next morning, and bowed his head as he spoke. "Your highness, we delivered the Princess Kafni to Wantilla in Lahore and received the lingam in exchange, but now it is lost and the Rajkumar is missing. I beg to offer my resignation. I have completely failed you.'

'Chandra, you are one of my most loyal and trusted members of staff. I do not wish to hear mention of your resignation. We must have faith that both will be found and I now need your help.'

'*Shukriya Hazrat,* I am totally at your service.'

'Right! Then come with me. I believe the *dewan* has some news for us.'

'A retired sapper jemadar was arrested by a police patrol last night,'the Dewan reported, 'and in the early hours of this morning, a sahib calling himself Major Vernon was found by the palace search party. They managed to stop him shooting himself with his revolver. Both these prisoners now await your interrogation, Major Chandra.'

'*Shukriya, Dewanji,* they will be questioned intensively, and the results handed over to the state prosecutor. Have you any news of the Rajkumar Rindi, or the lingam?'

'A search party of thirty men left at first light this morning. The *subadar* in charge has instructions to follow the flood and search the course of the Alaknanda River. It is a hazardous task- the ravines are deep and inaccessible and the rock faces steep and treacherous. The first man who finds the rajkumar will be rewarded with a thousand rupees. '

'Have we any information about the lingam and the Bentley? The driver is one of my most trusted soldiers. I am sure he will return soon.'

'Yes, we have had some news, but I'm not sure how reliable it is. The Bentley was last seen travelling very fast through the outskirts of Saharanpur in the early hours of the morning. The report said there was only *one* person in the car.'

Further information came that afternoon. The Bentley had been found abandoned outside a village near Ambala, eighty miles north-west of Saharanpur. In the car was the body of the Kushnapur driver, with fatal knife wounds in his back and chest. There was no sign of Narajan, or of the crate containing the lingam, but the police had found a note.

"*I have been kidnapped by Muslim extremists who have threatened to kill me if their ransom demand is not paid. They say they will make contact.*"

Narajan Ram.

Chandra was sceptical. Why had it been written by Narajan? This was no normal ransom note. But these were not normal times. Why would they need to ask for a ransom when they had one of the most valuable treasures on the Indian subcontinent? He could only hope that they would make contact soon and didn't decide it would be easier to break up the Kushnapur lingam. Maybe they hadn't even discovered what was in the wooden crates.

The police at Ambala opened a murder inquiry and ordered Narajan Ram to be detained for questioning. A *havildar* and a small party of Kushnapur sepoys were dispatched to honour their dead soldier driver and collect the Bentley. Their mood was angry and vengeance against Muslims was uppermost in their minds.

The Alaknanda Valley, 29th July 1947.

The early morning sunshine burnt its way through the last traces of the dawn mist as Rindi stumbled along the ravine, a few feet above the raging water. Around him were small branches, twigs, loose reeds and a silt line showing the high point that the flooded river had reached during the night. He vaguely recalled being caught on the branch of an overhanging tree and dragging himself from the river. Beyond that, he remembered nothing. Now scanning the sheer rock faces, he saw, about fifty yards ahead, a *nullah* running down into the ravine.

He staggered on, hoping he had found an escape route; his head throbbed and his body ached with bruises. Reaching the *nullah,* a small waterfall forced him to cling to the rocks as he started his hazardous ascent.

For two hours, Rindi struggled up the steep damp slope, frequently sliding back on his hands and knees, where the rocks defied his grasp. Pausing to regain his energy he felt a gentle breeze carrying the scent of wild rock plants, making him aware that he was nearing the top. Intensely tired, he relaxed his concentration and lost his footing on a wet boulder. Unable to save himself he fell and crashed his head against a jutting rock.

Slowly regaining consciousness, Rindi became aware of a gentle swaying motion, the scent of grain and the pungent aroma of hessian gunnysacks. He heard the bleat of a goat, and propped himself up on his elbows. He was lying on sacks of corn and rice on the back of an ox cart. Staring at him two feet away was a kid goat and beyond it a young boy not more than eight-years old.

'Father! The man's awake,' cried the boy.

The driver stopped the cart and spoke to Rindi. '*Namaste,* sahib. *Ap kaise hain?*

'*Namaste.*' responded Rindi.

'We are taking you to our home to give you food and a place to rest.'

'*Shukriya.* How far is your home?'

'Two hours more. We live at Rikhali village, near the *Chota.*'

Wondering how he might reward their kindness Rindi reached into his pocket to see if he had any rupees. His fingers felt a few wet notes. Memories of the scene in the gorge now came back to him with painful clarity. His only solace from these bleak thoughts was that Chandra had managed to get away and had hopefully been able to return the lingam safely to Kushnapur. He needed to urgently contact the palace to tell them he was still alive. Before he could act on this thought he slipped back into a semi-comatose state. He did not know how long he'd slept but when he awoke the ox cart driver was leaning over him checking to see if he was still alive.

'Good morning, sahib.'

Rindi attempted to respond but only produced an incoherent grunt.

'Where is sahib coming from?

The driver clearly had no idea who he was. As Rindi gathered his thoughts he decided it was better to maintain his anonymity for the present.

'My family live near Kushnapur City. Do you know where I can get a bus to go there?'

'There is a bus from our village this afternoon that will go to Kushnapur.'

'Good. I must return home as soon as possible. I also need to contact my family to tell them where I am. Is there a telephone in your village?'

'Yes, sahib, at the village general store.'

Two hours later, whilst waiting for the bus, Rindi went into the village store to enquire about using the telephone. He glanced down at the pile of newspapers on the counter and was surprised to see a photograph of himself on the front page. He was then shocked to read that he was suspected of having murdered Lord Chalvington and there was a three-thousand rupee reward for information leading to his capture. Fortunately in his dishevelled state he bore little resemblance to the picture of him well-groomed in army uniform.

The store manager asked him what he wanted and Rindi said he would like to use the telephone. The manager explained that the telephone was out of order, but that he hoped it would be working again within two days. He told Rindi that there was a telephone at the Post Office in the next town. If he wanted he could take the next bus, which would take him there. Rindi thanked him and left the store hoping he had not been recognised.

His wait for the bus seemed interminable and when he finally boarded it he breathed a sigh of relief. He had sufficient slightly damp rupees to buy a ticket to the next town, from where he would telephone the palace.

Any comfort that Rindi may have felt at not being recognized was short-lived. The village storekeeper had indeed recognised him and had acted rapidly to claim the reward. As the bus stopped at the Post Office, two plain-clothes detectives boarded the bus and asked him to accompany them to the local police station. At first Rindi resisted suspecting them of being bogus policemen. This did not endear him to them and he found himself treated like a common criminal. His request to make a telephone call was denied. As he sat in a dark cell, enduring the pervasive stench of urine, he wondered how long it would be before word got back to the palace that he was in custody.

CHAPTER TWENTY SEVEN

The Punjab, 1st August 1947.

To the Kushnapur soldiers, news of the pre-independence human chaos in the western Punjab was extremely disturbing. Reports of Hindus and Sikhs fleeing for their lives, or being persecuted, raped and murdered in cities like Lahore and Rawalpindi, soon to be embraced into Islamic Pakistan, inflamed their desire for retribution.

Having collected the Bentley from the police, they drove to the town of Kurukshetra, where they had been told that thousands of Muslims were passing through the railway junction on their way to the northern Punjab.

At the station, led by their *havildar*, the party climbed out of the shooting-break and walked through the booking hall and on to the platform. The train standing there was awaiting the arrival of an Up train on the broad gauge single line from Delhi and Panipat junction, before being able to proceed.

As the Kushnapuri soldiers reached the carriages they heard the most pitiful wailing, and looking through the windows the reason was all too evident. In almost every compartment were Hindu men, women and children with horrific injuries. Two army doctors and four nurses from the cantonment at Ambala had joined the train, and were giving first aid and emergency treatment. Many casualties were beyond the scope of their limited facilities and needed urgent hospital surgery. The best they could do was to stem the haemorrhage of severed limbs and lacerated bodies. In the guard's van were the bodies of those who had not survived, several hideously mutilated. Two young women had their breasts slashed off and another had a gaping abdomen with a dead foetus spewing out.

'Memsahib-nurse, where did this happen?' cried the *havildar*. She looked exhausted with her blood and sweat soaked uniform clinging to her body as she abandoned another victim who hadn't made it.

'The train was halted and attacked last night at Raiwind Junction, half-an-hour out of Lahore,' she replied wearily. 'The soldiers guarding the train couldn't control the mob. There were hundreds of men and women armed with knives and swords, screaming for blood.'

A young army doctor shouted an order at her. 'Quick, go to the end compartment. There are two boys there who've had their penises cut off. Have we any morphine left?'

'Probably half a dozen shots.'

'Just give 'em a quarter shot each, their systems won't take more than that. When you have dealt with them, please come back immediately, I need help with a leg amputation. A few more hours in this heat and gangrene will set in.'

The *havildar* saluted the doctor. 'Is there any help that my men can give you, Captain-sahib?'

'Thank you, sergeant. Are any of them trained in first aid?' he asked wearily.

'So sorry, Captain-sahib, they are not.'

'Then the best thing is to get them away as quickly as you can. We're waiting for that damn train to come up from Panipat junction. We need the single line clear so that we can get this train through to New Delhi and the General Hospital.'

Just then, a breathless Anglo-Indian stationmaster came up.

'Not much longer now, Captain-sahib. The refugee train went through Kanal Station seventeen minutes ago. It will be here in fifteen minutes. I've ordered the signalman to give it a clear run through the station without stopping. We don't want to risk any trouble; there are fifty Muslim families on board.'

'God help them if their train gets stopped.'

'Is there no end to this madness, Captain sahib?'

The doctor looked at his bloodstained gloves and medical gown.

'For two hundred years Hindus and Muslims have lived happily side-by-side under British rule. Now they are being allowed to run their own countries and all they can think about is slaughtering each other.'

'How can we stop the massacres?' the stationmaster pleaded.

'Just try and keep them apart.'

The *havildar* had seen enough. He saluted and left abruptly. He instructed his men to follow him. He was thankful that they had not overheard mention of the imminent arrival of the Muslim laden train. Before there was time for their anger to foment further he reminded them that any acts of indiscipline would result in the severest punishment Major Chandra could inflict. Mercifully this was enough of a real threat to ensure they contained their rage. Returning to the vehicles they set off in subdued silence on their return journey to the palace.

Kushnapur, 2nd August.

At the palace, events had been no less dramatic. Vernon had been subjected to hours of intensive questioning by Chandra. At first, he had been taciturn, claiming that he was only subject to the authority of the British and had requested access to a lawyer. Chandra had consulted the dewan, who had agreed that for many reasons it was important that Vernon remain in their custody. There was, of course, the problem of MacDonald, the British Resident in Kushnapur. He had already been given the initial report of the blasting at the lake. He could hardly have missed it; almost everyone in the state knew about the deluge, but he had not yet been informed of Vernon's capture.

Chandra needed more time. He calculated that to avoid being ordered to hand over Vernon to the British authorities three factors would serve his purpose. The first was that no charge had yet been made against Vernon; the second that Vernon might be persuaded that it would be in his own interests to voluntarily remain in their custody. And finally, as MacDonald was due to leave his post when it became redundant after Partition, he was unlikely to wish to get involved, unless circumstances absolutely demanded it. Chandra and the dewan intended to make sure that nothing should arise to draw his attention to Vernon's arrest.

As the flood subsided, the Kushnapur police had found the body of Lord Chalvington. Macdonald was notified, and he instructed it to be handed over to the British police at Saharanpur. They immediately opened a murder enquiry. Forensic tests revealed that Chalvington had been shot. The bullet had passed right through the body and the calibre was not easily identifiable. This process was further frustrated by the fact that no weapon and no bullet had yet been found.

Armed with fresh intelligence, Chandra returned to interview Vernon.

'I must tell you, Major Vernon, that there have been certain developments which may cause you to reconsider your request to be moved from our custody to that of the British Indian police.'

'Police? Who said anything about the police? I'm a retired Indian Army officer.'

Chandra ignored this. 'Lord Chalvington's body has been found, and by order of the British Resident has been handed over to the police at Saharanpur. They have now opened a murder enquiry.'

Vernon looked stunned. 'Murder! Why do they suspect murder?'

'Chalvington was found to have been shot and that rather than drowning was almost certainly the cause of death.'

'Good God. They don't think that I did it?'

As Chandra had correctly anticipated, Vernon was rapidly changing his attitude. The prospect of being accused of the murder of an English peer opened an ugly aspect to his situation, albeit that Vernon knew he was innocent. Proving it was another matter.

Chandra now played his trump card. 'Your *jemadar* sapper has also been picked up and is now in our custody. He has been very co-operative.'

The colour drained from Vernon's face. He had hoped that the *jemadar* would have got clean away to enjoy his rewards.

'What do you propose I do?'

'You were captured on Kushnapuri soil. Pending charges being made against you, you could voluntarily place yourself at the pleasure of His Highness the Maharajah of Kushnapur; ostensibly to advise on dealing with the devastation caused.'

'Why would I do that?'

'For many reasons. The most important is that I am the only person who knows positively that you did not shoot Lord Chalvington.'

'Of course I didn't shoot him; I was miles away. Anyway, how do you know I am innocent?'

'I was there and saw him die. Just before the wall of water reached him he shot himself.' Chandra lied but knew that only two people had witnessed exactly what had happened, and the other person was still missing.

'Holy Jesus! He never told me that was his intention. It was simply agreed that we would never meet again. What do you want of me?'

'Subject to the approval of the *dewan* and the maharajah, you will be given a document to sign. It will state that you are indebted to his highness and undertake to serve and advise him, without reimbursement, in any professional capacity that he may direct. And further, you undertake not to leave the precincts of the palace grounds without the written authority of the *dewan*.'

'Does this mean that I am to be a permanent prisoner here?'

'We intend that you will devote much of the rest of your working life to supervising the reparation of the damage you have done.'

There was a pause as Vernon absorbed what he had heard, his mind sifting through the grim predicament facing him. Could he ever extricate himself from this nightmare?

'It seems I am in no position to bargain with you.'

'Finally I must tell you that fifty of the maharajah's men are now searching the ravines for the Rajkumar Rindi. You should pray, as we do, that he is still alive, because if he is dead you will certainly be charged with causing his murder.' With that, Chandra left the room.

Next morning when Chandra responded to the chief minister's urgent call, he found him in considerable distress. 'Have we any news of the rajkumar, dewanji?'

'Indeed we do, and every piece of it is bad. Those idiot police in Saharanpur have issued a warrant for the arrest of the Rajkumar Rindi on suspicion of murdering Lord Chalvington. Our search for him has so far proved unsuccessful. This gives us some comfort that he may still be alive but it has made the police even more suspicious. Those fools are not fit to be detectives; they should be shot for even thinking that Rindi is a murderer.'

'Can't the Resident help us? He must know that the Rajkumar would never do such a thing.'

'Sir Iain says his authority is rapidly waning but has promised to talk to the police as soon as Rindi is found.'

'Would the Resident be prepared to see me so that I can explain what really happened?'

'I think he'd say the same thing. Come and see me when Rindi has been found. You should bear in mind that the Resident would want to know why he had not been told before and exactly what you witnessed. He might also be curious about why the lingam had been stolen and why he had not been told. We must certainly avoid that.'

In another part of the palace in her private quarters the Princess Puhella sat gazing out of the window. Her eyes, red and swollen from crying, were making it difficult for her to focus. Except to visit her mother, she had not left her room since she heard that Rindi was missing, and may have drowned. That was two days before.

'Have patience and faith,' her mother had said. 'No body has been found so there is hope that he is still alive.'

Since then, Puhella had devoted herself to almost continuous prayer. Now her *ayah* had come with more distressing news.

'How could they think Rindi guilty of such a crime? Have they forgotten his bravery and his medals?'

'Do not lose hope *Rajkumari*,' her *ayah* said trying to comfort her.

She turned back from the window, and looked at her *puja* box with its rich trappings of Hindu devotions. Two days of prayer had brought her little solace. She knew that her God Shiva worked in strange ways; he could both destroy and create. But all she could see now was destruction.

She knelt on the prayer rug and bowed her head. 'You have taken my sister Kafni to a far away place. *Meharbani karke Shiva,*' she silently begged her God, 'please not my beloved brother as well. Kushnapur now needs him more than ever.'

The ayah came and knelt behind her mistress, and murmured, 'Perhaps Lord Shiva wishes us to do something ourselves, or to find someone who can help us.'

Puhella turned to her servant with a new look of resolve on her face. 'Yes, maybe you are right, Rashni, and I know someone who would know what to do. But he is in Egypt.'

'Who could possibly help us from Egypt, Highness?'

'Rajkumar Rindi's very best friend, Cullworthy-sahib. He is now a burra-sahib.'

'But how can he help us when he is so far away?'

'He will find a way. He is very clever and brave like our *Rajputs,* and has many awards for gallantry. He will know how to deal with these people, and he will help find Rajkumar Rindi and the...' she stopped herself saying "lingam." Its loss needed to be kept secret, even from the faithful Rashni. She now knew there were unscrupulous people who would go to any lengths to steal this priceless treasure. She must not make her servant vulnerable to these people.

'Rashni, you must go to Delhi. I know that Cullworthy-sahib has a friend at GHQ in New Delhi called Brigadier Mercer. I shall arrange for a uniformed *chaprassi* to accompany you. The guards will not permit a woman, without a pass, to enter GHQ, but they will not question a uniformed *chaprassi*.'

'When do you wish us to leave, Highness?'

'You must be ready to go in two hours. Do you have relatives in Delhi?'

'I have two aunts there, your Highness.'

'We will have to say that one of them is ill and you need to go and see her urgently. For the present, no one here must know the real reason for your visit to Delhi. The dewan might not permit one of his *chaprassi* to travel so far in these dangerous times. The *chaprassi* and your *dasi* will not be told your actual destination until you reach New Delhi.'

She realised how dangerous this mission was at this turbulent time but she also knew they desperately needed help. She gave instructions for a *chaprassi* to be ready by noon to accompany Rashni to Delhi. Train seats were reserved and a car ordered to take them to Saharanpur station.

Puhella spent two hours drafting a letter. She knew how important it was to get the wording right, if it was not to be dismissed as the whim of some lovesick Indian woman. The palace headed notepaper that she now wrote on should lend sufficient gravitas to her letter. Nevertheless, what would really count was how good a friend of Adam's was this Brigadier Mercer.

Egypt, 4th August 1947.

Adam felt a frisson of pleasure as his signals officer told him he had an international call coming through from GHQ.

This could only mean one thing; Sarah must have changed her mind. It was not easy to get an ordinary trunk call, so it must have taken a bit of clout to get an international call put through. But then with the influence of that minister of hers, it would not be too difficult.

As Adam sat waiting for the call, he began to feel a trifle conciliatory towards Ivan. Perhaps he had a soul after all. As the telephone rang he was poised, brimming with charm to respond to her.

He picked up the receiver and was surprised to hear an Indian-accented voice addressing him as Colonel-sahib, and asking him to hold on for Brigadier Mercer-sahib.

'How's married life treating you, Adam?'

'Fine, thank you,' he lied.

'And how are things with you? I thought you were heading back to Oxford.'

'That was the idea and I've been offered a Chair in History at New College but events here have rather scuppered that plan.'

'Yes, I hear it's not going as smoothly as hoped.'

'That's the understatement of the day.'

'But I assume this is not a social call.'

'Sadly not, Adam, the reason for the call is that I've had a letter from a Princess Puhella Debrahm. Do you know her?'

'I do indeed, she's one of Rindi Debrahm's sisters.'

'Yes, I gathered as much. Well, she seems to be very worried about her brother. The letter was brought to Delhi by her ayah and a *chaprassi*. They're asking for your help and insisting on a reply.' Bob read Adam the letter.

'This sounds serious.'

'Yes, Adam, but I'm not sure there's much *you* can do about it. What shall I tell them?'

Adam made a quick decision. 'Tell them I'll come to India. I can be there within three days.'

'You can't be serious.'

'Yes, Bob, I'm deadly serious. I know the family they wouldn't ask for help if they weren't in real trouble.'

'But how can you help them? And how do you plan to get here?'

'I'll have to decide what I can do when I arrive. Getting there should not be a problem; BOAC now have three flights a week that land in Cairo and go on to Karachi and Delhi. I'll get on one of those. I've got quite a bit of leave due so I should be able to be there by Sunday.'

'You amaze me. This family really must mean a lot to you.'

'Yes, they do.'

'Cable me your flight number and I'll get someone to meet you at Palam Airport. And I'll book you into a hotel.'

'That would be extremely helpful, thank you.'

In a way this dramatic development was an effective counter to his disappointment that the call was not from Sarah. It may even have spurred him on to go to India.

10th August 1947, Delhi.

On arrival at Palam Airport in Delhi he was met by Bob Mercer's *naik*. He informed Adam that Brigadier Mercer had been called away to Ambala Cantonment but that he had made a reservation for Colonel-sahib in the Imperial Hotel.

Adam gave the hotel telephone operator the Kushnapur Palace number. After what seemed an age his call came through.

'Sorry, sahib,' said the palace operator, 'the Rajkumar, he is not available. Major Chandra-sahib will speak with you.'

Chandra came on the line. *'Namaste*, Colonel Cullworthy-sahib. I hope you are well. Did you have a good flight?'

'Yes, thank you, major. Where is Rajkumar Rindi?'

'I am afraid the news is very bad. He's been arrested.'

'Whatever for?'

'They're accusing him of murdering Lord Chalvington.'

Adam took a minute to digest this piece of news.

'Hold on Chandra. Why was Chalvington even in India? And why would anyone think Rindi had murdered him?'

'It is a complicated story Colonel-sahib, best not to discuss on the telephone.'

'When did this happen?'

'Two weeks ago. There have been some terrible events here. Can you possibly come to Kushnapur?'

'Of course I will.'

'If you can take Monday night's Frontier Mail to Saharanpur, I'll be at the station to meet you.'

Kushnapur, 12th August 1947.

Chandra was at the station to meet Adam and by the time they had reached the palace he had given him the full story as far as he knew it. Adam found it incredible that the Debrahms would exchange Kafni for the lingam and indeed that she would agree to go to Wantilla whom he knew she reviled. He couldn't express these thoughts to Chandra who was a loyal servant of the family and who presented Adam with this news very matter of factly.

'You may wish to speak to this Vernon yourself,' said Chandra interrupting Adam's thoughts. 'He thinks his status as a retired British army officer gives him privileges. Maybe he will be more co-operative with you.'

The name Vernon meant nothing to Adam.

'Where is this chap now?'

'You could say he is a long-term guest of the maharajah.'

'I see, and what is his connection with Lord Chalvington?'

'He was in the Bengal Sappers and I gather Chalvington used his engineering skills to execute the destruction of the dam.'

'I still find it incredible that he would cause such devastation just to kill one man.'

'And he even failed to do that.' Chandra said trying to appear sanguine.

'So where is Rindi being held?'

'We have been informed that he is in the custody of the Indian Police. They're beginning to flex their muscles on the eve of Independence, and I think they're rather enjoying having an excuse to hold the son of a maharajah.'

'So who can authorise his release?'

'The District Magistrate, or the police themselves if they've insufficient evidence to charge him.'

'What about the British Resident? He must have plenty of clout.'

'At his last meeting with Sir Iain, the maharajah had to defend his right to the *gaddi,* so he was reluctant to get him involved particularly as it might give Mahavir another opportunity to lay claim to the *gaddi.*'

'Does the Resident still hold power locally?'

'Oh yes. Whilst Mountbatten is in Delhi, the Resident's wishes will be adhered to.'

'Well, perhaps I should try and have a meeting with him. How easy is it to get to see him?'

'It would normally take about a week.'

'That's hopeless. We need to get Rindi released as soon as possible.'

Before pursuing this idea further Adam decided that it would be sensible to consult the maharajah. He knew well enough that Rindi's father would not let protocol stand in the way of any action that might secure Rindi's release, but Adam did not want to interfere with any initiatives that he or his *dewan* had already planned.

'Adam how very good of you to come to our aid at this very distressing time.'

'When I received Puhella's message I came as soon as I could. I only hope I can be of some assistance.'

'Puhella should not have requested you come as I am sure you have important duties to fulfil with your battalion. But I must say I am very relieved that you did. I am sure your influence will be helpful.'

The maharajah had arranged for the court astrologer to attend their meeting. He greeted Adam and gripped his hand and said, 'your presence here is most propitious, Colonel-sahib. The day after tomorrow is the fifteenth of August, the day my fellow astrologers have chosen for the Independence of India. You will find some success on that day.'

Before dinner, Adam had a less formal meeting with the maharani and Puhella, both of whom thanked him for coming to India at such short notice. Whilst Rindi's release and proving his innocence was foremost in their minds, neither of them seemed prepared to talk about Kafni's absence from the palace. Whether this was because of their own discomfort or to avoid causing him further distress he never knew.

After dinner Adam telephoned the Resident's secretary. He was a crusty major, seconded from the Indian Cavalry. 'Why the devil are you disturbing me at this time of the night?'

'Sorry, Major, I'm afraid it is extremely urgent. My name's Cullworthy, I am the C.O. of the Second Wessex stationed in Egypt. I flew in from Cairo the day before yesterday. I am a guest of the Maharajah of Kushnapur and now his envoy in the matter of the arrest of his son the Rajkumar Rindi.'

'Yes, I've heard about it. Rather a tricky one that shooting of Lord Chalvington.'

'Steady, Major. The rajkumar has not even been charged. There is only the flimsiest of evidence against him. I know with absolute certainty that he didn't do it. I would very much appreciate an opportunity to discuss this matter with Sir Iain as soon as possible.'

'Well now, it's very short notice and as you can appreciate the Resident has a packed agenda ahead of the Independence day.' There was a pause followed by the sound of pages being turned.' I think I can fit you in for a brief meeting early tomorrow. Shall we say nine o'clock?'

The Residency Kushnapur. 14th August 1947.

Adam found Sir Iain to be an astute Scot, able to rapidly assess the situation. The major had been as good as his word. The Resident was so well briefed that he knew exactly where Rindi was being held and on whose authority. Whilst he listened carefully to his explanation

Adam sensed he had already made a judgement on the matter.

'You've come a long way, Cullworthy; you must think a great deal of your friend. Let's see what can be done.' He picked up the telephone, and gave an instruction to the operator. As they sat waiting, there was a silence that he obviously didn't feel inclined to fill. Adam glanced around admiring his book-lined study of splendid proportions and the grand entrance through double doors with their ornate gilt handles. As he contemplated the grandeur of the Residency his thoughts turned to Wantilla. If it wasn't for him none of this would have happened and here Adam was using the influence with the British Resident "to interfere" as Wantilla had put it, in the affairs of the Princely State of Kushnapur.

After only a few minutes the telephone rang, and the Resident was put through to the Collector in Saharanpur. There was an exchange of greetings and a reference to a recent successful *shikar* before Sir Iain came to the reason for his call. He gave the Collector a clear and incisive summary of the case and then hung up.

'He's going to call me back,' and after a pause he said, 'you've come at an interesting time, Cullworthy.'

'Yes, indeed, the last day of the British Raj. It seems the transition to Independence is not going as smoothly as hoped.'

'I am afraid you are right, the situation in the Punjab is appalling, and it's getting worse by the day. Three hundred women had their breasts cut off in Jallandar and Amritsar, and yesterday two thousand dead arrived on a train into Lahore. Slaughtered in retribution by the Sikhs. What a terrible price to pay!'

The telephone rang and Sir Iain had a brief conversation. 'Right, Cullworthy, your friend is being released immediately, no charges or conditions. The Chief Magistrate is also making enquiries as to who put up that reward money. Whoever it is will have a lot of explaining to do.'

'Thank you, Sir. I know the maharajah will be very grateful.'

The Resident put out his hand. 'Good luck, Cullworthy. You'd better be careful on the roads today if you are going to pick up your friend. You know, Colonel, I've rather enjoyed this.'

It was possibly Sir Iain's last use of his legendary powers as the Resident of Kushnapur.

Later that day. Saharanpur.

Adam arrived at Saharanpur police headquarters to find Rindi being treated with great respect by the local police chief. Doubtless, he was ingratiating himself after the dramatic turn of events.

'Adam, I cannot begin to tell you how grateful I am for your coming to my rescue. I just know that we wouldn't have had the same result if the family had represented my case to the Resident.'

'Sadly I think you are right. It is amazing how doors open if you can get to the right people.'

On their return journey Rindi related his version of the encounter with Chalvington.

'Extraordinary that those events on the boat were still tormenting him all these years later. I bet you wished you had come clean about Wantilla's involvement.'

'Well, as you know Adam it wasn't as simple as that at the time.'

'So, Chandra told me the lingam was stolen. When did that happen?'

'It happened when we were all away attending a family wedding. Of course Wantilla was also there and so claims he could not have had anything to do with it.'

'How on earth did they get in to the temple? If they went through the palace they would have had to pass endless guards and even then they must have had a key.'

'We found some rope and an abandoned pulley so we think they came in over the roof and through the skylight.'

'But they can't possibly have got the lingam out through the roof it weighs far too much.'

'That is still a mystery. One theory is that they used the subterranean river but no one could swim that far carrying the lingam without sophisticated kit.'

'It almost sounds like a military exercise.'

'Yes, and that's why we come back to Wantilla. He had those sort of connections. Whoever it was knew all about our security arrangements and knew we would be away.'

'How did they get past Sheba?'

'I'm afraid she was poisoned.'

'How tragic.' Although Adam still bore the scars of the cheetah's attack, he knew how much she meant to the family.

'Yes, it was,' Rindi replied with a mixture of sadness and anger in his voice.

'So how long was it before you discovered it was gone?'

'Puhella discovered it when we got back. She would often just go down and see Sheba. She really loved that cat and still hasn't recovered from losing her'.

'And where did the lingam turn up?'

'The local police were hopeless as you can imagine. And then two weeks later Wantilla casually announces that through his sources he has recovered the lingam.'

'Didn't the police query how he had traced it?'

'Adam, you underestimate the power of his political connections. In any event we were thankful that it had been found and were keen to get it back as quickly as possible. And as you know he agreed to return it on the condition that Kafni consented to be part of his household.'

Even though Adam had heard this information before from Chandra, he found myself gripping the seat in anger. It was the word "consented" that stung him this time.

'Are there no limits to the depths to which this man will sink? And I can't believe Kafni would consent to effectively be his concubine, or frankly how you could let her be?'

'Adam, I know you find it inconceivable that she would agree to go and live with someone she loathes, but you underestimate the importance of the lingam to the Debrahms and the unquestioning duty Kafni feels in helping to recover it for the sake of the family.'

He was right, even after years of following their customs Adam still found it difficult to fathom this level of devotion to duty and honour.

'I don't understand why would he want to exchange it for Kafni? Surely the power lies in possessing the lingam.'

'That's the clever bit about his plan. He knew that if he held on to the lingam he would remain a suspect in the eyes of the authorities. For reasons that you know he was keen to impress the Resident that he was a responsible member of the Debrahm family. By returning this valuable object in exchange for what seemed like an almost charitable gesture of taking a widow into his household, he suddenly becomes the hero of the hour. As you also know he has been obsessed with Kafni for years and sees having her as a stepping stone to his ultimate objective.'

Adam suppressed his rage which he knew to be driven by a deeper emotion.

'Rindi, I want to offer my services to try and retrieve the lingam, and Kafni if possible. Please let me help.'

'You have already helped us more than you can imagine by securing my release before the balloon goes up tonight. I know you have feelings for Kafni, but I am afraid she and my father have made an agreement with Wantilla. However strange it may seem, they will honour this and nothing you say will dissuade them from doing so.'

'Well what about the lingam?'

'Recovering that is our first priority.'

'Where do you think it might be?'

'I am not convinced that Narajan is totally innocent in this matter. He has ambitions beyond being his uncle's lackey. Wantilla would love to get the lingam back again and Narajan wouldn't pass up an opportunity to possess such a valuable card in this high-stakes game. If we find Narajan I think the lingam will not be far away. It could well be in Lahore by now.'

'Why Lahore?' Adam asked trying to make sense of this 'game'.

'That's Wantilla and Kafni's last location.'

'Could I not go to Lahore and try and find Narajan?' said Adam, expressing his frustration.

'Half of India is on the move Adam, and the route to Lahore is highly dangerous at the moment. We could not condone sending you up there on a speculative mission at this time.' Rindi said with a degree of finality.

'And what about Pratap? with Kafni gone what is to become of him?'

'He will remain at the palace and be cared for and tutored under our guidance. He is nearly five now and is less dependent on his mother.'

Adam found this impossible to comprehend. How he would love to be a proper father to his boy at this distressing time, but he knew this could never be.

15th August 1947.

Adam returned to Delhi, where he boarded the BOAC flight to take him back to Egypt. There was a night stop in Karachi, where they were driven to a hotel in the airline's bus. It wove its way slowly through crowds celebrating the new independent state of Pakistan and everywhere they looked there were huge posters of Mohammed Ali Jinnah, the new Prime Minister. Adam wondered just how long the euphoria would last and had it been worth the price in human life? With the British gone how long would it be before corruption and rivalry reared their ugly heads. A good night's sleep was impossible. Makeshift bands were endeavouring to play marches in a discordant clash of instruments.

As he lay awake on his bed in the sweltering heat, he reflected on the events of the past week. He could claim some credit for getting Rindi released, but that would have happened sooner or later. He knew he was leaving with so many problems unresolved. The lingam was still missing and his beautiful Kafni was being held captive heaven knows where, a hostage to her family's fortunes.

Adam reflected on his final meeting with the maharajah. The rejection of his offer of further help had been clear in the maharajah's statement: "Adam, I think you should now return to Egypt; to your career and to your wife."

This was a stark reminder that there was a limit to his involvement with their family and that his honour and duty lay elsewhere. But just when he had resigned himself to being excluded from the family they surprised him with a touching gesture.

'Once more we are in your debt, Adam, and as a token of our gratitude I have something for you,' the maharajah had said handing him a small flat box covered in pale blue leather. Inside, Adam found a large star-shaped platinum brooch in the centre of which was a sapphire the size of a dove's egg. Surrounding it were a dozen small diamonds and below was an inscription.

'Why are you giving me this, your Highness?'

'As a token of our gratitude and to remind you, that you, Adam Cullworthy, are an honorary Rajput. It is inscribed in Sanskrit with our family motto. *"The successful perpetuation of human life lies not in the quantity, but in the quality of its procreation"*.

Adam remembered that these words were inscribed on the lingam. Turning the brooch over he found his name engraved on the back and realised that this was no passing whim.

'I am deeply honoured to receive this.'

There was one last thing he desperately wanted to do before he left.

'I wonder if it might be possible to see Pratap before I leave.'

'Of course. I will arrange that for you.'

Adam was with the maharani in her private sitting room when Puhella brought him in. It was immediately evident that this handsome and delightful little boy had inherited his mother's grace and beauty not least those bewitching violet eyes. Proudly, Adam took credit for his broad shoulders.

As soon as he saw his grandmother, he ran to her and raised his arms to embrace her. How wonderful it would be to be greeted like this, Adam thought, in full knowledge of who he was. Puhella walked over to her mother and took Pratap by the hand.

'Come and meet Uncle Rindi's great friend, Colonel Cullworthy-sahib, who has come all the way from Egypt.' The prepared words, which Puhella was obliged to say, only served to exacerbate his heartache.

There was a look of recognition in the little boy's eyes as he shook his father's hand and said, 'Good morning, Sir.'

That was the last time Adam was to see him for more than ten years.

CHAPTER TWENTY EIGHT

Canal Zone, Egypt, January 1948.

Adam had written to Sarah when he returned to Cairo making it clear that he resented being a lower priority in her life than her political career and asking her how she ever thought they would have a family if they never lived together like a normal married couple.

It may have been this letter or the fact that she had spent Christmas with her parents that jolted Sarah's conscience. Her letter in reply, dated New Year's Eve, gave Adam some encouragement that she had been missing him.

"I can't wait any longer, darling. I'm taking two month's leave and coming out to join you. Ivan is paying my airfare to save on travelling time.'

It was wonderful news. The only reservation Adam had with the letter was the "two months leave" part. Never mind; if all went well she would be attending the ante-natal clinic before she was due to return to England.

A week later, at 08.00 on the Sunday morning, Adam was at Cairo Airport to meet her. Despite Sarah's pallor after a winter in London, she had retained her lovely English rose looks. They took a taxi to Shepheard's hotel, had an excellent breakfast and then at midday caught the train to Ismailia. A driver was at the station to meet them and from there it was a short drive to the Moascar Garrison.

Thus began two of the happiest months of his life. Sarah was relaxed and contented and even gave up smoking. With this happy state of affairs, Adam had almost forgotten that she would be returning to England at the end of March. He had hoped so much that she might have become pregnant which may then have resulted in her changing her plans.

'We don't seem to be having much luck getting me pregnant. Perhaps I am just not destined for motherhood.'

'Oh, darling, don't be downhearted. I am sure it will happen sooner or later. It would of course help if we saw a bit more of each other.'

'I suppose you'd like me to abandon my career?'

'Not if you don't want to. But I do miss you and it would make it easier for us to start a family.'

Sarah's disappointment was manifest but she was reluctant to share it with Adam. Outwardly she maintained an air of cool control but he knew this was a cloak that disguised a vulnerable girl within. How he wished that she would let him love that inner girl. It didn't help that Adam knew that any infertility was not on his part, and that he could not share this truth with her.

Sarah had enjoyed the break from the cut and thrust of the political frontline and was a great success within the Garrison. She brought a whole new dimension to the repetitive life of the other wives and their husbands. Adam hoped she would take to the role of Commanding Officer's wife as fluently as her mother had but he knew that having been a senior officer herself, playing second fiddle to him was not her preferred status.In the absence of children it was only a matter of time before she would get bored.

After a couple of months of tennis, bridge, sailing and dinner parties with the same people week in and week out, the prospect of returning to the rollercoaster of life in Westminster became increasingly attractive.

'Darling, my leave is up next week and I need to go back to London.'

'Do you really have to? You have become such an indispensible part of our lives here. I can't bear the thought of you being so far away.'

'I did promise Ivan that if he paid for my ticket I would return.'

'Will you at least promise to think about coming back out here? Maybe for longer next time.' They both knew that meant her giving up politics and they both knew how unlikely that was.

'I will think about it.'

She flew back to England, leaving him feeling desolate.

December 1948. England

Although the regular letters between Sarah and Adam were affectionate, she had taken up her parliamentary post again and made no mention of returning to Egypt but asked whether there was any chance of him coming to England for Christmas. With this encouragement, Adam applied for leave and travelled on a forces special-rate sea trip from Port Said to Malta. From there, he booked on a commercial airline to London.

With parliament in recess, Sarah was thankfully free from her political work. They divided their time over Christmas between his parents in Sussex and Sarah's parents in Bayswater. The General had retired from active service and now had the time to read the newspapers from cover to cover. He took particular interest in the Death announcements, not out of morbid curiosity but as a reminder of his own mortality.

'Adam, did you see that Sir Julian Westbury had died? You knew the family quite well, didn't you?'

'Yes, I knew them through the Debrahms, they will be very sad to hear that.' The brief comment by the General transported Adam back to that day they had all gone to lunch in Richmond. How much had changed since then. The rather obscure conversation he had had with Sir Julian with it's far reaching implications. And then of course there was Tina. He still found it difficult to think of her as being romantically involved with Rindi, if indeed she still was.

This sad news prompted Adam to contact Jardeeson and Nina.

'How wonderful to hear from you, Adam. Where are you now?'Nina's effusive manner always made Adam feel like the prodigal son returning.

'I am just back from Egypt for Christmas. I am staying with my wife Sarah's parents in Bayswater.'

'Will you please come and have lunch? Both of you. We'd love to meet her properly.'

'I'm not sure whether Sarah will have the time, she's very busy at the moment.' This was partly accurate, but in truth Adam wanted to see them on his own. 'Perhaps I could come over tomorrow?'

'Jardeeson won't be here and I know he would love to see you. How about the day after?'

'Very good, I'll see you on Wednesday and I'll try and bring Sarah along if I can.'

Queens Gate Gardens

'What happened to Sir Julian? He was only sixty five. I rather feared one of his past cases might have caught up with him.'

'No, nothing as dramatic as that. He had a heart attack. Years of gin drinking in India finally took its toll.' Nina gestured despair with upturned hands.

'What news of the rest of their family?'

'As it happens Tina is coming round after lunch to discuss the memorial service with Jardeeson. He will be doing one of the readings.'

Adam didn't know whether he was emotionally prepared to meet with Tina. What would they say to each other? It was bound to be very awkward.

'I see.'

'You know she and Rindi have been walking out for a while?'

Adam loved Nina's delightfully old-fashioned way of describing lovers.

'Yes, Rindi told me.'

'His parents don't think it's a good idea at all.'

It hadn't really occurred to Adam how complicated this would be for Rindi but now that it did it was obvious that they would object to their son marrying anyone but an Indian princess.

'He's not engaged to her, is he?'

'No, but all the time he is involved with her he studiously avoids meeting anyone his parents line up as suitable candidates.'

Having been resentful of Rindi and Tina's relationship for so long, Adam now found himself strangely sympathetic to their plight. By the time Tina arrived after lunch Adam had composed himself and was surprisingly pleased to see her.

'Adam! What a wonderful surprise. What brings you to Kensington?'

'I am so sorry to hear about your Pa's death.' They embraced each other. 'You were always his favourite.'

Tina struggled to find words and let out an almost inaudible sob. 'Oh, Adam, it's ghastly. He has left such a big hole in our lives.'

Adam found the tears welling in his eyes and felt Tina clinging to him with greater urgency. Nina tenderly reached out for Tina's hand and she reluctantly let go of Adam and turned to hug Nina instead.

'We will all miss him terribly, my dear.' Nina tried to comfort her.

It was not the time or the place to discuss her relationship with Rindi even if he had had the courage to talk about it. But Adam felt a great sense of relief that even without words they had somehow reconciled themselves to what had happened in the intervening years.

September 1949

Adam spent the next nine months in Egypt living a bachelor life yet always hoping that Sarah would change her mind and join him again. However, in September, she was officially adopted as a Labour candidate for a constituency in the West Midlands. Adam knew that, for the immediate future at least, she would not want to leave England. He applied for leave and flew home for the month of October.

Adam insisted that Sarah take a fortnight's holiday so that they could go to Scotland. His motives were twofold: to try and recapture some of the romance of their honeymoon, and to get her a long way away from Westminster. He never underestimated Sarah's achievements in her political career but he also resented what he felt certain was the main obstacle to them having a family. They had some idyllic days when everything seemed perfect between them but neither of them was going to give up their career, so their only hope was that he would get a long period of duty in England.

Adam returned to Egypt with greater optimism, believing that with patience his marital problems would resolve themselves. The Second Wessex would be due for a period of service at home the following year. Until then he would continue to shape the battalion into the finest infantry regiment in the Middle East. It was ironic that this efficiency, whilst benefiting his career, would result in a further stumbling block to their marriage.

Prime Minister Clement Attlee called a General Election for 23rd February 1950. Sarah had hoped that Adam would be there to help canvas for her as he had promised but he had no leave due. In the event she won her seat with a comfortable majority, and gave up her job with Ivan. Labour had won the election, but by such a narrow margin that they found it difficult to govern and were obliged to go to the country again the following year. The Conservatives won this election by a small majority and Churchill returned as P.M. Sarah had retained her seat and Adam cabled his congratulations, happy in the knowledge that he would soon be back with her in England.

In response, Sarah wrote to thank him but also to tell him that Ivan's wife of 30 years had been tragically killed in a motor accident. She told him how much Ivan had appreciated the comfort she had given him as he came to terms with this sad loss. Knowing how supportive

Sarah had been of Virginia, when faced with her predicament, Adam gave no more than a passing thought to this comment.

By November his regiment had returned home and was in barracks in Exeter. Not as near to Sarah as he had hoped since she was living with her parents in London during the week and travelling to her constituency on the Shropshire border at the weekends. Adams career was equally inconvenient to Sarah who needed support from a husband. Her constituents expected her to attend events with her spouse but this rarely happened.

January 1952.

In the New Years Honours list Adam was awarded the Distinguished Service Order.

"We are very proud of you," wrote his father-in-law, "you've really earnt it and you have a great future ahead of you."

Two days later the Military Secretary told him that he had been recommended to fill the vacancy for a general staff officer 1st grade at the War Office. His record in the Middle East placed him first in line for the job, but it meant that he was to become a victim of his own success.

A war was still raging in the Far East, with intense fighting against the Communists. In June 1950 North Korean troops had advanced into South Korea and President Truman had sent air and sea forces to support the South Koreans. War continued to escalate and by the beginning of July, American troops had landed in South Korea. General MacArthur was designated Commander-in-Chief of United Nations forces in Korea. These were soon joined by British troops, who went into action in September. By October, the U.N. forces had crossed the 38th Parallel and captured Pyongyang, the North Korean capital. But this was a short-lived victory. In November, vast Chinese Communist forces swept down from Manchuria and in December they re-occupied Pyongyang.

Things had become more aggressive and bloody. Even the Russians at the United Nations – no doubt sensitive to the massive Chinese involvement - appealed for a settlement. With no sign of this happening, the British government anticipated requests to send out more troops. One battalion earmarked was the Fourth Wessex, strategically placed in Hong Kong. However, an inspection by the GOC revealed that they were unfit to go into action, and their CO was sacked. War Office immediately looked around for a lieutenant-colonel urgently to lick them into shape. Adam's reputation was still fresh in their minds and he was given orders to fly to Hong Kong and take over the battalion. It was a bitter blow to his hopes of a period of duty in England.

King George VI died on 6th February aged 56, two days before Adam received his orders to go to Hong Kong, and his departure was delayed for a week to enable him to attend the funeral, not in his own capacity but as the spouse of a sitting M.P. Ten days later he exchanged the chill grey days of an English February for the agreeably warm 60 degree winter of Hong Kong. Under different circumstances, it would have been a welcome posting. Now the Fourth Wessex was training to move to a war theatre where no families were permitted. As far as he was concerned, this did not alter things. Sarah would not be able to leave England whilst she was still an M.P. Rather selfishly he secretly hoped she would lose her seat so that she could be with him in the Far East.

Two months of rigorous and intensive exercises brought the men to peak condition. The battalion was fit and ready to take up their active role. But changes were taking place in Korea, with massive raids by U.S. aircraft having their effect, and their move to Korea was put on hold.

Adam was already formulating ideas for Sarah to fly out and spend the parliamentary summer recess with him, when the GOC telephoned from HQ 'Your replacement is on his way out, Cullworthy. You are to hand over and proceed by air to London. It's confidential, but you're to be in the Queen's Birthday Honours List for a C.B.E. I just need your confirmation that you will accept it.'

It was not always necessary to receive this honour from the Queen herself so Adam had the feeling that the GOC knew more than he was saying. But he was not about to object when events seemed to be favouring his personal life for a change. The timing of this event meant that he would also be home in time for the Coronation. This had the added benefit that he might get to see Rindi who he knew had been invited to attend the Coronation to represent his father who was now too ill to travel.

Adam cabled Rindi suggesting they could meet when he was in London.

Rindi's reply was brief.

REGRET UNABLE ATTEND CORONATION DUE DEATH
OF FATHER STOP LETTER FOLLOWS ADDRESSED YOU IN
LONDON STOP RINDI.

Those few concise words set off turbulent thoughts which
constantly inhabited a parallel consciousness in Adam's mind. The
happy anticipation of seeing his friend once more was instantly turned
into disappointment, then deep sadness and then a strange sense of
relief, followed finally by feelings of resignation. The sadness was for
the loss of someone who had embraced him as a son and been a pillar
of a whole new world to which his son had introduced him. The sense
of relief was a less obvious feeling. Somehow the maharajah's death
gave Adam a feeling of hope that a barrier had been removed and that
perhaps he was one step closer to the girl he loved. In the context of
where his life now was this was a completely irrational thought and
the cold reality of the situation quickly returned.

As his plane came in to land at Heathrow, he wondered what
fresh surprises lay ahead of him. He did not have to wait long. A driver
from the Adjutant-General's Department was there to meet him and
handed him a letter. It informed him that he had been gazetted as full
Colonel and acting Brigadier. This meant he had bypassed the normal
year or two as a full colonel. This was more like wartime promotion,
which though flattering was not likely to lead to the London staff job
he was hoping for.He had ten day's leave before he was due to report
for his briefing and he spent most of this time with Sarah in the West
Country . Their break was enjoyable enough, but due to their long
separation, he was aware of an aloofness in her. The uncertainty of his
future did little to help the unresolved issues in their marriage.

On the Tuesday after their return Adam found himself in the
Department of the CIGS wondering what they had in mind for him.
There were three brigadiers' posts, one in military intelligence and
two more in military operations. Any of these posts would be ideal.

Adam was greeted by one of these brigadiers. 'Good morning
Cullworthy, the D.M.O. is expecting us.'

He knew that if the Director of Military Operations was dealing
with his appointment, he was destined for an active service role.

As they entered the D.M.O.'s office Adam saw a small immaculately
turned out man in a full General's uniform scrutinising a map of South

East Asia. He turned and directed Adam to a chair in front of his desk.

'Cullworthy, I'll come straight to the point. We have a special assignment on the Malayan Peninsula and we think you are just the man for the job.'

'Right, Sir,' Adam tried to sound enthusiastic, 'perhaps you could tell me what this role will involve?'

'Indeed. You probably already know that General Templer went to Malaya last year as High Commissioner and Director of Operations in the peninsular. A very serious situation has developed there, and if we don't deal with it effectively we'll lose the whole bloody country to the Commies. Templer wants another brigade to deal with the emergency and has asked us to send out a commander with the right sort of experience.'

There was a moment's pause whilst Adam stared at the map and let the news sink in. The General must have read his thoughts, as he added. 'You're probably wondering why you, a brand new brigadier, is being sent out?'

Adam was deep in thought, but the slight movement of his head was sufficient acknowledgement for the General to continue.

'It's an entirely new type of warfare. The Communist terrorists have substantial bases in the remote jungles, and they've developed very successful techniques. Not least, their ability to force the villagers into helping them. We have to learn new methods of dealing with these people. That's why Templer wants officers who are readily adaptable and not hide-bound by their old methods. His standards are extremely high and he's very demanding.'

'So I've heard, Sir.'

'The Malayan jungle is bloody hot and humid all the year round; the temperature seldom falls below seventy-five even at night. Operating there is a dirty and sticky job. You'll be expected to see front-line conditions for yourself to know what your men are up against, but this doesn't mean taking unnecessary risks. Your experience fighting the Japs in the Burma jungles should prove useful.'

Adam left the briefing with mixed emotions. He was flattered that the top brass had thought him worthy of such a challenging role, but it was far from what was needed as a panacea to his struggling marriage.

He telephoned Sarah and suggested they meet for lunch at a small Italian restaurant just off Berkeley Square. It was hardly the occasion for a celebration. Sarah's reaction to his news was ambivalent. She wanted to be more enthusiastic about his appointment but for her it meant another prolonged period on her own. This made her more vulnerable to the attentions of her male collegues in the House many of whom weren't even aware of Adam's existence. As one of the few female members of Parliament there was a level of expectation beyond that of her male colleagues. However, she had always possessed perseverance and persistence and in some respects Adam's absence allowed her to work longer hours than other women in the House who had families to manage as well.

Shortly before Adam left by air for Malaya, Rindi's letter arrived. The one he had promised in his cable. It was much more formal than the normal letters from him. Understandable perhaps as it had been written a week after he had returned from the sacred duty of lighting his father's pyre on the banks of the North Tons River. His father had been ill for a while but his death was nevertheless unexpected. He told Adam that they had not heard from Kafni for six years and feared the worst. Rindi wrote that he thought his father had died of a broken heart. His favourite daughter had left without a moment's complaint and he could never forgive himself for having sent her away. Adam found it almost unbearable to read these words. Their anguish was palpable and he so wanted to be there to provide solace to his friend. Rindi had made no mention of Wantilla. What could have happened to their arrangement? And where on earth was Kafni now? The thought that Kafni was still unaccounted for left him feeling desolate. He could hardly bear to think of that beautiful girl alone somewhere - or even worse, dead. How powerless he felt. *"I also feel I have failed Father and the family,'*Rindi wrote, *'because I have still not recovered the lingam."*

This was a further shocking revelation. How Adam wished he had been allowed to go on the quest, which the old maharajah had forbidden him to undertake. Perhaps he would not have been successful in either task, but at least he would not have the sense of frustration which now enveloped him.

"Pratap is well and enjoying his school lessons at the Palace. He is now nearly eleven and already fluent in three languages. He is at present under the guardianship of my mother, who adores him. But soon he must go away to boarding school to study a wider range of subjects and away from the indulgence of the palace servants."

Adam relished this news of his boy but wondered how he was

coping without either a mother or a father.

Rindi was now the Maharajah of Kushnapur, although strictly speaking the authority of the *gaddi* was incomplete without the Kushnapur Lingam. The new Indian government had permitted the princes to retain their titles, even though these no longer carried any power. All income taxes and customs duties were paid direct to the Federal centre, although the State Governments did have an income from the sales tax and land revenue.

> *"Finally my friend I must inform you that I have submitted to the wishes of my parents and have married a princess of their choice. Her name is Alisha and she is a fine woman who I hope will bear us many children. I would have asked you to the wedding but what with father being ill it was felt propitious not to delay the marriage which took place last month three weeks before father died. I look forward to your meeting her in the near future."*

Adam had always thought that this would be the most likely marital conclusion for Rindi but he couldn't help wondering how and when Rindi had ended his relationship with Tina. Had it been before or after Adam had seen her in Queen's Gate Gardens? Rindi hadn't mentioned Tina at all in the letter, almost as if it was too painful a subject. How difficult this decision must have been for both of them, but he always knew that duty would ultimately prevail in the Debrahm family. What had happened to Tina? He remembered how desperately she had clung to him in the hallway of Queen's Gate Gardens. Was that expression of grief only for the loss of her father?

Rindi's letter left Adam with many more questions unanswered. Why had they still not traced the whereabouts of the lingam? Had they ever found Narajan? Where was Wantilla? And how was it that Kafni was missing?

Malaya, June 1955

Although Adam had only been able to leave the Malay Peninsula once in two years, it was, by 1955, permissible for wives to join their husbands out in Malaya. Sarah as an M.P. had been reluctant to leave England, but when she lost her seat at the General Election in May

1955, that problem was removed. Thus, after some prevarication, Sarah came out to join Adam in George Town on the island of Penang, where the British Army had taken over the Runnymead Hotel. There were two serious drawbacks about getting to see her. The first was that leave was restricted to one week every three months and the second was that travelling there involved a tedious rail journey of two days and two nights.

Sarah was determined to make the best of it and the easy manner which had made her such a good M.P. meant that she quickly made friends with both the army wives and some of the local dignitaries. She was able to keep herself busy for a while but secretly she resented the seemingly effortless way the other wives produced children. Sarah had always got what she wanted when she wanted it so failing to get pregnant was the ultimate frustration. This was something beyond her control. Adam knew from various conversations he had overheard between Sarah and her mother that they wondered whether Adam was the one lacking fertility. Adam had to suffer this conjecture sure in the knowledge that the problem was not his.

Eventually the colonial life palled and Sarah asked Adam if he would mind her returning to England for a few months.

'Why do you want to go home, darling? I know it must be boring at times, but I thought you were reasonably content here.'

'I have been, but I also feel I'm just marking time and I want to get on with my life.'

'Do you want to stand for election again?'

'I'm not sure whether they would still want me but I do miss being an M.P. If I was offered a safe seat I would be very tempted.'

Adam loved having Sarah around because having grown up in an army environment she was so at ease with the way of life. But he always felt he was caging her and that she resented playing only a supporting role. It worried him that the further they advanced in their chosen careers the more incompatible their lives became. The only advantage that the army offered over politics was the predictability of employment.

CHAPTER TWENTY NINE

London, Sunday 10ᵗʰ May 1959.

It was not until three years later that Adam was recalled from Malaya. He was asked to report to the Vice CIGS at the War Office and the predominant thought in his mind was where they might send him to next. That was until the Britannia landed at Ciampino Airport in Rome and parked on the apron next to a Super Constellation of Air-India International. A party of Indian women, looking striking in their colourful saris, walked from the steps of the plane into the bright sunshine, immediately transporting him back to India. He visualised the magnificent Kushnapur Palace glistening in the sunset, its great walls standing like a giant sentinel in the foothills of the Himalayas.

Beneath this serene memory lay the tormented thought that there was still no news of Kafni. Wantilla had eventually confessed to Rindi that Kafni and her ayah had escaped from his custody whilst they were visiting Lahore. The prospects for two unaccompanied Hindu women in Pakistan were grim indeed. Hindus had continued to be routinely murdered well after Partition. He wondered what might have become of that beautiful gentle girl.

At Heathrow, a corporal from the War Office met Adam at the immigration desk and gave him a letter telling him that he had an appointment with General Festing the CIGS at Whitehall the following morning. This made it necessary for him to stay the night in London.

He declined the corporal's offer of a lift into town and waited to look round the arrivals area hoping that Sarah might be there to meet him. As he was about to leave, he saw his sister Sue's genial husband striding towards him with his hand outstretched.

'Adam, so glad to see you old chap.'

'Oliver! How good of you to come and meet me.'

'It's the least I could do. It's so long since we've seen you. What's your programme? Sue wondered if you could come down to Sussex and have lunch with us. I've got my car here.'

'Afraid not, Oliver, I've an important meeting tomorrow morning, so must stay on in London.'

'That's a pity. She was hoping to get your parents over to join us; they'll be disappointed, they........' Oliver's hesitation suggested that there was something a little awkward coming.

'What is it?'

'Well, you know, they are concerned for your marriage. We all are.'

'And the fact that she chose not to meet me at the airport after months apart tells you a great deal about the state of it.' Adam said with resignation in his voice.

'They're very fond of her, you know. Speaking as an old friend and not your brother-in-law, I think the trouble is that you're both very strong-willed and of course it doesn't help that you both have demanding careers.'

Adam was a little too weary to cope with Oliver's eagerness at that time in the morning. He glanced round the concourse and shook his head. Oliver must have sensed his chagrin and did not probe further.

'Look, old boy I'll talk to you about it sometime; not just now, if you don't mind. Were you planning to drive straight back to Sussex?'

'That was the idea. But I'd be happy to take you anywhere you like.' He grabbed one of Adam's bags. 'Where will you be staying?'

'I think it'll be the Army and Navy Club, if they've got a room.'

'That's Pall Mall, isn't it? Let me drop you off there.'

'If you don't mind, that would be kind of you.'

They walked out to the car park and minutes later were on the A4 heading into London.

'Oh by the way have you seen the morning papers?'

'Not yet.'

'Then you'd better have a look at mine, it's on the back seat.' Adam reached behind him and picked up the copy of the Telegraph.

'Take a look at page four. But I expect you know all about it anyway.'

He opened the paper and quickly located the article by Chapman Phillips.

"New Tactics in Warfare"

"Brigadier Adam Cullworthy, the talented military tactician, returns today from Malaya where he has served with such distinction under Field Marshal Sir Gerald Templer. He is due to be briefed on his new post by the C.I.G.S., General Sir Francis Festing and sources say he is tipped to become our youngest peace-time major-general."

'Sources indeed. Bloody amazing! The first I learn about my future is in a newspaper!'

'Well, Phillips' sources are pretty reliable. Is it too early to celebrate?'

'Certainly is, 'war box' will doubtless want me to jump through several hoops first.'

Adam had not anticipated staying in London so after Oliver dropped him at the club, he made a call to Nina and Jardeeson. Nina sounded more relieved than surprised to hear from him.

'Do please come and have lunch,' she insisted.

Shortly before midday Adam found himelf at the door of the house in Queen's Gate Gardens, where so many times in the past twenty-six years he had been received with such warm hospitality. This time he was nagged by an anxiety that something was seriously wrong. Nina had tried to sound her usual cheerful self on the telephone, but she had not succeeded in hiding a tone of distress in her voice. Their only contact in recent years had been an exchange of Christmas cards. The last three had contained the same message: "please come and see us as soon as you return to England." But Adam had attached no urgency to these comments; their invitations to visit had always been so freely issued.

He felt a huge sense of relief when the door was opened and he was greeted by the familiar face of Jandah. Butlers had become scarce since the war - although he could never imagine this household without its *khitmager*. Though the beard was now white and the face more lined, it was still proud and inscrutable. The modern-day egalitarian trends could not ruffle the dignity that he attached to his post.

'*Namaste*, Brigadier Cullworthy-sahib.' The polite smile he gave Adam as he placed his palms together in greeting was his acknowledgement of an old friend of the family. Adam well remembered the awe he had felt when, as a schoolboy, he had encountered him for the first time.

'The sahib has no luggage?'

'Not this time, Jandah. I'm only here for lunch.'

Closing the door after Adam, he led the way along the hall and up the Regency staircase, which rose gently and curved round towards the drawing room on the first floor. It would have been churlish of Adam to suggest that he knew the way, and deprive Jandah of the pleasure of announcing his arrival.

The reception room Adam now entered looked smaller, maybe there was more furniture in it or maybe it was just his memory telling him it had seemed grander when he had visited before. The view of the gardens which formed the Square was unchanged as were the pictures on the wall. There was a feeling of stability and continuity in contrast to a world outside that had changed so completely in recent years - especially his own.

He turned to see Nina come into the room and walk towards him in the graceful way that few but Indian women are able to achieve. Her rich blue sari, tastefully patterned with small white and cerise lotus flowers, edged with a broad gold border, conveyed the elegance she always managed to capture.

'*Namaste*, Adam.'

'*Namaste*, Ninaji. It must be more than five years since I was here, but nothing seems to have changed.' But as he spoke he looked at Nina and realised that it was she who had altered. She looked frail and there was now a good deal of grey in the hair that framed her fine features.

'I'm so glad you have come, Adam.'

'My pleasure. I hope you and Jardeeson are both well.'

'Oh yes, of course, and he apologises for not being here but he had urgent business to attend to at the Foreign Office.' There was distinct apprehension in her voice. 'I suggest we have *tiffin* straightaway then we'll have plenty of time to talk afterwards.'

Over *tiffin,* as she still rather quaintly liked to call lunch when with those familiar with the East, they chatted light-heartedly, but Adam was aware that she had something pent up within her..

'When were you last in India? Adam enquired, 'I imagine you must miss it.'

'I have recently returned from a visit, and yes India will always be a part of me, especially my family home at Alwar. But I've become too anglicised to live there now.'

'Has much changed since Independence?'

'Yes, a great deal, although in many ways India is timeless. But politically...' Nina shook her head and appeared unsure how to express her thoughts.

'Did you go to Kushnapur?' He had to ask; though he knew that Nina would not have visited India without going there. Adam had not been to Kushnapur for twelve years and he wanted to know how she had found it.

'There are problems in Kushnapur, Adam. Wantilla is now a member of the Legislative Assembly for the State of Uttar Pradesh'

Just the sound of his name after all these years was enough to insense Adam.

'He seems unassailable,' Nina went on. 'He's even trying to buy his way into the *Rajaya Sabha* in Delhi. My God, how money corrupts. Fortunately, there's no chance of him succeeding in becoming a national M.P. of the upper house. It's quite a different proposition from buying off a few thousand State votes from the poor and illiterate. Things will never be right in Kushnapur until the honour of the Debrahm family is restored.' There was a catch in her voice, as she broke off, clearly wishing to change this painful subject. 'We can talk about it after lunch if you like. Now tell me about yourself. We read in the papers of your success in Malaya. Weren't you commanding one of the Commonwealth Infantry Brigades?'

'Yes, I was very fortunate to be given that command; they were a damn fine bunch of soldiers.'

'Jardeeson tells me you're up for promotion.'

'Yes, so the papers tell me, but I'll know more about that after I've been to the War Office tomorrow.'

'How is all this fitting in with your married life?' She asked the question without guile, though Adam thought she may have suspected problems.

'I'd be less than honest not to admit that there are difficulties.'

'I'm sorry to hear that.' Nina appeared to accept his answer without needing to pursue the matter further.

After lunch they were served coffee in the study. For a few moments she sat without speaking, then got up from her chair and walked over to the writing bureau. Opening a drawer, she took out a photograph and brought it over to him. Although he was much older than when Adam had last seen him, he instantly recognised the handsome face of Pratap, her great nephew. The determined look and firm jaw belied his young years.

'His father would have been very proud of him.' Nina said.

'Yes, I'm sure he would,' Adam responded almost reflexively.

'You knew, of course, that his father was Prince Ranjhalla Singh. Tragic that he was killed so young.'

Although Adam nodded, it was inconceivable to him that after all these years Nina had not been told the truth. Clearly it was still considered important that only a few people should know.

'Yes, but I heard they awarded him a posthumous Military Cross. He must have been quite a soldier.'

'Fortunately, Ranjhalla was the second son of the Maharajah of Sirmur and not the *rajkumar*. That's why Pratap was permitted to remain at Kushnapur with his mother.'

Adam listened but his mind was elsewhere. It was as if he was watching a Shakespearean play, the plot and cast of which was only known to three or four people. Would the truth ever be told or was his part destined to be a secret footnote in history.

Nina saw Adam look again at the photograph and then said, 'it's about Pratap that I want to talk to you.'

Adam could feel his pulse quicken.

'Why does that concern me, Ninaji?' he said somewhat ingenuously.

'How much do you know about the Kushnapur lingam, Adam?'

He might have known that it would concern the *lingam*. Both it and Wantilla were at the root of so many of the Debrahm family's problems.

'Quite a lot. Has it been found yet?'

She shook her head. 'No, I'm afraid not, and you will then no doubt be aware of its significance to the Debrahm family.'

Nina's words brought the whole saga rushing back along with the painful memory of Kafni's disappearance. Had she been found? That was more important to him.

'Is there any news of Kafni?' he asked tentatively.

'No news I'm afraid. The last time I was in Kushnapur was just after Pratap had left on his mission.'

'What mission?'

'Pratap and his friend Gopal have gone to find the lingam and to look for his mother.'

Adam was briefly struck silent. 'Isn't he a bit young to set off into the Punjab?' he asked trying to supress the anxiety he felt on hearing this news.

'He is sixteen and very determined and I must say quite mature for his years. And let's be honest, having already lost his father in battle, he must have felt that there was no more important task in life for him than to find his mother.' Nina spoke softly, with the pathos in her voice that she had tried to disguise on the telephone that morning

'Rindi, as his uncle and his guardian, was particularly reluctant to let him go, but finally relented on the condition that he was accompanied by Gopal, the son of Major Ram Chandra whom I think you know. Gopal is two years older, and, like Pratap, a *Rajput* of the *Kshatriya* warrior caste. Having consulted the astrologer, they set off on the 26th December last year, that being the first full moon of the Hindu year 2015, and the *pittithi* of his birth.'

As he listened to Nina, Adam visualised that part of northeast India that he had come to know so well. A mixture of pride and anxiety swept through him as he imagined these two young men setting off to Pakistan.

'The lingam has now been missing for over ten years and we are particularly concerned that it may have been broken up for the value of the gold and the gems.'

Adam found it difficult to share this deep concern when all he could think about was Kafni missing and his young son doing what he should have done twelve years before and should be doing now.

'We have tried to keep its disappearance a secret as any knowledge of its whereabouts would lure collectors and fortune hunters. We cannot even ask for the help of the government of India as they might seek to claim it as bounty and restrict our legitimate efforts to retrieve it. We are also anxious that it should not fall into the hands of Wantilla again who will use it to try and legitimise his claim to the *gaddi*. You asked me why I'm telling you this, Adam. It is because you are Rindi's most trusted friend and I do believe he would now want you to know. He is particularly concerned that there has been no news of the boys' whereabouts for nearly six months.'

Nina, being unaware of the truth, could not have known the profound effect this statement would have upon Adam. In her elegantly understated way Nina had made him realise where both his heart and his duty lay. He looked again at the photograph, and then handed it back to Nina. He was overdue for leave and in those moments was already formulating a plan to return to India.

'I'll be busy most of the day tomorrow, but will Jardeeson be at home on Friday?'

'Yes, he'll be free all day. Come early and stay for lunch. I'm sure you'll have lots to talk about.'

Adam returned to the Army & Navy Club that afternoon with his mind trying to make sense of the disturbing news that Nina had given him. But this was no time for impulsive decisions. This was at an extremely important juncture in his career and he needed sound advice. After a few phone calls he managed to track down Bob Mercer. As his Commanding Officer during the War, he was someone that Adam much admired and respected. After the war he had chosen to return to Oxford to take up a professorship at New College. They had corresponded regularly but not spoken for nearly four years.

'Adam! How the devil are you? I hear you might be bumped up to General.'

'Yes, quite possibly. Never thought I would ever outrank you.'

'I was only talking about you the other day. Do you remember Hugh Archibald on the boat out to India?'

'Archie, yes of course.'

'After he finished his post graduate degree he was offered a place as a don at Christchurch.'

'Small world. Send him my best when you next see him.'

'So are you planning a trip to Oxford? It would be good to catch up.'

'No, sadly not, but I do need to talk to you about something fairly urgently. I don't suppose you are going to be in London in the next couple of days?'

'I'm giving a lecture at the British Museum tomorrow afternoon but I might be able to squeeze in a quick lunch before that.'

'That will suit me fine. I will be needing a drink after my meeting with Festing in the morning.'

Bob was waiting for Adam at the club when he returned from his War Office appointment. Over lunch they talked about the Malaya campaign and life in general during the intervening years since they had seen each other. Adam suggested that they take coffee in the library which was situated at the rear of the club. An oasis of tranquillity with its dark blue, deep pile carpet and heavy matching curtains which absorbed most of the traffic sounds from Pall Mall on the other side of the building, making it ideal for a more discreet conversation.

'So what did old Festing have to say to you, Adam? Do you know what job they're giving you?'

'Yes. It's a new department to deal with insurgencies and inter-tribal conflicts in various parts of the world. I haven't been given all the details. I'll be briefed before I go to the Imperial Defence College. In the meantime I've been given some leave.'

'Well, you said you had something you wanted to discuss with me. I can't think you want to pick my brain about a military matter, I've been out of the loop far too long to be of any value on that score.'

'No, not military advice but your understanding of army protocol will be useful. You see I think I might have committed myself to an assignment in India'

'But not with the Army?'

'Correct'

'You say you might have committed yourself? Tell me more.'

'Do you remember a school friend of mine called Rindi Debrahm?'

'Yes. Maharajah's son, had some palace in the foothills of the Himalayas. Did you ever sort out that problem he had with the police?'

'Yes I did and thank you for your help on that front.'

'So what's his problem now?'

'Well his father died recently so he's now the Maharajah of Kushnapur and he has something of a crisis on his hands.'

'What sort of crisis?'

'He has lost a sculpture of considerable value to his family and they would like me to help them get it back.'

'I see. And what form does this sculpture take?'

'It's a lingam, a golden phallus.'

'Ah. Interesting,' said Bob. 'Do they have any idea where it might be?'

'Somewhere in Pakistan.'

'When did they lose it?'

'It was stolen about twelve years ago.'

'Excuse me asking - but do they really need a serving British army brigadier for this assignment?'

'No, they don't, it's really a matter of honour. I feel I owe it to the family to help them in their hour of need. Rindi cannot leave Kushnapur for fear that his rogue of a cousin will usurp his throne in his absence. He has sent two young fellows to the Punjab to investigate. But that was six months ago and unfortunately since then there has been no news of them.'

'How long did you say your leave was?'

'Just over three weeks.'

Adam felt that Bob was cross-examining him like a prosecution counsel but he needed to have the facts.

'So you have to comb the Punjab for some religious artefact that disappeared a dozen years ago and be back on duty by the 4th June?'

'Correct.'

'The phrase "wild goose chase" comes to mind. Have you asked Sarah about this?'

'I'm afraid things are not good on that front.'

'Oh, sorry to hear that,' said Bob, pausing for thought. 'Have you considered the implications to your career if you are AWOL on the 4th June?'

'Court martial?'

'I think that is pretty unlikely as they seem impressed with you but they would take a pretty dim view and it might mean your promotion not coming through. But you don't seem that concerned. I sense the heart ruling the head.'

'Well, it is a bit more complicated and there is a woman involved.'

'It wouldn't be anything to do with the Indian girl who sent me that letter in Delhi?'

'No, not her but her older sister. She is the mother of one of the boys sent to find the lingam. She too has been missing for several years and I also need to find her.' Adam wished he could be more open with Bob about Kafni and Pratap but he had been sworn to secrecy.

Bob drew on his pipe and his bright blue eyes assessed him in silence. Adam knew that matters of romance were not his strong suit.

'Do you think I am mad?' he asked his old friend.

'Candidly, yes, but I think you have already made up your mind and I am now wondering how I might be able to help. You'll need a good team. Have you had any thoughts?'

'You're right; I can't do this on my own. The need for secrecy is also paramount. I shall be up against some ruthless and greedy individuals. Not least Wantilla, Rindi's treacherous cousin. Fortunately, I should have good support from the Palace staff in Kushnapur.'

'Yes, that will help but if you are short of time you'll need a good wing man.'

'After our conversation yesterday I had a thought that our American friend Hugh Archibald might just fit the bill.'

'Not a bad idea. He'd be a good man to have alongside in a tight spot.'

'You'd know better than anyone what his academic commitments might be.'

'Not a bad time of year. Exams are largely over and most of Oxford is just partying. It may be that he will head back to California soon but you might just catch him.'

'Perhaps you can tell me where I might get hold of him.'

'I can certainly do that. Keep me informed, and call me if there is anything else I can do. Given your time constraint you're going to need more than a little luck, old boy, but I can't think of anyone more qualified to undertake such a venture.'

After Bob had left Adam reflected on his comment about 'your heart ruling your head.' He had been right in thinking that Adam would not have been so keen to embark on this venture if he had not still been yearning to see Kafni again.

Queen's Gate Gardens.

Jardeeson was waiting for Adam in the library when he arrived at Queen's Gate Gardens the next morning. 'Adam, how good to see you. How did your meeting go with the top brass?'

'Very well thank you, Jardeeson. It looks like my next job will be that of a major-general.'

'That is splendid news. When do they want you to start?'

'Well, I am long overdue for some leave and they have given me three weeks.'

'And what do you plan to do with that time?' he asked with more than passing interest.

'I'm planning to go back to India. It sounds as if Rindi really needs some help.'

'Adam, I cannot begin to tell you how much it would mean to us if you could help us at this difficult time.' He looked as if a great weight had been lifted from him and his relief quickly changed to energetic enthusiasm. 'We have no time to lose. Let's go and study the maps.'

Jardeeson lifted his hand, indicating to Adam to lead the way. Neither of them spoke as Adam studied the maps on the wall. One of them he had seen years before when Rindi had first told him about India. Now, beside it was another map, and across the western Punjab was over printed in bold letters the word: PAKISTAN.

'I shall need your advice and help, Jardeesonji.'

'I'm sure you will. In England I can help, but it is in India that you will need reliable friends. You must find people that you can trust implicitly. Friends, whose knowledge and capability can meet the challenge, and who are preferably already in India, or are willing to go there with you.'

Adam did not intend his laugh to be cynical. 'That's quite a tall order.'

'I'm well aware of that, Adam, but without the right help, you have no chance of success. There is, of course, Major Harish Ram Chandra. As you know he has a personal interest in the venture beyond his duty to Kushnapur. I will cable him to stand by for your call.'

'Excellent. I know Major Chandra well. I'd trust him without question.'

Adam was well aware that in India Chandra's knowledge would be invaluable. He knew the whole situation better than anyone, was totally dependable and highly respected in army circles.

'Now, Adam, although I've said that there is not a great deal I can do for you in India, there is something vital that I can do from here. I think you know that Nina and I look upon you almost as a son. More than anything else, we want this quest to succeed. If I were younger, I would not hesitate to go myself. As I cannot, I trust you will permit me to finance this whole expedition. When my father came over to England in the nineteenth century, he brought a large sum of money, which he left here in trust for me until I came of age. I am now a very rich man, and we have no children. To what more noble cause could I give my support?'

Adam knew that he would be offended if this offer was declined. He also understood why Jardeeson had never written to give the news about the boys' mission whilst he was still in Malaya. There might have been a danger that he would have gone straight to India and without substantial funds and the right people to help him, Adam would have had little chance of success.

'Very well, Jardeesonji, I'll accept your offer.'

'Nina will be very happy to learn this news, because I must tell you that she now knows the truth about your involvement with the family.'

'That is a relief. It was becoming awkward to maintain the deception with her.'

'Yes, I am sorry about that. Now, regarding the financial arrangements. I will authorise my branch of the Bank of India in Delhi to open an account there in your name. Here in London, I will instruct Coutts to transfer funds to your own bank, so I will need your bank details. There will be your own airfare and those of any others that you wish to go with you, as well as compensation for their loss of earnings, and other expenses. Then I will arrange a further facility in Delhi. You will be short of time but there will be no need for you to be short of funds.'

'That sounds remarkably generous.'

'Generosity doesn't come into it. I am so grateful to you for agreeing to help us.'

Adam nodded his acquiescence as he shook Jardeeson's hand to seal the arrangement. Already he was evaluating the daunting task ahead of him.

'May I stay here until I leave for India? It will be easier than trying to organise things from the Club.'

'Yes, of course. We still have many things to discuss and please use the second telephone line in the study if you have any calls to make.'

'That's splendid. I'll need to call my parents as there won't be time to go and see them. I also need to tell Sarah what I am up to.'

'I think that is a good idea, Adam. You do not want to go off leaving any loose ends.'

Adam was not sure what was in his mind, but knew Jardeeson had his best interests at heart.

'Time's short, Jardeesonji. I ought to be on my way to India within a week.'

'That will be cutting it pretty fine-we've a lot to do. I'll arrange finances tomorrow. If you need any help with air bookings, I can get on to it. I know BOAC has a Britannia flight to Delhi on Mondays, and there's a Comet on Wednesdays and Fridays.'

'I think it will have to be the Friday flight.'

'Have you any thoughts who might be able to help you? We'll need to book them a flight too.'

'Yes, I do. But I need to make a few calls to see whether he is available.'

'Good. I'll leave you to get on with it, Adam. Let's speak again over lunch.'

His first call was to Sarah. Her response was cordial but she did not offer any excuse as to why she had not been at Heathrow to meet him. Nor did she ask why he had not been in contact earlier.

'Is it true what I read in the papers about your promotion?'

She had become very remote but was still well informed. Her next comment took him by surprise.

'Are you going away again, Adam?'

'Yes, very shortly.'

'Then I would like to see you as soon as possible.'

'What about dinner tonight?' he said.

'I would prefer lunch tomorrow.'

It seemed so strange arranging to meet his wife for lunch having not seen her for months but such was the formality of their relationship now. 'How about the Savoy Grill?'

'That sounds fine.' She then added somewhat unnecessarily, 'Adam, we really do need to talk.'

'Yes, we do. Shall we say twelve thirty?'

'Right, I'll see you there.'

Bob had given him Archie's number in College and he only hoped he hadn't already left to go back to California for the summer.

'Could I speak with Dr Archibald please?'

'I'm afraid you might have missed him,' the efficient sounding college porter informed him.

'Has he left for the summer?'

'Oh, Lord no, he's gone down to the river should be back in an hour,' Adam remembered what a keen rower Archie was but couldn't imagine he was still doing it himself. 'Shall I leave him a message sir?'

'Yes that would be kind. Please tell him Brigadier Cullworthy rang.'

'Very good, sir. Do you wish to leave a number?'

Adam left his number and hung up, relieved that at least he wouldn't be having to make long distance calls. An hour and a half later Jandah informed him that there was an American gentleman on the line for him.

'Hey, buddy, how are you doing? 'I hear you are running the British army now.' Adam had forgotten how infectious Archie's enthusiasm for life was.

'Not quite yet.'

'So what are you up to? Bob tells me you still have business in India.'

'Not exactly business, but it was about India that I was calling you. Do you have any plans for the next month?'

'This week I'm training the college boat. They have a big regatta this Saturday. After that I had planned a little fishing trip to Scotland.'

'Well, I have a big favour to ask of you.'

Adam gave him a brief summary of the venture.

'Sounds interesting but what would you need me to do?'

'To be honest I am not entirely sure. I am still formulating the plans so have no specific role at the moment. What I do know is that I need someone I can trust who will be adaptable to whatever unexpected hurdles we encounter.'

'And a little crazy too.'

'I guess your right. But if you can survive a Japanese prisoner of war camp this should be walk in the park.'

'I won't be able to leave before Saturday morning but I can probably rearrange the fishing trip.'

'Thank you Archie, you are a real brick.'

'What about flights?'

'Rindi's uncle will get your flight and paper work sorted. I will be leaving a day ahead of you.'

'OK, buddy so let's speak before you leave.'

'Oh, one more thing Archie. Would there be any chance of your getting hold of some U.S. Army maps of Northern India? They are so much better than any others.'

'No promises but I'll see what I can do.'

The Savoy Hotel, London, Tuesday 12th May 1959.

It was several months since Adam had last seen Sarah and as she walked towards him in the restaurant he was struck by her elegance. As an MP in the House of Commons, she had favoured slim tailored suits. Their well-cut lines hugged her curves and complemented her tall figure to perfection and it reminded Adam of the time when she was in uniform. Happier times. He stood up to greet her and they kissed rather formally on both cheeks. She wore her hair up, gathered in a neat blue felt hat with a black feather to complete her elegant outfit. As long as he had known her she had always worn Joy, her little extravagance, the scent of which triggered a flood of memories in Adam. The slight suntan she had had when in the Tropics had gone. What, he wondered, lay behind the pale and serious expression she now wore?

Emboldened by a gin and tonic she came straight to the point. 'It's not working, is it?'

'Do you want it to work, Sarah?' he responded gently touching her hand. It seemed strange not to be calling her "darling", and even though there was a distance between them that had not previously existed he still felt a strong attraction to her. Sarah withdrew her hand and tried to maintain a formality in her attitude.

'Perhaps it's just our careers that are incompatible. I have tried Adam but I really don't think we make each other happy any more.'

Adam knew she was right but something in him wanted to cling on to what they had or was it what they had had. But it felt like it was slipping through his fingers.

'I had so hoped that you would be like your mother and adapt to being an army wife but you always had more ambition than that. I respect you for what you have achieved in your career but I can't pretend I don't resent it slightly as well.'

'It may have been different if we had had children.'

'Or it may just have been even more complicated.'

'Let's not tear each other apart, Adam.'

'So what did you have in mind?'

'Ivan has asked me to marry him.'

'I see.' He was not expecting this but with hindsight perhaps he had been naïve. 'So how long has this been going on?'

She did not answer and the look she gave him made him feel the question was unworthy of a response.

'Do you love him?'

'Not in a starry-eyed way. We just get on well together. It has been a while since his wife died and I think he still misses her. But he also needs me.'

This comment really hurt Adam but he felt it was pointless saying he had needed her too.

'Then is it mainly companionship?'

'It's not just Ivan and me, Adam. It's you and me. For the past few months, we might as well have been divorced. Are we tying ourselves together for the sake of appearance, in a marriage with no permanent happiness for either of us? Can you honestly say your heart is still in it?'

Her words touched the truth of the matter. Faced with this request he knew they had been living a lie for some time. A relationship perpetuated by convention and social norms. There was a structure which held their professional lives together. His by the solid walls and disciplines of the army. Hers by the expectations of her constituents and fellow MP's. But love offered none of that security, when it was real it was as strong as any physical structure but when it was gone it left only crumbling memories and confused regrets. Were it not for the stark reality and hopelessness of his desire to be with Kafni it could so easily have been him asking to be released. Was it fair of him to deny Sarah the opportunity of a happier future that apparently he could no longer give her?

'Have you discussed this with anyone?'

'Only Ivan, and he will not mention it to anyone until you and I have reached some sort of resolution.'

'This is a bit of a bombshell, Sarah.'

'I realize that only too well. You're going away and when you get back there's your big promotion and doubtless a whole basket of new responsibilities. I'm asking you in the meantime to consider it. Perhaps we can get together again when you get back.'

As ever, Sarah had approached the situation in a level headed and practical way. Prevarication at this point would serve no purpose. She deserved a straight answer.

'Well, if that's what you really want. I won't stand in your way,' he paused, 'I would like to meet Ivan sometime.'

Sarah gently nodded her head.

They sank into pensive contemplation of what the future held for them both. There seemed little more to say on the subject. Adam eventually broke the silence.

'Have you seen anything of Virginia?'

'Yes I have actually. We had lunch a fortnight ago.'

'How is she fairing? Simon's death must have been a bit of a shock.'

'She's a bit of a lost soul if I'm honest. Still as beautiful and serene looking but very sad.'

It seemed easier to talk about the failure of someone else's marriage than examine the reality of their own.

'What happened to her little boy?'

'Tristan.'

'Is that what they called him?'

'Tristan Arthur Chalvington.'

'So why Chalvington?'

'Simon never actually signed the papers disinheriting him and no one else has ever challenged his legitimacy. He is also much fairer now than when he was a baby.'

'How come you know so much?'

'She's asked me to be a Godmother.'

'Well that's an honour.'

'I suppose it is but she doesn't seem to have that many good friends, poor girl, and many of them abandoned her. What with questions over the child and then Simon's suicide.'

'So has she admitted that the baby was Wantilla's?'

'No not really and she refuses to rule out the throwback possibility.'

'I still think that rascal had her at his beck and call.' Adam said with barely disguised indignation.

'Yes he certainly had a hold over her but bizarrely she talks about Rindi with rather more affection. But that may just be because she feels bad about Simon trying to kill him.'

'I think Rindi certainly felt sorry for her after the incident on the boat. That rather threw them together.'

'You don't think there could have been any truth in Simon's conjecture?'

'No I really doubt that.' Adam said with conviction but the thought that Rindi had not always been entirely honest about his romantic life niggled him.

'So where are you off to this time?' Sarah asked.

'I have been asked to go back to India.'

'By the army?'

'No, by the Debrahm family. They have some very tricky problems that they need some help with.'

'And you are the most appropriate person to sort them out?' she said with a hint of scepticism reminiscent of his conversation with Bob Mercer.

'It seems so.' Adam replied blandly not wishing to go into it in any detail and Sarah didn't seem inquisitive to explore the matter further.

'I never did make it to Kushnapur, but you seemed very protective of your relationship with Rindi and his family.' She said with more than a suggestion of jealousy.

'They asked me to be a trustee you know, so I felt I should offer to help.' Adam replied knowing that this was the least of his reasons.

'Well good luck with it. Will you call me when you get back?'

As they parted Adam felt a strange sense of liberation tangled up with a feeling of vulnerability. The sense of failure and the fear of the changes it would mean to the way he had lived his life for the last sixteen years pervaded. Not for the first time, he felt that he was not in control of the direction of his love life.

CHAPTER THIRTY

New Delhi, India, Saturday 16ᵗʰ May 1959.

As Adam came off the plane at Palam Airport, the heat, the glare and the familiar cocktail of earthy smells assaulted his senses. His lightweight suit was already damp with perspiration by the time he passed through the terminal building and three Sikh taxi drivers were vying for his custom.

The driver he chose looked briefly crestfallen when he spoke to him in Hindi and asked to be taken to the Hotel Imperial in Queensway. His fare obviously knew the city and would suspect any inflated charges but, regaining his self-esteem, he said, 'Sahib, these Congress politicians, they are changing the name of Queensway to Janpath.'

Just before Connaught Circus, the taxi drew into the palm-lined drive of the Hotel Imperial. Although Jardeeson had suggested that no expense should be spared, this older, less fashionable hotel suited the low profile that Adam intended to keep on this visit. It was a good central location and from here he knew his way around. Much had changed since his last visit. Many of the street names had changed to reflect the new independent status. With the British no longer in control there were noticeable changes in the diplomatic enclave with the Russians competing with the Americans for the size and impressiveness of their embassies.

He registered at the hotel simply as "Mr" Cullworthy. The arrival of a high-ranking British officer would attract the wrong sort of attention. He had reserved a large room on the the first floor overlooking the garden where he could conduct his strategy meetings in private. The furniture was a reflection of the Colonial past with heavy mahogany chairs, a writing desk, a solid table bearing Indian magazines and a very wide bed. On the wall hung a painting of the Red Fort in Delhi and a ceiling fan spun like a frustrated propeller attempting to reduce the searing midday heat.

Apart from a few key changes, like the addition of Archie to the team, Adam's plan was much as he had envisaged it twelve years before. The first call he made was to Chandra. Jardeeson had done his stuff and Adam was told that Chandra had already left Kushnapur and would be in Delhi by the following morning.

Sunday 17th May

Adam was shaving when the the hotel waiter knocked on his door the following morning.

'Chota hazri, sahib.'

Adam had requested coffee rather than tea.

'Sorry sahib, no coffee. No coffee for six months.'

This was the first indication that things had changed since the British had left India. It was also the dawning realisation that getting things done in a hurry was no longer possible. Had he totally underestimated the time it would take to complete this task? This whole venture now seemed like a complete act of folly. Was it too late to change his plans and return to London? He couldn't do that. All these years he had been tormented by the frustration of being deprived of the chance of fulfilling this mission. Too much was now riding on his leadership and too many people were already committed and expecting him to deliver on his promise.

There was a knock at the door and Adam opened it to be greeted by the beaming smile of Harish Chandra. Any swirling doubts he had been harbouring now vanished. Even out of uniform he had the dignified bearing of a distinguished soldier. Maybe it was because he was thinner but he seemed taller and his neatly trimmed moustache less prominent.

Namaste, Brigadier Cullworthy-sahib. Thank you for coming to India. The Maharajah sends you his personal regards.' It was strange to hear Rindi referred to by his title. 'He agrees with your reason not to come to Kushnapur for the present. Wantilla's spies would soon hear of your arrival.'

'Yes, and for that reason I've also registered here as "Mister" Cullworthy, so perhaps you'd bear this in mind if you call me.'

'A wise move, Brigadier-sahib, I will remember that'.

Monday 18th May 1959.

The following morning Adam left early to avoid the New Delhi rush hour and was at the airport to meet Archie. It was six years since they had last met in London, when Archie came for a Rhodes Scholars' reunion. As he came into the arrivals hall, Adam recognised the big bear of a man, his thick blond hair still unkempt, but now with a few grey hairs round his temples. In his white linen suit and Panama hat he had assumed all the mannerisms of an Oxford don. That was until he opened his mouth to speak.

'I'm feeling a bit bushed, old buddy. I could do with a shower and a kip. From what you tell me we've got one hell of a job to do, so I'd better be in good shape.'

'You can do that when we get to the hotel.'

'This is quite a turn up for the books, eh, Adam. A Yank university lecturer comes to India to sort out a British brigadier's problems.'

Adam smiled. 'Let's hope you can, Archie, we're up against something very tricky here.'

'Oh and by the way, I got you those maps you asked for.'

'Excellent work, Major Archibald,' Adam said reinstating his old rank in jest.

Two hours later Archie and Chandra convened with Adam in his room to prepare their strategy.

'Can I start by saying I think we should all use first names from now on.'

'Sure,' said Archie, 'but I'd prefer Archie to Hugh if that's OK.'

'I am Harish,' Chandra said with less conviction.

'OK, so the objectives of this mission are to find the lingam, find Pratap and Gopal and if possible to locate Princess Kafni.'

Adam could see the anguish on Chandra's face at the mention of Gopal and only wished he could confide in him that they were both in the same boat.

'We now have two and a half weeks to achieve what previous search parties have failed to do in twelve years.'

'Crazy odds,' said Archie 'but I'm in.'

'We can do it, sahib.'

'It's Adam now Harish. And for what it's worth I think you are the best team I could ask for.' Adam took a sip of one of the cold beers he had asked to be sent up to his room.

'Now gentlemen given that time is of the essence we need to avoid wasting too much of it by pursuing three different searches. The key as I see it is to first find the lingam. The boys are also intent on finding the lingam so if we find it I suspect they will not be far away.'

Archie and Chandra nodded in agreement.

'So the last time we had a reliable sighting of the lingam was twelve years ago when Narajan left you Harish to contend with Chalvington in the gorge. Wantilla has subsequently admitted that Narajan was with him in Lahore albeit before he then disappeared. Jardeeson told me that Narajan's body was found badly mutilated so it was assumed that he was the victim of a sectarian attack. The trail seems to have gone dead in Lahore and so I suggest that is where we start our search.'

'What else did they get out of Wantilla?' Archie asked.

Adam looked to Chandra.

'He claimed that after Princess Kafni was endowed to him, she refused to consummate their arrangement until she had made her pilgrimage to the Hindu Kush. Then after completing the pilgrimage she claimed the right to consult a diviner of the divine will, who would decide the *muhurtam,* the auspicious time, for the consummation. However, before that could happen she and her ayah absconded from their residence in Lahore.'

'Is all that really likely?' asked Archie.

'About the pilgrimage and consulting the diviner? Yes, perfectly possible. Even Wantilla would respect those customs,' Adam confirmed, 'but I'd like to know where exactly they were in residence when they absconded.'

'These were dangerous times for Hindus,' Chandra continued, 'so Wantilla decided he would avoid another night in a hotel. He knew about Kashmir Bhavan on the outskirts of Lahore, a great house belonging to the late Maharajah of Kashmir, a proud if rather careless Hindu who had not foreseen what might happen in Lahore after partition. Although he had personally never lived in the mansion, relatives and friends visiting the city were often entertained there. Wantilla and his entourage moved out there and the Princess and her ayah were given accommodation in adjoining suites in the *zenana*. The next morning, despite an extensive search, neither of them could be found.'

'So what did Wantilla do then?'

'By all accounts he was furious because Kashmir Bhavan was built like a fortress over three hundred years ago and was meant to be impregnable.'

'And was that the last news you had of the Princess?' Adam asked. Chandra nodded.

'So if this lingam is so valuable why have the authorities not been asked to help recover it? Archie asked.

'Because if the Indian government recovered it they might well claim it as a national treasure, which would be bad enough. But if the Pakistan government got hold of it, they might break it up and dispose of the jewels.'

'A son-of-a-bitch scenario.' Archie chipped in.

'But wasn't it Wantilla's responsibility to find Kafni?' asked Archie.

Harish shook his head. 'His pride demanded that it was *her* duty to come to him. We know that he despatched several spies, but these were more likely to have been searching for the lingam. If he could find the lingam again he knew that would be his strongest hold over Kafni.'

There was a knock at the door and initially Adam looked surprised. Then after a moments reflection he said 'Ah yes, of course, that will be our curry. Gentlemen, I thought we might need sustenance so I ordered dinner to be brought to the room. Apart from not wishing to waste time I think the less we are seen together in public the better. Archie, you will be pleased to hear I have ordered an extra hot curry for you.'

'Excellent, the hotter the better.'

Two waiters wheeled in a trolley with an impressive selection of curries, vegetables and chutneys. Adam suggested they continued their discussion over the meal.

'Harish, when exactly did the boys set off on their mission?'

'The twenty-sixth of December, last year.'

Archie nodded. 'So five months ago, and no news since then?'

'None. But communications with Pakistan are difficult at the best of times. I am sure that if they had found anything they would have sent news.'

'Wouldn't two young Hindu boys attract the wrong sort of attention?'

'Unfortunately, you are right which is why they planned to assume Parsee attire just before they crossed the Pakistan border,' Chandra said in confirmation.

'Adam, I am still puzzled as to what we can do to find the lingam that hasn't already been tried,' said Archie.

'We do have several advantages that those lads don't have. The most obvious of which is money. But you are right, there is little point in covering old ground. No, we will need to use an entirely different approach.'

'Sounds interesting.'

'Your role, Archie, is to take the guise of an extremely rich American who's very interested in antiquities. With your knowledge, you should have no difficulty in befriending museum curators and the like. Most of them have modest salaries and will be glad to receive a little financial inducement in return for advice on where to purchase antique jewellery and precious stones. As we are short of time I want you to make a couple of extravagant purchases. We need the word to get out that there is a big spender in town. '

'I think I can do that all right, but I know what some of these things cost. Even with the help of your rich friend in London, surely we don't have access to that sort of dough.'

'We have enough to fund the teasers and if things work out as I've planned I hope not to have to part with any serious money. The lingam will certainly have been stolen, and assuming it is still in Lahore its present holder will probably be ready to sell at well below its true value. In any case, if we find it I intend to frighten those concerned into releasing it and only giving them a modest reward for their trouble.'

'Do we have any contacts in Lahore?' Archie asked.

'Fortunately, yes, Jardeeson Debrahm gave me two contacts and both should be helpful to you, Archie. They are men he knows well, and who see him regularly in England. There is a Behan Boolajee, a trustworthy and successful Parsee businessman connected with shipping. He's highly respected by the Pakistan government and would never act contrary to their interests. On the other hand he would wish to see a stolen treasure returned to its rightful owners.'

'Does he know about this golden phallus?'

'Not at present, and it may avoid embarrassment for him if he's never given any precise information about the lingam. Boolajee will also be your financial guarantor, should you need one. He has opened a current account for you at the Chartered Bank in Lahore. And Jardeeson has already transferred funds there from London. Boolajee will take you to the bank to introduce you and get your signature registered, so that the account can be activated. I too shall have an account at that bank, though we shall be quite unconnected there. Your second contact is Zaki Ibrahim, an oriental carpet dealer who has several shops in the Northern Punjab. He is described by Jardeeson as a likeable rogue. He came from Egypt with his father on a purchasing expedition in 1939 during the British Raj and never left.'

'Am I expected to make a foray into the oriental carpet market as well?'

Adam laughed. 'Only if you want to take some back to America. No, Zaki's business interests cover a wide field, and I'm told he has an amazing network of contacts.'

'Sounds useful.'

'Yes, he certainly will be. Now, Harish, you will be our anchor man here in New Delhi. There is not enough time to set up our own office but Jardeeson has arranged for us to have a room in a friend's legal practice. Our cover will be that we are setting up an export business. This will explain your overseas calls. Oh, and by the way, I think that you should continue to use your army rank. There's still a high regard for your old regiment.'

Adam saw a visible change in Chandra's posture in acknowledgement of the pride in his regiment.

'You will have to keep in daily contact with the *dewan* at Kushnapur; Jardeeson in London; Archie and Boolajee in Pakistan; and me, wherever I may be. I'll give you code names for the lingam, Kafni and Wantilla, but it would be better if we don't mention them at all when we are on the telephone. This is particularly important when making calls from the hotels. A bored switchboard operator is always tempted to listen in. One of your telephone lines must be reserved for incoming calls. You'll need to engage a secretary for your letters and to answer the telephone.'

'So what exactly are you going to do?' Archie asked.

'I was about to come to my part in the operation. I intend to go first to Islamabad to look up some army officers that I met during the war. Some of them are quite senior now.

Given the devious characters we are up against we will need all the influence we can muster.'

'Good thinking, bud. So how do I fit in with you in Pakistan? Am I supposed to know you?'

'Just a polite nodding acquaintance. To ignore each other completely could arouse even more suspicion. We shall not meet very often and we'll rely mainly on Harish for our daily updates. Now, I suggest that Harish books you on a flight from Delhi to Lahore, leaving tomorrow. I'll leave the following day. Did you get your visa for Pakistan?'

'Yes, all fixed up at the U.S Embassy in London. I think your friend Jardeeson had smoothed the path as you say.'

'Right, then there should be no travel problems. Well, gentlemen, if there are no further questions I suggest we all get a good night's sleep. Archie, I'll see you in Lahore the day after tomorrow. We won't see you, Harish, until we return to Delhi, hopefully with mission accomplished. Good luck my friends.'

Faletti's Hotel, Lahore, Pakistan, Tuesday 19th May 1959.

Archie and Adam arrived separately in Lahore. Archie booked in at Nedoos, a big sandstone hotel, built by a successful Anglo-Indian family and Adam thought it wiser to stay at a different hotel. His decision to choose Falletti's Hotel was also motivated by the happy memories he had of his time there with Sarah. In the evening, they would go to the Gymkhana Club in Lawrence Gardens for cocktails and dancing to the Police Band and then move on to Falletti's for dinner and more late night dancing. The last glorious days of the Raj.

The same old black hair furniture was still there but the atmosphere had changed. The absence of those laughing officers, snatching a few days pleasure with their wives or girlfriends, before returning to their regiments and the front line, left a poignant void. The difference now served to remind Adam that he was not here on a sentimental sojourn.

As soon as he had unpacked, he made three telephone calls. The first was to Boolajee, who invited him for dinner that night at the Punjab Club. The second was to a Pakistani brigadier who he had met in Delhi during the War. His response was friendly and encouraging. 'I'm just off on manoeuvres for a week,' he said, 'but as soon as I'm back, come to Jhelum and stay a few days and meet my family.'

It sounded agreeable enough, but the delay ruled it out so Adam declined the invitation. The brigadier expressed his regret and then gave Adam his private telephone number.

'Ring me, Adam, if you find you can spare time to come, or if you need help with anything whilst you are here.'

The final call was to a Lieutenant-General Mohammed Malik, a contact General James Elliot at GHQ in London had given him. His response was cordial and Adam accepted an invitation to spend the weekend at his residence on the outskirts of Lahore. This high-ranking contact would certainly justify the use of his valuable time.

Wednesday 20ᵗʰ May 1959

Before the weekend he had two days available, and the first thing he did was to locate Kashmir Bhavan, the residence from where Kafni and her *ayah* had disappeared. This proved easy enough; the hotel taxi driver knew instantly and took Adam straight there. The difficult part was to get inside.

Enquiries revealed it to be unoccupied and that it was being retained as an asset to meet a bogus claim against the late Maharajah of Kashmir's estate.

Adam now had to find a good excuse to get in. Normally, a modest bribe to the *chokidars* would have been enough, but not this time. Other callers, probably Wantilla's agents, had made clumsy attempts and queered the pitch. No one was now allowed through the gates without the written authority of the lawyers handling the claim. However, to approach them, he needed the influence of someone like his brigadier friend; or better still perhaps a letter from General Malik.

At Falletti's Hotel, that evening, Adam got into conversation with some of the guests. Most were just passing through, but others who resided permanently at the hotel indulged in nostalgic memories. One of them was a Mrs Gascoyne, the widow of a retired colonel who had insisted upon staying on in Pakistan when the British left. She and her husband, being well known and respected, had been offered permanent residence at Falletti's. They had been there during the massacres of August and September 1947 and Adam listened as, with obvious distress, she related some of her experiences.

'It was quite terrible,' she said. 'Every day some unfortunate creature, caught up in the turmoil, would come into the hotel and beg for our protection or ask for help to escape to India. Some were quite badly injured.'

'And were you able to help them?'

'Not much, I'm afraid. The resident nurse gave them first aid and a doctor made a routine call every morning. The hotel was very good, I thought, but they couldn't possibly encourage these people to take refuge here. There were so many of them. My husband did manage to get his old regiment to provide two army lorries and an armed escort to take some of them back to a temporary refugee camp at Ambala. It really was a tragic time. And you know, the killing went on for several weeks.'

She sighed, and then continued, 'William loved it here; India was in his blood, that's why he could never leave. He's buried here in the cantonment, and now I can never leave.'

'Have you ever thought about going home?'

'Yes, I did once. My friend Dorothy Manning, the District Commander's widow, wrote and asked me to go and live with her in England. I suppose I ought to have gone then, but I could never have settled in Cornwall.'

She gazed across the room pensively, perhaps wondering if she would have been better off in England.

'Dorothy was such a caring person,' she continued. 'She was visiting me here one day in August 1947 when two unfortunate young Indian women were brought in. A British Army corporal driving his Jeep along Nicholson Road had been stopped by one of the women, who had begged for his help. The hotel was the nearest place of safety the corporal could think of. The younger woman was in a terrible state of distress, with blood streaming from her arm and face. I remember the incident well; she spoke such beautiful English. The woman with her said that she was the *ayah* and that her mistress was some sort of princess. Of course, these people have such vivid imaginations and tend to exaggerate. Perhaps they just wanted our sympathy.'

Adam felt the blood drain from his face as he mentally wrestled with the cruel possibility of this coincidence. His throat went dry and he found it difficult to frame the words. 'What happened to these two women?'

'Oh, the nurse bandaged up the woman's injuries, and then of course dear Dorothy, ever the Good Samaritan, took them home with her.'

'Presumably they were Hindu. Did Mrs Manning help them get back to India?'

'Well, that's the strange part about it; a few days later when they had recovered, William offered to help them get to India. They politely declined his offer, and instead, asked if they could possibly be taken somewhere up country.'

'And did she arrange that?'

'Oh, yes, William located an army transport going near to where they wanted to be taken. As far as I know, they got away safely.'

'Have you any idea where it was?'

'Afraid not. Why the particular interest?'

'It is vaguely possible that one of those women is the sister of a great friend who was at school with me in England.'

'Really? Sounds most improbable.' Mrs Gascoynes assertive manner reminded him of Lady Roberts, ever the *Burra Mem-sahib*, 'there were millions of refugees around at that time,' she continued, 'in any case, if it were your friend's sister, she would surely have been keen to get back to India.'

She was right it would be a remarkable coincidence but Adam had to pursue it however unlikely it was. It would have been too complicated to start to explain the background to Mrs Gascoyne, and pleasant as she was it was prudent to tell her as little as possible.

'Is there anyone here who could possibly know where those two women went?'

'I shouldn't think so for one minute. William probably knew the place, and certainly Dorothy did, but then she's in England.'

'Do you have her address?

'I've got it somewhere; she usually sends me a Christmas card. She might have moved; she did say a couple of years ago that the house was now too big for her, but then that may have been her way of hinting that I should go and live with her.'

'Do you think you could look out that address for me?'

'This all sounds like a wild goose chase, and I'm not sure that I should give you my friend's address,' she said doubtfully.

'I quite understand your hesitation, Mrs Gascoyne, but although I'm travelling in mufti, I can prove to you that I'm a serving brigadier in the British Army.'

'If that is in fact the case I may be able to help. Is that why you are here in Lahore?' she said, still slightly sceptical of his motivation.

'It is one of the reasons I'm here,' Adam said, hoping not to be drawn into further detail.

'Well, I think it seems rather hopeless after so long.'

Thursday 21st May 1959.

The next morning Mrs Gascoyne duly produced Dorothy Manning's address and Adam passed these details on through Harish to Jardeeson in London. He requested urgent contact with Mrs Manning in the faint hope that she might be able to remember where the women had been taken.

CHAPTER THIRTY ONE

Punjab Club, Thursday 21ˢᵗ May 1959.

That evening Adam dined with Behan Boolajee. When he arrived at the Punjab Club, Adam told the porter he was a guest of Mr Boolajee and was directed towards a large man lying prostrate on a leather club sofa, his hands clasped over his stomach.

As Adam approached the figure raised his head and gave an inquisitive glance in his direction. Whilst still remaining in this prone position he said. 'Ah, the Brigadier I presume? Welcome to Lahore.'

He slowly elevated himself and smoothed back thick tufts of silver grey hair. He was wearing a pair of dark rimmed spectacles, which gave him an owl-like appearance and his beautifully cut dark blue suit helped to disguise a well-nourished figure. He barked what sounded like an Urdu insult at a club servant, who hastily disappeared, then reappeared minutes later with a tray on which there were two glasses and a bottle of scotch.

'My dear boy,' he said in a perfect Oxford accent. 'How can I be of help to you?'

Before Adam could reply, he proceeded to tell him that he had already arranged bank accounts for Archie and Adam at the Chartered Bank.

It quickly became evident from the attitude of passing staff and members that he was a highly respected figure. Clearly, he was amongst the good and great of this Club, whose membership included anyone of significance in Lahore. Aware of what Jardeeson had said about Boolajee's standing in Pakistani society, Adam was a little reluctant to disclose too much detail about the exact nature of his assignment. However, when he left him after dinner, he was in no doubt that he would prove invaluable to them.

Dinner with Boolajee had finished early and, keen to pass on his news about Mrs Manning, Adam took a taxi to Nedoos where he hoped to contrive a meeting with Archie. At the hotel, he walked casually through the lounges, and then into the dining room where he spotted Archie with a guest who he suspected was Zaki Ibrahim.

The headwaiter came to over to him to suggest a choice of table, and he indicated one where Archie could easily see him. Reassured by Archie's glance, Adam moved on through to the Kashmir Room where he ordered a whisky and soda. He had chosen a table near the entrance and a few minutes later Archie walked in with his guest. By prearrangement, he had placed a copy of the New York Herald on the arm of his chair, and as he passed Archie paused, looked down at the paper and said, 'Excuse me, Sir, would mind if I have a look at your Herald? I'd like to see what's going on back home.'

'Certainly, please take it. I've finished with it.' Their charade being for the benefit of any inquisitive guest or possible informer.

'Thank you, that's kind of you,' responded Archie. 'Perhaps you'd care to join us?'

'Why not?' Adam signalled the waiter to transfer his scotch and followed them to a secluded corner of the room.

'I have explained to Mr Ibrahim here that I am seeking a very valuable religious sculpture.'

His guest smiled at Adam and said, 'I think it is better that you call me Zaki. Only people who owe me money call me Mr Ibrahim.'

He was a short slim man with a shiny bald head, his darting black eyes were separated by a beak that hooked over a mean little moustache. Unlike Boolajee, he wore traditional Pakistani dress, and his quick elegant fingers subconsciously shuffled a string of jade beads. He exuded a very distinct aroma, a melange of musk and Turkish tobacco. If he had not come with Jardeeson's blessing Adam would have judged him as being a highly suspect character.

He stared at Adam intently and then surprised him by saying, 'Mr Cullworthy do you have any idea who you will be dealing with in this venture of yours?' Before Adam could respond he continued, 'I fear you are too much of a gentleman to handle these unsavoury characters.'

'I know Wantilla well enough and I doubt whether they could be more unscrupulous than him.'

'Your courteous English manner may be very useful as they will think they can out-fox you. Fortunately you will have a rascal like me to prepare you for their tricks.'

He did not respond to Adam's comment about Wantilla, but appeared to be thinking aloud. Adam liked his no nonsense approach and was glad that he was on their side. They chatted on together for the next hour and were amazed to discover that Zaki was almost as knowledgeable about precious stones as he was about carpets.

Archie, who had made a considerable study of the subject and could make a reasoned judgement, was now constrained to ask, 'How have you come to be so well informed Zaki?'

'My education in jewels started as a necessity,' he said in his heavy Middle Eastern accent. 'My family are now happily settled here, but there was a time when we might have had to move quickly. Carpets are not easily portable wealth, and even gold is heavy. Precious stones were the answer, but when the situation changed and our position in Pakistan was settled, jewellery became my hobby and I returned to my true love, carpets. A fine carpet is not merely a thing of beauty or a useful floor covering; it has its own tale to tell. It starts its life through the devotion and skill of the carpet maker and then gathers history and a personality over hundreds of years with different owners. I have many carpets that I would consider to be family heirlooms but I know that they will outlive me. I am merely a custodian for my lifetime and of course, ultimately, gentlemen,' he said with a cheeky grin, 'everything has its price.'

'Tell us a tale of one of your carpets,' said Archie, clearly amused.

'Carpets need to be seen and felt to be fully appreciated but tomorrow I will show you a magnificent Ziegler. It has beautiful designs in green, rust, blue and brown and they are no longer made. It is product of European brain and Persian handicraft and it is one of my great favourites. If you're looking for tales of adventure and intrigue, even corruption, few can surpass the Ziegler. The family came from Manchester to Sultanabad in 1860, and began importing cotton fibres for their industry. When problems arose, they turned their skills and abilities to other enterprises. Spying was one, and another, equally disreputable, was shipping opium to China. Their activities quickly attracted the attention of the British Government of the day, and the Zieglers were enlisted for espionage work. I like to think my Ziegler has travelled the world and witnessed many clandestine assignments. But enough of my trade.' He leaned closer. 'I want to know more about your assignment.'

Adam decided to defer disclosing his news about Mrs Manning and left it to Archie to fill them in on his progress. He had visited two museums that afternoon and struck up a friendship with one of the curators, whose special interest was archaeological art objects and gemstones.

'We were thinking Archie might buy a few quality gems to 'smoke out' the lingam.'

'Excellent idea and I know just the man. A jeweller who is notoriously indiscreet.'

Zaki continued to captivate them with his tales of famous jewels that had been fought over, and treasures that had been buried or lost during retreats across the Punjab.

'Frankly, I must admit that I am occasionally asked for an opinion on an object of dubious origin.' A gleam came into his eye as he continued. 'There is now a new breed of customer. The sheiks in the Middle East are becoming rich from oil revenues, and their wives are competing for material displays of a husband's devotion. Nothing enhances a woman's prestige in the seraglio as much as the spectacle of a beautiful gift. If it is a jewel with a provenance of romance and daring, so much the better. As an Arabic speaking Egyptian Muslim, I understand their psychology, and I am well placed to take advantage of this business.'

'You've given me an idea, Zaki.' Adam sketched out his plan to them.

Zaki seemed satisfied with the scheme. He said that he would think it through over night and suggested that they all meet at his Anarkali premises, as soon as Adam returned from his weekend with General Malik. Adam suggested that whilst he was away, Archie might visit the jeweller and make a purchase extravagant enough to attract interest. He then recounted his conversation with Mrs Gascoyne.

'Ah, honour and love, it's worse than I thought,' Zaki said moving a few beads along the string. 'I prefer it when people are motivated by greed, they are so much more predictable.'

Adam was surprised at the speed with which Zaki had jumped to the conclusion that there was more to the story of the Hindu women than Adam was letting on.

'Fortunately, Adam, I think the men we will be dealing with are driven only by greed.' He spoke with relish.

To maintain the subterfuge, Adam parted company with Archie and Zaki in the lounge. They then walked through to the reception area of the hotel where they conducted their separate farewells, before leaving in different directions.

Sunday 24th May.

Adam's stay with General and Mrs Malik was a curious mixture of pleasure and anxiety; always at the back of his mind were thoughts of Kafni and Pratap and how little time he had to find them. The Malik's home was beautiful and their company delightful, but he knew that he was enjoying the benefit of his hosts out of respect for their friend General Elliot. Clearly Malik had been assessing Adam's integrity and when he left he handed Adam a letter of personal recommendation addressed simply "To whom it may concern".

On his return to Falletti's Hotel, he had a note to call Mr H. He rang Harish in Delhi and was disappointed that he had no news of Mrs Manning from London. He then called Archie at Nedoos who confirmed their meeting with Zaki the following evening, in Anarkali.

Zaki's salon, Anarkali, Monday 25th May.

'Welcome to Anarkali and to my emporium,' Zaki greeted them enthusiastically.

'Did you know the name Anarkali means "pomegranate blossom"? It was the name of a favourite girl in Emperor Akbar's harem. Unfortunately she smiled at Jahangir, the Emperor's son, and in a flash of fury he ordered her to be buried alive. The grieving Jahangir raised a cenotaph to her, carving upon it the lines:"*Ah, if I could again see the face of my beloved, To the day of judgement I would give thanks to my Creator."* '

Adam prayed that Kafni had not suffered a similar twist of fate. 'Where is the cenotaph?' he asked.

'Here in Lahore but after the British annexed the Punjab in 1849, they converted it into the church of St. James.'

He ushered them through the outer showroom, past rack after rack of fine oriental carpets, into his private office.

'So, Zaki, where is this Ziegler then?'

'Yes, yes, all in good time,' he said like a father protecting his most beautiful daughter. Walking over to the nearest carpet he ran the back of his hand over it. 'Moghul Kashmir: the weave is so tight that only the strongest eyes can count the knots.' He gently passed his hand over the next two.' Kerman; Isphahan; lovely.' Then on to the next, 'Heriz; just come and feel the silk; look at that fine geometric design and that blend of soft palette colours: rust, green, yellow and orange-red. A thousand years blending have gone into creating those shades.' He moved on, 'Turkoman Bokhara, - the real thing, not one of those copies from Iran, or Pakistan - these are some of the most classic carpets ever made. That's why they are so often imitated.' He shook his head disapprovingly. 'Sometimes however, the influence is absorbed with great sensitivity. Look at this Afghan with its clean reds and blacks, a coarser wool, but beautifully woven. It will last forever. But as you can see gentlemen I can talk for hours about carpets. Tell me, what developments?'

The casual observer, seeing them drinking their mint tea, might well have concluded that their business was solely concerned with carpets.

Archie had discovered from his curator friend that an offer of rubies and sapphires of unusual design had been made to the museum. Inspection of the gems was proving difficult because contact had been made through a dealer. Archie's keen interest, and a tempting commission in the offing, had enticed the curator to try and arrange for Archie to see the stones as soon as possible.

'I just hope that if I get to see them, I'll be able to assess their quality. Obviously, what I want to learn is the provenance of the stones. There's no time to waste chasing the wrong thing. It's a pity no one has ever photographed the lingam. By the way Adam, I do have one problem: before this character sets the thing up, he wants some sort of evidence that I have adequate financial resources. Understandably, he doesn't want to lose face. What do you suggest?'

'Boolajee has agreed to give you a letter as assurance of your sound and substantial assets. That should do the trick.'

Zaki nodded to show his approval of Boolajee as a guarantor.

'Now, Zaki, have you thought over my plan?'

'I've not only thought it over, I've taken the liberty of putting it into action. I've sent telexes to my agents in the Middle East. They will know which of the sheiks and princes would be interested. Names are important you know, because without them, how do you say it? Someone might sniff a rat.'

'Aren't you putting your own reputation on the line, Zaki?' asked Archie.

'I think I can deal with that. I shall say that I was in it for the money. No one around here would begrudge a merchant such a business opportunity.'

Zaki ordered two more trays of hot sweet beverage, the last of which was a concoction with chips of nuts, rather too potent for Adam's palate.

'Shall we meet again tomorrow evening?' asked Zaki. 'There is no respect for anyone who would purchase an expensive carpet without many hours of bargaining. I'll have three excellent carpets set aside for your inspection tomorrow.' This charming yet shrewd merchant was clearly enjoying himself.

Tuesday 26th May 1959.

Next morning Adam took a taxi and called on the lawyers handling Kashmir Bhavan to seek permission to visit. He presented the letter from General Malik, and the effect was remarkable. He was ushered into an elegantly furnished office, greeted by the senior partner, who asked him to wait. A few minutes later there was a knock on the door and a middle-aged Indian entered and introduced himself as Shri Shastri. It was immediately evident that he was a fastidious dresser. His cream suit was well made albeit probably by a local tailor. He wore a plain white cotton shirt with a stiff colour and a blue tie with narrow diagonal white stripes. He had a very serious demeanour and Adam thought he was probably a legal clerk with aspirations to become a qualified lawyer. He told Adam he would be his guide and that he had a car waiting to take them to visit Kashmir Bhavan.

At his hotel, Adam had taken the precaution of putting one fifty-rupee note and two twenty rupee notes into one envelope, and another fifty-rupee note into a second envelope. He now took the first of these envelopes from his pocket.

'Shri Shastri, will you be kind enough to thank the *chokidars* at Kashmir Bhavan.' and then handed him the envelope. Knowing it was implicit that the reward for his own services were included, Adam added, 'A small appreciation of their services.'

On arrival at the *bhavan*, they were greeted by the two *chokidars*, and Adam noted their respect for Shastri when they opened his car door first. He hastened to cover his embarrassment as Adam heard him snap out, '*Voh hai burra-sahib.*' Thereafter, it was Adam, who received the preferential attention.

As they entered the house, Adam felt a brief moment of uneasiness, visualising how Kafni and her party would have arrived that night in 1947. Nevertheless, he was not here to reconstruct her reception; it was the method of her departure that he had to discover.

Shastri and the *chokidars* conducted him through a maze of impressive reception rooms, three dining rooms, and two kitchens. Dustsheets had been laid over all the furniture, with the exception of the dining and kitchen tables. Although these were bare, they were spotless, probably cleaned regularly by a wife of one of the *chokidars*.

At first, Adam displayed an interest in some of the main rooms, then he became impatient and asked to see the *zenana*, knowing well enough that this mansion would have exclusive women's apartments. The *chokidars* exchanged a few words in Punjabi with Shastri who turned to Adam and said, 'I am sorry sahib they do not have the keys to the *zenana*.' Adam then took out the second of the envelopes.

'I really am sorry to be taking up so much of your time, Shri Shastri, but I must see the *zenana*, perhaps this will take care of some of the commitments that I'm causing you to neglect.' Adam handed him the envelope.

His change of attitude was, Adam assumed, in response to his reward, but he would later learn that this reasoning was misplaced. He was immediately conducted back through one of the reception rooms and into another, where a door leading off was opened for him by Shastri himself. The rooms here, although fewer in number and slightly smaller, were not dissimilar to those in the main part of the house, and there was yet another kitchen and a dining room. On the first floor were four bedrooms, each with their own bathroom, with elaborate mosaic floors. On the second floor, set out in inter-connected pairs, were eight servants' bedrooms of more modest proportions.

Although these could be reached from a landing and a back staircase leading to the ground floor, there was another interesting arrangement. It was a facility that acknowledged the very personal relationship between an *ayah* and her mistress: Each pair of servants' bedrooms had a private staircase down to a passageway, from which a private door gave access to the mistress's bedroom.

Adam carefully inspected room after room, finding no clue to his quest. Little wonder, he thought, that the means of Kafni and her *ayah's* escape remained a mystery.

'Have I seen everything, Shri Shastri?'

'I am quite sure that the burra-sahib has looked well at the house.'

'That does not answer my question. Now, Shri Shastri, I have no time to footle around. I'm sure that General Malik would be disappointed to learn that I haven't seen all I wish to see.'

Inwardly Adam was amused, knowing that General Malik would not have the slightest interest in the architectural investigation that his introduction had facilitated.

'Perhaps, if the sahib could tell me what he is looking for, I could be of more service to him.'

Adam wondered if he was being unreasonable but he had the distinct impression that Shastri did not want to reveal anything more than was entirely necessary. By the same token, Adam was also reluctant to reveal the exact purpose of his enquiries. However progress was vital. 'Shri Shastri,' he said, 'the sister of an Indian friend of mine was a guest in this house one evening in August 1947. The following morning, neither she nor her *ayah,* could be found. I'm here to try and discover what may have happened to them.'

'Thank you, sahib for telling me that. May I propose to the sahib that we again inspect the *ayah's* quarters which serve the Royal Suite.'

'Which one is that?' Adam asked, no such suite having been previously identified.

'It is the end suite at the corner of Bhavan, overlooking private gardens. I will show the sahib.'

Shastri led the way back to the second floor, along the landing and into the servants' end room, which Adam had twice inspected. He then descended the private stairs and at the bottom, walked on a few paces and opened a door.

'This is the Royal Suite, sahib,' he announced.

Adam was curious as he was sure that he had already seen this room but before he could say anything Shastri looked back along the passage to see if anyone was following them.

'Sahib will come with me.'

He walked back along the passage, past the foot of the stairs towards what looked like a stair cupboard. 'This might be what the sahib is looking for,' he said, opening the tall angle-topped door to reveal a wide stone staircase.

At first glance, Adam could not understand why there was sunlight falling on the staircase. Then passing through the doorway, he looked up and saw a wide window on the exterior wall, high enough on the outside to afford just an innocent view of the stone ceiling.

As he went down the steps followed by Shastri, he noted that the masonry soffit was set at an angle to deflect the daylight down the steps and into a long wide passage. This was about seven feet wide, skilfully constructed, with a vaulted stone ceiling, and, judging by the absence of dampness, must have been well ventilated.

'Where does this tunnel lead to?' he asked

'One is travelling more than half a mile to reach the Old Walled City, sahib.'

'Is there an exit to the Walled City?'

Shastri shook his head.

Adam followed him along the passage until they reached an archway cut into the side of the tunnel. Peering into the gloom, Adam was able to make out some sort of room. 'What is this place?' he asked.

'I am not sure, sahib. Some say that it is where the eunuchs waited to accompany the concubines returning to the other *zenana.*'

'There is another *zenana?*'

'*Han, sahib,* there is another tunnel which joins this. It is said, that hundreds of years ago, before the Maharajahs of Kashmir bought the Bhavan, there was a *seraglio,* a harem, in a secret apartment in the *makan,* at the end of the second tunnel.'

'Why would that be necessary?'

'Perhaps to avoid the women fighting and quarrelling.'

'Fighting?'

'*Han, sahib.* A Muslim *Nawab,* was allowed to have four wives, but he would be wise to keep them apart from his concubines.'

'I can understand his reasoning. Is this *makan* still there?'

'Oh no, sahib. That exit was closed and hidden before the house in the Walled City was pulled down. A cinema was built on that site.'

'How do you know this?'

'There are pictures and writing on the wall.' He gestured through the archway to the room, but it was too dark to see any detail. 'The old *chokidar* who spent most of his life here at the Bhavan has told me many things. His wife was an *ayah* in the *zenana,* and she also is telling him very much.'

'Would it be possible to see her?'

Shastri looked surprised. '*Nahin,* sahib, she was killed by a mob seeking vengeance in the September of 1947.'

'And what about the old *chokidar?*'

Shastri shook his head, and with sadness in his voice said, 'The old man is dying five years past.'

Adam felt a surge of frustration. He was now convinced that Kafni and her *ayah* had left the *zenana* by one of these tunnels, but it seemed that the only people that knew the secrets of this place had died.

'I want to go to the Walled City at the end of the tunnel. Will you please take me there?'

'Does not the sahib think that he will be wasting his time?'

Adam felt Shastri was being obstructive. 'Is there any reason why you don't want to take me there?'

'My instructions are to show the sahib whatever he wishes to see,' Shastri responded more compliantly.

'The sahib is excusing me. If we are to go there, I must obtain a torch from the *chokidars*.'

Two minutes later, he returned with a torch and they continued along the tunnel. At first it became darker, then after a while daylight became visible. Reaching the source of the light, Adam saw that the vaulted ceiling had tapered into a stone lined shaft. At the top he could see a small oblong patch of sky.

'Where are we now?'

'It's one of the shafts for air, sahib, and is coming out in the gardens of the *bhavan*. It is disguised as a shrine to Parvati, because she is benevolent no one is looking to disturb her.'

'Are there other ventilation places?'

'*Han, sahib,* there is another just before we reach the Walled City.'

They walked on in silence for some ten minutes. Adam was glad of Shastri's torch as the dank, dark, narrow passage was making him feel entombed. Gradually a blurred pool of light formed in the distance. As they approached, Adam could hear street noises. The light from above revealed a stone spiral stairway leading up out of the tunnel. Daylight flooded the centre of the stairway as it curved up and round, hugging the outer wall of the shaft. Adam mounted the bottom steps without hesitation, and as he did so, he felt the gentle movement of warm air.

'There is no way out there, sahib.' Adam heard Shastri calling, but continued up ignoring his comment. The stairs wound on and on, with only the increasing daylight and traffic noise to confirm his progress. To his disappointment, the steps ended at a stone platform, about ten feet from the top where he could see sunlight streaming in through a line of narrow stone beams. The vertical wall offered no foothold to climb higher, and he felt obliged to concede that Shastri was probably right.

'What's up at the top there? Surely it must be accessible from the outside?'

'*Nahin, sahib.* That is at the top of one of the ancient stone walls that were built round the old city by the great Emperor Akbar. It is not possible to get there.'

'Are you sure?'

'I think no one is interested to find it. It is not near the many gates and looking down those small spaces a man would only see darkness.'

'There must have been more to it than this, Shastri.'

Once more Adam felt foiled in his attempts to unravel the mystery.

'Perhaps, sahib,' he said, without conviction.

'I'm coming back down,' Adam said, and Shastri hurried ahead of him.

'Shall we go back now, sahib?' he said hopefully.

'Not yet. I would like to have another look. May I have the torch?'

'Certainly, sahib, but I do not know what you are hoping to find.'

Adam climbed back up the staircase, carefully looking at each step and stone as he passed. Nothing aroused his suspicions until he reached the last flight. Then, in shadow, just below the top stone platform, he saw it: a tall stone in the wall with a slot along its edges. At first glance it appeared that the mortar had just crumbled out due to age, but on closer examination, he found that he could insert his fingers between the joints.

He could feel air passing between the stones. He pushed hard at the stone, without effect. Then he noticed next to it a smaller stone, also without mortar in the joints. He pressed gently, and it moved inwards exposing a handle set into the side of the tall stone. Reaching forward he gripped the handle and pulled eagerly. The stone swung round so easily on its central pivot, that he had to take two quick steps backwards to avoid being knocked over. A slim entrance had opened. Before he could pass through it Shastri ran up the stairs. 'Wait, sahib! Wait! Please do not go through there.'

Adam paused.

'What's your game, Shastri? Are there more secrets you're keeping from me?'

'Please, sahib, I can explain.'

'You bloody well better, Shastri, and make it quick.'

'Sahib, there is someone to whom I have given my word that I will not expose this secret, even to a sahib. This person will be in danger if anyone finds out about this exit. If you go out that way in daylight the truth will come out.'

'What truth might that be Shastri?'

'I will explain everything to the sahib, and I am sure that I can help you to find out what you wish to know. But I am now please asking the sahib to return to the *bhavan* with me. If the sahib is not satisfied with my explanation, I promise to bring sahib back here, whenever he wishes.'

'How can I be sure that you'll keep your word?'

'The sahib can be quite sure of that. My employers do not know about this secret entrance, and trouble for me would be most serious if they are ever knowing.'

Adam could see the fear and sincerity in Shastri's eyes. He was now fairly sure how Kafni and her ayah had escaped from the *bhavan*. Perhaps it was better that he use Shastri's sense of obligation to gather more information. Who was it, for instance, that was in danger? How had Shastri become his or her confidante? It couldn't be Kafni as she would have left long before Shastri had become responsible for the *bhavan*.

'Very well, I agree to your proposal.'

Shukriya, sahib, shukriya.' He spoke with genuine gratitude and relief in his voice.

Once they were back in the *zenana* and alone Shastri told Adam that a young Indian, calling himself Jalla, had come seeking employment at the lawyers where he worked. Being well educated, he had been given employment as a junior clerk. Then some three months later, Jalla had confided in Shastri that he had come to Pakistan in search of his mother. He had taken the post only as a means of gaining access to Kashmir Bhavan. For it was there that his mother and her *ayah* had last been seen eleven years earlier. Shastri, having assured himself of the sincerity of Jalla's quest, had agreed to help him.

The disappearance of the women in Jalla's story had not surprised Shastri. He had learnt about the steps and passage from the old *chokidar,* who had shown him that the secret exit led into a room at the back of a cloth merchant's *dukan.* This shop was part of a block of old buildings in the walled city, and although this was also owned by the late Maharajah of Kashmir, just who knew about the secret entrance remained a mystery.

The cloth merchant, Vikram Das, who had a long lease on the *dukan,* certainly did know. When he was killed in August 1947, his son Samvat took over the business. However, Samvat only learnt the secret years later, when Shastri brought Jalla there to introduce him.

That evening Adam made his way once more to Zaki's place. When he arrived Archie was examining some carpets that had been laid out for his inspection. He gave Adam a knowing smile as he lifted the corner of one of the carpets and with barely disguised enthusiasm he said, 'Come into Mr. Ibrahim's office, we have business to discuss.'

Zaki welcomed them into his room and closed the door. 'Archie has some news for us I think.'

'Yes, indeed I do. Through my museum curator contact, I've been offered some unusual jewels and, what's more, I've been taken to see them. This curator took me and introduced me to a goldsmith in the Walled City.'

'Why a goldsmith?'

'Well, this fellow is an expert in designing and remounting ceremonial and state jewels. He even claims to have sent a phallic love stone to Paris for the Duke of Windsor. It had been worn on the wrist of a *nawab* who had managed to satisfy a hundred wives.'

'So who was this name-dropping goldsmith?' Adam asked impatiently.

'He was introduced to me as Jamal.'

'Ah, that will be Jamal Shah. It would have to be something very valuable for him to bother with it.'

'Well, it certainly was. I first had to give them sight of Boolajee's letter of credit guarantee. I was then shown two matched rubies the size of hens' eggs, and a pair of sapphires as large as pigeons' eggs. Jamal said that they were priceless, but he could probably arrange for me to purchase them for forty lakhs.'

'That's four million rupees,' said Zaki, 'about three hundred thousand pounds sterling. Quite a sum, but if they are faultless, they would be worth much more than that; which indicates that they have probably been stolen.'

'Very interesting,' Adam said, 'it certainly sounds like the jewels from the lingam but it worries me that they have been removed from the sculpture. We can only hope it hasn't already been broken up. So then what did you say to him?'

'I said that what I really wanted was the whole original piece intact. Initially he seemed taken aback and asked, "What makes you think that they're part of a larger piece, sahib?" To which I replied that gems like these would be unlikely to not be set in some serious work of art. He said I was very astute but that he had no knowledge of such a piece but he could arrange for them to be set in a piece of jewellery of my own design. I told him that my clients would only be interested in the stones in their original setting as that would increase their value. I suggested that maybe he would like time to think it over. Then as I made a move to leave, he held up his hand and said, "If there is such a piece, as you suggest, it would be very expensive. I would need a guarantee for a crore of rupees."'

'I wasn't quite sure how much that was at the time, but I said that I would have a letter for him within twenty-four hours. By the way, Zaki how much is that?'

'A crore is one hundred lakhs; that's ten million rupees, three-quarters of a million pounds sterling.'

Archie gave a soft whistle. 'Is Boolajee good for that sum, Adam?'

'I'm quite sure he is; his family own a shipping line. We'll see him in the morning and ask for another letter. You've done well, Archie, but I think we need to move quickly now. When do you next see Jamal?'

'He said it would take about a week. I rather think someone's having to do some re-setting. He'll telephone me at the hotel when he's ready.'

'We could have done without that delay; our time is so short. Now Zaki, would you be willing to go along as Archie's expert adviser? We cannot risk him being duped with fakes.'

'I think that Archie is wiser than you give him credit for, Adam, but I would be happy to assist. What I want to know is, if these jewels are what you are looking for, just how do you propose to pull off this purchase?'

'That, Zaki, is a subject for another time. But for now, I have something very interesting to tell you about Kashmir Bhavan.'

That night when Adam got back to Falletti's there was a message for him to ring Harish. It was almost midnight, but he put a call through and Harish was there waiting in the office. His first piece of news was very good: Mrs Manning had been located and she had remembered that the two Indian women had been taken to the town of Lala Musa, about eighty miles north of Lahore. The bad news was that Brigadier Williams had telephoned Jardeeson to say that the C.I.G.S. had not approved an extension to his leave.

Bloody Williams again! He was probably still smarting over Adam's imminent promotion and the fact that he had been passed over. Until Adam's promotion was gazetted Williams was still his senior and in a position to make things awkward for him. Adam needed to speak to the vice-C.I.G.S. himself at the first opportunity, but with the five hours time difference and a long wait for telephone calls, this would be very difficult.

Wednesday 27th May.

The following morning, Shastri collected Adam at Falletti's and drove him to the Walled City. He had thought over Shastri's story. Was it too much to hope that he had actually met Pratap? The coincidence, timing and circumstances fitted exactly. So it was with rising expectation that he entered the cloth merchant's *dukan*.

The *dukan* had a dazzling array of merchandise, with scores of bolts of cloth in dozens of colours. He passed through the entrance and was addressed by a man of about thirty.

'*Namaste*, sahib, can I show you material for dresses for memsahib?'

Adam did not answer immediately, but picked up the edge of an attractive piece of silk cloth that reminded him of a sari he had seen Kafni wearing.

'That one make very beautiful dress for missisahib.'

'Yes, your right.'

Sensing Adam was weakening he pushed for a sale.

'Last roll, very good price. I am finding excellent *derzi* who is sewing for sahib.'

'Thank you. I'd like to look round first.'

'Please see what you wish.'

Two walls were covered with shelves carrying bolts of cloth and other materials, and in front of one ran a counter with brass measures set into the edge. At the end of the counter, there was an open archway, through which he could see more bolts of cloth. 'May I see these?' he asked, indicating through the arched entrance.

'Sorry, sahib, materials in there most unsuitable.'

But before he could say anything further Adam had passed through the arch into the room. On the far side, a youth in his late teens was sitting at the top of a short flight of stone steps. Behind him hung a large, faded tapestry of the Garden of Shalimar in Kashmir. He stood up as Adam entered.

'*Namaste*, sahib.' He seemed a little uncertain about what he should do next, but in the absence of further directions from the proprietor, said, *'Ap ko kis ka intzar hai, sahib?'* Adam would like to have told him exactly what he was looking for, but decided that it would be premature to do so.

'I may find something here that I like,' and continued to look around.

With a tone of resignation and waving his hand toward the rolls of cloth, he said in English, 'Please,' and sat down again.

Adam turned and smiled at him and said, 'Thank you,' whilst carefully examining his features.

Because of his high expectations, he felt a pang of disappointment that this was not his son Pratap, although there was something familiar about him. Then, as the young man reciprocated with a smile, showing white teeth beneath his black moustache, he saw the likeness. The features were unmistakably those of Harish Chandra. This must be his son Gopal.

His first thought was to introduce himself, but he knew that this must be done with circumspection. He had not been to Kushnapur for nearly twelve years, and Gopal would be unlikely to remember him. His purpose in the store was certainly more than that of a sales assistant; and the reasons for his mission would make him wary of strangers. Shastri had already made it clear that there were others nosing around. Wantilla would have his well-paid spies, and he would know that Pratap and Gopal had left Kushnapur on a secret mission.

'You've a splendid selection of cloth here.'

Han, sahib.'

'I'm on a visit from England. I'm looking for something unusual to take back'.

'The sahib is understanding Hindi very well.'

'I served in India during the war.'

'In what regiment did you have the honour to serve, sahib?' The correct form of his question indicated a knowledge of the military.

'The Second Wessex Regiment.'

His manner now became relaxed, as he proudly said, 'My father served with the Indian Army; he held a *King's* commission; he was a major with the Fourth Punjabi Rifles.'

'An excellent regiment,' Adam said, 'I think perhaps I know him. Is his name Harish Ram Chandra?'

The look of pride on his face quickly turned to shock. He cautiously asked, 'What is your name, Sir?'

'Cullworthy.'

'Cullworthy', he repeated, almost to himself, then asked, 'Are you a colonel, Sir?'

'I was a colonel.'

'Then I have heard him speak of you, Sir. I am sure that my father knows you well.'

The tension had now gone and Adam felt he could get down to the true purpose of his visit. He looked over his shoulder to make sure the proprietor was not listening.

'Indeed he does and he will be pleased to hear I have found you.'

'But how did the sahib find me?'

Adam looked back through the arch, into the *dukan,* and saw that the cloth merchant was dealing with another customer. 'Is it safe to talk?'

'Oh yes, sahib, the *saudagar,* Samvat Das, is now our friend.'

'If I tell you that I know about the Kashmir Bhavan, and its connection with this cloth merchant's premises and that I also know that behind that Kashmir tapestry is a door, which leads into a tunnel to Kashmir Bhavan.'

'Then the sahib knows well indeed. How can I be of assistance?'

'I have been sent by the Maharajah to try and help find the lingam and also to find Princess Kafni. I know that you and her son are on a mission to find them so it would be useful to know what progress you have made.'

'I can tell you that the Rajkumari Kafni is at Lala Musa, but she calls herself *Shrimati* Ranjhalla. She is English teacher there.'

Adam's heart leapt with this news. Kafni was alive and, as he had hoped, <u>was</u> the girl Mrs Gascoyne had told him about.

'Why did the *rajkumari* go to Lala Musa?'

'Samvat's grandmother lives there. Her son, Vikram Das, was the cloth merchant at the time the *rajkumari* went there in 1947. I believe that he took her to Lala Musa, but was sadly killed in a motor accident on his way back to Lahore.'

'That is sad.' Adam said distractedly, his thoughts still on Kafni, 'And where is Pratap?'

'Pratap is working for a very rich *bania,* a businessman, writing letters and translating documents. This *bania* is buying and selling precious stones, and lending money. He is not paid well, but he is finding out many interesting things.'

'Anything that might lead us to the lingam?'

'Pratap himself must tell you that colonel-sahib, he is responsible.'

'Of course, I understand. When can I see him?'

'Tomorrow afternoon he will come here. Today he is travelling with the *bania* to collect diamonds and sapphires in Multan in the North-West Frontier Province.'

'All right I'll come back tomorrow, but now I must go urgently to Lala Musa. Do you know where the *rajkumari* is living?'

'I do not know, sahib. They say it is safer that I do not have that information. Samvat will give you the address of his grandmother in Lala Musa. She will know where to find the Rajkumari Kafni. I'll ask Samvat to give you a letter.'

CHAPTER THIRTY TWO

Lala Musa, 29th May 1959.

With Samvat's grandmother's address now in his wallet, Adam hurried out of the *dukan* into the narrow street to look for a taxi. The first one he found was rather ramshackle, but it got him back to Falletti's Hotel, where he asked for a reliable long distance taxi with a good driver. Twenty minutes later he was crossing the Ravi Road Bridge on the outskirts of Lahore city heading north towards the Grand Trunk Road on his eighty-mile journey.

A generous incentive to the driver to reach their destination as fast as possible, invited perils. The cluttered highway was not conducive to speed with any degree of safety. However, it was with a self-satisfied smile that three hours later the driver drew to a halt outside Grandmother Das's house in Lala Musa.

Shrimati Das appeared at her door even before he had reached it. Adam introduced himself then handed her Samvat's note and waited for her to read its contents. 'What do you wish me to do, sahib?'

'I shall be most grateful for your help, Shrimati Das. Please could you tell me where I can find Shrimati Ranjhalla? I have an important message for her.'

She looked at him and then at the driver standing by her gate. His polite smile, and respectful *"namaste"* greeting with a tilt of his head, must have overcome her hesitation. She beckoned the driver towards her and gave him detailed directions in Punjabi.

Adam did not fully understand, but the driver told him that he knew where to go. It was quite near. Adam could hardly contain his excitement at the thought that he would soon be seeing Kafni.

'Drive into town,' Adam told the astonished driver, 'and find the nearest flower market.'

Fifteen minutes later, laden with flowers, they pulled up at a low neat bungalow with a short colonnaded verandah. Three stone steps led down to a path, arched over with purple bougainvillaea. The property with its small garden, obviously well tended, may have been a legacy of the Raj and was now a perquisite for a schoolteacher.

He could feel his heart beating as he waited at the door, clutching the flowers and thinking of that lovely face. He wondered how she might have changed. It was nearly fifteen years since he had last seen her that blissful September in 1944.

There was no immediate response to his knock. Then the door slowly opened, and she stood there facing him; an attractive woman with dignity and a gentle manner, as she responded to his *namaste*.'

How incredibly she had altered, he thought. Then he realised that this was not Kafni. It was Mandira, Kafni's devoted ayah, someone who knew so many of his most personal and intimate secrets.

She stared at him in disbelief and tears came to her eyes as she quickly bowed her head to hide her emotion.

'Ram ram, Namaste, Adam-sahib, *ana men,*' she said with respect and warmth, then led the way through into a sitting room where she took the flowers from him. She indicated to one of the large cushions and then offered him tea. Adam sat down and readily accepted, hoping that this would give her time to compose herself.

A few minutes later, she brought in a tray with the tea and a plate of small cakes. She filled one of the cups and handed it to him, then said in her clear English, 'The Rajkumari Kafni is teaching at the school, she will come home at five o'clock.'

Adam looked at his watch. A quarter to three. After fifteen years he could wait another two hours. There were so many things he had to ask Mandira before then. He excused himself for a minute and went outside to give the driver money for tiffin, and asked him to return at six o'clock. He needed to be back in Lahore that night as there was still so much to do.

'There is very much to tell you, Adam-sahib. I am sure you know that the Maharajah Rindi, when he was still the Rajkumar, took Kafni and me to Rawalpindi.'

'You met with Wantilla?'

'Yes, we met with him and some of his men outside the city. The lingam was handed over to the Rajkumar and his escort and in exchange Wantilla then took the Rajkumari.'

Adam had a burning question that had troubled him all these years. 'I still don't understand how she could bear to have gone with Wantilla.'

'This was a most difficult time for the *rajkumari* because as you know she detests this man. She was prepared to make a sacrifice for the sake of restoring the lingam to Kushnapur.'

'But how could she leave her son and everything else she loved?'

'Leaving Pratap was the hardest thing for her. We both hoped that somehow, in time, we would return to Kushnapur. Every day she talked to me about how we might escape from Wantilla.'

'Where did he take you?

'He took us to his suite in the Rawalpindi Hotel. He tried to discharge me, but my mistress strongly objected. She insisted that her personal servant must always be with her or in a communicating room to hers when she was sleeping and he reluctantly agreed.'

'That night I heard Wantilla enter my mistress's room and heard her protesting. A few minutes later, I heard the door slam. Next morning she told me she had rejected Wantilla's advances, saying that she must first exercise her right as a Hindu noblewoman to make her once in a lifetime pilgrimage to the Debrahm ancestral home in the Hindu Kush. He was very angry but eventually agreed, knowing that he could not deny her this.'

'Was that really her reason? Or was it just a delaying tactic?

'No, the pilgrimage was of great importance to the *rajkumari*. She had wanted to undertake this spiritual journey and invoke her own special god ever since her son...' She hesitated and looked at Adam, 'and *your* son, was born.'

The poignancy of her words gave him a strange feeling of melancholy. Noone else among those that knew the secret had ever referred to the truth. He was not even a surrogate father. It was as if, by omission, his part in the arrangement would quietly disappear, and the late Prince Ranjhalla Singh would become the acknowledged father of Kafni's son.

His thoughts flashed back to their intimate relationship. How magical had been their union and how he had hoped there was someway they could be together. But it was not to be. "It must be a closed chapter," Rindi had said firmly at the time; and for the past few years, it had been just that. Now, circumstances had lifted the lid on these memories.

Mandira's voice brought him back to the present.

'Perhaps the sahib would like to know what happened to us.'

'Yes, very much.'

Rawalpindi- N.W. Frontier. August 1947

It was a sullen Wantilla who sat next to the driver as his Rolls Royce drove out of Rawalpindi City, having grudgingly conceded to Kafni's wish to make her expedition. In the rear seats were Kafni and her *ayah*, with their tiffin boxes, flasks of cordial and a change of clothing. It was going to be a long and tedious journey of 250 miles. They would spend the night at the village of Drosh in a superior dak bungalow. Wantilla would remain there whilst at dawn the next day the driver and a sentry would take Kafni and Mandira to her revered destination. Wantilla saw no reason for him to endure those last fifty tortuous miles of the journey along the Chitral river valley.

The ancestral castle of the Debrahms' had been built in the Hindu Kush, beyond Chitral, where a tributary of the great Indus River rose. It was also his ancestral home, but some years before, he had chosen to make a quite different, pilgrimage. His journey had been to the seat of the Mahavirs, who had married into his branch of the family. The Mahavir dynasty was even reputed to have descended from the Sun God, whose maharajahs had ruled their state in Rajasthan long before the first Moghul set foot in India.

His grandfather, Debrahm Singh, had married a favourite Mahavir princess, and she had brought with her a dowry of incredible riches. Thereafter his grandfather's descendants had all added "Mahavir" to their names. In the absence of a direct male descendant, who better than he, whose great-grandfathers on both sides had been maharajahs, to claim the Mahavir *gaddi*.

As a result of his impressive and opulent arrival at the Mahavir palace, with a uniformed escort, riding in his father's ivory and gold *howdah*, on the first of six richly caparisoned elephants, the Maharajah of Mahavir had sent a dispatch to Wantilla's father proposing a marriage between Wantilla and his eldest daughter. Although no great beauty, this Rajasthani bride had proved a compliant and faithful wife to him. Apart from her considerable dowry, her best asset was her good humour and tolerance of Wantilla's philandering. Her one shortcoming was that she had not borne him a son.

This journey to Chitral, although tiresome, was something that he had to tolerate. Kafni, his prize, would get this pilgrimage over with and out of her system. Whilst he had originally suggested, mainly to insult his cousin, that Kafni as a widow would only be worthy of being his concubine he had now come round to the idea of having her as his second wife. Which would mean that if she gave him a son he would become his legitimate heir.She had after all already produced a son. But for the moment he only had lustful thoughts and couldn't wait to indulge them.

Chitral, The Hindu Kush, August 1947.

Next morning, relieved to have left Wantilla behind, Kafni was deep in thought as the Rolls Royce lurched round each bend along the Chitral Valley. Even the suspension of that beautifully crafted limousine could not completely compensate for the potholes and loose stones that plagued the route. Not that Kafni was aware of any discomfort; her mind was too pre-occupied with her long-awaited visit to Paropamisus Castle. Three hours after leaving the village of Drosh she at last caught her first glimpse of the castle. 'There! Look up there!' she said breathlessly.

One hour later Kafni and Mandira were climbing the granite steps of the castle in search of the secret part, known only to the Debrahm family. There on the vaulted rock ceiling of the lower ground floor, inscribed in Sanskrit was the history of her ancestors. A feeling of pride ran through Kafni as she thought of the part she had played in perpetuating a virile and dynamic dynasty. If she must now subject herself to a course in life that she would never have chosen, that mattered little.

Fortified by her pilgrimage, Kafni travelled back, resigned to her fate to be dutifully acquiescence to demands of Wantilla. They returned to Rawalpindi and to the Palace Hotel. Wantilla was in the process of convincing the receptionist that he must have the best suite, when his driver hurried into the foyer and asked to speak to him on a matter of urgency.

'Well? What is it, man?' he demanded impatiently.

'H*azoor,* this is very, very serious. Before five minutes are passing, this Punjabi major is arriving in staff car. He is walking over and looking at the Kushnapur crest.'

'Of course, they all do. Why should that concern me?'

'He is writing down number and then speaking to his driver. Then he is coming into this hotel. I am going quickly to this Punjabi driver, giving him respectful greeting and packet of cigarettes.'

'Yes, yes, now get to the point, man.'

'He is telling me that the major sahib has been reading in the newspaper about big trouble in Kushnapur; important sahib murdered; maharajah's family must be arrested.'

'Are you completely mad? Where has this major gone?'

'Driver says he is staying in this hotel and will await orders.'

'That does not sound good,' mumbled Wantilla. 'Get the women and the bags back in the car.'

He returned to the reception desk, and gave the nonplussed clerk a smile of resignation, 'Sorry, *babu,* change of plan, one of the ladies is feeling ill.' With that he sauntered out of the hotel.

'Get back to the Grand Trunk Road as quickly as possible and head for Lahore!' he ordered the driver. He knew exactly where to go to receive a cordial welcome and be safe from intrusion. He should have thought of it before. The Debrahms had been friends of the Maharajahs of Kashmir for centuries, and Kashmir Bhavan in Lahore, although never occupied by the maharajah, was renowned for its lavish hospitality. Few in Pakistan would wish to offend the Maharajah of Kashmir. Pakistan's leaders were still hopeful that the maharajah would commit his vast mountain state to become a part of their new nation.

Unfortunately, Lahore was 175 miles away so after two hours Wantilla agreed to stop at a hotel in Jhelum. Tiffin boxes were ordered from the restaurant and Wantilla bought a copy of the Times of India. He carefully scanned the newspapers and found the item he was looking for. Lord Chalvington had been murdered in Kushnapur; the prime suspect was a member of the Maharajah's family.

He was baffled by the story. Why was Virginia's husband in Kushnapur in the first place? and why on earth would his cousin want to murder him? It all sounded very improbable. He was not in the least bit sad to hear of Chalvington's demise and although he relished the thought of Rindi being arrested, he was furious at the inconvenience it was causing him.

Firozpur, Pakistan-India Border, August 1947.

Wantilla was not the only one reading the papers. His nephew Narajan, with even more reason to keep a close eye on events, was now looking through the morning editions as he ate his *jalpan*. He had spent the night at Firozpur, a few miles from the soon to be created state of West Pakistan. The van he had hired in Ambala was safely locked in a private garage at the back of his hotel. A pity, he thought, that he had been obliged to kill that idiot driver of the Bentley. The bloody fool should have accepted his bribe and driven him to Rawalpindi where he hoped to catch up with his uncle Wantilla.

With the lingam safely crated in the back of the van, he had an unexpected feeling of power and he meant to use it. An opportunity like this would never come again. He might even be able to outwit his uncle who had dominated his life for as long as he could remember, and who had abused him whenever it was convenient. What had he got out of it? A few trifling favours. Well, this time it would be very different.

Things were going his way; even the daily massacres were a convenient diversion. The travelling money he had lifted from the driver's wallet was very useful, and that note he had left in the Bentley was an inspiration. If things did not work out with Wantilla, he could return with the lingam to Kushnapur as a hero. He would then claim Puhella as his bride. As for the police, they would be much too busy dealing with mass slaughter to bother about the murder of one Hindu driver.

In this assumption, Narajan might well have been correct, had there not been a connection with the death of Lord Chalvington and he read with some concern that the police at Saharanpur were looking for witnesses to the shooting.

He had not in fact witnessed the incident, but the police would certainly know that he had been there at that time. Perhaps the note had not been such a good idea. He must now lie low until the Chalvington affair had dropped out of the news.

Where best to go? Narajan was twenty-five miles from Lahore. He racked his brain for a possible safe haven and came to the same conclusion as his uncle; Kashmir Bhavan. His grandfather had once taken him there and they had been treated like Royalty.

Narajan had signed into his hotel under a false name and hoped that this would buy him some time. The following morning he headed north, facing two hours of hazardous driving conditions on crowded roads. When he reached the Sutlej River Bridge, he encountered heavy congestion of vehicles, animals and a mass of Muslim refugees desperate to reach safety in West Pakistan. This reduced his progress to walking pace and before he knew it the rear doors of his vehicle were wrenched open and about ten refugees clambered in with their meagre bundles of possessions. A further three migrants forced themselves into the cab beside him. As a Hindu travelling on his own he thought it better not to object and in any event his load of Muslims would ensure safe passge into Lahore City.

He drove to Stadium Road, where he managed to persuade them that food and temporary accommodation awaited them. Unburdened of his uninvited passengers he was relieved to see the crates containing the three parts of the lingam still in the back. He now headed for Kashmir Bhavan.

As he drove up to the gates of Kashmir Bhavan his reception was not as warm as he had expected and he found his way barred by a uniformed *durwan* guarding the entrance. A single travel-weary driver in a hired van was not like the normal distinguished guests they were accustomed to receiving and the sentry needed a great deal of persuasion by Narajan to convince him that he really was a Debrahm. When he finally threatened to report the man to his uncle he was taken aback to be told that Wantilla and his party had arrived there the night before and were now guests at the *bhavan*. Whilst this ensured entry and a renewed level of respect from the sentry it was contrary to his carefully thought out plan.

He knew that Wantilla would soon realise that he had the lingam and take it back off him. He announced to the surprised sentry that he needed to go back into the city to buy gifts for his uncle. He then drove to a hotel, booked-in, berthed his van safely in a lock-up garage, changed his clothes and ordered a taxi to take him to Kashmir Bhavan. This time, he was given immediate entry and then asked by the resident *khitmagar* to report to his uncle's quarters.

Narajan found Wantilla relaxing in his suite, smoking a hookah. As usual he treated him with contempt. 'Bastard! What the hell are you doing here?' he said puffing out a cloud of smoke.

'I could ask you the same question, uncle.' Narajan decided it was now time to start asserting himself.

'Mind your manners, you insolent bugger.'

'Wouldn't that be a more appropriate description of yourself, uncle?'

Wantilla flung down the mouthpiece of the hookah and stood up. 'One more remark like that and you'll wish you'd never been born. Have you completely lost your mind?'

'Quite the contrary, uncle. I have an interesting proposition, but first tell me, have you slept with your little prize yet?'

Wantilla's mouth twisted and his eyes narrowed as his handsome face took on an aspect that, in times past, would have frightened Narajan into compliance with any demand. Narajan now stood defiantly as Wantilla moved towards him and grabbed the collar of his *achkan*.

Narajan quickly parried, as he raised his arm and stepped aside, breaking Wantilla's grip, then snapped out, 'Let go of me, you bully. I think you'll listen to me this time. I have the Kushnapur Lingam!'

'I suspected as much. Where the hell is it?

A triumphant smile came over Narajan's face. 'That's my secret.'

'I demand that you hand it over to me. Immediately!'

'Not so fast, uncle. You can have it for the same reward that you yourself demanded. I want Kafni. She must be unconditionally consigned to me as my property and concubine. I don't care whether you've bedded her already.'

Wantilla took in a deep breath and his face again contorted with anger. 'You filthy little upstart, what makes you think I'd ever agree to such a thing?'

'Because if you don't, I'll return the lingam to the maharajah, and claim Princess Puhella as my bride; at least she's still a virgin.'

'You slippery bloody toad, you'd never get away with that. They'd have you executed as soon as you set foot in the palace. Haven't I taught you more sense than that?' Wantilla paused to change tack. 'Now don't be a foolish fellow, I'm sure we can find a tempting alternative. If it's a nubile virgin you want, my friend Isher has a beautiful young sister. Be a sensible chap and bring that lingam to me and I'll see what privileges I can negotiate for you.'

'Privileges?' Narajan spat out, 'what are they this time? More buggery, a few trinkets and a bazaar watch, or if I'm lucky a second-hand Ford?'

'You ungrateful little bastard. I don't know how you got hold of the lingam, but it's obviously gone to your head. Without my help you'll never be able to negotiate it. I'll give you just twenty-four hours to make your mind up. After that I'll see to it that you're thrown out of Kashmir Bhavan. And if I'm not mistaken, the police are very interested in your whereabouts.'

'Careful, uncle. You'd better make sure that nothing happens to me; I know far too much. Don't forget I know exactly how and when the lingam was stolen. How long would you keep your seat in the legislature if that came out and there would be no chance of ruling Kushnapur, however rich you become.'

'Get out, you insolent sod! Now! Before I change my mind and have you forcibly ejected.'

Narajan left the room, muttering, 'we'll bloody well see about that.'

CHAPTER THIRTY THREE

Kashmir Bhavan, Lahore, August 1947.

Narajan was not unduly disturbed at the thought of having to leave Kashmir Bhavan now that Wantilla was there. He had already planned to quit the place as soon as it was convenient. His only reason to remain was the prospect of claiming Kafni for himself.

Along the corridor, his altercation had been heard by the dignified *khitmagar*. As resident butler, he was anxious to distance himself from any such dissension between guests. It was his duty as head of staff to ensure that this household was run in a harmonious and orderly manner. He now addressed Narajan, politely, but with an air of authority. 'May I show you to your room, sahib?'

Narajan gave a nod of assent, and a curt '*shukrya*', then followed the *khitmagar* to another part of the house.

In his room, Narajan sat down to consider his options. Although stung by the cavalier treatment he had received from Wantilla, it was not unexpected. However, there was more than one way of skinning a tiger. He would lure Wantilla's prize from under his very nose; and as far as Kafni was concerned, he had the irresistible bait of the lingam.

Narajan would like to have seen Kafni personally, but this was not feasible for two reasons. Firstly, she would certainly be in the *zenana* and would only leave there at the behest of Wantilla; secondly, even if he could meet her, she would require proof, not just his word, that he had the lingam. The solution was to use her *ayah* Mandira as the go between. There was no time to waste; Wantilla might be getting ideas of his own. Narajan went downstairs to the drawing room and ordered one of the servants to find Mandira and bring her to him immediately.

Mandira did not appear to be in any hurry to respond to his demand. Narajan paced back and forth whilst the servant handed him a succession of cups of tea, frequently consoling him with, 'she is coming, sahib.' When, after half an hour, Mandira finally appeared, she treated his complaint with disdain. 'I was attending my mistress, Her Highness, the Princess Kafni. I trust that this is a matter of importance.'

Narajan wished to speak in private and waved his hand to dismiss the servant in the manner he thought Wantilla would have done. He then jerked his hand towards some cushions in a corner of the room, and said to Mandira, 'over there, ayah'.

Selecting the largest of the cushions he sat down and then tossed the smallest cushion available in front of Mandira. His intention to make her feel subservient was unsuccessful as she deliberately chose another larger cushion and gracefully seated herself on it.

Narajan couldn't help admiring Mandira both for her beauty and her sense of pride. It was a pity she was a 'Vaishya'. His brief preoccupation with her good looks almost subverted his intention to be curt. If his plans reached fruition, this woman could be useful, but it was best to let her know where she stood from the start.

'I shall be brief. I do not know whether your mistress is aware that there has been a disaster at Kushnapur. An evil English lord had the banks of Lake Kushnapur dynamited resulting in a great flood in which the precious lingam was almost lost.'

'The Rajkumar Rindi? Is he safe?' She almost choked on the anxiety of her words.

Narajan raised his hand, as if to dismiss the subject, then said, 'Undoubtedly, he will be, but we'll deal with that later. Now to continue. Due to my skilful driving and my complete disregard for the danger of that towering wall of water racing through the gorge behind me, I was able to save the lingam. My thoughts were then totally for its safety. I knew that its whereabouts must be kept secret from the Indian Government and unscrupulous dealers who would willingly commit murder to possess it. You will understand that it was at great personal risk to my life that I brought it to Lahore.'

Mandira gave him a look of disdain. 'It would seem that the Debrahm family owe you a debt of gratitude, Shri Narajan.'

'Indeed they do,' he said imperiously. This servant, he thought, must learn to address him as 'sahib'. Plain 'mister' was not sufficient for a great grandson of two maharajahs.

'And where is the lingam now?'

'I had hoped to store it here at Kashmir Bhavan but then I discover my Uncle Wantilla is already in residence and up to his old tricks.'

'But, Shri Narajan Ram, I thought you were a faithful kinsman of Wantilla?'

'It only appears that way. I have to protect my mother from his treachery. She is a widow and relies upon his beneficence,' he lied. 'As soon as I learnt from the sentry that he was here, I took the lingam to a place of temporary safety. We must now make urgent arrangements so that the Princess Kafni can be released from her bondage and returned to Kushnapur with the lingam. Secrecy is vital. If Wantilla gets even a hint of our plans he will try to stop us. I'm sure he has already bribed some of the staff to spy for him.'

Mandira was tempted to ask why he had not taken the lingam back to the palace but she could guess the answer and did not want to antagonise him further especially if there was now a chance that he might help them escape from Wantilla.

'Perhaps, although I think that the servants in the *zenana* favour Princess Kafni. They would not spy on her or act against her interests.'

'That's good, you may need their help.' Narajan paused, and softened his voice in an attempt to ingratiate himself with her. 'I do hope you have been well looked after on your travels.'

'I cannot say that we have enjoyed the experience.'

'Now tell me, Mandira,' his voice took on a solicitous and confidential tone. 'Have they..? Has he? You know?' He spread out his fingers and twisted his wrist from side to side.'

'I'm not sure what you mean, Shri Narajan. You would have to ask Princess Kafni herself, though if it is of a personal nature, I doubt that you would receive an answer.'

This woman could become tedious, he thought. 'Tell your mistress that she must make a plan for you both to escape from this place. We can then go into hiding until the maharajah sends an escort to take us back to Kushnapur. She no longer has any obligation to Wantilla. I now have the lingam, so she must listen to <u>my</u> proposals.'

He looked at his watch. 'It's just after four. Come back here at six o'clock and tell me her plans. Invent something, or say she is ill and must be taken to hospital.'

'Wantilla would not be fooled by that, he'd first send for a *hakim* to medically examine my mistress.'

'Yes, probably. Well you think of something, but make it quick.'

A smirk of satisfaction passed over Narajan's face when he found Mandira already waiting for him ahead of the appointed time. They were learning who was calling the tune. Had it not been for the danger of alerting Wantilla, he would have insisted that Kafni herself came.

'Princess Kafni is shocked by your news. Wantilla must have known what happened in Kushnapur but kept it from her. She is prepared to consider your plans but only once she has seen the lingam.'

'Have you worked out a way of getting out of here?'

'No, not exactly, but the head *chokidar's* wife Rashmi, who is in charge of the *zenana,* says she knows a way to get us out.'

'Oh? And just how will she do that?'

'She did not say exactly, but we trust her. I believe she has a great regard for Her Highness.'

'So when will this happen, and where will you go?'

'Rashmi says that she can get us to the city without anyone knowing that we have left the *bhavan.* She suggested that you meet her husband with your vehicle and the lingam at a rendezvous chosen by you in the city. It must be at exactly five o'clock, just before dawn. He will then take you to meet with us.'

'Can I trust him? And how shall I know he is the right man? I don't want any bloody tricks.'

He will come to your room early this evening with a *chitthi* written personally by Princess Kafni. You may be quite sure that if you have the lingam, she will do nothing that might endanger it.'

Narajan waggled his head in confirmation.

'Tell the *chokidar* to come to. ..' He stopped. Even now he was suspicious that something might go wrong; better that no one knew where he had left the van.

'Tell the *chokidar* that I will meet him outside the west entrance to Lahore Junction Railway Station. I happen to know that the Awam Express from Karachi gets in at twenty minutes past five every morning. There will be many people meeting that train so we shall not arouse any interest. I will be driving a pale blue Chevrolet van with "Vanhire" painted on the side.'

'I shall pass on that information,' said Mandira, and then left, her heart beating fast with anxiety for what lay ahead.

The *chokidar* duely came to Narajan's room with the note from Kafni. He knew her hand well because she always personally wrote her greetings to family and friends at *Diwali.* Out of habit he tipped the man, looked furtively either way down the corridor and then said. 'I will see you tomorrow.' The *chokidar* nodded and slipped discreetly away.

Narajan took his meal in the dining room that evening. He wanted to be seen around the house until as late as possible, knowing that Wantilla was probably having him watched. Making a display of tiredness, he ordered *chota hazri* for eight o'clock the next morning, and then retired to his room. Half an hour later, he slipped over the balcony of his room, into the garden and across the lawns. He crossed onto the drive at the last bend and walked up to the sentry.

'I have to go back to my hotel to collect something important for my uncle Wantilla,' he said, in the manner of giving an order.

'Han sahib,' acknowledged the sentry, as he stood up and moved to open one of the gates.

'I shall be returning tomorrow morning, will you be on duty?'

'Han, sahib. The gates are locked at midnight and opened again at six in the morning. If the sahib arrives before that time, the driver can sound his horn and I will come from the guard room and open the gates.'

'Shukriya,' said Narajan, as he handed the sentry a ten-rupee note, and walked through the gates. Once he was confident that he was not being followed he hailed a taxi.

Wantilla had called the *khitmagar* to his suite to discuss the menu for dinner that was to be served in his room. He had no wish to encounter that callow nephew of his until he had been brought to heel. He could not be sure that Narajan did have the lingam; though his truculent manner certainly indicated that he did. That was something which would be thoroughly investigated in the morning. Contrary to his threat to have Narajan ejected, he would have him detained in Kashmir Bhavan. Narajan would soon disclose the lingam's whereabouts, knowing that if it fell into the wrong hands all his advantage would be lost.

The irritating thing about this unfortunate development, was that it necessitated altering his immediate plans for Kafni. If she got wind of the fact that the lingam was not safely back in Kushnapur, she was unlikely to honour her side of the bargain.

Wantilla had taken the precaution of instructing that no newspapers were to reach the *zenana*. He had also given orders that under no circumstances was the Princess or her *ayah* to leave the *Bhavan*. But he had underestimated both the guile of his nephew and the loyalty of the staff in the *zenana*.

Once Narajan had been effectively dealt with, and the lingam was in his possession again, Wantilla could revert to his plan for a leisurely consummation. He had intended to have the staff prepare the Royal Suite, and then request that Kafni be brought to him. Thereafter, he would instruct the *khitmagar* that they were not to be disturbed. This time there would be no meddling *ayah* to call upon in the next room. Kafni would be totally his, for as many days as it would take to indulge himself through the whole amorous gamut of the *Kama Sutra*. No position of sexual union or gratification would be neglected.

Wantilla lay back on the silk cushions, reflecting upon the pleasures that he must now postpone and flicked open the flies of his cream twill jodhpurs to relieve the tension. He moved his hand down under his scrotum, approving its weight. No wise Hindu ever wasted his semen. This delayed encounter was going to be even sweeter.

Kafni and Mandira, with the help of Rashmi the head *chokidar's* wife, had made their own meticulous plans. They had taken supper early and then waited anxiously all evening, expecting a call from Wantilla. Had it come, Mandira was ready to explain that her mistress was experiencing her moonphase, and it would not be seemly for her to come into the presence of her new conjugal master. The resident *dai*, as a trained nurse, had willingly conceded to confirm Kafni's condition. Thankfully, this had not been necessary, and as there had been no word from Wantilla by ten o'clock, Kafni and Mandira decided to get some sleep.

At four in the morning when all was silent and the house still in darkness, Mandira was awoken by Rashmi. 'It's nearly time to go,' she whispered. 'Please wake your mistress and wait for me in the Royal suite. My husband has already left to go and meet Narajan-sahib, so we must leave soon.'

Shukriya. Rashmi. We appreciate the risks you are taking for us.'

A few minutes before five, as the first rays of the early morning sun crept up over Lahore, still sultry from the August heat and dust storms of the previous day, an agitated Narajan drove up to the west entrance of Lahore Junction Railway Station. Although satisfied at the way things had gone so far, he was ill at ease. He would be a lot happier when the next few hours were over. He trusted no one. There was precious little loyalty in life that money could not buy, and he was quite prepared to see Wantilla or one of his agents lurking in the shadows. This old *chokidar* would be able to live in luxury with his family for the rest of his life on the money that Wantilla would be prepared to pay for information.

There were always precautions that could be taken against

treachery, and Narajan had learnt most of them. Tucked into the seat and half-hidden, was a razor sharp dagger, long enough to be thrust under the ribs and pierce the heart. He had been obliged to murder one foolish bastard, so if this *chokidar* looked like trying any tricks, he would have to go the same way. After a couple of circuits round the station he was satisfied that the *chokidar* was on his own and there were no obvious characters lurking in the shadows. Keeping the engine running he drew alongside the man who quickly hopped into the van.

'Han, sahib, I'll direct you.' The *chokidar,* addressed Narajan as "sahib" to keep him in good humour, not out of respect. 'Take the next turn right at Shara Habibullah, and head back to the city,' instructed the *chokidar.* They drove a short distance along Mayo Road, passed the deserted Rex Cinema. 'Straight on now, sahib, across Nicholson Road and into Fleming, that will take us to Circular Road.'

They drove on in silence until reaching Circular Road, where the *chokidar* had indicated a left turn, and now they were running along in line with the old city wall.

'Which gate?' snapped Narajan.

'The Bhati Gate, sahib. I will tell the sahib when we get there.'

A few minutes later they were driving through the narrow streets of the old city, now slowly coming to life. Their progress reduced to a walking pace as they entered alleys barely wide enough to permit passage of the van. Some early risers emerged from the *souks* and *dukans* and squatted in the time honoured Muslim manner to relieve themselves in the open drains, before removing the shutters and opening their shops.

'Are we nearly there?'

'Not too far now, sahib,' said the *chokidar,* aware that Narajan was becoming suspicious and impatient, as they negotiated the early morning merchants rolling carts loaded with great bunches of bananas, sacks of oranges, and fresh vegetables. Sugar cane was piled high ready for the syrup presses.

Narajan drove on, passing the workshops of silversmiths, leather workers, shoemakers, tailors, woodworkers, ivory carvers and heavily barred *dukans* selling arms and swords. None was yet open, only the garish illustrations and descriptions above the shops revealed their wares.

'We are here now, sahib, this is the *gali.*' The *chokidar* indicated that Narajan should turn into a cul-de-sac with just three shops on one side. On the other side, a blank wall ran down to the end to join a very high, ancient stone wall. On the corner was a bakery already preparing loaves and *chupattis* for the oven, then a shop whose closed shutters advertised lacquered trays and plates decorated with brightly coloured enamels. Next came a stone archway closed off by tall wooden doors, adjoining which was the last shop in the lane.

As the van drew level with these doors, the *chokidar* raised his hand. 'Stop here, sahib.' He got out of the cab and walked towards the adjacent *dukan* where the cloth merchant, a middle-aged Indian, was sitting. Behind him, through un-shuttered windows, Narajan could see an array of bolts of vividly coloured cloths.

'*Namaste*, Vikram Das,' said the *chokidar*.' Has my wife arrived?'

'*Han, mitra purana*. Rashmi is here, more than one hour, and also your guests. That van must park in the old *gadhakhanna*, I'll go inside and open those doors.'

Narajan parked the van in the old donkey stables next to Vikram Das's own van as instructed. Ever suspicious, he insisted on reversing into the stables; he calculated that if things went wrong he could always crash his way out.

'I'll take you to meet your guests, sahib,' said Vikram Das politely.

He led the way through a low door at the side of the stables, across a well-stocked storeroom and into an office. Sitting on the far side was Kafni, partially veiled by her sari held across her face. Standing next to her were Mandira and Rashmi. Narajan felt relieved and amazed that Kafni was there in the flesh.

'*Namaste*, cousin,' he said. Then, recalling the tortuous route that he had just travelled, asked, 'How on earth did you get here? Did you come last night?'

Kafni let her sari drop from her face, and put the palms of her hands together to return his greeting. '*Namaste*, Narajan,' she said impassively, not responding to his question, leaving him to believe that perhaps she *had* arrived during the night. The *chokidar*, who had followed them in, now spoke to his wife. 'We have to go, Rashmi. You must be back before the staff come on duty, otherwise you will be missed.'

Although Narajan must have heard this, his attention was so fixed upon Kafni that he gave no thought to ask how they intended to return to Kashmir Bhavan. Even when Rashmi quietly said, 'goodbye' to Kafni and Mandira, and left the room with her husband, Narajan could not take his eyes off the beautiful face of his cousin. He stared in disbelief. He had finally outwitted his uncle. Was this lovely creature now really his?

Narajan, finding himself alone with the two women, again posed his question. This time he looked accusingly at Mandira. 'Well, how did you get here?'

Kafni made no response, and Mandira, feeling any reply might be less suspicious than silence, said, 'It would be better that you do not ask, sahib.' She moved her eyes and nodded towards the shop, to imply that Vikram Das did not share their secrets.

'Perhaps for the moment, you are right. Anyway, I shall learn soon enough.'

Narajan would have preferred to discuss his proposals alone with Kafni, but it would be difficult to get rid of Mandira, and time was pressing. He wanted to be quickly out of the Punjab and much nearer Delhi, in a place where he could safely cache the lingam, and detain Kafni at his pleasure, until she accepted his terms.

'Cousin Kafni,' he began, 'it is my dearest wish that the lingam shall be returned to its proper place in Kushnapur, and I shall need your help to achieve this. We must move fast, to prevent Wantilla getting his hands on it again. The sooner we can get out of the Punjab and into the United Provinces, the safer we shall be. From there we can send a message to His Highness, your father, to dispatch an armed party to escort the lingam and ourselves back to Kushnapur Palace.'

'That is also my wish, Cousin Narajan. You can be sure of my co-operation.'

The last word was the most encouraging he had heard.

'But,' she continued, 'I think that the first thing we should do is examine the lingam to ensure that it is intact and not damaged.'

'Of course, Hazrat,' he replied as a reflex action, then instantly regretted that he had addressed her as a superior. Wantilla would never have slipped into that error. He would need to re-assert himself.

'We shall go and examine the sculpture now. Come with me, Kafni. Mandira, you will stay here to see that this merchant fellow does not observe what we have in the van. Do whatever is necessary to keep him occupied for the next twenty minutes.'

'Why so long?' Kafni said. 'Are we not in a hurry?'

'Yes, but we must open up the packing cases and then carefully re-pack and seal them, so that they can travel securely.'

'I understand.'

Leaving the office, Narajan led Kafni across the storeroom to the stables whilst Mandira walked into the *dukan* and began talking to Vikram Das.

Narajan went to the van, unlocked the cab door and took out a pair of pliers, a strong screwdriver, and from under the seat, a blanket.

'Would you like to wait here, Kafni? I'll go and open up the cases and tell you when I'm ready.'

Kafni climbed into the cab without comment, whilst Narajan went round to the rear, unlocked the doors and walked up the low rear steps into the van. He then started carefully to lever open the first of the three wooden cases. Interesting, he thought, they are still packed exactly as they were when first stolen.

Narajan had played a small part in that removal and admired the astute way Wantilla had planned the whole operation. The cases had 'FRAGILE! CHINA & GLASS' stencilled on the outside and then inside each case, a wrapping of brown paper covered a layer of wood shavings mixed in with a few worthless china plates. Underneath these, white cotton sheeting was wrapped over several layers of black velvet, protecting parts of the lingam itself.

Narajan had never before seen the lingam let alone touched it. His fingers trembled as he drew back the folds of velvet to reveal the jewel-encrusted head of the phallus. Its glittering spectacle surpassed anything he had imagined and now the thought that he possessed it infused him with a feeling of immense power. Perhaps it was true that it possessed its own aura.

Wantilla had explained that the lingam comprised three skilfully interlocking parts: the golden base decked with alternate tiers of purest white diamonds and emeralds; the scrotum of platinum, patterned with a thousand sapphires; the phallus of pure gold, traced with rubies along its shaft and headed with a pair of enormous, faultless rubies, inter-set with diamonds to display their full brilliance. Every generation a maharajah had added his contribution to the treasure, and for this reason one component of the lingam could be dismantled and taken to the palace *kandukan* - the workshop, of the royal jeweller, Even he would not be allowed to gaze upon the complete lingam.

Narajan folded the blanket and laid it beside the crate he had opened, intending to take out the first of the three parts of the lingam for Kafni's inspection. Now, as he knelt down, he could not take his eyes from the jewels, and without moving his head, called to Kafni to come and see.

Acknowledging his call, Kafni slid across the seat to get out of the cab, and as she did so, her body brushed against a hard object. Putting her hand down to investigate, she felt the dagger in its scabbard. She pulled it out from between the seats and briefly examined it. Whilst puzzling over its purpose, Kafni heard Narajan call again. She dropped the dagger on the seat, climbed out of the cab and went round to the back of the van.

Narajan had not moved and was unable to take his eyes off the treasure. When he heard her footsteps, he glanced over his shoulder. 'Come up here, it's ready for you to see.' As he spoke, he still held the black velvet to one side. Mesmerised by the splendour of the jewels, he could not bring himself to lift out the phallus, and waited whilst Kafni came up into the van.

Looking down, she gasped, knowing that this was indeed the Kushnapur Lingam. She had seen it many times but now wanted to be sure that it was not damaged. She knelt down on the blanket to examine it more carefully. She was so close to Narajan that he could feel the warmth of her body, and see the curve of her breast beneath her sari. He felt invincible. He possessed the lingam and now he wanted to possess this beautiful woman. As the blood raced to his loins he knew he could no longer control his desire to have her. There would never be a better moment. He slipped his hand across Kafni's back, and pulled her to him. She reacted with revulsion struggling to free herself from his grasp, but he tightened his grip, and put his other arm underneath her.

'Kafni, *ladla, darling,* you see what a wonderful thing I have done for your family. You now need never go back to Wantilla; he has broken his promise to restore the lingam to Kushnapur. Now I am the only one who will do that great deed. Am I not worthy of you now?'

As he said this, he held her tightly and tried to kiss her, but she turned her head sharply away, sweeping his face with her long glossy black hair.

'No, no! Nothing! I can agree to nothing until the lingam has been restored to Kushnapur, and my father has given his consent.'

'Do you not realise, foolish woman, that unless you consent now, Kushnapur will never see its lingam again. I can bribe my way to Karachi and take a ship to Zanzibar. Possessed of such a treasure the Sultan will shower me with gifts and beautiful women.'

'Such threats are meaningless, you would never succeed.' She tried to wrestle herself free but his hold was too strong.

'You overlook man's greed, my dear Kafni. Stop playing hard

to get. You're not even a virgin, just a widow only fit for *suttee*.'

'You're mad!' Kafni was now getting angry and no longer chose her words carefully. 'Do you think that I'd be idiotic enough to get rid of a jackal, only to replace him with a snake?'

Her words stung Narajan, and abandoning all sense of reason he gripped her viciously, turning her round on to her back and pushing her down on the blanket.

'You loose-tongued bitch. I'll teach you never to speak to me like that.'

Narajan's brain was now churning with hate and anger at being spurned. Once he had raped her, shame would compel her to remain totally under his command. He gripped one of her arms and forced it under her back, then, despite her frantic punching and scratching with her one free hand, he began to tear off her sari.

Kafni screamed, realising that she could no longer reason with this beast. His response was a stinging slap across her face.

'Shut up, you silly bitch! Don't think that anyone will come to your rescue. That servant of yours will never let that merchant get a glimpse of this treasure. He would take it from you and sell it immediately.'

'They will come,' Kafni sobbed breathlessly, with tears of pain and anguish streaming down her face. 'Vikram Das is a good man.'

'If they do come, they're going to witness you being fucked. You'll never be able to face your family again. I've coveted you, Kafni, for a long time and now I'm ready for you.'

Then, fired with lust and beyond caring what risk he was taking, he snarled, 'I've fought and killed to get this lingam. Now you're going to feel my lingam thrust into you.'

He had unbuttoned his trousers as he spoke and the adrenaline of lust pumping through his body, he tore at the last of Kafni's underclothes. Her resistance was now rapidly ebbing away and kneeling between her legs, he forced them apart. He then ran his hand down between her thighs, savouring his moment of triumph.

Kafni tried to isolate her mind from the ghastly reality of what was happening. She listened to the traffic in the distance and the calls of ambulatory merchants seeking their early morning customers. Turning her eyes up to the roof of the van, she wondered what fate her gods had predestined for her. Had she offended them? Her fervent prayer begged to be answered. Should she resist until the end; was it more pleasing to her deity to die in the struggle, or should she submit to Narajan? Were his more violent gods rewarding him?

Beyond Kushnapur

A convulsive gasp from Narajan made Kafni look at him just as he fell forward on to her, grasping her throat in a final reflex action. His fingers fell slack and he suddenly weighed heavily on her. She struggled to move from under his lifeless body and then as she rolled him off her she saw Mandira standing there. 'Princess! My princess, what has he done to you?'

Kafni saw the handle of the dagger she had found in the cab was protruding from below Narajan's ribs, buried up to the hilt. A watery rattle came from his mouth and blood began to ooze out.

'My God! You've killed him.'

'Yes, Rajkumari, I had to do it. I was afraid he would strangle you.'

'Thank you' Kafni spluttered, 'but I think we may be in terrible trouble now. We desperately need help.'

CHAPTER THIRTY FOUR

Anarkali, Lahore, August 1947.

With intense revulsion, Kafni moved out from under Narajan's body. Shivering with shock, she was helped to dress by Mandira. Both of them were now in a state of distress as they climbed down from the van and returned to the *dukan.* There they found Vikram Das busy serving a customer. All were too pre-occupied to notice the unsavoury-looking character loitering in the street outside. In different circumstances, Vikram would not have missed the surreptitious way the man was examining the contents of the window, yet paying far more attention to activities within the shop. Vikram would soon have identified him as an opportunist thief and given him a warning glare that would have sent him on his way.

With her heart still racing, Mandira waited until the customer had left, then spoke breathlessly to the cloth merchant. 'Shri, Vikram Das, something terrible has happened, we need your help.'

Her eyes pleaded with him, as she said, 'Narajan-sahib tried to rape and murder my mistress and I have killed him.'

'You've killed him!

'*Han, Babu*'she said respectfully, 'he was a *bhoot,* a demon. I am not ashamed of what I have done. He was poisonous like a viper. I am sure that my God Shiva willed me to do this.'

Vikram Das nodded in agreement and contemplation. He knew that Shiva was a destroyer, as well as a creator. A Hindu whose behaviour is unworthy, and who ventures beyond the precepts of his religion, must receive his just desserts.

'Young woman, I can believe that it was Shiva's will that you saved your mistress. As soon as I saw that man, I felt sure there was something evil about him.'

'Thank you for understanding, Shri Vikram. Will you help us?' begged Kafni.

'Certainly. First you must choose a new sari and use the hand basin at the rear to wash yourselves. In the meantime I must attend to something myself.'

The man outside the window had now moved nearer to the open doorway and Vikram walked over to intercept this prospective customer. Barely glancing at the man, he said, 'I am sorry, Shri, we are closing this morning. One of my cousins is feeling unwell.' He closed and locked the door, and walked back to the women.

'We must act quickly and carefully. I will go and see what we have to deal with.'

'We will come with you, *Babu,*' said Kafni, addressing him as a Hindu gentleman, 'It is our responsibility.'

The man outside then saw them leave the *dukan* through a side door and as he walked away along the street past the stables, he glimpsed a movement of someone through a crack in the tall wooden doors. Obviously, he thought, there is something very interesting in there.

Vikram Das climbed up into the back of the van and dispassionately viewed the body of Narajan. He was quite satisfied that this man deserved to die. He must give these unfortunate women all the help he could.

'This body and the van must be removed from here as soon as possible. It is too risky to do anything in daylight; I will come back tonight and drive the van to the other side of the city where I will abandon it. With so much killing going on, the police are unlikely to pay much attention to one more murder. The dagger can be left in to show how he died; I'll wipe the handle.'

He rolled the body over, and saw that Narajan's trousers were still unbuttoned and his genitals exposed. 'We'll leave the dog like that,' he said to Mandira, 'It will explain why he died.'

He pulled the blanket over the body, and as he did so, looked at the open crate beside it. The black velvet had fallen back over the lingam and only shavings and two or three plates were exposed. 'Is this of any value?' he asked.'

'Yes, *Babu* Vikram, it is of great Hindu value and of tremendous importance to my family. We will forever be in your debt if you help us to return it to my home.' She stopped, and then said quietly, 'My father is the Maharajah of Kushnapur; I know he will reward you richly for your kindness and great help.'

Vikram Das raised an eyebrow in disbelief and turned to Mandira. 'Is she really a princess?'

'She is indeed, but in these turbulent times it must be kept a secret. She has only told you, *Babu* because she trusts you completely.'

He looked at Kafni in wonderment. 'You may be sure that I shall honour that trust, and help you all I can; but there will be great difficulties and risks. The city is a dangerous place these days; many thieves and cutthroats are lurking around to take advantage of the situation for their own ends.' Glancing round the interior of the van, he spotted two more crates, both still sealed. Are these also valuable?'

'Yes, they are all part of the same treasure,' Kafni responded , 'Perhaps you would be kind enough to open them both for me so that I can check that nothing is damaged or missing.'

Kafni and Mandira watched anxiously whilst Vikram Das carefully released and lifted the lid of each case. He then moved aside to enable them to examine the contents. Uncertain how much should be revealed, Mandira looked at her mistress to know what she should do next.

'Please take out all the covering shavings and plates, Mandira so that I can examine all parts of the lingam. And I want Shri Vikram Das to see everything.'

Mandira nodded silently, took out the superficial packing and lifted off the white cotton sheeting. She then carefully folded back the layers of black velvet and as each piece of the sculpture was uncovered Kafni made her inspection in silence. Still shaking from her recent trauma, she ran sensitive fingers along each section of the lingam. Behind her Vikram Das watched in amazement, gasping and shaking his head in disbelief at what he was witnessing.

'I can see nothing missing or damaged. Shri Vikram is there anything more you wish to know before we repack the crates?'

'No, nothing, Shrimati Kafni; if I may address you as that, your Highness?'

'I would rather you didn't if you don't mind. It is best that nobody knows who I am.'

'As you wish. Not even my own family shall be told of your true identity until I know that you and the lingam are safely back at your home in Kushnapur. '

'Thank you, Babu, you will understand how greatly indebted we are to you. I look forward to the day when I and my family can truly express our gratitude.'

'Then we must urgently repack this lingam and take it to a place of safety.'

'Where do you suggest, Shri Vikram? We are in your hands.'

'I'm sure it will be safe at my family home in Lala Musa, eighty miles from here. We can go there together on Sunday, when my *dukan* will be closed. But you cannot remain here.' He paused. 'My cousin owns a flower shop about half a mile away. She has a spare room now that her daughters have left home. I'm sure you will be able to stay there. She is very kind; I will take you there this morning in my van. She also knows Rashmi, so we can truthfully say that you are her friends.'

After Vikram Das had nailed back each of the lids he leant forward to lift up one of the crates. 'My God, they're heavy. I will transfer them to my own van when I come back. I live only a few streets away and usually walk to and from home. Now, I must take you and introduce you to my cousin. It's only a short distance away.' Vikram looked at the canvas bag Mandira had beside her. 'Are those the only things you have?'

'Yes, that's all. The *chokidar* asked us to bring the very minimum.'

Shortly after midnight, Vikram Das went back to his shop to get rid of the van and Narajan's body. He took out his key to open the door, but saw by the light of the street lamp that the door was ajar. Checking with his hand, he realised that the lock had been forced. Cautiously he entered, lest there was someone still inside.He walked slowly through to the storeroom, listening out for an intruder. The door to the stables was open, and he could hear someone moving around. Feeling his way through the doorway, he saw a man in the back of the van holding a flashlight. He was kneeling beside an opened crate intently examining the contents. The door creaked as Vikram pushed it open. The intruder looked up and shone his torch in the direction of the sound. The beam caught Vikram before he could hide. With no weapon, Vikram was at a loss to know what to do. He prayed that the man would leave quickly without taking anything. He dodged away from the doorway, and moved round to the other side of the van to give the burglar the chance to escape. But the thief had no intention of leaving empty-handed. Holding the torch in his mouth the man lifted the jewel-encrusted phallus from its crate. He grabbed at the blanket to wrap up his booty and in so doing revealed Narajan's dead body. He let out a flow of obscene Punjabi oaths followed by 'You filthy bloody murderer, so that's how you got this loot.'

Stepping out from his hiding place Vikram Das shouted at him.

'Get out of my shop immediately!'

'Or else what?you will call the police? I don't think so.'

He picked up the heavy jewelled sculpture and despite its weight ran out through the storeroom, grabbing a piece of cloth on the way to wrap it in. Vikram hurried after him into the darkness, but it was hopeless; the man was younger and faster. Calling for help outside in the street would be risky; there were too many secrets to hide.

Panic-stricken and distraught, Vikram rushed back and looked into the open crate. Only the black velvet cloth remained and he was filled with remorse. He had failed the princess's trust. Now it was vital to safeguard the rest of the treasure. He opened up the second crate and lifted out the massive jewelled base of the sculpture and staggered with it to his office. Where could it be safely hidden? Yes, that was it, the stone coffer, only *he* knew about that. It slid into the wall at the back of the secret chamber leading to the tunnel; he had always wondered what it had been used for. He returned to the van for the last piece; the bejewelled scrotum but realised there would not be enough space for this piece in the coffer so he decide to leave it in the crate and took it into the *dukan* and hid it beneath some bolts of cloth. The urgent thing now was to get rid of the body, another few hours and it would begin to smell and there was no knowing who the thief might tell.

Having secured the front door of the shop. He opened the double doors at the rear and drove Narajan's van out into the street. He returned and bolted the doors from inside then left by the shop door. Still under cover of dark he drove to the other side of the city and abandoned the van in a deserted alley. On his walk back, he picked up his own van from his house and drove it back to his *dukan*. The quicker this hazardous operation was over, the safer it would be for all concerned. He looked at the remaining crate. Where could he hide it? It was much too dangerous to leave there. Sooner or later the burglar would come back and look around the *dukan* for more loot. No, this part of the treasure must be taken far away. A safe place would be his parents' home in Lala Musa. It would be unwise to wait until Sunday. He must act now and explain things later to the princess and her ayah. He loaded the crate into his own van and set off. He would hurry back in time to meet them as previously arranged. He would have to confess to his terrible shame in losing part of the lingam and then pledge himself to do everything possible to recover the stolen piece.

The Old City, Lahore, August 1947.

An anxious Kafni and Mandira walked back to the cloth merchant's *dukan* early on the Sunday morning. Their few possessions and a change of clothes were in the canvas bag carried by Mandira.

Entering the store, they were curtly greeted not by Vikram Das, but by a young man in a state of distress.

'*Namaste*,' he said, 'I am sorry, we are closed today.'

'We were expecting to meet Shri Vikram Das here this morning, do you know what time he will arrive?' asked Kafni.

'Who are you? Why do you want to see my father?'

'Shri Vikram was to take us to Lala Musa this morning. Why is he not here?'

The young man paused and then looked away to hide his emotion. 'My father is dead.'

'How could that be?' Mandira asked in astonishment.

Tears came into his eyes as he continued; 'He was killed in a motor accident on his way back from Lala Musa yesterday morning.'

'Oh my God!' said Mandira, 'How dreadful.'

Kafni gasped, unable to speak as the tragedy and its implications registered. Then regaining her voice she said, 'We're so very sorry; he was a fine gentleman. Do you know why he went to Lala Musa on Friday instead of today?'

The young man seemed impatient with Kafni's question. 'Late on Thursday night my father left the house saying he had to attend to something very important here at the *dukan*. He would not tell me what it was. That was the last time I saw him. The next morning his van had gone, and he left a note. It said that he was taking a crate of china goods to my grandparents' home. If he was not back by Friday night, I must open the *dukan* for him on Saturday morning.'

The young man walked over to a chair and sat down, choking back a sob. 'On Friday evening the police came to tell me that my father had been killed near Lala Musa. I am waiting for my uncle to take me in his car for the funeral. He has gone to buy the oil for my father's pyre.' He sobbed again, 'now I have to carry out my sacred duty at my father's funeral.' He thumped his fist on the counter. 'He should never have died. The police say he was driving too fast. He ran off the road and hit a tree. Why did he have to go so urgently? Why was he racing to get back?'

He turned to look at the women as anguish and spite welled up within him.

'You! It's all your fault. It was for you he went to Lala Musa. You tempted him and were meeting him to repay him with your shameless bodies.'

'No, no! That is not true. Please believe us, it's nothing like that,' said Mandira, but the young man was oblivious to her plea.

'Why couldn't he tell me what he was doing? 'You've corrupted him. You are whores. Get out!'

Kafni, seeing that the young man was distraught and beyond reason, left the dukan followed by Mandira. Even when they reached the corner shop at the end of the lane, they could still hear him shouting from the doorway of his *dukan*,

'Whores, filthy whores! You've killed my father.'

Highly embarrassed, they began to run, and after a few yards, attracted by the shouting, a small crowd of Muslim men gathered round them. They pushed their way through and continued to run, until three of the men overtook them and blocked their way.

'Leave us alone, please leave us alone,' said Mandira with all the authority and dignity she could muster. 'We are not prostitutes. My mistress is a respectable lady.'

'Mistress indeed! Respectable?' The man who was speaking made an obscene gesture.

'Then why are you running away, and why did that young cloth merchant call you whores? Would he not pay your price?'

'He does not know us. He has made a great mistake.'

There were jeers, as another of the men taunted them.

'You're just a couple of loose Hindu women, tempting devout Muslim men who keep their wives in purdah.'

'Let us deal with them like the Hindus treated our own Muslim women in Ambala,' said one, rushing forward and starting to rip off Kafni's clothes. Mandira dropped her canvas bag and made a brave effort to stop the man, clawing at his face and screaming, but with little effect. Then taking from her waist-band a small knife she had bought in the bazaar the day before, she lunged at him shouting, 'leave her alone you filthy brute.'

The man whilst maintaining a hold on Kafni, grabbed Mandira's hand and trapped the knife. He grappled with her and attempted to turn the weapon back towards Mandira. In the mêlée, the open knife blade slashed Kafni's neck, arm and breast. Mandira tried to ward off the man, but he was too strong and she was thrown to the ground.

'You're going to get the same treatment in a minute, you fiery bitch,' the man spat out in Urdu as he ripped the last garment from Kafni's body leaving her standing naked. She felt defiled. She told herself she could never be a wife, a concubine or even a mistress; she was so degraded, only fit to be a whore.

Mandira scrambled to her feet, picked up part of Kafni's torn sari and attempted to cover her mistress, but it was scant protection. A man from behind pushed his way forward and called out in bitter anguish, 'I've come from Jullandar where these bastard Hindus came and slaughtered our women, slashing their breasts and cutting out their unborn babies.' He almost choked with grief as he spoke.

A murmur of sympathy passed through the group as he pulled out a knife and advanced towards Kafni. 'She's a Hindu and not from these parts. Allah has given me this chance of retribution.' He had almost reached Kafni when a great hulk of a man put up an arm and restrained him.

He leered at Kafni and grunted, 'A quick death is too good for her; some of us should have her first.'

A stallholder standing next to him grabbed Kafni's arm and pulled her towards his stall. Mandira, now frantic, looked desperately around for help. Not one face showed any trace of sympathy or compassion. A short distance away, she saw an old man, and she knew by his dress that he was an imam. She rushed up and knelt in front of him, and whilst the others watched and listened, she spoke in Urdu and begged him to intervene.

So passionate was her plea that he walked forward to the man holding Kafni's arm and in a sonorous voice ordered the stallholder to release her. Then turning to the group of men said, 'One of Allah's greatest gifts is mercy. These women do not appear to have committed any crime. Allah does not countenance vengeance upon innocent victims, most especially defenceless women; even those unveiled. Leave them to go on their way.'

The men began to disperse, suddenly anxious to dissociate themselves from their disgraceful behaviour. The stallholder, who had been holding Kafni's arm, slunk behind his stall to escape the accusing stare of the Mohammedan priest. As the imam looked around, he saw a woman standing in the doorway of a dress shop. He beckoned her and told her to take the women and let them dress in the privacy of her *dukan*.

Mandira recovered her canvas bag and gathered up the rest of Kafni's underclothes and sari, a piece of which was covering her mistress's bleeding body. Together they followed the woman into the dress shop where Kafni quickly changed into the spare sari from Mandira's bag.

'You are injured, you need medical attention,' the woman said, looking at Kafni's neck and arm. 'My son is a doctor, I'll send for him to come and dress your wounds.' Kafni just shook her head, and Mandira understanding her message, said, 'Thank you for your kindness, Shrimati. Please don't call your son, we must leave here immediately.' She did not need Kafni to tell her that even though she was injured, they had to get out of the Old City straightaway.

The streets and alleyways felt hostile to Kafni and Mandira. Not for them the joy of celebrating the Independence of Pakistan. Kafni, in considerable pain and still bleeding, held the end of her sari to afford some protection to the wounds on her neck. Then, brimming with anger at the injustice of their treatment and half blinded with tears, she dimly perceived the Mochi Gate; their way out from the city. Minutes later they passed through it and were heading down Fleming Road, not knowing where they were going, wishing only to escape their persecutors.

By the time they had reached Qila Gujjar Singh Square, Kafni was exhausted, bleeding profusely and losing the will to survive. Mandira looked around that great intersection of roads for a refuge, but the only seat she could offer her mistress was a low stone wall. Desperate for help, Mandira scoured the traffic hoping to see a friendly face. Vehicles of every description were roaring by, yet who could she dare to trust?

As she stood at the roadside with her heart anxiously beating their plight seemed hopeless. Then coming up Nicholson Road from the direction of the Railway Station she saw a Jeep with a British Army corporal at the wheel. Without hesitation she rushed into the road waving her arms. The Jeep stopped. 'Can I help?' the corporal asked.

'My mistress has been badly injured, she needs urgent help. Please, please take us to a hospital, or somewhere safe.'

Kafni had seen Mandira stop the vehicle, and she staggered over to join her, fearful lest the corporal drove off again. The corporal looked at her in her wretched state. Blood was running from the cuts on her neck and arm and seeping through her sari from the wound above her breast.

Beyond Kushnapur

'Holy Christ, Missus you're in a right state, we'd better get you somewhere quick. I don't know about a hospital, but Falletti's Hotel is nearby. There must be someone there who could give you first aid.' He put his hand out to help the women into the seat beside him, and then drove off rapidly down Montgomery Road.

CHAPTER THIRTY FIVE

Lala Musa, Wednesday 27ᵗʰ May 1959.

Adam sat listening to Mandira, and saw the tears run down her cheeks as she relived the agony of their last terrifying days in Lahore that August of 1947. How he admired this devoted servant. Could he ever express the gratitude he felt for how she had cared for Kafni in those dark times. His dear Kafni, the beautiful mother of his son.

He stooped down beside Mandira and took her hand. 'I can never take away the torment that you and Princess Kafni have suffered, but I can tell you sincerely that if in the future you are ever in need of help, you must call me wherever I am.'

Mandira leaned forward and looked at his hand holding her small fingers. She nodded to acknowledge Adam's words, yet hesitated to breach the barriers of convention to show her appreciation with a more intimate gesture.

'I knew that you had been taken to Falletti's Hôtel, even before you had told me,' said Adam.

'How could you? No one else knows.'

She then listened intently as Adam explained what had led him to Lala Musa.

'Mrs Manning was so very kind to us,' Mandira said,' even though her husband was a burra-sahib. Some of the memsahibs were rude and objected to us being in the hotel. That is why Mrs. Manning took us to her own house. As you know the other memsahib's husband arranged Army transport to bring us to Lala Musa.'

'So what did you do when you got here? Did you have any money?'

'Thankfully I had kept some hidden and we were also able to sell the little personal jewellery that the princess had brought from Kushnapur.'

Lala Musa, August 1947.

After the army transport took them to Lala Musa their first call was to the house of the parents of Vikram Das. They were kindly, but suspicious and still mourning the loss of their son.

Vikram had told his parents that there had been an incident at the *dukan* but fortunately had not given them any details apart from telling them that he had helped two women in distress. When Kafni tactfully asked them whether he had brought any crates with him on his last visit they confirmed that he had left some china with them for safekeeping. They knew that the "china" did not belong to him but he had not told them who it did belong to or the value of the contents.

Kafni was disappointed but was relieved that the crates were at least safe. She felt that this was not the moment to reveal the importance of the contents or to lay claim to them.

In time she hoped she could gain the confidence of the Das grandparents, but patience would be required. In the meantime she must remain incognito and keep a low profile, to avoid the attention of Wantilla's agents and spies.

She decided the best way to do this was to present herself as a teacher. Many English teachers had left with the Raj and with her level of education she felt she could fill one of these vacancies.

Calling herself Shrimati Ranjhalla, she found temporary lodgings for herself and Mandira and applied for a position in a local school. In addition to her knowledge of English literature and poetry she spoke Hindi, Punjabi, and Urdu, the national language of Pakistan. Despite not having any formal qualification to teach she was given the post. She was allocated a staff bungalow vacated by a departing junior official of the Raj. Her respectability was soon established as a cultured schoolteacher; a widow with her own maid to wait upon and cook for her and a *mali* to attend to her garden. Some months later with restored confidence, she and Mandira again called on the Das parents.

Kafni identified herself as a member of the Debrahm family and told them that the crates contained a religious family treasure that had been stolen from Kushnapur. They were sceptical about her description of the contents but were sufficiently impressed by her sincerity that they agreed to unpack it in her presence. To Kafni's horror they revealed that there was only one crate. When this was opened it contained the scrotum part of the lingam. The Das parents were staggered by its magnificence.

'Are you sure this was the only crate? Kafni enquired anxiously. 'There should have been two more crates containing 'the other two parts to the sculpture, the base and the golden phallus itself are missing.'

'Are you suggesting that our son stole them?' said the old lady, indignantly.

'No, I cannot believe that, *Mataji*,' said Kafni using a respectful form of address. 'He was a good man. He may have hidden the other pieces elsewhere for safety reasons. Something serious must have happened to make him bring this crate up to you without waiting for us to come with him.'

'You know, *Mamaji*,' said the old man, affectionately addressing his wife, 'I do believe that this treasure does belong to the family of this young woman; she knows so much about it.'

'Is that knowledge proof enough?' his wife replied.

'Frankly no, it is not... But Vikram made it clear that it did not belong to him and I think that if we find no other instruction left by Vikram, we should consider this lady's claim. Perhaps if she is able to find the other two parts of the lingam, this piece should be handed over to her.'

'That sounds very fair,' said the old lady, who realised the religious significance of the jewels and now looked at Kafni for her reaction.

Kafni moved her head gently in acknowledgement, still pondering what might have happened to the other two parts. In the absence of any evidence to support her claim this proposal seemed reasonable enough. She would now have to find the rest of the lingam, a bewildering task given that the only person who might have had any knowledge of their whereabouts was now dead. She felt a sense of shame that having regained the lingam she had lost it again. She felt honour bound to find it. There would be little point in contacting her family as given the state of chaos in Lahore they would be unlikely to make any better progress than herself. She knew that she could not ask Rindi to come to Pakistan, the risks were too great. The responsibility was hers and she knew she had little alternative but to accept the Das grandparent's proposal.

'Thank you, Shri Das, I will do as you wish. We shall not prevail upon you again until we have made progress with this formidable quest. May I ask you, Babu, to please let us know if you receive any further information that might help us. Could I also request that you be very careful not to let anyone know about this treasure. You will understand that given its great value there are many who would like to acquire it.'

404

'You may be sure that we shall do that, Shrimati; we wish you God's guidance.'

'Shukriya, your kindness and trust will not go unrewarded.'

It was a near impossible undertaking that Kafni and Mandira had agreed to and with no one to consult or confide in, they were at a loss to know their best course of action. Their greatest hope was that old Babu Das might come across something that would give them a lead. His grandson Samvat would have been a useful pair of eyes and ears to have in Lahore city, had he not been so hostile towards them. She wasn't even sure whether his grandparents would decide to involve him.

In the absence of anyone else they decided to contact Rashmi; she had been so kind and would certainly wish to help them. She had known Vikram Das and they had shared the secrets of the tunnel. Their fear that they would encounter Wantilla was removed after they read in the newspaper that he was back in India and was amongst the list of candidates for the parliamentary elections. It was nevertheless thought wiser that Mandira would make the journey to Lahore alone.

On arrival at Kashmir Bhavan she found the gates locked and she was refused entry. The situation had changed dramatically. Since Independence, a border war had flared up between India and Pakistan over the state of Kashmir. The Pakistan government contended that because ninety percent of the four million population of Kashmir were Muslim, it should be part of their nation; the "k" in Pakistan standing for Kashmir. The roots of the conflict lay in the procrastination of Sir Hari Singh, the Maharajah of Kashmir, who wanted his state to remain independent after Partition.

The Maharajah, a Hindu ruler, continued to prevaricate on a decision to join either India or Pakistan. More than two months after Independence, he still vacillated, nurturing hope of continuing to reign over an independent Kashmir with its beautiful valleys and lakes. This territory swept across four hundred miles to the Himalayas and borders of China and Tibet. Its summer capital of Srinagar with the Mogul Gardens, trout streams and houseboats on Dal Lake, had become very popular with the Raj, but was also the envy of its neighbours. The Maharajah of Kashmir's hopes were rapidly overtaken by events. The Muslim troops of his army at Srinagar mutinied, and a hundred miles away, a column of thousands of ferocious Pathan tribesmen crossed the border, intent on capturing the capital and the Maharajah himself. The war for Kashmir was on.

One upshot of this war was the freezing in Pakistan of the assets of the Maharajah and in particular the Kashmir *Bhavan*. Immediately this became known, a host of financial claims appeared, many of them bogus. To deal with these, the District Legal Administrator appointed a firm of lawyers, and Kashmir *Bhavan* was locked and placed under their control.

It was an employee of this firm of lawyers that Mandira encountered when she arrived at the *bhavan*. She explained that she was there to visit a friend. When she gave Rashmi's name, she was told she had been killed in a skirmish in the city one night. In a cruel twist of fate, she had been mistaken for the wife of a Sikh and stabbed to death. Horrified at this news, Mandira asked whether Rashmi's husband was still employed at the *bhavan*, only to learn that he was away at his home up country, no doubt mourning the loss of his wife.

Lala Musa, January 1958.

As the years passed, Kafni became increasingly resigned to the fact that she and Mandira might have to stay in Lala Musa indefinitely. She had become an accomplished teacher and life was comfortable for them. She missed her family and in particular Pratap but feared that if they were to return to Kushnapur her presence would only antagonise Wantilla and he was bound to cause trouble. She had also not given up hope of recovering the lingam.

Ever alert for information that might help them, they regularly scanned the newspapers, and through the local library, had access to copies of Indian newspapers. It was in the Times of India that they read of the death of Kafni's father, on the 18th of January 1958. A deep sadness welled up inside Kafni; she had so much hoped that the lingam would be returned to the palace before her father died. Perhaps there was more she could have done.

Later that month Kafni learnt that Grandfather Das had died. And although Kafni was sure that his widow would wish to honour their agreement regarding the lingam, there was a fresh problem. Samvat, his grandson, had now become head of the family. His first responsibility after lighting his grandfather's pyre, was to sort through his belongings. He had opened the crate and was amazed to find jewels of such splendour. His first reaction was that they should be sold. However, his grandmother insisted that they did not belong to their family. She would send for a lady whose family, she believed, did own the jewels and she could explain everything.

When Samvat saw that the "lady" was none other than one of the women he had expelled from the *dukan* ten years before, his anger flared.

'Grandmother, I am sure this woman is a prostitute who seduced and duped father into taking the dangerous journey which killed him.'

'Samvat! I will not hear you speak like that about this lady. She is a respectable school teacher from a very good family.'

Samvat looked suitably rebuked but still unconvinced.

'Where could they have procured such priceless things? These jewels must have been stolen.'

'Your grandfather was convinced she is telling the truth that these jewels do belong to her family and that what we have seen is only one part of a sacred lingam. In any event if these jewels have been stolen then they certainly cannot be sold.'

'Well, then, somewhere there must be a large reward to be claimed.'

Kafni gazed across at the old lady and as their eyes met, a silent confirmation of trust passed between them.

'Your grandfather and I made an agreement with Shrimati Ranjhalla that if she could find the other two parts and prove to us that this was in fact an ancient religious treasure then we would hand over the part in our possession. He would wish you to honour his word. As far as a reward is concerned

I do believe that this lady's family will express their gratitude.'

'Gratitude. Is that enough for my father's life?'

'We were not responsible for your father's death, Shri Samvat Das,' said Mandira who until that point had kept silent in the background. 'That was a tragic accident. We are deeply sorry about what happened; he was a fine gentleman. Believe me, his association with us was totally honourable.'

'I'm quite sure it was,' interjected the old lady, 'and I think we should do everything we can to help them find the missing parts.'

'Perhaps I will,' Samvat said somewhat reluctantly. He turned to address Kafni. 'When did you last see the other parts of this lingam?'

'It was in your father's stable. All three parts were there when your father took us to lodgings with his cousin.'

'Cousin. What cousin?'

'She runs a flower shop.'

'Ah, then I know her. She is highly respectable. My father would never have taken you there if he had doubts about your morals.'

Kafni was relieved that he had not asked who her family were or questioned her identity and in accordance with her previous request, Grandmother Das was the essence of discretion. Their safety continued to depend on them remaining anonymous within the local community.

'Have you been searching all this time?' Samvat asked.

'We started a few months later, after we had been to see your grandparents.'

'That is a long time ago. Have you made any progress?'

'Very little I am afraid, but we remain hopeful,' Kafni replied wearily.

'I'm still not happy about this, grandmother. I think that somehow these jewels did belong to father. Perhaps they had been hidden for hundreds of years and he found them,' Samvat said somewhat wishfully.

'Why then would he have told us that they belonged to someone else?'

Samvat Das drew himself up and took a deep breath.

'Very well, in deference to my grandparents and to show that I am not without compassion, I will give you one more year to find the other parts of the lingam.' He looked at a calendar on the wall. 'It is now the twentieth of April. On this same day in 1959, exactly one year from now, if the other parts of the lingam have not been found, I shall sell the treasure in that crate. That will be the end of the matter.'

Kafni made no comment, her only sign of acquiescence was a gentle nod of the head and a polite farewell "*namaste*" to Samvat Das and his grandmother as she and Mandira left their house.

One Sunday morning in late March of 1959 Mandira responded to a knock on the door of their bungalow to find Samvat Das standing there. She was quite sure that he had come to warn them that they had only one month left before the treasure would be sold.

'May I please see your mistress,' he requested very formally.

With her heart thumping, anxiously anticipating the crisis that they were approaching, Mandira led Samvat Das through to the sitting room. She left the room and returned a few moments later.

'Shrimati Ranjhalla will be here shortly. She asks if you will kindly wait a few minutes. May I offer you tea?'

Samvat shook his head, deeply preoccupied.

'Please sit down.' Mandira indicated the sofa, and he accepted her invitation. They waited, the silence broken only by the ticking of the pendulum clock that had been left hanging on the wall by the departing Raj civil servant.

Mandira sensed his unease. Then as Kafni entered the room he sprung to his feet and Mandira was surprised at his deferential 'Namaste' and bow of his head.

'Rajkumari, Kafni, I have done you a grave injustice. I owe you my deepest apology for the things I have said.' His head remained bowed. 'My behaviour was despicable, your highness. It would be presumptuous to ask for your forgiveness, but perhaps it is not too late to make amends.'

Mandira listened with astonishment as he spoke. Kafni glanced at Mandira then back to Samvat.

'How do you know who I am?'

'From your son Pratap.'

Kafni's gasp betrayed her astonishment, then gaining her composure she asked, 'How could you have met my son? Where did you see him?'

'I think it would be more appropriate if Pratap himself explained everything.'

'What is going on, Shri Samvat? Is my son here?

'Nahin, Hazrat, he is not here.' Samvat smiled as he prepared to deliver the news he was sure she would be happy to hear.

'He is working today but he will come to visit you tomorrow.'

'Tomorrow!' Mandira hurried forward and put her hand on Kafni's arm.

Unable to conceal her joy at the news, Kafni turned to face her. 'Did you know about this, Mandira?'

Mandira shook her head, the lump in her throat preventing her from answering as the tears of relief and happiness ran down her face.

As Samvat turned to go, he said, 'As for your treasure, Hazrat, I shall do everything I can to help find the other two parts of the lingam and get it back to Kushnapur. Please also be assured that there is no longer a time limit on finding the other parts.'

He placed the palms of his hands together and bowed his head as he said, 'Namaste,' then quickly left the sitting room and let himself out of the front door of the bungalow.

Pratap was only five and a half when Kafni had last seen him in July 1947, more than eleven years previously. She did not know what information or explanation had been given to him about the absence of his mother and her status. She had left Kushnapur as a widow and agreed to escort Wantilla in return for the restoration of the lingam, but what would he think of her as a mother. How could a child understand the imperative of her sacrifice?

Kafni had followed one tenet of the *Vedas*, that one should live life to the best of one's ability and if achievements were not always those desired, then there was comfort in the knowledge that at least she had made her best endeavours. She did not therefore have a fatal belief in preordination. Worthy behaviour could merit its own rewards and she was sure that avoiding consummation with Wantilla and her rescue from Narajan's attempted rape were the justice of a compassionate God. Whilst she still felt unworthy of returning to Kushnapur, she was excited at the prospect of becoming a mother to Pratap once more and hoped he would forgive her the years of neglect.

The two women debated Pratap's means of travel to Lala Musa and correctly deduced that he would arrive by the Awam Express, the first train out of Lahore Junction that Monday morning. Mandira had delivered a message to the headmaster that Kafni could not attend school that day. *Jalpan* was prepared and eyes were fixed intently on the front gate. At eight-thirty a taxi drew up outside and a tall youth alighted, paid the driver and strode up the path.

'It's him! It's him!' Mandira's excited cry must have been loud enough for their visitor to hear. She rushed and opened the door, then stood back so that Pratap could enter the hallway. '*Namaste*,' she said breathlessly, 'Your mother is waiting, please come through.'

Pratap paused whilst Mandira closed the door, and then followed her into the sitting room. He was carrying a bunch of white roses and two brightly coloured packets of *halwa*, a sweetmeat, tied up with ribbon. These he placed on a brass top bamboo table, just inside the door, freeing his hands to greet his mother.

'*Namaste*, Mataji. *Namaste*.' Pratap bowed his head in deep respect; amazed at the sight of the mother he had not seen since he was a young child.

'*Namaste*, Pratap.'

These were the only words they spoke as they faced each other, both feeling the poignancy of their meeting. Kafni saw before her a handsome young man wearing a high collared cream silk *achkan* reaching below his knees and emphasising his height of over six feet; his bright violet eyes framed by a warm tanned face; his serious countenance reflecting the demands of manhood and heavy responsibilities which circumstances had thrust upon him. Her gaze of pleasure and admiration was surpassed only by the wonder that Pratap felt as he looked at his mother. His only images of her had been the paintings and photographs at the palace. Her good looks and delicate features had impressed him. Now he saw a woman whose beauty had been enriched by maturity; this was the true image; the photographs had not done her justice. Her lovely eyes, enhanced by long lashes and a trace of make-up, gave the only evidence of the sadness Kafni felt, knowing the reason that occasioned their meeting.

The rest of that day was spent exchanging experiences. Pratap talked about his education; conditions at the palace and the restoration of the lake after the flood disaster. He had wanted to come on this quest when he was fourteen but the maharajah had forbade him. Only after his sixteenth birthday did his Uncle Rindi, the new Maharajah, finally grant permission on the condition that he took with him Gopal Ram Chandra. Now, the heartening news for his mother was that a good man named Shastri at the lawyers' office had agreed to help them find the lingam.

Pratap described how he had come to Lahore and obtained work as a clerk in the office of the lawyers administering Kashmir Bhavan. It was there that he had met Shri Shastri, a babu whose kindness and trust had led to his discovery of the same tunnel that his mother and Mandira had used for their escape. He was sure that it had more secrets to divulge, even clues perhaps to the missing treasure.

Kafni recognised that Pratap's success was due in no small measure to his charm and sincerity. He reminded her so much of his natural father. Where was Adam now, she wondered. He had married that general's daughter and would probably have other children by now. Would any of them be like Pratap? No, she must not think about it; her father had ordered it to be a closed chapter.

There were so many questions they wanted to ask each other but many of these would evoke painful memories.

Kafni was thankful that Pratap did not refer to his assumed father, Prince Ranjhalla. He had been killed before Pratap was born and although he had heard accounts of his bravery as a soldier it was difficult to miss a legend. His Uncle Rindi had assumed the father role in his life. But his mother, that was different, he had fond memories of her and still found it hard to understand why she had left when he was so young. Why had she not at least told them she was alive? Throughout the post Partition period they heard reports of Hindus being massacred and when they heard nothing they feared the worst. The uncertainty had been terrible.

Kafni's disclosures were limited and discreet. This was no time to elicit sympathy or motivate vengeance that would merely deflect Pratap's efforts from his objective. One day perhaps he could be told everything. Everything? No, some secrets might have to remain.

Pratap and Gopal arranged that they would take it in turns to visit Lala Musa on alternate weeks to discuss any developments. Gopal, on his first visit, reported that Samvat was conducting a detailed search of every inch of the *dukan*. He was now certain that for good reason, his father must have hidden the other parts of the lingam. Two days later, Pratap made an unexpected visit to tell his mother that they had found the second part of the lingam: the base, with its magnificent array of jewels.

'How wonderful, where was it found?

'In a secret coffer which was part of the old *bhavan* building.'

'Surely it can only be a matter of time before you find the third part of the lingam.'

'I fear it may not be so simple, Mataji. Samvat has told us that about a year after his father died, a man had called at the *dukan* making enquiries about jewellery. Were there any for sale? The man would pay an exceptionally high price for the right items. "This is a cloth merchant's *dukan*," Samvat had told him. But the man had persisted, "I was told that your father sometimes dealt in rare jewels, with no questions asked."

Indignant at the implication of dishonesty, Samvat firmly told the man that he was seriously mistaken; there were positively no jewels there nor ever had been. He had thought no more about the matter until the week after his grandfather's death. He had returned from the funeral, and a few days later another man had called at his *dukan* making a similar enquiry about jewellery. This man's words had been more discreet with no suggestion of impropriety. He had even left a visiting card with an address in the city where he could be contacted.

Samvat had once more dismissed this second caller as having been misdirected but when he had discovered the contents of the crate at Lala Musa he began to think this was too much of a coincidence. Initially he thought this may be a good avenue for selling the lingam once the women had failed to find the other parts. The subsequent revelation that Kafni was in fact a *bona fide* princess and his resolve to pursue every angle made him think this visting card may be a valuable lead.

Pratap took the train back to Lahore that afternoon, and the following day Gopal secretly conveyed the newly discovered base of the lingam to Lala Musa. This was then carefully hidden in Kafni's bedroom at the schoolteacher's cottage. When Gopal returned to Lahore, he and Pratap set about the next stage of their search. Their plan was to visit every jeweller and merchant in the Lahore area who dealt in precious stones. They were convinced that someone in the district had that missing part of the lingam. Any experienced jeweller would know that if the other parts of the sculpture could be found and re-assembled it would be worth a king's ransom.

Justifying their reason for visiting these merchants presented a problem. At their age, no merchant would accept them as serious buyers; they therefore posed as students of mineralogy, doing research. But this needed preparation if they were not to be exposed by their ignorance of the subject. They started visiting libraries and museums, and after many hours of intense study, they tested each other's knowledge by cross-questioning. At the end of the week they felt confident enough to venture forth.

One of their early calls was to the address on the card that Samvat had been given. It proved to be a small shop on the other side of the city, where they were greeted by a smooth talking, obsequious *wyapari,* a trader, who proved to be little more than a street hawker who could only show them poor quality gems.

The ploy adopted by Pratap and Gopal was to refer to a rich uncle, who was interested in adding to his collection of unusual jewels, especially rubies and sapphires. When they tried this contrivance on the *wyapari,* he suggested "that for such valuable items he could put them in touch with a Mr. Khan". Sensing that it may be premature to meet this Mr Khan at this stage they said they would return once they had established the level of their uncle's interest.

They met a variety of different characters in the course of their research many who just smelt the irresistible combination of money and inexperience. But there was one man by the name of *Shri* Dastur Ramiyar, a respected Parsee businessman and an expert in precious stones, who recognised their innocence and decided they needed protection from the unscrupulous types that proliferated his trade. After their third visit to his showrooms and workshops he was so impressed by Pratap's enthusiasm, his knowledge of languages, and his natural charm, that he offered him work drafting letters to overseas customers and translating business documents. Ramiyar then proceeded to tutor Pratap. This employment and the increased knowledge that came with it gave him legitimacy in his quest. A friendship with his employer developed, and occasionally Pratap would be invited to go with the merchant to make notes on jewel collections to be purchased or valued. One such visit was scheduled to examine and give a valuation on some very unusual precious stones.

CHAPTER THIRTY SIX

Lala Musa, Wednesday 27th May 1959.

For two hours, Adam had been sitting listening to Mandira give her account of what she and Kafni had endured since they had left Kushnapur twelve years before. At times, the pain of remembering those experiences had forced her to stop and dry her tears. Adam sat choked with anguish, visualising these events and wishing he had been there to help them before.

His mind scanned the names of those responsible for the suffering of these women: there was Narajan, who had received a fitting retribution for his vile behaviour. Kafni's father and brother. How had the maharajah and Rindi consented to a course of action which, had placed her in such a vulnerable position? Adam found it difficult to understand how they could do this to someone they loved. Although-given that until the previous century, a Hindu widow would have willingly thrown herself onto the funeral pyre of her dead husband perhaps their culpability was more understandable. Then there was Wantilla, who had been responsible for the original theft of the lingam and had contrived the whole wicked plan. Even ignoring the fact that he had previously tried to murder him, Adam could never be at peace until he had settled with him.

The clock on the wall struck five. Hoping it might be fast, Adam looked at his watch.

'She should be here very soon,' Mandira said, sensing his concern.

He got up, walked round the room and glanced out of the window towards the gate.

'Does Kafni always come the same way? I could go and meet her.'

'Perhaps not, Adam-sahib, it may surprise her too much. I think it would be better to greet the *rajkumari* here in private.'

'Yes, of course you're right.'

At twenty minutes past five they heard the click of the gate and Mandira stood up.

'That will be her now,' she said as she walked to the window.

'No, it's one of the *chokidars* from the school.' There were hasty steps coming up the path and Mandira hurried through the hall to the front door.

Adam could hear an agitated conversation. He made out "Shrimati Ranjhalla", and "motor car." He heard Mandira say *'idhar thaharo,'* asking the man to wait. She then rushed back into the sitting room in great distress.

'Oh my God, Adam-sahib, Princess Kafni has been abducted; they've taken her.'

Adam leapt to his feet and ran through to the front door to confront the *chokidar*.

He explained that he had seen Shrimati Ranjhalla walk away from the school as she did every day. When she reached the corner of the road a car had driven up beside her, and a man jumped out and grabbed her. Hearing her scream he ran to help her but before he could get there the abductor had forced her into the back of the car, which then sped off.

'And the car?'

'It was a dark blue Ford with a Lahore number plate.'

This could only be the work of Wantilla. Adam wondered at what stage he had picked up their trail. Perhaps his spies had followed Chandra as far back as Kushnapur or maybe it was just a chance discovery at the hotel by one of his informants. They had underestimated him and it was a shattering thought that despite all their precautions Adam had actually led him straight to Kafni.

It would be pointless to report the matter to the police, as Mandira had suggested. If anything, it would add complications and delays. Adam's fury at being out-foxed by Wantilla was mixed with bitter disappointment at having come so close to being reunited with Kafni. He was concerned for her safety, but he knew that she was just a pawn in Wantilla's scheming. The *king* in this sinister game of chess was the lingam. If he had come all the way to Pakistan he would not leave without trying to find it. Where would he have taken Kafni? It was unlikely that he would stay in Lala Musa; it was more probable that at that moment he was heading for Lahore.

It was difficult to be sure how much Wantilla knew, but Adam concluded that he probably did not know where the lingam was or even that the parts had been separated. Adam hoped that he did not know about his own contacts in Lahore, or the involvement of Archie. Great circumspection would have to be exercised if he was to keep things that way. Kafni would doubtless be offered her freedom in exchange for information. Whilst Adam knew that Wantilla would not balk at torture, his most likely gambit would be to use Kafni to lure someone who did have useful information: Pratap, Gopal or himself – and then, of course, there was Mandira.

It was unlikely that he knew where to find Pratap and Gopal, and it was essential that he did not locate them. Their part in the operation to recover the rest of the lingam was vital. He and Mandira had been located and would be the first targets. Given his time constraints, Adam decided to make it easier for Wantilla to contact him. There would be risks, but the consequences of delay could be even greater. Kafni was very vulnerable but would prevaricate because at this stage she didn't know that Adam was in Pakistan.

Adam told Mandira to be very careful and be wary of any suspicious characters. He then returned to Lahore. By the time he had reached his hotel his plans had crystallised. He would play Wantilla at his own game. He knew that he could only get information about Adam's movements if he was in touch with his agent, who in turn would need a contact at the hotel. It would need to be a subtle approach if the trail back to Wantilla was not to go cold. If well paid, there would be no lack of willing recruits; not only had spying been endemic in the sub-continent of India for thousands of years, it was positively relished.

There was no time to spare; a small display of largesse would push things along. Adam telephoned the front desk and asked the manager to come up and see him. He arrived promptly and Adam told him that he wanted information about tours and travel. Also advice on purchases and restaurants, but that he did not want to be pestered by touts or agents. Was there anyone on his staff who could arrange these things for him?

'Of course,' he said. To ensure that he was taken seriously Adam showed him the letter from General Malik. He was duly impressed and said that the general had dined at the hotel on two occasions. Adam handed him a hotel envelope with four hundred Pakistan rupees inside.

'This will cover any unforeseen expenses you and your staff may encounter.' The manager nodded appreciatively.

'There is one other thing: my time is short, could you arrange for me to have a priority service on outside telephone calls?'

Yes certainly sahib, I will personally attend to this.'

His faint smile of satisfaction and waggle of the head implied that he also understood that his calls were not to be monitored.

Adam telephoned Archie, who told him that on his side things were nearing finality. He expected that the 'viewing' would probably take place in the next seventy-two hours. On the strength of this Adam asked him to lay on a meeting with Zaki for the following evening. Zaki would decide on the time and place; it must be a discreet rendezvous, and would he please ask Boolajee to be there as well.

'I will also be bringing three other people with me. Will you call me this afternoon with the exact location?'

'Roger to that old boy.'

Adam was about to turn off the light when the telephone rang. It was Harish with two messages from London. The first was that Jardeeson had been asked for and had given further financial guarantees to the banks in Lahore. The second was from Williams, requesting confirmation that Adam would be back for the briefing session on the Monday 1st June.

'Shall I tell him you are out of reach for the moment?' Harish suggested.

Adam was not due back until the 2nd so he felt sure this was a ploy to put him in conflict with his superiors at the War Office. However he was anxious not to antagonize Williams unnecessarily.

'No, send a message that I cannot get on a flight for another week and would he mind delaying it until Monday 8th June.'

'Very well, but are you sure your 'tour' will be completed by then?'

'With a bit of luck. Oh, by the way, I met a splendid young man the other day. His father would be proud of him.'

'That is good news.'

'And I think we are getting close to locating the item we have been looking for.'

'Are you still hoping to meet as planned in two days time?'

They had previously agreed that Harish would reserve hotel accommodation back in India at Amritsar and that he would stand by with two cars at the border post at Wagah.

'Let's hope so.'

Thursday 28th May. Faletti's Hotel.

The following morning after breakfast, the manager sent two employees to Adam's room. They arrived separately to be vetted by Adam. One was a waiter, the other a commissionaire. The commissionaire was a retired *daffadar*, a sergeant in the cavalry, and Adam felt sure of his trustworthiness. However, this was not Adam's primary concern. The waiter, Fikry, seemed more mercurial and would better serve his purpose. He had a demeanour that positively thrived on intrigue and he looked surprised when Adam sent for him again.

'The services I require are rather specialised,'

'Certainly, sahib, I am well understanding. Is the sahib wishing the special services to be brought here to hotel? Or is sahib preferring to visit palaces of pleasure? All very young, all very beautiful. I can make good arrangements.'

Adam listened with amusement, not wishing to dampen his enthusiasm.

'Thank you, Fikry, but that's not what I had in mind. What I need is information.'

'Information, sahib?'

'Do you think you could do that for me?

'Does the sahib want me to do *jasus* work? I am knowing this surveillance business very well.'

As Adam suspected spying was right up Fikry's street. He gave him a hundred rupees and told him he was interested in locating a man called Wantilla Debrahm and a woman called Shrimati Ranjhalla. There would be more reward if he was successful and time was of the essence.

That evening after a final briefing for what was to be a complicated and delicate operation Adam ran over in his mind the diverse characters involved. Each of them had a crucial role to play and each of them had his own reasons for wanting a successful outcome. For Archie it was an exciting challenge; Zaki Ibrahim loved the merchandise and the intrigue; for Behan Boolajee, it presented an opportunity to do a service for his old friend Jardeeson Debrahm. Shri Shastri, the lawyer's *babu*, had at first, seemed an unlikely candidate for the team, but his admiration of and loyalty to Pratap had convinced Adam that he could be trusted to play a crucial role. Gopal and Pratap had already been prepared to risk their lives on this mission and now had valuable influence and expertise. It was not as Adam would have planned the first meeting with his son for twelve years. How strange it felt to have Gopal introduce Pratap to him with both the boys oblivious to the significance of the moment.

'The brigadier knows my father well,' Gopal said proudly, as Adam shook hands with Pratap.

'I've heard my Uncle Rindi speak of you, sir. I know you were at school with him, and of course you've been to Kushnapur Palace.'

'I certainly have, several times. And I've met you before, but you were too young to remember.' His grip was firm as Adam took his hand and held it for a moment, suppressing the urge to put his arm round the boy's shoulder. Equal in height, Adam stood facing him, endeavouring to disguise his pride in his son's fine physique, handsome face and distinctive Debrahm violet eyes.

It was a strange sensation to be meeting his son. Was it right that he would never learn that Adam was his father? Or at least not until his grandchildren had married and fulfilled their part in the Debrahm genetic plan. By then, Adam would be long since dead. Seeing him as a man for the first time, and talking to him, those niggling doubts returned: had he really come to terms with his secret role in this family?

His taxi, now in Cooper Road, slowed to cross the intersection with Montgomery; a couple minutes more and he would be back in the hotel savouring a *Jheenga Masala* curry. His precaution of changing taxis halfway on each journey and walking down side streets to pick up another taxi, had been effective. He was confident no one had followed him.

They turned off Egerton Road and into Falletti's Hotel entrance. As the taxi drove off, the commissionaire came up to Adam and saluted. 'Message from Fikry, *Huzoor*.'

'Yes, what is it?'

'That car over there, sahib.' He pointed to a large dark blue Ford V8 on the far side of the hotel approach. 'Fikry is saying that the driver brings important message for sahib.'

Adam hoped this would be news of Kafni, and he followed the commissionaire across the drive. As they reached the car the front door opened and a thickset woman looking like a well-fed muscular cook, got out. The driver remained at the wheel staring ahead. The sheer size of him would have dissuaded Adam from accompanying them.

'*Namaste*, Killwerty sahib.' The woman greeted him with raised hands that looked capable of delivering a karate chop.

'Shrimati Kafni sent me. She say you pay me well if I bring you to her house.' Adam did not think Kafni would have said quite that, but accepted it as a typical ploy to get *baksheesh*.

'Where is she? Is she with Wantilla?'

She seemed uncertain how to answer. 'Ah, sahib, I think that is brother of Shrimati. He gone out; excellent time for visiting. We can take sahib, not too far travelling. This driver good man.'

After his previous experience with one of Wantilla's drivers Adam was not about to repeat the mistake of getting into a car with strangers.

'Thank you, but I think I will follow you in my own car.' Adam handed her a ten-rupee note thinking it wouldn't do any harm.

'*Shukriya,* Killwerty Sahib.' She sounded nervous as she took the money and looked dismayed that she had not persuaded him to come with her.

Adam walked back to to the hotel where Fikry was waiting on the entrance steps. Adam asked him to get a taxi and told him that if he was not back in an hour he was to find out where the taxi had taken him and pass the details on to Dr Archibald at Nedoos Hotel.

His taxi followed the blue Ford out along Egerton Road and left into the Mall, past the grounds of "Governor's House" and past the playing fields of Aitcheson College, or "Chiefs", as it was called, due to the number of princely rulers' sons who attended it, including Rindi. At the end of the War he had shown Adam around the bungalows that had been built by maharajahs so that their sons could be privately accommodated with their own domestic staff. The bungalow where Rindi had lived was a large T-shaped, sprawling residence with outbuildings for servants. Adam now recalled that it was in fact owned by Wantilla's father, Mahavir and suddenly it all made sense where they were going.

The large well fed woman turned out to be the housemaid and wife of the *khansama*. Adam remembered having met a retired French couple who were the housekeepers and he wondered if they were still there. His answer came when the door was opened by an old Frenchman with a nervous disposition. He briefly acknowledged Adam's greeting, then led the way along the entrance hall and through to a small reception room, where he asked Adam to sit down. A moment later, Wantilla entered the room as if he was coming on stage. Adam jumped up and moved towards him.

'Where is she? Where's Kafni? I want to see her. Now!'

'Calm down, she's quite safe... and she'll be a lot safer if you co-operate.'

Adam had no intention of calming down or co-operating, and

reached out to grab him by the throat.

'I wouldn't do that Cullworthy.'

From behind Wantilla the heavy bulk of the driver appeared menacingly.

'Come and you can see for yourself.' Adam followed him into a broad passage, at the end of which was an open door revealing a richly furnished room. To one side there was a seated woman, partly screened by the housemaid. As Wantilla entered, the maid moved aside, and Adam saw that it was Kafni tied and gagged in a heavy teak chair.

'Kafni!' Adam pushed Wantilla aside and started towards her, but instantly felt his shoulder roughly jerked back. A stab of pain followed as the "heavy" took one arm and twisted it viciously behind his back. He propelled Adam swearing and protesting back down the corridor, through a side archway and across a scullery, where Wantilla un-bolted and kicked open a door. The next moment, Adam was shoved into semi-darkness. He stumbled down steep wooden steps on his hands and knees and came to an abrupt halt when his head hit the stone wall beyond the bottom step. In his dazed state he vaguely heard the door slam and the bolts shoot across. He was in total darkness and lay for several minutes reeling from concussion. Staggering to his feet the groped his way around his prison. His hand made out some type of shelf, and as he ran his fingers along it he heard a squeak and felt a creature move over his arm and heard others scurrying away.

The place smelled musty and dirty. Even in this subterranean prison it was uncomfortably hot and airless. There was a clatter of metal as his shoe kicked a galvanised bucket. Bending down to move it aside, his hand came across a lavatory roll. This primitive sanitary arrangement confirmed Wantilla's confident anticipation of Adam's capture.

Mahavir bungalow, Aitcheson College, Friday 29th May 1959.

As dawn broke next morning, a glimmer of light filtered through the sole fenestration: a small window just beyond Adam's reach, heavily barred on the outside to prevent anyone getting in. For the present, it would certainly stop him getting out. His overnight incarceration had clearly been intended to soften him up and weaken his resistance to Wantilla's demands.

About an hour later he heard the bolts being drawn back. As the door opened Wantilla's silhouette appeared at the top of the steps. 'Are you ready to talk, Cullworthy?'

'No, not with you, and certainly not in this stinking hole.'

'You'd be wise to think about it, and make it quick: this place will be a picnic spot compared to where I'll put you if you don't co-operate!'

'What do you want from me, you devious bastard?'

'Careful with that tongue of yours, our friend here can get very nasty.' He jerked his head half sideways and Adam could see the unsavoury looking driver standing behind him.

'It's quite simple, Cullworthy; I want to know who has the lingam, and where it is. I'm pretty sure you know. Give me the information, then you and the princess, can be on your way.'

'You'd better not harm her.'

'Oh, how touching to show such concern. Do I detect that you are fond of the little bitch?'

His salacious laughter made Adam shudder. If he hadn't been at the bottom of the steps he would have given him a good kicking but insults and threats would be wasted on this scoundrel. He and Kafni had to get out of this place fast. The complicated plan he had set up on the previous evening needed to be implemented. Every minute was precious. Fikry was obviously unreliable and so there was no chance that a message as to Adam's whereabouts had got through to Archie. There was no prospect of being rescued.

Adam made no further comment and Wantilla called to someone behind him. He then stood back to let the khansama pass with a small tray that he carried down the steps. *Jalpan, sahib.* Adam was tempted to reject the tray of food but he had missed his curry the previous evening and knew that a soldier works better on a full stomach.

Wantilla called down, 'Perhaps you'll be ready to talk when you've had some breakfast.' The door slammed again and he heard the bolts shoot across.

Adam broke off a piece of the chapatti and rolled it round part of the cold omelette. It reminded him of a breakfast he had had in a foxhole when visiting front-line troops in the stinking heat of the Malay jungle. He nibbled at the food, ignoring the rats and the fetid atmosphere.

Predictably, after half an hour, Wantilla sent his brute down to coax him. With the cellar door closed and bolted, the semi-gloom afforded Adam an advantage. The driver aimed a series of vicious blows with the base of his open hand, intended to inflict the maximum pain, with the minimum evidence of physical damage. Most of his lunges had simply fanned the air, or struck the wall behind Adam's head as he weaved and dodged around the cellar. The blows that did make contact were painful but also sent the adrenaline racing through Adam's body. He snatched the handle of the sanitary bucket, swung it round, urine and all, and crashed it hard against the side of the brute's head, knocking him off balance. He fell; giving Adam the chance to deliver two carefully aimed kicks. His screams of agony as he scrambled to crawl up the steps, were pure music to Adam. Once back at the top, he pounded and shouted for Wantilla to open-up and Adam flung the remainder of the piss over him.

As brute force had failed Wantilla resorted to a callous form of persuasion. The cellar door was pushed open and he heard screams of protest. Kafni, with head bent down, was at the top of the steps, her arms twisted behind her back. Close beside her stood Wantilla with a red-hot poker held near her cheek. He moved the poker up to singe her hair and as the fumes of her burnt tresses drifted down to Adam, Wantilla lowered it near her cheek.

'I'm sure you wouldn't like to be responsible for some ugly brand marks on this pretty face. And don't think I won't do it,' he said. Then to make his intentions clear, he touched her bare shoulder with the still glowing poker. She winced and screamed with agony.

Imagining her excruciating pain, Adam flung himself up the stairs. 'You filthy coward, how dare you torture her! You'll pay for this, you *unspeakable bastard!*'

But as he reached the top of the steps, the door slammed in his face. Adam could still hear Kafni's cries of desperation and longed to be able to comfort her.

'It's time to stop fucking about, Cullworthy,' shouted a furious Wantilla through the closed door. 'Are you ready to talk?'

'How do I know that you'll release her when you've got what you want?' Adam shouted back.

Wantilla gave a cynical laugh. 'You don't know, except that I'll be delighted to see the back of both of you. Anyway you're in no position to bargain with me, Cullworthy. I'll be back shortly, so think about it.'

Adam remembered what Chandra had said about Wantilla

wanting to marry Kafni to improve his claim to the gaddi and doubted whether he would ever let her go.

By the time Wantilla returned, Adam had a plan.

'Let's get this over with quickly,' he spat out. 'I've got a job to get back to.'

'Oh yes, I too read the newspapers. It would be a pity to bugger up that promotion of yours, wouldn't it? A good general always knows when it's time to retreat. So let's have it, Cullworthy, where's the lingam?'

'It's hidden at Kashmir Bhavan.' Adam's laconic statement triggered a flow of invective and then a series of questions to test the veracity of his story.

'That isn't possible. How was that possible? How do you know this?'

Adam's explanation was made easier because much of it was based on actual events, some of which were already known to Wantilla. He told him that when Narajan had come to see him at Kashmir Bhavan, some of the staff had overheard his conversations. They had learnt that Narajan possessed something very valuable which he was prepared to exchange for Kafni. They did not trust Narajan to deliver his side of the bargain. So partly out of a sense of loyalty to the princess and partly because times were tough and they felt there was something in it for them, they joined the conspiracy to get hold of the lingam. Narajan was followed back to his hotel. He'd been made a tempting offer, and lured into taking the lingam to a secret rendezvous in the old city, where he believed it would be exchanged for Kafni.

'She and her ayah were taken prisoner, gagged and secreted out of Kashmir Bhavan.'

'That is just not possible.'

'Of course it was. Why do you think that the next day no one could tell you where the women had gone? Obviously all of the staff were in cahoots. With such rich pickings at stake there was plenty for everyone.'

'Then why did the exchange not take place? And who killed Narajan?'

'The idiot tried to renege on the deal, there was a quarrel and a fight and he was stabbed in the heart.'

'The impertinent little runt thought he could outsmart me and got his bloody comeuppance. So what happened to the lingam?'

'The crate with its contents was taken to a house belonging to one of the conspirators.'

'Not taken to Kashmir Bhavan?'

'No, that happened only after you had left and it become too risky to leave it in the old city.'

'You seem to have all the answers, Cullworthy. Are you sure you're not making this all up?'

Wantilla stalked up and down the room furious at the explanation he had heard and Adam was helped by the fact that Wantilla wanted to believe it was all true and that he would soon have the lingam back in his possession.

'And Kafni and that bloody woman of hers?' A note of impatience had crept into his voice.

'They were held captive until you had left Pakistan, in case they came running to you for help. The conspirators knew they would be in real trouble if you discovered what had happened. So they took the women up country to Lala Musa.'

'And what happened to them after that?'

'Once you had left the country they were released. Kafni felt she could never return to Kushnapur without the lingam so she sold her jewellery to pay for food and accommodation, and got a job as a schoolteacher.'

'But if the treasure was safe at Kashmir Bhavan, why was it never sold?'

'At first, they did try to sell it, but were unable to find a dealer who was prepared to pay the price they were asking and also take the risk of handling something so valuable in those troubled times.'

'And when things quietened down why didn't they try again?

'They did, but unfortunately the treasure could not be found. The *khansama* at Kashmir Bhavan who had hidden the lingam had been killed in a riot. Then, shortly after Pakistan's independence, there was another development.'

'Oh? What was that?'

'A number of claims were made against the estate of the Maharajah of Kashmir. Many of these were bogus. The late Maharajah may have had his shortcomings, but failure to honour his debts was not one of them.'

'What difference did that make?'

'Pending settlement of the matter, the Regional Civil Court placed Kashmir Bhavan under judicial control, closed the place to all visitors and appointed a firm of supervising lawyers.'

'Yes, those bastards wouldn't let my agents into the place. So how the hell did you manage it, Cullworthy?'

'I had a personal letter from General Mohammed Malik: it opened many doors.'

'You cunning bastard. I suppose that's what you call the "old boy network." And how did our clever brigadier discover where the lingam was hidden?'

'That had already been done before I arrived.'

'Been done! By whom?'

'By Pratap and Gopal.'

Wantilla let flow a tirade of abuse about his incompetent agents who had failed where a couple of callow youths had succeeded.

'So that's your source of information.'

His false assumption was very convenient and Adam did not disabuse him.

'And where are those two runts now?'

'I should imagine Pratap is looking for his mother.'

'In that case, the quicker we get this over with the better. I hope you're not planning any tricks, Cullworthy; I'm warning you I have some pretty nasty contingency plans.'

Adam did not doubt that for one moment.

Two hours later, sitting in Wantilla's car on the way to Kashmir Bhavan, Adam felt thankful that at least the first part of his plan was working. But there were still many things that could go wrong. In the seat in front of him was a thickset, surly, dark-skinned character. His loose-fitting brown woollen cap was set well back, revealing slightly balding black wavy hair above a short forehead and an aquiline nose. He, and an equally unpleasant looking accomplice, who might well have been his brother, had been brought to the bungalow by the driver that morning. The thug had been left at the bungalow, and with the help of the burly housemaid would doubtless ensure that Kafni was securely detained. The ageing French couple had retreated to another part of the bungalow, anxious to dissociate themselves from events that might prejudice their continued permanent residence.

Adam had suggested it would be helpful if Kafni accompanied them but Wantilla was having none of it. She was too valuable an asset to risk on such a speculative venture. Adam had intentionally been given a brief sight of her whilst being frog-marched through to the back of the bungalow. Their eyes had met but no words were spoken. A multitude of thoughts must have passed between them.

Adam's stubborn reluctance to reveal any information had in the end worked in his favour as Wantilla believed his coercion had finally worked and borne fruit.

CHAPTER THIRTY SEVEN

Kashmir Bhavan, 29ᵗʰ May 1959.

Wantilla's car drove up to the gates of Kashmir Bhavan where a *durwan* in a pale blue uniform and matching *puggaree* stood guard. Beside him was Shri Shastri, immaculate in a double-breasted pale grey suit. As their vehicle came to a standstill, Shastri, with great dignity walked over to Adam's side of the car and he lowered the window to speak to him.

'*Namaste*, Shri Shastri, thank you for coming.'

'*Namaste*, Brigadier sahib, I am arranging this quickly after your driver brought me your message.' He inclined his head towards the driver.

'I am sorry it was such short notice, Shri Shastri, the burra sahib here has to return to India very soon, and wishes once more to see inside the beautiful Bhavan that he had the pleasure of visiting some years ago.'

Whilst Adam was speaking he looked straight at Shastri and slowly closed and opened one eye. He was sure that when Shastri received the letter that morning he must have guessed that something was amiss. The note had been brief and in itself would have aroused no suspicion; Wantilla had ensured that when he had collected a sheet of headed notepaper from his hotel, dictated what Adam should write and then examined the letter before giving it to his driver to deliver to the lawyers' offices. But Shastri would have been suspicious receiving a letter from Adam rather than a telephone call. He also knew that with time so pressing, Adam would be unlikely to engage in an unnecessary visit.

Shastri formally greeted Wantilla: '*Namaste, burra-sahib*, I am pleasured with your visit.' He signalled to the *durwan* to open the gates, then said, 'I will meet you up at the house.'

Their car passed slowly up the drive, all passengers maintaining the ominous silence that had prevailed during the journey. At the carriage porch they were confronted by a *chokidar* standing at the door of the house, holding a formidable looking *lathi* similar to those used by the police to control rioters. He made no move until Shastri had joined them and issued his instructions. A pseudo-military salute was then given and he came forward to open Wantilla's door. Everyone got out and Shastri led the way up the short flight of stone steps to the portico.

Adam needed to convey a delicate and urgent detail to Shastri without attracting any unwanted attention from Wantilla and his party. As part of his plan, he had written a second note; quite different from the one delivered to the office. It had not been easy, but he had managed to pocket a pencil and a scrap of paper at the bungalow whilst writing to Shastri at Wantilla's direction. Fortunately, he had been returned to the cellar whilst the driver delivered his letter to Shastri, where he had written the second note. It was now vital that he passed it to Shastri.

'May we start with the reception rooms, Shri Shastri?' Adam asked. Although he was playing for time, he knew that Wantilla was entirely dependent upon him for this part of the operation. It had been agreed that Adam would show him exactly where the lingam was hidden then contrive to keep the staff occupied whilst Wantilla assessed the best method of removing it. They would then return to the bungalow where Wantilla would put into action a carefully planned burglary. As he was stealing something that was already stolen property it was unlikely that the theft would be reported to the police. Once he had the lingam back in his possession he felt confident that he and his party could make a quick exodus from Pakistan.

Shastri led the way through the ground floor rooms followed by Wantilla and Adam. The creepy driver and the sinister companion were behind them, denying Adam the opportunity of passing the note unobserved. Following at a discreet distance, came the female servant, a kind of chatelaine. Adam deduced that she was in attendance for Shastri's purpose rather than part of the *bhavan* staff.

Although Wantilla wanted the visit to be over as quickly as possible, he had agreed that by viewing most of the rooms, they would allay suspicion about the reason for their visit. Adam's motive for suggesting this had been quite different; it was more time that he needed. The presence of the chatelaine now gave him an idea of how to get things moving.

He drew level with Wantilla and in a conspiratorial whisper said, 'I'll try and get rid of this woman; I'll send her to make tea for us.'

Keep an eye on Shastri.' Before Wantilla could demur, Adam turned and walked back towards the woman, giving the two thugs a nod of complicity as he passed, implying that it was all part of the plot.

Walking straight towards the servant, he obliged her to stop barely an arm's length from him. He hoped that the others were continuing with the tour, but did not dare to confirm this by glancing round. He also prayed that this woman could understand English; he had a lot to say in the briefest possible span and there was no time to verify. It was vital that she displayed no fear or distress and he said in a low voice, 'Don't speak *Shrimati,* just listen. I am in great danger from these people. Take this note, then go and pretend you are getting us tea. After a few minutes, call Shri Shastri and tell him he's wanted on the telephone.' She calmly took it and muttered, 'I understand.' A moment's pause, then she said, 'Careful, sahib, one man is coming back.'

She turned away, and Adam called after her, *'Yah jaldi lao,'* indicating that she must be quick. It was the driver who had come back to check up, and Adam ignored him as he hurried to draw level with Wantilla who frowned at him and hissed under his breath, 'I hope we are nearly done here, Cullworthy.'

Adam nodded and they continued their tour. After about five minutes the chatelaine reappeared and hurried up to Shastri. 'Your office is on the telephone, Shri Shastri.' she said, just sufficiently loud enough for the others to catch the message.

'Can't it wait? I'm busy; I can't leave my guests.' Adam silently held his breath wondering if there was something wrong, Shastri was reluctant to leave him alone with these people. Thankfully, the woman spoke again.

'They said it was urgent, Shri Shastri.' Then, seeing a young *khitmagar* appear at the door carrying a tray, she added, 'your tea is ready, gentlemen. Will you take it in here?'

Adam nodded his assent, and she directed the *khitmagar* where to serve the tea, then left the room. Shastri followed, excusing himself and saying that he would be back soon.

'Are we nearly there yet, Cullworthy?' Wantilla said impatiently, as soon as the *khitmagar* had left the room.

'It won't be long now,' Adam said trying to reassure him. 'It would be a mistake to rush things. If Shastri suspects anything, you've not a hope of getting a "lease" on this place.' Adam stressed the euphemism and made a slight grimace, implying that he was not sure how much the others knew.

'Well, maybe you're right, but I don't want it to take all day.'

Shastri rejoined them quicker than Adam had anticipated and he only hoped he had stayed long enough to lay things on. It was of some reassurance that his assistant did not reappear and might well be playing a part in the plan.

As they moved from room to room, Adam could feel the tension rising. Wantilla's contrived interest in the splendid decor began to wane. Shastri, now fully aware of the predicament, was ignoring this moderation in his guest's attention. He was endeavouring to prolong the tour by describing the period and style of some of the architecture. Wantilla nibbled distractedly at one of his finger nails wondering how much longer he would have to endure this bore.

They progressed upstairs and were approaching the Royal Suite. This was where Adam would have to make his move and there was no margin for error. Adam and Shastri, and his loyal staff would be no match for this ruthless bunch. Adam hoped help would come soon. Shastri waited for all five of the party to assemble in the Royal Suite before starting his oration. Adam tried to look attentive but he was distracted by the gentle crunch of vehicles on the drive. Unobtrusively, he positioned himself near the door leading up to the ayah's quarters on the second floor and, crucially for him, down to his escape route. He could see two neat bolts on the door affording the occupants privacy from their servants, but of no use to him. What he needed was the key which was there sticking out of the lock. He turned his back to the door and was about the feel for the key, when he realised that the hawk-nosed character was watching him. Adam gave a sheepish grin and looked across at Shastri hoping to divert the man's gaze away from him. In the distance, Adam could hear the heavy tread of footsteps coming up the stairs beyond the landing. The hawk-nosed man heard them too and turned his head to the main door and in that instant; the key was in Adam's hand.

Simultaneously the woman servant burst into the room through the other door.

'Sahib! Sahib! The police are here! What shall I do?' The near hysteria conveyed by her voice brought instant reaction from everyone in the room. Shastri responded with a well-prepared exclamation.

'Tell them I'm busy. Do what you can to get rid of them!'

'I couldn't stop them, Shastri-sahib, they're coming along the landing now.' The woman was still speaking with evident distress.

Adam saw the driver reach to an inner pocket, and half withdraw an automatic. Wantilla saw it too.

'Put that away, you fucking idiot,' he hissed.

Wantilla seemed momentarily at a loss to know how to react to this totally unexpected development. Adam was in no such quandary. 'My God, the police! They mustn't find me here: that would be the end of my career.'

Adam couldn't work out whether the look of disbelief on Wantilla's face was at his statement or just the fact that the police were about to enter the room but there was no time to delay. He pushed open the servants' door and gave a parting shot. 'I must get out of here!' Just before the door shut behind him, he saw several plain clothes and two uniformed police burst into the room. Feeling for the lock, he put the key in and turned it. If Wantilla did hear him lock the door, he might just believe that fear for his career was driving Adam to escape.

Adam had suggested in his note to Shastri that the police could excuse their sudden visit by implying that they were looking for spies. The military situation between India and Pakistan was still simmering because of the Kashmir dispute so the *bhavan* might well be harbouring agitators. If Wantilla believed that Adam might also be the target of the detectives, so much the better.

How long Wantilla and his henchmen could be detained, he did not know. He was not a man to be intimidated by the authorities. The absence of a valid visa or a firearms permit might involve a visit to the police station, confiscation of their weapons and a magistrate's spot fine, but that need only be a matter of hours. There was not a moment to lose.

Adam raced down the steps and pulled open the angle-topped door, stepped onto the wide stone staircase, and closed the door behind him. Seconds later, he was in the tunnel and hurrying past the archway of the room reputed to have accommodated the eunuchs. The light was now fading and having no torch he was obliged to keep one hand on the side of the tunnel to check the direction. It became lighter again as he reached the ventilation shaft; then two minutes later he was in complete darkness once more. He ran on, awkwardly trailing his hand on the wall and hoping he didn't encounter any unexpected obstacle.

Although convection of the air prevented the midday heat finding its way down into the tunnel, he was dripping with perspiration by the time he reached the shaft under the old city wall. He skipped up the bottom three steps of the spiral staircase, and with heart pounding started the climb. The steps seemed to go on endlessly, and then above his head he saw the stone platform and it all came back to him. There was the tall stone with clear joints. Beside it was the smaller locking stone, the key to the exit.

He pushed hard and the stone swung inwards with a thud, exposing the neatly recessed handle. He snatched at it. Nothing moved and he pulled it again. His urgent tugging almost wrenched his arm from its socket. What could be wrong? Why did it not open like before? Taking a deep breath he tried to remain calm. He pushed the stone back into position and repeated the process, this time more gently, but the result was the same. There had to be some logical explanation for the malfunction. He really could do without being trapped at the end of this tunnel. The thought of an ignominious return to the *bhavan* was unbearable.

He leant back against the stone door taxing his brain for an answer. Something was preventing the door moving and with the locking stone still open, he began to search.

He pressed his head hard against the slit at the side of the stone door to listen for other sounds. A thin draught of air brushed his ear and with it came the sound of voices. If he could hear them, then why not the reverse? If only he could attract their attention, they might be able to release the door from the other side. He cupped his hands against the slit and repeatedly shouted the names of Pratap, Gopal and Samvat.

He paused to get his breath back and to look at his watch. Half an hour had passed since he had left the *bhavan*; it seemed like an age. He must have been calling on and off for about five minutes, when he recognised the voice of Gopal.

'Is someone there?'

'Gopal, it's me the brigadier.'

The door was released and an astonished Gopal welcomed Adam into the storeroom.

'So what went wrong with the door? Why couldn't I open it?'

'That's what happens when the locking stone is pushed too hard. It tilts the safety stone on the inside. There is a trick to correct it.'

'You must show me sometime, though I hope I never have to use it again.'

'How ever did you come to be here, Brigadier-sahib? We thought you were at Fallettis Hotel.'

'Yes, I realize that. But we have to move fast. I'll explain as we go along. Where is Pratap?'

'He's gone to see Ramiyar to arrange things for tomorrow's meeting.'

'Yes, I thought that's where he might be. We must get hold of him immediately.'

They went through the *dukan* and Adam was greeted by an incredulous Samvat.

'Brigadier-sahib, I thought...?'

'I'll tell you all about it later.'

Leaving a speechless Samvat, Gopal and Adam rushed out into the street and hailed a taxi.

An hour after leaving Samvat's *dukan,* they had made three calls and Pratap was now with them.

'Head out of the Old City towards Aitcheson College,' Adam instructed the taxi driver. 'We want to go to the princes' bungalows. From the Mall, I'll direct you where to go.'

He could not personally appear at the bungalow. As the captors knew him, Adam asked the taxi driver to drop him off one street away. The taxi then drove on to the bungalow where Gopal was dropped off. He walked up the drive and knocked on the door. It was opened by a housemaid. Gopal said, 'I am a student training to join the Foreign Service and have been told that there is a lady here who gives French lessons.'

'I am afraid she is resting and is not receiving visitors. Can you please call again in a day or two?'

'It really is very important, Shrimati,' Gopal said, giving the woman a little more status than her position justified. Having ascertained that the Frenchwoman was at home, he now gently persisted. 'If I could just have a word with the madame, I may be able to make an appointment.' Gopal gave a slightly pained expression. 'I have to give an answer to my professor. Please, Shrimati.'

Over the woman's shoulder, in the entrance hall, Gopal saw the heavy figure of a man lumbering towards them. He spoke coarsely in Urdu. 'What's going on here? What does this wallah want?'

Just the look of this man would have intimidated most people, but not Gopal, albeit that out of the corner of his eye he had seen Pratap coming up the drive. This new arrival served only to further provoke the ruffian.

'Get out of here, you two, *jaldi*! You are annoying my housemaid. Make it quick, before I put a bullet up your arse.'

Adam had made his way round to the service lane that ran along behind the bungalows. A thick hibiscus hedge screened him from the buildings as he walked along the lane. He waited behind the hedge a short distance from the back gate until he heard Gopal talking to the woman and when he heard the gruff voice of the man shouting abuse at the boys this was his signal. He hurried along the hedge, through the gate and up the short path to the back door. As anticipated, it was unlocked, and he slipped inside.

Reaching the door leading to the retired French couple's quarters, he found it ajar. Strains of classical music emanated from within. To make sure they were kept out of the action Adam carefully felt behind the door, removed the key, closed the door and then locked it from the outside. He moved cautiously into a passage and saw that there were four more exits. To the right were two archways: the first went through to the scullery with its dank cellar that he knew only too well; the second led to the butler's domain. And at the end of the passage was the ornate inlaid door of the princely suite where he expected to find Kafni. The snag was that to reach it he had to pass the wide archway leading into the entrance hall.

Both the servants were now involved in the noisy altercation at the front door. Adam slipped past the archway unobserved; returning would be the trickier. The thug and the housemaid had their back to him as he passed, but he hoped that the boys would have seen him pass.

He quietly tried the door of the suite. It was locked and predictably there was no key in the door. The housemaid must have it with her. As loudly as he dared, he whispered Kafni's name.

'Is that you, Adam?' she replied somewhat hesitantly.

'Stand back, I'm going to shoulder the door.'

He briefly wondered about damaging that beautiful door with its turquoise and gold inlay but then moved back and charged. It didn't seem to budge, so he took a longer run. This time the door flew open with a tremendous crash.

Kafni was standing ready as soon as the door swung back and he took her arm and pulled her through the doorway. He turned and was about to run with Kafni to the other end of the passage, when they saw the ruffian come through from the hallway waving a heavy revolver. At that range, the point four-five Colt would have blown a hole in Adam the size of a man's fist. But before the brute could take aim, they ducked through the nearest archway, into the butler's quarters, and slammed the door. They heard rapid foot steps, a thud and then a noise which sounded like a bull in agony. Through the door they heard the reassuring sound of Pratap's voice. 'Are you there, Brigadier? We have the situation under control.'

Adam opened the door to see him standing there smiling, holding the Colt. He glanced behind Adam to Kafni.

'Are you all right, mother?'

Before she could answer, he went up to Kafni; his six-foot frame towering above her, and briefly put his arm round her.

'Brilliant work,' said Adam. 'What happened to that brute?'

'Take a look through there.' Pratap pointed towards the archway with the pistol and Adam hurried through into the passage. There on the floor face down was the thug, now their prisoner, his arms securely held by a grinning Gopal with one foot on the man's back. 'He went down like a ninepin,' said Pratap, 'Gopal landed his shoe right in the middle of his back.'

'We must be quick,' Adam said, 'Wantilla and his mob could be back at any minute.'

The housemaid, now cowering in the hall, looked pleadingly at Kafni. 'I didn't want to do it, *Hazrat;* they forced me. They threatened to injure my son.'

'I understand,' Kafni assured her.

'Take your mother out to the taxi, Pratap. Get the driver to turn down the first street on the right and wait there. Gopal and I will tie up this wallah, and then we'll come through the back way and meet you there.'

Adam ripped the flex from a table lamp, and tied it tightly round the thug's wrists, then took a tea towel and gagged him.

'Are we going to leave him here, Brigadier?' Gopal asked

'No, I've a much more interesting billet planned. Take hold of his other leg.'

Ignoring the muffled protests they dragged him to the cellar, opened the door and unceremoniously rolled him down the steps before closing and bolting the door.

The housemaid had stood immobile, witnessing the activity.

'I think we'd better tie you up as well. Otherwise Wantilla will want to know why you let us get away. And where's your husband?'

'He's gone to the market for meat and vegetables, sahib.'

'Well he can untie you when he gets back. But I suggest you leave our "friend" in the cellar for as long as possible.'

The music was still emanating from the French couple's quarters.

No one stirred; had the occupants really been oblivious to the violent drama that had just been enacted? Adam replaced the key in their door but decided to leave it locked so they too would not suffer Wantilla's wrath. The haunting melody of Pietro Mascagni's beautiful opera rose to an appropriately thundering finale as Adam and Gopal made their escape.

They emerged from the rear gate of the bungalow and two minutes later they had joined Pratap and Kafni in the taxi and were heading rapidly back towards town. Adam looked at his watch. Just after four, still time to catch the bank. 'Straight on along the Mall to Bank Square,' he told the driver, who seemed unphased by any of the changes to their destination. He did, however, point to his meter. Gopal, sitting beside him, reassured him of the brigadier's ability to pay, and with an expression of equanimity the driver turned the taxi away from Aitcheson and into the Mall.

Sitting in the back of the taxi with Kafni next to him and Pratap on her other side was a strange feeling for Adam. It was the first time in Pratap's adult life that he had been with the two of them: a son who did not know him, believing instead that his father had been killed in battle; and the woman he had been refused permission to marry. Her beautiful profile still sent his heart racing; those lovely eyes with their long dark lashes, and the faint blush on her almost flawless skin. Only a small scar on her neck as a reminder of the ordeal she had endured twelve years before. They sat without speaking, lest the words betrayed their emotions.

Leaving Gopal to look after Kafni, Adam asked Pratap to come with him into the bank, where he drew a large sum of money. He handed Pratap a wad of bank notes.

'You'll need this. I want you to take your mother by train back to Lala Musa.' Pratap looked at the notes and shook his head. 'Why will I need so much, Brigadier?'

Adam longed to remove the formality between them but knew he couldn't.

'You'll understand why when I tell you what I want you to do. Your mother and Mandira must pack all their belongings and stand by to leave their bungalow at an hour's notice. Mandira must tell the school that your mother is indisposed and cannot take her classes at present. There's another thing: every morning before breakfast, then again after supper, Mandira must telephone Dr. Archibald at Nedoos Hotel.'

Adam wrote down the number and gave it to Pratap.

'He will tell her if there's any change of plan. And now, as soon as your mother is back at her bungalow with Mandira, you must go and see the Superintendent of Police at Lala Musa. Ask him please to arrange for two police reservists to be on guard at the bungalow for the next few days. Two men must be on duty there every hour of the day and night.'

'Will he agree to that?'

'I plan to call on the Divisional Commandant in Lahore this afternoon, and using General Malik's letter, ask him to call the superintendent and request his co-operation. To further smooth the path you will hand over sufficient funds for his men to be paid treble their normal rate.'

Pratap smiled and nodded.

'Now, we must get you down to Lahore Junction Station.'

There were the usual long queues at the booking window, and when Adam finally spoke to the clerk he regretted that there were no seats in Air Conditioned or in First Class. 'Too many people travelling Peshawar, sahib.' Adam flashed a couple of bank notes, and told him that he would be happy to compensate whoever might have to give up their seats.

'I would also like one seat reserved on the 6.30am train returning from Lala Musa tomorrow morning.' He slid more notes forward on the counter. 'I'll come back in half an hour, *babu*, I hope you can help me.'

Adam knew that Kafni and Pratap could always fall back on the slow train, but time was valuable and he had a lot to do. Getting them an air-conditioned compartment on the Khyber Mail express with only four brief stops was the least he could do.

When Adam returned to the booking-office clerk, his smiling face told him that all was well. 'One A.C. single to Lala Musa and one A.C. return sahib. Booking on 06.29 hours tomorrow, confirmed. Sixty-two rupees.' Adam paid and took the tickets.

'Two passengers pleased to help me for sahib; they are taking night train.'

'I'm very grateful, *babu*. Please give them this to pay for their extra meals.' He gave him another twenty rupees and received a "shukriya" on behalf of the imaginary passengers.

In the waiting room, Adam ran over arrangements for following day with Pratap. He would meet him off the train back at Lahore Station next morning at 09.00 hours. They would then go together to Samvat's *dukan* in the Old City to join Gopal.

Pratap excused himself to go and telephone his boss Dastur Ramiyar to confirm arrangements for the following day. It was a measure of the high regard Ramiyar had for Pratap that he had agreed to help them with their plan, even at some risk to his reputation. After delicate negotiations, and further reassurance from the bank as to his financial surety, they had arranged for Archie to see the "valuable piece" the following day. Pratap's anxiety was apparent.

'How can we be sure that it's all there? Only you and mother have ever seen the complete lingam.'

'At this stage we can't even be certain that it is the missing piece. Archie and Zaki have a detailed description, and if they are in any doubt Archie will say that he would like to think about it for twenty-four hours. If this looks too risky, we may have to carry on with just what's offered. To set things up a second time may be precarious.'

Pratap nodded. He seemed deep in thought, but satisfied with Adam's answers. Kafni, like Gopal, had sat listening in silence. Adam could not help wondering what was passing through her mind. As he looked at her he was suddenly overwhelmed with the desire to speak to her alone.

'Pratap I need to discuss some things with your mother, I wonder if you and Gopal wouldn't mind...'

'Of course,'said Pratap before Adam had even finished his sentence.

On their own at last Kafni gazed at Adam with studied expectation. He reached out and held her hand.

'I'm sorry about that. I hope they don't feel dismissed but I just needed to say something,' everything was moving so fast that he was finding it difficult to make sense of the turbulent feelings he had at that moment, 'I know there is no hope for us but I still love you very much.' She squeezed his hand and looked down in an attempt to disguise her emotions. 'In fact, you are the only true love I've ever had.'he said in conclusion.

'But what about your wife, Adam?'

'She's asked me for a divorce.'

'Oh, I am sorry.'

'Don't be. It never really worked. She was far too interested in her political career and anyway there is another man in her life now.'

'Did you have children?'

'No. We tried for years but to be honest we were never together in the same place long enough.'

'That didn't seem a problem for us,' she said, letting her guard down for a moment.

'I'm very proud of our boy. I only wish I could tell him.'

She gave a deep sigh and said, 'I don't know how to thank you for coming to find me and the lingam. I can scarcely believe it, but I feel I can go home now.'

'We haven't got it yet.'

At that moment Pratap and Gopal returned.

'Right then you had better be getting on that train and I need to go now,' Adam said. 'I must see the Divisional Commandant, and also get hold of Shastri before he leaves the office. I'll see you in the morning, Pratap. Do you want a lift in my taxi, Gopal?'

'No, thank you, Brigadier-sahib, I'll wait and see the Rajkumari and Pratap onto their train.'

Adam looked over at Kafni and smiled, suppressing his overwhelming desire to kiss her.

'*Namaste*, Kafni, we'll see each other again soon.'

'*Namaste*, Adam, I hope so.'

So much more that could have been said and Adam would happily have listened to her gentle voice for hours.

Falletti's Hotel, Lahore.

'There are telephone messages for you, Cullworthy-sahib.' The reception clerk handed him his key and a sheet of notepaper from pigeonhole "C". He returned the key.

'I'm not stopping, I just want the envelope I left in the safe yesterday.'

'Of course, Brigadier-sahib.' He opened the safe and took out the envelope with General Malik's letter inside. 'You did not return to the hotel last night, sahib. Is your room and our service satisfactory?'

'Yes, very satisfactory, thank you. I was just delayed for the night.'

On his way to the Commandant's office, he looked at the sheet of notepaper the receptionist had given him. There were messages from

Harish and Archie and then a number he didn't recognise. Back in his room he called the number. A woman answered, then Shastri came on the line. He had left the office early, and knew that Adam would want an update as soon as he returned to the hotel. He confirmed that Wantilla had been charged with both illegal possession of a firearm and entering Pakistan without a visa, and that after paying his fines he had left the police station in a blinding rage.

Adam knew that Wantilla would now pull out all the stops, even to the point of recklessness, but he was determined to stay two steps ahead of him. There was also just a possibility that he still believed the lingam was at Kashmir Bhavan.

Adam called Archie.

'Boy, am I pleased to hear you. Where the hell have you been?'

'It's a long story which I'd rather not tell you now. Can we meet in my hotel? Say in half an hour.'

There were things he deliberately wanted to have overheard, but the events of the past twenty-four hours and the plans for the next twenty-four hours needed to be discussed beyond snooping ears.

They met for tea in the garden at Faletti's where they could be certain they would not be overheard. Adam brought him up to date on the kidnapping and escape.

'Wow! that was a close call, Adam. Well, everything is set up for tomorrow. With all the people now involved we can only have one shot at this. I hope you've been practising your American accent, old buddy?'

'Shoor have, buddy. I'd even paas on Maayne Street, Stamford Connecticut.'

'I shouldn't think those hoods will stop to question it; they'll be too preoccupied with other thoughts,' commented Archie. 'By the way, I've got your passport back, and the documents from our "friend." I had to pay extra for an A.C. train fare on the Quetta Express because he'd had to send a man up to Rawalpindi to acquire some headed notepaper from the minister's office. I'm afraid they skinned me on the price but what do you expect. The mug shots came out well; the old crook claimed that even the Chief of Police himself wouldn't be able to fault the documents.'

'Well, I hope to God he's right, Archie. We're skating on very thin ice here. I'll send Gopal round in the morning to pick them up on his way to the theatrical costumiers.'

After Archie left Adam called Harish, who, sanguine as ever, confirmed all the arrangements had been made as planned. 'Your son's done an excellent job here, Harish. I am sure you will be pleased to see him again.'

'Yes, I will.' Chandra replied, not revealing any emotion.

'Anything else from your end?'

'Yes, I am afraid your man Williams in London has sent a telegram with a request from General Festing that you to make urgent contact.

It seemed improbable that the General had personally made this request, yet Adam did not think that Williams would stick his neck out without any grounds. But with Williams in his present frame of mind, one could never tell. A brigadier, who had been passed over, was hardly the most unbiased person to be dealing with a younger brigadier who was about to be given early promotion to major-general. With the uncertainty of the next thirty-six hours, Adam would have to tough it out. To invent a temporary illness would be a dangerous course to take, inviting a gruelling examination, both verbal and physical, on his return to England.

Adam showered and changed. He had two painful bruises from where he had hit the wall and the stairs when thrown into the cellar. Fortunately neither of them were visible. In the hotel dining room he enjoyed a long awaited *Jheenga Masala* curry, both the surroundings and the food a great contrast to his last meal shared with the rats in the cellar.

CHAPTER THIRTY EIGHT

Anarkali, Lahore, Saturday 30th May.

Zaki and Behan Boolajee had done a remarkable job. They had organised a private auction. Zaki had convinced the seller's agent that in this way they would get the best price. 'Once they have seen the jewels,' Zaki had said, 'they will be falling over themselves to bid. And there are several other parties interested: at least two oil sheiks have given me authority to put in bids for them, so your rich American will not have it all his own way.'

Because they knew that the vendors would wish to cash their cheque immediately after the sale, the auction was set for 2.30pm, allowing them time to get to the bank before it closed at 4.30pm.

The venue chosen was the special showroom at the rear of Zaki's private offices. They were away from his main business premises and used only for exclusive customers. These were generally rich clients who did not wish to be seen visiting his public showrooms. The displays would be laid out beforehand, and the employees would leave before the arrival of the customers, who preferred not to draw attention to their wealth. The only staff exceptions were the burly *chokidar,* who would remain outside, and a trusted staff *khitmagar* who made tea and coffee and served cakes, biscuits, and *halwa.* The seller's agent had had considerable reservations about the privacy and security of the venue for the auction. But Zaki had taken him on an inspection tour of the premises, and convinced him that the rare rugs and carpets in his salon were nearly as valuable as the jewels which were to be auctioned. Zaki had his own reasons for wishing to keep the jewels well out of the public eye.

The auction was to be conducted by Dastur Ramiyar, Pratap's employer. Boolajee had confirmed that he was a jeweller of high repute. He was already well known to Zaki, but there was another advantage: he was a successful fellow Parsee business associate of Boolajee, who trusted him completely. When after tactful soundings Boolajee had taken Ramiyar into his confidence, he had been only too pleased to help his young protégé. And to justify Pratap's presence at the auction, Ramiyar would bring him as his clerk and assistant.

The seller's agent had no hesitation in accepting Ramiyar as the auctioneer. Not only did he meet the criteria of competence; his reputation would lend an element of respectability to the disposal of these items, thus screening their dubious provenance. His commission for conducting the sale was therefore readily agreed by the agent.

The seller, who did not wish to be identified by name, *would* be in attendance at the auction, but would be represented there by his agent, who, somewhat reluctantly, introduced himself as Jamal Shah.

There was to be one other member of the seller's party, a Mister Khan. His rôle, as it was described, was to co-ordinate with Shri Ramiyar on behalf of the vendor and, if required, give a second opinion on values. Mr Khan had also reserved the right to bid on his own behalf for the jewels. This last facility appeared to present a conflict of interests and when Gopal was told about the arrangement he became suspicious. It rang a bell in his mind; where had he heard the name Khan before? And then it came to him, it was that unctuous *wyapari* in that little shop in the city who had mentioned the name. After a suitable sweetener Gopal had learnt that from time to time the *wyapari* acted as a fence for Khan. It took a second sweetener for Gopal to learn that Khan had already bought a part-share in the lingam jewels, and that his real motive for taking part in the auction was to discover who had the other parts of the sculpture. This confirmed to Gopal that the seller knew that the jewels were only part of a more substantial treasure. From this he also deduced that Khan was either the original thief or was closely associated with him.

There were now three prospective customers: Archie, and two sheiks whose letters of authority and bank credit guarantees were held by Zaki. The sheiks' credentials were genuine enough, but Zaki had been told in separate communications from them that both were only interested in unusual individual stones for their own royal jewellers to mount. This had intentionally not been stated in the letters of authority, nor did Zaki intend to acquaint the vendors of that fact. Archie had already seen and examined some of the stones which had been removed from the sculpture, probably in a crude attempt to disguise their origin. Only the temptation of huge sums of cash had lured the vendors to put the complete phallus into the auction ring.

The Auction. Zaki's salon, Anarkali.

Shri Dastur Ramiyar and Pratap had arrived early so that they could run over the intended procedure for the auction. It had been a smiling Zaki who greeted them. He conducted them through to the air-conditioned private display salon where a long, highly polished mahogany table graced the centre of the room. On each side of the table were four high-backed chairs upholstered in rich deep-red velvet, and at the near end was a matching carver with a blue and gold crest woven into the back. Beyond the table were about a dozen superb oriental carpets draped on tall racks to display their splendid colours to full advantage. Even Pratap, who had been surrounded by beautiful rugs and carpets all his life, was struck by the excellence of these exhibits.

Ramiyar, himself something of a connoisseur of oriental carpets said, 'You certainly have some magnificent specimens here. I wonder what tales they could tell.'

'You may indeed wonder, Shri Ramiyar. We shall probably never know their true stories. Most of them have been lost in the mists of time.'

'Tell me about this carpet,,' Ramiyar asked, pointing over to the great Mamluk that hung in pride of place in the centre.

Zaki smiled as he responded facetiously, 'Ah, so you noticed?'

'I could hardly miss it. It's the biggest carpet here.'

Zaki turned to the carpet with its velvet pile reflecting the dark shades of moss green and blue. 'This is one that I could never part with. It has very personal associations for the family. My father searched Egypt for it for years. He had been commissioned to find a Mamluk by the Maharajah of Bhatinda, but unfortunately on our arrival in India my father found the Maharajah facing bankrupcy. At the time, no other buyer could be found and it has remained in the family as a sort of insurance against hard times.'

'In which case I hope you never find yourself in the position of having to sell it,' said Ramiyar

Zaki looked at his watch, 'I'm afraid we have run out of time to talk about carpets. The other guests should be arriving soon.'

Walking back towards the table, Pratap looked around the room. Oil paintings of the cities of Teheran, Tabriz, Kashan and Shiraz, in splendid gilt frames, hung on the walls. And at the far end, gazing out at the Mamluk carpet was the portrait of the inscrutable founder: Zaki's father. The surroundings conveyed an aura of opulence conducive to lavish spending.

Pratap had come equipped for the part. He was wearing steel-rimmed spectacles, giving the effect of a studious junior *babu*. He carried a portable goldsmith's balance,a jeweller's eyeglass, gemstone reference manual and a black velvet display cloth, which he laid out in the middle of the table.

The vendor, his agent, and Mr. Khan arrived together a few minutes after 2.00pm. There was a perfunctory introduction of themselves, with mumbled names and no handshakes. They were then taken through to the viewing salon and seated at the table. It was not surprising that the seller declined to offer his hand; it was too earnestly occupied clutching a leather Gladstone bag. Even as he awkwardly drew a chair up to the table, he was unwilling to surrender his grip on the handle.

Shri Ramiyar took the seat at the head of the table and placed a baize-backed cream-coloured board in front of him. He then produced a small rosewood gavel, a watch and a notepad, and laid them on the board. His demeanour and self-assurance conveyed professionalism; he was ready for business. The *khitmagar* came through bearing a tray of small cups of Turkish coffee: strong and very sweet. He placed one beside each person at the table and alongside it a glass of water. Pratap walked to the last chair on the left where he set up his scales, then with a studious air laid his manual and eyeglass on the table, and sat expressionless facing the swarthy countenance of the vendor and his agent Jamal, who was already perspiring heavily.

Boolajee and Archie were the last to arrive for the auction. Zaki acted out their reception and then brought them through to the viewing salon. There, after brief introductions, he suggested their seating. His casual manner obscured the careful prearrangement: Archie next to Pratap; then Boolajee; Zaki himself next to Ramiyar.

As soon as everyone was seated, Ramiyar opened the proceedings. His proficient manner and air of detachment was most impressive. 'I have,' he announced, 'been appointed by the owner's agent, Shri Jamal Shah, to auction privately certain valuable and very rare jewels. Some of these I have already had the privilege of examining. And I believe that you Dr. Archibald have also seen these fine specimens.'

'I sure have,' responded Archie, 'but I'm hoping to see a lot more than that today.'

'I do not think the doctor will be disappointed.' Jamal Shah articulated well, but was unable to mask his unctuous lisp. This was the first positive indication that they were going to actually see the missing part of the lingam and all the jewels.

'Before I ask Shri Jamal Shah to display the objects for our inspection, will those who wish to bid please present their credentials and client authorisation with their bank letters of credit worthiness. These, as I'm sure you know, must have been endorsed and stamped with today's date by a bank here in Lahore, confirming that the amounts stated may be drawn in cash, immediately after the sale.' As he said this, Jamal Shah nodded his concurrence.

'The conditions of sale,' continued Ramiyar, 'are that I shall give an opinion on the quality rating of the gems and jewels being offered; beyond that, they are to be purchased as seen; the vendor reserves the right to confirm or reject the final price after the fall of the hammer. The bidding shall be in rupees, stated in lakhs, and crores. Upon completion of the auction, I shall take temporary charge of the merchandise, then proceed with the vendor and his agent in their own car to the nominated bank, where we shall meet the purchaser and make delivery within banking hours. I understand that those of you who intend bidding have arranged with your bank to have the use of a private office for the money to be counted. Are there any questions so far?'

There was a murmur of general approval and nodding of heads at the thoroughness of the arrangements. The trace of a smile crept over the vendor's face.

'There are two other conditions which I believe are of equal benefit to buyers and sellers. In the interests of security, the auction must be completed within thirty minutes of my declaring it open; and the successful purchaser must give his solemn oath on the Vedas, the Bible or the Koran, that no publicity will be made until the elapse of thirty days after the purchase.' Again there were voices of approval.

There followed a flurry and interchange of letters and papers handed first to Shri Ramiyar for his examination and notation. They were then passed on to the seller and his agent for their scrutiny. This procedure completed Ramiyar then announced the names of the four parties he had approved to enter the bidding: Mr Khan, Dr. Archibald and two Sheiks from the Gulf States, both to be represented by Shri Zaki Ibrahim. Ramiyar looked across the table, 'We are ready for your presentation, Shri Jamal Shah.'

Jamal Shah looked round and muttered something in Urdu,

whereupon the seller placed the Gladstone bag on the table, took a key from his pocket, unlocked and then opened the bag. There was complete silence in the room, followed by muted gasps, as the seller removed from the bag, two superb blood-red Burmese rubies and a group of matched Kashmir sapphires, then the dazzling sculpture of the phallus itself. As he reached out and placed it on the black velvet cloth in the centre of the table everyone seemed stunned by its splendour. Row upon row of faultless rubies ran up the shaft, their deep rich colour and transparency skilfully enhanced by the thousands of facets of the pure white diamonds that interspersed them.

The agent reached over to adjust its position, causing a brilliant ripple of light to run along the sculpture as it caught the beam of the spotlights. It was now possible to see clearly where the rubies and sapphires had been removed from their original settings in the golden phallus. Ramiyar stood up and made a brief examination with his eyeglass. He then commented upon the beauty and artistic construction of the sculpture and assessed the quality and purity of the component gems. He accurately identified each group by their source and rarity, drawing particular attention to the Burmese rubies.

Ramiyar resumed his seat. 'Gentlemen, I shall first invite bids for the whole collection of jewels which you see displayed. If the vendor declines to accept the highest bid, the jewels will be offered in three lots: the rubies, the sapphires, and then the sculpture.'

Despite the air conditioning, Archie began to sweat. They had rehearsed every detail of the plan but something could always go wrong. He had in front of him a pad setting out the amounts in rupees, lakhs and crores, and their approximate equivalents in sterling. A lakh of rupees was one hundred thousand; a crore of rupees, one hundred lakhs, which was ten million rupees. His credit facility had been given by the bank at two crores - more than one and a half million pounds sterling - this was a genuine facility. Archie's mind boggled at the credit rating of Jardeeson. Holy shit, he thought, he couldn't commit that sort of money. Suppose something went wrong and he was forced to actually make the payment? Could he shoot his way out? That automatic in his waist belt might be the real thing, but he'd only intended to use it for effect. And he didn't doubt that Khan and Shah would be similarly armed and equally prepared to use their shooters. One thing was for sure: he was not going to bid to the full extent of his credit on the first round.

'Who will open the bidding on the total collection, gentlemen?'

Complete silence. Archie could feel his heart thumping; this was worse than waiting for a Jap ambush in a Burmese jungle. Then Khan spoke, 'Fifty lakhs.'

Zaki now bid: 'Sixty lakhs.' That's funny, thought Archie, he was only supposed to be interested in the stones - must know what he's doing. Maybe he was making intervening bids in the early stages to keep them guessing.

'Seventy lakhs,' blurted Archie.

'Eighty lakhs.' Khan again.

'Ninety lakhs,' Archie continued getting into the rythym of things.

'One crore!' Khan once more.

So, we know they want more than that, Archie thought, this bugger already owns part of it.

'One crore, one lakh.' Zaki, this time. He must be confident they won't sell at that, thought Archie.

'One crore, two lakhs.' Archie.

'One crore, three lakhs,' Khan.

'One crore, four lakhs.' Archie.

'One and a half crores.' Khan.

This is where I pause to see what happens, thought Archie. He had another half crore in hand, but he wasn't going to push it. Let Jamal Shah sweat, he won't want Khan to buy it.

Ramiyar looked at Jamal Shah. 'Are you selling, Shri Shah?'

Jamal turned to the vendor, who, Archie knew must decline. There was a shake of the head.

'Any more bids, gentlemen?'

Silence around the room.

'Very well, gentlemen, we will break for five minutes, then I will offer the three separate lots.'

Everyone relaxed. All stayed seated except the seller who got up and left the room.

What's he up to, thought Archie; probably gone for a piss; hope the bugger's not gone long. Two minutes later and he was back in his seat. Archie looked at his watch; the sale was about to re-commence.

Ramiyar tapped the ivory board with his gavel. 'I'm asking for bids for the matched pair of rubies. I believe my assistant has an approximate weight. Pratap?'

'*Han, sahib.* Four hundred and fifty carats each.'

'They are superb stones. May I suggest an opening bid of two lakhs?'

Zaki nodded.

'Two lakhs, fifty thousand rupees.' Khan was bidding.

There was a knock at the door, and the *khitmagar* entered.

'I told you that under no circumstance were we to be disturbed.' Zaki had stood up and there was an angry tone in his voice.

'Very sorry, Ibrahim-sahib. They are insisting that they must attend sale.'

Pratap detected considerable unease on the faces of the three men sitting opposite him.

Ramiyar banged his gavel down, and, with high indignation, said. 'This is outrageous. I will not be interrupted in the middle of a private auction. Get rid of them!' There was momentary relief on the faces of Khan, Shah, and the vendor. But it was only fleeting; the *khitmagar* was pushed aside, and a middle-aged man entered. He was dressed in a well-cut khaki drill suit and wearing a pure white *puggaree*.

'I'm afraid he cannot do that.' The man spoke in Urdu and with authority.

'Who are you?' Zaki asked, echoing the indignation of Ramiyar.

'I am Detective-Inspector Shastri from Special Branch, Rawalpindi.' A smartly turned out uniformed constable now came in and stood beside him. Shastri continued, 'I am sorry to disturb you, gentlemen.' His tone was intended to put them at ease, and he looked around with a benign smile. The vendor attempted to respond but only the lower part of his jaw operated, producing an apish grin.

'If we can get this over with quickly, gentlemen, you may resume your business.'

'Before we do any talking, where's your authority and identity?' Zaki's manner displayed a command of the situation.

'Of course, sahib.' Shastri produced a suitably worn-looking leather wallet with a plastic window, behind which was a Police Identity card. He handed it to Zaki together with a letter typed on Police Headquarters headed paper. Zaki studied both of these intensely, waggling his head in approval, the set of his jaw clearly indicating that they were in order. The documents were handed on to Ramiyar, who gave them a dignified examination, then passed them over to Khan on the right of the table, where they were scrutinised simultaneously by Jamal, Khan and the vendor.

'May we proceed, gentlemen?' Shastri spoke in a tone that brooked no dissent.

Whereupon Zaki walked quickly over and collected the

documents, then took them to the other side of the table and held them to give Archie and Boolajee a perfunctory glance. The implication was clear: if they were acceptable to him, the proprietor of the salon that should be sufficient.

'Thank you, Detective Inspector.' Zaki handed the wallet and letter back to Shastri.

'Thank you, sir. Now that you have seen my authority, I would like to introduce Chief Inspector Poole from the Washington office of Interpol.'

Archie pushed his chair back and looked uneasy as he glanced around for an exit route.

Chief Inspector Poole sauntered into the room, dressed in a lightweight grey suit that hung loosely from his tall thin frame. 'Who's in chaaarge here?'

Zaki came towards him with a look of studied indignation.

'These are my premises. How can I help you?' he said tersely as he flicked another jade bead along its string.

'You wanna see my paypers?'

'I certainly do. And I shall have some strong words to say to the Commissioner of Police about you barging in here like this.'

'Yeah, why don't you do that, Sir, I've got his signature here.' He handed Zaki an American passport and a headed letter signed by the District Police Commissioner.

Zaki looked quickly at these, shaking his head with disbelief and annoyance. He passed the two documents to Ramiyar. 'I must apologise, Shri Ramiyar, the police are going to hear a lot more about this!'

Ramiyar offered the documents to Khan, who looked at them, but seemed too dumbfounded to concentrate on their contents. Shah also glanced at them, and the vendor gave an impatient and dismissive wave of his hand, implying...get on with it. His hand moved towards the jewels and he picked up a corner of the velvet cloth, doubtless intending to flick it over the dazzling display; but there was insufficient spare material. Shah's right hand reached over to restrain the vendor's arm, and his stern look implied... *That's a stupid move.*

Inspector Poole walked up to the head of the table and stood beside, Ramiyar. 'Sorry about this, Sir, it shouldn't take long.' He took a document from an inside pocket and opened it, then looked at Archie. 'James Arthur Strickland, alias Doctor Hugh Archibald, I have a warrant here for your arrest. You are charged with the theft of jewels from a suite in the Waldorf Astoria Hotel in Noo York on 25th January 1957. Enna thing you say...'

Archie stood up. 'This is ridiculous!'

Poole continued ... 'will be taken down and may be used in evidence against you.'

'Not so fast, Poole, you haven't got me yet.' Archie took the automatic from his waistband. He pointed the weapon round in a menacing sweep, and then edged from the table to be in a position to cover everyone in the room. He looked across the table. 'Get up! Get yer hands above the table.' His manner was so menacing and his glare so sinister, that Khan, Shah and the vendor instantly struggled to their feet and moved back from the table. 'Now the rest of you, on your feet. I'm ready to use this shooter, so back off, Poole.' Archie had now moved round a few feet and was directing the automatic straight at Poole. 'Let me get out of here, and no one will get hurt.'

'This is outrageous!' Ramiyar remonstrated. 'Didn't you thoroughly check him out, Boolajee?'

Poole now spoke, 'Back away everybody, he's dangerous.'

'Move aside, Poole, It's time for me to leave this happy gathering.'

In the brief second that his concentration was directed at Poole, there was a movement to his left. He swung round, but it was too late. Pratap's flying tackle overbalanced him, simultaneously knocking the automatic from his hand. Archie hit the floor emitting a flow of obscene American oaths, as Pratap followed him down, grappling to prevent him retrieving the weapon. The young uniformed police constable ran forward and grabbed one of Archie's arms.

'Quick, put the cuffs on him, constable.' The command came from Shastri.

Moments later, Archie was dragged to his feet, his hands securely handcuffed behind his back.' Pratap had picked up the automatic.

'Well done, Pratap,' said Ramiyar.

Shastri gave a huff of appreciation as a murmur of relief passed round the room. The vendor returned to his seat at the table, and appeared about to make another attempt to cover up the jewels. Again Shah dissuaded him, this time by a grunt.

'Well, that seems to have dealt with what we came for.' Shastri gave a token bow. 'My apologies, sahibo, we'll leave you to get on with your business. You, Strickland, are coming with us to the station. You'll have the opportunity to make a statement and call a lawyer.'

'Not so bloody fast, Inspector. Someone here's dropped me in this shit, and if I'm going down, that fucking rat is going down with me.' He glowered at Boolajee.

'No, No! You're wrong, I was nothing to do with this.' Boolajee whined like a cornered Judas. 'I'm a respectable businessman. You must have tricked my friend in London into trusting you.' Regaining his composure he straightened the lapels of his beautifully tailored blue suit.

Archie gave a chilling laugh. 'Listen to him, Inspector. Who's going to be the next son-of-a bitch to try and scuttle out of the sinking ship.'

'Come on, Strickland. You're not making things any easier for yourself.'

'Oh no? Well, just listen to this buddy: *THOSE JEWELS ARE STOLEN!* I even know just where they came from.'

A look of horror passed over the faces of the vendor and his agent. The vendor's hand moved down to his waist to feel the reassuring bulge of his revolver. Was this the moment to use it, or could he bluff his way out? No, there were too many people in the room. Let agent Shah come up with something; that's what he was being paid for.

Khan's eyes narrowed as he mentally searched for the wisest course of action. A nonchalant stance was required; there was after all nothing to connect him with the origin of the jewels. He leant back in his chair apparently quite unconcerned.

Pratap, relieved of his captive by the police constable, moved unobtrusively round behind the carpet displays and reappeared close to the vendor. The look he gave the vendor could have been interpreted as reassuring and protective. Pratap had, after all, just a few moments before, courageously intervened to prevent an ugly situation. The vendor, however, drew no such conclusion; he would have preferred Pratap to remain on the other side of the room, especially as he was still holding the automatic.

'What's this that Strickland is saying?' Inspector Shastri addressed Shri Ramiyar. 'Who is offering these jewels for sale, burra-sahib?'

Ramiyar looked across the table to Jamal Shah. 'You're the vendor's agent, Shri Shah, who actually owns these jewels?'

'They belong to my client here...' He indicated to his left, 'whose interests I represent.'

The vendor looked very uneasy. This was not the clever answer he had hoped for. He mumbled something in Punjabi to Shah, which Pratap understood as, 'In the name of Allah, think of something more to tell them.'

Shah spoke again. 'The vendor has reminded me that he is the trustee of a private collection of family treasure, whose beneficiaries have asked him to find a suitable buyer.' The vendor looked satisfied with this explanation.

Shastri nodded his head in contemplation, 'In that case, you will be able to produce proof of ownership and an authority to offer these jewels for sale?'

The vendor looked unhappy again. Perhaps it was not such a clever answer to have given. He half turned his head toward Shah.

'Yes, certainly, Inspector, I have both those documents in my office.'

'If you believe that, Inspector, you'll believe the moon's made of cheese,' Strickland interjected.

'Inspector, can't Chief Inspector Poole and your constable take this unpleasant fellow away?' Khan had decided to intervene in a pseudo-cultured manner. 'I'm sure we can then sort this out quite satisfactorily.'

'You see, that hood wants me out of the way, Inspector. He's probably part of it.'

'Just keep quiet, Strickland,' Poole said, 'we don't need any advice from you.'

'Constable, take Strickland into the other room whilst I deal with this business,' said Shastri reasserting himself.

'*Han Inspector-sahib.* The constable reacted immediately, firmly leading his handcuffed prisoner out of the room.

'Under the circumstances,' Shastri continued, 'this becomes a matter for the Lahore Police. It is therefore my duty to take charge of these jewels and hand them over for safe keeping to the superintendent of Lahore C.I.D. I shall issue an official receipt and they can be returned as soon as the correct documents are presented at his office.'

The vendor looked extremely unhappy, and muttered to his agent, again in Punjabi, 'I don't like this; do something.'

Jamal Shah framed a protest, but as he opened his mouth to speak Ramiyar pre-empted him. He stood up and raised his hand. 'Wait! I'm not satisfied with this.' Some relief showed on the face of the vendor, but his misery returned as he listened to Ramiyar. 'I have been lawfully appointed to conduct this auction. I therefore formally declare this sale is postponed but I feel I should be responsible for the safe custody of the jewels. Inspector, I'm sure this is a misunderstanding and that the vendor and his agent will be able to quickly produce the papers you have asked for.'

There was a nod and murmur of agreement from Shah. 'These are valuable jewels, and will have to be sealed in a container to ensure that they are not tampered with. My reputation is at stake here. I assume you have a good safe here, Shri Ibrahim?'

Zaki nodded, 'Yes, we have a modern Chubb.'

Khan, seeing his investment at risk now intervened. 'As a professional jeweller I think the jewels would be safer in my custody. I'm sure these gentlemen would agree.'

Verbal concurrence was given, and, in the fleeting hope that this might be agreed, relief showed on the faces of Shah and the vendor.

'I could, of course, take charge of the goods myself,' said Ramiyar. 'This would be the normal course at a public auction. So, we now have four possibilities for the safe keeping of the jewels.'

'I am afraid my chief would not approve of any other alternative,' Shastri interjected, 'the jewels must be impounded at the police station.'

'Just a moment, Inspector Shastri,' Ramiyar said, 'there are a couple of things I'd like to clear up. First of all, this was a very private auction. Just how did you know when and where it was to take place?'

In that brief moment of silence before Shastri replied, many eyes were cast round the room. If the inspector was not going to tell them, perhaps the informer would in some way betray himself.

'It was not too difficult.' Shastri spoke in a calm and confidential tone, 'Chief Inspector Poole has been shadowing Strickland for weeks, and our branch of Interpol in Pakistan has been assisting him. As time went on Strickland became over-confident and careless on the telephone. We tapped his calls.'

'I see,' Ramiyar continued, 'So you are from headquarters in Rawalpindi. We would have to confirm with the Police in Lahore, that you have authority to take temporary charge of such valuable items. Shri Shah perhaps you or Shri Khan, would you care to telephone the Chief of the C.I.D?'

This comment was a calculated gamble, and in case they should toy with the idea of faking the telephone call, Ramiyar added, 'Inspector Shastri can go into the office with you and get through to the number.'

Shah's confidence in Ramiyar was now at a high level. He clearly was not intimidated by the police. Shah himself was not keen to offer his own name to the police, it might well arouse suspicion. The fewer names that were mentioned, the better. No, let Ramiyar do it and use his name; these Parsees were usually well in with the authorities. But he decided before answering that he must get the agreement of the other two. If it came to the worst, they could forge the documents, and collect the jewels in the morning. 'May I just consult my client?'

'Of course.'

Shah got up and the other two followed him to the end of the room where the carpets were being displayed. They whispered briefly, but Pratap did manage to catch the words, "...easily make up some documents." The three returned to the table.

'We think that you, Shri Ramiyar, as the auctioneer, should telephone the police.'

'As you wish, Shri Shah. Shri Ibrahim may we use your telephone?'

'With pleasure, Ramiyar-sahib, it's through in my office.'

At that moment, the *khitmagar* entered. 'Excuse please, Ibrahim-sahib, Lahore police are telephoning; they are wishing to be speaking with Inspector Shastri.'

Zaki looked at Shastri with disdain. 'Why are they telephoning here? This is a private number.'

'Very sorry, Ibrahim-sahib. We've been co-ordinating with them; they'll wish to know if Chief Inspector Poole wants an additional escort. We arrived in a taxi to avoid arousing Strickland's suspicion; he is a wily man. I must go and tell them to send another car.'

'Then make sure it's an unmarked car. I do not wish to have any sirens or police cars arriving at these premises,' Zaki said.

'Understood, sahib.' Shastri turned to leave the room, but was intercepted by Ramiyar. 'Wait, Inspector. I will first talk to the police; I have some questions to ask. You can speak to them afterwards.'

'Yes, Shri Ramiyar, you must speak to them,' Khan concurred, confident that he would effectively deal with this matter.

Ramiyar left the room, and two minutes later, after again apologising to Zaki, Shastri followed him.

Five minutes later Ramiyar and the Inspector returned to an expectant silence, as everyone waited to hear the result of the telephone call.

'It was the C.I.D. Superintendent. I am afraid he insisted that the jewels must be held by the police. He has confirmed that Shastri is authorised to issue a receipt and take custody of the jewels. However, to ensure that they are not tampered with, they must be sealed before being handed over. Can that travelling bag be locked Shri Shah?'

Although Shah approved of this official procedure, his disappointment was obvious as he confirmed that there was indeed a key. He had no choice but to accept the situation. There was an armed man standing behind him, Shastri would certainly draw his police revolver at the first hint of trouble; and there were two more policemen outside. To willingly co-operate with these police officers would be viewed favourably by the authorities and allay suspicions. In twenty-four hours' time this unfortunate intervention would be over and they would have regained possession of the jewels. They could then make a quick sale to one of Zaki Ibrahim's sheiks: Shah had already seen their purchase authorities so he knew the money was available. He turned to the vendor who nodded reluctantly.

Under the watchful eye of everyone, the vendor carefully placed all the jewels in the Gladstone bag, and with trembling hands took out a key, turned it in the lock, and returned it to his pocket.

Zaki had produced some sealing wax, a miniature methylated burner, and a length of stout cord. Shah wrapped this round the bag, under the handle, and heated the wax ready to seal the cord ends. 'Do you have a seal, Shri Shah?' asked Zaki.

A brief conference ensued and the vendor produced a small crested dagger, the engraved head of which he used to mark the wax. Shastri wrote out a receipt on a sheet of his notepad rubber stamped with "Police Headquarters" at the head. 'You will be able to collect this tomorrow morning at Central Police Headquarters, as soon as the Chief Superintendent has seen your authority from the family trust,' said Shastri, as he handed over the receipt to Shah and lifted the heavy Gladstone bag.

The *khitmagar* entered the salon and announced that the car had arrived for the inspector. Zaki nodded and then instructed the *khitmagar* to make tea. He then addressed his guests, 'Gentlemen, you will please join me in refreshments after this unpleasant interruption.'

'Yes, most unfortunate,' complained Boolajee, 'I shall now probably have to appear in court. I was guarantor for that villain on behalf of my friend in London.'

Whilst he was speaking, Shastri had quietly left the room. The vendor had stood up and was moving towards the door, but his agent gently put his hand on his arm to detain him. Pratap caught the mumbled Urdu words, "useless" and, "tomorrow."

'Gentlemen, I think we should accept Shri Ibrahim's invitation.' Ramiyar addressed the six who remained in the room; it was almost a command. 'Certainly I need some refreshment after that episode.'

In the background, Pratap heard a door close, and a car drive away. The immediate danger was over. He returned to his seat.

CHAPTER THIRTY NINE

The Punjab, Pakistan, Sunday 31ˢᵗ May.

Eighteen hours later as Adam sat in the taxi heading for the Pakistan border post at Wagah, he had mixed feelings. So far, events had gone according to plan. It was no mean success. But they were not out of the woods yet. He needed to telephone the War Office and try to speak to the Vice-C.I.G.S.or if necessary, General Festing himself, but as it was Sunday this would not be possible. He was confident that Jardeeson had personally delivered his request for an extension to his leave until the 8ᵗʰ June. However, he was also fairly sure that Williams was putting the worst possible face on the situation and time was running out. He had five days in which to deliver Kafni and the lingam to Kushnapur and then get back to Delhi to pick up a return flight to London. Adam was beginning to wonder if furthering his army career was really that important to him. Years of responding to army rules and protocol had confused his sense of priorities. What he now knew was that he was with the people he loved and nothing was more important than this mission.

Sitting beside him, Archie was enjoying in retrospect his role as Strickland in the escapade. If Shah and Khan came looking for him, Boolajee would claim that he too, had been duped.

Shastri had one final task to perform for them: to telephone the police using a false name and address, and warn them to be on the alert next day for two or three criminals who might produce bogus documents relating to some jewels. He had played his part faultlessly. Adam was feeling happy about the arrangement he had made for Shastri and Samvat Das. Boolajee would pay both of them a substantial sum of money out of the funds transferred by Jardeeson. Behan Boolajee himself and Zaki Ibrahim had refused to accept a single anna, being only too glad to be of service to Jardeeson, their respected friend and legal adviser in London.

As Adam looked at Gopal sitting in front of him beside the driver, he could decern a contentment that he had not seen in him before. His police constable guise had been most convincing. The treasure was now locked in the boot of their car together with two more strong leather bags containing the other parts of the lingam. Stout, well-worn bags had been purchased, to distract attention from the value of their contents. Gopal had good reason to feel pleased with himself, and his father would be justifiably proud of him.

Occasionally Gopal glanced at the taxi that was following them. In the front seat of that vehicle was his friend Pratap. Its other two passengers owed their presence to his recent dash to Lala Musa. Mandira had on the previous morning made her routine telephone call to Archie at Nedoo's hotel and learnt that today was the day. She and Kafni were collected that evening by Gopal using Zaki's car and driver. The same "police car" that had arrived at Zaki's salon the previous afternoon to collect Shastri, Chief Inspector Poole and his prisoner.

Samvat Das's grandmother had been true to her word and had handed over the bejewelled scrotum, once she had seen the rest of the lingam. 'I know this is what my son would have wanted,' she told Kafni.

Kafni had embraced her and replied, 'I shall never forget your kindness, Shrimatiji.'

They were relying on Harish for the next stage of the operation: to get them through the border posts and customs. But what was preoccupying Adam now was the ominous absence of any sign of Wantilla. Fikry, Adam's spy in the hotel had proved unreliable by failing to get a message to Archie when Adam had gone missing but in an attempt to redeem himself he had managed to uncover the source of leaked information to Wantilla. One of the *dhobi wallahs* was spying for Wantilla. He was in an ideal position delivering and collecting laundry at any time of the day - or night - with an excuse to be in almost any part of the hotel. These suspicions were confirmed by the other spy in Adam's pay, the commissionaire, who said he had seen the *dhobi wallah* making regular contact with the baker. This would allow him to pass on information without leaving the hotel. Bread deliveries were made at six-thirty each morning and again after lunch. Adam calculated that Wantilla probably received his information within the hour. There was going to be a lot of information to pass on today and by making a very early start, Adam hoped to ensure that it got there too late for Wantilla to interfere with their plans. If he knew that Adam now had both Kafni and the Kushnapur lingam, it was inconceivable that he would not try to pursue them. This thought made him wish that Kafni was in his taxi.

Wagah border post was only twelve miles east of Lahore, and as Adam had sight of the long low buildings of Pakistan Customs and Immigration, his watch showed it to be a few minutes before 6.30am. Their taxis pulled up at the Douane barrier, they unloaded and paid the fares, whilst the other three men carried their own bags into the customs hall. There were several coolies waving their porter's badges, and Adam engaged four of these. Two would carry the women's luggage, which was innocent enough, and the other two coolies the bags containing the lingam. These he would claim as his own luggage. He knew that he would have to play it by ear depending on the turn of events and what questions the customs officers asked.

In the hotel they had re-packed two of the bags with some insignificant ceramics on top, but the Gladstone bag, although relieved of its seal, was still locked. If humanly possible he had to avoid them looking inside any of the bags, especially that one. The lingam was rightfully being returned to Kushnapur but the Pakistan authorities might take a different view.

All the luggage was placed on the long examination rack, and their party was approached by two uniformed customs officers, the younger of whom started to question Archie. Pratap and Gopal were standing beside him with their own luggage, then Adam with the three precious bags in front of him, and finally the two women. The second customs officer, a man of about fifty with a touch of grey at the temples, addressed Adam with the usual questions. Was he a tourist on holiday? From England? How long had he been in Pakistan? How much money had he taken into the country and how much had he spent? Adam had anticipated these questions and had his answers ready.

He then asked Adam if he knew it was an offence to take Pakistan currency out of the country. He said that he did and that he had been using traveller's cheques, but that he had some Pakistan rupees left to pay the porters and any other contingencies. Although he had not asked, Adam flicked open his wallet and showed him about a thousand rupees in various denominations, and asked if it was permitted to carry this out of Pakistan. He hesitated, and Gopal who had been listening, now respectfully addressed Adam as Brigadier-sahib, and reminded him that they would need cash to pay the coolies to take the luggage over to the Indian side of the border. This had the effect intended.

'You are British Army, Sir?'

'Yes, but I served in India during the war.'

'I am fighting in Indian Army with Balluch Regiment,' the customs officer said proudly.

'Very interesting. I had friends in that regiment.' Adam pointed to the ribbons on his uniform. 'Where were you serving?'

'My company was in Waziristan. I was *havildar*; then Pakistan came and they gave me good job, customs officer. You are with this party, Brigadier-sahib?'

'Yes, I am accompanying my friend's sister and her son, back to India.'

He appeared about to mark the bags with chalk and signal the coolies to take the bags, when Adam heard the younger customs officer, who had moved along from Archie, address Pratap with the standard questions. It may have been to impress his junior, but Adam was taken by surprise when his customs officer said, 'I'd just like to look inside your bags.'

Endeavouring to be nonchalant and trying to stop his fingers from shaking, Adam took the keys from his pocket, undid the locks of two of the leather bags and opened their lids. The underneath section of both bags was protected with a canvas flap which had to be separately unstrapped. Fortunately this was not immediately evident, although it would not have missed the keen eye of a customs officer. Adam was going through the motions of selecting a key for the Gladstone bag whilst the customs officer was starting to look at the first of the open cases, when suddenly there was an anguished cry beside him.

Adam turned to see Kafni collapse into the arms of Mandira; her head was tilted back and she was gently moaning.

'Is she alright?'Adam asked anxiously.

'She is just exhausted and needs water urgently.' Mandira said, attentive to her mistress's needs.

'My God,' Adam exclaimed, in genuine shock at this un-rehearsed incident. 'The journey's been too much for her.'

The customs officer leant across the counter and looked at Kafni's pale face, sharply contrasting with the scarlet and silver of her sari.

'Is there somewhere she can sit down and rest?' Adam asked.

'Of course, Brigadier-sahib, there is a Ladies Room at the back.'

There were several people queuing up behind them, and Adam asked, 'May the porters take these bags now?'

He moved his head in vague consent, his eyes still gazing at the beautiful face of Kafni, resting on Mandira's lap.

'Bring her this way,' he instructed Mandira, and led the way through to the rear of the building. Adam quickly closed the lids of the bags, and locked them. The younger customs officer, whose attention had been briefly interrupted by the incident, was now marking Gopal's bags, and as he came level with him, Adam gestured with his hand, 'These have been cleared.'

The customs officer looked at their coolies hovering close-by, waiting to pick up the luggage. He seemed to hesitate, then, without further comment, marked all of the bags including those belonging to the women. Ten minutes later, the women re-joined them and the party completed emigration formalities. There was a hiccup when it was discovered that Kafni and Mandira had no passports and could have been accused of entering Pakistan illegally. They were, of course, already in the country before Partition, so had had no need of passports then. The problem was quickly resolved when, for the very last time, Adam produced General Malik's letter.

They walked with their bags across the border to the Indian Immigration Buildings where Adam paid-off the porters. A smiling uniformed clerk greeted them and handed out Indian Customs and Immigration forms. For the others, the long list of questions could be answered with a clear conscience. For Adam, however, there was a grave risk that he would commit to paper something which could be used as evidence of his intent to deceive the customs, and risk having the whole lot confiscated. The obvious course might be to explain the true facts: he did have Rindi's letter, written as the maharajah, who had commissioned him to recover the lingam. However, this was a high risk strategy. The lingam would quite possibly be impounded pending investigation, and although there was a good chance that it would eventually be restored to the maharajah, this could take months. In the meantime, there was always the chance that the Department of Antiquities would claim the jewels. He could have tried bribery to get the customs officer to look the other way but not all of them were corrupt. In Pakistan he could always resort to General Malik's letter but it was of no use here in India; it would in fact be counter-productive. Their best hope was Harish and of him, there was still no sign.

'That was a bit dicey back there, buddy,' whispered Archie. 'Have you decided how we're going to handle this one?'

The truth was that the whole party was deeply enmeshed in the plot and each of them would happily do anything Adam cared to propose without considering the consequences for themselves. This implicit trust was admirable, but it did mean that he had to get it right.

'I think the best strategy is for me to take the three bags entirely as my own. I'm going to put down on the form: "Hindu artefacts retrieved from Pakistan." That should at least arouse their nationalistic sympathies.'

'Yes, and of course it's perfectly true.'

The Immigration Officer stamped their forms one by one. They were instructed to take the forms through to the customs section and present them with their luggage which they would need to carry themselves.Once they were through customs there would be a fresh batch of coolies to help carry them once more. In the meantime they had to share things out. Archie and Gopal each relieved Adam of one of the lingam bags, whilst Pratap helped his mother and Mandira carry their luggage into the customs hall. There were four examination bays, two already in use. Gopal dropped his own luggage on the bench at the head of the third bay, which was unattended. They took up their positions as before and Adam found himself facing four pieces of luggage.

The building, of prefabricated construction, would have been hastily erected after Partition eleven years before. Three ceiling fans were making a vain effort to circulate the stifling hot air rolling down between the rafters. Above these, a flimsy roof offered little protection from the morning sun, already pushing shade temperatures into the upper nineties. There would be no relief from the oven-heat until the monsoons broke towards the end of the month.

As the tension increased Adam could feel the sweat soaking the armpits of his lightweight suit, and he longed to get under a cold shower. Archie mopped his brow and tried to appear unruffled. Kafni gave Adam a reassuring look; everything was going to be all right. Her hand reached for his and gave it a comforting squeeze. She appeared to have recovered from her fainting fit and her smile conveyed trust and confidence that Adam would be able to handle the situation. He would have felt more confident himself if Harish had turned up. He had last spoken to him on the telephone at his hotel in Amritsar the night before, and they had confirmed the plan to meet at the Indian border post. So where the hell was he?

A customs officer carrying a clipboard walked across to their inspection bay and started speaking to Archie. Adam took a deep breath and contrived to appear relaxed. Archie was smiling, though the babble of voices masked his words. It looked like he was intentionally engaging the officer in conversation and playing for time. Beyond Archie were two pairs of swing exit doors with glass observation panels, and to his great relief, through one of these Adam saw the face of Harish. As he caught his eye, he gave a broad smile and a thumbs-up signal, and then was gone, leaving Adam nonplussed.

A moment later Harish entered through one of the double doors, followed by the towering figure of a Sikh in army officer's uniform. He was at least six feet six tall, immaculately dressed and wearing the insignia of a major. Clearly he was well known to the customs officer who was speaking to Archie, because as they drew level, this official stood to attention and put down his clipboard. The Sikh major said something to Archie, and then gestured towards the rest of the party with his swagger cane. Harish walked towards Adam and addressed him politely in Hindi. 'Namaste, Brigadier-sahib. May I introduce Major Karni Singh, the District Customs and Immigration officer.'

The major and Adam shook hands. He then announced, doubtless for the benefit of the customs officer, that he wished to interview their party in the private reception lounge. In response to his instruction to the customs officer, the porters instantly appeared and their luggage was taken through to a moderate-sized room furnished with a number of service issue armchairs and small low tables.

'Do please sit down,' Major Singh invited. 'I'll order some refreshment.'

Major Singh called a *chaprassi* and ordered tea, then walked across to speak to Adam.

'It's a great pleasure to meet you, Brigadier. Harish tells me you're a friend of the Maharajah of Kushnapur.'

'Yes, we go back a long way.'

'Harish and I also met a long time ago when I was a second-lieutenant in his company in the Punjabi Regiment.'

'I had the feeling you knew each other rather well.'

By the time the tea arrived Archie had joined them. Harish then took Major Singh over to meet the women, and when Adam heard Singh address Kafni as *"Hazrat,"* he wondered how long it had been since she had been addressed as "Highness."

Major Singh left the room, and then a few moments later returned holding some customs forms and quietly spoke to Adam. 'Brigadier Cullworthy, I see that according to this form you are importing some Hindu artefacts.'

Adam's heart beat quickened. Was this going to be the inspection he had been dreading?

'Yes, that's right. But strictly speaking, I'm not importing them. They were stolen before Partition, and I'm returning them to their owner, the Maharajah of Kushnapur.'

'That's what Harish has told me, but as you are the person carrying these items, I need to ask you whether there is any possibility that they will ever be sold, or re-exported?'

'To the best of my knowledge, there is no possibility of that happening.'

Major Singh gave an order to the *chaprassi* standing by the door and almost immediately an examining officer came into the room. 'Please take these custom forms; everyone in Brigadier Cullworthy's party has now been cleared; send in a couple of porters to help with their luggage.'

Harish had booked all of their party into the Amritsar Hotel in anticipation of an afternoon arrival. However it was still only nine in the morning when they arrived there. A revision of plans was necessary for several reasons. For Adam, the next six hours would be wasted if they stopped at Amritsar. As it was Sunday the vice-C.I.G.S would not be available so the logical course was to drive on the 155 miles to Ambala which was within a day's journey of Kushnapur.

One snag about contacting Whitehall at this juncture was that once Adam had given an undertaking - or more likely been given an order to return on the first available flight - he might have to abandon the journey to Kushnapur. But he could not do that. He was sure that Wantilla would try to intercept them on their journey. He could not leave India without making sure the lingam and Kafni had reached the palace safely

They had a brief conference, then Harish paid the hotel a cancellation fee, and they were on their way. Adam decided they would travel on to the military cantonment five miles to the southeast of Ambala, where he might get some help with a priority telephone call. His confidence was not misplaced. He and Harish called on the District Commandant, and his signals officer booked a call to London for the following afternoon. Their whole party was given comfortable accommodation in the officers' staff bungalows, with a Brahman *khansama* to prepare their evening meal.

Ambala, Monday 1ˢᵗ June.

The call went through to the War Office as arranged. As soon as Adam had identified himself, the sergeant in charge of the switchboard came on the line to politely advise him that General Festing was away for the following two days, but could he please hold the line. Before Adam knew it, he found himself put through to Brigadier Williams. His instinct was to hang up but time was short and he decided to tough it out.

'You do know that you are due back here tomorrow! The Army Board have been asking the General why you have not appeared at the Imperial Defence College.'

'But you knew that I was delayed and had requested an extension.'

'They were not amused by that Indian turning up at the War Office to ask for an extension to your leave. We sent a message the next morning to tell him that it had *not* been approved.'

Adam noticed the use of "they" when he was certain it was Williams who had been unamused. Previously he wouldn't have hestitated to voice his own contempt without hiding behind the top brass. Adam had not received any such a message and he was starting seriously to distrust this man.

'Who actually dealt with it?'

Williams' reply was deliberately evasive. 'That is really not important. But if I were you Cullworthy I would get myself back here sharpish if you want to avoid some serious consequences.'

Adam felt sure that Williams was overdramatising the situation but he was also perfectly capable of "poisoning the water" with the senior ranks at the War Office.

The line was crackling and Adam was now becoming incensed with him.

'I'll get back on the first available flight.' Adam put the phone down without waiting for a response.

It was inconceivable that his request for a further week had been rejected out of hand. What was now clear was that his future was likely to rest upon the explanation that he would give on his return. His war record, and more importantly, his operational successes in Malaya would count in his favour. But there was a limit to the tolerance of the establishment, some of whom felt that his career was already advancing too rapidly and Williams was clearly trying to make trouble for him. As for his explanation, he would have to work that out: the truth would sound too bizarre.

It was now imperative that Adam was back at the War Office no later than Monday the 8th of June, the date on which his requested leave extension ended. He telephoned the British Overseas Airways office in Bombay to check on flights from Delhi to London. There was a twice-weekly service for both the Comet and Britannia aircraft. He made a reservation for the Saturday which gave him just enough time to go to Kushnapur and get back to Delhi in time to catch the flight. With these arrangements settled, Harish had the pleasure of telephoning Kushnapur to alert the *dewan* of their imminent arrival.

Their journey next morning would take them first to Saharanpur, and although this town was only fifty miles from Ambala, just an hour-and-a-half on the train, the road journey was a very different matter. It was necessary to leave the Grand Trunk Road twenty-five miles south of Ambala, head across country and then turn south-east over the Western Jumna Canal Bridge. Further on they must cross the long Jumna River Bridge with its constantly shifting riverbed.

Taking into account the crawl through numerous villages and the probability of being stuck behind ancient buses and bullock carts, it would be optimistic to allow less than three hours. A good night's rest was needed to prepare them for an early morning start and a very long day.

CHAPTER FORTY

Ambala Cantonment, Tuesday 2ⁿᵈ June.

Their dawn departure from Ambala Cantonment had gone smoothly enough, and they reached the Jumna River without incident. But Adam knew it was a race against time. Wantilla would have been informed of their departure from Lahore and would be on their trail. He had been unable to intercept them before they reached the Indian border and Adam pondered what his next move might be.

Although he would have been at least four hours behind them it was conceivable that he could have made up this time if he and his gang had driven through the night. But if Adam knew Wantilla the discomfort of such a journey would not suit him. It was more likely that he would attempt to overtake them by flying to Delhi and taking a train up to Saharanpur. Even this would require a series of smooth connections. The most likely scenario was that he would arrange some of his more unsavoury employees to intercept them somewhere en route.

What tricks Wantilla might have in store for them was anyone's guess but it was always safer to assume the worst. If their luck held, he would have insufficient time to arrange any serious ambush before they made it back to the Palace. Harish had already taken the precaution of sending a request for a platoon of the palace guard to stand by.

They reached Saharanpur around mid-morning, and Adam decided to call at the station to make a few enquiries. These confirmed that a Bentley from Kushnapur with a Mahavir crest had picked up a passenger early that morning.

Before turning in the night before, Harish and Adam had studied the map and made an assessment of possible places where they would be vulnerable to interception. They had eliminated the Jumna River crossing because there would be too many people. Logistically the next likely site was much nearer Kushnapur. It was along the palace road, shortly after leaving the main highway into Kushnapur City, where a plantation of deodars offered good cover. This was about a mile and a half before the defile where Chalvington had come to his tragic end. Wantilla might risk using the gorge which could be cut off at both ends but it was also near the palace with its availability of soldiers.

Adam told his party to be prepared for the unexpected. Their defensive strategy had to take into account the fact that they were armed only with Archie's automatic and Harish's service revolver.

If anyone had to do any shooting, it was to be Harish and Adam. Archie had given him his automatic, which he kept ready and loaded. He would travel in the first car with Gopal and Archie; Harish would be in the second car with Pratap, Kafni and Mandira. Then when they reached the Dak Bungalow a few miles before the turn-off, Harish would telephone the Palace. An armed party would come and meet them to accompany them the rest of the way. In the event of trouble, Harish's car would turn round, and go back to the Dak Bungalow. It was important to get the women away from any action, to avoid the risk of them becoming hostages.

After they had driven for about two hours they noticed in the distance a car being driven at great speed towards them. It was not the Bentley but it was taking up the middle of the road. Adam ordered the cars to pull over and be prepared for the worst. The car shot past, leaving them relieved but covered in dust.

By mid-afternoon they had passed many of the vulnerable points on the road. There was a light-hearted mood amongst the party as they were now within an hour of the palace. Kafni could not believe that she was actually returning home and with the lingam safely in the boot of the car. But the longer they went on without incident the more nervous Adam became. Perhaps he had overestimated Wantilla's ability to catch them up. They still had the deodar plantation and the gorge to negotiate. Maybe Wantilla had decided that it was futile to try to intercept them at this late stage and would simply try to reassert his claim to Kafni from his home base. That was wishful thinking because without the lingam, he had no bargaining chip. Anyway, they would soon be at the Dak bungalow where Harish would telephone for the armed escort.

Their confident mood was further boosted a little later when Gopal saw a car that he recognised, coming towards them. 'That's from the palace, Brigadier-sahib, shall we stop it? We can ask the driver if he has seen anything unusual on the road.'

'Good suggestion, Gopal.'

They pulled over to the side of the road and Gopal got out and waved down the oncoming car. The driver recognised Gopal and stared at him in complete bewilderment. Then he saw Major Chandra get out of the second car and knew he was not dreaming.

'Where are you going to?' Chandra asked.

'I am taking this *naik* to Bawar village, Major Chandra-sahib. His father has died and he has to light the funeral pyre.'

Harish glanced at the sad looking corporal sitting in the back of the car, then asked, 'Have you seen any suspicious looking men or vehicles on the way down from the Palace?'

No, nothing, Major-sahib,' came the reassuring reply, and the driver was sent on his way.

After a further half an hour's drive they reached the Dak Bungalow. They turned off the main road into a circular drive lined with bushes, and parked about twenty yards from the house itself. Rindi had told Adam that the bungalow had been built as a stopover between the Palace and Saharanpur in the days before motorised transport. It was seldom used to stay over any more but still maintained a small staff of a *chokidar*, a gardener and a house maid. There was nothing grand about the single storey building which had a verandah across the whole of the front. It had a beautifully maintained garden and two bougainvillea plants framed the front of the house, one with white flowers at one end and one with pink flowers at the other end.

They were all weary after the long drive made worse by the constant anxiety of wondering when they might encounter an ambush. Adam was feeling exhausted from the pressure of keeping the show on the road ever since they left Lahore. It was a great relief for everyone to be able to stop and regroup before the final leg of the journey. The bungalow was a tranquil haven and to Kafni in particular a reminder of happier days and gave her the comfort of knowing that she was nearly home.

Gopal accompanied the women up to the house, Archie chose to explore the lower garden and stretch his legs, Pratap remained in the car examining the map, the drivers disappeared to find refreshment in the servants quarters at the back of the building and Adam and Harish stood on the front lawn admiring the view up into the hills in the direction of their ultimate destination.

'It seems very quiet,' Harish said. 'I wonder where the staff are.'

'Yes, it seems deserted, but I suppose they weren't expecting us. You'd better go and make that call to the palace.' Adam replied wearily.

'Very good' said Harish heading towards the front door.

'If you find the *chokidar* ask him to prepare some tea and cakes for us.'

Adam realised what an invaluable person Harish had been on this venture, and one who had also become a good friend. He strolled slowly along the front of the building enjoying the relative coolness of the hills, admiring a bird of prey which drifted menacingly over the trees. As he got to the end of the building he saw a sight which punctured his state of calm and sent the adrenalin surging through his body. Just visible at the back of the house like the tip of an iceberg was the familiar sky blue bonnet of the Bentley. He froze knowing the full implications.

'A particularly nice colour don't you think?' came the mocking tone of Wantilla as he emerged from the deep shadow of the verandah. Adam turned on his heel and reached for his gun.

'I wouldn't do that, Cullworthy.' And from alongside Wantilla there came the sound of a rifle being cocked. As his eyes adjusted to the shadows Adam could make out the ominous shape of one of the heavies.

'Be a sensible chap and drop your weapon on the grass.' Adam complied reluctantly.

'Admit it, Cullworthy, you have been well and truly out-foxed this time.'

Adam could not believe what a complete fool he had been not to have considered the Bungalow as a possible ambush point. How could he have allowed himself to be so blatantly out-manoeuvred?

'You won't get away with this you bastard. Chandra will have called the Palace by now and as we speak there will be an escort of guards on their way.'

'I don't think so, my friend. Your Major Chandra will be enjoying the hospitality of my men and as for the call, we cut the lines as soon as we arrived.'

Adam was so tired he was at a loss to think how he could extract himself from this situation. All those in the house would now be captive. But where was Archie? and would Pratap have noticed what was going on?

'You see, Cullworthy, I now hold all the cards. Once you have handed over the lingam I will be in a position to make my claim to the *gaddi* of Kushnapur and you won't be able to go squealing to the Resident for protection this time.'

Adam was at a loss for words. He wondered where Kafni was.

Had he in the final event failed her and the Debrahm family?

'Oh, and in case you were thinking you will keep the princess you should think again. I don't intend to make that mistake twice. This time I will finally get my wicked way with her. Still a delicious piece of fruit, I am sure you will agree, Cullworthy? And one I shall relish peeling.'

Adam felt physically sick at the thought of this vile creature possessing his Kafni. At that moment the car door opened and Pratap got out still oblivious to the encounter taking place at the end of the verandah. They both looked across at Pratap as he stood folding the map.

'He's a fine boy,' Wantilla said admiringly, 'and tall. But I seem to remember Prince Ranjalla being a rather short chap. I must say, Cullworthy, he bears a remarkable likeness to yourself.'

Adam didn't like the way the conversation was going, particularly as Pratap, who was leaning against the car, looked puzzled as if he might have overheard what Wantilla had said, although as he and his bearer were still in the shadows it was unlikely that he had seen them.

'Now that I think about it, Cullworthy, it all makes sense. Those frequent visits to the palace and your obvious affection for the princess.'

'You are a complete fantasist, Wantilla. You know what you're suggesting is unthinkable.'

'I think you protest too much, my friend. Perhaps I have yet another pawn in this game?'

At this point Wantilla removed a Mills bomb grenade from his pocket which he held threateningly by the triggering pin.

'Now enough of this idle chat, tell me where you have stashed the lingam.'

Wantilla's raised voice made Pratap start. Finally realising what was going on, he began to walk towards them.

'Stay where you are,' Wantilla shouted at him and the heavy with the rifle stepped into the light to reinforce the command. Wantilla looked at Pratap and then back at Adam who wondered what he was thinking. The menacing way he was twirling the grenade made Adam very nervous. The crazed look in his eyes made Adam realise this was not just about the lingam or Kafni, this was about revenge. Payback for all those times Adam had got the better of him, culminating in the realisation that Adam may have plucked his ultimate prize before he could have her.

The crack of a rifle shot broke the silence. Wantilla fell like a sack of potatoes. The heavy stood dumbfounded at the sight of his dying master. Adam strode towards the prostrate figure anxious to get the grenade off him. But it was too late. Lying on his side with blood oozing from his mouth he gargled. 'You bastard, Cullworthy, you're coming with me.' and with a final jerk of his finger he pulled out the pin and the live grenade rolled down beside his inert body.

Adam turned and ran a few paces before the blast hit him and threw him into the azalea bush where he lay dazed and deafened. He could just hear the muffled sound of Harish shouting commands. He felt too weak to move and closed his eyes wanting to sleep but when he opened them again he saw Archie and Pratap bending over him.

'Are you OK, buddy?'

'I'll be fine.' Adam croaked without much conviction.

They helped him to his feet and Adam could smell the cordite and see the swirling dust and the shattered glass of the car windows. The aftermath of the explosion. Pratap had minor cuts from the flying glass but was otherwise unharmed. The heavy lay dead at his master's side.

'So, who fired that shot? Was that you, Archie?'

'No, I assumed it was Harish as I heard the shot come from the house as I was walking back.'

Having taken command of Wantilla's men with ferocious efficiency Harish now came over and joined in their conversation.

'It wasn't me,' he confirmed.

'Who the hell was it then?' Adam spluttered.

'Whoever it was has saved the day,' said Archie.

'Let's go inside,' Adam said, and they walked towards the door where they were intercepted by the distraught *chokidar* shouting, 'The memsahib! The memsahib!' Signalling them to follow him, he led them through to a front bedroom. The door was locked. The spare key was found and the door opened. To their astonishment, sitting on a chair beside the shattered window, was Virginia Chalvington with a service rifle across her lap.

'Virginia! My God, what are you doing here?'

Archie who had followed Adam said. 'Jeepers, Virginia did <u>you</u> shoot Wantilla?'

Adam had forgotten that Archie and Virginia had met previously.

The *chokidar* had retreated, not venturing to enter the room. Archie came in and closed the door. Virginia was staring out of the barred window. Adam went over and put his hand on her shoulder.

'Tell me what happened?'

She continued to stare at the scene in the drive and offered no resistance when Adam took the rifle from her. After a few moments, she responded in a flat quiet voice.

'He locked me in here and all I could do was listen to him telling you how he was going to have his way with Kafni. I couldn't stand his taunting any longer; he pushed me beyond the limit. I found his rifle in the cupboard and....oh dear what have I done? '

Her head dropped and she started to sob uncontrollably. 'I loved him so much. All I wanted was to be with him,'

'Was it love or obsession?'Adam responded finding it hard to believe that anyone could love such an evil character.

She drew a desperate breath, 'I wanted him to acknowledge his son.'

'You mean Tristan?'

'Yes, did Sarah tell you about him?'

'She did but she also said you hadn't been certain that he was the father.'

'I did have doubts early on but Tristan is so like him in many ways.'

Adam shuddered at the thought and hoped she meant only his physical attributes.

'So where is he now?'

'At school in England. I wanted to bring him to India but Wan..' she tried to say his name and then sobbed, 'but he wouldn't agree to it.'

Adam put his arm around her and gave her his handkerchief to wipe the small trickle of blood from a cut on her forehead.

'I gather Tristan inherited the title after all.'

'Yes fortunately Simon never followed through with his threat to disinherit him.'

'And yet you still wanted him to be acknowledged by Wantilla?'

'My roots are here in India, Adam. As you know my father had Anglo Indian blood. I would have given everything up to come back and live here.'

'What I don't understand is why you are here now?

'I came out on my own hoping that we might rekindle something. I wouldn't even have minded being just his mistress, if I could have been the only one, but he continually taunted me with his exploits with other women. He once even left the bedroom door ajar so I could witness him with a young Kashmiri girl.'

'But why did he bring you here? ' Adam persisted.

'I had gone to his house uninvited which was not a good idea in retrospect. He arrived back in Kushnapur early this morning and I have never seen him so angry and he was clearly appalled to see me. He told me that he was taking me to Delhi to put me on a flight back to England, but said he had some business to attend to on the way.'

All this time Archie had been sitting in the corner, mesmerised by Virginia and her tragic story.

Harish appeared at the door. 'I think we should get the Rajkumari and the lingam back to the Palace before the police get involved. I will stay here with Gopal and give them an explanation of what happened.'

'What about Lady Chalvington?' Adam asked, handing him the rifle.

'I don't think we need to involve her. If you see the mess the grenade made of his body,' Harish said, matter of factly, 'you will realise that there is no evidence of a bullet wound.'

Virginia winced and bowed her head.

Both cars had lost windows in the blast, which made the last leg of the journey to Kushnapur hot, dusty and noisy. No one spoke partly because of the noise of the wind and partly because each was lost in their own thoughts about the rollercoaster of events of the previous twenty four hours.

Adam had an immense feeling of relief combined with a confused sense of loss. The man who had caused them so much torment over the last twenty years was dead. Killed by the only person who truly loved him. Adam should have been feeling euphoric that they were finally returning Kafni and the lingam to Kushnapur. Instead he was feeling the anticlimax of an adventure ending and a mission fufilled. He now faced the prospect of leaving once more the woman he loved and returning to an uncertain future in England. Within five days he would have to 'face the consequences', as Williams had put it.

His reverie was disturbed by the crunching of the tyres on the gravel as they turned into the lower courtyard of the palace. He thought of his first visit to Kushnapur; meeting the elephants and seeing Kafni for the first time emerging from the warm waters of the pool on that fresh December morning. So much had changed in their lives since then and just as Rindi had warned him all those years before, he had surrendered his soul to India.

Rindi, Alisha, Puhella and all the senior members of the household were there to greet them, and despite their being exhausted, blood-stained and covered in dust, it was an emotional reunion. Puhella flung herself at her sister and then turned and hugged Adam.

'Oh, Adam you are our saviour!' The exhuberance of her youth still there.

Behind her stood Rindi, every bit the Maharajah of Kushnapur and with a confident air Adam had not seen in him before.

'Adam,' he said clasping his hand and then setting protocol aside embraced him.'It's so good to see you. Chandra called from the police station to tell me what happened. It must have been horrific. I am eternally grateful to you for all that you have done.' And then pointing to the blood on Adam's shirt he added, 'You haven't been fighting cheetahs again, have you?'

He introduced his wife Alisha, who was petite with an engaging smile.

'Welcome back to Kushnapur, Adam. I do hope you will be able to stay for a while,' she said.

'Sadly not, in five days time I have an urgent appointment at the War Office in London.'

'I hope you haven't jeopardised your career for us, Adam,' Rindi said gravely.'

'I hope so too, but whatever the outcome, this mission was one of the most important things I have ever done.'

He was now aware of the curious look Rindi was giving him. Without realising it Adam had put his arm around Kafni's waist. To avoid any further embarrassment he guided her towards Rindi saying, 'Anyway, here is the other part of your family treasure.'

'No, Adam, I think she is now your treasure.' There was a twinkle in his eye as he spoke. Only when Kafni had hugged Rindi and then returned to kiss him on the cheek did Adam realise the full significance of his statement.

Taking Adam's hand she said, 'I must go and see Mother. Will you come with me?'

'No. I think that after all these years she will want to see you alone.'

The second car had now pulled into the courtyard and Archie and Virginia got out. Even with tear-stained cheeks and dusty hair she was still the beautiful woman that Rindi remembered.

'How lovely to see you, Virginia,' he said calmly and kissed her hand tenderly. Then turning to Archie he said, 'How can I begin to thank you both for what you have done for us?'

'Well, a shower and an ice cold drink would be a good start,' replied Archie to everyone's amusement.

Kushnapur Palace, Wednesday 3rd June.

The next day, the Maharajah of Kushnapur held an extempore *durbar* in the Durbar Hall. It was attended by the *dewan*, ministers of the State of Kushnapur, and officials of the palace and their wives. Everyone was in court dress; Adam's own attire having been produced overnight by the palace *derzi*. It was a dazzling occasion. The Kushnapur Lingam had been carefully reassembled and cleaned. Many seeing it for the first time gasped as it was unveiled. The *durbar* was hastily planned out of necessity as Adam was the guest of honour and had to leave for Delhi and London in the morning.

There were four ceremonies. The first was to present 'swords of honour' to Pratap and Gopal, both of whom were simultaneously commissioned as ensigns in the service of the Kushnapur State Regiment. The second ceremony was to bestow the Star of Kushnapur upon Major Ram Chandra, and to promote him to the appointment of Colonel of the Kushnapur Guards Regiment. The third ceremony was for Archie. He was appointed a Commander of the Himalayan Sapphire Order. The ribbon proved too short to fit over his large head of tousled hair and was therefore pinned to his chest.

In the final ceremony, Adam was introduced by the *dewan* as Honorary Rajput, Brigadier Cullworthy-sahib, and he was asked to kneel in front of the *gaddi*. Rindi, magnificent in his mauve and cream turban, stood to address his court.

'Adam, you have done us a great service in returning the Kushnapur Lingam and the Rajkumari Kafni to us. There are few who know the true extent of what you have done for the future of the Debrahm family. It is for this reason that I have decided to bestow upon you the Satrap of Kushnapur, a title descended from General Craterous himself. This honour makes you the third most important person in Kushnapur after the Maharajah, and the Rajkumar.'

With this he took a broad mauve and cream silk ribbon bearing the jewelled crest of Kushnapur, and hung it around Adam's neck. The crowd cheered and Puhella jumped to her feet and clapped her hands in a spontaneous display of appreciation.

'Wait!' continued Rindi, raising his hand to calm the euphoric mood. 'I have not finished. It is not customary for us to acknowledge, publicly, the efforts of our women but I cannot conclude this *durbar* without showing recognition to my sister Kafni for her selfless endeavours and the personal sacrifices she has suffered in her quest to recover the Kushnapur Lingam. She has courageously and loyally endured so much torment for the sake of our family. Now she is entitled to her own happiness. I therefore wish it to be known that I shall bestow upon her the status of *noble munificence.* This privilege, which she so richly deserves, will remove from her all those limitations by which a Kshatriya widow is normally proscribed. If she so wishes she may now re-marry and to someone of her own choosing.'

Kafni sat serenely beside him, a vision of beauty and elegance and for the first time in public her violet eyes held Adam's gaze, unashamedly.

The *durbar* was followed by celebrations with traditional dancing and musical entertainment.

The next morning at breakfast, Archie was in surprisingly high spirits.

'This is a style of life that I could easily get used to, Adam,'he paused, 'I should tell you that I have been persuaded to stay on for a few weeks.'

'Who persuaded you? Harish? Or was it Rindi?'

'No, as a matter of fact it was Virginia,' he said rather coyly.

'Well, you are a dark horse.'

'I thought she could do with some company after all she has been through. Anyway there's no rush to get back, I've another three months before I am due back in Oxford.'

'Has she told you that Rindi has given her a grace and favour house on the estate? His uncle Ashok lived there until he died last year.'

'No, she hadn't told me that.'

'Rindi said she could live there on the one condition that she never disclosed the real father of her son.'

'Yes, I can see that might complicate things.'

'Well, Archie, you could do a lot worse than Virginia, she is a remarkable woman. They would love her back in California.'

'That's for sure. Now how about you, buddy?'

'I would love to stay longer in Kushnapur but there are several things in my life that I have to sort out before I can think about the future.'

Queens Gate Gardens, Kensington, 18th June 1959.

Jardeeson had listened intently to Adam's account of his adventure.

'So how did you avoid disciplinary action? Your leave extension had been declined, and so you must have been absent without leave.'

'Ah, that's where you are wrong. My request for an extension of leave had not been declined because it had never been submitted.'

'But I submitted it myself, in person, to that Williams fellow. I gave you the copy of the submission which he had signed in acknowledgement.'

'Yes, and it was that document which was my saving grace and Williams's undoing. He never processed the request and must have hoped that no one at the War Office would query his word. As soon as I produced your document signed by him the Advocate General dismissed the action.'

'And Williams?'

'Taken early retirement.'

'Good riddance I'd say.'

Nina entered the room and they both briefly stood up as she took a seat on the sofa.

'And your promotion to Major General?' Jardeeson continued.

'Yes, that has been approved.'

'So what now, Adam?' Nina asked.

'Well, to be honest I am not sure that I want to continue in the army and once my divorce from Sarah comes through there seems little to keep me in England.'

'I think perhaps your heart lies elsewhere.'

'I have a yearning to go back to Kushnapur.'

'Are you sure it is Kushnapur that you yearn for?'

Adam looked at them both wondering how best to answer her perceptive comment.

'Did you know that Pratap is being sent to Rockton to complete his schooling?' she asked.

'No, I didn't. That is excellent news.'

Jardeeson broke his silence.

'Adam, Nina and I have decided that we wish to make Pratap our sole heir.' He paused to allow this to sink in. 'You look surprised.'

'Frankly, I am astonished.'

'Well, as you know we have no children and are not getting any younger. We also cannot think of anyone who has done more for this family and been more like a son to us, than you have. By giving Pratap a reason to spend time in England we felt it was probably the best gift we could give you.'

'I don't know what to say.'

'You could say, "Thank you,"' he said with a mischievous grin.

Adam laughed, shook his hand and then went across and kissed Nina.

'This is such a thoughtful and generous deed.'

'If you don't mind, we would like you to be the Trustee of the estate until he is twenty one.'

'I would be delighted.'

'There is one more small favour we have to ask of you. We have a guest staying who would love see the sights of London and we wondered if you could be their guide?'

Before Adam could reply the door opened and there stood Kafni, radiant in a green and red sari. She ran to him and they embraced. Neither of them spoke as no words could describe how they felt at that moment but Adam knew that the years of waiting and hoping had been worth it. There was now a future for them, beyond Kushnapur.

THE END

Glossary

Achka	Tight fitting three-quarter length coat
Adytum	Innermost chamber of temple
Angrezi	English
Ankus	Goad for guiding elephants
Ap kaise hain	How do you do?
Arahat	Saint
Apke-wastu	Toady (lit. at your honour's command)
Afreet	Evil devil in Mohammedan mythology
Ayah	Nursemaid or lady's maid
Baba-log	European Children
Babu	Indian clerk;Hindu gentleman
Bahadur	Hero or champion; suffixed to name as "gallant officer"
Bai-sa	Term of respect
Baksheesh	Gifts; a tip or reward
Banias	Traders; bankers; money-lenders
Banyan	Merchant
Ben	Sister; also used as a general term
Bhavan	Pavilion or large residence
Bhai	Brother
Bibi	High class woman
Brinjal	Aubergine
Butchcha	Baby
Burra khana	Big dinner party celebration
Burra-peg	Double tot of whisky
Byah	Marriage
Caravasieri	Desert rest houses
Chapattis	Unleavened flat bread
Chaprassi	Office messenger; (name refers to brass belt-buckle)
Chai-wallah	Tea boy
Chitthi or Chit	Note
Chokidar	Night watchman
Choli	Under bodice

Beyond Kushnapur

Chota	Small or little
Chota-hazri	Early morning tea; little breakfast
Coolie	Native porter
Crore	Ten million (one hundred lakhs)
Daffadar	Indian sergeant, in cavalry
Dai	Nurse/Midwife
Dak	Post; Mail
Dak Bungalow	Rest house for travellers
Dandy	Open sedan chair
Dasi	Maidservant
Devi	Goddess
Dewali	Popular Hindu festival of lights
Dewan	Chief minister of a prince's court
Dhobi	Laundryman or washerwoman
Dhooly	Covered palaquin
Didi	Elder sister
Doob	Indian lawn grass
Dukan	Shop
Durwans	Guards
Ek dum	At once
Gaddi	Throne. (lit. cushion)
Gadhakhanna	Donkey stables
Gali	Lane
Ghari	Horse-drawn vehicle
Ghati	Ravine
Gussal-khana	Bathroom
Halwa	Sweetmeat
Han	Yes
Havildar	Indian sergeant in infantry
Hazrat	Highness
Hetaerism	Open concubinage
Hill Station	Hot weather stations (above 5,000 feet)
Howa khana	Rest, breather
Howdah	Palaquin on elephant
Hukam	Term of respect

Huzoor	Exalted form of address
Izzat	Prestige; honour
Jaldi	Quick
Jalpan	Breakfast
Janjal	Forest or wood
Jasus	Spy
ji	A respectful suffix
Jotish	Astrology
Jotisha	Astrologer
Kamdukan	Workshop
Khama	Deed; law determining rebirth
Khana	Meal; dinner
Khansama	Cook or cook/butler
Kharab	Bad
Khitamagar	Butler or waiter
Kshatriya	Warrior cast among Hindus
Kumari	Miss
Kurta	Long tunic shirt, usually white
Kutta	Dog
Ladla	Darling
Lakh	One hundred thousand rupees
Lathi	Long heavy cane
Macham	Camouflaged hunting platform
Madya	Central
Maharajah	King (Hindu)
Maharajkumar	Crown prince
Maharani	Great Queen
Mahout	Elephant driver
Maidan	Long parade ground
Makan	House
Mali	Gardener
Manji	Respectful address for mother
Mandapa	Large open hall or porch
Marg	Road; avenue
Masalchee	Scullion

Mataji	Mother
Meharbani se	Please
Miltha	Sweet
Mirador	Belvedere or raised turret
Mistri	Head servant
Mitra	Friend
Mofussil	Up country
Moucharabya	Auspicious time
Murkh	Fool
M.L.A	Member National Legislative Assembly
Nahin	No
Naik	Indian corporal
Nala	Small valley or dry ravine
Namaste	Greeting for all occasions
Nautch-girls	Professional dancing girls
Nawab	Muslim princely ruler
Pilkhannas	Elephant stalls
Pitaji	Father
Poodle-faker	Womaniser
Pradesh	Place/ District
Puggaree	Turban
Pukka	Out and out good
Punj	Buddhist monk
Punkah	Fan
Purana	Old
R.A.S.C	Royal Army Service Corps
Rajaya Sabha	National Parliament, Delhi
Rajkumar	Prince
Rajkumari	Princess
Rajmarg	Ruler's avenue
Rajput	Hindu warrior of Kshatriya caste
Ram	Form of greeting
Ram Ram!	Hindu prayer intoning name of God
Rasoighar	Kitchen
Salwar	Trousers

Sarraf	Banker
Saudagar	Merchant
Sekos	Sacred enclosure in ancient temple
Sewak	Waiter
Shikar	Hunting, usually big game
Shikari	Experienced hunter
Shri	Mr.
Shrimati	Mrs.
Shudra	Lowest of the four main castes
Shukriya	Thank you
Sikundar Delkan	Alexander the Great
Sirdar	A noble
Souk	Bazaar
Subadar	Viceroy's commissioned officer
Swaraj	Home rule
Syce	Groom, stableman
Thaharna	Wait
Talab	Lake
Taza	Friend
Thakur	Minor nobleman in Rajputana
Tiffin	Luncheon
Tonga	Light two-wheeled vehicle
Tulwar	Indian Sabre
Utta	North
"WACKEYE"	Slang for (W.A.C.(I) (Women's Army Corps (India)
Wallah	Man
Wyapari	Trader
Zenana	Women's secluded quarters in high caste families
Zemindari	Landowner's estates

Acknowledgements

We would like to express our sincere thanks to the following people, whose help and advice in their field of expertise, as noted, has been invaluable.

Major-General, James Elliot, *Tiger hunting*

Major Stephen Anderson, *New Delhi*

John Cowasjee, *Pakistan & North-West frontier*

Captain David Whitehead, *Sea convoys & Cape Town*

Field Marshal Bevhoor, *Indian Princes and Poona*

Elsa Constantine, *Lahore*

Brigadier Gerald Thubron, *Age related Army ranks*

Percy Broughton, *Calcutta*

Mary Charlton, *Simla*

The Maharaja of Jodhpur *Life in an Indian Palace*

We would like to give special thanks to Sue Carpenter, Charlotte Fry, Jan Henley, Jacqueline Goodhart, Virginia Graham and Emma Stewart-Smith for their invaluable editorial assistance. We would like to thank all those of you who have read the manuscript and given their support and encouragement and in particular to Nina Toller and Christopher and SallyAnn Neame. Thanks also to Katie Isbester at Claret Press for her guidance on publishing in all formats and to Caroline Mills and Petya Tsankova for their design input. Finally a big thank you to our family who have shared the long journey to publication of this book.

About the Authors

This is the first novel for father and son writing team Peter and Mark Flawn-Thomas.

Peter was born a year after the end of the Great War and the Second World War started the day after his twentieth birthday. After the war he lived in Southern Africa where he witnessed the unravelling of the British Empire at first hand. He subsequently spent time in India and Pakistan travelling extensively where both personal relationships and painstaking research provided the material for this atmospheric saga. Peter died in 2015.

Mark has also travelled widely and after a career in finance has devoted much of the last twenty years to writing and painting. He lives in London with his wife and two children.

Peter contributed his military and colonial experience and Mark has brought to life a cast of authentic characters and a captivating romance. Together they have crafted a thoroughly gripping story.

Lightning Source UK Ltd.
Milton Keynes UK
UKHW012233111119
353329UK00002B/51/P